Orpheus C. Kerr

Avery Glibun; or, Between two Fires

A Romance

Orpheus C. Kerr

Avery Glibun; or, Between two Fires
A Romance

ISBN/EAN: 9783337008253

Printed in Europe, USA, Canada, Australia, Japan

Cover: Foto ©Andreas Hilbeck / pixelio.de

More available books at **www.hansebooks.com**

Avery Glibun;

or,

Between Two Fires.

A Romance.

BY

ORPHEUS C. KERR.

NEW YORK:

G. W. Carleton & Co., Publishers.

LONDON: S. LOW, SON, & CO.

MDCCCLXVII.

ROCKWELL & ROLLINS, STEREOTYPERS AND PRINTERS,
122 WASHINGTON STREET, BOSTON.

PREFACE.

"AVERY GLIBUN" being my first essay in sustained fiction, it seems remarkably prudent to say no more about it.

O. C. K.

COTTAGE-ON-THE-WAYNE, 1867.

In

GRATEFUL RECOGNITION

OF

THE INDIVIDUAL SYMPATHY, ENCOURAGEMENT, AND GENEROUS PRAISE

EXTENDED TO THE AUTHOR

AT A TIME WHEN HE REALLY NEEDED SUCH

DISINTERESTED HELPS;

AND

REQUIRING NO AUGMENTATION TO MAKE THEM SURPASSINGLY WELCOME,

WHEN, TO A CERTAIN EXTENT,

SUBSEQUENTLY JUSTIFIED BY MORE OR LESS OF PUBLIC APPROVAL;

THIS

EXPERIMENTAL COMBINATION

OF

THE OLD AND NEW SCHOOLS OF FICTION

IS

AFFECTIONATELY DEDICATED

TO

NOBODY.

CONTENTS.

VOLUME I.

VOLUME II.

AVERY GLIBUN;

OR,

BETWEEN TWO FIRES.

VOLUME I.

CHAPTER I.

THE HOUSE THAT JACK BUILT.

His face was all in rags, with a huge and tangled red beard, and, as he bent over me, holding the dingy little jail of a lantern aloft in his right hand, I noticed that his deep-set eyes glistened in the bleared light like window-glass at night.

Yes! there he was, just as my most horrible and delightful story-book had been so particular to describe him! That very same obese and hairy Dwarf, who only needed the true love of the adorable Princess of China to make short work of his evil enchantment and restore to him his original matchless legs and surprising feathers. In a vague and shadowy way I took exception to the lantern, which seemed something of an innovation; but, then, it might be one of those magic lanterns I had heard mentioned. Yes, it was the Dwarf at last, and no mistake. Indeed, I had commenced to speculate upon the propriety of asking him some polite question about the Princess of China, whom I believed to be celestially fascinating in a pink velvet dress and a perfect dog-collar of a gold crown; when a sudden and pungent taste in my mouth caused me to open my eyes more widely, and, in an instant, I comprehended that the figure at my bedside was *not* the Dwarf.

Out went my dream under a curdling flash of terror, and, with a shrill scream, I attempted to start up.

Quick as thought the creature's left hand was upon my mouth and held me fast to the rickety cot.

"Hold your noise, you brat!" he growled hoarsely; and inclined his head still lower, as though to listen.

Terrified as I was, I could but listen, too, in a petrified, helpless way; and I heard a dreary sort of thud! thud! accompanied by an intermittent splashing sound, apparently coming from some place beneath us.

"All right!" muttered the man, at last, nodding at something in the air, and setting down the lantern just beyond me on the cot; "but don't try that again, my little man, or I'll have to give you to the booboos."

Notwithstanding the threat, there was something so roughly kind in his tones, and in his manner of removing the hand from my lips to my hair, that the first fear of him left me, though the terrors of a strange place still made my poor little heart throb violently.

"What house is this?" I cried, sitting up in the bed, and staring affrightedly around.

He had been resting upon one knee, but now he took a seat upon the cot, and patted my shoulder very good-naturedly. "I wouldn't tell everybody," said he; "but this is the House that Jack built."

"But where's the Cat?" asked I, momentarily diverted by this realization of a favorite fiction of mine, and triumphantly sure that I had him there.

"Oh!" he said; "you mean the Cat that killed the Rat that ate the Malt? Why, she's down cellar."

"And where's the Rat?" I went on, growing more interested, and beginning to feel quite at home.

"Well," returned he; "I suppose I must be the Rat."

This speech frightened me again, and I commenced to whimper piteously.

"I want Elfie!"

The man looked anxiously into my staring eyes, and resumed his patting.

"Did she bring you here?" queried he.

"No, no, no-o-o!" I sobbed, petulantly pushing away his hand; "nobody didn't bring me here. Go 'way!"

He had moved his head nearer to mine, and now suddenly caught my face between his hands and drew in his breath.

"Phew!" exclaimed he, after a moment's pause,—"laudanum!"

The word was strange to me; nor was my

Increasing fright mitigated by three thoughtful nods of the bearded head, which was all that I could see of him.

"Where's your father, boy?"

The question brought before me the figure of a tall, dark, black-whiskered, handsome man, of whom I was very much afraid. Here, again, I thought of Elfie, who was always telling me that he was my father, and once more I cried distractedly, — "I want Elfie!"

"It's queer," said the man, lifting the lantern in one hand, while with the other he thoughtfully fingered my blue merino coat and the woman's cloak which was thrown over me; "it's all a mess of queerness to me." Then — noticing that I was intently listening to him — "Lay down again, my cherub, and see if you can't sleep in the House that Jack built. This is the Cat that killed the Rat that ate — hark!"

The exclamation came so sharply that it seemed to drive the breath out of my body; and, for the second time, I heard the dreary thudding and splashing below us.

"What's that?" whispered the man.

There had been a sort of snapping sound, away off somewhere; and, as I remembered how the milkman used to crack his lash at me when I went out on the sidewalk with cook to get the milk, I said, —

"It's a whip."

"One of the joists cracking, I guess," he muttered, drawing a long breath and not heeding my explanation. "The whole shanty'll be going overboard some of these fine nights, I'm thinking."

Not understanding this talk, I began to cry again, which recalled his attention to me.

"What's the matter now?" he asked.

"Oh, I'm so afraid," whimpered I. "Why don't Elfie come?"

Then I thought of the splashing down below, and a new terror came upon me.

"Is this the boat?" I asked him, in a kind of alarmed wonder.

"The boat!" ejaculated he, quickly, — "oh, you mean — yes, to be sure it's a boat; it's Noah's Ark."

"But where's all the animals, then?"

"The animals? Why, they're down cellar; but you shall see them when you wake up in the morning. One of them's a rat, too."

I was interested again in my story-book world; but declined to welcome the rat, which I suspected and openly accused of a disposition to bite.

"Not this rat, though," said the man, quite earnestly, — "not this rat, though, my little man. He's not allowed as much cheese as would keep a mouse, and he's been kicked about some, and had cruel traps set for him; but still there's nothing vicious about him. He wouldn't hurt you no more than I would. He's in the cellar till morning."

I was not sufficiently critical to note the incongruity of a cellar to a boat; and, as any immediate view of the menagerie seemed out of the question, I tired of the Ark at once, and peevishly resented a pungent odor which tickled my nose and throat.

"You smell smoky," said I.

"I've been smoking my pipe to-night," he responded with great good nature; "but left it downstairs in the big store-room, on an old barrel. You shall see it to-morrow. It's such a nice, handsome pipe, you know, with a Turk's head — Hello!"

There certainly was some peculiar noise this time besides the thud! thud! and splashing; a cracking, splintering noise, as though some distant door were yielding slowly to a strong and steady pressure from without.

Instantly the lantern was extinguished, and the huge, hard hand was upon my mouth again.

"Not a sound, you young imp! Not so much as a wheeze, or I'll strangle you!" was hoarsely whispered in my ear. "Keep still; it's only the rats, and they won't hurt you. Hunted down at last! Hunted down at last!"

In all my fright, I could hear the beating of his heart as he leaned across the cot. Finding that I made no effort to move or speak, — for I was too much terrified to do either, — he cautiously withdrew his hand and sat motionless beside me.

Crackle, crackle came the sound, more and more distinctly through the thick darkness, as though that relentless shoulder against the door were growing stronger; and it seemed to me that even the thudding and splashing waxed louder than before, in an irritable rivalry with the fitful September wind which had begun to moan bitterly outside. Then there was the snapping of the milkman's whip again; and then the splitting, cracking, and splintering from where it left off before; and they all began to associate themselves unaccountably in my mind with the hairy Dwarf and the beautiful Princess; and I was fast slipping back into the old idea of having the enchanted Prince at my elbow, when an awful something — thick, heavy, and invisible — wafted down upon me in the gloom, and I sprang convulsively up in the bed, choking and coughing violently.

In vain I clutched at the thickening air all around to find the man. He was gone, and, as I turned to look for him, there suddenly appeared, not far from my resting-place, what looked like three sides of a very thin frame of light. The man apparently caught sight of it at the same moment; for he fairly leaped to the cot again from wherever he had been, and the hand he laid upon my shoulder trembled.

"Don't be scared," he whispered.

I opened my mouth to answer, when hundreds of needles seemed to prick my throat and nostrils, and I shrieked aloud with pain and terror.

With wonderful celerity the man dashed open a solid wooden window-shutter at the head of the cot, with his fist, letting in the cold air and the noise of waves, and letting out the strangling demon that had assailed me; then he bounded away from me, and in an instant the three-sided frame of light flashed into an open doorway, all radiant as morning!

"On fire! my God, on fire!" shouted he, standing fully revealed on the fallen door, and staring across the great room in which he stood, at a stairway, up which a single sheet of livid flame seemed leaping over its own bright cataract.

Wild with excitement, I took in the whole scene at a glance : the cheerless, bleak place I was in, with its cobwebbed beams overhead, and the boarded floor so worn that the heads of the nails in it shone like silver; myself upon the cot in a corner, right under the open window; the extinguished lantern resting on a barrel about four feet from me; a basin-shaped hat on the ground near it, and my strange companion standing like a statue in the full glare of the outer room, with his back toward me.

Ding dong! Ding dong! clanged a solemn bell from somewhere in the air, and ding dong! ding dong! responded other bells all around; just as a whole neighborhood of dogs will answer the first one that scents a thief in the night.

At the opening peal, the man disappeared from before the door so quickly that I could not see which way he went. In fact, I did not care; for all my fears had given place to a feeling of intense exhilaration; even the smoke, which completely hid the beams from sight as it moved slowly toward the open window, only enlivened me the more, as I associated it with the fireworks I had once seen at Vauxhall Garden; and my chief inclination was to handle the lantern upon the barrel.

Scrambling from the cot, I eagerly laid hold upon the coveted prize, and was soon so deeply engaged in fathoming its mysteries that even the sounds of loud voices and a kind of measured thumping, which began to blend with the clangor of the bells, did not divert me from my amusement. I had managed to get the bottom out of my novel toy, when a pounding at the open window drew my attention thither, and I could see something glimmering and moving along the sill from the outside. Taking the lantern in my hand, I mounted the cot and looked out, just as the moving object, which proved to be a wet oar, was drawn down. I could both see and hear water right under the casement, and a gruff voice, which seemed to come out of the very waves, asked, —

"Is that you, Wolf?"

Before I could speak, I was roughly thrust from the window, by my companion of the night, whose reappearance with such abruptness quite took my breath away.

"Got the boat there?" he asked, hurriedly.

"Yes," said the voice. "How did you ketch fire?"

"My pipe, I suppose — it's all in the storeroom yet — wait a minute."

He was gone again as quickly as he had come, vanishing, as before, into the outer room, and I followed as far as the door to look at the fire. The white flame was still flaring up the stairway, and, as I gazed with wondering admiration, it changed with a hot burst into lurid red, and a huge black cloud, all spangled with sparks, swept full upon me. At the same moment there was a crash in the room behind me; a scraping and scuffling of many feet, and some one dragged me, all choking and panting, to a near window, through which many dusky figures were swarming, with a great wet serpent of a hose.

Hastily wiping the tears of strangulation from my eyes with as much of my elbow as could be conveniently twisted into that service, I looked fearfully up along the arm of the hand grasping my left shoulder, and found that it belonged to a being in a firecap and a red shirt, whose peculiar countenance, as it appeared in the firelight, somehow suggested to me a street-corner with a grocery store upon it.

I looked at him and he looked at me.

"Why, whose kid are you?" said he.

"Sir?" said I.

Here the fireman was gently touched upon the arm by a smooth-faced gentleman, who had just glided in through the window, and bore some resemblance to a benignant sexton in a full suit of rather cheap black.

"Excuse *me*," said the gentleman, cheerfully; "but, as you are engaged in a perilous occupation, I almost feel it to be my duty." Here he dexterously whipt a little book from one of his coat-tails, and said he, — "Life is uncertain at any time, you know, and if you *should* want to insure your life, I can recommend the Salamander Mutual Trust Company, of which I am agent. You will find the system of dividends, et cetera, all laid down in this small book, which I will leave with you."

With the agility of a monkey this pleasant gentleman glided out through the window again before another word could be said, and, as the men with the hose came confusedly backing into the room, with much vociferous talk about some danger somewhere, my friend lifted me swiftly to his shoulder, and I found myself being rapidly carried down a ladder into a great mob of shouting, surging humanity. Right after us came the others with a reckless speed which made the ladder spring again, and then I was borne irresistibly through a fierce crush of shoulders and fire-caps, to where a grim-looking machine was throbbing spasmodic life into a leathern artery stretching to the burning house. Upon the box part of this machine my bearer seated me, and, after giving some roaring direction about "working her lively," to the score or more of his own exact likenesses who were toiling up and down at the long rails on either side, he tapped me encouragingly on the head with his trumpet.

"Hey! there goes the crib!" burst from

a hundred throats, when a bright glare fell suddenly on us all.

Something between a cheer and a howl rent the air, as I looked up and beheld the flames gushing furiously forth from the side window through which we had so recently descended. Out they came, whirring and crackling under a heavy canopy of folding smoke, making an awful torch to evoke from the black bosom of night a pier washed on either side by lurid waves, and swarming with red and black shapes in every conceivable attitude. Along the dry wooden gutter and up the peaked roof went lashes of light, as though to show the way, and then followed the scathing, livid scourge in tottering rises and falls, laying open the miserable old tenement to the very bone in fiery gashes, and swinging up to heaven a low, continual moan, to the symphony of cracking tendons and the hisses of blistering joints. Ten thousand mimic fires danced in miniature upon the polished brass-work of the steadily thumping machines on the pier, and half a dozen threads of prismatic water sprang from amid the sea of fire-caps and arched into the seething bowels of the conflagration like lofty feathers of frosted glass; but the breath of a furnace drank them mockingly from the air, and fresh banners flashed up everywhere to join the burning hosts. The advance of the infernal legions crested the sinking roof at a bound, and straightway the sails of two or three anchored sloops came pallidly out of the darkness of the river beyond, like spectres of lost shipping. It broadened toward the chimney and flared higher, and a whole ocean, with all its commerce, seemed to redden and sparkle away from it. It fluttered, swirled, gathered a dozen concentrating flames to itself, hurled up, with a dull burst, its giant vitals of black smoke and embers, and, with a noise like thunder far underground, the roof and front of the glittering mass fell away from it, as a body from a soul.

Up swept a hoarse cheer from the dazzled swarm on the pier, to greet the new revelation; but still the whole rear wall and one of the sides were standing. Half a floor up there, too, seemed to be suspended miraculously, with an open window toward the river; or perhaps it rested on that stairway which, though flaming, yet sustained itself.

Quicker grew the thump—thump, thump, thump—of the great opposing machines, and the one upon which I was sitting shook so violently under the muscles of its tireless workers that I could hardly keep my seat. Louder swelled the wordless roar of the excited multitude; for, now that the mask was off, man fathomed all the designs of his old enemy, and felt sure of speedy victory.

But, in a moment, there came a sudden hush, like a caught breath. Every eye had seen a something moving in the fire, and not with the motion of the scrolling and tottering things around it; a black and bearish thing, which was crawling, as it were, from the very heart of the great, glowing skeleton of the furnace. It gained the unburnt end of a fallen beam, arose to an upright position upon it, and then flitted toward the blazing stairway. A pause for a second, and then up it went right through the flames, and leaped through a shower of sparks, like a maddened ape, to the sill of the open window. Framed by the casement, it stood erect for a minute—turned half around—swiftly wrapped about its head and shoulders what looked like a woman's cloak, and—bounded from sight.

Then burst from hundreds of eager lips a speaking yell,—half-wondering, half-familiar,—

"Hi! hi! Did you see the Dock Rat?"

<hr>

CHAPTER II.

WHAT HAPPENED THEREAFTER.

HALF sick with excitement, and thoroughly chilled by the cold night air, I was not sorry when my new protector lifted me from the box of the engine, and silently led me by the hand until we reached the street bordering the river and halted under a lamp. Several other firemen had followed, vivaciously discoursing the merits of a recent spirited single combat with which the question of precedence at a hydrant had been satisfactorily adjusted, and they now formed an inflamed ring of red shirts around us.

"I say, Hosey!" said one of them, stooping to get a closer view of me, "is this here the young tarrier you was a coughin' about?"

Hosey nodded an identification of me with the fanciful and poetical canine object concerning which he had expressed himself in that peculiar manner; at the same time intimating a lively inclination to concede his boots immediately to that sagacious person who should tell him what to do with me.

This generous offer excited the cupidity of a gentleman with a colored lantern and a pair of spectacles, who promptly brought a pale-blue glare to bear upon me, and advised my expeditious removal to the hospital.

Thereupon, still another gentleman, who, by dint of an inordinate seal ring and a vast amount of watch-chain, asserted his fashionable proclivities, wished to be instantaneously informed as to the tendency of the last speaker's "cackling," and ironically besought a detailed account of the bodily injuries qualifying me for public medical treatment. He likewise addressed his friend by the facetious title of "Old Top-lights," and earnestly counselled him to exhibit no further moisture.*

Mr. Top-lights' irascible disposition, somewhat aggravated in this instance by a cold in his head, caused him to receive this flight of humor imperiously. With great deliberation of manner, and in awful silence, he at

* You see, the real words were "Dry up!" but public taste in this country is too refined to stand any such language in a book.

once passed his lantern to a speechless individual near him. With impressive care he placed his fire-cap upon the walk, and his spectacles within it. Then he carefully untied the black silk handkerchief girding the neck of his red shirt, and added it to the contents of the casket. After which he commenced rolling up one of his sleeves with studious elaboration, at the same time asking, in a terrible voice, if his fashionable friend wanted anything of *him?* His fashionable friend was not prepared just at that moment to assert any pressing need in that direction; whereupon Mr. Top-lights consecutively resumed his full costume with the same unspeakable gravity as before, and reclaimed his lantern with an air of moral grandeur well fitted to adorn the triumph of a virtuous cause.

At the conclusion of these absorbing solemnities, which he had witnessed with great admiration, Hosey became conscious that I was shivering with cold and should have some attention.

"Did you belong to that Dock Rat, up there?" he asked me, pointing with his trumpet toward the pier.

"No, sir," said I, with chattering teeth; "but I waked up there, and saw a great big man with a light, and he said it was the House that Jack built, and Noah's Ark; and it wasn't, — was it?"

"He's been stole!" ejaculated Hosey.

"Take him home with you to your old woman for to-night — why don't you?" murmured Mr. Top-lights.

"So I will, so I will," said Hosey, with sudden decision. "You just take my trumpet to the Truck House, and I'll lug the youngster right home, and see what turns up to-morrow."

Raising me to his shoulder with one hand, he stalked abruptly away from them, across the street, and up another street, at such a pace that I clung to his neck and arm with anything but a sense of safety. Poor, bewildered little creature that I was, my heart fluttered under my soiled jacket like a frightened bird, and I only took such cognizance of my journey as might be involved in a succession of glimpses at what fragmentary patches of first floors the dingy street-lamps feebly illuminated. Now and then, the motionless figure of a watchman appeared at a corner, like a fixture, and was silently left behind. Not quite silently, though; for the boots of the fireman kept up a steady clink-a-clink on the pavement; and the sound first soothed, and then tempted me into counting; and finally I was conscious of hearing it less distinctly, as I gradually slid down upon my bearer's red breast. Then for a moment I heard each footfall distinctly again; and then once more they seemed to be going away from me, mixed with a murmur of words that were kind; and I knew no more.

O sweet oblivion of our earliest sleep! thou leafy shadow of the Tree of Life, to woo the fair young spirit to its rest, and from its sorrows plume the birdlike dream! How look we back regretfully to thee, when after-years have brought us such repose as unto thine is like the brackish sea unto the still, sweet-watered woodland spring! How look we back, all longingly to thee, when care unsleeping journeys with the soul, and slumber's but the sightless moving on through a black tunnel cut 'twixt day and day!

The warm kiss of a woman awoke me; and, as I stared again into the active world under the mild spell of her eye, I became duly aware that my couch was a haircloth sofa, and that I was in a cheerful, whitewashed room, with a picture of some kind hanging over the mantel-piece. Candlestick in hand, my friendly fireman was sitting upon a chair near my feet, while at my head stood a light-haired, pleasant-looking little woman, attired for the levee of Morpheus, and just recovering from the attitude she had taken when saluting me.

"Hosea Waters," ejaculated the little woman, looking very intently into my eyes, "it's a boy!"

I have since had reason to believe that my other features, all blurred with smoke as they were, had suggested to her only an indefinite abstraction of humanity, both idea and distinction of sex having come to her simultaneously with the raising of my eyelids.

Mr. Waters nodded approvingly, and deftly snuffed the candle with his fingers. "All right, my tulip," said he, with floral grace; and there was a pride of property in the look he gave her which taught me instinctively that she was his wife.

"To think of such a little young thing being alone in a house afire, with such a creature!" she pityingly soliloquized, gently pushing my hair back from my forehead with her hand. "Lay still, dear, you're safe now."

I had attempted to rise; not in fear at all, for I felt safe enough now; but from a precocious sensation of awkwardness at reclining in the presence of strangers.

"Where is your father, my dear?"

"He lives way over there!" answered I, pointing over the back of the sofa in the direction of a window.

"What is your name?"

"Avery Glibun."

She saw that I was growing uneasy under her questions, and put the next one stooping smilingly beside me.

"And where is your mother, my dear?"

"She was putted into the ground," said I, with a memory of a steepled van, and a procession of carriages before me.

The little woman placed a plump arm around my neck, and, as she kissed me and for a moment pressed me to her, my young heart caught a glimpse of a new sympathy; an intuitive consciousness of something deep being kindly stirred. For, as I subsequently discovered, she had been mother to a little one, who, like a cry from God entering one ear of the world and passing out at the other, had died with the night of birth.

Mr. Waters took such an interest in this demonstration, that he permitted the candlestick in his hand to assume an angle in range of his chin, when the sensation and smell of burning whiskers produced a quick reaction. "Come," said he, rising to his feet, while a distant bell sounded from the street; "it's two now, by the watch-house clock, old woman, and we'd' better be getting some sleep; for I've got to be at the shop by seven, you know. Let young brass-buttons sleep on the sofa, there, and we'll leave our door open. Come."

Placing his fire-cap upon the mantel-piece under the picture, so that I could see it from where I lay, and pointing to it as though to assure me that my contemplation of such an object must naturally be a source of great comfort to me, he placed the candlestick upon the chair he had vacated, nodded pleasantly to me, and passed through a door leading into an adjoining room.

"I'll be back in a moment, pet," said the little woman, as she softly followed him.

Immediately reappearing, with several quilts and a blanket in her arms, she proceeded very expertly to convert me on the sofa into a child in a snug bed, and I presently found myself confounding her with Elfie, and feeling very much at home.

"Now go to sleep," said she, "like a good boy, and I'll leave the candle until you do so. That's my room, right over there, and I'll leave the door part way open; so you needn't be afraid. Now kiss me, dear."

I turned my mouth full towards her this time, for I already liked her very much; but hardly had her lips touched mine when she drew quickly back.

"Who gave you laudanum?" she asked.

I only looked at her in a startled way.

"Well," said she; "no matter about it to-night," and kissed me thoughtfully on my cheek.

"Now say your prayers, dear, and go right to sleep. Good-night."

She moved noiselessly into the other room, and I was half-minded to cry, and feel afraid at being left alone; but, as my roving eyes gradually took in the whole apartment, with its spotless walls and ceiling, its clean striped carpet, and simple furniture; its picture over the mantel, showing like some sort of map now that the light was right under it; the cylinder stove, and the ticking of a clock sounding from the next room, —all these things had something so peaceful about them, that they quieted me before I knew it. Upon one thing, however, I was resolved: she was coming after the candle when I had gone to sleep, and I was resolved, therefore, not to go to sleep at all. Filled with that resolution, I fixed my gaze with great intensity upon the candle, and awoke at sunrise precisely, next morning.

Wonderful changes had been effected in the mean time. A fire was crackling briskly away in the stove, a little square table, all spread for a meal, stood in the centre of the room, and, by the tender, early light coming in through the muslin-curtained windows, of which there were two, I could see Mrs. Waters adjusting a teakettle on the top of the cylinder. She was dressed so plainly that she looked even prettier than before.

As I stirred, she turned her full face my way, and smiled a good-morning.

"Want to get up?" she asked.

"Yessum," said I, timidly.

She came over and helped extricate me from the bed-clothing, kissing me as I stepped upon the floor, and turning me to the light, so that she could examine the clothing I had on.

"Why!" said she; "brass buttons; and what a nice coat!"

I fingered the buttons, and looked at her from the corners of my eyes with that ingenuous bashfulness which is believed to indicate excess of childish innocence.

"Who made such a nice coat for you?" she asked, stooping to inspect the sewing.

"Nobody didn't make it; but Elfie bought it for me," I replied, without a presentiment of Lindley Murray.

"Is Elfie your sister?"

"No'm; she's my nurse."

She turned the lower edge of my jacket outward and inward upon her forefinger a few times, and then asked, —

"Did Elfie take you to that old warehouse, where Mr. Waters found you last night?"

"No'm," said I, very positively; "nobody didn't take me there; but I woke up and saw the man."

After this reply she gave a few turns to the edge of my jacket again, and finally brought very noiselessly from the other room a wet towel and a comb.

"Let me fix you for breakfast," she said, in a motherly tone, and soon I was freshened and combed into something like my tidier self. Then she looked closely at my face again, kissed me once more, and told me to look at the picture on the wall, while she got the fish ready.

The work of art in question represented a very long-legged company of military-looking firemen allowing their machine to follow them down a glorified street of nothing but churches and domed palaces, while the entire sky overhead was of that red-hot tint which realizes the very ideal of a popular conflagration. The picture gave me great satisfaction by its high colors, and I was dwelling fondly upon the figure of the fireman, who seemed to be pressing a bright yellow trumpet with both hands to his lips, as a last desperate means of escaping an imminent fall upon his face, when Mr. Waters arrived safely from bed.

"Well, young three-foot," roared Mr. Waters, in a tempest of amiability, "how are you now?" and he at once took my weight upon the sides of his hands by lifting me unceremoniously in the air by my arm-pits.

"Milly, old woman," he continued, "let the banquet be served."

Mrs. Waters promptly served him with a kiss, by way of a relish, and then dished the mackerel, whose odorous smoke had for some moments lain heavy on my lungs. There were a chair and plate for me, and we all sat down to a meal which might be eaten with a knife without overturning society.

"Now, Hosea," said the little woman, after the first emotions were over, "you must tell me what to do, you know, while you are away."

"You jest lay low," responded Mr. Waters, with an air of conversing on some extremely private family matter quite unknown to me,—"you jest lay low and see if anything comes up."

As this sounded like a scientific direction for some kind of gardening, I was about to make inquiries as to what was most likely to come up, when Mr. Waters checked me by throwing himself very far back in his chair, and looking regretfully from me to his wife.

"Ah-h!" sighed Mr. Waters, abstractedly loosening the upper button of his gray cloth vest, "if ourn had only a lived, he'd be about four inches taller than him."

Milly put down her teacup and looked at me very sadly.

"I always intended that fine, scrumptious boy for the Department," resumed Mr. Waters, in deep affliction. "I intended him to carry a trumpet in the Department, and be a credit to that Department. He should a made the machine, which is the pride of our lives. so much immortal that nothing in the Department could a been more bilious. Methinks I see him now, a sittin'—on the reel—at par-a-a-de!"

Here Mr. Waters' lower lip twitched so that he could say no more just then, and he wrinkled his forehead so severely, to keep something back, that I was quite frightened at him; while Milly held the skirt of her dress to her eyes, and suffered her spoon to fall upon the floor.

"But this here's downright weakness, you know," said Mr. Waters, leaving his chair with a boisterousness much too demonstrative to be real. "We'll make young three-foot think that we're a couple of play-actors. I must be off, too, old woman; so here's a go."

He kissed her on top of her head. for she still kept her face covered, patted me on the arm as he passed to the door. and then I heard him going downstairs very slowly.

The little woman remained behind her skirt until I began to writhe upon my chair, and then cast it away from her and started up as though suddenly called to some pressing duty. Bidding me go to one of the windows and see if I could find the milkman, she commenced to clear away the table very briskly; and as I discovered that she had no inclination to talk, it was only left for me to obey her direction.

Toddling to the nearest window, and climbing into a cane-bottomed chair thereat, I was enabled to look down into a narrow and not very clean street, near the centre of which a dreadfully thin and tattered old woman, with a great bag on her back, was gleaning with an iron hook for rags. It was quite amazing to see the expertness with which she whipped each fresh capture into her bag without so much as looking up, and I had cultivated quite an admiration for her, when my attention was attracted to a milkman who had just driven up to a house on the other side of the way, and was uttering his shrill call in great enjoyment of his own voice. A woman, who wore her sleeves rolled to her elbows, and carried a white pitcher in her hands, appeared as by magic on the edge of the curb beside the wagon; and as the milkman dipped the milk from one of the tall tin cans between his knees and the horse, he evidently made some humorous remark; for she looked up at him from under one of her hands and laughed. Satisfied that he had produced an impression and given good measure, the milkman drove dashingly away, leaving the reins loose upon the cans for a step or two, as though to assure the whole block that there was much gentlemanly ease about such a business as his. The woman, with her pitcher between her hands, stood looking rather vacantly after him, until the violent tapping of a hand, which seemed to grow out of a muslin curtain, on a pane in the basement window behind her, made her retreat precipitately down an area and under a front stoop. From the point where she disappeared. I ran my eye up the front of the house to the roof, where a pair of old-maidish dormer-windows stuck out like a couple of monstrous bonnets. Then I looked at the houses on either side, which were just like the first one; and then I looked down to the walk again, where a fat little boy, with checkered sleeves over his coat-arms, and a basket of meat swinging under one of his elbows, was leaning against an area railing, deeply absorbed in the study of a family breakfasting in the basement below him. While he thus attained some knowledge of life, there came along a boy of the same description, but one size larger in all his departments, who was suddenly stricken with a staggering affection and reeled heavily against him. This produced a face-to-face match of an animated character, the parties taking turns in crowding each other around in half circles and mingling bitter sneers.

I was watching them very intently, when the voice of Milly made me turn my head; and when I looked again both boys had vanished.

"Here. Avery," said Milly, "come and look at the pictures in this pretty book, on the sofa."

She had brought a large, leather-bound

volume from the back room, and, as it proved to be a Bible full of pictures, I was soon engaged in exploring its leaves. Between this book and the window I spent several hours, the little woman working about me from one department to the other, and promising to tell me about the pictures as soon as she sat down to her sewing. The latter she was finally preparing to do, when a bell tinkled somewhere downstairs, and presently we heard some one coming up. Next came a knock at the door, which Milly opened half-way, and I heard a familiar voice say, —

"Good-morning, madam. The woman downstairs informed me that a fireman named Waters occupied these rooms."

"Mr. Waters is my husband, sir," answered Milly; "but he is not at home now. Won't you walk in?"

She opened the door more widely, and before I could make up my mind whether to hide behind the sofa or not, my father had entered and seized me by the arm.

"I have found you at last, have I?" he said, with a sternness that made me cower. "I beg your pardon, madam, but this is my son; my name is Glibun."

"He has been a very good boy," replied Milly, evidently not knowing just what to say.

"He was stolen or ran away from his home during my temporary absence," continued my father, still retaining his hold on me, "and upon almost the first move of the police this morning, at my instigation, it was discovered that a well-dressed child was saved from a burning building last night by some fireman, who proved, upon inquiry, to be your husband. I hardly expected to find the child here; but, since he is here, perhaps you can tell me under what circumstances your husband chanced to discover him."

"Well, sir," said Milly, "it was at an old warehouse on some dock, where the fire was, and my husband says that he found the child upstairs in one of the rooms, just as the fire was getting hottest. He carried him down the ladder and put him on the engine until the fire was out, and then brought him home here."

"Was nobody with him? Whose warehouse was it?" asked my father, biting the rim of his hat and looking fixedly at her.

"My husband said, sir, that the warehouse is not used by any one at this time of year, and there was nobody with the child. Oh! I do recollect now, though, that my husband spoke about seeing a rough-looking man jumping out of a back window into the river, just as the roof fell. Have you any idea, sir, how the little boy could have got into such a place as that?"

"Who took you there, sir?" asked my father, holding me off from him so that he could see my face.

"Nobody didn't take me there," said I, beginning to cry and feel very miserable; "I woke up there."

"I shall, of course, find out all about it on my return home," observed my father to Milly; "and now, madam, what is the sum of my indebtedness to you and your husband for your kindness to my son?"

"Nothing! sir!" came like a shot from Milly.

"But I must insist. You have had much trouble, and perhaps some expense."

"Let the little boy come to see me sometimes with his nurse, — that's all we ask," responded Mrs. Waters, very shortly.

"That he shall certainly do," assented my father. "Come, sir, you must go home with me."

He did not free my arm, even when Milly stooped to kiss me, and I had barely time to note that she had immediately turned and gone into the other room, when I was half hoisted, half dragged downstairs and bundled into a cab at the front door.

"Where's your cap, sir?" asked my father, as he took a seat beside me, and the vehicle drove off.

I don't know what answer I made; but I do know that his glittering gold watch-chain, with which I had never been permitted to play, seemed to my infant eyes the insignia of a power to be dreaded rather than loved.

<hr>

CHAPTER III.

MY FATHER DOES HIS DUTY AS A PARENT.

THE driver of the cab was also the proprietor of a carriage, with which he frequently called for my father just after nightfall. Hence, we knew each other by sight; for often had I befogged a certain pane of glass in one of our basement windows with staring at him by the half hour, as he paced reflectively to and fro upon the sidewalk, in waiting for his patron. To this day I am utterly uncertain as to what his age was; whether he was a young man rendered prematurely serious by reverses in horse-flesh, or a middle-aged person with a past experience to hold him in perpetual reverie. A black velvet cap drawn far down over his ears, and a grey scarf wound far up his chin, were among the devices with which he defied chronological speculation at every season of the year; and the fact that he transacted his entire business with my father, so far as observed, with coughs graduated to all the degrees of inquiry, and nods adapted to all the shades of intelligent assent, would have established his reputation as a phenomenon of immaculate speechlessness, but for the qualifying legend of an actual conversation he had once held with me. Early one summer evening, when I had climbed through the opened basement window into the front area, and was taking a nearer view of this profoundly thoughtful man, our cook suddenly presented her head and bust in the casement behind me, and desired me to come in. I was trying to obey her by climbing in backwards, — for I could not bear to lose sight for an instant of one in whom my interest had become absorbing,—when he unexpectedly diverged from his usual walk at an acute angle, and came directly to the area railings. His hands were in his pockets, his whip was under his right arm, and a voice of fabulous hoarseness said to me, —

"Is that one married?"

In dense confusion I hazarded the random response, —

"I b'lieve so."

There came a muffled sigh as from under several layers of woollen goods, and the voice said, —

"They're all so."

After which the owner of the voice gave a thoughtful look skyward, as though that was the only place, after all, and moved heavily back to the curb.

From thenceforth, however, there was an understanding between us; and the familiarity of past associations might have been cited as his justification for making sounds upon his box, on the way home, as of an infant being severely chastised, and otherwise conveying to me within the cab his conception of the penal incident likely to occur in my immediate future.

Not a word spoke my father in all the ride; but from time to time he brushed down his black mustache between his lips, and looked at me, sitting, or crouching, opposite, in a way which made me feel, somehow, as though I were being sternly considered in a position altogether apart from the present one.

The cab had crossed Broadway, and rattled and bounced through one street and another, until it finally stopped before the door of the house known to me as home. Descending from his lofty seat, with a red pocket-handkerchief, curiously knotted, between his teeth, the driver leisurely ascended the stoop and rang the bell. Returning to the cab, he opened the door for our exit, and, as we ascended the stoop, I noticed that he had laid his knotted handkerchief across the palm of one hand in the likeness of a goblin babe, and was applying the other to it in a series of soundless slaps not to be misconstrued.

Dear old cook answered the bell, and was not to be deterred from clasping me immediately to her ample chest, and exclaiming, —

"Ah, then, you've found him, sir, as I was hoping; and not hurted, either. Where was it you strayed to, Master Avery, that myself and Mrs. Elfie were next door to thinkin' yon'd been stolen? And where's the cap of the child —"

"There, Mrs. Fry, that is enough, if you please," said my father, hanging his hat upon the mahogany stand in the hall. "Is Mistress Elfie in?"

"She's up in her own room, sir."

"Be good enough, then, Mrs. Fry, to let her know that I have found this runaway boy again, and that I desire to see her for a few moments in the back parlor, on business."

"Yes, sir," answered cook, relapsing into her usual helpless awe at the sound of that cold, supercilious, unimpassioned voice.

I started to follow her upstairs; but his hand arrested me at the first step.

"I want you with me, sir, for a few moments."

He led me into the back parlor, pointed to a sofa between the door and a window, and then turned the inside blinds of the latter so that the light should fall upon me and upon the door. Between an oak sideboard and the chimney on the opposite side of the room was a large haircloth arm-chair, which he drew to a position near the grate fire, where its occupant would be partly in shadow. He had lifted another chair, of the ordinary sort, and was bringing it toward where I sat, when there came a knock at the door.

"Open it, sir," said he to me.

Tremblingly I obeyed, and Elfie came quickly past me into the room. I had thought she would take me in her arms and carry me straight away from him; I had thought she would hug and kiss me, and be crazy to hear about the man in the House that Jack built, and all the other strange things; but she passed me by without a look, and went straight to where my father was standing. He bowed, and placed the chair for her; but she neither returned the salutation nor seated herself. Motionless she stood where she had paused at the moment; her face rigid and colorless; her pale-yellow hair looking almost as white, in the rays pouring over her from the window; and her tall, stately form instinctive with a defiant dignity in its drapery of lustreless black.

"Well?" she said, very sharply.

"Won't you be seated, madam?" asked my father.

"Well?"

She did not move a muscle. The word had the lightning of passion in it, and seemed to come from her eyes rather than from her lips.

"If you will not take a seat, madam," said my father, coolly, "perhaps you will pardon me for not following your example, as I am rather tired."

He deliberately seated himself in the arm-chair by the fire, brought his hands together under his chin, and, with his great, dark eyes fixed upon her face, continued, —

"It is useless for me to tell you, madam, that the recent disappearance from home of my son there, is not such a mystery to me as it might have been to another parent. Here he is again, you perceive. I flatter myself that my measures for his recovery have not indicated on my part any of that frenzied apprehension or hasty alarm which might possibly be natural in a person wholly unprepared for such an exigency. I have not asked the boy to tell me anything. I have not asked him to explain how he — my son — chanced to be in a deserted warehouse at the dead of night; nor how it happened that I found him this morning in charge of a common fireman's wife."

Ellie started, and a deep flush passed over her face. I put my right hand in one of hers, and she squeezed it spasmodically, and held it.

"I have no wish," continued my father. "to know the details of the affair. It is enough for me to thoroughly understand its entire meaning, to clearly comprehend its instigating purpose, and to be capable of readily identifying the hand whose cunning would forget every obligation of trust and gratitude, to make me childless."

The tears of a woman are either prayers or curses, and those which now wet Ellie's cheeks were one or the other.

"You speak of trust, of gratitude!" she said, in a suppressed voice, bending slightly toward him. "Are human trust and human gratitude, at their best, superior to all that is sacred and holy toward the Almighty? If *you* know so much, do not *I*, also. know something? Do *I* not know — God help me! — what you would do with this motherless child? Do I not know —"

"The child is present, madam," interrupted my father, rising from his chair, as though he would send me from the room; "surely you forget yourself."

"Let him stay!" she ejaculated, waving him off and drawing me closer to her; "let him stay! I shall be calmer if he is here; I will not hear you without him. He reminds me of all the good there is in me, and you of all the bad!"

She fell upon her knees beside me on the carpet, and pressed me to her throbbing heart in a transport of uncontrollable grief. "My darling, my darling," she sobbed, "you will never believe anything wrong of me, will you?"

Suddenly her arms dropped from me, and she arose to her feet, at a touch from my father's jewelled hand. There was an expression, almost smiling, on his darkly-handsome face, which held her spellbound.

"Is it a kindness to the boy to make me hate him?" he asked, very slowly. "Is it a kindness to the boy to place him before me in such a light, that when you leave him — as leave him you must! — he will be odious to my sight? Ellie, that boy is mine. This house is his home. My wishes and my will must control him; and whoever comes between those wishes and that will and their object — whether man or woman — must go down!"

She looked straight at him now, breathing heavily through her dilated nostrils; and, although her face was flushed, her lips were like ashes.

"Yes!" she said, throwing a whole breath into the word, and clutching the hand I had again placed in one of hers. "Your will! I know what it is, — who should know better? I am not weak, and it has been a relentless tyrant to me; he is but a child, and it will be the destroyer of his soul. You know it! — as you stand there so calm and smiling, you know it!"

"Madam," — his tone was clear and unemotional as that of a silver bell, — "the time has passed when you and I could discuss that topic to any useful end. Whatever I have been, or may be, to others, to you I have ever been, or tried to be, a friend. In so far as you have trusted me, I have proved no traitor. To your care I gave my dying wife;" — here my father paused for a moment; — "to your care I have hitherto confided my only child. My house has been free to you as your own home; you have commanded here; and yet (such have been my precautions) no breath of calumny has assailed you under this roof. I do not speak boastfully of performing obligations which the chivalrous instinct of any gentleman must suggest as due from the most illustrious of his sex to the lowliest of yours; but it seems necessary to remind you that I have at least given you no provocation for an enmity which should deliberately seek to deprive me of my own flesh and blood."

Again she sank upon her knees; but this time her arms were not for me; she extended them toward him,.as he stood there to torture her with his sinister and studied words, and her hands were clasped in supplication.

"Forgive me! I have acted wildly, foolishly, not knowing what I did, and I ask you what I have never dared to ask Heaven, — forgive me!"

He breathed upon a brilliant diamond which flashed from a ring on one of his fingers, and did not even look at her.

"Do you see me here on my knees to you?" she said, in a voice so harshly unlike her own that I shrank from her in terror. "Do you hear me, man? I say I have acted madly and would be forgiven. Do not make me leave this child. Trust me once more; put me to any test; I ask, I *beg* of you."

"Madam," came the measured response from the lips above the diamond, "where I have been once deceived, I never trust again."

That taunt, of all others, is the one which no living woman can hear from man, without realizing that there is a devil in her. Whether it comes as a despairing imputation upon the unswerving truth which she knows to be hers, or bursts upon her as an accusation made hourly familiar in her own conscience, there is a maddening lash in it which reaches down to the very quick of that deathless woman-instinct which knows no modifying circumstance, and draws blood to the eye and murder to the heart.

Springing to her feet like a tigress under a blow, her blue eyes scintillant with passion, her thin nostrils dilating and contracting, and her hands tearing into her heaving breast, the kneeling supplicant of a moment before advanced with one fierce stride upon her judge, and *made* him look at her.

For a moment, as they stood thus closely face to face, there was a startled look in his eye as though his heart might be hastening its pace under a coward sensation. It was only for a moment, however; and then over all his features deepened an expression of concentrated and despotic command, to make innocence shrink beneath a greater steadfastness, and guilt cower before a darker daring.

I saw the woman sinking under it like some broken, withered thing; I saw her put out her hands as though to ward off some yet-to-be-spoken reproach, and then bow her head between them and burst into a piteous, helpless wail.

My father smiled into his former self again, at her first sob, breathed once more upon his diamond, led her by an elbow to the chair he had placed for her at first, and stood looking down upon her bowed head without the slightest sign of emotion.

"Elfie," he said, "I would spare you if I could in justice do so; but I must perform my duty as a parent. Since you have such an inordinate liking for the boy, I will not say that you shall never see him again. Indeed, you will probably see much of him some day or other, and I would have you take the spirit I am now compelled to display regarding him, as a guide for yourself then. I shall place him temporarily in charge of Mrs. Fry, and, at the same time, keep such an eye over him myself as will prevent any further adventures with firemen. He is old enough now to be out of nursery leading-strings, and your departure need cause no particular comment amongst those who chance to notice it. I will try to think that you were indeed mad, as you say, when you undertook to perpetrate the astounding folly just frustrated, and you must not go away thinking that I have any permanent anger against you. Such is not the case. I shall always remember how much I am in your debt for the past, and feel honored to call myself your very good friend. No more need be said, I think, on the subject."

"Has Elfie got to go 'way?" I asked, speaking for the first time since my return home.

My father seemed unconscious that I had spoken at all, and Elfie raised her head only to look vacantly toward the door.

"You are right, sir," she said, in a listless, weary way, — "yes, very right. It is certainly for the best that I should leave this house at once — at once. I will go soon. I will go to-day."

She arose from the chair, and moved in the direction of the door, like one walking in a dream. My father stepped before her, opened the door, and bowed. She paused on the sill, glanced earnestly at me for a moment, and then threw back her head impatiently.

"Why," said she, turning half toward him, but addressing herself to something above her, "why should I fear for myself, or for anything that I love, now? Why should I not disobey him?"

Their eyes met again. His had the glitter of steel in them, and his upper lip worked curiously upon his gleaming teeth.

"Because you dare not!"

Her head drooped at the sound; she moved slowly into the hall, and he stood staring after her with that look upon his face until we heard the door of her own room upstairs close upon her. He touched a bell-pull on the wall, and cook quickly made her appearance, in great trepidation.

"Mrs. Fry," said my father, "Mistress Elfie, the nurse, is obliged to return unexpectedly to her family, and I must confide Master Avery to your especial care until I can make suitable disposition of him. He seems to be so valuable that people are ready to steal him, and I must caution you to keep him always in sight. Do this faithfully for a short time, and do not permit your assistant to gossip about this matter of his being lost. It will be as well, also, for you not to let him say a word about it himself from this time forth. You hear what I say, sir? Now take him downstairs with you."

The kind-hearted cook trembled very perceptibly as she led me to the kitchen stairs, down which we had not progressed very far when the front door closed after my parent.

In the kitchen we found Mrs. Fry's assistant, a rather slouchy young girl with weak blue eyes, reddish locks, a frock chronically flapping open behind her uneasy shoulders, and a habit of walking which cook not unfrequently described as "scuffling." Her nature was not exactly an emotional one; in fact, she possessed an equanimity of disposition alike significant of an incorrigibly philosophical mind, and of no mind at all; but, upon catching sight of me, as I was led in by Mrs. Fry, she exclaimed, "Oh, good gracious!" and let fall into the water a dish she was washing.

"Now just see here you!" cried Mrs. Fry, leaving me and pouncing upon her. "there's nothing to be said about it; and if you go to hystericking over the recent denoument, there's a certain person — I will not say whom — will wreak his vengeance into the very kitchen, even."

"Oh, good gracious! Is it anything like that one about 'The Nobleman's Vow,' or 'The 'Sassinated Hair,' ma'am?" asked the young woman, gazing askance at me.

"Does the Hair look as though he was 'sassinated, you poor, half-witted creature?" queried cook, contemptuously. "Isn't he back again in the halls of his ann-sisters, and without his entail cut off?"

"Oh, good gracious, yes!"

"Well, then, don't be talkin' like a false caitiff," added Mrs. Fry, impatiently; "but go sweep the basement and keep a palsied tongue in your head. The mystery is not for the likes of us to solve; and we're forbid to open our mouths about it."

The false caitiff seemed to understand this speech to the full extent of its subtlest meaning; for she responded to it by promptly taking down a broom from beside the dresser, and "scuffling" thoughtfully away into the front basement.

By this time I was sprawled on the floor, by the range, fondling my old friend, the cat, and cook felt it incumbent upon her to round a period for my especial instruction before resuming her interrupted work.

"Master Avy," said she, pointing in the direction of upstairs, with a saucepan, "what's past cannot be remedied; but the future is before us, when the wrong shall be righted, as will be shown in our coming chapters. Myself and others have got our orders to say nothing about where you've been the while; and you've got your orders, from one whom I won't name, to tell no tales. So ask me no questions and tell me no adventures, for fear of the vengeance of them that can see through stone walls and hear through dungeon doors."

"Can he hear away down here?" asked I, perfectly comprehending her reference.

"Oh, to be sure, dear, he can."

"But he couldn't if we was in the cellar, could he?"

"Every word and whisper," responded cook very emphatically.

This assurance only added to the unspeakable awe I already felt toward my father, and effectually frightened all thoughts of seeking a confidant out of my brain.

It was about an hour after this when cook's young girl returned from an excursion upstairs, to inform me that Mrs. Elfie wanted me in the front hall. "And oh, good gracious! she's going away, ma'am," added she, in feeble bewilderment.

Mrs. Fry was in the middle of an indignant rebuke to this further effort of her subordinate to interfere with the interdicted mystery, when I slipped past her to the entry-way, and hastened up, on all-fours, to the hall.

Near the street door, with her hat and shawl on, and a carpet-bag in one of her hands, stood Elfie, apparently undecided whether to turn the knob at once, or to wait inside for something.

I ran to her with my little arms outspread, and she dropped the carpet-bag, and stooped to me with arms to meet mine.

"Dear, dear, dear child!" she exclaimed, passionately embracing and kissing me; "you won't forget Elfie when she's gone away?"

"No!" answered I, manfully; and immediately added, "but I won't like father, though, for making you cry so, and sending you away."

"Hush, darling!" she whispered, kissing me again; "you must not speak so of your father. He has done right, my pet, and you must honor him and obey him, no matter what he does. You are too young to understand all you see and hear, and if you love poor Elfie, you will be a good boy to your father. You do love me, — don't you?"

She put a hand upon my forehead as she asked this question, and looked mournfully and anxiously into my face.

I could only reply with a nod and a whimper; for I now began fully to realize, for the first time, that she was actually going to leave me.

"You love me enough to answer me one question, and never tell anybody in the world that I asked it?"

Another nod from me.

"Avy, my precious boy," she said, close to my ear, "where is that cloak of mine, — the one, I mean, that I always fold so carefully and put under your head, between the beds, every night?"

She spoke in an awkward, uncertain way, not usual to her, and for a moment I was bewildered. Then, like a flash, came a consciousness of what she meant.

"Why," said I, all vivacity at once, "it was on the bed in the House that Jack built!"

"And where — where is it now?" she asked hurriedly, unconsciously clutching my neck with one hand, and pressing the other upon her heart. "Tell me at once, child! where is it?"

"The man took it," answered I, in some alarm.

"Are you sure of that, child? Are you sure the people in that fireman's house didn't have it?"

I was sure of that, and told her so.

For some minutes she smoothed my hair and seemed lost in thought. Then my head was drawn close to her shoulder, and her cheek pressed upon mine, as she softly and distinctly uttered these words, —

"Avy, I am sorry to leave you, but know it is for the best; and when you are older you also will know that it was for the best. I have tried to be kind to you, and you, again, will better understand that kindness when you are older. If I have ever said anything to make you think your father an unkind man, — and I don't remember having done so, — you must believe that I was naughty in such talk, and should have been ashamed of myself. Only obey him in everything, and keep away from his room except when he sends for you, and he will treat you well. If you are good, I shall see you again, some day, as he says. He must think a great deal of you, because you are his child; and if he ever looks crossly at you, or does not answer you when you speak to him, it is all for your good."

She paused an instant, drew a heavy sigh, and went on, —

"Take down some of those nice books from my old room, and get Mrs. Fry to read them for you, as I have done. Don't let her read her foolish papers to you, but ask her to read about the fairies in your books. She is a very kind woman, and I shouldn't wonder if she would be willing to help you on, too, with your spelling and multiplication-table. If *any one*, no matter who, — remember, my dear, any one, — should ask you, even in the street, where Elfie has gone, say that I have gone home —"

"Aint this your home, Elfie?" I suddenly asked, in greater surprise and confusion of mind than can be described.

"Say that I have gone home; that is all. Now give a good-by to Mrs. Fry and the girl for me. It's all I have to leave them. Kiss me once more, dear, and God bless you, may — God — bless — you!"

The benediction was uttered in a kind of moaning voice, and, as it ended, the speaker stood upright, and turned from me to recover the carpet-bag. After that, too, she kept her back toward me; and when I helplessly sought to take her disengaged hand, she drew it away from me, placed it against the door, and bowed her head upon it.

It has since occurred to me that she may have felt in that moment an unanticipated sense of some turn in her destiny, more ominous than the mere suggestion of her present situation. She may have felt a presentiment of something before her, from which she would gladly have turned had she but known just how it took its growth from the house she was leaving.

"Elfie," said I, timidly, "mayn't I go with you, too?"

Without answering, she straightened herself impatiently, opened the door, and would probably have fled with all speed, had not her carpet-bag been dexterously spirited from her hand at the instant, and carried gravely down the steps to a cab at the curb. The deed had been achieved by one who wore a velvet cap on his head and a gray scarf about his chin, and who now stood holding open the door of his vehicle as though nothing could be more natural and usual in the world than for my nurse to take an airing at that particular hour of the day. Whether he had been there ever since bringing home his employer and me, or had come freshly by a mysterious appointment, none other than himself, or his master, perhaps, could say.

Elfie started at the sight, and irresolutely stepped back a pace or two; but in the next moment she pulled down her veil and walked directly to the cab. The stolid driver made sure that she had taken a seat, and thereupon mounted to *his* seat without a word. Intuitively, or from the instructions of some invisible mentor, he evidently knew whither to convey his lonely passenger.

So she left me; never looking back after giving me God's blessing. Heedless of the cold air, and careless that the door had blown-shut behind me, I sat miserably down upon the stone steps, and cried bitterly; for, neglected and desolate as my whole young life thus far had been, there fell upon me, as the cab rolled away, the chill of a sterner neglect, a deeper desolation.

CHAPTER IV.

The house in which my earliest years were spent is still standing, and as the worthy piano-forte-maker now occupying it with his family may be fully satisfied with such fame of residence as accrues from honorable note in Mr. Trow's Directory, I will omit mention of both its street and its number. I may state, however, that it presented, and still presents, a complacent countenance of brick to the street, and was considered pretty well up-town in those days. Starting from a substantial foothold of basement and kitchen, half above and half below the level of the outer pavement, it discovered two parlors and a hall at the first ascent; two large and two small rooms above those; and finally went to exhaustion in two dormer bedrooms and an open loft over all. Its front windows, excepting those of the basement, were always covered with shutters, giving it a folded-arms and closed-eyes sort of aspect, expressive, so to speak, of lethargic resignation under neglect; and the very pigeons, occasionally parading on the peak of its precipitous slate roof, assumed a magisterial gravity of demeanor quite depressing to behold.

As I look back to my days passed there, and fancy myself once more perched on a bench at Elfie's knee, in her room on the second floor, listening eagerly to her as she reads aloud to me from "Kris Kringle's Tales," or some more advanced story-book, a bell tinkles sharply in a lower hall, and we discard the book and adjourn to the stair-landing outside, on a mission of inspection. Mrs. Fry, or the girl, is opening the door, and a voice, which is neither gentle nor harsh, utters some brief remark in apparent accompaniment of a polite nod of recognition. The door is closed, the servant returns noiselessly to the kitchen, and a series of measured footfalls ends upon the heavy carpet of the back parlor. My father is at home. He has been away a week, perhaps two weeks; for his returns are very irregular and never by specific appointment; but now, at any rate, he is in the house, and my nurse and I go back to our room with very little taste for further reading. Had my father brought two or three elegant-looking gentlemen home with him in the carriage, as he sometimes did, we should feel more at ease; for then there would be dining and wining downstairs until midnight, and we should be left entirely to ourselves; but, as he is alone, this time, we know what will come next. It does come pretty quickly, in the shape of a stereotyped message by the girl, —

"If you please, ma'am, the master sends his compliments, and you and Master Avy will take dinner with him."

The books are summarily put away upon their shelf over the open fireplace, my nurse washes and brushes me in blank silence, and I experience a fear of speaking, which the mere knowledge of that back parlor having an occupant is always sufficient to give me. At last I am properly primmed, Ellie has impatiently smoothed her yellow hair and donned new cuffs and collar, and at a summons of the girl we finally repair dismally (on my part) to the presence.

An oblong table laid for three stands in the centre of the room, and, although the opening of blinds and shutters at the two windows would admit quite enough light for the meal, a couple of wax candles, in tall silver sticks, burn whitely at either end of the board and illumine a handsome array of gilt china and substantial silver.

As we enter, my father arises from his arm-chair by the mantel, and greets me with a "Well, sir," and Ellie with a stately bow. Two fingers of his right hand are given me to shake,—one of them sparkling with a solitaire in black enamel, which is supposed to be an inconsolable widower's badge of mourning,—and a hope that her health continues good is courteously addressed to my nurse. She replies, "Oh, I am always well, sir!" and does not appear to feel at ease until Mrs. Fry and the girl bring in the soup and claret, and we take our seats at the table. My father presides at the head, and we two face each other at the sides; and I, in my uncomfortable confusion of spirit, am very likely to at once start the conversation by making a noise with my soup, or curiously entangling my elbow with my spoon until the latter falls to the floor.

"Master Avery," my father says (he generally addresses me thus), "is that behaving like a gentleman, sir?"

A glow of guilt pervades my whole physical system, and I am disposed of for the meal.

Ellie darts an indignant look at him, which he is sure to meet with a pleasant smile, and then he goes through the regular form of offering her the claret and begging her to excuse *him* for the eccentricity of coloring his soup with it. Her stiff refusal of the offer produces another pleasant smile, and, like as not, a gossipy little discourse about the lighter foreign wines and their assimilating properties, in which he manages to display no small amount of curious information. As he talks on, in this sprightly style, about wine, or about anything else, Ellie's face gradually lights up with an expression of pleased interest, and by the time the meal is on she is questioning and answering with the greatest vivacity. I am permitted to blunder joylessly over my plate unnoticed, and find myself often wondering how Ellie can dare to talk and laugh in such a presence. Finally, coffee is served by the girl, whose last official act is to hand my father a decanter of brandy from the sideboard in the room and an exceedingly small glass. He knows from custom that he must drink this alone (the brandy, I mean), and waits until the coffee is gone before filling his glass. It is his signal that the sitting is finished, and he contrives to make it follow some grave topic which he has been discussing in low, musical tones,—a strong contrast to his tones and manner previously. Without losing the fixed and luminous gaze which he has thus magnetized to himself, he lifts the tiny glass chin-high, bows to Ellie, nods to me, and drinks.

This is our regular dismissal, and even I feel that there is something imperious and abrupt about it after the preceding genialities. I slip at once from my chair, Ellie and my father arise simultaneously from theirs, and we are escorted to the door, and dismissed with a bow of singular complacency.

My feelings upon leaving the back parlor on such occasions are always those of relief, blended with a certain nightmareish sensation of returning suddenly from evening into day. Somehow, I associate my father with the idea of Night, and have that same vague fear of him which children generally have of darkness.

We regain the room upstairs, and Ellie undertakes to read for me again until my bed hour; but the reading is listless, and I am so far from resuming my interest in it that I presently fall asleep on my bench. Then I am prepared for bed, and the process so thoroughly awakens me that I lie for some time quietly watching the movements of my nurse, who is so changed from her proper self that she pays no heed to me at all. She paces to and fro for a while, with her head down, and then stands for some moments by the window farthest from the bed, apparently looking out. I know that there is nothing to be seen there save a quadrangle of withered yards, bisected by cat-paths or fences, and I wonder what she can possibly see to interest her. Before I can settle that point in my own mind, she has turned suddenly to a small card-table in the corner, seated herself beside it, and is alternately writing upon and destroying bits of note-paper. By the light of a candle, which stands upon the table, I can see her face in profile, and it has just the look she gave my father when we were first at the table. Watching the face, I slowly go into a doze, from which I am partly roused, presently, by the creeping of an arm under my neck as she lies down beside me. So we both go to sleep.

In the morning all is right again, and the back parlor is vacant and unminded. We go down to our breakfast in the basement; I chatter and Ellie talks, and we no more mention the event of the day before than if it had been duplicate dreams, which each was bent upon keeping from the other. I take a lesson in spelling and primary arithmetic, from my nurse, and then go out on the walk in front of the house for a little while, to play with our neighbors' children. I can go half way to the corner of the block, in either direction; but not one step farther if I do not wish our young girl to come reprovingly upon me and convey me ignominiously in-doors for the day.

This young girl, by the way, is known to us as Sirrah, which may be either a corruption of Sarah, or an arbitrary application of a term very generously sprinkled through the favorite reading of her superior, Mrs. Fry.

Even now I laugh when I remember how ardently our plump and ever-amiable cook used to read the Sunday papers, and how fervently she took to heart all the surprising romances in those exciting sheets. She had a mania for such stentorian literature, superinduced, no doubt, by the long seclusion from society, incident to her veteran service with us; and not only did she firmly believe in it as a miraculously true reflection of the only sort of life worth living, but adopted many of its more striking phrases for her own conversational uses. For want of higher intellectual sympathy, she admitted the young girl to a share in her weekly banquet of aristocratic fiction; and, whether they jointly arrived at the conclusion that the frequent Sirrah was a general name for an indulged inferior, or whether the young girl's real name was Sarah, and she had passively accepted Sirrah (she was an orphan from the country) as the city reading of that appellative, she was certainly called Sirrah, from the first, by cook, and was thus known to the rest of us.

To go back again: these two are the familiars of our lowest floor, and it is in their department to see that I never go beyond a certain distance from the house, unless accompanied by one of them, or by my nurse. Nor are their other duties light; for it is a standing rule to have full dinners prepared every day, in order that my father may never go amiss in bringing friends home with him, nor ever fail to find a proper table for himself. This rule involves considerable expense and a greater waste; but there seems to be no stint of money for it, and mendicant seekers after cold victuals bless the days which first brought them to the most hospitable of basement doors.

I do not know what it is to have a mother. Lifie has told me, though, that I once had one, who died when I was but a few days old, and was carried away, to be put into the ground, in a shiny black van with little steeples on the top. A funeral procession passing the door is pointed out by way of illustration, and from thenceforth such processions have a particular interest for me, and I believe my mother to be the subject of each. Possessed of this idea, I have a dignified sense of superiority over all boys whose mothers are living, and not unfrequently experience an elevated sensation in observing to my playmates on the walk, as we all stand still to see some hearse and carriages pass by, "That's my mother in there."

As I look up the street, who is this that I see coming toward me, satchel in hand, on his way to school? It is Noah Trust, whose father (firm of Trust & Fayle) keeps a large grocery store on the nearest avenue, and whose pockets always abound in condemned almonds and questionable dried peaches. I find that I do not like Noah, and have, upon occasions, openly doubted his rather extravagant descriptions of the Malaga grapes, oranges, citron, and sugar crackers, which he represents to be fabulously plentiful in his house. He smells of brown sugar, too, and is reported to make a corrupt use of his almonds and peaches at school in procuring the solution of his sums by mercenary pencils.

That other boy, dodging behind the tree-box yonder, is Upton Knox, much celebrated for a precocious skill in pugilism, and believed to be equal to at least three public-school fighters. He is the champion of his own " Select School " around the corner, against any reasonable number of presuming publics, and is now on the watch for a butcher-boy of three times his size, whom he intends to insult and defeat for a wager of two apples. I have liked Upton ever since the day when he protected me from the insults of a great lout of a fellow, by threatening to " bring his fellers; " though I am to this day sceptical as to the existence of those " fellers " elsewhere than in a lively imagination.

An ice-wagon goes by, and there clings to its footboard a youth, in a full suit of pepper-and-salt, who wafts me a complicated salute, as he passes, in derision of the unconscious driver. He is Ben Beeton, whose father is a clergyman, and who is a favorite with all the boys. Ben is of an original turn of mind, his originality tending chiefly to the invention of novel amusements involving more or less peril of paternal wrath. He has caused more boys to come to extremities with their parents than any other lad of his age in the ward; yet the boys seem to like him all the better for it, thus resembling certain metaphysical soldiers, whose devotion to their general deepens with each overwhelming defeat he manages to blunder them into. By way of illustrating his originality, Ben Beeton once induced a whole school of little fellows to range themselves symmetrically on the curb, with their feet in a Croton-running gutter; and the after-clap was, that, from nearly every house on two adjoining blocks, that night there issued the sounds associated in the minds of all men with their very earliest reverses in life.

I am looking earnestly after Ben, as he rides gratuitously away, when something hits me stingingly upon the cheek. Instructed by past experience, I look directly across the street to the house facing our own, and detect a brown-haired head, and a section of green coat with pearl buttons, endeavoring to dive below the sill of an open window. Finding themselves discovered, the head and coat arise fully into view, accompanied by a hand carrying a long tin tube, through which pellets of paper can be dexterously puffed, to the utter surprise and mystification of all passers-by. The marksman is Gwin Le Mons, the best-loved of all my boy-acquaintances, and the lightest-hearted son of a widow, that ever knew how far a widow's might could go. There is good reason to believe that Gwin takes his daily castigation very much as other boys take their lunches, and would feel as much lost without it. Thus familiarized with affliction in his youth, he has, with all his irrepressible buoyancy of disposition, a certain softness and kindliness of manner not to be resisted, and I think so much of him that I am always tempting him to stay on my side of the way until he is sure of a flogging when he goes into the house. In this respect I am not greatly unlike some young men of a larger growth, in their friendships for chosen comrades.

Gwin Le Mons has a sister, about two years younger than himself, with curly hair, distracting pantalets, and a doll resembling an angel. It is needless to say that my whole heart is eternally hers, and that I am capable of distorting my frame into the most supernatural squirms of manliness, when I believe her to be covertly surveying me from the window. Her name is Constance, or Conny, or Con, according respectively to her mother, her playmates, and her brother; and even in his rendering of that delightful name, my luckless bosom friend contrives to earn for himself an extra misfortune. It is at the "Select School," which he attends with his angel-sister, that she finds the teacher's pencil upon the floor, and gives it to Gwin for conveyance to its owner. Conscious of an important mission, my bosom friend marches unceremoniously from his seat to the awful desk, and boldly says, —

"There's your pencil, sir; Con found it."

"WHAT?"

"It was on the floor, sir; Con found it."

Thereupon, my hapless bosom friend is whipped for swearing, and is audible some moments after in a passionate wish for death.

Gwin and I, with the other boys, have met together one day on our walk for some playful purpose, and are just wavering between the equally ingenious projects of encouraging a battle between Noah and Upton, and overturning an ash-barrel before a neighboring door, when my friend is suddenly reminded of a positive appointment, and starts briskly across the street. At the opposite curb he pauses, to shout, as cheerfully as possible; "Just wait a minute, boys; I've got to go in and get a whipping."

After a lapse of three minutes there is a sound of orthodox punishment; and then Gwin comes out to us again with his eyes full of tears, and proposes an all-handed game of Duck on a Rock.

How I regret to dismiss these few joyous memories of my boyish days, trifling and absurd as they seem! They are all I have left to remind me that I was once really a careless and play-loving boy, with all a boy's harmless follies and romping acquaintance-ships. They come to me now, as I look back through succeeding years of self-dependence and sophistication, like the pleasant dream of a first sleep, oblivious to the wearying day before, and unprophetic of the troublous visions to follow.

CHAPTER V.

I MAKE MY FIRST APPEARANCE IN SOCIETY.

SIRRAH found me on the door-step. From such a dark corner of the kitchen entry as an assassin of Sunday romance would have chosen for his most sinister act of overhearing, she had listened to the hum of my last interview with Ellie, and came hurriedly up, shortly after the opening and shutting of the front door, to ascertain what had become of me.

Stricken speechless at beholding my attitude of grief, she stood staring at me until cook's voice sounded a recall, when she led me into the hall by my jacket collar and comforted me all the way downstairs by vigorously washing one of my hands with her apron. That, she felt, was the least she could do, at such a very thick stage of the plot.

Four days after this, my father came home again in the carriage, and went away again the same night without seeing me; but he had held a brief consultation about me with Mrs. Fry, the conclusion of which seemed to be that my sphere of amusements was to be extended. At any rate, when Mrs. Le Mons' girl came over one afternoon to inquire very kindly if she might take me, along with Master Gwin, to a tent menagerie in Tenth Street, Mrs. Fry gave answer that she herself would go with me.

In less than an hour from thence, my favorite comrade and I, guarded as above, were revelling in the wonders of the menagerie, which had managed to gain quite an aristocratic patronage by advertising itself as the "World-renowned English Caravan of the Desert," and announcing, in blue letters composed of gymnastic snakes, that it had "given zoological soirées before the Royal Family of Great Britain."

Measureless was our delight at the great, canvas-covered plain of sawdust, encircled with cages full of beasts and birds, — not to mention two elephants and an invalid ostrich. To maintain a specific superiority over a rival establishment showing upon a "vacant" lot on Broadway, and to intensify the English idea, I suppose, there was a talking showman on hand, disguised as a lecturer, who improved the intervals between the tuneful agonies of an elevated brass band near the entrance by expatiating oratorically upon the animated marvels of the exhibition. His name was William Henry Al Reschid, "a converted Mausoleum," as Mrs. Fry read it to us from the bills, and his calico dressing-gown and red smoking-cap gave a truly oriental veracity to what he said.

Those two Elephants, ladies and gentlemen, were captured after a struggle of two days in the jungle of Seringapatam, whose ivory was used for knife-handles and articles of virtue. In their wild state they sometimes ate up whole villages; but soon became tame after being captivated by the natives, or mamelukes, and subsisted on straw beds and an occasional keeper. The only other elephants mentioned by Cuvier, Buffoon, and your own immortal Audubon (great applause) — whom the Royal Family of England mentioned to me (prolonged cheers) — was the sacred White Elephant of the Ganges; so called, because he was brown.

That Ostrich was seized while scouting in the great desert of Sarah by a party of English sailors, in the very act of sticking his nose in the ground. This habit of the ostrich was very curious, and was occasioned by his believing that if he hid his head nobody could see him (Much laughter) — just like some human beans. (Uproarious mirth.)

In the large central cage was the royal Bengola Tiger, which sucks the blood of his victim in a wild state. When found, beside the Euphrates, he was eating the skeleton of a woman, whose tongue, horrible to relate, still moved. When this circumstance was told to the royal family of England, they refused to look at the Bengola tiger, and asked to have the shutters put on to his cage. The royal family were as kind-hearted as women, and permitted no one to abuse the Americans in their presence. (Enthusiastic applause.)

That strange creature in the smaller cage to the left, was the first specimen ever seen of the Hypochondriac of the Andes, a blending of the leopard and the domestic cat. If you went boldly up to it and patted it, there was no danger; but if you seemed to be afraid of it, it would turn and rend you just like a human bean.

The bird now uttering cries for food to the extreme right was the English Parachute, or barnyard Moslem; a variety of the Turkish nation. It was frequently eaten for food in the British empire.

In the two cages near the lions' den were a Cinnamon Bear and a spotted Incubus, both from Labrador, where they roamed eternal fields of ice and fed upon the farmers' grain. The Incubus cried like a child at night, so that travellers often stopped in their carriages to give alms, and were never heard of again. The cinnamon bear inhabited the highest icebergs, and lived on sailors so exclusively, that at the present time he preferred a dose of salts to any other food.

The grand van, or den, yonder, held the Aurelian Lion, Lioness, and whelps, whose howls upon the coast of Africa rendered night hideous. But no more need be said about that, as Professor Dening would now demonstrate man's sublime power over the beasts that perish.

Then came a malevolent crash from the brass band, and the sudden slipping into the lions' den of Professor Dening, in exaggerated soldier-clothes, who twirled a bar of iron rather overbearingly, and stamped imperiously to attract the attention of the broken-hearted beasts around him. Contrary to our fearful expectations, the Aurelian monsters did not dismember him on the spot, but crouched ingloriously as close to the bars as possible, and betrayed cowardly anguish when compelled to stand on their hind legs.

After this, three military monkeys were lashed upon the backs of as many ponies, and took a series of nervous rides around the sawdust plain, to the especial glory of a red-coated gentleman with a whip, whose facetious remarks convulsed us all. I asked Gwin, in confidence, if he had any idea who this gentleman was, and he confidently assured me that it was the King of England.

It needed not the somewhat compassionate tone in which this piece of information was given, to show that Gwin had something of an elevated character on his mind. On the way to the menagerie, his manner had been constrained, if not offensively supercilious; and upon such little girls as we passed he had bestowed glances that were rakish beyond his years. At the exhibition, too, he was supernaturally sedate over everything, and it was not until we were near home that he let me into the secret of his new importance. We were permitted to walk on just ahead of our watchful attendants, and I was in the middle of an arbitrary theory to account for the failure of the lions to bite Professor Dening, when he abruptly interrupted me with the question, "What do you think, Avy Glibun?"

Slightly discomposed by this sudden change of subject, I came very near drawing one of my hands from my pocket (a sure sign of discomfiture in a boy), and answered that I did not know.

"Me and Con are to have a party to-morrow night, and mother's going to play the pianner for us!" exclaimed Gwin Le Mons, relapsing into his old self in a moment, and surveying me with a gleeful smile.

"Will it be a big one?" asked I, much dazzled.

"Oh, I'll bet you it will!" said he, with glowing emphasis, — "as big as a room! We're going to have cakes, and oranges, and candy; and we're going to have Knox, and Becton, and Trust, and a lot of more boys and their sisters; but we aint a going to ask you, though."

My eyes had been dancing until the last

phrase was reached, but that paralyzed them like a flash. I tried to look defiantly unconcerned, and, as that effort did not succeed, I am afraid that tears came.

"Well, I declare!" laughed Gwin. "if you aint took it in earnest! I was only in fun, Ave Glibun. You're to come, you know, at six o'clock. Why, Con said she couldn't have no party at all, if you didn't come."

If ever the gentlest of motives inspired the most flagrant of fabrications, that assertion regarding the sentiments of Miss Le Mons was the latter. I swallowed it, however, with a sensation of rejoiced sheepishness which actually made me weak in the knees, and ran excitedly back to ask Mrs. Fry if I might go.

To be sure I might! Mrs. Le Mons' girl had been telling her all about the coming event, and she had consented to take me over to the party, and herself pass the evening in the kitchen with said girl.

This was sufficient to make the remainder of the walk home a dream to me, and, by the time we reached our respective houses, all thoughts of the menagerie had been swallowed up in delightful anticipation of the new treat ahead.

Cook and I were just turning to go down through the area to our basement door, after parting with our company, when she stopped a moment to remark, "I wonder, Master Avy, what that old man wants there, looking up at our windows?"

She referred to a shabby-looking man at the edge of the walk, the rim of whose seedy, slouched hat nearly covered his whole head and face, and who had been glancing from one to another of our windows, until the notice of Mrs. Fry caused him to look another way.

"He's a beggar," I suggested, without much interest.

"He looks like an emissary, my child," said cook, in the full spirit of Sunday romance.

As the man walked on just then, there was no demand for further argument about him, and we went in-doors to regale the spasmodic Sirrah with accounts of our afternoon experiences.

I was put to bed that night, in the cot prepared for me in cook's own room, to go through a series of visions devoted principally to Miss Le Mons, who appeared to me in the velvet dress and gold crown of my favorite enchanted Princess, and not only let me kiss her, but fairly kissed me in return!

All the next day I neglected my story-books and arithmetic, and took no pleasure in anything save staring across the street at the Le Mons mansion, which I now regarded in the light of a fairy temple. The other boys of the neighborhood, too, lingered before the door on their way to and from school, and were fitful and feverish in their conceptions of the splendor preparing within the walls. Noah Trust did, indeed,

attempt a complicated sneer, founded upon his knowledge of Mrs. Le Mons having purchased some oranges at his father's store that morning, and taken the " mixed " kind, which were two shillings cheaper than the " Assorted;" but Upton Knox very shortly settled him, by innocently wondering if any dried peaches had been included in the bill! Also, whether any almonds had been bought, and if they had worms in them!

Toward six o'clock, the labors of my toilet were undertaken by Mrs. Fry, who was not quite as apt with buttons as Ellie had been. She succeeded, though, in turning me out to pretty good advantage; and when I got upon a chair and consulted a mantel mirror, after receiving the last touch, I saw reflected the figure of a slim, pale-faced boy of about six or eight years, with chestnut hair curling all over his head, and dark, large eyes, not very strong in expression.

My dress on that occasion was, if I remember rightly, a claret-colored suit, fancifully planted with steel buttons, and finished with spotless collar and cuffs. Thus attired, decked in a tasselled cap, and with a finger in my mouth, I was dragged sideways across the street by cook, Sirrah looking admiringly after us from the area. To tell the truth, I was the least bit frightened at this crisis, and felt no better when my name was asked of cook by a little colored boy, whom Mrs. Le Mons had engaged to announce her childrens' guests, and whose complacent occupation of a purple and red breakfast jacket belonging to that distinguished lady, made him resemble an imp in some pantomime.

Upon ascertaining my title, this vassal galloped from me to the further parlor door, opened it with a rush, proclaimed " Mister Every Gibbons," and was past me again for the next arrival before Mrs. Fry had fairly added my cap to the already extensive assortment of its fellows on the gothic hall-chairs.

My first appearance in society was not impressive. I have a dim recollection of stumbling into it over an unnecessarily high door-sill, and immediately walking into a corner with my face to the wall. Finding myself there, and burningly realizing the horrors awaiting me if I moved, I desperately refused to come out of it. A chorus of laughter, and an outburst of sarcastic invitations from voices not unknown to me, were not the treatment best calculated to check a supernatural perspiration with which I had been suddenly attacked; and even an assurance, in the thin, languid voice of Mrs. Le Mons, that "the little girls wouldn't bite me," inexplicably failed to put me entirely at ease.

"Nettie Beeton, dear, go and kiss him," were the awful words next audible to my scorching ears.

There was a general fluttering and shuffling toward my corner, and my agony reached a climax when a really dear little arm went pitilessly around my neck, and a dimpled chin began crowding over my shoulder.

Flesh and blood couldn't stand this. With a frenzied convulsion I turned face to my tormentors, put out my arm as a protection from Nettie, and slid down to the floor in reckless despair.

Fresh laughter and sarcasms hailed my new phase of wretchedness, and Miss Beeton's advances were becoming more deadly, when some one sharply exclaimed, "You just leave Avy alone, you hateful thing!" and Conny Le Mons appeared for my rescue. Nettie retreated to the side of her brother Ben, and Conny stooped to inform me that I "mustn't mind them," and that she wanted to show me her new tea-set. I ventured to look shyly up at her, and came near being overcome again by her pink dress and curls; but when she partially fulfilled my dream of the night before by kissing me exactly on the top of my head, I suddenly grew courageous and scrambled resolutely to my feet.

"Come and see Gwin," said Conny, exchanging defiant glances with Nettie Beeton.

I surveyed the ceiling, the candles on the mantel-piece, and the company, with what was meant for a haughty look; but, as I followed Miss Le Mons to her brother, I was painfully conscious of a wrong spirit in my legs, and, when I addressed Gwin, my voice sounded as though it came from somewhere above my head.

Gwin wore the eternal green jacket with pearl buttons, and had been stationed, by his mother, directly before a pier-glass between the windows. His sister had been at his side before she came to me; and in such high state they had awaited the successive greetings of their guests, according to what Mrs. Le Mons firmly believed to be the higher European style.

That lady, attired in saintly white, occupied the piano-stool before the instrument, and beamed softly upon fashionable society with a sweetly-tolerant air. Upon the wall opposite her seat hung a gilt windowful of the late Mr. Le Mons, in oil colors; and to this she occasionally threw up her sleepy gray eyes, in a manner to express that her children were now the only ties binding her to an unloved world. The departed had been a scion of Louisiana planter-stock, — so the legend ran, — though his married days were profitably devoted to the sale of molasses on commission in New York; and he left his widow and babes fairly provided for. Possibly his distinguished descent had imbued his wife with those aristocratic instincts which she perpetually indulged, and which could scarcely have been coeval with her own early days in a milliner's shop; for she certainly had social tastes of a lofty order, and took milk of a man who charged three cents more a quart for his ware than the other families in the block paid to their coarser milkmen.

Such was the maternal being who presided over the scene of my first dissipation, and I shook hands with her under a deep sense of her superiority.

"Avery, child," she said, after languidly kissing me, "did your nurse come with you?"

"No'm," answered I; "cook brought me."

"Is nurse sick?"

"No'm; she wented away."

I commenced working away from her as I made this reply, fearful that she would ask something which the command of my father had forbidden me to speak about; and with the thought of my father came a chill of dread, making me uncomfortably timid again.

By that time Gwin and Conny were permitted to discontinue the reception ceremony, as most of the invited ones had arrived; and my friend and I were presently entertaining knots of fashionables with rival stories of the menagerie. Lemonade, not remarkable for strong individuality, was handed around in wine-glasses by the girl, and I was growing quite fluent in a description of the cinnamon bear, when the colored Mercury tore wildly into the room, with the announcement: "Mister Ben Poore and sister, and Mister Luke Hyer and his other sister."

These parties, being especially select, had made a point of coming later than the rest, and Mrs. Le Mons' marked demonstration of welcome inaugurated the flutter of the whole company over such distinguished arrivals. Ben and Luke were gentlemanly fellows enough, and displayed no other arrogance than might be involved in a certain heavy air of wearing new boots; but Miss Poore was not long in attracting a host of suitors by exhibiting a bright two-shilling piece as her property; and the well-authenticated report that Miss Hyer's father had been twice to England (as a purser's clerk) soon placed in her train a majority of the remaining eligible youths. This last report, too, operated irresistibly in Luke's favor when he wooed Miss Le Mons from my side with a promise to show her a top, — greatly to my disappointment.

Gwin engaged Nettie Beeton in a discussion upon the ability of her brother Ben to contend with Upton Knox in single combat, provided there were "no strikings in the face;" Upton and Noah Trust were both climbing over the sofa after a crop-haired lady in blue, whom the latter had just tempted with a bunch of inferior raisins from his pocket; and, as all the other favorites of the fair sex seemed to have found mates, I wandered disconsolately across the room to where a misanthropical assemblage of neglected gentlemen were chasing the heavy hours away with scientific experiments in heat.

Upon joining this thoughtful association, and turning up my collar, as they had theirs, to produce the effect of manly maturity, I united with them in the curious and absorbing occupation of freely moistening slate-pencils in the mouth and then applying them to the stove; thereby producing a sound favorable to meditation, and dispensing an odor not aromatic.

Nine o'clock brought an opening of the folding-doors to the front parlor, by the girl and the colored vassal, discovering a table tastefully spread with cakes, nuts, and fruits, and a supply of motto candies heaped around a candlestick in the centre. By direction of his mother, Gwin excitedly arranged us in couples of male and female, and to the music of "Bonnie Doon," played by Mrs. Le Mons with great solemnity, we all marched in to the banquet. In this movement I was so happy as to have Conny for a partner, and became so infatuated when she tendered me a half of her own orange, as to openly and madly hug her!

Crimson with blushes she extricated herself from my unexpected embrace, but not before everybody had noticed the inexcusable proceeding; and Gwin demanded, from the opposite side of the table, that I should just look out what I was about.

The Misses Poore and Hyer tossed their heads, as though really unaccustomed to witnessing such vulgarity in positively good society; and Noah Trust, whose natural gloom of disposition had been intensified by a recent decisive snub from the lady in blue, was emboldened to say, "She's his sweetheart!"

Promptly thereat, Conny began to cry hysterically into the second breadth of her pink skirt, and I called Noah "A nasty grocery boy!"

"My children! quarrelling!" exclaimed the voice of Mrs. Le Mons, as the matron broke hurriedly through the ring around the table; "Gwin, I heard your voice, and shall punish you for this."

"It was that Ave Glibun," said Noah.

"Avery, child," she said, turning to me, "are you such an ill-bred boy? And Constance crying?"

"He hugged her right out before everybody!" roared Noah.

"Yes, so he did!" cried a dozen voices.

Gwin could have spoken for me, I think, but for the low-spirited condition into which he had fallen at finding that even such a festal day had the usual whipping in store for him. As it was, even Upton Knox seemed to be against me.

"I — I — couldn't help it," stammered I, with quivering lips, and quite beside myself with dismay.

Down went Conny's skirt from her eyes, and, looking her mother straight in the face, she said, —

"I wanted him to do it, ma!"

"Daughter!" ejaculated her ma, recoiling.

"Yes, ma, I wanted him to do it!"

There may have been — probably there have been — greater sacrifices made for others in this world, than the one that little girl dared to make for me then; but many a lesser act of self-devotion has surely been celebrated by a more illustrious chronicler.

"Constance Le Mons, I am ashamed of you!" said her mother, angrily. "The idea! wanting a boy to hug you. Now go right up to your room, miss, and stay there."

Dear little Conny! She walked right to the door, and left the parlor without a word.

I was glad to see the door opened again almost immediately, and hear the colored vassal declare, "Mr. Every Gibbons is wanted."

My departure from the party was as ungraceful as my advent had been; for I unhesitatingly ran out of it, to rejoin Mrs. Fry in the hall. To that good woman's inquiry as to my enjoyment of the evening, I made but vague replies, and greatly surprised her by my entreaties to be taken home. Such was my haste to get away, that I went out to the street ahead of her, while she paused to finish something she had been saying to Mrs. Le Mons' girl.

The night was dark and foggy, and I was stepping carefully down from the stoop to the pavement, when an arm caught me up in a twinkling, and before I could utter a sound a hand was upon my mouth, and I was carried swiftly to the other side of a tree-box on the walk.

"Don't be frightened," whispered a man's voice; "I won't hurt you, my lamb, and I'll let you go in a minute, if you'll tell me who that is with you, up there. Now who is it?"

The hand was withdrawn long enough for me to say, "It's cook." Then it silenced me again instantly.

"And where's your nurse? Where's Elfie Marsh?"

I remembered what Elfie had told me to say, and, as the hand lifted again, I unhesitatingly said, "She's went home."

"All right. Good night," said the voice, and with magical quickness I was set down upon the very toes of Mrs. Fry, and the man had disappeared.

"Master Avery!" ejaculated cook, who had just come down the stoop, and thought I had stumbled against her, "is the shadows of the night upon you?"

"Come home," I said, pulling at her shawl.

And after we were safe in her room, and I was being made ready for bed, I told her what had happened to me both at the party and in the street.

"Oh, the mystery of these doings!" said she, lifting up both her hands, and bringing them down hopelessly upon her knees; "the mystery of kidnappings, and governesses going away, and emissaries a gagging the son and hair in the public street; and no one allowed to speak of it! O me, O me, what a denooment it is, what a denooment it is!"

I went to sleep without telling her who the man was. For, though at first having only a confused idea of knowing him in some way, and not feeling very much frightened while in his arms. I had soon made out in my own mind that he was identical with him whom we had seen looking up at our windows the day before,—the man in the slouched hat.

CHAPTER VI.

ANOTHER PARENTAL DUTY DONE.

SPEECH, reduced to one of its simplest offices, may be termed the safety-valve of memory; carrying off and diffusing much that would otherwise develop in the latter faculty a morbid retentiveness for everything, and conveying back to the more important impressions, permanently retained within it, a wholesome and rectifying fresh air from the expressed impressions of others.

To the tyrannical habit of silence imposed upon me in the more youthful days of my life, I attribute my vivid recollection of every little event in that period;—a recollection so unwholesomely distinct, that it renews to me now the very sensations of my abused boyhood, and, with a power of retro-identification, under which I suffer afresh all the slights, repressions, and loneliness of that most miserable time.

Repression rather than oppression was the characteristic of my father's sententious rule, and I cannot help believing it to be the harder to bear of the two. Under its smothering omniscience, my natural amiability of temper and affectionate disposition withered by degrees into an artificial secretiveness and suspicion destined to influence sinisterly my whole future character. Forbidden, not so much by words as by an indescribable dictation of manner, to exchange views and confidences with others, I at last became moody by habit, and wandered uncomfortably hither and thither within the narrow limits of my liberty, like some odd little word whose whole language afforded no rhyme for it.

Still, there were occasions, as I have shown, when my instinct, as it were, would drive me into making some feeble attempt to draw from those around me an explanation of experiences and events which that same instinct taught me could not be common to every household. One day, in particular, when Mrs. Fry sat knitting in her room, I terminated a rather lengthy contemplation of her profile by suddenly asking,—

"Cook, my father don't keep a grocery store, does he?"

"Why, of course not, child," she answered, turning over her work and going more briskly on with it.

"Well, he don't keep a doctor's shop, then, does he?"

"Bless my heart! no, Master Avy. What ever put such an idea into your head?"

I was sitting on the floor, and entered into a profound and rather distorting examination of the heel of my left shoe as I asked the next question,—

"Well, he aint a milkman, is he?"

There was something so grovelling in this idea, to a mind accustomed to weekly familiarity with the highest circles of Europe, through the mediumship of Mr. G. W. M. Reynolds and other court novelists, that Mrs. Fry felt compelled to pause in her knitting and eye me with severity.

"Your father, Master Avery," said she, pointing at me with a needle, "is a gentleman bred and born; and that's what you'll be when you come into possession of your man's estates. But you shouldn't ask too many questions while you are so young, Master Avy; because too many questions corrupt good manners and breed contempt."

The information and apt lesson in morality, thus conveyed to me, were of that complicated character which requires more or less speechless cogitation to duly digest it, and I remained silent for fully five minutes. Then I resumed my examination of the witness.

"Cook, why does other little boys' fathers send them to school, and take them to church, and let them play tag in Washington Parade Ground? Aint other little boys' fathers gentlemen?"

The good woman was aghast at my inquisitive pertinacity, and resolved to make an end of it.

"My child," she said, earnestly, "there is a skeleton in every house, which is a thing made entirely of bones and a ghost; and they have skeletons in their houses, and we have one somewheres; though I don't know where it is, and I—"

"I know where it is," cried I. "it's hid away down in that iron box in the wall in the back parlor!"

"That's only the safe, Master Avy, where your father keeps his papers."

Rather impatient at such an abrupt coming down to the commonplace, cook started her needles again, and I relapsed into temporary silence. My mind was all alive, though, in its novel burst of freedom, and I soon began afresh,—

"Cook, why don't you never go out to see people, like Gwin's mother's girl? She goes out ever so often."

"Why you see, Master Avy," said she, speaking quite freely this time, "all the people that I know, live way off in the country, where I came from when I came here, four years ago."

"Has Elfie gone there?" asked I, much emboldened.

She shook her head, and knitted faster.

"Aint this Elfie's house, cook?"

She pointed the needle at me again, and said almost sternly, "I want to knit now, and you mustn't talk to me so much, or I shall never get done. Mrs. Elfie never did live here for good, child. She was here nearly a year the last time; but don't you remember how she used to go home before that, and then come for a while again, and then go again? Now you've made me drop two stitches."

I have since thought that Mrs. Fry's use of romantic phrases had originated with her inability to get along well in ordinary language when attacked with subjects upon which she felt (not knowing exactly how, perhaps) enjoined to secrecy. I think so, because I recollect that she generally talked in an ordinary way about other matters.

I remembered perfectly well the goings and comings of Elsie before her final establishment with me as my nurse, as she was called; but a few months seem a long while to a child, and I could not help feeling as though there was something unnatural in her last going from me.

"Cook," asked I, "what made him say to her—"

"Master Avery, not another word about it,"—Mrs. Fry shook her finger as she spoke—"not another word about it! One whom I need not mention will not have it."

I knew very readily what she meant. There was no more talk for me about home; and, after picking at the carpet a moment or two, I got up and went to my picture-books.

The one not to be mentioned came home that same afternoon, and held an hour's interview with Mrs. Fry after dinner. From this interview the good woman was seen to come with tears in her eyes, and that night she told me I was to be sent to school immediately.

"I had to tell him about that man the other night," she said, with a sigh; "and how could I help it when questioned by such as him, dear? He trusted me as one faithful to his house, Master Avy, and I was true to his heritage. Yes, dear, I told him, when he asked, how the man picked you up in the shadows of the night; and he said, —so gentlemanly, too, —'Of course, Mrs. Fry, you will agree with me that such things must be guarded against in future. You will at once prepare my son to leave home, as I shall send him immediately to the boarding-school of an old friend of mine, where he will at least be safe from vagrants.' Those were his words, Master Avy, in modulated tones; and I've got to part with you."

She cried, and I cried; but my weeping was rather to keep her company than from any poignant grief at what I heard. It was one of the compensations of my generally loveless lot, that no one had been sufficiently engrossed in my intellectual and moral welfare, to make the future school a wholesome terror to my infant days. Motherless and insignificant as I was, no one had thought it worth while to encourage my imagination with that finely nervous ideal of the coming school-master which causes very little boys to regard learning as the expiation of crime, and the multiplication-table as a distracted formula prior to the scaffold. Thus, destitute of educational premonitions, the idea of being sent to school grew pleasanter to me every moment; and when cook became calm enough to romance upon the gentlemanly glories of learning how to read, write, and understand everything in the papers, I needed only her farther prophecy of my early proficiency in writing letters, to send me to bed in raptures.

On the following morning cook invested Sirrah with supreme authority for the day, to the intense and exclamatory amazement of that languid maiden, and commenced her own new office by making a trip to the nearest avenue. On her return, she was accompanied by a loquacious young man, who bore a black leather trunk upon his shoulders, and made much of himself in the hall, before Sirrah, by elaborately explaining the mysteries of lock and straps.

How curious it is, by the way, that a man always *does* make a fool of himself when an unknown woman appears to be looking at him! It is man's hysterics.

The trunk, I soon ascertained, was to contain my clothing, and be sent with me to school. This piece of knowledge brought on such blissful excitement that I felt impelled to seek the front stoop at once, and see if Gwin Le Mons was to be hailed; for I desired an impressible witness of my grandeur. It was Saturday, or no-school day, and my bosom friend happened, at that very moment, to be drawing a demoniac conception in charcoal, on his own sidewalk; so I called him over, and made him observe the interment of my cloth and linen mortal coils in their short home.

Upon being informed as to the purport of what he saw, Gwin Le Mons fell into a state of great admiration at my good fortune; but rather bewildered me by the tendency he had to regard my condition in the light of an approaching dissolution from earthly enjoyments. He wished to know whom I should "leave" my peg-top and marbles to, and demonstrated his own right to a legacy by insidiously trying-on my choicest paper soldier-cap. Really, he made me quite uncomfortable by taking that view of the situation, and it required all the sanguine eloquence of Mrs. Fry to cheer me up again, when he finally ran briskly home to be whipped for his exploits in charcoal.

Mrs. Fry certainly did not expect to see my father again before Monday, at the earliest, as he had only gone away that morning; great, therefore, were her surprise and confusion at his return before four o'clock that very afternoon, accompanied by a strange gentleman. The twain went into the back parlor, dinner was ordered; and, furthermore, an order was dispatched by Sirrah for me to dine with them.

Between the bustle of preparing the meal, and her nervousness about the half-finished packing, poor cook had little chance to brighten me for the table; and, as a consequence, when Sirrah at length led me into that dreaded room, my personal appearance was no counterbalance of my awkward and timid air.

My father, darkly elegant as before, occupied his usual seat at the board, and unconcernedly greeted me with the words : "Master Avery, we dine early to-day. Take this seat beside me."

I obeyed him, as a cowed poodle might obey a whip-tap from its owner.

The guest was a short, stout man in black, with smooth red hair and sparse whiskers of the same hue; a pale-faced, sleek man, and not unlike a depressed clergyman in general effect. He glanced thoughtfully at me, for a moment; but at once understanding, apparently, that I was not to be noticed yet, looked quickly back to his plate and sipped softly.

My philosophical parent, indeed, had no idea of taking me into conversation just yet, and I was left at liberty to enjoy as many spasms of horror as there were spoons, knives, and napkin-rings near me that *would* jump off the table, while he entertained the visitor.

. "Mr. Birch," said he, "let me offer you these olives. You need them to sharpen your appetite, I see."

"Yes; thank you, Mr. — ah — Glibun; they are very fine," was the answer, in a mild voice.

"By the way, Mr. Birch, I suppose that post-office appointment at Milton was satisfactory to your friend? The salary is not so very inconsistent with the burthen of the duties, I should say."

"Ha! ha!" laughed Mr. Birch, wiping his lips, and then suddenly becoming sadly meek again. "*Our* friend — for you have now made him yours — has no reason to complain. Four letters have gone through his office in — a month. Ha! ha! — hum."

More talk of this kind passed between them; and, despite Mr. Birch's devout aspect and mildness, his part of it had a disingenuous sound. His entertainer's, on the contrary, aided by continual bright looks in every direction but mine, only suggested the graceful freedom of a controlling mind's relaxation. At last, when the brandy-decanter was brought from the sideboard, and Sirrah had withdrawn for good, my father very suddenly put a hand upon my shoulder, and said, abruptly, —

"You see here is the lad, Mr. Birch. Avery, you are to go to this gentleman's school."

I had not dreamed of this, and probably betrayed fright in my looks, for Mr. Birch leaned over very quickly to shake hands, and say I must not be afraid of him.

"You and I shall be the best of friends Master Avery," said Mr. Birch, in the tone generally adopted to soothe a startled cat; "I have other young gentlemen like you under my academic caves near Milton, and you will find them good company, both in class and at play."

"Mr. Birch," said my father, turning my face half-way toward him, and looking musingly at me, "do you think he and I resemble each other at all?"

"Very strongly," responded Mr. Birch; "or, that is to say, he seems as though he might be a mixture of father and mother."

"Meaning," said my father, taking his hand from my chin, and raising his glass to the light, "that you prefer not to answer that question definitely, until you know just what answer I expect."

"Ha, ha! Mr. — hem — Glibun; you are quite a Juvenal."

"Or a Persius, perhaps," observed my father; "for I can detect the 'old woman' in a man at sight."

He said this with cheerful carelessness, still looking through his glass; and the school-master answered with another short laugh, as he tipped the raised glass with his own. My father nodded, drank, and looked at his watch.

"Mr. Birch," he said, drawing back from the table, and at once assuming the stern air by which I knew him best, "you have left orders at home for the preparation of quarters for the lad, I presume? You are aware that I wish him to return with you to-night."

"Yes, sir; your — ah — dispatch was to that effect. Master Glibun will chum with a boy near his own age."

I was all in a flutter at this short and sharp disposition of me; and so was Mrs. Fry when she came to answer my father's immediate touch upon the bell.

"Mrs. Fry, this gentleman, Mr. Birch, will take Master Avery home with him, to school, in a few minutes, and you will be good enough to bring down his cap, overcoat, and so on, immediately."

"To-night!" ejaculated cook, lifting her hands; "why, your lord — I mean Mr. Glibun, his trunk aint half-packed."

"I did not suppose it was," said my father, coolly. "It can be sent by express next week."

With a despairing glance at me, and then at Mr. Birch, cook made a stiff courtesy, and disappeared.

"Now, Mr. Birch," continued the peremptory master of the situation, lighting a cigar and simultaneously extending the open case to the school-master as he spoke, "you probably understand that I shall hold you strictly responsible for the lad's safety until I recall him. Of late I have scarcely known what to do with him; for I cannot look after him myself, it is not proper that he should be with servants all the time, and the very ruffians of the street seem inclined to meddle with him. I have already told you my chief reason for sending him to you earlier than I formerly intended; and I now tell you that I shall hold you strictly responsible for his safety. Watch him. That is all you have to do."

"But, Mr. Glibun," said the school-master, rising from his seat with considerable animation, "suppose a certain party should still be inclined to act nonsense with the boy. I'll do all I can, you may be sure; but how is one to manage a raving tiger?"

"By naming me, possibly," said my father, smiling rings of smoke from his mouth into the air.

Mr. Birch did not seem to relish this prescription altogether. In fact, something like anger shone in his eyes for a moment; but it passed quickly away again, and he sighed.

"Well," said he, "there doesn't appear to be anything more to say about it, and we must be moving, or we shan't catch that stage. I'll write once a week as agreed."

Here Mrs. Fry came in with my cap, coat, and comforter, and proceeded, without a word, to jerk me into those articles. I should have been entirely confounded by such treatment from her, had I not soon discovered that she was silently crying. Tears were coming upon my checks, too, when she hurriedly threw on my cap, gave me one frantic hug, and actually ran from the room.

"Good feeling there," said Mr. Birch.

"A good woman, I believe," said my father.

The school-master, after an uneasy pause of a moment or two, was mechanically leading me toward the hall, when my father stepped hastily over to us, and at a motion from him Mr. Birch dropped my hand and went out into the passage. Then he who should have loved me best of all the world bent down and kissed my cheek. A blow would not have surprised me more, and, as I looked yearningly up into his face, I saw that it was changed.

"My son," he said, gently, "you must not think me too unkind in sending you away. It is my duty as your father. I am sorry for you, my poor boy; I wish you had a mother. Good-by. Now go with him."

He turned from me, folded his arms, and paced thoughtfully toward the mantel. The school-master had me by the hand again, and led me hastily out to a hack at the street door; and the first period of my life closed with the crack of a whip.

———◆———

CHAPTER VII.

A TRAVELLER'S STORY.

As we rode to the Jersey Ferry, my spirits improved apace; for, although I had felt a momentary stagnation of heart as the hack started from our house, and experienced an inclination to cry for cook, there was a novelty about my new situation and prospects which presently stirred my thoughts to all-forgetful excitement. As we turned the first corner I saw upon it Upton Knox and Ben Becton just finishing the last round of a lively combat, wherein Ben seemed to have been severely punished in the cap. I impulsively shouted Ben's

name as we whirled past, whereupon the battle prematurely ended, and, as I looked back, I could see both the gladiators walking in short circles, with their faces upturned, as though hopelessly bewildered by some spectral salutation from the air.

Mr. Birch watched me awhile, until we neared Courtlandt Street, when suddenly the spirit of the school-master came strongly upon him, and he bade me tell him what I knew.

"For instance," said he, "do you know, Master Glibun, how a fly can climb up a wall?"

The question had never occurred to me before, but I was prompt to express the opinion that the fly's legs were sticky.

"That's very good for a guess, sir," observed Mr. Birch; "but you will have a different light on the subject after becoming familiar with the laws of cohesion. *Docendo discimur*—which means, you will improve at my establishment."

Not being qualified to criticise a classical application which I have since had reason to regard as remarkable, nor feeling any passionate interest in the laws of cohesion, I kept silence.

At the ferry the hack came to a stoppage with great éclat, by overturning an applestand near the gates; and the speechless driver liberated us upon the implied condition of our immediately leaving the State. His whole manner was that of releasing two prisoners whose time had expired, and he wore the jailer air of one, too long familiar with the incarcerated depraved to be moved by such a trifling incident as the present. I think Mr. Birch was rather struck by his judicial aspect; for he stood looking at him until the hack door was closed again, and the oracular whip pointed to the ferry entrance. As we went through the gates, I lingered and looked back, and there that unspeakable man in a velvet cap still stood, a perfect wall of inarticulate philosophy, against which the vivacious remonstrances of an outraged apple-vender were being hurled in vain.

The ferry crossed, we got into the last stage for Newark, as there was no railroad thither in those days of natural deaths. Only two other passengers were going; a tall, lean travelling agent with a carpet-sack full of specimen knobs, and a short, thick gentleman, whose red face was quite a setting sun in a clouded west of gray mufflers.

The school-master made his legs and me an excuse for occupying a whole seat of the clumsy omnibus, and composed himself at the start for a nap; but the other two seemed disposed to sociability, and both instructed and amused me with their talk. We were about half-way up Bergen Hill, when the knob man observed, that he preferred a steamboat to a stage for night travel, if he knew himself.

"Well, it's hardly night just yet," responded the muffled gentleman, "and perhaps you *don't* know yourself."

"Don't know myself!" ejaculated the knob man; "well, if I don't know myself by this time, it's too late to be introduced. I've been thinking to the contrary of that for nigh onto thirty-eight years."

"Yes, everybody thinks he knows himself from all the rest of the world," answered the muffled gentleman; "and yet it's very possible to upset the theory. I could tell you a story that *would* upset it, I think."

"A story!" exclaimed the knob man. "Let's have it whether or no. I hope it's nothing that will offend our clerical friend—but he's asleep, though,—and if it won't do for the boy, he can be set out with the driver."

"Do for the boy? Nonsense!" said the muffled gentleman, petulantly.

"Beg pardon, sir," returned the knob man; "but I'm tender of what children hear. I can't help remembering that my own mother was a woman."

This last revelation of a family secret seemed to be rather unsettled in its connection with the rest of the sentence; but the muffled gentleman cordially approved the general sentiment advanced, and observed, that as *his* own mother had also been a woman, he should be the last to disregard the moral interests of childhood.

"You must understand," continued he, "that my story relates to the two twin daughters of old Othello Chandler, of Broad Street, who had the good luck of Plato Wynne himself, in clearing out a whole warehouseful of speculative commodities for cash in the war of 1812, just before the news of peace came so suddenly and ruined a perfect army of other operators."

"If he had the luck of Plato Wynne," murmured the knob man, "he *was* lucky."

"Possibly you know old Othello?"

"Heard his name,—that's all," answered he of the knobs.

"And a very curious, ridiculous name it was, sir! What could ever induce civilized American parents to give a son such a play-acting affliction of a name as that, I can't see," said the muffled gentleman, irascibly; "but they did give it to him, though; and if he lost respect for the old ones before they died, who could blame him? Well, sir, after losing his wife, he went to live with his two twin daughters in a house of his own in Pearl Street. You are probably aware, sir, that one of those twins married, and the other didn't?"

The knob man scratched his head reflectively; but couldn't pick out that fact especially from the bewildering number of his fashionable recollections.

"Well, no matter about that," went on the muffled one; "**such** was the upshot, and I'm going to tell you how it came about. The girls — I knew 'em when I was a spark — were named Minerva and Cleffy, and looked and dressed so much like each other that they resembled a hopeless inebriate's duplicative view of the same woman. The gentleman who, upon his late return from an important whig meeting, politely offered to escort home that 'other lady' whom he found with his wife, did not see before him more perfect duplicates.

"These young misses, then, were very much alike in person; and matched equally well in dispositions, until there came along a dashing young spark who had travelled in Europe, and could speak enough Paris French to break any woman's heart. Him they both selected as the most eligible catch in the gold-fish tank of society, and as he happened to make the first demonstration, of a wish to be hooked, to Miss Minerva, the twins became inharmonious at once, and made hysterical amends in private for every time they were compelled to address each other as 'dearest darling' in company.

"Miss Cleffy might have borne an ordinary defeat in such rivalry with some patience; but when it came, at last, to being addressed at least once a week as 'Minnie,' by mistake, and that, too, by the mistaken spark in question, it was too much, you know. So they made their father's life miserable by insisting upon separate apartments and servants, and threw water on each other's lap-dogs to such an extent that a howl was in the air pretty much all day long.

"Finally the vital spark of heavenly flame blazed up at the feet of Miss Minerva at an assembly ball, one night, and made a precious ass of himself,—as we all do, you know, on such occasions. It was in the interval of a cotillion, and he was softly referred to her pa. But this would not do for the spark, and he was man enough to acknowledge that he hadn't quite as much money as he seemed to have. In fact, that visit to foreign courts had used up the only eight hundred dollars he ever had in the world, and it struck him that old Othello Chandler might not think a thousand-dollar clerk in a merchant-tailor's store the most promising stock to invest a daughter in. He was man enough to confess all this, and his audacious honesty helped him; for girls can't help liking that sort of thing, even when it sounds like impudence. Well, she pretended to be indignant; played fast-and-loose with him all the evening, and, at last, when he was helping to cloak her for home, consented to receive a note from him next day. That is to say, he thought she did the latter; but she didn't at all; for it was Cleffy that he had helped to cloak, and Cleffy had answered with 'Yes' to his whispered request of the privilege. Next day there came a note for 'My cruellest of Minnies,' frantically beseeching an elopement; and as it incidentally mentioned her last evening's consent to hear from him by mail, and as Cleffy had been unusually high with her that morning, she put this and that together and saw how the cat had jumped. Possibly the irritation of the discovery decided her to act as she did, indignation against her sister being stronger than her pique at the young spark. At any rate, she wrote a properly romantic consent to the proposition, and notified the suitor that she should attend a party in State Street, with her sister. It was a fashionable party, and he was there, and at the first convenient opportunity they arranged the details of their escapade. She was to have a week to 'get her things ready;' then he was to come early in the evening with a carriage and invite her to go with him to the Battery for a moonlight promenade. Once in the carriage, they were to drive straight to the residence of a previously engaged clergyman and be married. Then he was to take her back home again, and leave her to break the secret to old Othello, and bore a pardon for him. It was a delightful arrangement, and the young spark avowed himself incapable of expressing more than half the joy he felt. Later in the evening, however, he felt equal to the other half, and, accordingly, imparted it to Cleffy, whom he saluted as 'Almost my own.' She understood, then, why *she* had not got the note for which her permission had been asked, and, at the same time, she also comprehended the direction of the cat's jump, and, instantaneously determined to take desperate steps. She would not tell all to pa. Oh, no! for that could only cause Romeo to be forbidden the house; — a consummation not to be thought of. She would do quite another thing.

"For a week, Minerva was out shopping every day, followed by Cleffy's maid in disguise; and whatever Minerva bought, was exactly followed in the maid's succeeding purchases. Duplicate bonnets and what not were thus obtained almost simultaneously; and as the maid acted as a surreptitious spy upon Minerva's dress-maker, duplicate dresses were also got ready.

"Well, on the afternoon preceding the momentous evening, Cleffy gained access to Minerva's dressing-room, while her sister was temporarily absent, and smuggled in a corrupted footman, who, by her orders, hastily removed the boards and all the quicksilver from the back of the only mirror in the apartment, — a large cheval glass, swung in a frame. This done, she dismissed the footman with the rubbish, and, in her new dress, and with the new bonnet in her hand, carefully drew over the front of the glass the curtain employed to protect it from flies and dust, and then cautiously crouched herself in a corner of the room close behind the same mirror.

"There she waited, and waited, and waited, and continued to wait, until, through a lapping of the curtain, she at last saw her sister enter, dismiss her maid at the door, light a gas-burner, and begin hurriedly to array herself in those new things of hers. A woman, you know, must dress herself expressly for every occasion, even if it's the funeral of her grandmother. That's what makes a wife cost so much, you see. So, as I was saying, the girl be-

hind the glass could see all this; and when her sister put on her bonnet and gloves at last, she also put on *her* duplicate bonnet and gloves, and stood up.

"Being all fixed, Minerva approached the glass to take one parting look at herself, drew back the curtains abstractedly, and contemplated the figure before her, in a careless way. She was really thinking about something else at first, and didn't look very sharply; but suddenly it flashed upon her that the face in the glass was Cleffy's, and not her own. Involuntarily she raised one hand, and opened her mouth. So did the figure. She took a step forward. So did the figure. She took a step backward. So did the figure.

"'O mercy!' thought Minerva, 'can I be awake? That's my bonnet, and my frock, and my gloves, and yet it isn't me! It must be that I'm — but no! I certainly am not dreaming. O me! I must be going mad! He'll be at the door in five minutes; and if I *should* happen to be Clef instead of myself, and be crazy in thinking that I am myself — !'

"It was all plain to her in a moment. She was *not* herself, at all; she was Cleffy, and was preparing to get ahead of herself in going off with Romeo. She, *herself*, was not in the room at all, but must be somewhere else — purposely drugged, perhaps! And she was not herself at all, but her sister, and was just on the point of shamefully passing herself off for herself to the only man —

"She flew from the room; tore wildly upstairs to another room; locked the door and threw the key out of the window, to make sure that she *could not* pass herself off for herself; and fell fainting to the floor.

"Then Cleffy slipped from behind the mirror, went softly down to the front door, and was whirled away to the parsonage in mistake for her sister; which proves, I think," said the muffled gentleman, "that it's barely possible to mistake yourself for somebody else."

The dreadful confusion prevailing in the latter part of the muffled gentleman's story had caused the utterly disordered knob man to actually paw at the air from sheer intellectual vertigo; and the sudden winding-up of the whole thing positively made him pant.

"Law!" said he, feebly.

"Curious affair, wasn't it?" asked the muffled gentleman.

"Extrawnary!" gasped the knob man, "and true in the time of it, I daresay. Excuse me; but this must be Newark we're in, aint it?"

"Newark it is," said the muffled gentleman, as the stage turned the corner of a street, and the dim light of a curb-lamp came in upon us. "It's Newark, and I suppose I must stop here all night; though, to tell the truth, I'd rather be at home with my good woman."

"So would I," yawned the knob man, innocently.

"Eh?" ejaculated the muffled gentleman, with such sharpness that even Mr. Birch roused up.

"Of course I meant with *my* own good woman," explained the knob man, pitiably abashed.

Here the stage stopped before a low wooden tavern, and the two got out together, leaving the school-master and me with bluff good-nights.

With a stretch and a sigh Mr. Birch brought himself to realize where we were, and then languidly conducted me from the vehicle to the ground, and from thence to an irregular rim of stones intended. I suppose, for a sidewalk. Not far from this landing-place there stood a mud-splashed rockaway wagon, with a drooping grayish horse in the shafts, and some one occupying the driver's seat.

"There's Old Yaller," said Mr. Birch, pushing me before him toward the wagon, "and after one more ride we're home. Yaller!"

"Yes, Misser Rod'rick," answered the figure on the seat.

"All ready to start? Got the groceries I told you about?"

"Everything, Misser Rod'rick."

"Then into the wagon with you, Master Glibun," said Mr. Birch, summarily lifting me into the rockaway, and himself taking a seat with Old Yaller.

We were travelling on a country road again before I found chance to fairly realize that there had been any break in the journey; and, as I clung to a seat of the vehicle and stared at the two half-figures between me and the still darkening sky ahead, my thoughts took continuity once more from the appearance of our driver. By the light of a lamp before the tavern I had briefly noted that he was a black man, and had a stoop in the shoulders suggestive of age; but now, as my eyes became accustomed to him in the transparent shadow of night, he seemed to grow more erect and lose all signs of particular infirmity, though having a shabby look.

"Anything new since I left this morning?" asked the school-master.

"No, Misser Rod'rick," returned the black; "because there aint been no time for it."

"No questions about the new boy?" queried Mr. Birch.

"Yes, Misser Rod'rick, I believe the madam did call me in from choppin' wood to know about that yar. Says she, 'Yaller, do you know who the boy is that Misser Birch's gone after?' and says I, 'I aint not the least idevar.'"

"H'm!" said Mr. Birch.

No more words passed in my hearing; for I fell into a doze after that, and did not awake until shaken from my seat by the stopping of the wagon. Upon being lifted from the latter by the school-master, I found myself in a straw-strewn lane, as I may call it, bounded on either side by a line of dilap-idated picket fence, and terminating at the upper end in a small wooden shed, or stable. The rising moon, and an old tin lantern which the black had drawn from under his seat, gave light enough to discover these objects pretty distinctly, and my glance also took in a dingy building of some description not very far inside the pickets to the right.

Upon receiving the lantern in one hand, the school-master took one of mine in the other, and led me through a broken gate, and up a path paved with clam-shells, toward the dingy house.

"Is this school?" asked I, boldly.

"Yes, sir, this is the school," answered he; "and a nice, quiet, pleasant place you'll find it, my boy. See how still everything is. Just the place for sleep, isn't it? As Virgil says: *Hic secura quies, et nescia fallere vita, dives opum variarum.* Which means: Here we have a quiet, easy life of it, with opium in every variety. The opium in case of sickness."

This speech made me certain that he was a Dutchman; it being a singular peculiarity of our earliest instinct, as it is of our later reason, to associate anything particularly incomprehensible with the German; and I felt creeping over me a stronger repugnance.

Ascending two or three rickety wooden steps, to a door painted green, the school-master produced a large iron key from his pocket and opened the way to a hall, or entry, in which stood a long wooden table with rush-bottomed chairs ranged on either side of it. At the farther end of the table, and with a lighted candle and several books before it, sat a shapeless figure, which moved and half arose as we entered. As it moved, a clumsy wrapper of some sort fell away from its head and shoulders, revealing a boy, about fifteen years old, apparently, with a crown of golden curls, and a face so tender and beautiful in tone and expression that I stared at it with open-mouthed admiration.

"Ezekiel Reed," said the school-master, "you should not be sitting here without a fire."

"I wrapped myself up for it, sir," answered the boy, mildly, "and have been too much interested in reading to feel the cold. The boys are all abed, and, as I knew you expected to bring a new boy home with you, I told mother that I would be here when you came, and show him where he is to sleep for to-night."

"Is there a fire in the kitchen?" asked Mr. Birch.

"Yes, sir, and something kept warm for you against the fender."

"We want nothing to eat," said the school-master; "for we had dinner late. Are Bond and Vane in the school-room?"

"No, sir, they're in their own rooms, writing or reading, I suppose."

"Well," said the school-master, "I'll go into the kitchen for a while; but you had better show this boy to bed. His name is

Avery Glibun, and his clothes will be sent next week. Take him along."

Mr. Birch advanced to a door under a flight of stairs, as he spoke, and concluded by disappearing through it with his lantern and going heavily down some steps unseen.

Throwing his wrapper entirely aside, Ezekiel Reed came, candlestick in hand, to take a look at me; and while he, for a moment, was silently surveying my bundled-up little figure. I had a fairer view of him. He was quite as tall as Mr. Birch, and looked supernaturally slender in his close black jacket; but his easy motions greatly lessened the latter promise of boyish awkwardness; and his face, set off by a broad white collar at the neck, was delicate and smooth as that of a pretty girl.

"Is this the school?" I asked him.

"Part of it," he replied. "This is where we eat, and upstairs is where we sleep. You must come after me now, and go to bed."

He turned and went to the foot of a flight leading up from a farther corner of the hall, —the same under which the master had retired; but, not hearing me behind him, he shaded the candle with one hand and looked back.

"Aren't you coming, Glibun?"

"No!" said I; "I'm 'fraid."

"All right, then," returned the boy. "Perhaps you'll feel better if I leave you in the dark;" and he commenced going up the stairs unconcernedly.

This treatment had its effect in causing me to take a sudden start after him at once, and I was clinging timidly to his jacket when another hall was traversed by us and a second flight of stairs commenced. This flight led again to a third hall, of irregular shape, on reaching which I was startled to hear. at first a scattered kind of whispering and then a sharp "H'sh!" The sounds seemed to come from beyond some half a dozen doors along the hall or corridor, and Ezekiel pushed open the nearest one and looked in.

"The parson!" said a voice in the room, loud enough to be heard over the whole floor; and then came a sound of tittering all around.

"That's you, Dewitt," remarked Ezekiel, drawing back from the door, "and I'll report you to-morrow. Here's your room, Glibun."

I followed him into a small, whitewashed room, containing two cot beds, a painted bureau, two yellow chairs, and a curtained window. The ceiling slanted down toward the window with the roof, and upon the wall over one of the cots was a colored print of the Flood.

My companion placed the candlestick upon the bureau, and then proceeded to relieve me of my cap, comforter, and overcoat, regardless of my evident inclination to stand still and stare about.

"That's your bed, over there," said he, indicating the farther cot; "and you must get into it as soon as you can, for it's cold up here. Do you want me to help you?"

I nodded mechanically, and presently found myself between a pair of chilly sheets, hardly knowing how I had got there.

"Don't you say your prayers?" asked Ezekiel, as I lay shivering and miserable before him.

Of course I did not.

"Then I will read a chapter in the Bible to you," said he; and, taking a book from the bureau, and a seat near the candle, he read me to sleep.

CHAPTER VIII.

MY FIRST DAY AT SCHOOL.

Some one had slept in that other bed. I was sure of it, because the pillow, counterpane, and sheet were rumpled. That bed was so narrow, though, that it must have been split off from my bed, and it was funny to have my bed seem so narrow, too, that one of my hands was part way over the edge, and felt cold. But how did there come to be two beds in the room at all? And what made the room seem so small? Why!—

As I turned upon my pillow I opened my eyes widely at last, and remembered where I really was.

The sunlight was streaming in through the white muslin curtain of the window, spanning the chamber with falling rafters of dusky gold; and in the full glow of the space between the bottom of the curtain and the termination of the window, sat Ezekiel Reed, book in hand. With a heavy shawl drawn over his shoulders, and his head so inclined that the full light should fall upon the volume and not into his eyes, his resemblance to a pretty girl seemed stronger even than it had the night before, and I lay gazing at him as though he had been a fascinating picture.

Presently, a rustling that I accidentally made caused him to look up and around from his book; and, seeing that I was awake. he placed the latter upon the bureau and turned his face to me.

"Good morning, little Glibun," said he, in a soft, pleasant voice; "how have you slept?"

I assured him that I had done pretty well in that line, as indeed I had.

"I should think so," he went on: "for that is my bed, yonder, and I didn't hear you move once. You went to sleep while I was reading the Testament to you last night."

He made this remark with so much gravity that I felt a vague consciousness of some indefinite wrong-doing, and probably betrayed it in my face, as usual.

"You will learn better than that, I hope," said he, "and get as fond of the Testament as I am. I've been reading it more than an hour this morning."

He now threw off the shawl, showing me that he was dressed in a neat suit of mixed gray, and told me that I must get up. The washing-bell, he said, would ring very soon, and then I would have to go down with him and wash for breakfast.

Upon this hint I scrambled reluctantly to the floor; and, as he resumed his Testament again, and hinted no offer to assist me, I made a desperate shift to dress myself, and succeeded, after a fashion. Not a moment too soon, though; for scarcely had I awkwardly adjusted the last button, when a bell sounded from the roof above us, and Ezekiel immediately left his book, and conducted me downstairs.

Going through the first hall, where the voices had sounded the night before, I noticed that all the doors were thrown open, disclosing small rooms with two rumpled cots in each, and trunks between them. The other boys slept there, my companion told me, and I would sleep in one of them, myself, to-night, my last night's lodging having been only temporary. In the lower, or main entry, the long table was covered with a figured oil-cloth, on which Old Yaller, assisted by a ragged and sickly-looking little white boy, was placing rows of white plates and pewter cups. The black nodded and grinned at me, and his rickety little assistant stuck his tongue into his cheek; but Ezekiel Reed hurried me along through the front door into the open air, and then around the house to a sort of shed, where my future school-mates were already at their ablutions. This shed, which seemed to be a partitioned extension of the kitchen, was paved with clam-shells, and had a low shelf all along one side of it, set out with tin basins, in which about a dozen boys of various ages were drenching their faces in water from the well just outside the door.

"Mr. Bond," said Ezekiel, leading me up to a thin, red-faced man, with gray hair and whiskers, who seemed to be superintending the scene, "this is young Glibun, you know. Father wants you and Mr. Vane to look out for him to-day."

"Yes, certainly, — all right, Master Reed, I will see to it," answered Mr. Bond, in a weak, dispirited kind of way. "I'll attend to it, Master Reed, — certainly."

He gave me a listless, tired look, as though quite weary of everything in the shape of a boy, and then introduced me publicly thus,—

"Young gentlemen, here's Master Glibun, a new school-mate for you. I wish you'd make room amongst you for him to wash."

The eyes of all the young washers were already upon me from behind their fingers and towels; and, as Ezekiel hustled me up to a basin which some one had deserted for me, a hum of indistinct comment went round. They were all dressed in mixed gray, like Ezekiel, so that my blue jacket with brass buttons made me rather conspicuous; and it was very palpable that I should have been criticised pretty boldly, but for the restraining presence of the old gentleman.

After directing me to wash my face by rubbing it with wet hands, as the others did, and pointing to where a brush and a comb were suspended by a chain under a looking-glass on the opposite side of the shed, Ezekiel Reed left me, and I managed to make an imitative toilet before a second ringing of the bell announced breakfast.

"Two-and-two, now, young gentlemen," said Mr. Bond, with the profoundest melancholy. "Master Dewitt, stop those capers, if you please, and take your place by Master Glibun. He's to chum with you, I believe."

Whispering and laughing (I knew well enough that it was about my jacket), the boys formed an imposing procession behind Mr. Bond, a sharp-eyed, iron-faced lad, with his black hair cropped close to his head, unceremoniously dragged my left arm under his right, and to the sound of this lad's suppressed whistling, we all marched around the front of the house, to the hall.

The table was spread, and on either side of its head sat Ezekiel Reed, and a dark-haired, handsome young man, in a light cassimere suit, whom the boys addressed as Mr. Vane. Mr. Bond having reached the seat at the head raised his hand, whereupon we all took chairs as we came to them; and Old Yaller served coffee to Reed and the two elders, and boiled eggs, biscuit, and well-water, to us. Then Mr. Bond arose to his feet with a very miserable look, closed his eyes, and observed, with much anguish: "For what we are about to partake, make us truly thankful,"—after which we were all at liberty to eat in silence, while our superiors sipped coffee (they had already breakfasted), and talked with each other.

The new sensation of being at table with boys, gave me a confidence hardly possible under such circumstances to a child ordinarily trained. My future school-mates, without an exception, were older than myself, and had older manners than my street acquaintances at home; but they were boys; I was their equal; and an immediate grasp of that fact so nicely weighted or balanced me with self-appreciation, that I felt myself steady enough to master a whole meal without once dropping knife or spoon. I am particular to mention this effect, because I often think of it, even now, as an odd proof of the inversion my youthful character had already received from an unnatural mode of life.

The boys were prohibited from talking at breakfast, save in answer to questions from the head; and as the privileged conversation from the latter direction was not distinct enough to serve for general entertainment, they varied the monotony of the meal for themselves with covert crumb-shots at each other, and divers fragmentary combinations of knives and egg-shells in tasteful bridges. Willie Dewitt, though, showed his original turn of mind by constructing a chaste Greek temple from the halves of a biscuit; but I doubt much that the Pythian Apollo would have approved the bread ball with which the dome was tipped.

At the rising of Mr. Bond, Mr. Vane, and Ezekiel Reed, we also quitted the table, and, after clustering for a moment or two around a stove in one of the front corners of the hall, were called by Ezekiel into a large room adjoining. This was the school-room, and extended the whole depth of the house. On either side an open space, which ran from the door to a platform with three desks and chairs, were regular rows of desks and benches. One or two maps, and a large blackboard, adorned the walls, and over a Franklin stove at the end of the room hung a rusty musket. The central space I have mentioned as terminating with the platform had a continuous seat, or long wooden settees, up both sides of it, and there we took our places, while Ezekiel and Mr. Bond ascended to chairs on the platform. The former read aloud a chapter from Genesis; the other plucked up animation enough to question the boys in their catechism, and then the negro brought down our caps and great-coats from the dormitory upstairs, and we were formally marshalled for a walk to the village church in Milton.

Smoking at the mouth, for the air was chilly, we filed through the hall, out of the door, and down a shell-path to the road; and I had time to see that the school-house was a great, square, red building, in the middle of a lot and on the spur of a high hill, with a slatted little bell cupola upon the peak of its mossy roof. I also discerned the faded traces of white lettering across the front, and was informed that it had read "Oxford Institute," before repeated rains had nearly erased the inscription. Why it was called "Oxford" Institute I do not know to this day, but suppose a scholastic fancy had something to do with it.

The distance to the village was about half a mile; so we had time to talk on a variety of subjects by the way. At first I was the favorite subject, the boys nearest me being unanimous in the opinion that I belonged to the army and was about to establish a military professorship at Oxford Institute. I protested earnestly against such a mistake; but my brass buttons were held to be proof positive of my martial calling. The idea being insisted upon until I was sufficiently miserable, Dewitt changed the topic by wondering whether "Old Rufus" would pass us before we reached Milton?

Upon my inquiring who "Rufus" was, he expressed the belief that I must be green not to know that, and informed me that the title had been borrowed from royal English history for Mr. Birch, whose red hair fully justified the application. I was also informed that the principal of the Institute to which we belonged, always went to church in the rockaway, if he went at all, accompanied by his wife and Mr. Vane, and that they might be expected to drive past us at any moment. This explanation led to still further news. I learned that Ezekiel Reed was step-son to Mr. Birch; that he had a sister living somewhere, and that his mother, a widow, had been Mr. Birch's first wife. Reed was monitor, or head boy, at school and was a great favorite with the clergyman at Milton, in whose church he had a Bible-class; the boys, however, looked upon him with a dislike for which there seemed no very just reason, and saluted him as "the parson." Finding me an excellent listener so far, Dewitt went on to tell me that no one knew just when "Rufus" had married his present wife; but it must have been before he turned school-master, for the oldest fellows at school knew her to be there when they came. The fellows didn't know much about her, though, Dewitt said, as she never appeared in the boys' part of the house, and might as well be a hundred miles away for all they saw of her, except once in a long while at church. "Rufus" lived on the second floor of the Institute, and no one was ever allowed to go into a room on that floor except the parson, or the other teachers, Bond and Vane, who took their meals there. But what surprised me more than anything else that Dewitt told me, was his positive assertion that the school-master often went to the village of an afternoon to meet a parcel of political cronies there, and upon returning home, late at night, drunk, had been heard, by the boys in their rooms, to rave around downstairs by the hour and abuse his wife awfully. One night, two of the boys had started to go downstairs, thinking that murder was going on in the house, but they found Ezekiel Reed in the hall, all dressed and listening, and he drove them back, and reported them next day for being out of their rooms. Didn't they get locked up in the cellar for awhile, though! You bet they did!

Inspired by the recollection of that celebrated event, and greatly flattered by my breathless attention, the iron-faced lad immediately proceeded to confide to me his utter sickness of school and vague intention of writing his father very decisively to that effect. He guessed* he wasn't the only one sick of it, either. There was Vane, the teacher of Latin, Greek, and Algebra, who'd just as soon leave as not, and treated Old Rufus so uppishly that the fellows were always expecting a row. He took things easily enough —oh, didn't he? —and used the nag and rockaway as if he owned them. Old Bond, the English and Writing teacher, didn't dare do so; in fact, Old Bond was tame as a cow; but the boys liked him, though. Old Yaller was a trump, too, and never reported the fellows for hunting eggs in the stable. He was a slave and belonged to Old Rufus, and it was a shame for that fellow, Cutter, over there, to call him names the way he did.

* *Guess* is the American for *suppose*. This explanation may be necessary in case any genuine Briton should peruse this biography.

By this time we had reached the village, where all talking must cease and the boys assume that gravely meditative air which properly advertises the dignity of scholastic pursuits. The expected school-master had not passed us yet; nor was it until we had been settled for some moments in the rear pews reserved for us in church, that Mr. Birch walked softly up the centre aisle, accompanied, or followed rather, by a tall, veiled lady, in deep mourning, and Mr. Vane in his unseasonable suit. They went to a seat far from us, and near the pulpit, the lady entering it first, with a haughty sweep past the school-master, and Mr. Vane immediately following her.

It needed not a nudge from Dewitt to make me look towards the three as they sat stiffly there, with vacant spaces between them. I was old enough, and realized enough of family estrangements, to be greatly interested in persons of whom I had just heard so much, and the officiating clergyman had given out the first hymn before my attention became sufficiently general to notice that Mr. Bond was already nodding, and that Ezekiel Reed had taken his place in the gallery with the choir.

Church was another novelty to me. As my mind echoes that sentence I go over it again with my lips, and a chill is at my heart. I had never been in a church before, God pity me! No prayers at a mother's knee for me; no child's altar at home, no mother's unwritten Bible there for me. It all comes back as I sit here, and in the feeling it awakens I am more than thankful to recognize a proof that what might have been is not!

The prayers, the sermon, the singing, were to me like the dream a younger child might have wandered into from the murmuring of a shell at his ear; and when the last word of the benediction was said I went out through the throng with my companions as though unconscious of their presence.

"Here, Glibun! we've got to hold on here a minute," said Dewitt, catching me by the shoulder.

Looking up, I saw that the boys were standing in a group on the green, to let Mr. Birch pass to his wagon, and the school-master almost stumbled against me on his way to the tree under which Yaller was watching the gray horse. At his side, but without taking his arm, walked the lady, and just behind the two lounged Mr. Vane.

With childish curiosity I stared straight at Mrs. Birch, until I was abashed at seeing that she was evidently returning my stare from behind her veil. At least, there was something in the rigidity of her head which made me think so; and Mr. Birch probably thought so too, for he stopped a moment, and motioned impatiently with his finger for me to go in amongst the boys.

Dinner at Oxford Institute was but a heartier repetition of breakfast. Between that and sundown, however, we were allowed the liberty of the school-room, on condition of being quiet, and I then had some opportunity to become acquainted with my future fellow-students. Willie Dewitt, who had taken me under his special protection, soon made me familiar with all around by the ingenious expedient of stealthily sticking a pin into one after another of them, and unblushingly referring to me as the offender in each instance; and, although the plan subjected me to a variety of embarrassing interviews with irritated youths, I am bound to say that it made me acquainted with everybody in much less time than would have been consumed by any other process.

The new sense of freedom which I experienced in such company inclined me to like them all. I had shades of preference, though, and I may say that I liked Hastings Cutter least of any. He came, as I afterwards learned, from South Carolina, where his father was a planter, and the boys had a story that he had been sent from home for nearly killing his mother's cook with a carving-knife. He had the wide nose, heavy under-lip, and slightly Africanized intonations of speech often noticeable in the South, and his dark complexion, small black eyes, and closely curling hair helped to constitute an aspect anything but gentle. He was about two years older than I, and, owing to defective digestion, was so chivalrous in disposition that no younger companion was safe with him for an hour. This, of course, I was to discover subsequently; but my first impression of Cutter was not entirely sympathetic.

Cassius Streight was a pale, slender lad, from Roxbury, Massachusetts, whose eccentric bearing and general severity of countenance left the ordinary observer in hopeless speculation as to his age. He had straight auburn hair reaching to his collar, and sidled about when he walked, as though the upper half of his body suspected itself of being carried on strange legs. But Streight's large brown eyes laughed at me when all the rest of his face was stony, and I liked him particularly.

In short, as before intimated, I liked them all. My very strongest liking, though, had settled upon Willie Dewitt, because I felt best acquainted with him, and I was pleased enough when Mr. Bond and Yaller went up to the sleeping-rooms that night and arranged for me to occupy the second cot in his room. The room was smaller than that in which I had passed the previous night, and the chairs and bureau much shabbier; but I did not mind that, and Dewitt said he was right glad to have me for a chum.

After we had both retired, and Ezekiel had been around to see that all the lights were out, Dewitt whispered from his cot,—

"Say, Glibun!"

"'m 'm?" queried I.

"I say, Glibun, when you was coming up with Old Rufus, did he ask you why a fly could creep up a wall?"

I whispered a weird affirmative.

There came a strangling giggle from the other cot, ending in a rapturous whisper of "He gets that off on everybody!" A brief silence followed to enable my vivacious room-mate to produce a sound with his finger and lip like the popping of a cork, and then came the further question, —

"But you don't mean to say that Old Rufus cracked any Latin gibberish on you, — do you?"

In whisper I expressed the belief that it was Dutch.

Pop! pop! went two large corks, followed by an effervescence of giggle, and then were poured out the words, "He gets it off on everybody! He don't know any more Latin than Old Yaller does! But I say, Glibun," added Dewitt, "are your daddy and mother going to keep you here long?"

"I aint got no mother," answered I.

"Why, Glibun, you don't mean to say she's dead?"

"Yes."

"But, Glibun," — I think he arose upon his elbow and peered at me through the darkness, — "haven't you really got any mother at all?"

"No."

The boy seemed unable to believe in such a state of things. I was falling asleep, when he aroused me by getting half-way off his cot and feeling across my pillow with one of his hands.

"Glibun!"

"Hey?"

"Haven't you really got any mother? Upon your word and sacred honor?"

"No, I haint!"

"I think," said the voice of Willie Dewitt, retiring from me as he laid softly down again, — "I think I'll write to my mother to-morrow."

———◆———

CHAPTER IX.

Goodman & Co. were merchant-princes, and received vast annual tribute from their innocent vassals, the provincial retailers of the South and West. Their principality was a goodly brick building of three stories and cellar, not far from the Bowling Green on Broadway, and it was significant of their royal dignity that they had passed through all the upward grades of lessening signs, and attained the mercantile altitude where it becomes the duty of the world to know just where the Establishment is, without aid from vulgar sign-boards. To call such an edifice a store would be truly rural and unworthy a refined republic. Stores must have signs, from the mere pimple of a black and gilt tin card in the show-window, to the fully developed disease all over the front. Establishments are severely unlet-tered from roof to street, as becomes the familiar haunts of princes; and the house of Goodman & Co. went so far in republican simplicity as to have the names of the august firm printed in smaller type on its bill-heads than any other line thereon.

The interior of this Establishment, on all its floors, was studiously devoid of the common aspects of sale. There were the importations, sternly stacked on endless tables and mathematical shelves: Broad-cloth and silks, first floor; laces and embroideries, second floor; cotton and woollen, third floor; Yankee-notion department, front cellar. In an atmosphere tempered to churchly twilight by an arrangement of blue shades on a central skylight, the importations loomed funereally to the eye whichever way it turned, and asked nobody to buy them. There they were; they were to be obtained for so much on draft. To buy them for money was out of the question; they were not that sort of article, at all. This was *not* a store.

The importations thus lying in state were sincerely mourned by sombre beings in decent black, who wandered around them in all the dignity of the most respectable despair, and could only be cheered by the arrival of frequent sympathizing inferiors from the South and West. Forgetting, in their genuine grief, all distinctions of rank, they would take these inferiors from place to place, to look upon what was there, delivering a brief funeral discourse at each stopping, and ordering certain undertakers, or porters, to "lay out" the bill. There may have been young men among these bereaved mortals, but their manners were toned down to the solemnity of their calling, and they dressed by rank, from the rigid black post of a man with an inverted triangular mosaic of white shirt-bosom, who mourned the Yankee notions in the cellar, up to the senior watcher whose ruffled mosaic, mourning-ring, and substantial gold fob-chain, were the highest grade of memorial insignia, before arriving at the magnificent firm themselves in a sash-bound private burial-ground in the rear of the broadcloth and silk mausoleum.

Away up with the cottons and woollens were half a dozen little mutes, with feather-brushes in their hands, continually turning to dust. Something of the outer world, though, crept into the shades of the first floor in the persons of a cashier and the first and second book-keepers, all of whom wore figured vests and abstruse masonic breast-pins; but if you wanted to see the volatile outer world itself, you must descend to the remoter half of the cellar-floor, where a perpetual gas-light, aided by a conical shade of green paper, threw its pallid radiance over a standing desk and a manly form writing thereat.

Mr. Benton Stiles, entry clerk in the Establishment of Goodman & Co., had seen better days; or, at least, he had seen lighter days; and that fact was evident in the gentlemanly, forward slant of his well-oiled black hair, and the pertinacity with which he wore a mercilessly-brushed dress-coat and the most rakish of silk hats. Upon his linen front of scattered pink vines appeared a horse's head sculptured in cornelian, and on the little finger of his right hand blazed an enormous locket-ring containing Her portrait. His face derived vivacity from a pair of twinkling black eyes and a prim goatee; and a small heap of peanuts on his desk, just beyond the large book in which he was writing, indicated a philosophical temperament.

In the glow of another light, some distance off, with a pile of varied importations before him on a detached counter, stood Mr. Charles Spanyel, eye-glass on nose, and curly brown wig on head. Short and natty was that gentleman, with large features, ample collar, and the dress of one of the mourners upstairs.

"All ready now for this bill, Stiles?" asked Mr. Spanyel, after an admonitory cough.

"Drive on, my jockey," responded Mr. Stiles, dipping his pen into the ink with a flourish.

"One piece, broadcloth, number two nought seven," proclaimed Mr. Spanyel.

"One — piece — broad — cloth —

"'And there was mounting in hot haste; the steed,
The mustering squadron, and the clattering car,
Went pouring forward with impetuous speed,
And swiftly forming in —'

number two — nought — seven. Drive ahead."

"Two pieces, ditto. Number three five nine."

"Two — pieces —

"'The glories of our blood and state
Are shadows, not substantial things;
There is no armor against fate;
Death lays his icy hand on —'

ditto. Number three — five — nine."

"Got that down? Six gross Coates's cotton, assorted numbers."

"Six gross — you said six? —

"'Where Solitude, sad nurse of care,
To sickly musing gives the pensive mind,
There madness enters; and the dim-eyed fiend,
Lorn Melancholy, night and day provokes —'

Coates's — cotton. Assorted — numbers. Well!"

"Twenty pairs elastic suspenders, with patent buckles. And send by express."

"Twenty — pairs — elastic —

"'Know'st thou the land where citron-apples bloom,
And oranges like gold in leafy gloom;
A gentle wind from deep blue heaven blows,
The myrtle thick, and —'

suspenders — with — patent buckles —

"'Know'st thou it, then?
'Tis there! 'tis there!'

Send by — express."

"We'll call that bill back, and give the prices, after we've been to dinner," said Mr. Spanyel, coming toward the desk with his hat in his hand. "You're to dine with me to-day, you know; for I shan't go up home until the last train. By the way, Stiles," added Mr. Spanyel, looking admiringly at that gentleman, as he smoothed his silk hat with a coat-sleeve, "is that a play I hear you repeating to yourself so much?"

"A play!" ejaculated Mr. Stiles, contemptuously. "No, sir! Modern plays are dimd nonsense. It's poetry, sir; it's the only thing that keeps me from going mad! when I think of myself reduced down to taking three hundred and fifty a year for such degradation as this! Who was the top-sawyer at Niagara four summers ago? He stands before you now, a miserable devil!"

Here Mr. Stiles clenched one of his fists, and went through the motion of stabbing himself to the heart.

"Don't give way, my boy; don't give way, my boy," urged Mr. Spanyel, patting him soothingly on the back. "A man of your ability is sure to come out all right. I've always recognized your abilities; and if some of the others upstairs —"

"They're snobs, sir!" interrupted Mr. Stiles, passionately. "They're snobs!"

"And if the Yankee-notion man in front there —"

"He's a beast!" sneered Mr. Stiles, glaring toward the front of the cellar.

"Well, no matter for them," purred Mr. Spanyel; "you'll rise to your proper level yet. I don't know but I can help you myself. What do you think of such a man as General Cringer?"

"I think," said the victim of circumstances, eating a peanut, "that Cringer is immense. He's Augustus, Mecænus, Talleyrand, and Richelieu, all holding the ribbons at once. I came near knowing Cringer several times when I was a top-sawyer."

The recollection of that period so deeply affected Mr. Stiles that he shook his head like an oracular mandarin, and abstractedly buttoned his coat up to the very neck.

"Stiles, my boy," whispered Mr. Spanyel, rubbing his hands, "General Cringer wants a Secretary, and you're the very man for him! You must meet him."

"I will!" exclaimed the late top-sawyer. "Shake hands on it, Uncle Charley, and see me visibly improve, sir, at the bare idea. I go, and it is done!"

Mr. Stiles slid his right foot forward, stamped twice with it, and stabbed the air with a ruler.

"And now let's try some dinner."

The reduced gentleman and his patron emerged from the sepulchre of Yankee notions into the broadcloth and silk Cimmerio, by means of an iron stairway; and he not only committed the unparalleled sacrilege of swaggering on the passage to Broadway, but actually indulged, near the door, in a dissipated whistle.

The place selected for the banquet was a fashionable but retired restaurant in Warren Street, known as "the Frenchman's," and in a crimson-curtained box of the same, on either side a marble-top table, were quickly seated Mr. Charles Spanyel and the late top-sawyer.

"Now, then, where's the *gamin?*" queried the former, vivaciously polishing his eye-glass with a handkerchief, prior to cultivating his mind with the very thin morocco-bound bill-of-fare.

"Gammon!" called Mr. Stiles, projecting his head from the box.

Promptly at the summons appeared a middle-aged sprite, in a white apron mapped with gravies, who at once dashed at the table with his pocket-handkerchief, and stood the castor in Mr. Stiles' silk hat on the seat, while he obliterated a mustard stain.

"Francois," said Mr. Spanyel, "how are your cutlets à la Maintenon to-day?"

"Ah, sure, they're splindid, sur," responded Francois, tastefully equalizing the map of Europe on his apron by scraping its coast line with the salt-spoon.

"What do you take, Stiles?"

That gentleman paused in the middle of a learned chapter on "Made Dishes," which he had been perusing with the liveliest satisfaction, and pronounced in favor of bean soup for "a breather," and tenderloin with vegetables for the "second heat."

"And, Francois," said Mr. Spanyel, meditatively, "bring me Consomé soup and some bread — *pain*, you know, — first; and then a couple of coo-te-lets. — *Savez?*"

"Yaysur."

"What's your appetizer, Stiles?" inquired Mr. Spanyel with deep interest.

Mr. Stiles at once laid back in his corner, placed a thumb in the arm-hole of his vest, and glanced imperiously at the chapter on wines in the volume before him on the table. His turn to show some knowledge of high life had come.

"Gammon," he asked, "have you any Chateau D'Or?"

"Nawsur," answered Francois, with great confidence; "but the pig's fate is splindid."

"Any Vando Porto, Gammon?"

"All out, sur; but the biled crabs might do ye."

"Waiter!" thundered Mr. Stiles, in a sudden burst of the vernacular, "bring me a pony of Otard."

That one touch of nature made the whole waiter kin. For several years he had been in an artificial France, had the waiter; the spirit of the culinary Gaul had weighed upon his breast like a domesticated nightmare; and under the accumulation of Parisian phrases, in the carrying about of which in plates and dishes full three fourths of his life were spent, he had been smothered at last into a feverish dream that he was really a Frenchman.

"I'll do that, sur!" he exclaimed, beaming with joy at his temporary awakening to Anglo-Saxon identity; and having received Mr. Spanyel's order for Sauterne (which threw him into a relapse at once), he slid from sight.

Mr. Spanyel now exhumed from the several pockets of his coat, a small phial containing brown liquid, a pill-box, and a leather case of powders, and arrayed all three on that edge of the table which touched the wall. Some men are said to be worn out by the energy of their minds; but Mr. Spanyel's too energetic organ was his stomach. The disposition of that organ for exhaustive research into everything edible, at every time of day and night, compelled its owner either to put some restraint upon it, or to stimulate it with nostrums; and he chose to do the latter.

As he took his first powder, preparatory to eating, Mr. Stiles made an effort to save his own appetite from banishment at the spectacle, by hastily plunging into conversation.

"That about General Cringer, you know," said he, with a laborious swallow, — "what's your idea? Couldn't you give me a letter to him — 'Perfectly reliable young man — first circles — abilities crushed to earth, but will rise again — immense advantage of literary knowledge' — eh?"

"I'll tell you how I've arranged *that*," replied Mr. Spanyel, softly shading his phial; "we are going to have a little gathering at my place to-morrow night, — a *conversazzioney* as my cousin in Europe would call it, — in compliment to an English sea-officer of our acquaintance. The general has promised to be there, and you must be there to see him, my dear boy."

"Let's see," said Mr. Benton Stiles, looking up from his soup, "your place is Toadville, aint it?"

"Toe-der-veal," ejaculated Mr. Spanyel, majestically, — "Toe-der-veal. — T, o, d, e, v, i, double l. e. We take the name from a seat near Paris which resembles it, my cousin in Europe writes. But, as I was saying, you must be there to meet the general at our *conversazzioney*. To tell you the plain truth, my dear boy, I've already mentioned you to him."

"My friend!" murmured Mr. Stiles, "you've done me a great favor. If you ever have two of your own wheels taken off, just hail me and see how I'll pull up."

"I don't doubt it," responded Charles Spanyel, deeply touched, "and I'll certainly call on you if I ever find myself in that situation. You'll pardon me, Stiles, if I take a little of my mixture before trying those canned tomatoes?"

"Don't speak of it. A *conversazzioney*, you say, —

    "'Who riseth from a feast
   With that keen appetite that he sits down?
   Where is the horse that doth untread again
   His tedious measures with —'

Will there be many there?"

Mr. Spanyel merely paused long enough to recover from the shudder occasioned by the exceeding bitterness of his mixture, and then responded,—

"Oh, we shall only have a few. Besides the general and you and the English officer, Mr. Lord, there will be my former landlord. Mr. Wynne, who has promised to come with his old friend, the general; and perhaps half a dozen others."

"My wardrobe, you know, isn't up to the mark of a regular splurge," hinted his friend.

"You only want a plain evening dress," explained the other. "There's none of your mushroom aristocracy about us, my boy. You take the Harlem car at seven o'clock, from the City Hall over here, and you'll find the carriage waiting for you at the first station up-town. Perhaps I'll meet you there myself,—I shall go up at noon, you see,—if my daughters don't keep me back to help them in some of their preparations. By-the-by, Stiles,—you've seen some good life in your day, and ought to know.—I wonder what would be my best plan for procuring a good governess for two of my girls? I want a thorough lady,—a reduced lady, so to speak, and not a professional. You don't know of any reduced lady?"

"None whose pride would admit of the direct proposition, sir," said Benton Stiles, loftily; "none who could be approached on such a subject by a common friend, Mr. Spanyel, without suddenly kicking over the traces and obliging that common friend to take a back seat. I, myself, know what such pride is; and if any man had come to me a few years ago, just as I commenced to go down hill, and asked me to enter another man's employ, no bonds of friendship could have restrained me from punching that man's head against his own shifting-top! No, Charles Spanyel!" said Mr. Stiles, with great fervor, "don't think of trying friendship to that extent. You must advertise."

"But that will bring out the professionals, won't it?" urged Mr. Spanyel, sipping his wine.

"It will, sir, undoubtedly;" and Mr. Stiles balanced a fork on his thumb as one who weighed his words. "It will bring out those strong-minded trainers who wear spectacles and alpaca, and will undertake to break girls to harness by dint of an eternal sulky, —which is better, perhaps, than an eternal giggle,"—interpolated Mr. Stiles, with great appreciation of his own humor. "But it will also bring out your reduced ladies, sir, who may be willing to negotiate with strangers through advertisements, though their pride would shrink from such negotiation through those who knew them in better days. A dusty thing is pride, Mr. Spanyel; and I've got plenty of it myself, though three hundred and fifty a year scarcely support it."

"You're right, Stiles!" exclaimed Charles Spanyel, his eyes twinkling in sympathy with the wine he was drinking. The same favorable opinion was evidently entertained by Francois, who stood leaning into the box from a stand-point not far outside, and rendered himself interesting to view by industriously dressing his hair with a pocket comb.

"You're right, my dear boy," said Mr. Spanyel, "and, let me tell you, I have a high respect for that sort of pride. And I respect it in you, too, Benton Stiles; I respect it in everybody, and would not wish my daughters to have a companion and instructress without that kind of pride. What is such pride? Why, it's the style of article that distinguishes true gentility, even in rags, from the agrarian vulgarity of the mob,—the rabble, sir,—who rule this country."

To preserve himself from injury after such an explosion of honest aristocratic wrath, Mr. Spanyel hastily washed down a pill with his last glass of Sauterne.

As the two gentlemen arose to quit the box, Francois skimmed at them with a whisk brush in his hand, and committed so many complicated assaults from one to the other that a dime from each was the very least that could be offered to buy him off.

"That's enough, *mon ami*," panted Mr. Spanyel.

"Thank ye, sir," responded his *ami*, pocketing the silver tribute, "it's wan loaf of bread that'll put into my childers' mouths."

"What's that!" ejaculated Mr. Stiles, with sudden and violent emotion. "Your children's mouths? Are you, then, so poor that—" Here Mr. Stiles seized Francois by the arm and walked him away some paces. "Tell me, poor gammon, can I—" Mr. Stiles fairly walked him into a corner, this time; and, while Mr. Spanyel paid the bill at the bar, was seen to hold confidential discourse in that position with the unhappy father.

"Come, Stiles," said Mr. Spanyel, touching him on the shoulder, "let's be going."

"Eh! Going?" exclaimed Mr. Benton Stiles, turning about in great surprise. "Now, Spanyel, you haven't been paying for everything, again?"

"Don't mention it."

"If you get ahead of me in that way again, I shall really be offended,—I shall be seriously offended," said Mr. Benton Stiles.

"Stiles,"—Mr. Charles Spanyel uttered this remark very abruptly, as they wended their way back to the great Establishment of Goodman & Co.,—"Stiles, I've made a strange mistake."

"Confide in me, my friend."

"Why, I called that waiter a *gamin*, when I meant all the time to say *garçon*. How curiously a man will get his words confused sometimes."

"You got your lines crossed," was the reply by which Mr. Stiles intended to indicate his exact appreciation of the lapsus; and its exceeding horseness might also have served, in the hearing of a shrewd third party, as a clue to at least one of the causes by which a man of Mr. Benton Stiles' figure had been brought down to three hundred and fifty a year.

CHAPTER X.

A CONVERSAZIONE AT TODEVILLE.

HUCKLEBURY-ON-HARLEM is called by a different name nowadays, and boasts four liquor-shops and a church more than it did then. It has also a singularly pale-looking daily paper of its own, that may have grown livid from the rage with which it continually and injuriously assails the heavier journals of the metropolis; and, furthermore this improved suburb possesses a leading politician whose lungs may always be depended upon when the country is in danger. In the time to which this chapter refers, however, Hucklebury-on-Harlem was not insignificant, by any means. Being quadruply underscored by the rails of the Harlem Railroad it had become much more than *Italicized* in its own estimation, and set itself up as a tempting spot for men with large capitals.

By the romantic aid of a mellow autumnal moon, which glows like a druggist's yellow jar in the middle of a transfixed explosion of silver pills, you can behold Hucklebury-on-Harlem as it appeared on the night of Mr. Spanyel's *conversazione.* Not that Todeville was an immediate *imperium* in the Hucklebury *imperio;* for Todeville was full half a mile further up that majestic haunt of the sunfish known as Harlem River; but Todeville led the fashions of Hucklebury all the year, just as Saratoga leads the fashions of New York in early summer, and the gayeties at the "place" of Mr. Charles Spanyel were ever a source of exquisite interest to the Huckleburials. Did not the Spanyels do most of their marketing in that village? Had not the project of sending Mr. Charles Spanyel to the Legislature been more than once advanced by the affable and popular blacksmith, and as often approved by mine host of the "Spanyel Arms?" Was it not perfectly well known by all the deepest thinkers of the village, that the solemnly great Establishment of Goodman & Co. could never get along without Mr. Charles Spanyel and that a withdrawal of Mr. Charles Spanyel's immense and aristocratic business connexions would cause that establishment to totter at once?

You'd better believe it!

Consequently, from certain windows of all the houses, small and great, of Hucklebury-on-Harlem, anxious heads were stretched that night to notice who drove through to Todeville; and on the covered stoop of the "Spanyel Arms," right across from the little railway platform and station-house, a quartette of local celebrities, with red noses, criticised the horses, which, at long intervals, drew past a city top-wagon, or hack coach, in the direction of the "place."

Near the tavern horse-trough, stood a rickety, two seated open wagon, whose shafts sustained an inexpensive, yellow horse; and the driver of this equipage was observed by the quartette to straighten himself and take a more decided hold of the lines as the whistle of an approaching train sounded spitefully close at hand. When the train stopped at the station, he became still more on the alert, and at the vision of a person issuing from the crowd of passengers on the platform and coming straight toward him, he even urged the yellow horse forward a pace or two. The person mentioned wore a black silk hat, knowingly slanted over locks tending unswervingly to the front, and the defiant swing of his Talma cloak, as he crossed the road, indicated a character not to be abashed.

"Are you Mr. Spanyel's groomsman, or coachman, or whatever you call it?" asked this impressive personage, on his arrival at the equipage.

"Yes, sir," responded the coachman; "are you Mr. Stiles, sir?"

"That's my card," said the gentleman; "but haven't you got to wait for anybody else?"

"No, sir; the rest of the company drive up, or are brought up in carriages."

"I see how it is," muttered Mr. Stiles, climbing into the wagon, "I'm to do the poor relation business to-night. I'm to be the poor but deserving young man who had to take the cars. Oh what a fall mine is! Right over the dashboard into the mud! — Drive on with your crab, there."

The Spanyel coachman executed a sharp turn with his animal, for the edification of the tavern critics; and Mr. Stiles, after a hasty scrutiny of the plodding steed, was resigning himself to a reverie, when the clattering of hoofs on the road behind, caused him to look back. A light wagon and span, were coming up at a brisk trot, and the spectacle instantaneously fermented the blood of all the Stileses.

"Lay on the gad, there," said Benton Stiles to the coachman, with great animation; "those chaps are getting ready, now, to pass us. Come! quick! Start up, now!"

"Sir?" exclaimed the sober driver of the yellow horse, "sir?"

"Confound it! g'long, there! — be in a hurry now! — here they come! —"

"Why, dear me, sir! I —" The coachman did not finish his sentence; for, in the very middle of it, Mr. Stiles pounced upon him from the back seat, snapped the reins from his hands, and uttered one of those cheerful howls which are believed to be infallible inspiration to horse-flesh.

"Hey, there! g'long! hi!" roared Mr. Benton Stiles, his cloak flying from his shoulders in the likeness of wings, and his locks flapping back from his temples and ears in oily pads. "Hey! Go it, boy! Here! where's a whip? where's a stick? This umbrella under the flap'll do! Hi! hi! Giddap."

Whack! went the umbrella on the back of the yellow horse, while that thoughtful beast literally astonished himself by the rate at which he hopped along under such exciting auspices. His fast gait was a series of delirious hops, was that yellow horse's; and the team behind found that it wouldn't be quite such easy work to pass him, after all.

"Whoop! w's't! w's't!" hissed Mr. Stiles. — Whack! whack! — "Hi, boy! hold on to the seat, coachy, if you won't holler. I don't see myself being passed by any livery team, even if I'm in a funeral! Hi-yi! whoop!" — Whack! whack! — "Oh, *would* you?"

This pungent question had reference to the rival span, whose driver was evidently ready to make a final push for the lead.

"Oh, *would* you?" was the sarcastic screech of Mr. Benton Stiles. "WOULD you?"

It was beautiful to behold how that unprotected young man circumvented the livery-team in the very moment of their fancied victory. It was wonderful to witness how he plied the old umbrella (which had already assumed the appearance of a huge and crazy skeleton-bird), and made that rejuvenated yellow horse zig-zag all over the road, to the entire and exclusive occupation thereof. Frantically clutching the front seat with both arms, the horrified coachman bounced and bounded as though two thirds of his frame belonged to somebody else. Houses and autumn-fields appeared to be jerking about in all directions in the moonlight; and the fore-hoofs of the rival team threatened every moment to be in the Spanyel wagon.

"Up the next road," gasped the coachman between two agonizing bumps.

"All right!" shrieked Mr. Stiles, as the vehicle swung around a curve in three awful skips, and skinned the nose of one of the livery-horses. "Now then, hip! Here we are! whoop! — "

The moonlight deceived Mr. Stiles that time. He went just a trifle too near the hitching-post in front of Mr. Charles Spanyel's door, and he and the coachman were shot out upon the stoop of the mansion with a noise which brought every occupant of that mansion to the scene with surprising quickness.

The light streamed through the doorway, and over the heads of Mr. Spanyel and his startled family and guests, upon the figure of Mr. Benton Stiles prostrate on the mat, and that of the coachman sprawling on the upper step. It also illuminated one side of the wagon, and lingered lovingly upon the well-defined left ribs of the yellow horse; for the sagacious thorough-bred had jumbled himself to a full stop on the instant.

"By Jove! Stiles," exclaimed Mr. Spanyel, stooping low and advancing a lighted wax candle to that gentleman's nose.

"Is he dead? Oh, ask him if he's dead!" screamed the eldest Miss Spanyel.

"It's utterly absurd!" trembled her elder sister.

"How ridiculous!" warbled the youngest.

"Sensitive natures!" murmured a chorus of male voices in the background.

Mr. Stiles deliberately arose to a sitting posture, pulled off his hat, and ruefully surveyed its fractured crown for a moment. Then he gained his feet, cleared his face of his cloak, which was mostly twisted around his neck in the manner of a giant muffler, — retired a step or two to have room for a graceful movement, and bowed devoutly to the astonished and shivering company.

"Ladies and gentlemen," said Mr. Stiles, "you must pardon me. I had a little brush with a party on the road — ah, here they come."

Two gentlemen were indeed coming up the steps as he spoke, and one of them, as he stepped into the light, doffed his hat, and said, gravely, —

"I 'ope no one is 'urt."

"Mr. Lord!" cried Charles Spanyel, seizing his hand, "I'm delighted to see you. And you, Mr. Seaman. No, there is no one hurt, I am happy to see." (The coachman was by this time sitting up, at the edge of the stoop, and scratching his head in a state of hopeless amazement.) "But come in, gentlemen."

Back to the warm parlor flocked the reassured *conversazioners*, the new arrivals leaving their hats and coats in the hall, as they passed in, and finally resigning themselves to their host for the requisite introduction.

The building stood in, a short distance, from the Harlem stage-road, with which it connected doubly by means of a semi-circular private drive, and was the smallest of some four or five tree-girt residences in that particular locality. Constructed of wood and painted white, it had a rather staring effect by daylight; and its rigidly square shape and dead-green shutters were not entirely poetical in their suggestions to the eye. The front piazza, however, with its row of quaint white steeples on top, and delicate lattice-work at either end, was a saving clause in the architecture of the edifice, and looked quite attractive that night as the light from the windows defined it in a subdued illumination.

Two years before, Mr. Charles Spanyel had bought the house cheaply from one Mr. Wynne, a gentleman resident in the city; and a sense of ownership was not the least element of his enjoyment as he stood with his back to a mantel in the parlor and smiled immeasurable welcome to everybody. The large collar in which swayed his wigged head, the white vest emphasizing his hospitable heart, the springy eye-glass bestriding his substantial nose, and the white kids making his hands genteelly ghost-like, were all so many auxiliaries to the luminous expression of hostliness exhausting his countenance. He flattered himself that his parlor looked like the parlor of a thoroughly refined home that evening, even if there was no vulgar show about it; — that the candelabri in ormolu on the two mantels were gentlemanly; that the piano between a front window and door was ladylike; that the oak-and-green carpet with chairs to match were chastely genteel; and that the hard-finished walls adorned with portraits and fancy pastels did not frame a scene altogether plebeian. Could his cousin in Europe refrain long enough from the upholstery business to view the said scene for a moment, he might possibly be convinced that the American branch of his family was not without a certain progressive degree of social culture.

Such was the state of Mr. Spanyel's mind before the eccentric arrival of Mr. Stiles temporarily disturbed his complacent equanimity, and into that state did he relapse on regaining his position of receptive dignity on the rug before the mantel.

"Mr. Lord," said he, bowing in unison with that stout, red-faced, and sandy-whiskered Briton, "let me assure you again that I am delighted. You see, we have a few of our friends here, whose respect for your country — *our* noble mother-country, permit me to say — makes them all the more happy to meet you. Mr. Seaman" (bow), "you are very kind, sir, to accompany our friend, Lord, and will bear in mind my telling you to make yourself quite at home on the occasion of your last informal visit here with him. Gentlemen, my friend, Mr. Stiles, with whom, I daresay, you feel slightly acquainted already, after your late match against time. Ha! ha! Mr. Lord, Mr. Stiles; Mr. Stiles, Mr. Seaman."

Mr. Lord and Mr. Seaman both said that they were 'appy, they were sure, on being thus introduced; and as they chorused the same phrase all through the other introductions, and repeated it to Mrs. Spanyel and her three interesting daughters, there could be no doubt of their consummate bliss.

The first-mentioned lady, in a blue silk dress and with a coronet of braided black velvet resting on her still black hair, presented a plump and meek appearance on the sofa opposite the piano; where, with her hands comfortably crossed and a perpetual gleam on her face, she admired her artless children and answered friendly questions about their health.

Those three maiden Spanyels did not group very often; for, as there were only three or four other ladies present, they felt it incumbent upon them to scatter judiciously through the company and take turns in leaning upon the piano. There were moments when it was appropriate to their gentle characters for two of them to stand affectionately by a window with their arms about each others' waists, or for each of them now and then to kiss her mother in passing; but these were merely beautiful fragmentary instances of that exquisite feminine softness which explains much of man's premarital infatuation, and did not involve any stated combination of the three together.

Miss Spanyel proper — that is to say, Miss Flora Spanyel — exactly resembled her

sisters in her blonde locks with rosebuds and leaves in them, and her blue waist and white skirt; but her mouth, nose, eyes, and manner were larger than theirs, as became her superior years, and her steps were more like sailing — less skiffy, so to speak — than theirs.

Miss Rose and Miss Lily were specimens of the same hearty beauty in successively younger grades, and played as prettily with their lace handkerchiefs as Flora did with her mirrored fan. In fact, all the Misses Spanyel were mild-eyed charmers, though it seemed a pity that their features lacked the clear delicacy of outline which should sustain their papa's tendency to rank himself and his with the finer porcelain of humanity.

No amount of artificial aristocracy will give the profile of a Medici to a Smithers; nor will full dress and a gaudy carriage for a White-House reception substitute the physical legacy of progenitors in broadcloth for that of remote and immediate ancestors in corduroy.

Mr. Lord, the British sea-officer, in whose honor the *conversazione* raged, was purser of a Liverpool steamer, and had given the honor of his acquaintance to Mr. Spanyel from the day when the latter went aboard the "John Thomas" to secure a state-room for Goodman & Co.'s European buyer. During that transaction, Mr. Lord's lofty and distinguished manner of repeating the phrase, "Commercial Traveller," had excited Mr. Spanyel's profoundest veneration; and the proffer of a glass of Scotch porter in the cabin (it being for the interest of a freight steamer to cultivate such shippers as Goodman & Co.) cemented a friendship and evoked a respectful invitation at once. The invitation to go up to Todeville some evening with Mr. Spanyel, while the ship was in, had been accepted by Mr. Lord both for himself and for his assistant, Mr. Seaman; and the consequent visit produced the offer of an honorary entertainment to the British sea-officer when next the "John Thomas" should reach New York.

Mr. Seaman, the purser's clerk, was a smooth-faced, dapper little man, with weak blue eyes, bushy brown hair, and an intense belief in the social majesty of his superior.

Both gentlemen displayed their easy independence by appearing without gloves; and moved about with that cautious shortness of step which is equally characteristic of seamen in rough waters and landsmen in slippers too large for them. Furthermore, both gentlemen concentrated on Miss Spanyel, in whose homage they dropped enough nitches to make a Jacob's ladder.

General Cringer, in his most benignant and tolerant mood, stood upon the rug with Mr. Spanyel and permitted all the company to see that he could, like any ordinary man, mix familiarly with the bright herd in their little festivities. Prominent features had the general, and his wealth of iron-gray hair, trained with bristling precision from nape to temples, gave the bald summit overtopping it the implication of an extra forehead. General Cringer was there because he considered it politic to favor his friend Spanyel occasionally; not because such an assemblage had any particular congeniality for him. He had found Mr. Charles Spanyel not disinclined to stand for the legislature from Hucklebury-on-Harlem when the proper opportunity should offer, and for this reason he felt it politic to cultivate him.

"You say," said General Cringer, in the course of a conversation with Mr. Spanyel, "you say, if I comprehend your full meaning, that this young man possesses the abilities requisite for the proper and effective performance of those duties which facilitate public business in a subordinate employ like mine?"

"Subordinate employ *you* may call it, general," returned Mr. Spanyel, with elaborate propitiation of manner; "but the world don't think it so, sir; the newspapers don't think it so. A man who can elect congressmen and senators, as though they were his workmen, can scarcely be called a very subordinate power."

"Oh, nonsense, my dear Spanyel," retorted the great man, roguishly; "the public tongue will tell you more of me than I know of myself. I will not deny," said General Cringer, resting an elbow upon the mantel and smiling benevolently, — "I will not deny that I may have facilitated the selection and election of certain appropriate persons, on occasions, for responsible offices; but as for anything farther — the public tongue really honors me too much."

"The President never consults you, I believe?" queried Mr. Spanyel, in an ecstasy of knowing equivocation. "Congressmen never call at your hotel for a few hours whenever they are in town? For instance, now, *you* of course had no idea of who was to be collector, last week?"

Upon arriving at this point of humorous inquiry, Mr. Spanyel had got his head so knowingly on one side that his eye-glass tumbled from his nose. It was the most insinuating and arch cock of a head ever seen in private circles.

"Heh! heh! heh!" laughed the general, qualifyingly, "you are as bad, Spanyel, as one of the journals. But this young man, if I fully understand your former expressions in regard to him, has some literary facility; some gift with the pen, perhaps."

"I shouldn't hesitate to recommend Benton Stiles to you, general, as a man who can use a pen as cleverly as — well, as cleverly as he can a whip."

The young man thus richly gifted may have known instinctively that he was being discussed on the rug; for early habits on the race-track and in other debative localities had rendered him singularly intuitive as to the currents of the knowing ones' thoughts; but such consciousness did not immediately disturb the graceful flow of his conversation with the artless Miss Rose Spanyel on the other side of the room. Possibly he would

7

have enjoyed the interview quite as well if one Mr. Barlow Wapples had been less inclined to intrude his remarks without invitation. It happened, though, that Mr. Wapples seldom troubled himself about invitations at any time; he was the family grocer at Hucklebury, and had come unsolicited, with his portly wife, to the *conversazione*, on the strength of having furnished lemons for the occasion. He was a tall, lank, good-natured judge of flour, and frankly treated all his regular customers as equals and friends.

"Now, Mr. Stiles," simpered Miss Rose, "it's utterly ridiculous for you to say I look like pa; because everybody says that Flo's his likeness."

"I may be mistaken," growled Mr. Stiles, in a sentimental bass; "but it's pleasant for me to think so. Your father, Miss Rose, has been such a true friend to me that everything related to him suggests him personally to my heart. When you and Miss Lily called to see him at the store that day, and you asked him for some money, I knew you must be his child, even before he was kind enough to introduce me. Ah, Miss Rose, there was a time when you could have seen me first in other spheres. There was a time when I was familiar with such scenes as this at least twice a week, and went after boned turkey and orange ice for one who much resembled thee."

Mr. Stiles sighed, and unconsciously placed his right hand with its locket-ring in the bosom of his coat.

"Hor! hor!" laughed Mr. Wapples, coming genially up, "I hope three don't spoil company,—does it, Miss Rose? Let me look at that ring of yours, Mr. Stiles, if you don't mind. I was noticing it a few minutes ago when you had your hand behind you."

In a manner not studiedly untheatrical, Mr. Stiles swept the coveted hand to the grocer, and permitted a tender melancholy to usurp his features.

"Yes, you may look at it," murmured he. "The original of the picture in that ring cannot mind it now."

"Who did she marry?" asked Rose, sweetly.

"She is — no more!" ejaculated Mr. Stiles, shaking his head wofully.

"How utterly absurd!" exclaimed Miss Rose, sympathizingly.

"Why!" said the grocer, with a start, "I've certainly seen that face somewhere. Just let me hold your hand a little higher for a moment. I'm sure I know that face. — Let me see! It was never on a prune-box, was it?"

"Mr. Wapples," hissed Benton, sternly withdrawing his hand and malignantly eying the thoughtful grocer, "such a supposition could only originate in a mind rendered vicious by familiarity with cheap prints."

"Don't be offended, Mr. Stiles," urged Mr. Wapples. "The first woman *I* ever loved was on a jar of grape jelly."

"It is wholly immaterial to me, sir, what

—" Mr. Stiles was not destined to finish this scornful sentence; for, as the throng just beyond opened for a moment, his look of indignation gave instant place to one of unlimited amazement. — "Miss Rose! who is that person talking to your mother, over there on the sofa?"

"Why, how ridiculous! It's Mr. Wynne."

"Wynne? Bless me!"

"He's the gentleman pa bought our place of."

"The — gentleman — pa —

"'Oh, who can tell ? not thou, luxurious slave!
Whose soul would sicken —'

— pa — bought — the — place of," maundered Mr. Stiles, in the first stage of idiocy.

It was really extraordinary that the presence of such a subdued, and perfectly undemonstrative gentleman as Mr. Wynne should ruffle the tranquillity of the most nervous being; much less of such a well-seasoned personage as Mr. Benton Stiles. Positively gentle was the expression of Mr. Wynne's fine face, with its dark eyes and whiskers; and quietly deferential was his coolingly self-possessed manner, as he bent from his chair toward Mrs. Spanyel's sofa, and unostentatiously gave her that courtly attention which makes no distinction of age or condition in its chivalrous dedication to the whole sex.

"And while I am flattered, Mrs. Spanyel," he was saying, "by the honor you do me in remembering the circumstances of my first acquaintance with this house, you must also do me the honor to believe that those circumstances could not find a more harmonious continuation in my memory than from the pleasant scene around us to-night."

"Flora was afraid it might jar on your feelings, Mr. Wynne, and that's why I spoke of it."

"Miss Spanyel's consideration for others is hereditary."

"Oh, thank you! Do you think Flora is looking as well as she did, Mr. Wynne?"

"She is your own daughter, madam."

"You're very polite, sir, I'm sure. But I feel a little anxious about Flora. She appears to have no appetite for anything but confectionery."

"Sweets to the sweet," commented Mr. Wynne, with a bright smile and an airy bow toward Flora.

The while that plump object of maternal solicitude was laboriously yielding to Mr. Lord's strongly aspirated entreaty that she would evoke the witchery of music from the piano-forte; and as meltingly favoring Mr. Seaman's request that she would comply with the wish of Mr. Lord.

"Allow me to 'and you for'ard," said the distinguished British sea-officer, offering his arm and escorting her to the instrument, as he might have escorted an interesting female-passenger to the cabin-stairs on the first morning of a voyage.

"Allow me," said Mr. Seaman, making short steps along deck to the piano, and placing the piano-stool.

"It's utterly ridiculous; but I'll try," prettied the angelic Flora; and she made those dabs at her skirts without which no attractive woman can give seated attention to anything, and languished the usual truant glance of meek resignation at the adjacent Mrs. Wapples.

All the somebodies, and a variety of guests of whom it was easier to tell who they were not than who they were, immediately gravitated toward the piano, and Miss Rose audibly asked Miss Lily if their sister wasn't the darlingest creature?

Tum! — that is to say, ti-tuin! — Diddle, diddle, diddle, diddllle, did — dle — di! Dr-rr-rr-rr — rumtie! And repeat, con expressione.

Plump white right hand with a turquoise ring, seeing plump white left hand sprawling luxuriously on the spotless sidewalk, cheerfully challenges it to a little race up the street, and practises two or three false starts as an incitement. The left makes an impatient move to crawl away from its tormentor, which the latter takes for an artful feint. Away gallops the right, and gets near the end of the block before discovering that left is indignantly going the other way. Back it comes, then, on a sharp run, tearing up the pavement here and there on the way and throwing it tempestuously after the unsociable left, which thereupon turns irascibly about and hops rheumatically after the agile wretch. Up a convenient side-street darts the latter and bounds gleefully to the top of the first fence; from which it skips tantalizingly to the tops of several others, with a taunting delight not to be borne. Thoroughly in earnest now, and madly exasperated, the left makes a flying leap for the fences; but goes 'way beyond them; at which down scampers right into the main thoroughfare again and rattles zig-zag down-town. More provoked than ever, left bears down in hot chase and quickly brings right to bay, when the tumult becomes frightful and culminative. — Dum, di-dum-dum! Diddy — diddy — yi-yiyi — yum! Yi — yum! Diddy-yi, diddy — diddy yum!

Charming! Wonderful facility! Such a brilliant touch! Everybody was delighted and made as many demonstrations of applause as gentility would allow. As for the British sea-officer and Mr. Seaman, they would never consider St. Cecilia peerless again.

"Hor! hor! hor!" laughed Mr. Wapples, from the farther end of the enchanted instrument; "we ought to have a good song now before we put up the shutters."

The remark was coarse, and grated horribly upon all refined ears. Mr. Spanyel turned deadly pale with the thought that it would prove a mortal shock to the acute European sensibilities of the British sea-officer and Mr. Seaman; but the former quickly relieved him by boldly approving the idea.

"If you would hoblige us with another treat—?" hinted Mr. Lord, bowing to Flora.

"Hanything," added Mr. Seaman.

"Oh, I couldn't, Mr. Lud; it would be so perfectly absurd."

"Perhaps Mr. Lord himself will favor us with a *chanson*," suggested Mr. Spanyel, from the rug.

"Oh, do, Mr. Lud; I do so love English songs."

A murmur of general approbation following, the British sea-officer looked at the piano, looked at Mr. Seaman, and couldn't help yielding.

So down sat Mr. Lord at the instrument to vocalize "The British Tar," and hammered out a rasping nautical melody with one stumpy fore-finger of each hand. From a tasteful habit of accompanying his notes in alto with exactly the same notes in the bass, this gifted performer was enabled to invest his symphony with a solemnity of effect not otherwise attainable; and his seafaring tones reached all hearts at the words, —

> " I 'ave an 'aven, 'ouse, and 'ome,
> Though in a nut it be,
> Wherhever 'angs Old Hingland's flag,
> And 'earts of hoak are free."

Mr. Seaman lent additional volume to the stirring strain by loudly humming the melody all through; and, at the conclusion, Mr. Spanyel impulsively came up to shake hands with both of them, and Miss Spanyel positively shed tears.

Nothing could have stopped the congratulations of the company but the noiseless invasion of two gliding female domestics in pink, who brought coffee, lemonade, and iced cakes, on trays. This pleasing incident threw the assemblage into general conversation again, and gave Mr. Spanyel a chance to conduct General Cringer and Mr. Stiles to his "Library" upstairs, where several glasses, and bottles of port and brandy, awaited them on the table.

The Spanyel Hall of Learning boasted one mahogany bookcaseful of miscellaneous knowledge, to which the general at once referred, before taking a seat:—

"Small, but select," said he, affably. "No trash there, I'll warrant; but all standard authors in their best editions. The other day, at Washington, I was talking about books with one of the President's secretaries, — young Upperton, — when he remarked, that a gentlemanly library should never contain more than one hundred volumes. Perhaps you know Upperton?"

"I've heard of him," returned the host, striving to look as though his failure to know the gentleman personally had just escaped being a frequent success. "He's quite intellectual, I believe?"

"A perfect philosopher, sir," returned General Cringer, seating himself.

Mr. Stiles, who had previously taken a chair in close proximity to the brandy, was observed to fix his eyes intently upon the latter, and shake his head in vaguely mournful commentary.

"Perhaps *you* know young Upperton, sir?" queried the general, surveying their youthful friend with some interest.

"Ah!" sighed Benton Stiles, without raising his eyes, and still wagging his head, "it's a pity he drinks!"

The great man could only murmur, "Yes, indeed, yes, indeed," and give the feeling moralist a glance of approbation, before accepting a glass of port and entering upon business. Something more than ordinary notice was due to one so well acquainted in upper circles.

At the return of the trio from their secret and momentous interview, which had resulted in the engagement of Mr. Stiles as secretary to the great man, from the first of the ensuing month, the said future secretary thought it prudent, considering the stimulants he had taken, to indulge in a turn on the front piazza before returning finally to the heated parlor and saying adieu. Seizing his damaged hat in the hall, and donning it cavalierly, he slipped silently out at the door, and instantly found himself in company again.

For there, near the first square pillar of the piazza, with his hands crossed upon his breast, his back to the house, a cigarette between his lips, a white, soft hat tilted over his eyes, and the full moon bathing his whole figure in watery light, stood Mr. Wynne.

"The King of Diamonds!" was the dramatic exclamation of the startled Mr. Stiles.

The figure turned sharply about at the sound, and took a swift stride toward the speaker.

"Long live the King!" said Mr. Stiles, bringing his hands together over his head, and making an exaggerated oriental obeisance.

"O Stiles! I did not recognize your voice," remarked Mr. Wynne, indifferently. "Fine night;" and he tipped the ashes from his cigarette and sauntered coolly back to his pillar again.

"You have a hearty, affectionate way of saluting an old friend!" pursued Mr. Stiles, going after him. "It's quite affecting to see you. It beats anything I knew of you when I was a top-sawyer."

Mr. Wynne kept his eyes mildly fixed upon the leafless branches of the trees across the road below him until he had whiffed two or three light clouds from his lips, and then turned musingly to his old friend,—

"Mr. Stiles, did it ever occur to you that the porches or vestibules of houses are so called, because the ancient Romans used to erect statues in their porches to the goddess Vesta?"

"No, sir!" returned the other, considerably nettled; "that style of thing never does occur to me; but it *has* frequently occurred to me, so please your majesty, that if I had never put foot in *your* porch, I might be driving my own span now!"

"Do you know, Stiles," went on Mr. Wynne, with unruffled serenity, "do you know that I have a peculiar liking for this place? Here I first saw my wife, and right here, where I now stand, she said 'Yes' to my question. The moon is now throwing my shadow right, over where she stood then."

"Yes; to be sure, —

"'See where the moon sleeps with Endymion.'"

Mr. Stiles was superciliously trying to retaliate upon his highly unsatisfactory friend by retorting his coolly inconsequent style of remark; but his friend did not propose to give him further opportunity for that.

"Shall we go in now?" asked Mr. Wynne, throwing away the end of his cigarette.

"I follow your majesty," answered Mr. Stiles, with a very vain effort to appear entirely ironical; and the curious pair were presently in the parlor to take leave of host and hostess.

To speak plainly, the combined effects of the compact celebration in the "Library," and the interview on the piazza, were too much for the habitual assurance of the late top-sawyer. His parting bow to Miss Rose was mechanical, and, in a staring, dreamy way, he greatly alarmed Mr. Lord, in the hall, by unexpectedly seizing and wringing that sea-officer's hand.

"Forgive me, sir, for that little brush we had coming up," said Mr. Stiles, with a stony stare at his hat. "I bid you good-night, my lord; a long good-night, —

"'Twelve years, twelve tedious and inglorious years,
Did England, crushed by power and awed by fears,
Whilst proud Oppression struck at Freedom's root,
Lament her senates lost, her Hampden mute.'

May good digestion wait on appetite, and health on both."

"Dear me!" exclaimed Mr. Lord.

"Good gracious!" chimed Mr. Seaman.

He was gone before they could say more. Regardless of the yellow horse, which Mr. Spanyel had placed at his disposal to convey him to the "Spanyel Arms" for the night, he stalked rapidly down the steps, passed windingly through the snarl of horses and vehicles awaiting their owners and hirers, and strode out to the road for Hucklebury-on-Harlem.

As, one after another, the wagons and hacks overtook and passed him on his lonely way, he held down his head, and drew his cloak up to his chin, until Gen. Cringer and Mr. Wynne drove smartly by. Them he looked furtively at and curiously after.

And when all the lights of the Spanyel place at Todeville were out, and the whole aspiring family were soundly sleeping away the bitterness of such powders and mix-

tures as they always thought it judicious to take before retiring, Mr. Benton Stiles sat up in his bachelor bed, on the second floor of the "Spanyel Arms," and muttered fragmentary conjectures about the King of Diamonds.

<hr>

CHAPTER XI.

I PURSUE MY STUDIES AND SEE A GHOST.

It was J. J. Rousseau, I think, who said that all education bestowed upon a child before the age of twelve or fourteen is like so much breathing upon a glass, or metal surface. I may not remember the comparison accurately, but of the sense I am sure; and my purpose in citing the idea at all is to combat it in a degree by what I recollect of my own earliest acquisitions at Oxford Institute.

Not only did my very first lessons in that scholastic place of exile sink into the most retentive grasp of my quickened intelligence, but the process was like eating snow to allay thirst, and made me the more eager for the river beyond the spring. The careless, fragmentary way in which I had been taught at home made the regular system of the school an inciting novelty for me, and I plunged into my studies with a hungry enjoyment not to be easily sated. As I recall the feelings I had then, I can account readily in my own mind for what has been esteemed marvellous precocity in the youthful erudition of certain men of genius. From nature and choice they were as secretive and self-contained in their opening years, as I had been from perversion and compulsion; and with their first taste of the Pierian spring came that tireless ardor to drink deep, which I, from the same preceding circumstances, both felt and exercised.

Mr. Bond soon singled me out from the rest of the boys for my earnest heed of his generally mechanical course of instruction, and from thenceforth appeared to take a special interest, and experience a kind of melancholy pleasure, in my rapid advance. Patiently, and with the gentleness of a woman, he steadily caught and corrected all my rasping crudities of speech, giving a simple grammatical or rhetorical reason for each correction, and making me understand it, too; with judicious care he inducted me to fresh studies as often as I displayed a capacity for attempting them without confusion to those already in hand; and, although his face never wore a really cheerful look, my ambitious mastery of some knotty problem in the books would often call to his eyes a beam from his setting sun.

The old man's wrinkles were the dimples of his dead youth deepened into the graves of its smiles, from whence the wan ghosts of old laughs would sometimes flit forth for a moment.

The handsome and indolent Mr. Vane, from his aristocratic office as chief of the lower and higher classics, occasionally stooped to notice me kindly; but he gave to all of us that patronizing condescension which answers better with children and servants than positive kindness might, and I did not feel myself especially distinguished by him. I had a stronger sympathetic relationship with him in my thoughts, though, than with Ezekiel Reed; for that young St. John, and most girlish of monitors, treated Cassius Streight, Willie Dewitt, and me, with a meek toleration, provoking what I may term a cowardly dislike.

As for Mr. Birch our principal, he did little more than sit behind the central desk on the dais, opposite the blackboard, all day long, and either silently supervise the recitations to his assistants and monitor, or devote himself to a book or paper. He was the judge, Bond and Vane were the lawyers, Reed was, to all intents and purposes, the jury; and, if a case went against any of us boys, the court proved that it had some alacrity in the penal department at all events.

One day I was punished for fighting. Yes, I actually fought Hastings Cutter in the wash-house, after school, for pulling my hair, and asking me to beg his pardon for it.

"Say 'I beg your pardon,'" said he, holding me painfully by an ear, while the fellows crowded eagerly around.

"You hurt me," pleaded I, as the tears came into my eyes.

"Say. 'I beg your pardon,' then, little Yankee."

"I beg—"

"Hush up, you little coward!" exclaimed Streight, angrily; "what do you want to ask pardon for? Here, you Cutter! just take your hand away from his ear, and stand where I put you. You haven't got your knife again, have you?"

"No," said the Carolinian, sullenly; "Old Rufus keeps it in his desk."

"You shan't cut another boy, you know, as you did poor Little, that day," continued Streight. "Now, Glibun, tell him you won't."

"I wo-n-'t! bawled I, hysterically.

On the word, he flew at me grinding his teeth, and my whole body tingled with the fiery sting of his full right hand on my cheek. The flash of that degrading blow, gave instant combustion to a something wicked in me that I had never felt before; and, with a blind fury that fairly had a tiger leap in its own birth, I hurled myself at the bully and bore him crashing to the ground. Utterly reckless of what I did, and almost suffocating with the new devil struggling madly in my breast, I fought him there with both hands and feet, feeling his blows no more than if they had been made with paper, and growing madder every second with an instinctive ferocity to seize him with my *teeth.*

The boy must have read something of the wild animal in my face, for he at once burst into a series of frightened screams, and tried to defend himself with his elbows. His screams, the expostulations of Streight and Dewitt, and the cries of astonishment and alarm from the other boys, sounded without meaning in my ears. I dug my bleeding hands under his head, and was dragging his face irresistibly to mine, when strong hands suddenly tore me from my prey, and I struggled desperately in the grasp of Mr. Bond and Ezekiel Reed.

"Avery Glibun!" exclaimed the former, pinioning my hands behind me with a sharp twist. "Can it be possible that this is you?"

The reaction came with his words, and I stood perfectly still, panting and ashamed.

Streight and another boy, both pale as death, lifted my adversary to his feet, and were evidently much relieved by the fresh howls he uttered on seeing the teacher and monitor. Beyond a cut lip and some bruises on his legs, he was not really hurt; but he blubbered stentorianly in answer to all questions, and left it to be inferred that his injuries were mortal.

"Glibun," said Reed, "you are a bad boy. Mr. Bond, as father has gone to the village you will have to send this young Cain to his room, I suppose. Cutter, you go to Yaller and let him brush your clothes and give you plaster for that lip."

"Cutter began it, Reed," said Streight.

"Of course he did," added Dewitt and several other boys; "he's always fighting."

Mr. Bond had released my hands, and looked at me with an expression of sad inquiry, as though expecting and wishing me to say something in my own defence; but, as I remained stubbornly silent, he said to the monitor,—

"Master Cutter is a quarrelsome boy, you know. Perhaps I had better send both boys to their rooms until Mr. Birch gets back."

"Glibun," asked the monitor, surveying me with sorrowful gravity, "will you beg Cutter's pardon? That is, if he is made to beg yours?"

"No, sir," said I; "he struck me first because I wouldn't beg his pardon for nothing. and I won't do it now."

"Then, Avery Glibun," exclaimed Mr. Bond, very quickly, "you are certainly a bad boy. and I shall lock you in your room. Come with me, instantly."

Taking me roughly by an arm. he pushed me out of the wash-house before him, and around the front of the house to the main entrance. There he paused a moment.

"Master Glibun, will you ask it, now?"

I shook my head doggedly.

He said no more, and I was taken to my own room and locked in.

With a fever burning in my veins and a swollen sensation at my heart, I sat down upon one of the cots and at once began to chafe bitterly at what I considered the outrageous injustice of my treatment. So far was I from regretting what I had done, that I fought the battle over again in imagination with redoubled fury, and passionately writhed upon the bed and bit the pillow and counterpane in my renewed rage against my enemy. I was in the very middle of this paroxysm, when the door of the room quietly opened and Mr. Vane entered. Had it been any one else, the intrusion would have wrought me up to a still higher pitch of desperation; but, as he came coolly to the bedside and seated himself upon my trunk, my fury subsided in a moment to a kind of respectful defiance, and I pretended to be arranging the pillow and sheets.

"Glibun, my lad," said he, eying me with some curiosity, "what has got into you to-day? I should as soon have expected to hear of a sheep biting a dog. You might have killed Cutter."

"I wish I had!" said I, drawing a hard breath through my nostrils.

"You young wolf! what ails you?"

"He slapped me right in the face for nothing. I didn't do him any harm, and he slapped me right in the face. I wish I had killed him! Oh, I wish I had!" and I panted again.

"Now see here, my boy," said Mr. Vane, seating himself by me on the cot, "this spirit will never do for a child like you. Cutter deserves to be horsewhipped half a dozen times a day; but if you are going to do your school-fighting in this way you'll have everybody against you. Mr. Birch would have punished you severely had he been at home this afternoon; but if you'll take my advice and shake hands with Cutter to-morrow morning, before school, you may be saved from further penalty. Do you understand? You seem to have a very good friend here."

I thought of Mr. Bond, and better feelings began to overcome me. I remembered how kind he had always been to me, and softened at once.

"I'll shake hands with Cutter, sir," I said whimperingly; "and I wish you'd tell Mr. Bond that I'm sorry he's mad at me. I wouldn't have fought at all if I hadn't been hit first for nothing."

"I'll tell him what you say, Glibun, and I'm sorry that I can't let you go down to supper. I'll be your friend after this; so you'll have two good friends in the house."

He left me as quietly as he had entered; and, in a more comfortable state of mind, though feeling strangely tired and nervous, I laid down upon the cot and tried to fall asleep. I did drop into a hazy doze, and took a troubled and chilly imitation of rest as twilight gradually crept over the room. It was anything but sleep, though; and when I started up at the entrance of Dewitt for the night, and heard Yaller bidding him good-night after restoring the key to the door, it seemed as though he had been on a long journey and was returned unexpectedly.

By way of making his intended proceedings the more secret and plot-like, my friend blew out his candle as soon as he discovered my position, and then hastened to tell me how all the boys felt about my case. They were all down on Cutter — so he expressed it — like a thousand of brick, and were bound to shut him out of all future larks and refuse him all further privilege of fishing sums from their slates. My victory had been glorified by Cassius Streight until the fellows were ready to do almost anything to Old Bond and the parson for locking me up, and Streight had sent me an egg as a convincing proof of his entire approval of my conduct.

Dewitt gave me this egg, which Streight had obtained surreptitiously from the stable; and, although its uncooked state was something of a bar to its immediate utility, I received it in the dark with much emotion and felt proud of such a subtle tribute of esteem.

Having duly discharged his seditious mission and avowed his own complete satisfaction with the swollen aspect of Cutter's upper lip, my room-mate lost no time in getting to bed, and thereupon eagerly inquiring whether I had been "to my shell-house" during my imprisonment.

This shell-house was Dewitt's Spanish chateau, from the model of which he had induced me to build a rival establishment for myself in our nightly kingdom of whispers. Having once seen a miniature castle made of shells, in the possession of an early playmate, he had mentally adopted it thenceforth as an ideal palace for all the beautiful curly girls and regal adventures of his waking dreams; and from the night when he first minutely described its magical splendors to me, I had exulted in an exactly similar palace of my own, and taken thither all the imaginary curly girls and captive giants he could spare me from his seraglio and dungeons. Until overpowered by sleep, night after night we were wont to relate marvellous tales to each other of the latest dazzling events in our respective shell-houses; and as each invariably finished his present narration with the couplet —

"The curtain dropped and the play was done;
The curtain rolled up again and another play begun,"

there was always a very positive pledge of continued activity in the shell-house business until the curtain should be worn out.

"Have you been to your shell-house, Glibun?" asked Dewitt, before his head had fairly pressed the pillow.

I mendaciously affirmed that I had made the journey, and, on my knightly trip thither, had rescued a beautiful girl with golden curls from the clutches of a mountainous giant, and conveyed one under either arm to my shell-house.

"Not *golden* curls?" hinted my rival.

"Yes; pure gold," said I, in sheer perversity of spirit.

"No, they weren't, Glibby," whispered

Dewitt, very anxiously; "because, you know, the golden ones are all mine. You're to have the black curls."

"I've got her in my shell-house, anyhow," responded I, with petulance.

"I'll come with my army and take her."

"You can't!"

"I can't, hay?" He hissed this with a bitterly ironical inflection on the "can't" and a taunting prolongation of the "hay" "I *can't*, ha-a-ay?"

"No-o-o!" I blurted.

Down went his head into his pillow with a savage thump, as though words were incapable of expressing the rage he felt; but the words had to come at last, and he burst out with, —

"Oh, won't I punch you to-morrow, though!"

I felt too sullen to make any reply; and, satisfied with his supposed victory, Dewitt triumphantly went to sleep.

I tried to sleep, also, and never felt more weary; but there was a curious and deadening sense of fulness in my head that made me miserably uneasy the moment I closed my eyes. With it all, too, there was an inanity about me that I cared not to combat even to the extent of undressing myself; so I rolled wretchedly from one side to the other, and envied every other boy in the world, and thought confusedly of my battle, and drearily longed for morning.

I cannot say just how long I laid thus before my ears caught the sound of hoofs and crunching wheels near the house. The top of our window was lowered to ventilate the room, and I could hear the measured stepping and creaking as distinctly as though the whole still world had been my ear of shell to them. The very turning of the road was unerringly defined in the sound, until the latter suddenly ceased. Dead stillness for a moment, and then a shuffling, stumbling noise on the shell-walk in front of the house. A door creaking open, and shutting with a dull reverberation. Thump! thump! thump! thump! upon the hall-stairs.

The act of listening must have relaxed my nerves in some way and won me to sleep for a few moments. At any rate, I seemed to be awakened by a voice first heard in sleep; for at the instant I sprang up in my bed there was no sound save a soft flutter of the window-curtain at the top. In another instant, though, I heard a voice — two voices — from somewhere under the floor. I could not detect the words; but the voices there could be no mistake about; and, in a kind of dream, I slipped quickly from my cot and put my head through the half-opened doorway.

"—— creeping along by the fence! He must have seen me, I tell you, Zeke; and I saw him, and knew him! I'd wake her up and curse her if she was a devil! Let me go! Curse —"

"You only imagined it, I tell you, father!

Now go into your own room. Settle it in the morning. Hush!"

"My own room? — take your hand from my mouth — my own room! Aint she my wife? I *will* have her up, I tell you, and *make* her tell me what — he — wants!"

"Hush! hush!"

"—— hands away, or I'll murrer you! 's she my wife? and her room mi-ine? What's he doing creeping 'long fence? Take your hands —"

"Hush! Here's the door, now."

I stood stupefied by it. My head seemed to be bursting. A thousand wild things whirled in my brain and seemed ready to lift me off my feet. There was a light coming up the stairs, I thought; but it flashed out as though it had never been more than a flash, and I heard something fall with a thick, fluffy sound.

"Now, father, come in again;" — this voice was very low, but familiarly clear; — "you've fallen again, and we'll have all the boys awake next. Come, get up."

"Call her, then, Zeke," — *his* tones were husky enough, and even whining this time — "call her to her husband, 'tell you! 'm drunk, eh, my good woman? Drunk, eh? *In vino ver-ver'tas!* I know all about it! Vane, too! You and Vane, eh? Knock on that door, Zeke, for your mis'able hush — father, I mean. Ask her what he wants — not Vane, but that old tramp creeping 'long er fence. Knock! kick —"

"Father, get up, now, or I'll make you! Come!"

"Take y'r hands —"

Ezekiel Reed must have dragged him into the room by main strength and left him drivelling on the floor; and must then have crawled stealthily upstairs.

I saw a light really, this time; and it illuminated the golden-crowned St. John face, with its soft blue eyes peering along the hall from the head of the passage, to see if all was still with those who should not know the midnight secrets of the house.

Mechanically, and with my breath burning hot in my mouth, I fled noiselessly from the door to the window. A piece of stout ladder-work, bearing a heavy grape-vine, slanted from the sill of the latter to the ground outside, and there was a dull, dogged instinct in me, at the moment, to escape down it to the cold sod beneath.

With fevered hand I was drawing aside the curtain, from where it hung in lifeless transparency between the dark room and the watery sky, when the glass took an awful life to my first breathless glance, and I saw, pressed against it, a ragged, bearded human face!

The rising horror suffocated me before it could become a shriek; ice touched my heart; and as, with clenched hands, I threw myself backward, the world sank from beneath me. . . . . . .

CHAPTER XII.

MY FIRST ILLNESS.

THE washing-bell, thought I, must have rung long ago, and the monitor will give me a mark for being late. I wonder if old Dewitt is up yet? He might have called me, I should think, when he knows that another mark will take away my "Best Reading." I don't feel as though I had been asleep at all, somehow. I'm as tired as anything; and my head feels as if it were sticking out of the window. What's that! Oh-h, I see how it is; old Dewitt hasn't gone down yet; but he's dressing himself on tiptoe and thinks he'll give me the slip. I won't let him know that I hear him, though, until he stoops down for his shoes, and then I'll jump out all of a sudden and tilt him over. . . . Oh, my head! . . ."

"Pulse better — great deal better."

"Less fever, doctor?"

"Much less, Mrs. Birch."

I opened my eyes then, I should think! I opened them in startling proximity to a fat, sunburnt, double-chinned little man, one of whose stubby hands was grasping me by a wrist, while the other held a staring silver watch. I looked blankly at him for a moment and then instinctively turned a startled glance toward the foot of the bed.

"Elfie! Dear, dear Elfie!"

She started from the chair with uplifted hands, and had her arms around me before the little man could make quite sure that his watch had not been swept from his palm like a feather.

"Am I home, Elfie, am I home?" I asked, suddenly conscious that the whole scene around me had been changed, and that my voice was strangely weak.

"No, dear child, not home. You have been very, very sick, Avy, for several days. This is Doctor Pilgrim, who's trying to make you well again. Now put your head on the pillow again, like a dear, or you'll have the wet towel off. Don't be afraid; I won't leave you; I'll sit right here."

I let her do with me as she pleased. It was so delightful to have her by me that I felt perfectly happy.

"Is this your house, Elfie?"

"It's the school-house, pet, and I live here."

Another question was on the tip of my tongue; but the little doctor wouldn't have it.

"Ta — ta!" he said, shaking a fat forefinger at us and wagging his bald head, "you mustn't talk now, my little man, you've done enough talking in the last week to serve for a year. Such talking, too! — ghosts — wagons — fights — all sorts of things. Mum's the word now, until you've had a nap. Brain fever kills little boys when they talk too much. Now let's see what must be done for you to-night. You haven't got a bit of Helleborus Niger about you, Mrs. Birch, — have you?"

Curious to relate, Oxford Institute happened to be out of the article just at that critical time.

"Nor the least grain of bryonia?"

Unusual misfortunes never come singly; and there was none of *that*, — astonishing to say.

"Oh, well, well," said the doctor, with infinite toleration, "as the *congestio ad caput* is not so strong now, you might try a little of your lachesis, then, in some water. A teaspoonful every hour."

"Would Doctor Pilgrim write a prescription, that Yaller might go to the village for it?"

"None of it in the house, ma'am? *You* don't say! Well, if that's the case," said the doctor, pleasantly, "you may keep the wet towel on his head, and don't let him eat any rich broths."

With which necessary admonition he went affably out of the room, and Elfie and I were alone together.

"My poor Avy," she said, noticing that I was about to speak, "you must not try to talk until you are stronger. Your fighting that afternoon — O Avy! — with that bad boy, and your being so long in the cold room upstairs must have made you sick, or thrown you into some kind of fit. At any rate, your room-mate found you lying upon the floor, under the window, next morning, and I had you brought right down here to my own room. You've been delirious with fever ever since, until now; and I was afraid at one time, Avy, that you would die. But you're much better, now, and will soon be well if you keep perfectly quiet. I shall be with you much of the time until you *are* well. Mr. Birch, Avy, is my husband."

I started at the word.

"Keep still, child; I tell you all this, so that you need not talk this afternoon. Now try to sleep for a while."

Without a thought of disobeying her, and satisfied to the very centre of my heart in having one of my hands clasped in one of hers, I laid quietly as she had placed me and looked dreamily up at her through lids nearly closed. From the school-room below us came the hum and murmur of the boys at their last arithmetic-lesson for the day; and, as I slowly realized what the sounds meant, there crept gradually over my mind a vague memory of my encounter with Cutter and what followed.

"The man at the window, Elfie!"

The recollection and the exclamation were simultaneous, and I spoke with revived affright.

"Hush, dear! You shall know about it after you have slept. Now do try to sleep, or I must leave you."

She was certainly disturbed by my outburst of terror, and spoke with nervous impatience; but my pitiable look of appeal softened her again immediately, and once more I laid quietly at her hand and looked at her through drooping lashes.

There she sat to love and guard me, as I

had so often seen her at home; a soothing, cooling, tender presence, with just that pensive beauty in the pale face, rising from the gloom of her mourning-robes to the eternal sunlight of her hair, which calms the watching soul in a medium of trustful rest between instinctive melancholy and instinctive delight; a presence so real to me even now, as memory brings it back, that I can slowly close my lids and fancy it fading tenderly away as then, beyond the thickening veil of sight, like some beautiful vision of a mother's care from eyes that never knew a mother's truth.

It was night when the sound of voices, low as they were, recalled me to consciousness. Possibly the involuntary and spasmodic variations in the pressure she gave my hand had some agency, also, in breaking my stupor sufficiently to make me sensible to sound. At any rate, I became aware that two persons were conversing near me in suppressed tones, and felt no disposition to do more than passively listen.

"Mrs. Birch," were the first words I heard, "your contemptuous manner of receiving what I have said, might be more of a rebuke to me, but that I know my motives to be wholly worthy your respect. Since I first came to this dreary place, I have never been hypocrite enough to affect ignorance of the state of affairs between you and your husband, and to act upon such an affectation now would be a pretence of delicacy which could be instigated by nothing higher than such pity as you would scorn to receive. Why, then, madam, do you look at me so contemptuously when I beg of you to let me be your representative at this boy's bedside, for a day at least? Did I not come in here with your husband last night, and did I not hear what he rudely said to you?"

"Oh!" came like a wail from Elfie, "can I go nowhere to escape this persecution? Isn't it enough to bear the tyranny of the master, but I must also be hunted and insulted by the insolence of the man? O Heaven!"

"Mrs. Birch," — I recognized the voice now as Mr. Vane's, — "I will not allow myself to be offended by what you say in your present temper. I cannot believe that you are so unjust as to really mean what you have just said. I have ever treated you with perfect respect, and it is only a refinement of such respect that I am showing you now. The boy cannot be of such consequence to you — I must speak plainly if I die for it — that you should risk the violent resentment of a violent man, for the sake of giving him that mere attendance another might give as well. To speak still more plainly, what I ask is as much for my best interest, madam, as for yours; for if your remaining here provoked another of those unmanly outbreaks which I know to be not uncommon, I will not allow it to pass without my vigorous protest. Not intrusively on your account, Mrs. Birch, but for the sake of my own manhood!"

8

He spoke thus, in a quick, energetic way, and I felt Elfie's hand tremble violently, as she bent to see if I still slept. Satisfied upon that point, apparently, she cautiously loosed my hand from hers, and answered him.

"Do you know, honorable sir, *why* the man you speak of commands me not to do what I wish?"

"I am not in his confidence, Mrs. Birch, and can only conjecture. He probably has a private reason for it."

"It is because he is *jealous*, sir. Do you understand me? — jealous of that child."

"There must be some other reason also."

"I say he is!" exclaimed Elfie, fiercely; "I say he is! he is! jealous of that child! jealous of the air! jealous of a dog! jealous, Mr. Allyn Vane, even of his hirelings, — of you!"

In the wildness of her rage, the immeasurable depth of her scorn, she threw all care of me to the winds, and recked not if I was awake, asleep, or dead.

Cut to the quick by the cruel lash so savagely laid upon him, Mr. Vane so far forgot himself as to lash blindly back, —

"And he may have reason to be jealous, by Heaven! All the house knows of that boy's ravings about a man's face at the window."

"It's false! A sick child's fancy!"

I was staring right at them then, and saw her standing at the head and him at the foot of my bed. By the light of a candle on the table near by, I could note that Elfie's nostrils and lips were working as I had seen them work once before.

"A sick child's fancy!" repeated Mr. Vane, tauntingly. "Could that break a stout bar of frame-work outside the window, and leave footprints on the ground below?"

With that leaping stride of hers she reached him while his lips were yet sounding the last word.

"Dog! Spy! Pitiful—"

I thought she was about to strike him; and he thought so, too, and stepped quickly aside; but, with arms raised and hands clenched, she swayed slowly from him, uttered a choking, gurgling sound, and fell, rigid and insensible, across my feet.

The unspeakable terror I felt, as I started up in bed, was fully reflected in the colorless face of Mr. Vane. He actually wrung his hands. Sounds of feet on the stairs changed his whole aspect, though, in a second, and, glancing hurriedly about him, he came close to me.

"Say she has fainted," he whispered. "Don't mention me to them, if you love her. Not a word!"

He ran from the room with a something so guilty and cowardly in the motion, that even my boy nature was filled with a contempt temporarily overpowering all other feelings.

Scarcely had he disappeared, when the feet outside sounded close at hand, and Mr. Bond and Ezekiel Reed entered the door.

"My dear little fellow," commenced Mr. Bond, hastening forward with both hands outstretched. "Why, look! Glibun — Master Reed — what is this?"

The monitor caught sight of what he meant, and darted past him to the bedside.

"Glibun!" exclaimed he, recoiling, "what does this mean?"

"She has fainted," cried I, falling back upon my pillow, too weak and exhausted to utter another word.

There was on the mantel a bottle of powerful hartshorn which had been used during my illness, and, with marvellous quickness, the monitor seized it from its place and applied it to the nostrils of the prostrate woman. The effect was startling; a deep, agonizing sigh followed the very first inspiration; a tumult of sobs succeeded it, and Ellie arose, first upon an elbow, and then upright. But oh, what a change was there in her aspect from the grave calm, or even the resistless tempest of a few moments before! Her hair was all down on one side, her face was hotly flushed from brow to chin, and her bloodshot eyes streamed with unrelieving tears.

Mr. Bond bowed his gray head. In his broken spirit there was still a true chivalry that forbade him to look upon a woman thus naked of her womanhood.

"Mother," said Ezekiel, with the air of a pitying angel, "you are ill. Let me help you to another apartment."

The walls rang with the blow she struck him full in the face, and rang again with her harsh, unnatural laugh, as she flew from the room!

"Master Reed," said Mr. Bond; and there was a tear on his cheek as he spoke, "let me apologize to you, sir, for her. She is sick, sir. She is not herself. I apologize for her as for myself!"

The red mark of ignominy upon the monitor's girlish face faded into the pallor extinguishing its usual delicate bloom, and the smooth brow relaxed from the frown it had for a moment worn.

"I hope I am Christian enough, Mr. Bond, to forgive my enemies. Glibun, are you better?"

If I was better than I had been, I certainly was not so well as I might have been. The scenes of that miserable evening had passed jarringly through my head, as though the latter had been a phantascope, and they the glass slides bearing distempered images. I could only answer, —

"Oh, my head! my head!"

"I am very sorry for you," said Ezekiel, "and so is my father; and so are all the boys."

Mr. Bond dismally patted my shoulder with the hartshorn bottle, until he happened to discover what it was; and then he very gently removed the towel from my throbbing temples, wet it anew with cold water, and replaced it as before. It was kindly and thoughtfully done, and I was glad when he sat beside me, as another had, recently, and took one of my hands. His only words were, —

"I will remain by you to-night, my boy."

The monitor seated himself at the table, where the candle was, and drawing his faithful Testament from a pocket in the breast of his coat, began to turn the leaves.

"Glibun," he said, as he did so, "if I acted unfairly toward you about your fight with Cutter, I want you to forgive me. I thought I was doing right; but, maybe, I took too much upon myself. Don't try to speak. I know that you'll forgive me when I'm sorry for it, and ask you. I shall stay here, too, to-night; and now I'll read you something."

I could not like Ezekiel Reed. To some natures systematic goodness is always precocious; and precocity is more likely to excite wonder and admiration than to win affectionate sympathy. It generally has this effect in the estimation of the mature, and still less is its sympathetic attraction for the young and quick-blooded. Yet, as the youthful monitor sat there on that eventful night, like an embodied benediction after an unholy tumult of the worldly passions; the light shining through his golden hair until the latter seemed irradiate with a saintly essence, and his voice rising from tremulous monotones to a full melody in the ascending heavenward passages of the sublime Sermon on the Mount, I felt a cloud rolling away from all my waking senses as though touched with the luminous tranquillity of a purer world than this; and the figure of the reader, growing lovelier to those senses as they sank lingeringly away from it to the dying music of its own voice, dwindled first to a gentle star, and then to the gentler starlight of my untroubled sleep.

The morning sun was far toward the zenith, and all traces of both storm and rainbow had passed away, when I awoke once again to the bustling presence of Doctor Pilgrim, and resigned my wrist in painless languor to his scientific grip.

"Ay! ay!" was his cheerful salute, "here's improvement! A little weak yet, but regular as a clock. A perfectly quiet night and abstinence from rich broths have brought you round, my little man, as I knew they would — as I knew they would! Let the allopathists say what they please," said the doctor, glancing triumphantly around for a hearer, and suddenly frowning eruditely upon Old Yaller, whom I now saw sitting meekly near the door, — "I say, let the allopathists say what they please, there is nothing more efficacious in a majority of serious cases than rigid abstinence from rich broths!"

"That's so, Doctor Pilgrim, — h'yah! h'yah!" responded Yaller, with obsequious mirth; "the anabaptists don't know nothin'."

The doctor looked very serious for a moment, and chewed a bit of calamus with thoughtful gravity; but I recalled his attention to me by feebly inquiring for Ellie.

"You mean Mrs. Birch?" said he, soothingly. "Why, you see, my young friend, that lady is a little under the weather herself, this morning. She's been too much devoted to you, and is paying for it with a sick-headache. You must get along without her for a while, now, and let her have some rest. You don't feel any cravings for rich broths, do you?"

"No, sir."

"That's clever! You'll be up in a week."

He shook hands with me upon that pleasant prospect, and, having carefully charged the admiring Yaller to give me a teaspoonful of the thirty-fourth dilution of aqua lactea, in case I should have any pain during the day, went majestically away in a *similia similibus* manner.

Contrary to what might have been expected, the excitement of the evening before had conduced to secure for me the long and refreshing sleep by which I found myself so greatly benefited; and when Old Yaller, with many grotesque expressions of sympathy, placed a tray of toast and water on the bed beside me, I managed to eat a little, and felt still better.

During the noon recess, Dewitt, Streight, and several other fellows, came up to see how I was getting on, and the former gave me a boisterous description of my discovery under the window on the morning after the fight.

He himself had seen me lying there, when he arose from his cot to ascertain why I did not answer his question about the washing-bell, and had fled affrightedly downstairs to report that I was dead. Mr. Bond, Mr. Vane, and Mr. Reed hastened back with him to our room, into which the whole school flocked presently, and all seemed paralyzed at my death-like appearance. Yaller made the first attempt to account for the affair, by asserting, with awful solemnity, that he had found a fresh egg on my cot; but before the assembled minds could debate upon this abstruse explanation, the boys at the door were scattered right and left, and Mrs. Birch came hurriedly into the room. In silence they all made way for her, and, after stooping beside me for a moment, she impatiently desired Mr. Bond and Mr. Vane to carry me downstairs to her own private room, and as impatiently ordered Yaller to ride hotly to Milton for the doctor. She looked only at those to whom she gave these imperious directions, and at me, and followed my bearers through the hall and down the stairs like a solitary mourner at a funeral.

There was great excitement about the whole thing, in school that day. Some of the boys imagined they had heard a sound of quarrelling during the night, and believed Old Rufus had come home drunk and beaten me; others expressed the equally bright idea that I had received some mortal injury in my fight with Cutter; and they all agreed to cut the latter dead until I should be well.

It was thought strange that Mrs. Birch should show interest for any boy, much less for the latest scholar; and Mr. Vane's solicitude for me was quite as surprising; but Dewitt had a perfectly satisfactory theory of his own, to wit: I had been frightened into a fit by seeing a ghost, and both Mr. Vane and Mrs. Rufus couldn't hear enough from me about it.

"Did you see anything of the sort, though?" put in Streight.

With an aptness of concealment to which my whole childhood had been trained, I told him that nothing but fever and faintness had been the cause of my fall; and his positive disbelief in spectres made him completely content with my answer.

"You're getting better, Old Glibun,—aint you?" asked Dewitt.

I said I was; and all the boys gave me three hearty cheers just as the bell rang for a resumption of their tasks.

Old Yaller closed the door behind them, remaining by it until the last footstep had sounded on the stairs and the hum of voices in recitation became audible. He even put his eye to the keyhole for a moment, to make sure of necessary security, and then came on tiptoe to my bedside with such a curious look on his sable countenance that I raised my head to gaze at him.

"Misser Glibun," he said, "thar's one queshun I've been wantin' to ask you all this yar mornin', and I want to ask without no 'fence. Who was it that made the madam sick las' night? I want to know that yar, Misser Glibun. She don't done go and get crazy like that yar, without some abuse."

"She fainted," said I, in considerable alarm.

"Now jus' you see h'yar, Misser Glibun — was it Misser Birch?" The old black bent toward me with an earnestness of look and gesture not to be disregarded. "You'll jus' tell me Saviour's truth, Misser Glibun, — was it him?"

"No, it wasn't, Yaller."

"Bekase if it was, Misser Glibun," exclaimed he, standing erect in his rags, and shaking his black right fist slowly over his head, — "if it was him that did that yar; though I b'long'd to his father 'bout three hundred and fifty yea's ago, and danced him on my knee, Misser Glibun, when he was like you, — if he was to do that yar, I'd kill him! — by the blessed Book, I would! I've stood 'tween Misser Birch and the madam befo' now, to keep him from doin' what would make him worse than the angels of hell; and I've took blows from him that I wouldn't give to the cattle on a thousand hills. I'd stan' by him if it was for death, and say 'This old nigger aint no use; take him and let mars'r go;' but if he was to do *that* yar, I'd KILL him! — by the blessed Book, I would!"

CHAPTER XIII.

I OVERHEAR A CONVERSATION.

WHEN I reappeared at my desk in the school-room Mr. Birch was kind enough to come down from his throne to me, and ask, mechanically, if I felt like going to work again. He looked differently, in some way, from his former self, and I soon observed that he had suddenly grown careless in his dress (the sleeves and collar of his coat were plentifully streaked with dust), and had blue circles around his eyes. His manner, too, was more sluggish and abstracted than before; and, instead of looking at me while speaking, he kept his heavy eyes fixed vaguely on a corner of my desk. After my answer to his question he raised his voice so that all the boys might hear, and went through a forced kind of speech about the wickedness of fighting and the disgrace it was to both scholars and school. But for my sickness, he said, he should have punished Cutter and me very severely for our violence! but, as I had suffered in another way, and Cutter had declared himself very penitent, he would overlook the offence for once.

I looked over to Cutter's seat, as he said this, and was favored with a malevolent glare that indicated anything but penitence. I think that Cutter even shook his fist under his desk; but perhaps he was stooping only to pick something from the floor.

Having finished his magisterial duty with me, the master walked stiffly back to his dais, and the usual studies were renewed again with the usual inattention from him.

Mr. Bond was more gentle than ever, I thought; and Mr. Vane returned such glances as I threw his way with no signs of any closer recognition than if he had never seen me out of the school-room.

At the noonday recess I made it a point to go directly up to Cutter and offer him my hand.

"I'm sorry that I fought you, Cutter," said I, "and hope you're ready to make up with me now."

"That's fair enough," said Streight, in a cheerful, wholesome way. "Why don't you shake hands with him, Cut, and make it up?"

"Oh yes; you'd like to see me do it, I reckon!" sneered the other, drawing sullenly away from me. "Hadn't yer better go and get Parson Reed to make me do it? Didn't you, and Dewitt, and the rest of yer, do all yer could to make Old Bond lock me up?"

"Let's make it up," said I, trying to smile at him, and again holding out my hand.

His black beads of eyes snapped with spite at my amicable offer.

"I'll make it up with you, I reckon, when I've paid yer back for cutting my lip open. I'll fix *you* yet."

"Bah!" said Streight, tossing back his auburn locks with a jerk of his head, "you'd better go and throw stones at the poor nigger, again, if you want to hit somebody that won't hit back. Come away from him, Glibun."

Streight's report of this affair made my school-mates more friendly to me than ever; but they all agreed that I must be on the look-out for stones in the air.

Several months rolled on after this without incidents worth recording, if I except the common rumors of Mr. Birch's reckless dissipation at the village on frequent nights, and an occasional hint amongst the boys that Yaller had seen mysterious figures hovering around the school-house after dark. I saw no more of Elfie after the strange scene in my sick-room, and I gradually began to associate her presence there, even, with the vague images of my feverish delirium. My strong liking for study during the day and profound interest in the continued rivalry of shell-houses with Dewitt at night, gave me plenty to think of in the present, without recurring to the past at all; and a year or two of such congenial employment might have purified my developing character of the unwholesome elements left in it by the experiences I have related.

It was not destined, though, that my course should run smooth long enough for such a result as that; and scarcely had pride in my own budding abilities began to engender in me a boy's natural aspiration for a future, when the August vacation brought a sudden cessation of my dream.

The delight of the other boys at the idea of going to their homes for a month seemed curious to me; for when Mr. Birch curtly notified me to make ready to accompany him to New York, I experienced but a small degree of the pleasure boisterously exhibited all around me. I did feel some gratification in the promise of seeing Mrs. Fry and Sirrah, and rather more than a willingness to meet Gwin Le Mons, Constance, and my other playmates, once more; but the figure of my unsympathizing father loomed so repellantly over the whole prospect, that I could not echo the bustling homeward enthusiasm of my school-mates.

Mr. Vane was the first member of the establishment to leave; going, as it was understood by some of the elder boys, to visit certain relatives in Boston. It was the last day of the term when he left, and his cool way of ordering Yaller to hitch the horse and carry him to meet the Newark stage from Milton, caused even Mr. Bond to look at Mr. Birch, in whose disrespected presence the order was given, as though expecting from him some rebuke of such assurance.

The master, however, only glanced up from his book, for an instant, at his younger subordinate, and then went on reading, or pretending to read. Ezekiel Reed, who was finishing the yearly "Certificates of Merit" for the scholars, at his desk, turned a flushed face upon the arrogant teacher of the classics, and the boys lounging about the benches suddenly stilled their conversation to hear one of the monitor's moral addresses; but the face bent again to the desk without speaking, and the horse and wagon were presently heard at the gate outside.

Mr. Vane did not seem to have any baggage to trouble him, nor any other preparations for travel to make than were concentrated in the careless putting on of his hat in-doors.

"Mr. Birch, Mr. Bond, Reed, and boys, by-by until we meet again," he said, from the hall.

"Good-by, Mr. Vane," the boys chorused after Mr. Bond.

"Good-by, sir," said Mr. Birch, very shortly.

"I shall be back by the first, Mr. Birch; perhaps before."

"Very well, sir."

"I will give the stage-driver orders to stop here in the morning for a load to Newark, and in the afternoon for another."

"Very well, sir!"

Mr. Vane sauntered off to his usurped vehicle whistling a fanciful tune, and such of us as went to the door saw him riding away with a lighted cigar in his mouth.

Toward evening Mr. Bond started on foot for Milton, where he was to overhaul and write-up the books of an insolvent mill company; and when Streight, Dewitt, and I accompanied him to the gate, and gave him three cheers at parting, his half-smiling, half-tearful pride in the demonstration was very different from the insolent self-possession of his junior.

That night, Dewitt and I took farewell trips to our celebrated shell-houses, and disported ourselves before our numerous fair captives, or refugees, in a manner to reflect eternal honor on the valor of knighthood. Being in my usual yielding vein on that occasion, I voluntarily surrendered the girl with the yellow curls to Dewitt; who, not to be outdone in generosity, promptly confided to my protection a matchless creature with black curls, for whose rescue he had just slain several miles of fiery dragon. And

"The curtain dropped and the play was done;
The curtain rolled up again and another play begun."

In the morning, the Milton stage made a detour by Oxford Institute, and, by dint of crowding inside like herring, and clinging to the steps, roof, and driver's seat like flies, all the young Oxforders managed to go in one load; leaving me at the gate, with many ironical congratulations upon the probable delights of my coming journey with Rufus. While Ezekiel Reed was explaining to the driver that he need not call again in the afternoon, Hastings Cutter, from his seat on the stage-top, dashed a handful of pebbles into my upturned face; but, as I cleared my eyes with my coat-sleeve, and the lumbering vehicle turned into the main road, I had the satisfaction of beholding my enemy pinioned by one ear, while the right hand of Cassius Streight boxed him vigorously on the other.

Neither Mr. Birch nor the monitor paid the slightest heed to me until about eleven o'clock, when the former called me, from wandering around the lonely school-room, to put on my cap and come out to the rock-away with him.

"Now, then, you Glibun, come on!"

Ezekiel Reed was standing in the doorway, and, as I passed him, I looked hesitatingly into his face and said good-by.

He took a step after me, shook me by the hand, and said: "Take care of yourself, little Glibun."

The master waited for me on the shell-walk, some feet from the house, and when I joined him he motioned for me to go on ahead. I stopped, however, when he began to speak.

"Ezekiel Reed," said he, more loudly than seemed necessary, and with a quick glance toward the end of the building, as though intending a hearing for some one unseen, — "Ezekiel Reed, you will bear in mind what I have told you about letting no one in until my return?"

"Yes, sir; I will mind."

"If a tramp, or suspicious character of any kind, should try to force his way in, on finding that there is no dog (I wish I had one!) about, you can take down the old musket from over the stove in the school-room, and use that to him. You understand?"

"Yes, father, I do."

Mr. Birch then hurried down with me to where Yaller and the wagon were awaiting us; and, without another word, we were quickly on our road to Newark.

The dusty stage-ride to Jersey City was rendered instructive to us and the other passengers by the vivacity of a western gentleman in a white hat and bleached linen duster, who illustrated the thrifty habits of New Jersey by relating, that when, in the course of a fierce March gale, a vessel was wrecked off Long Branch, the Jerseymen stationed themselves along the shore with clubs, and would allow none of the swimming voyagers to come on land until they had first promised to pay ferriage. During the sail from Jersey City to New York, too, I, at least, found great edification in the melancholy strains of a blind minstrel with a harp, and could not but wonder at the supernatural sagacity with which he subsequently found his way around the cabin, hat in hand, and never once asked contributions from those absorbed readers who had devoted themselves intensely to their newspapers at the very commencement of his tour.

Just outside the ferry-gates, with his whip under his arm and his hands in his coat-pockets, stood that unspeakable creation, the hackman of my father, and I regretted the absence from his countenance of the least expression that might encourage me to address him. Roused by our approach from a deep study of two fighting cigar boys, he turned phlegmatically to the door of his carriage and opened it for us with automatic precision. His face, between the eternal velvet cap and muffler, was rigidly unemotional as ever, and if the slightest degree of specific meaning could be at all deduced from his sphynx-like aspect, it was to the effect, that he had known all along that we would soon be hauled-up again for something, and come back to be locked in the same cell once more.

"This is really very thoughtful in Mr.—ah—Glibun," ventured the school-master, experimentally; "he received my letter in good time, doubtless."

It wouldn't do. It was against rules to converse with the prisoners; so Mr. Birch retired hopelessly with me into confinement, and the carriage went dexterously over the projecting ferule of a blue cotton umbrella on which a middle-aged gentleman was leaning as he talked, and rattled at a smart rate up Courtlandt Street.

Upon reaching our house, the master briefly informed me, that I was to get out and ring the bell, but he should go further. Accordingly, when he opened the door of the hack and saw me descended to the sidewalk, he thrust his own head outside and said to the driver,—"Take me to Mr. Glibun's place." Whereupon, the driver, who had not thought it worth while to descend from his box, coughed assent, and drove off again without recognizing my existence.

Cheerless and deserted enough was the figure presented by me, as I climbed the stone steps of that desolate-looking house, after a hasty glance at its shuttered rows of windows and a not over-confident glimpse up the street for some familiar form. As I mounted the stoop a splashing sound from the area drew me quickly to the railing on that side, and, looking down, I was nearly cheered to see Sirrah languidly washing one of the basement sashes.

"Sirrah!" called I.

The maiden dropped her dripping brush, looked up at me for a moment with not a ray of expression on her face, and then,—

"Oh, good gracious!"

The way she clambered through the window after that exclamation was remarkable, to say the least of it, and revealed a confusion of slippers and stockings of which she could not have been aware. In another moment the door was opened and I was clasped vigorously to the heart of my poor old cook.

"Master Avy, come back again!" exclaimed the childless woman to the motherless child, "and growed so much that his head's above my elbow! When did you come, and how did you come, that there's no one with you?"

"Oh, I see him on the stoop, and it must 'a been his carriage that I heard stopping behind me, but I didn't look, thinking it to

be next door's milkman," chanted Sirrah, in a kind of triumphant dance behind us. "Oh good gracious, aint he got to be a scrouger, Mrs. Fry?"

Cook said she should think so, with an air of pride; and I felt proud, myself, of being a scrouger, though utterly unaware of what that might be.

To the kitchen we repaired, after leaving my cap on the stand in the hall, and when a generous lunch had been spread out for me on the table, I commenced to both eat and relate my adventures.

No ancient troubadour returned from the crusades ever had such interested auditors in baronial hall as had I in that kitchen; and though cook and her handmaiden heard no tale of chivalrous exploits, if I except Cutter's part in my story, their eyes stood out with as much excitement as the most ambitious minstrel of great deeds could have wished to cause, and made me feel rather surprised at my own power of working upon the emotions.

In a vivacious narrative, somewhat irregularly punctuated with knife and fork, and with parentheses of bites here and there, I gave my school experience to them without reservation, save one important portion of it, which I reserved for the last. When, at length, I reached the last, I moved back from the table, and said, with particular emphasis,—

"And what do you think, cook? That's where Elfie lives. I saw her when I was sick."

"Child! you don't say?"

My revelation had made her jump with surprise, and she spoke half incredulously.

"Yes," said I, enjoying my culminating triumph, "she's Old Rufus's wife too."

"It can't be, Master Avy!" ejaculated cook, earnestly; "Miss Elfie's last name was Marsh."

"She's his wife, anyhow," returned I, very positively, "and she don't like him, either."

"Oh what a plot it is!" said she, shaking hands and head despairingly,—"what a plot it is! Such a thickening and a disguising, and no signs of the *denooment* whichever way you look."

"Oh, good gracious, Mrs. Fry!" broke in Sirrah, "you don't think there's been a murder, do you?"

Whereupon that imaginative young girl was sternly ordered to go instantly and finish her window-washing; and cook, herself, proceeded to clear away the table.

Thus welcomed to the house I called my home, and with no other thought of my father than the relief I had always felt at his absence, my manners speedily took the stealthy tone of the place as before, and I wandered about between the rooms upstairs, the kitchen, and the sidewalk, with the old sense of repression and neglect.

On the morning after my return I espied Gwin Le Mons playing a game of marbles with himself on the stoop of his mother's house, and joined him just as he was about to win the very last "nib" he had. Having drawn a ring upon the stone with chalk, and being suddenly struck with the fact that its unique and cabalistical effect in that particular place might not find an artistic appreciation with his mother, he delayed shaking hands with me until he had erased as much of it as he could with one of his sleeves. Consequently, the arm he finally thrust at me was marked like a circus-clown's from the elbow down; but his greeting was as hearty as though I had not prevented the perfection of his victory over self.

I was answering his questions as rapidly as possible, when a mysterious voice from above pronounced his name as if throwing it at him, causing his countenance to grow blankly serious in the very middle of a laugh at Hastings Cutter.

"I do declare!" said Gwin; "if mother aint seen my sleeve from the window! I'll be out again in a minute."

He briskly pushed through the door, closing it behind him; and not only failed to come back to me at the appointed time, but presently burst into such violent notes of anguish somewhere in the remote depths of the house, that I concluded not to wait for him.

Thrown upon my own resources once more, I went back across the street, and, after idling in the area and basement for a few moments, wended my way aimlessly upstairs to the main hall.

The door of that memorable rear-parlor stood ajar; and, as I noticed this circumstance, and realized that there was no one on that floor to watch me, I became all at once seized with an irresistible curiosity to enter the forbidden room. Why I felt thus at that moment; why I felt such an unconquerable impulse to pry into a place which I had ever shunned before with shrinking fear, I cannot attempt to explain. Perhaps the strange influence vaguely named by us as destiny had something to do with it.

Confusedly, and with guilty caution, I sidled my way into the parlor, my imagination making the door appear to press resistingly against me as I rubbed past its edge. How dark a place it seemed after the full glare of the street! The table, sofa, sideboard, and chairs were ghosts of furniture in a ghost of a room, and there was that oppressive stillness in the air which gives a kind of awful presence to solitude. After two or three stealthy steps toward the table, I paused irresolutely and half determined to retreat; but objects were already growing plainer to me as my eyes became more accustomed to the shadowed scene; and as I became aware that some light was struggling in through the dusty shutters, my confidence increased apace. Going to the window near the sideboard, and finding it lifted a few inches, I carefully turned the blinds of half a shutter, and let in enough of the day to keep my courage up.

I could then see things distinctly enough. There, by the grate, was the hair-cloth armchair; in the centre of the room the table, with a crimson wine-cloth lying folded in the middle of it; between the first window and door stretched the black sofa, bearing two or three overcoats and a newspaper; and an array of decanters with silver labels, and goblets of white and colored glass, shared, with several fanciful cigar-stands, the shelves of the sideboard beside me.

Moving past the mantel to the space between that and the folding-doors, where a shallow but very strong iron box was let into the wall, my attention was at once attracted to a small mahogany quartette-table, on which laid a black leather case. After surveying the latter as it stood for some moments, I grew bold enough to raise the cover, and was thrilled with delight at beholding two long-barrelled duelling-pistols in a luxurious bed of red velvet. I did not remember ever having seen a pistol of any kind before, to know it as such; yet I instantly knew those two glittering things to be pistols, and hung over them with such admiring awe as young heathen must feel at the first sight of their fathers' favorite idols.

I was debating with myself whether to touch one of the pistols with just one finger, when a sharp, rattling sound in the hall made me suddenly drop the cover; and my heart leaped to my throat as I heard the front door of the house swing open, and the noise of feet on the oil-cloth.

The instinct to hide flashed through my every nerve in the track of a mortal terror, and I found myself crouching between the end of the sofa and the approximate window, without knowing how I had got there.

Not a second too soon, either; for my father entered the parlor at the same instant (how well I knew his step!), and not only my father, but also some one else.

"Sit down; sit down," were the immediate words of the former, spoken impatiently for him.

I heard the other person sitting down, — not on the sofa, luckily for me, — and then, after an interval of ungloving, I could also hear my father taking his seat by the mantel.

"Now, my good fellow," said the same voice, "I have brought you here, where we shall have no spies, to learn what you mean by dogging me, as you have been doing for the past few days! What do you want? What do you expect to gain by playing shadow to me in a public place where there might be those who would recognize you? Explain this new foolery in as few words as possible; for I must return immediately."

"Won't you give me that paper?" — how I started at *his* voice. — "Won't you give me the paper I set my hand to in an hour when the devil himself made me do it? Didn't I give you back, or send you back, the cloak, though I knew what paper of *yours* was in that?"

"You certainly did, my good fellow," came the answer, "and you might possibly have done it under any circumstances; but you seem to overlook the fact that I knew of your having it, and sent you a direct order for it by a person not accustomed to being refused. Wolfton, my man, you must never dream of playing any treacherous trick upon me; for you are so watched, my good fellow, that neither fire nor water can hide you for a moment. Do you suppose I was ignorant of that fine romantic affair of the warehouse? Why, I know every circumstance of that night as well as though I had been at your elbow the whole way through. I knew you had the cloak, and, of course, sent for it; and you very prudently returned it. Consequently, that gives you no claim upon me."

"I know how I'm hunted down," returned the other, with hopeless weariness in his altered tones, "and I feel more like a wild beast than a man. I know I've no claim upon you. But something tells me that there's harm hanging over the one I hold dear, and it's driven me to beg for that accursed paper once more, that I may feel free to come out as I ought. You've promised you'd give it to me sometime, sir, and if you'll give it to me now I'll swear on the Holy Bible never to trouble you in this world again."

"My friend Wolfton," ran the smooth answer, "you shall have that paper at the proper time; but not until then. You are the weakest man I ever saw, and I see weak men every day. If you want money you can have it; and I must say, that your disreputable habits of moping around the docks, wandering over the country, — oh yes! I know *that*, too! — and letting your beard and clothes go to rags, are illustrations of a disgraceful want of ambition."

"Ambition!" He laughed a doleful laugh. "What has such a wreck as I am got to do with ambition?"

The castors of the arm-chair gave an irritable little shriek as my father apparently arose to his feet.

"My good fellow, you know well enough that my will is settled in this matter. You have my word for it that the paper shall never be used against you, — the word of a gentleman. Beyond that, it is useless to waste words."

"Then, by Heaven! I'll have it yet, in spite of you! If I have to commit murder for it, I'll have it yet."

"Why, my good fellow, it would be a particularly weak thing for you to attempt anything desperate with me personally; for, aside from my general disposition to take the best of care of myself, I keep my documents and yours in this burglar-proof, let into the wall here. You see, I take this ingenious key out of my pocket, and apply it in this way, — there's a knack in it, though. Open comes the door; then open comes this iron curtain — (I'm afraid this box wouldn't stand fire, long, for all its iron complexi-ties) — open comes the iron curtain, I say, and here we have the valuables. That's the celebrated cloak rolled up in that compartment, just as you sent it to me; and I think we know of a certain young man who might give something to know what is written on that paper so nicely sewed into the lining. — That was a real woman's device. It seems a pity that I knew about it all the time. — The papers in these middle pigeon-holes and in the drawers are all worth something in their way, I suppose; though I've not looked over them lately. On that top shelf is your paper — no! don't trouble yourself to rise just yet — and a pistol. That pistol has cracked more than once over the Elysian Fields at sunrise; but the law is too sharp for it now, and there it rusts, — loaded. Now I shut the iron curtain again, close the door, turn the key, and then — take — the key — all — to — pieces. There! If any one steals the key from me, well and good. Do you see? The paper containing your secret is locked up there with the paper containing my secret, and we're both perfectly safe while a man of honor holds the secret of the key. Won't you have a little brandy before you go?"

I could hear the man rising slowly from his chair, and I heard a heavy sigh; but he said nothing.

"Then, if you are determined to be unsociable, my good friend, there is nothing more to say."

"Good-by, sir; good-by."

"*Au revoir.*"

Dragging steps resounded in the hall as he went out, and presently the front door opened and shut.

I knew not what to do. Just enough of the conversation had I understood to make me miserably alive to the danger of my situation; and a wild hope that my father would leave the house without discovery died of terror when I heard him sauntering measuredly to the very window beside which I was stooping.

Involuntarily I closed my eyes and held my breath. He was at the window; the skirt of his coat grazed my hair. In the full belief that his angry grasp was descending upon me, I looked up. He had turned the blinds of a shutter, and, with his nightkey whirling mechanically on one of his fingers, was staring frowningly at some object outside. I could no more have withdrawn my eyes from him than a needle could detach itself from a magnet, and the intensity of my fascinated gaze magnetically influenced him to drop his glance directly upon me.

His recoil and my terrified starting up were simultaneous; nor did his frightful change of countenance lessen the instinct of self-protection that had brought me spasmodically to my feet.

"I couldn't help it, sir!" I cried, hoarsely. "Upon my word and sacred honor, I didn't mean to listen at all!"

"You young devil!"

I turned sick at heart under the baleful glare of his blazing eyes.

"You — young — devil!"

"O sir, upon my word and sacred honor, I didn't mean to do it! I — I —"

"Sit down!" he thundered, pointing, with trembling finger, at the sofa. "Sit down there!"

Trembling in every limb, and scarcely breathing, I obeyed.

As he looked steadily into my pallid face, the fire in his eyes changed into a settled, smouldering glow, and a darkening, like the shadow of a hand, crept slowly over his whole countenance.

"Did you know him, boy?" He asked the question musingly.

"I didn't look at him, sir; but I know he was the man that was with me in the fire; and he was the one that spoke to me in the street, too."

He had given me a rallying point for my thoughts, and it made me stronger.

"How came you in this room, at all?"

His quiet manner calmed me still more, and I managed to explain that part of the business with tolerable clearness. Recollecting, too, his previous commands to secrecy in other matters, and thinking to excuse myself still further, I added, —

"I didn't mean to listen, sir; and I'll never tell anybody what you said."

Something in that speech went against me. I saw it in his face in a moment. He swept his beard with nervous hand, and looked to the floor for several moments in silence. Finally he asked, —

"Where's your cap, Master Avery?"

Filled with fresh apprehensions, I stammeringly said that it was hanging in the hall.

"Very well, sir; then you are all ready to go with me. Follow me immediately."

"Oh, where have I got to go?" cried I, miserably.

"Back to school," he answered, without looking at me; "only back to school."

I dared not hesitate to follow him into the hall, where he put on his own hat and passed my cap to me; and we went forth to the street together.

Sirrah was sweeping the sidewalk, and, after a single glance at us, dropped her broom and shuffled down the area as though bewitched. The girls working about the other houses we passed, and such persons as were at the windows, also looked curiously at my father; and I felt unhappily sure that they all knew me to be in disgrace, and were wondering what he would do with me.

Arriving at the first avenue from the house, my father called a cabman, gave him a direction I did not hear, and stepped hastily into the vehicle with me. During the ride he neither spoke to me, nor even looked at me, and when the cab finally stopped at the door of an obscure hotel in Courtlandt street, near the water, he sat abstractedly for some minutes, apparently unconscious that his destination was reached. Finally, on leaping from the cab, he gave the driver peremptory orders to see that I did not leave my seat, and I saw him go into the hotel with not the least idea in the world of what he sought there.

About half an hour went by I should think, and then, to my great astonishment, my father reappeared in the company of Mr. Birch. The latter looked shabbier and more dissipated than when I last saw him, and had a troubled, feverish air of being both unwilling and afraid.

"Now, Master Avery," called my father, "come out of the cab. You are to go at once with Mr. Birch."

I stumbled out quickly enough, feeling rather relieved than otherwise, and the school-master took me by the hand in a forced, despairing way.

"You understand my wishes, Mr. Birch," my father said, eying him sternly. "You shall be secured in any event, and I take the whole responsibility."

"Yes, yes — I understand," muttered the master of Oxford Institute — "I understand."

The ferry-gates were only a short distance off; and, upon looking back, as we passed through them, I saw my father still standing near the cab door, sweeping his beard with his jewelled right hand.

CHAPTER XIV.

MR. VANE DEVISES A REVENGE.

It was pleasant to be in the old red school-house once more, though my schoolmates were away, and neither the school-master nor the monitor could be called entertaining company for one like myself. It was pleasant to me, principally, because my gentlemanly father was not likely to make his appearance there, and, also, because Elfie was there.

When I made my way into the silent school-room, expecting to find it deserted, and intending to divert myself in solitude with slate and pencil, the first object that caught my eye was Elfie, who sat quietly sewing, on a bench near a front window. At his own desk on the platform, pen in hand and paper before him, was Ezekiel Reed; yet neither indicated any more consciousness of the other's presence than if they had been miles apart. The master's wife, with glance fixed steadily on her work, gave active signs of life in the motion of her hands only, and the low scratching of the monitor's pen was scarcely more assurance of the room's occupancy than might have been given to the ear by a gnawing rat behind the surbase.

Both must have heard the noise made in the hall by the entrance of Mr. Birch and myself; but my first steps on the school-room floor did not attract the least attention from either, and my immediate impulse to greet Elfie with a cry of pleasure died away when I observed that she did not look at me. What the sound of my coming had not effected, however, the sudden stopping of that sound accomplished; for, while I stood irresolutely looking from one to the other, both turned their faces upon me, and with equal apparent surprise.

"Little Glibun!" exclaimed the monitor. "Why, I thought it was Yaller's boy coming in!"

Elfie only rested in her work and questioned me with her eyes.

"How does this happen, Glibun?" continued Ezekiel Reed, leaning over his desk and surveying me from head to foot, "I thought you were gone for the vacation. Did father bring you back?"

"My father made me come back with him," answered I, with a guilty glow on my cheeks.

"Why?" It was Elfie asked this.

"Because he was angry at me for being in the back parlor;" and I turned to her as I said it.

"Don't worry the boy with questions, Ezekiel," interrupted the master, entering the door behind me like some evil spirit, and pushing me aside as he passed to the monitor's side. "Mr. Glibun thought his son would be better off here, for the present, than at home. That is the long and short of it. Master Glibun, go to your bench if you want to. Madam, I'm pleased to see you in this part of the house."

He tried to say all in a brisk, business-like way; but the manner was that of one striving to seem at ease when very much exhausted.

The short, contemptuous nod with which Elfie replied to his last sentence caused a momentary mantling on his sallow cheeks, and his fingers worked uneasily on the lid of the monitor's desk, as he again directly addressed her, —

"Perhaps, Mrs. Birch, I may take your presence here, with my son, as a sign of better feeling?"

"You may take it, sir, for what you please," she said, not looking up from her sewing, and with a seraphic softness of tone strangely at variance with the words; "but my purpose in leaving my own room was to spare your polite son the trouble of watching in the hall. Here, where he attends to his own affairs, he can obey your commands and watch his prisoner without inconvenience. The musket, too, is right at hand, here, in case I should attempt any violence!"

"Mrs. Birch! madam! How dare you treat me in this way? I will not bear it!"— He advanced a few paces toward her and leaned a hand against the wall, his voice trembling with excitement. — "You *know* that you are not doing right. You *know* that I am a miserable, ruined man, and yet do all you can to put me beside myself! You drive me to desperation, and then taunt me with the effects of it! What do you want? What do you ask? Have I not submitted to ignominy and disgrace in my own house for your imperious will? Am I not a husband without a wife, in the same house with my wife? Do you expect me to bear all my misery without ever once so much as reminding you of it? I will not bear this, I tell you! I will not —"

"Father! father!" exclaimed Ezekiel Reed, going to him in haste, and casting an indignant look at the unmoved woman who did not for a moment cease her sewing, nor again look up from it, — "you forget yourself, father; you forget your self-respect. Come away, now, with me. Come, poor father. I'm faithful to you. You're sick and nervous. Come."

At his caressing touch the master seemed to sink and shrink into a tottering, nerveless old man, and unresistingly permitted himself to be turned toward the door and slowly led away, shaking his bowed head and pitifully whimpering that he was ruined, ruined, and wouldn't, wouldn't bear it.

Having gone to my bench when told to do so, I sat looking intensely at my slate while father and son could be heard on their lingering progress up the stairs from the hall. Without particularly understanding what was the matter, I felt sorry for Mr. Birch, and hoped Elfie would tell me at once that she was sorry for him, too. I waited to hear her say so, and still kept my eyes on my slate; but when several moments had elapsed and she yet kept silence, I ventured to steal a glance at her.

"Elfie!"

She raised her head, as though expecting the most ordinary remark, and gave me the old, questioning look.

"What did you make him cry for, Elfie?"

An angry look came into her pale face, and she bit her lip with a sharp, hissing sound.

"You too!" she exclaimed, petulantly, "must you be a spy upon me, too?" Then, noticing my startled look, she added, more kindly, but still with some impatience: "These are nice scenes for a child, like you, to see, even after what you've seen and heard ever since you were born! No, Avy; don't come here. I can't talk to any one to-day. I'm not offended at you, dear; but you'd better go out and play on the hill. See if you can't find me a nice bird-nest. Won't you?"

Vaguely conscious of a something between us that had not always been there, and not at all deceived by the bird-nesting device, I straggled ungracefully into the hall, and from thence to the open air. I was hardly old enough yet to experience the reasoning and exquisite misery of knowing myself to be unloved, or cared for capriciously, only; but there is an instinct in the babe — even in the dog — which requires no intellectual process to make the spirit sorrowful in the only solitude thoroughly lonely. I loitered about the field in which the school-house stood, wishing by turns for cook, for my school-fellows, and for Mr. Bond; until, catching sight of poor Old Yaller, who was splitting wood in the stable-yard, I found somebody to tolerate my childishness at last.

It was a severe trial for me to be the sole occupant of a room at night; and so little familiar did anything seem to my sensations under such circumstances, that I could not even hold a recollection of the storied shell-houses in my mind firmly enough to lull the uncomfortable sense of strangeness. Leaping obstinately over the whole interval, my memory refused to be fresh with any later night than my second one at school, and of all Dewitt's nightly words to me, none came back so clearly as his sudden vow to write to his mother. I cannot say that I realized any particular application to myself in those words; yet they were the remembrance that diverted me gradually from my timidity at being alone, into a peaceful kind of stupor; and they inexplicably ceased, as it were, to be mere words, and were taking more and more a confused but pleasant bodily shape at my bedside, while I was falling asleep.

No washing-bell rang in the morning, and I did not awake until Yaller came to rouse me and deliver a message.

"Misser Glibun!" he called, from the doorway. "You 'wake, Misser Glibun? You's to take breakfast down h'yar in the madam's sittin'-room, with Misser Rod'-rick, and Misser Zeek'l, and the madam."

I knew the room: it was the one in which I had lain while sick. Dressing myself with all speed, and making a hurried trip to the wash-room for the final touches to my toilet, I duly presented myself at the door of the sitting-room, not sorry to take a vacation meal there, rather than with Yaller's rickety and speechless little assistant in the kitchen.

The three were already seated at a neatly-spread table, Elfie presiding at the tray of coffee-cups, and Mr. Birch and Ezekiel on either side.

"Good-morning to the young Prince of Wales!" was the master's salute to me, Elfie and Ezekiel only nodding to me and then turning their eyes to their plates. "This royal chair's f' you — for — you," he went on, speaking thickly, and placing a hand on a vacant chair beside him. "Here you are, little Glibby."

I took the seat in great discomfiture; for he did not present a reassuring appearance for a breakfast-table. His eyes were blood-shot and swollen, his hair looked as though it might have been tossed upon his head with a pitchfork, his face was flushed crimson, and one side of his collar was altogether lost behind his stock. From a bottle on the table he went on pouring some pungent yellowish liquid into his coffee-cup, although the latter was already overflowing into the saucer, and while addressing me he spilt much of the stuff on the cloth.

Elfie avoided my eye when she helped me, and I soon noticed that she, herself, was eating nothing; but the monitor was eating with apparent ravenousness; and I thought him the most suitable person to address first. Before I could speak, however, Mr. Birch thrust his bottle across the table, exclaiming, — "Have some, Zeke, — w — won't you?"

"No, father," and went on eating faster than ever.

"Mrs-is Birch! *you'll* have't?"

No answer to this; or, rather, something more than an answer.

"Two noes and no ayes," philosophized the master, recklessly standing the bottle on my plate, and resting his own elbow on the butter-dish, — "two noes and no ayes: referred back to C'mmittee on Fedel — on FedelLEral 'lations. Mrs. Birch! you've no idear, my dear, I fear. Ha — ha! Have you, now? Be honesht, mar'am, and tell me — have you, now? No idea what a night I've had. Plenny of brandy, and no company. But my own thoughts. But my own thoughts, mar'am. *Cogito, ergo sum.* I thought Mrs. Birch — "

A knock at the door cut him short, just as I made sure that Elfie was about to withdraw from the table. It was a single, confident knock, evidently not that of Yaller. At a motion from Ezekiel Reed I slid from my chair and opened the door, when Mr. Allyn Vane, hat in hand, stalked breezily into the room.

"Mr. Vane!" exclaimed the monitor, half rising from his chair.

"Mrs. Birch, your servant," said Mr. Vane, bowing to her, and coolly taking the chair I had just left. "Reed, you're looking well. Glibun, I thought you'd be at home. Mr. Birch, — excuse me for putting you last, — how are you, sir?"

The school-master stared at him. Elfie arose at once and went to the window.

"You're surprised to see me back so soon, I suppose, Mr. Birch, and Reed; but I will explain. I found my friends in Brooklyn just getting ready, as luck would have it, to go down to the sea-shore; and as my finances would not permit me to share in that sort of dissipation, I hardly knew what to do with myself. Finally, though, it occurred to me that I might as well come back here again and try a spell of rubbing up my Greek. I expected to find no one but Old Yaller here, and, of course, am agreeably surprised."

Still Mr. Birch stared speechlessly, and Mrs. Birch looked out of the window.

"Will you have any breakfast, Mr. Vane?" asked Ezekiel Reed, mechanically.

"I breakfasted in Newark, thank you, before hiring a team and driver to bring me up. Don't let me interrupt you, however, gentlemen. Yaller told me you were here; so I took the liberty of coming up."

"You're a scoundrel, sir!" burst with great vehemence from the school-master.

"And you're a good judge, Mr. Birch, —

if you happen to be pretty drunk and near a mirror," retorted Vane, with ready insolence.

The monitor sprang from his chair; but Ellie was quicker than he, and confronted the teacher of the classics with a suddenness that seemed supernatural.

"What do you mean?" she exclaimed, pale as death and passionately clenching her hands, — "What do you mean by addressing my husband thus, in my presence — you insolent — servant! Leave the room!"

He changed color, stammered an incoherent apology, and arose from his seat.

"Leave the room!"

Her flashing eyes drove him through the doorway as a flame might drive a feather.

Mr. Birch, somewhat sobered by the explosion, had managed to gain his feet, and stood leaning, with one hand upon the table, in a state of maudlin confusion. He comprehended only enough of what had so quickly happened to perceive that his wife had taken his part, and tried to put his disengaged hand upon her shoulder.

She shrank from him, and, as he commenced whimpering at the repulse, waved Ezekiel Reed and me impatiently to the door.

"Go, both of you," she said, imperiously; "I will take care of this man."

We went out immediately and silently, the door closing after us as though drawn with a spring; and while the monitor took his way thoughtfully to the stable, intending to ride to the parsonage at Milton, I left him on the shell-path and started for a ramble up the hill. So accustomed was I to scenes of passion, that to escape from one of them was to care about it no more.

The school-house, as I have already stated, stood in a lot, or field, at the foot of a hill. The latter began its ascent just beyond the stable, and bore grass, only, for some thirty yards. At that distance, however, a thick wood commenced and the ascent was more positive. Looking up to this wood, from the field, it seemed to reach and cover the summit, great piles of gray rock staring out, here and there, all the way up, and suggesting insurmountable obstacles to any human attempt at scaling the height. The fellows had been allowed the freedom of the grassy slope, from which a just-discernible footpath wound up amongst the trunks of the rising trees beyond; but the decided command of Mr. Bond and certain frightful stories of snakes from Old Yaller, deterred any one from trespassing further than the edge of the woods. I had never cared to play on the hill-side at all, being influenced to prefer the house-lawn and stable-yard by Streight and Dewitt, who always declared that there was something mean about a mountain that a fellow couldn't climb. Often, however, had I looked toward the rocky summit with childish speculation as to its probable wonders, and, after pausing on the slope that morning to see Ezekiel Reed

ride moodily out to the road on the gray horse, it came into my head to follow the footpath into the woods and see how far I could climb.

A single companion might have frightened me from the attempt by a very little snake talk; but, having no one to suggest ingenious perils to me, the instinct of adventure made me bold to explore, and confident in self-protection. It was a question with me from that day, whether fear is not purely a result of association; whether it is not a contagion spontaneous in communities, or suggested to the instinct by their herding together, rather than an inherent individual quality independent of extraneous creative influence; whether its prominence in children, sheep, deer, and wolves is not as much owing to the chronic herding of such creatures with their kinds, as its absence from manly men, dogs, tigers, and lions may be attributable to singleness of dependence? Whatever the truth of the idea may be, the thought of daring the wooded and snaky steep that morning came of my being all alone, and I clambered in amongst the forbidden shades with a little less than mischievous intent to do it because I never had done it.

The path narrowly marked in a trail of beaten grass wound snakishly upward between the trees farthest apart, and I made my way vigorously enough ahead until a huge boulder of rock seemed to stand directly across my road. A second look, however, showed me that the path made a turn around one mossy end of it, and with renewed ardor I followed the turn and was agreeably surprised, on passing the rock, to find myself arrived at a bit of open table-land some yards in width, beyond which the trees resumed their upward march. The path across this clear space, and into the shade again, was considerably wider than the part I had traversed, and revealed yellow sand and gravel here and there, as though rills from showers had washed it. I was trying to brush the grass-stains from my knees, preparatory to going on, when, to my great astonishment and alarm, I heard my name called, —

"Young Glibun!"

It was not unpleasantly said. In fact, it was lazily said, and from near by. I looked in the direction of the unexpected sound, and beheld Mr. Vane stretched luxuriously upon the fallen trunk of a withered tree, his head supported upon a hand and elbow, a cigar in his mouth, and a handkerchief thrown loosely over his head and brow to keep off the glare of the sun.

"What on earth brings you up here, youngster?" he asked, removing his cigar for a moment.

"Nothing," said I, hesitatingly, "only I thought I'd come."

"Well, that was pretty near my own reason for coming," remarked he, with a laugh, "and I shouldn't wonder if we were both more welcome up here than we were down there. Since we're so near alike that far, suppose you come and sit with me a while. I want to have a little talk with you."

His inviting manner made me willing to do what he asked; for, although I did not feel much real respect for him, his position of superiority as teacher compelled me to regard him as one whose attentions must do me some honor.

"Now, Glibun," said he, when I had seated myself on the turf near him, "I want to know how it happens that you and Mr. Birch are up here, instead of in New York?"

"My father told him to bring me back," I responded, not caring to be more explicit.

"Cutting capers, eh?"

"No, sir," said I, uneasily.

He looked at me through the smoke, with one eye just far enough closed to indicate a quizzical doubt.

"Oh, well," he drawled, "I suppose it's all right. You're about as much of a curiosity, in your way, as everything else down yonder is, in its way. I may be just as queer to you, too, and I daresay I am. — Why, what's this coming? A cow?"

A rustling, trampling sound came sharply from behind the boulder, and, as Mr. Vane sat up, and I got up, a human figure came running into view.

It was Elfie! Without hat or shawl. with her light hair flying in the breeze, her face white and distorted, and her hands outspread before her, she came flying up the path like one pursued by death to death. Catching sight of us, she stopped short.

"Mrs. Birch, for Heaven's sake what is the matter?" exclaimed Mr. Vane, rising from the fallen tree, and losing all his carelessness in a pallor scarcely less than hers.

Panting, and with her colorless lips apart, she looked at him like some timid creature at bay.

"Mrs. Birch, I — I am alarmed!"

"You — again!" she panted, dropping her hands to her side, and then suddenly clasping them behind her head. "You — again!"

"You are ill?"

He approached her nervously as he spoke, and held out his arms as if to catch her should she fall.

"Try to be composed. Upon my honor I am your true friend. Let me help you to a seat until you are better."

She groaned and let her hands drop again, and he led her to the tree unresistingly.

"There, sit there," he said, pityingly, "and, if you wish it, the boy and I will leave you. That is, if you will not tell us what has caused this."

"O me! O me! O me!" she moaned, rocking herself to and fro, wringing one hand within the other and staring at the ground.

"What *is* the matter?" he asked, vehemently, looking down upon her, and keeping me back with a gesture.

A fierce, terrified glance about her, and then the rocking and moaning again.

"Glibun." said Mr. Vane to me, measuredly, "Mrs. Birch appears to be very ill. Hurry down to the house, and tell Yaller to go to Milton for Doctor Pilgrim, instantly!"

"He struck me!" burst in a hoarse shriek from her lips. "That man struck me!"

"Your husband?" exclaimed Mr. Vane, starting back. "Then he shall answer for it this moment!"

"Stop!" — The word rooted him to the spot — "I had an avenger. His own degraded menial, his negro, struck him to the ground before my eyes!" She threw back her head and laughed in a dreadful way. "You would not have done it."

The taunt restored him to himself at once, and he even smiled as he folded his arms and took an easy, natural attitude.

"Glibun, hand me my hat from the grass, there, will you?"

I got it for him, and he placed it negligently on his head.

"Mrs. Birch, you are always so complimentary to me, that I cannot think of any new form of acknowledgment. In this case at least, however, I have in no way intruded upon you, and still you appear to feel resentful at some impertinence."

She arose from the fallen tree and pressed her palms to her temples as though to ease some throbbing pain.

"Can I never, never be alone? Must *you*" — and she looked him suddenly in the face — "always come between me and the last refuge of misery? You! who have even turned that child's heart against me!"

I was about to assure her that no one had done that; but he pulled me back before I could utter a word, and motioned me still further back with his hand.

"Madam," he said, returning her look, "you visit upon me the resentment you feel against the man who has misused you. I have never, intentionally, given you the least offence, and am not disposed to bear more of your unprovoked insults without the protest demanded by self-respect and —"

"Why don't you strike me then, too? Why don't you strike me?" she interrupted, smiling an instant and then glaring at him with insane wildness.

" — without the protest demanded by self-respect and a proper sense of the justice that even a woman should be compelled — that is the word, Mrs. Birch — *compelled* to observe. You cannot frighten me now. as you have done before this, by going into paroxysms of raving madness. I have a great advantage over you now; for I am perfectly calm and you are perfectly — otherwise. Consequently, Mrs. Birch, you may as well give up the contest."

He eyed her so intently that she dropped her own gaze, and went on, —

"Let me propose a point of compromise. You hate that man down there. You wish to be revenged upon him, — oh, I know it! — and thirst for a potent scheme; something to wring his heart as he has wrung yours!"

She raised her eyes slowly to his face again, and drew a long, audible breath.

"Anything but murder!" she said, in a low, concentrated tone.

"Walk with me to that rock, then."

She moved gradually away beside him to the place he had indicated, and when they stopped where the footpath turned, I marked him addressing her again. He bent his head to her, apparently speaking with great vehemence, and seemed to offer his hand; but I saw her make no motion to take it. Then he spoke anew, with several gestures toward the foot of the hill, and once more put out his hand; and she took it. Scarcely had she done so, however, when she threw it from her, and disappeared around the turning without another look at him.

He stood with his back to me for several moments, and leaned against the rock.

He will tell me, now, what she said, thought I; for his familiar manner with me led me to expect almost as much confidence as Gwin Le Mons or Dewitt might have given me under similar circumstances of trial.

"Glibun, come on down with me, now. It will not do for you to climb any farther to-day."

I went to where he stood, thinking that he spoke very composedly for one who had been treated so badly, and intending to learn from him whether Elfie was sick.

"What made her that way, Mr. Vane?" inquired I, taking the hand he held out to me.

"Glibun," said Mr. Vane, "you haven't got a match with you, of course? Well, no matter about it; I may as well throw this cigar away, at any rate. Toddle along now, or we shall have Mr. Reed coming to look for us."

<hr>

CHAPTER XV.

IT was about five o'clock in the afternoon when the monitor returned from the village; and, as I was sprawling upon the grass near the gate, with a book, when he called for Yaller to come and take care of the horse, I saw fit to join him in the stable-yard and inform him that the black had disappeared from the place. This necessitated some explanation, which I volunteered without his asking. In short, I told him that Yaller had struck Mr. Birch in the breakfast-room for striking Mrs. Birch, and had not been seen since.

My narration must have been next door to incoherent for a stranger, and I doubt that it conveyed a very distinct impression of the logic of what had happened to Ezekiel Reed; but, with his hand on the saddle from which he had just descended, he heard me through in silence, and made no other inci-

dental commentary than by slowly shaking his head and picking nervously at the leather.

"Is Mrs. Birch in the house?" he asked, glancing thoughtfully thither.

I said that I supposed so, though I had not seen her since my return from discovering Mr. Vane on the hill.

"Is he in the house?"

"There he is;" and I pointed to the figure of the classical teacher tilted back on a chair in the front doorway.

"I see him," said the monitor, looking that way again with a delicate but very expressive frown. "He is reading, I suppose. If Yaller is really gone, you cannot have had any dinner?"

I answered in the negative, and was very glad to have him think of that; for hunger was beginning to make me feel quite uncomfortable.

"Wait here until I attend to the horse."

He took off the saddle, led the animal into the stable, hastily poured some corn into the feed-trough, and then motioned for me to follow him through the gate and up to the school-house.

Mr. Vane arose to give him passage, and seemed inclined to speak; but Ezekiel Reed looked steadily past him with a rigidity of manner not to be mistaken, and entered the hall as though he had not seen him.

"Withers!" called Ezekiel, in a loud voice.

There was a sound of bare feet upon stairs, and presently the door under the stairway opened and the miserable kitchen-boy appeared.

"Put whatever there is to eat upon the table in the kitchen," said Ezekiel Reed, with a new air of authority about him, "and let the teacher and Master Glibun take supper there. If I do not come down in a few minutes, you come up to me, and I'll tell you if anything is wanted up there."

The little scullion vanished from sight like an imp in a pantomime, and the monitor, with his hat still upon his head, mounted the stairs. Even now, when I recall most plainly his appearance in so doing, I can scarcely decide whether his bearing evinced an inflexible indignation at the continued presence of Mr. Vane on the premises, or betokened an utterly dazed state of mind from the interpretation he had intuitively given to my disjointed report. Certainly his demeanor, from the time of unsaddling the horse, was either very deliberate or wholly mechanical, I can't say which.

I had heard him walk the second floor and turn into the room where he had breakfasted, when Mr. Vane called my attention to himself by throwing his book upon the school dining-table very petulantly.

"Pooh!" said he, looking up the stairs irritably, and snapping his fingers, "you'll have better reason for this sort of thing yet, my young preacher! Come, Glibun, let's go down and have a pick at the bones. We needn't fast because the rest of the people in this old lunatic asylum of a house choose to do so."

I said, very truly, that I was very hungry, and followed him down to the gloomy kitchen with an appetite for whatever might be found edible there. My companion seemed that way affected, also; and, although cold beef, bread, and milk were chief in the slipshod array of the kitchen-table, and the aspect of the deserted Withers was not calculated to stimulate the gastric juices, we both made a meal too hearty to admit of conversation, and returned to the hall again not much humbled by the rather ignominious circumstances of our banquet.

The monitor was descending the stairs as we emerged from under them, and paused upon the last step to hand Mr. Vane a folded sheet of note-paper. His girlish face was flushed, and his eyes, without losing their habitual gentleness, were sharp with the light of a strong feeling.

The teacher of the classics took the paper as lazily as though it had been a fan, and, throwing one knee over a corner of the table, proceeded leisurely to pull it open.

" Oh, of course," said he, glancing it over with perfect coolness, "I expected this : — 'Your services, as teacher of the classics at this school, are no longer required. The occurrences of this morning render it' — um —um — and so on. Yes, I see. You appear to have written this writ of ejectment yourself, Mr. Reed?"

" My father requested me to do so. He is too sick to-day to sit up," answered the other; adding, with a resolute look, "He could not have asked me to do a thing I would sooner do."

"'That remark is quite gratuitous," said Mr. Vane, turning on his heel and taking his hat from a chair. " I shall not be here to-morrow morning, and must charge you with my parting respects. Should your papa be asleep when you see ·him again, don't wake him on purpose, but I shall not excuse you if you fail to inform Mrs. Birch that I leave my P. P. C. for her with my compliments."

He laughed mockingly, and added, — " I'll take a parting stroll on the hill, now. For the novelty and exercise of the thing I shall walk to Newark this time, starting, say, at three o'clock in the morning, to have it cool all the way. You may not mind my sleeping here in the hall on a chair, until I do start?"

The monitor made no reply, but turned abruptly and went upstairs again. Thereupon, Mr. Vane tossed his hat upon his head, and, whistling the air of some song, sauntered out into the rich glow of the sunset. If he was going upon the hill, I wanted to go too, and I walked quietly after him as far as the picket-fence; but there he forbade my following further, saying that he wished to be alone, and would soon be back; and I stood and saw him cross the stable-yard, traverse the grassy slope, and disappear amongst the trees, on the footpath.

Like a troubled little ghost in the grounds of some deserted house, I wandered back and forth from the hall to the lawn, until night had closed in and the fire-flies began to sparkle in every direction like the ends of so many spectral cigars; and then I crawled timidly up to bed.

How I slept! I was still at the gate of the world, only; notwithstanding all that had swept hotly out, and around me and back again, and taken mould of me in passing. I was only at the gate yet, looking through now and then at some distempered scene and interested in one no longer than it took another to get ready for me. So, with the last scene of the strange show fading into the distant blur of its predecessor, and leaving no other impression upon me than a disinclination to talk, I slept dreamlessly where one within the gate would have dreamed sleeplessly.

Nor was my waking unworthy such a sleep, for the sun in his gentlest hour touched my eyelids as softly as a timid young prince, in the first day of his assured royalty, might touch the brow of him in whose first upward look he would catch the full trust of a willing allegiance. It was the pleasantest of all my wakings at school because it grew naturally like a blossom from the night and drew me unconsciously from the silence of darkness to the silence of light. Filled with the radiance of the morning I sprang boisterously from my cot, and scarcely had a thought until I found myself dressed and on the way to the stairs. Then the perfect stillness of the house struck me and awoke my first thought, that it must be Sunday. That can't be, though, either, reflected I, for yesterday was not Saturday ; and the thought and the reflection together kept me inertly confused as I passed down through the front hall and out to the wash-room, and heard no sounds on the way. On my return, after my usual ablutions and hair-brushing, it occurred to me that there was something strange in the front door standing wide open ; something peculiar in the noise my feet made ; something vaguely different from yesterday in everything.

Involuntarily subduing my tread, and wondering if Mr. Vane had gone yet, I went up to the room on the second floor, where I had breakfasted the day before, and tapped upon the door. No response followed; so I tapped again, more loudly; and again. Finally I turned the knob and walked cautiously in. No one was there; the table stood just as it did when I saw it last, with the soiled plates, cups on their sides, and remnants of the meal still upon it. A chintz pillow from a lounge was lying on the floor, and in some way gave me the idea that some one had slept on the carpet during the night. There I stood, looking at it, when quick, scraping steps sounded from the hall below, as though some one had entered the house in great haste, and was rushing frantically back and forth.

I turned to fly to my own room, with

some vague notion of robbers, when my alarm became positive at the unexpected sight of Ezekiel Reed, who, with his golden hair in all the disorder of his pillow, and his face white as that pillow, stood just inside the door behind me.

"Oh, what is that noise!" I exclaimed, doubly affrighted by his look.

"Hush! Hush!" he whispered, sharply, and with an aspect of breathless listening that brought midnight to the room.

The sound of a door swung violently open,—the door of the school-room; and those frantic footsteps in among the benches and back again.

"Gone! all gone!" came a hoarse, cracked voice up the stairs. "Gone!" it burst forth again, with the sound of some one leaping up the stairway like a frightened and heavy animal. "Gone! all gone!"

With a panted "O God, have mercy!" the monitor moved quickly back from the door, dragging me with him, and a frightful figure burst into the room.

"Gone! gone! gone!"

Each syllable was like the aimless blow from a maniac's knife, and came through lips trickling threads of blood over a quivering chin. The raving, livid creature was the school-master, a bandage tied about his head, and his dress bestrewn with carpet-lint and wisps of hay. In one hand trembled a piece of white paper torn nearly across, while with his other hand he grasped and wrenched at the bosom of his shirt.

"Do you know? do you know?" he howled, confronting his cowering son, and shaking the paper with fiercest vehemence, "all is gone! The horse and wagon!—and the gun! Gone! Stolen! all gone!"

He wrenched at his shirt so madly that his cheeks grew purple and the last word sounded like a shriek of strangulation.

"Father, dear father," murmured Ezekiel Reed, with trembling and colorless lips, "what has happened?"

"Happened?" screamed the miserable school-master, bursting into tears which seemed fairly to spring from his red and swollen eyes,—"Happened? Dishonor! Ruin! She has gone! Stolen away with that incarnate devil!"

"Oh!" came like the bursting of a broken heart from Ezekiel Reed, as he staggered, and fell upon a chair.

"Read what she left me—left on my face here while I was asleep;" raved the other," stretching the paper half-way toward him, and then furiously tearing it to pieces.—"No! you shan't read it! No one shall. And the gun gone! Look at me, with my head broken by a nigger, for her! I struck her, did I? That was why!"

He stooped to the floor and began picking up the pieces of paper, moaning as he did so.

I dared not move, and could only realize that Ellie had gone somewhere, and that the old musket was lost from over the stove in the school-room.

He was down upon one knee on the floor at last, picking up the pieces, and dropping them as fast, and still moaning miserably.

Ezekiel Reed's right arm was along the back of the chair, and his head resting on it, while his face, which was toward me, looked like the sickness before death.

"Go away," he said, faintly, and without moving. "Go, go."

Trembling at I knew not what, I went from the room on tiptoe, and hurried wildly downstairs, the moans sounding affrightingly in my ears until I reached the open air.

Going around the school-house to the rear, which contained the kitchen, I found the wretched little scullion cleaning knives on a board placed upon a reversed barrel, and entertaining himself with a very doleful sort of mixed humming and whistling as he worked. Always a shabby, sick-looking, tow-headed little nondescript was he, in baggy blue overalls and a marvellously creased sack of a linen coat, and had I met him elsewhere than in a school-house he would have been a wonder to me. In a school-house, though, I believed that all things must be different from things in other houses, and the spectacle of a negro and a shabby boy doing all the menial work of "Oxford Institute" might be in accordance with the general custom of boarding-schools. At any rate, Withers appeared to me in the light of a very inferior servant,—something infinitely below Yaller, even,—and a quite definite instinct made my manner toward him a continual assumption of superior gentility. This may seem strange when it is remembered what my enforced companionship at home had been, and that I never could have been trained to any kind of personal pride; but I put down the fact here because it *was* a fact, and am rather disgusted with myself at the irrepressible complacency I feel in so doing. Benvenuto Cellini, in his famous and every way curious autobiography, confesses to follies of the most extravagant kind, and even to murder, with all the pride a perfect hero might feel in frankly owning his own most creditable prowess; but after relating what is perhaps the only thoroughly good incident in his whole story,—his compelling one of his servant-men, who had ill-used a girl, to wed the latter,—he makes a merit of that confession to prove that he honestly tells the bad as well as the good of his life! With such an illustrious specimen of instinctive moral perversity before my mind's eye, I certainly feel less accusation of personal eccentricity in making my own admission just as I do. Its explanation I leave to the philosophers.

When I saw the scullion cleaning those knives, however, and simultaneously realized the two facts, that he and I were on an equality, for the time being, as related to our elders in the house, and that I was very hungry,—there came upon me a strong disposition to be friendly with him.

"Withers," said I, "you'd better get me some breakfast. Mr. Birch is awful mad upstairs, and I don't think there'll be any breakfast up there."

"Oh golly, what a row it is!" squeaked Withers, dropping the knife he was cleaning and entering into the boy-with-boy spirit immediately. "Old Yaller's flew the track; and Mr. Vane and the madam runned off in the night with the horse and wagon; and Mr. Birch slashing around in the stable with a towel on his eye. He asked me if I'd seen her," continued Withers, suddenly lowering his tone and looking at me mysteriously. "Wanted to know if I see Mr. Vane? I told him no; and then he cut out to the stable again like sixty! O jings!"

His manner was becoming too familiar, even for the privileges of the occasion. There was no possible connection between the domestic misfortunes of the family and the tassel on my cap; and when Withers followed his summary of the former by entering easily into a minute handling and examination of the latter, I severely desired him to give me something to eat, and am afraid that I called it "grub."

Shortly thereafter, I was going across the grassy slope, geography in hand, and up through the trees and brush to Mr. Vane's bower, intent upon making a luxury of study in that romantic retreat, and learning the exact number of inhabitants in Kamschatka. Arriving at the fallen tree, I stretched myself at full length on the grass, with my book before me, and was quickly upon my travels through Northern Europe, where gold, silver, platina, and precious stones do abound. Feeling somewhat tired when I got to Lapland, whose "inhabitants never use profane language, and observe the Sabbath very strictly," I thought it a good place for a nap, and took one. Awaking from that, much refreshed, I took a sharp turn and pushed for Stockholm, which has a safe and commodious harbor, and an extensive trade. At Stockholm, the royal palace, and the hangar, or great iron warehouse, attracted my particular attention; but the huge size of the latter, and the monotony of its contents, bored me so much, that I tried another nap before it.

Thus travelling and napping, I took no account of time, and was very much surprised when a sudden coolness of the air and a rapid lessening of the light upon my book made it seem as though evening were coming on. Closing the geography in haste, and looking upward, I saw that the coolness and the fading light were the effects of a vast black cloud across the sun; and while I gazed, a sharp, momentary puff of wind smote the tops of the trees in a way that brought a shower of leaves about my head.

The warning was sufficient. Tucking the book into the bosom of my jacket, and fixing my cap firmly in its place, I hurried down the shadowy hill-side for the school-house,

strongly impressed with the idea, that the storm was coming after, at a pace audibly quickening with my own. It was, therefore, with some mortification, that I saw the sun shining out clearly again, just as I crossed the stable-yard; and the faint rumbling of distant thunder did not change the belief that I had been needlessly frightened.

At the gate, Ezekiel Reed passed me without notice; but I inferred, from his Bible-class books under his arm, and the umbrella in his hand, that he was going on foot to the Milton parsonage, and expected rain on the way. He still looked really ill, and I should have asked some questions as to that, had he not so positively repelled me by his stiff, abstracted manner of going by.

I went on to the wooden steps before the front door, which remained wide open as before, and, seating myself on the lower one, devoted myself once more to the varied excitements of geography.

Again I was interrupted by the darkening of the page, and, as I glanced up toward the crest of the hill, a volume of thunder seemed to break from a heavy bank of clouds rising above it, and fall cracking and tumbling amongst the rocks. The awful sound had scarcely died away, when I heard heavy steps on the hall-stairs behind me, and knew that the school-master was coming down. An impulse to evade his notice was too late in defining itself; for, before I could slip from before the door, he had caught sight of me and called my name. Mechanically responding "Sir?" I remained where I was, and observed, as he came out to me, that he wore his hat over the bandage, and carried a large cane. His appearance, in fact, all rumpled and disordered as his dress and hair were, would have been ludicrous to a stranger; but to me, with my partial comprehension of what he had suffered, it was half pitiable, half frightful.

"Well, Master Glibun, these are lonely and hungry times for you," he said, rolling his hot-looking eyes from the clouding sky to me, and trying to speak naturally. "I didn't expect to find you so near the house; but it's all the better. I want you to take a walk with me before supper."

"Isn't it going to rain, sir?" asked I, as the thunder rolled again over our heads.

"Only a passing shower," he responded, in the same forced way, scraping a groove in the sod with his cane. "A few drops won't hurt us. We're neither sugar nor salt, and we won't melt. It's up that hill we're going."

"I've been there," said I, gaining courage.

"When? what do you mean?"

In some confusion I told him that I had been there once with Mr. Vane, and once alone.

He drove his stick into the ground at my mention of that name and gave me a savage look, but recovered himself directly.

"That's only a short distance up, my boy," he said. "I'll take you to the top this time; to the summit, where you can see the New York steeples."

"Can you see my father's house, too?"

He looked savagely at me again, and again recollected himself.

"No, you can't see that."

This negative did not lessen my willingness to go with him; and when he started down the shell-path and called me to follow, I obeyed readily.

Instead of crossing the slope, however, as I thought he would, Mr. Birch stalked down the stable-yard to the road, and along the latter in the direction of the little village of O——. He made no reply when I asked him if that was the right road, but walked quickly on ahead to where there was an opening in the wayside bushes, and a grass-grown wagon-track branched up that side of the hill. Taking me by the hand there, and turning from the road, he silently began the ascent with me; thunder continually muttering overhead, and clouds obscuring more and more of the sky.

Our way was tortuous and toilsome through an uplifted wilderness of trees and rocks; sometimes running steeply over a mossy ledge, and sometimes gravelly and pebbly as the bed of a lost stream. The increasing wildness of the scene, as turn after turn revealed new eternities of knotted trunks and rocks and tangled bushes in all the combinations of Nature massive and alone, filled my throbbing heart with an awe that smothered speech. Nearer and oftener came the peals of thunder, like dropping points of exclamation between the tree-spelt sentences of immemorial solitude; and, with darkness gathering in fold upon fold across the zenith, and all to the eastward turning a deeper green and gray under a slowly crawling shadow, the latticed branches and leaning colonnades to the westward let in great bars of tawny red from where the sun was setting in a continent of slashed and ruffled flame.

Something came down upon us like a mighty breath, to which the very mountain and all upon it seemed to bend and sink for one awful moment; and then, as it lifted, with a shrill rush and swirl, we both stood bareheaded and swaying in the midst of writhing trees and hurtling leaves and branches.

"Let's go back!" I screamed, in an agony of terror, as a blinding flash of light blazed with a crash upon the shadows.

"Not for a million!" shouted the schoolmaster, dragging me on.

"Some one is behind us!" I shrieked, maddened by a breaking sound near by, which I heard above the noise of the wind.

He grasped me by the coat, and dragged me onward with Herculean strength as though I had been a hare. Through brambles and over broken stone he dragged me on, running rather than walking, until, bursting through a line of thickest woods, he paused with me on an open floor of rock standing right in the eye of angry heaven.

One look I cast about me, and then clung with all my strength to the mad creature who had forced me thither.

The whole world seemed to be down, fathomlessly down below, there, with its fields, rivers, towns, and infinity of dwarfed possessions; all dimmed in a misty, lifeless twilight, through which came moving a mistier veil of rain. Arching up from the still lurid west loomed the black field of the storm; and dizzily pedestalled in the mid-air of the abyss, with heaven tottering in smoke and fire above them and the earth growing a blot beneath, stood a demented old man and a child clinging frantically to him.

"Let go! he roared, crushing me from my hold with his left hand, and keeping an iron grasp upon my coat.

I read his purpose instantly. Murder! was the meaning that came as much from the scene as from him; and from both in such pitiless immutability that my wild cry for mercy mocked my own ears.

"O sir, Mr. Birch, don't hurt me, sir! O, please, sir, don't hurt me!"

"It is your father!" he raved, striving to pull me to the verge. "It is your father!" and the tumult of the storm seemed to lash him into a fiercer insanity. "Your father's work. He wants you killed; and if he didn't, I'd carry you down with me for being his son! He has done it all; he made a devil of Her! Come on! Come on! Both of us together, and our blood be on his head!"

My swollen tongue refused to utter human sounds; but there broke from my lips the yell of an animal in mortal agony; and, as he lifted me swiftly from my feet, I struggled and kicked with all the strength of frenzy. Grasping blindly for something to clutch, I tore from his head the bandage, and saw, by the fading light and the glare of the lightning, that there was blood on his temple. The cloth fell over his eyes as I held it, and in the pause he made to draw his head back, my speech returned to me.

"Help! murder!" I screamed.

There came a sharp crack and a flash, that were not of heaven; and I felt myself slipping from his clasp; and I saw him fall away from me flat upon his back.

Bounding from the black line of woods came a man with something grasped in his uplifted hands, and, as he reached me on the rock, he cast it from him over the verge, — a musket.

"Hang to me for your life!" was the hoarse whisper, when a pair of strong arms lifted me again from my feet. "Heaven knows what I've done!"

<hr>

CHAPTER XVI.

I FIND A NEW FRIEND.

A VIVID consciousness of being borne headlong through crashing brakes of bush and branch was succeeded in my brain by an indistinct sense of riding at full gallop down swampy steeps beset with yawning pit-holes. With eyes close-shut, and a piercing crack ringing in my ears, I became possessed of the idea that I was hanging to the mane of a maddened horse, in frantic flight along the boggy edges of countless black chasms; and that each splashing plunge of the hoofs went deeper and deeper into yielding borders of destruction, until, finally, the hoofs fell upon air, and we went down, down, down, down into bottomless darkness.

When I opened my eyes again, all was rain and impenetrable gloom above and around me; but I was perfectly still then, and could feel that my head rested on some one's knee, that something damp and heavy was across my breast and arms, and that some one's face was bending over mine.

"Where am I?" was what I tried to call aloud; but my voice refused to rise above a husky whisper, and the exertion gave me a strange feeling in my head.

"Ah! you're alive," came like a sigh of relief from him whose knee supported me. "I was afraid you was done for, boy, and it's given me an awful turn."

I could discern the outlines of his head, now, with the slouched and dripping hat upon it; and his voice told me the rest. He was the man of the warehouse, of the street, and of that back parlor at home.

"I must have carried you three full miles after you'd fainted," he went on, while the storm beat upon both of us; "and then I laid you on the bank here, with my coat over you, and tried if the rain full in your face wouldn't bring you to. You've frightened me badly, youngster, and it's a dreadful night's business altogether. Now let me get you into that barn over there; for we can't go any farther in this storm."

As he raised me carefully again in his arms, I could see, at a short distance off, what looked like a standing shadow of a large house, and thither he carried me across the flowing road, with the coat still wrapped about me. After feeling carefully along the face of the building with his right hand, and trying in vain to pull open what felt like one of the main doors, he at last found entrance through a smaller door near the farther end of the barn, and bore me cautiously into an atmosphere redolent of horses and grain. In fact, we seemed to have come right upon the heels of several horses, whose stamping made my bearer edge closely along the boards as he moved forward with me. Very soon, however, he groped to a spot where heaped hay arrested his steps, and there he softly laid me down, and vigorously began to pile armfuls of the fragrant bedding upon me.

"Be still as a mouse, now," whispered he, holding me down and piling it on; "be still as a mouse, now, or we'll stir up the house-dog, if they've got one. We must sleep here till morning, and I'm covering you with plenty of hay so that you won't get cold. Hush! we mustn't talk a word here. Don't be afraid. I'll lay right alongside of you."

Bewildered, faint and weary, I felt no inclination to utter a word. To the extent that my faculties were alive, I felt safe with him; and to feel thus, after the events of the evening, was a solace for every restless emotion. So I laid quietly buried in the hay, with him beside me, listening blankly to the dull stamping of the horses in their stalls, and the monotonous pattering of the rain upon the lofty roof.

Daylight was shining on the man when next I looked toward him, and he stood, in his shirt-sleeves, looking attentively out through an open door just beyond the lower hay compartment in which I was literally planted. There were the tangled red beard and deep-set eyes of the Man in the House that Jack built; there was no mistaking them. The soft, black, shapeless hat was slouched over his pale, sharp countenance; his coarse blue shirt and mud-splashed corduroy pantaloons hung in wet folds about him, and it was his coughing, I think, that had aroused me.

The rustling I made to sit up caused him to look my way, and come to me with a cheerful smile on his face.

"So, lad, you've made a good nap of it, have you?" he said, in a broken, labored voice, rubbing his hands over my hair and coat. "And you're dried pretty well, too. See what a cold I've got, for lending you my coat all night."

I involuntarily grasped his hard hand as he stooped to me, and earnestly told him how sorry I was.

"Never mind it," said he, huskily, helping to extricate me from the hay. "One of the farm-hands was coming out from the house just now to get something from here, and I believe I've frightened him out of his wits. At any rate, he went back in-doors on a run, and will bring the farmer, I suppose. I shall say that you're my boy, and take care that you don't say anything to spoil my story, or I shan't be able to get any breakfast for us."

Sure enough, the farmer did come lumbering into our spacious bedroom, followed by a scared-looking big boy in a straw hat that had somewhat the effect of an aggravated halo around his unsaintly bullet of a head. A man of double-chin and much stomach was the farmer, and his manner of asking what business we had in his barn savored of the breeding natural to rural prosperity — in New Jersey.

"Why, you see, sir," explained my companion, hat in hand, "I'm a tailor, sir, from Morristown, and me and my boy there were on our way to Newark for work, — excuse my cold, sir, — when we got soaked through in that shower last night, and took the liberty of crawling in here among the hay-racks."

"H'm!" said the farmer, though not ill-naturedly.

"If you could be so good as to let us have a bit of something to eat, sir, — a little dry bread, and milk, say, — we'd be very grateful. We're wretched poor, and can't get anything this side of town, sir."

"Where's your boy's cap?" asked the farmer, not so good-naturedly.

"Oh, his — cap? Blowed off, sir, in the night. before we got here, and couldn't be found."

"We-l-l," — very slowly, — "I sup-pose I must. Go into the house, Dick, and bring out a couple of — let — me — see — bowls of that yesterday's milk, and a loaf of that ere last-but-one bakin'."

The big boy with the saintly head-dress obeyed this order with an alacrity quite surprising in one of such lethargic countenance, and the Morristown tailor and I fell-to with an alacrity to match. Having enjoyed but one meal during the day previous, I was ravenous, and the tailor certainly gave me much the larger share of the hard bread.

The farmer brought his large stomach and double chin to bear directly upon us while we banqueted, and drew several elephantine sighs as it became plainly apparent that no crumbs were to be left.

"We thank you, sir, very much for your kindness," said my companion, as we arose from the hay at last, "and I wish I could make some return for it. But we're miserably poor."

"Oh, no matter," murmured our obese host, heavily. "Is that a gold watch of yours? But it aint, I suppose?"

He was wistfully eying a common steel watch-chain dangling rustily from the other's waist.

"I don't carry a watch, sir, — I'm too poor for that; but this bit of chain was given to me by a gentleman from York, who got me to sew a buckle on. If you'd take the chain, sir, as some slight return — "

A chubby brown hand reached forth for the quaint bauble, and a thoughtful voice was heard to say, "We-l-l, I don't know but I *will* take that ere."

"There it is. Trot along, now, my boy," croaked my friend, with a sudden decrease of reverence in his manner; "we must be moving."

I briskly followed him from the barn to the road, leaving the farmer gloating over his prize; and we had gone some distance from both barn and house, when a violent pattering of feet behind made us halt and look back.

The pursuer was the big boy with the halo, and, before I could make the least motion to defend myself, he had torn the latter from his own head, and driven it excitedly upon mine.

"I'll be gosh-darned if 'twan't a shame!" roared the big boy, tempestuously, still pushing the hat upon my hair, and puffing with mingled wrath and hospitality; — "a darned wicked shame! But you just wear that hat until you get one for yourself, little 'un."

And the good fellow went racing back as swiftly as he had come, with a genuine halo won for himself at last.

The man looked after him for a moment, nodded his head several times at me, and we went on again hand in hand.

The sun was shining gloriously after the rain; the trees, the grass, the road, all had the fresh, clean, newly-washed appearance of renovated nature; and for the first half mile I hopped more than I walked, feeling too elastic of body and mind to entertain such ballasting thoughts as make us deepset and steady in the stream of life. Pretty soon, though, the sun grew hotter, and I grew less frolicsome; and then the scene on the rock came back to me, more and more heavily, until I abruptly reminded my conductor of it, and fearfully asked him if the school-master would ever come down from the summit again? The man quickened his plodding space, unconsciously, I think, at the question, and said, without looking at me, that no one could tell that, and we had better talk about something else. Very naturally, my curiosity became all the more anxious from his evasive reply, and, with my heart growing heavier every moment, I at once lost thought of everything in the world, save my recent escape from death, and became so importunate with him that he angrily dropped my hand and made a full stop in the road.

"Now look here, boy," he croaked, impatiently, swallowing to repress a cough, "I aint fit to talk — at all, — with such a cold — as this. You ought to know that. As for what happened last night, you saw it yourself, and had best be quiet about it. What I've got to tell you, I'll tell you in a few minutes, — not now. Hurry along."

I was mute at once, and sorry that he made no offer to retake my hand as he started off afresh. Indeed, I felt something of the same wish to please him that I had felt to please poor Mr. Bond; and it seems to me that such a wish is always the first symptom of affection, whether in child or man.

He walked a little ahead of me, keeping his eyes intently upon the fields to the right of us, for at least half an hour; but a wide, white-looking road becoming at last visible, at which the one we were travelling appeared to end, he slackened his pace so much that I presently found myself passing him; and I kept the lead until we both reached the wider and whiter road.

Turning to see in which direction he was going, I saw him quietly seating himself on the grassy bank, beside a rail fence, and beckoning for me to go to him.

"Sit down there," he said, when I had obeyed his gesture; "I must tell you something before we part."

I started, at his words, and was about to remonstrate in great alarm; but he shook his hand at me for silence, fixed his glance upon the ground at his feet, and went on, —

"I've got to leave you here, my boy, and look out for myself; for there's no knowing what that shooting business last night may do for me. I was dogged all day yesterday—I'm certain of that—just as I'm always hunted, God help me! So I must look out for myself, and take to the lots for the rest of to-day. All you've got to do is to keep straight along down this turnpike to Newark, and here's a dollar to take you from Newark to the city. Hold out your hand. There,—four quarters, you see. If you meet a load of hay, or a milk-wagon, on the turnpike,—and I daresay you will,—just offer the driver one of the quarters to carry you down a ways, and he'll be pretty sure to do it. When you get to the city you can soon find your way home,—if you want to go there."

The idea of being left alone there was so overwhelming, that I could only grasp his coat with one hand, and stare at the money in the other.

"I don't know of anything you can do but go home," he continued, his voice growing thicker and more whispering, "and that's enough money to take you there. It's nearly every cent I had, and I kept it from that farmer for you. I can't talk much more, and you mustn't act like a baby, and fret, because I've got to leave you. Let go my coat, now. If you should see Elfie any time, just tell her that I—you can call me Wolfton—looked out for you all right. Don't speak a word to anybody about that shooting, or you may get me into trouble."

Even then, when he arose to go, he did not look me in the face. Very few of those whom I had known could do that for any length of time; and he, like them, saw too much of God in a child's eye, perhaps, to dare the encounter.

"No! don't leave me!" I cried in affright, trying to catch one of his hands.

Heedless of the sound, or else hastened by it, he sprang over the fence instantly, and went running through a cornfield in the direction of a thick wood beyond. I also clambered frantically over the fence, screaming to him to come back, and went plunging in amongst the thick stalks; but the uneven ground tripped me up after a few wild steps, and when I got to my feet again I could see nothing of him.

Miserable little outcast that I was; tattered, dirty, and looking like a scarecrow; how I sat down and cried when I had crawled back to the roadside! All alone in the houseless, sandy, endless world; with not even a loving recollection to make my tears a spiritual companionship, even though of sorrow, with aught that was lost; and not a hope, however delayed, to make them a yearning for something to be found. If ever Despair, perfect because uncalculating, took the incongruous form of a child in this world, it was mine while I sat there crying.

But suppose some one should find the school-master lying on that rock, and come after me! I was up and walking again as though already pursued; for it was impossible to rest a moment after; and my rate of walking would have exhausted me in a few moments, had not a vision of my father suddenly come up, like an enemy in front. Mr. Birch had said that *he* wanted me killed! There was intuitive confirmation of that in my recollection of my father's looks and manner that day, before the hotel. I dared not think of going home! But where should I go? What, oh, what should I do?

The creaking and jolting of wheels caught my ear at that moment, and, looking a little way ahead of me, I saw two oxen drawing a heavy wagon upon the turnpike from a cross-road, and a man sitting on an improvised driver's seat, with a long "g'ad" in his hand.

The sight of a human being at that crisis gave me a vague delight, and I ran after the wagon. It did not require much speed to overtake it, for the animals only moved one pair of legs when the other pair were tired of one position; and my appeal awoke the driver from an unquestionable doze.

"Please, sir, give me a ride for a quarter?" I pantingly urged, with a beseeching look.

"Wo, haw!" he remarked to the oxen, giving the nearest one a mere satire on a blow with his goad; and the apathetic creatures desisted.

"Jump in. Gee!" he continued, in the same course of business; and, as I climbed into the clumsy vehicle, the latter took perceptible motion.

"Well, my cockywax, who are you?" inquired the driver, when I had reached his part of the premises, and let him see what I looked like.

With remarkable effrontery, in which the broad brim of my straw hat proved a convenience to disingenuousness, I assured him that I was a tailor from Morristown, on my way to Newark for work.

Thereupon, he became sufficiently interested and awake to turn fully around to me, and anxiously desired to be informed what I was charging for white silk vests with brass buttons. He also asked me how many men I kept at work in my shop, and whether I wanted a new hand of about his size to hold me up while I "tried on."

I gravely ignored the first questions, answering the last negatively; and my manner must have awed him, for he said no more on that subject.

Not to prolong his embarrassment, I inquired of him who lived in the house we were passing; and he told me that the proprietor was a particular friend of his, who would come rushing out and ask us to take dinner there, only he could see through the window that I was a stranger straight from York, and might think he was too free.

With such flattering local information did the agreeable driver satisfy my curiosity and beguile me from my troubles, until the oxen turned of their own accord into another cross-road, and I was told that the wagon had to go down there to "them salt medders" for a load of hay. Seeing no help for it, I handed the driver a quarter, with my thanks; but the former he wouldn't think of taking.

"I thought you meant a quarter of a mile," said he, kindly abashed. "I don't want the money, my cockywax. Put it up."

I felt very grateful, as I ran around to the front of the wagon to shake hands with him at parting; and it was a pity he had to alloy his generosity, after all, by calling to me that I might send him half a dozen of my best overcoats during the summer, and he'd see how they fitted. He laughed very heartily, though, as he turned to his oxen, and that made me think he might be only joking.

Feeling much the better for the ride and its talk, I renewed my walk briskly, with a vague idea that Newark could not be very far off, and that the next hill-top would at least bring some of its spires into view; but, as rise after rise commanded only the same interminable stretch of turnpike, field, and wood, I began to think wearily of my situation again, and grow confused under a sense of complicated perils. Here and there, at long intervals, red farm-houses with white window-casings, gave an inane aspect of possible humanity to the road;— yet I felt only the more an outcast for beholding them, and hurried past, lest some one should recognize me as my father's son. My feet were beginning to burn and smart, and I was moving onward slowly, and in a very disconsolate state of mind, when a bend in the road brought me unexpectedly into the neighborhood of what looked like a halt of market men. The lines of rail-fence, on the right, suddenly ended within a few yards of me; or, rather, took a turn across the country by way of change; and the green roadside at once swept smoothly in under the branches of countless trees, which commenced a wood running far back toward the horizon. Standing side by side upon the grass just off the road, and with their attenuated and leather-patched spans of horses grazing loosely around their fallen shafts, were three heavy and muddy wagons, or wheeled arks, with dingy white canvas tops. I saw them plainly through the trees, and thought I could hear human voices; but no human figures were apparent from where I paused to gaze, and it occurred to me that the owners of the wagons were, probably, inside the latter. Hardly knowing what I did, and impelled only by a desire to avoid being seen myself, I took to the roadside, in range of the first line of trees, and began advancing stealthily toward a closer point of observation. Fixing my eyes steadily upon the nearest wagon, I gave no heed to any minor object between it and me, and was almost on the verge of the mysterious encampment, when the sharp bark of a dog seemed to come from the ground at my very feet. In great affright, I jumped backward a pace, and simultaneously saw a black and yellow hound right at my hand, and heard a man's voice, saying,—

"Keep still, Mr. Mugses!"

Stretched on his back under a tree, not two yards off, with his arms clasped beneath his head, a Panama hat tilted over his eyes, and his elbows and knees at the easiest angles, was the person who had spoken thus. My intentness upon the wagons just beyond had prevented my seeing him before, and terribly was I scared to find myself so hopelessly caught sneaking. He did not move from his position, but turned his eyes sleepily in my direction, as I stood mutely fearful where the dog had stopped me, and I had time to note that he possessed a sly, comical face, and looked, somehow, like a shoemaker. The dog, to whom as it seemed, his words had been addressed, went and sat near his head, from thence to survey me blandly, and with more tongue than even medical curiosity might have demanded to see; and looked from one to the other in a pitiable, undecided manner.

Finally, however, I gave the lengthier stranger the exclusive benefit of the imbecile stare, which caused his smooth, sunburnt chin to move in unison with the words,—

"When you've taken my daguerreotype, young man, just let me know,—will you?"

"Sir?"

"I say when you've finished taking my portrait, be obliging enough to tell me."

Not understanding what he was talking about, I only stared the harder.

"Keep it up, Little Breeches!" said he, in a good-humored tone. "But while you're at it, you may tell me who you are. It's curious, by-the-by, to see a child like you prowling around in the woods here. Who are you, hey?"

I informed him, not without stammering, that I was a tailor from Morristown, going to Newark for work.

Apparently there was something in that account of myself to immediately wake-up everybody; for it had made the wagoner instantaneously loquacious, and now its utterance was followed by the abrupt sitting-up of the man who had so lately seemed tied to the ground.

"You—don't—say—so!" he drawled, letting his hat fall off, and uttering such a seductive whistle that the dog at once arose and began licking his face.

"Be quiet, Mr. Mugses!—So you're a tailor, are you? I'm blest if I thought such a little body could contain such a big lie."

He seemed to be getting up, and my guilty fear made me hasten to cry out,—

"I didn't mean to do it, sir; no, sir, I didn't. I ran away from school because Mr. Birch was going to kill me!"

"Mr. Birch!" he exclaimed with a start and a curious change of countenance. "Come here, out of sight of those wagons," he added, beckoning earnestly for me to approach him. "Now what's this about Mr. Birch? Tell me what you mean?"

Frightened into a revelation I had been forbidden to make, I stuttered a confused story about the school-master's attempt to throw me from the rock; but gave no other explanation of my escape, than that I had "run away."

The man bit his nails and stared thoughtfully at me, as though more attentive to his own ideas than to my awkward words.

"Well, see here, bub, what is your name?" asked he, when I ceased speaking.

"Avery Glibun, sir."

"Glibun? — Glibun? — where do your friends live?"

I answered, whimperingly, that my father lived in New York; but that he was very mad at me and I didn't dare go home.

"Where, in the name of Andrew Jackson, are you going, then, bub?"

"I — I don't know, sir," was my response, as my arm went to my eyes and the tears began to come.

He had risen to his feet and resumed his hat, and stood silently with his back to me and his face toward the wagons for several minutes. Then, turning to me again, and bending down, he asked in a low voice, —

"Avery, how would you like to stay with me and Mr. Mugses, and my friends over there by the wagons, for a while?"

"O sir," I exclaimed, eagerly, "if you'd only let me do it, I'd be so glad! I'm so tired and afraid."

"By George, you shall then!" said he, catching me by the hand and speaking with vehement decision. "Now come on and let me show you to my friends. My name is Mr. Reese, — you understand? — "

He strode quickly forward, pulling me along and followed closely by Mr. Mugses, and, before there was time to think, I found myself standing with him beside the grazing horses of the nearest wagon, and in full view of a curious assemblage.

Scattered upon the grass beyond the shafts, in various reclining attitudes, were four men and two women, all with very dark complexions and very black eyes, and attired grotesquely in the odds and ends of multifarious costumes. Leaning against a tree, with a clay pipe in his mouth and a torn velveteen jacket on his back was one of the party; a monkey dressed as a soldier capering at his side and trying to pull off his slouched hat. Farther on were two others, just as dark and tattered, playing at cards; and seated on a shaft of the last wagon was the fourth and oldest man, drinking something from a small tin pail. Of the women, who were sitting together mending a broken tambourine under another of the wagons, one was old and cross-looking, and the second young and sharp-eyed. They wore dingy striped shawls over head and shoulders, and paused in their work to look me through.

"This boy mine," said Mr. Reese, pointing to me and speaking authoritatively;

"he come to me, and I know him, and tell him to stay with us awhile. Confound the gibberish! I'm going to have him with me — you understand? — and that's the long and short of it. You, Juan, there, pass us something to eat."

All stared at us steadily enough to make me very uneasy; but no one spoke in reply to my new friend's extraordinary speech; nor did any one move, save the man on the shaft, who sluggishly reached an arm into his wagon in apparent obedience to the unceremonious order for eatables.

"Who are they, sir?" I asked, bewildered and scared at the strange spectacle.

My new friend threw himself upon the grass, as though entirely satisfied with what he had done, and replied, pulling me down to him, —

"They're good people, enough, — you understand? — Gipsies."

CHAPTER XVII.

If, as Mr. Leigh Hunt has fancied, houses have physiognomies, whereby the dispositions and prevailing moods of their inmates are outwardly expressed in the workings of such features of the architectural face as doors, windows, and blind-shutters, then did the respectable family residence, No. 50 Allouer Square, possess a brick countenance remarkable for its suggestions of mingled simplicity, reticence, and slyness. Its complexion, in the first place, was a quakerish drab, comporting with an idea of sober knowingness, so to speak; and the very narrow stone coping of the oaken front door, gave the latter a sharply-defined rigidity, as of habitually compressed lips. The parlor windows looked blankly upon Allouer Square in rectilinear draperies of white inner shades, drawn down to the sills, as though in meek deprecation of public notice; but as the observer's glance travelled up to the third floor, where one square window was closely darkened with its shutters, and another stood wide open, the effect was somewhat like that produced by the laborious shutting of one eye when its human possessor would concentrate an unusual amount of intelligent expression in its fellow.

B. Cringer was the legend on the plain, silver-coated door-plate, like a gentlemanly address on a genteel card, not without its idea of polished slipperiness; and the silvered bell-pull, protruding stolidly from the door-frame to the left, might have been the handle of just such a substantial cane as would fitly consult the nose of magisterial middle age.

A stranger entering that Metternich of a house for the first time, and without previous introduction to any of the inmates, — say a reflective burglar, for example, —

would have expected to encounter diplo-macy in the very servants, and complicated winks from what knowing children might be found therein. He would have expected words of salute, simple in their sound only, to cover some wonderfully shrewd design. He would have expected to behold almost any other figure than that of Mr. Benton Stiles, the sole living occupant of a goodly front room on the second floor. That room was something between an office and a law library, in fact; so the countenance of the building as a private residence was hardly answerable for it; and the solitary inmate's attitude and employment might be considered apart from the general foxy cast of that same countenance.

From a table-desk, confusedly strewn with books in sheep and writing materials, in the middle of the floor, Mr. Benton Stiles was leaning back in his armless maple chair, holding a small pocket-mirror in one hand, and endeavoring with the other to make a wiry forelock curl droopingly down the centre of his intellectual forehead. The while he labored to achieve this sentimental improvement in his appearance, he whistled a fashionable air, the whistle growing louder and more vigorous in the trills, as the obstinate lock exhibited a more perverse determination to maintain the curlless tendencies of all its straightforward associates. As the whistle increased in animation, it gradually evoked a humming echo from some other room in the distance, which echo was at first halting and incorrect, but presently followed with confidence and exact musical accord. Mr. Stiles thereupon stopped abruptly in his melody, and listened intently to the humming as it still went on.

"Lock my wheels, if she hasn't caught that tune, too!" ejaculated Mr. Stiles, nodding his head, and slowly returning the mirror to his pocket. "I can't whistle a neat thing, but the dusty old girl goes to humming it right after. I believe I've taught her half a dozen whole operas since I've been here, besides 'Rub 'em down and sheet 'em, John.' Go it, my adorable Miss Cringer! Go-o-o it! And now for the speech again."

The secretary turned his attention to the desk as he spoke, bringing down his chair upon its fore-legs, and mumblingly skimming over some writing on one of several written sheets radiating from the portfolio before him.

In a moment he arose and began scrutinizing the titles of a collection of sheep-bound volumes ranged on shelves along the fireplace-side of the room.

"Jefferson, — Jefferson," he muttered, pen in hand, — "for did not the immortal Thomas Jefferson say, —Thomas Jefferson say, — let me see; where is that Jefferson's Speeches, now? —Did not the immortal Thomas Jefferson say —"

Tinkle—inkle—inkle—'kl—'l—'l, sounded a bell from some remote depth, and Mr. Stiles was so dreadfully ill-bred as to stick his pen hastily behind an ear, glide stealthily to the door, noiselessly open the latter a few inches, and assume an aspect of breathless listening. Two other movements took place in the house simultaneously: a servant-girl moved along the lower hall to answer the bell, and Miss Cringer, crimped of hair and aged thirty-five, slipped from her room to the head of the second-floor stairway. It may be remarked of the latter personage, that the ringing of the street bell always suggested beggars to her, in search of cold victuals; and as she regarded such mendicants with implacable hostility, and had but one reply to their most artful entreaties, her practice was sometimes quite a novelty to visitors.

Thus, the moment the servant opened the door, and before Mr. Stiles could catch a sound of the new comer's voice, Miss Cringer made herself heard.

"Tell them we haven't got any!" called Miss Cringer to the servant, firmly convinced, as usual, that a demand had been made for cold victuals.

"It's a gintleman wants to see the Giner'l, miss," screamed the girl.

"Oh! show him up then," ordered Miss Cringer, not to be discomposed by such a trifling mistake; and back she swept to her room.

At the sound of boots on the stairs. Mr. Stiles darted to his seat at the desk. resumed his pen, and took upon himself an air of literary languor rarely excelled in the most approved portraits of our great writers.

"Come in," he intoned, when the expected knocking came; and there entered unto him a full and smooth faced gentleman in a complete and fashionable brimstone-colored suit, whose tightly-curled dark hair, very short coat, very baggy nether garments, yellow bamboo cane, and polka-spotted scarf, betokened an individual of distinguished tastes.

"How are you? How are you? General not in, eh?" said the brimstone stranger, tapping a glossy hat with his bamboo, and taking in the whole room in a sweeping glance of singular rapidity.

"Expect him in shortly," responded Mr. Benton Stiles, with an air. "He has been at the hotel all the morning with the Secretary of the Treasury, just on from Washington; but he'll return soon, now. Be seated, sir."

"Thank you, I will," returned the other, taking a chair and placing his hat and cane between his feet; "thank you, thank you. The General is arranging the collectorship now, I suppose?"

The secretary straightened up, as though in dignified menace of the visitor's unseemly want of delicacy, and brought his inestimable locket-ring into imposing prominence as he swept his goatee.

"The General, sir," said Mr. Stiles, "is probably attending to his own business, in his own way; actuated by no other motive than honest conviction may afford; desiring no higher reward than the applause of his own conscience, and seeking, simply as a private citizen, to facilitate the appointment of proper men to proper places."

It was a quotation from the last speech he had put into symmetrical shape from General Cringer's oracular suggestions, and he intended it as both a rebuff and an illumination to the presuming gentleman before him.

That gentleman, however, seemed neither abashed nor dazzled; unless a thrusting of the tongue into the cheek can be construed to indicate one of those effects. Indeed, something less than a microscopical examination of his round face would have detected something most reprehensibly like a leer thereon, and his words of response were inexcusably facetious.

"He! he! he!" laughed the brimstone stranger, twirling a pair of miniature golden handcuffs which hung as tasteful ornaments from his massive watch-chain; "just so; *of* course, and very right and jolly. Honest conviction, and all that sort of thing, is good. Facilitate, too, is *very* good. But what I like about the General, you know, is his independence; to-day with the Ebullition party, if they're in the right, and negotiating with the Demolition party for a compromise, to their mutual advantage; to-morrow with the Demolition party, if *they're* in the right, and negotiating with the Ebullitionists for ditto, ditto. That's what I call jolly."

Mr. Stiles was not favorably affected by this outburst of enthusiasm, and felt moved to assume a majestic coldness of demeanor, and ladle out a little more speech.

"The able and celebrated man, whose secretary I have the honor to be," said he, depressing his tufted chin to speak in deeper tones, "will, perhaps, explain his permanent political views, when so requested by those — if any such there be — who have a right to know them; always reserving for himself the American freeman's privilege to say, with the English poet, —

"'Thy spirit, Independence, let me share,
Lord of the lion heart and eagle eye.'

That independence, that constitutional liberty to think and decide in accordance with the dictates of his own unbiased judgment, he will ever maintain; unmoved by the temptations of corrupt political partisanship, and sternly regardless of those mercenary considerations —"

Mr. Stiles was brought to a full stop in his audible recollections of his employer's latest eloquences, by the extraordinary distortions of the stranger's countenance; a curious screwing-up of first one eye, and then the other, and a remarkable backward and forward movement of the ears by contractions and expansions of the scalp, being the most notable phenomena. At the words "mercenary considerations," the

11

motion of the ears became supernatural, and an outspread hand with projecting thumb was undisguisedly annexed to the nose.

Growing rigid in a moment, Mr. Benton Stiles stared malignantly at the astounding spectacle; whereupon the uplifted fingers fluttered piquantly, and one yellow eye snapped shut in an irresistible manner. Then Mr. Stiles' face began to undergo a peculiar change from the chin upward; the lower half, and especially the mouth, radiating an expression which just missed reaching the eyes at its very birth, and attacked the frown, hanging from the brow, with a twitching activity promising early triumph. During this progressive contest, too, Mr. Stiles' locket-ring hand wandered undecidedly around the goatee, like a vacillating bee about a coquettish flower; but in another second his eyes were imitatively screwed-up with the final defeat and flight of the frown, and the locket-ring hand leaped to his nose like a fantastic crab.

"Does your mother know you're out?" warbled the ingenious stranger, with much pretty finger-play.

"My eye!" chirped Mr. Stiles, adding his other fingers and thumb to his line of battle, and producing a doubly brilliant display.

This graceful ceremony involved each gentleman's entire recognition of the other's surpassing intellectual comprehensiveness; and the passwords exchanged by them will be immediately understood by all members of secret fraternal societies as equivalent to a mutual pledge of monetary aid, or funeral honors, in case of sickness or death on either side.

"He! he! he!" laughed the agreeable stranger, after that was over. "You ought to come in for something nice in the Custom House, one of these days; you're so jolly with the gab. The General has always wanted just such a jewel of a secretary as you are, Mr. Stiles."

"Hi! — you know my name, eh, Mr. —"

"— Ketchum — *of* the Independent Detective Force," put in the latter, with an insinuating nod. "I knew you the moment I put eyes on you, Mr. Stiles. You used to be a broker down in William Street, you know; but where I used to see you most was up at Woodlawn, with the fast crabs, and occasionally — only once in a while, you know — at the select family parties of the King of Diamonds."

The secretary came as near blushing as he ever had done since extreme youth, but instantly conquered the suffusion with a rakish wink.

"Then you're a friend of boyhood's sunny hour that I never saw before," said he, leaning back and putting both feet upon his desk, to appear fully at ease. "You knew me, then, when I was a top-sawyer, and also when my lynchpins began to work out; but you never knew me to cut-in before a friend, or break-up for a stranger — did you, Mr. Ketchum?"

"Not you" responded the detective, appreciatively.

"You never knew me to lay out more work for a nag than he could do, though nags and the king finished me?" pursued Mr. Stiles, in fond enjoyment of his own noble record.

"'Square' was *your* word!" corroborated Mr. Ketchum, infected with the prevailing enthusiasm of the moment.

Being lifted completely out of his official self by such tender reminiscences of a sunny past, Mr. Benton Stiles had parted his lips to narrate a brilliant runaway affair, in which one of the best fellows in the world had the top of his head taken off by being pitched against a stone-fence, when the sonorous closing of a door suddenly changed his mind and caused him to assume a more dignified attitude at his desk.

"There's the general," said he, and forthwith seized his pen and began to write with surprising industry.

Hat and cane in hand, Mr. Ketchum arose, just in time to take the extended hand of General Cringer, as that great man entered the room.

"Mr. Ketchum, I am happy to see you, sir," said the General, with large-sized geniality. "I hope, sir, that I have not kept you waiting too long; though, possibly, Mr. Stiles may have entertained you better than I could have done. What can I do for you, Mr. Ketchum?"

There was a mixture of benignant father and upright magistrate in his very manner of taking off his gloves, that made even the detective feel a certain reverence, as of Roman virtue.

"I haven't got a favor to ask this time, General," replied Mr. Ketchum, deferentially, "seeing that you have given my nephew that place in the Post Office. I've just dropped in to see if I can do anything for you at Albany, next week."

"Next — week, next week, sir," said General Cringer, placing his left hand in the breast of his coat, and pressing the forefinger of the other upon his lower lip. "Let—me—see, Mr. Ketchum. Is this week, sir, filled up with you?"

"Yes, General, I've got a country job to finish over in Jersey. I just got back from there this morning, after being a pedler, farm-hand, organ-grinder, and two or three other jolly humbugs, for the express benefit of a sort of half-cracked vagabond who's got to be tracked to town."

"Ah, I understand, Mr. Ketchum. A counterfeiter, I suppose. You've got a name, a deservedly great name, sir, for circumventing those foes to society. What a pity it is, Mr. Ketchum, that men *will* depart from the path of strict moral rectitude for the sake of money, mere money! — Mr. Stiles, you remember what I said about rectitude in that article I published to facilitate the harmony of a certain convention?"

"Oh, yes, sir," responded Mr. Benton Stiles, with great vivacity. "'As for the schemes of legislative corruption charged upon me by — '"

"Mr. Stiles!" interrupted General Cringer, with awful gravity, "that's not the one, sir!"

"Oh! I beg pardon," blurted Mr. Stiles in some confusion, "I know now: — 'Conscious as I am of the strict moral rectitude ever governing my own humble career as a private citizen of the republic, I would suggest to the gentlemen composing this convention the propriety of trusting wholly to that rectitude in themselves for a selection, at once honest and judicious, of the candidate for a public office so responsible and exacting. My friend, the incorruptible Dorgan O'Flannigan — '"

"There; that's sufficient," struck in the General, rather hastily; "if I have one weakness more extended than another, Mr. Ketchum, it's an indiscriminate rigor for moral rectitude. Next week, then, sir, you can go to Albany, you say?"

"On the nail," answered the detective; and instinctively stooped to gather some torn bits of written paper lying scattered on the carpet.

"Well, sir, then I may want you to go there — as a country constituent, of course; same as before — to look after the member from Cattawampus again."

"All right, general, you may depend on me. Adieu! Good-day, Mr. Stiles;" and Mr. Ketchum disappeared from the room like a shadow dismissed by the sun.

"Sharp fellow, that, Mr. Stiles," observed the great man, unbuttoning his coat, and combing-up his wreath of iron-gray with his fingers; "an invaluable man, in his way, sir. Now, Mr. Stiles, just make an entry, if you please: O'Shaughnessey, a thirty-five-hundred-dollar deputy's berth, Public Stores."

"O'Shaughnessey, a — thirty — five — hundred —

"'Well may your hearts believe the truth I tell;
    'Tis virtue makes the —'

dollar — deputy's berth — Public Stores."

"That's down, sir, is it? Any letters from Albany this morning, Mr. Stiles?"

"Only one, General, from that slow team, the Honorable Mr. Mulcahy. He says that bill of yours for the Atlantic Draining Company is so sure to pass, that you can commence selling shares right off."

"That's well, Mr. Stiles. Have you heard how O'Toole stands for the District Attorneyship, since our arrangement to give the assembly nomination to Mulligan to withdraw?"

"He seems to have a clear road ahead, and more than the pole for a start, General."

"*That's* all settled, then, Mr. Stiles; but you must keep stirring-up his workers, you know, to circulate the other side's tickets with his name nicely worked-in."

"Yes, sir."

"By the way — I nearly forgot it — there's our poor old Yankee friend, Pickering Lock, with his seven motherless children, and the rheumatism. Just make an entry: Pickering Lock, a night-watchmanship in the Custom House."

"Picker — ing — Lock —

"'My poverty, but not my will, consents—'

a night-watch — man — ship in — the Custom House."

Tinkle — inkle, inkle — 'kl — 'l — 'l. Thus sounded the bell downstairs once more; and — oh! undignified to confess — it was the great General Cringer himself who walked softly to the door this time, opened it noislessly, and unblushingly listened. Nay, he did more; he thrust out a hand and imperiously motioned Miss Cringer back to her room at the very moment of her appearance on the landing.

The tinkle of the bell was instantly followed by a sound of smart drumming on the door, by the knuckles of two parties, apparently; for the two distinct tunes of "The King of the Cannibal Islands," and "Old Dan Tucker," were both, distinguishably and simultaneously, drummed through before the horrified servant could get the door open. When the latter did open, there was a slipping, stumbling sound as though some one had been leaning unsuspiciously against it at the instant, and had at once gone down himself and painfully crushed the unprepared servant-girl between the door and the wall. But a tremendous cheer from half a dozen leathern throats silenced the intended remonstrances of the flattened menial, and General Cringer heard only a clatter of boots in the hall and a confusion of voice evidently surging into the first parlor.

"The ruffians of some club, I presume," muttered the General, glaring over his shoulder at the pretendingly busy secretary. "I'm glad the girl knew enough not to bring them up here. I'll go down."

"Will you want me, General?" asked Mr. Stiles.

"No, sir; not again to-day, Mr. Stiles;" and the speaker slowly buttoned his coat again, combed up his capillary wreath, and went-down to the parlor.

The sight meeting the eyes of the illustrious man when he opened the silver-knobbed mahogany door was not calculated to make a well-to-do gentleman desire its early repetition in his best reception-room.

Stooping to the open piano-forte, and dabbing at its keys with a merciless forefinger, was an individual dressed entirely in blue flannel, with pantaloons tucked into his boots and cigar in his mouth. Another gentleman, with steel spectacles on his nose and edges of red flannel showing at his neck and wrists, was intently admiring himself in the pier-glass, the while he rested a heavy boot on the slender marble shelf below it. On the satin-covered rosewood sofa sat a fat personage with his linen coat across his arm, removing one of his spacious shoes to discover what it was that

hurt his foot. Alternately rubbing a huge hand heavily over a valuable oil painting near a window, and looking to see if anything came off by the operation, stood an impressive figure in a velvet cap and gray muffler, neither of which did the owner seem to think of removing. Two other gentlemen, in blue overalls and linen coats were closely examining the cards in the marble receiver on the table by the sofa, as though anxious to discover how many of their fashionable intimate friends had called that day; and they completed the brilliant company.

A cold perspiration came out upon the shining brow of General Cringer, as it flashed upon him that the invasion of his home by such a remarkable collection of beings must have vastly astonished all his respectable neighbors; but what words shall describe his cold bath when the gentleman at the piano turned to meet him, and cried, —

"Fellers! three cheers for General Cringer!"

Where is the language to give the faintest idea of his inexpressible horror when those cheers were actually given, — awaking an echo from a gathering crowd outside the windows, and causing a nervous policeman on the sidewalk to rap with his club for reinforcements?

"Mr. Waters," said the General, recognizing his musical friend, and striving to appear benignantly gratified with his reception, "I am happy to see you, sir; and your friends — ?"

"Oh, that's Top-lights," said Mr. Waters, pointing to him of the spectacles; "and Lively Jim, over on that ere sofer; and the deepest cuss you ever see, over by the picture with the velvet cap; and them fellers at the cards."

The great man bowed to his guests, respectively, as they were thus admirably commended to his friendship, and remarked, patriarchally, —

"Happy to see you all, gentlemen, under my roof. May I ask, gentlemen, wherein it lies in my power, as an humble private citizen of the republic, to facilitate your wishes?"

"Take the pipe, Hosey, and play away," murmured Mr. Top-lights, in the chaste, metaphorical language of his native Fire Department.

"Well, then, General," said Mr. Waters, taking a saddle-seat on the piano-stool, and resting his cigar on the music-desk, "can we fellers depend on you as a member of the reg'lar, straight-out Demolition party?"

General Cringer, who had also taken a seat, rubbed his hands softly within one another, and answered, emollicntly, —

"Most assuredly, Mr. Waters and gentlemen, most assuredly."

Mr. Top-lights had, for the past minute, been eating peanuts from one of his largest pilot-cloth pockets, throwing the shells upon the carpet; but at this question he suddenly stopped his crunching, and directed the lambent fire of his green spectacles upon the gentleman of the house.

"The last time I heerd of you, General," said he, with great severity of tone, "you was a red-hot Ebullitionist."

"Ah, but that was a week ago, my friend," insinuated the General, with a glance of mild reproach. "You must remember, gentlemen, that my polar star is Principle, not Party; that my compass, as an humble private citizen of the republic, is the Constitution, — the Constitution of Thomas Jefferson and of Andrew Jackson."

Thereupon, the gentleman on the sofa, who had just got his stocking off, stamped agonizing applause with his disengaged foot, and emitted that ear-piercing whistle with which the more tasteful patrons of the Bowery theatres are wont to give piquancy to their acclamations.

"That being on the square," went on Mr. Waters, "there's no use of coughin' about it any more. We chaps are the Finance Committee of the O'Murphy Guard Target Company, and expect to turn out a hundred voters next week, — I mean a hundred muskets, — when we go up to Red House to shoot. We're named in honor of Mealy O'Murphy, Demolition candidate of the sixty-sixth district for Congress, and we want to know what kind of a prize he's likely to give us?"

General Cringer tapped his forehead with his fingers, in his most statesmanlike manner, and responded thoughtfully, —

"Well, truly, Mr. Waters and gentlemen, I am not banker to my excellent, honest old friend, Mealy O'Murphy, and I do not know just what his resources may be; but I should say that he would be willing to contribute a cheque for — say two hundred and fifty, to encourage good marksmanship. If my friend, Mealy O'Murphy, has a positive passion," said General Cringer glowingly, "it is for good marksmanship."

Here the speechless being in velvet cap and gray muffler, who had been introduced definitely as "the deepest cuss," suddenly ceased his experiments upon the painting, and began moving quite briskly about the room with eyes downcast, as though in eager search of some valuable article lost upon the floor. He looked under the sofa, the table, and all the chairs, paused a moment over the music-stand, as if in some doubt about it, and finally looked full at Mr. Waters.

"He's lookin' for your sand-box," observed the latter to the bewildered General Cringer; "don't you keep none in the shanty?"

The celebrated man understood the question, and regretted to say that the luxurious article desired was not numbered with his furniture.

"Spit out of the window, then, you deep cuss," said Mr. Waters; and the "cuss" proceeded promptly to do so, to the inexpressible indignation of a butcher having his boots blacked on the sidewalk.

"Two hundred and fifty will be the scrumptious thing," pursued the same speaker, reverting to the original topic and rising to his feet. "Now let's vamose the ranch, fellers."

Not that instant, though; for the occupant of the sofa, after hastily resuming his stocking and shoe, had these remarkable and cabalistic words to utter, —

"How much for Macginnis?"

Every movement was stopped at the sound, and even the two fashionables at the card-receiver suspended their attempts to loosen the marble birds from that Italian ornament.

"Considering that my friend Macginnis is a fellow-countryman of my friend, Mealy O'Murphy," answered General Cringer obligingly, "I should say that he might expect something handsome to compensate for half a day's free gift of wholesome beer to the deserving poor. Say, about seventy-five."

The sofa-man sat down again expressly for the purpose of sounding approval with his feet; and not only wore a hole in the carpet, but also repeated his dramatic whistle with renewed effect.

The General, in the fulness of his benignity, had to accompany his worthy friends to the street door, where the cold perspiration was again called to his martyred brow by the irrepressible enthusiasm of the O'Murphy Guard. No sooner were those genial gentlemen upon the stoop, than they broke into three hideous cheers for General Cringer, followed by three for Mealy O'-Murphy, followed by three for the Demolition party; and, as quite a mob was present in the street to join in their cries, the effect upon a quiet neighborhood was unique and exasperating.

Finally, however, the cheers were all given, the last bow was made, the Finance Committee and the mob retired to other localities, and the knowing face of 3. Cringer's residence looked down upon the deserted block, with one eye tightly shut, as before.

CHAPTER XVIII.

THE HYERS' NEW BOARDER.

If Mr. Luke Hyer, senior, had been content with the position of Purser's Clerk on a Liverpool steamer, affording him sufficient means to support his wife, son, and daughters, creditably, in half a comfortable house in Varick Street, — it would have been well for him. Had he rested satisfied with a flourishing retail dry-goods store in Broome Street, enabling him to remove his family to a whole house in Wooster Street and educate his children in all the modern accomplishments, — it would have been still better for him. But, as he undertook, upon the strength of small capital and large credit, to establish a great wholesale silk house, in which he failed, — it was bad for him. That is to say, bad when compared with the possibilities of the degree immediately preceding it; for a position, as minor salesman, even, in the imposing and solemn Establishment of Goodman & Co., yielded considerably more income than any honest purser's clerkship, and no living soul could impeach the integrity of Luke Hyer, senior. It was incomparably bad, though, in its domestic results; owing to the fact that the two elder Misses Hyer, their mother being no more, refused to descend from the social rank to which the silk venture had temporarily raised them, and persisted in retaining an expensive house and calling-list, to the great pecuniary embarrassment and misery of their remaining parent. Mr. Luke Hyer, though a plain, simple-minded person himself, liked to see his children dressed elegantly, and associating with people of culture, provided his purse could afford it; but when such dressing and associations were attained by such pretences, desperate devices, and debt-making, as his daughters were now resorting to, he felt ever the uneasy weariness of one who lives under a vague premonition of some coming trouble, and found his only relief in the cares and labor of his salesmanship. It was no real pleasure for him to go home in the evening to his stately residence on Fourteenth Street, near the square. To enter the house, was to be reminded of the large sum he must manage to raise against the next rent-day; to enter the brilliantly-lighted and luxurious parlors, was to be mocked with the reflection, that the coarse auctioneer's red flag might be flying at the door in another three months; to hear the thoughtless talk of his daughters about their "servants," their "maids," and their "jewelry preparing in Paris," was to be smitten to the heart with the thought that those most dear to him on earth were laboriously living a perilous lie; and so, when poor, soberly-dressed Mr. Luke Hyer, senior, reached home at night, he slipped guiltily down through the area entrance to the basement, for all the world like a belated bread-man, and moped alone in that part of the house until the hour came for him to glide upstairs, past the piano-ringing parlors, and betake himself to God's tenderest mercy, forgetful sleep.

The master, then, of that spacious and balconied house in Fourteenth Street was a doleful figure to meet on the premises of an evening; but there was always lively and modish company to be found in the richly-appointed parlors, and there can be no reasonable objection to trying an evening there.

Fine rooms were those parlors, with the square folding-doorway between them, and a silvered and glass-hung chandelier of four branches pendent from the ceiling of each. Illuminated by the flare of eight little fans of gas, the red damask curtains of the two pairs of windows, the red brocatel of the rosewood sofas, tête-à-têtes, chairs, and ottomans, the great red blotches of flowers on the Brussels carpet, and the radiating plaits of red on the upper front of the upright English piano-forte, all had a tendency to reflect a delicate bloom upon faces relieved against them in any direction, and gave a tone of sensuous warmth to the atmosphere. A large gilded harp in one corner, huge gilded mirrors over each mantel and between the windows, and a variety of ormolu statuettes upon brackets at various points on the wall, constituted the gaudy element; while several small marble-top tables loaded with petty china and papier-maché trickeries, and an entire absence of all pictures, save one sprawling, family-portrait, from the gilt-and-white papered walls, sufficiently indicated how far taste may be cultivated by accidental opportunities without becoming in any sense refined.

Posed upon a sofa toward the front windows, her dress of some very light silk, a gold-linked circle of little lava medallions about her fair neck, and her plentiful dark hair manipulated into such complicated braids, bands, scrolls, and frizzles, as only that form of woman's brains can compass, sat the eldest Miss Hyer, — Miss Caroline. At her side, like a puff of raw cotton with three black dots for a trade-mark, nestled the most malignant type of French poodle, blinking his weak and venomous eyes under the magnetic stroking of an exquisitely eatable hand.

On an ottoman not far off, and in a dress and coiffure nearly the same as those of her sister, appeared Miss Meeta Hyer, second in command, and a very pretty little brunette. To her belonged the harp, upon which she was taking three weekly lessons from a Polish refugee (late of the ferry-boats).

Miss Tillie Hyer, the youngest sister, had gone to a juvenile soirée at a neighbor's; Mr. Luke Hyer, junior, had gone with an older friend to witness some theatrical performance at the opera-house in Astor Place, and the two sweet creatures above mentioned had the parlors to themselves for the time.

There was an opportunity, then, for unreserved family talk, not to mention sisterly confidences; but while Carrie's dark eyes never turned from the poodle, whose name was Fleance, those of Meeta committed themselves unconditionally to the carpet, and neither seemed at all eager to begin a conversation. Smooth, delicate, transparent, young faces! what a pity those beautiful curves of brow, cheek, and chin, should ever sharpen to the plaintive angles of woman's household care! what a pity to see, even now, within those curves, the faintest shadow of the care that makes such angles!

Miss Hyer and Miss Meeta had cares, even if they did not let their fashionable friends know it. In fact, the most wearing and tremendous care they had was the care to make their fashionable friends believe they had no cares. To speak plain English, the Hyers let out one of the best rooms upstairs to a lodger who paid handsomely.

More than that, they had, on that very day, rented another room to a lady-boarder who had (it *must* be told at last) answered their disguised advertisement, for a boarder, in a morning paper. More than *that* — O print! dwindle to thy smallest — the sisters earned a little money by making chenille-buttons for a Broadway cloak house.

These very sly resources were not mentioned in connection with Mr. Luke Hyer, senior, for the reason that they were not his resources at all. The whole weekly sum derived from them went to the Polish refugee, a French hair-dresser, the dress-goods merchant, and the dressmakers; not one dollar being devoted either to the rent, or to those long-extended debts under which the father crouched miserably into himself, as though uncertain that anything beyond the mere mortal shell of himself was really his own.

The look on Miss Meeta's face grew graver and graver with an apparent intensification of what both were brooding over, until finally the young lady tossed her head impatiently, made a face at Fleance, and went to the piano. A couple of bleached frogs, making rival leaps on the key-board of that instrument, would have come as near the production of a melody as did the fair hands of Meeta; but music was not what the latter intended; she intended but to break her sister's silence; and she succeeded.

"Oh dear!" exclaimed Miss Hyer, with a fiery glance thither, "I do wish you'd stop that."

Back came Meeta to her ottoman at the word, with a gleam of entire satisfaction on her ingenuous countenance.

"Since you *can* speak to somebody besides the dog, Carrie," said she, amiably, "I wish you'd tell me how you think we'd best do if Miss Terry comes down this evening and there should be anybody here? I couldn't do less than ask her as I did, of course."

"I wouldn't be utterly silly if I was you!" responded Carrie, contemptuously. "I would try to have a little sense. Can't we introduce her without giving a whole history about it? I can, if you can't."

"Well, snap my head off, Carrie, will you? Sweet creature! You think everybody will be as obliging about being passed off as a visitor, as Mr. Stiles is; but I shouldn't a bit wonder if Miss Terry should come right out with something about where she boarded last, if she did board anywhere. Then you'd look nice!"

"There's no use of talking with any one so perfectly stupid," observed Miss Hyer, closing her fine eyes momentarily. "I don't see why you don't just have Mr. Stiles at once, Meeta, if you're so crazy about him."

"I couldn't break your heart in that way, you know," replied Meeta, smiling sweetly; "because then all your putting your feet out beyond your dress, Carrie, and wondering how anybody can help loving everybody, would be all thrown away."

"Oh, I do think!" ejaculated the elder sister, indignantly; and then she added something about a "hateful thing."

This vivacious little scene might have had still other piquancies, but for the arrival of Mrs. Cornelius O'Doricourt Fish, an acquaintance of much fashion, who thought she would call in for a few moments and see her dear friends, Carrie and Meeta, while Mr. Fish went around to the club for half an hour.

Mrs. Cornelius O'Doricourt Fish was a tall, gayly dressed, hazel-eyed lady, wearing her brown hair brushed straight back into a violet bonnet shaped like a church window, and displaying on her wrists above her gloves a pair of gold bracelets massive to behold. Without taking a particularly humorous view of life, Mrs. Fish was always laughing, to the great advantage of her admirable teeth; and the fact that she had lately presented Mr. Cornelius O'Doricourt Fish with a minute son and heir, baptized Phineas, gave the teeth a perpetual good time of it.

"My dear Carrie, he! he! I've been dying to see you for so long. My dear Meeta, too." Giggle — giggle.

Both young ladies made as much haste to welcome the visitor and conduct her to the sofa as elegant languor would permit. Carrie throwing an arm affectionately over her sister's shoulders and the two mixing much doting love for each other with their unanimous terms of welcome to Mrs. Fish.

The latter sank tittering upon the sofa; or, at least, was sinking upon it, when the air was suddenly rent with such deafening discord as might have burst forth had one taken a seat upon the upper octaves of an organ charged with air; for the lady had unwittingly subsided upon the temporarily lethargic Fleance, producing such an explosion of unearthly sounds and demoniac wrath as human philosophy would find extremely hard to reconcile with so small a body of matter. Lucky it was for Phineas Fish that he had not delayed his coming, or there is no knowing how his fortunes might have been affected by the surpassing agility with which his infatuated ma shot up to a standing position from that sofa. Her violet bonnet was jerked over one eye by the impetus of the shock, making her half blind for a moment, and the sagacious little dog took that opportunity to snap away the thumb of her nearest glove to keep himself steady while he barked.

"O you bad! bad! bad! little dove!" exclaimed Carrie, making his curly back a base for the infliction of as many ingenious back-handed blows at the air.

"Ne-ne-never mind it, my love, he! he!" panted Mrs. Fish, replacing her church window, and very nervously sinking upon a chair.

"Well, he *is* such a cunning dear!" exclaimed Carrie, catching up the household darling in her arms and sitting down to soothe him.

"Yes, Carrie darling; but maybe Mrs. Fish knows of a still cunninger little dear," said Meeta, with a glance of fond archness at her sister, and a fixed look of innocent quizzicality at the flushed guest.

"Now, girls, you ought really to see him," cried the mother of Phineas, thrown at once into her laughs again by the artless reference; "such be-yu-tiful legs, he! he! he! and eyes so full of intellect that I'm frightened by them sometimes; yes, really frightened. And such straight legs — I will say it, he! he! — and even my own family say he's handsome as any picture. In perfect health, you know, and such good legs."

With the aid of a dumpling, a pillow, and two black cherries, human art could have reproduced all the leading beauties of Phineas Fish, — except his legs; which was one reason, perhaps, why the proud young mother dwelt so gloatingly on the latter.

"And does he ask you many questions yet?" inquired the deeply-interested Carrie, as in beautiful maiden ignorance of the fact that babes do not usually converse volubly at three months old. She put the innocent query on her knees, too, in front of the visitor, and with her right hand stealing about her sister's waist.

"No, dear," responded the lady, giggling, "my Phinny does not exactly talk much, yet: but I am sure, from his looks, that he must think a great deal."

"Babies are such precious angels!" burst irrepressibly from the rosy lips of Meeta, — "aren't they, Carrie, love?"

"You know I've always said so, sweet," lisped the melting Caroline; "and how I wish our friend upstairs would come down, now, and hear Mrs. Fish tell about the darling creature. If she only would!"

"From the country, is she?" asked Mrs. Cornelius O'Doricourt Fish, with friendly interest.

"Miss Terry from the country!" exclaimed Carrie, looking incredibility at Meeta. "Why, Mrs. Fish, do you think all our friends come from the country? I declare, I've a great mind to send one of our servants right up to her, and bring her down before my maid's half done with her, after that! Meeta, my sweet, shall we?"

"O goodness, he! he! he! don't!" entreated Mrs. Fish, rolling her eyes and lifting her hands; "I wouldn't have you for the world. The idea!"

"She'll be down in a few moments, at any rate, and we can tell her then," said Meeta; and, unable to resist the temptation longer, she kissed the top of Carrie's head.

"But you don't expect any other company right away,—do you?" queried the visitor, in pretended fear of a very public exposure, — "no gentlemen, I hope?"

Carrie's head bent to hide what was intended to be a very traitorous blush, and Meeta simpered, —

"N-n-not more than w-w-one, Mrs Fish."

That lady was thereupon seized with a spirit of merciless roguishness only to be satisfied in the words: "Not that agreeable Mr. Stiles? You don't mean, he! he! to say that you are expecting him AGAIN?"

Reply was cut short by the opening, at that moment, of the parlor door nearest to the group, and the noiseless entrance of a lady, with light, smooth hair, and in a tasteful black silk dress, who paused, as her mild eyes fell upon Mrs. Fish, and became rigid.

"This is Mrs. Fish, Miss Terry," spoke Carrie, starting from her kneeling posture, after a brief paralysis, and making a gesture of introduction somewhat hysterically.

An inclination of Miss Terry's lustrous head, and an answering recognition from the mother of the legs.

"Take that chair, won't you, Miss Terry?" said Meeta, twitching her unexceptionable shoulders from no apparent cause.

"Thank you, I will," replied Miss Terry, in a pleasant voice; and she took the designated chair with a quiet ease much at variance with her demeanor a moment before.

"Do you know, Miss Terry," commenced Mrs. Fish, in immediate freedom and confidence, "that these wild girls, he! he! insist upon it that I shall tell you what a miracle of a little one I've got at home? And you being such a prized friend of theirs, of course I can't resist."

That was a dreadful instant for the sisters! a verge on which hung motionless in awful poise their whole precious character in society. *If* Miss Terry should ask — ! !

A scarcely perceptible glance at the breathless beauties did not disturb the serene beaming of those mild eyes on Mrs. Cornelius O'Doricourt Fish, nor give the slightest quaver to the low, pleasant voice.

"Our friends should not be denied that favor, Mrs. Fish, if you will only oblige me by conferring it."

Miss Terry had, evidently, fathomed the situation intuitively, and was willing to be merciful. The sisters breathed again.

"Did my maid please you, Miss Terry?" asked Carrie, with that startling boldness which often comes with the first reaction from mortal terror.

"All you have provided pleases me, Carrie," returned Miss Terry, with a boldness of address equally startling.

"My little Phinney does not talk yet, of course," struck in the mother, eager to be at it again; "but then, Miss Terry, he! he! he's so well-formed that you would scarcely notice his not talking. Oh dear, that must be my husband."

It was not her husband, though, whose feet were approaching in the hall; for, when the solitary servant of the house opened the door, the individual presenting himself was no other than the suppressed lodger, Mr. Stiles.

"Mrs. Fish" — with locket-ring hand on vest — "your most obedient and devoted..

Miss Hyer, *and* Miss Meeta," — shaking hands with them (as he always accommodatingly did when company was present) — "more charming than ever, if you will allow me to repeat that trite remark — "

"Mr. Stiles, Miss Terry," introduced by Carrie.

" — Proud, Miss Terry."

Mr. Stiles could not have played a part more congenial to his idiosyncracies than the one he was now inexpressibly obliging his landladies by assuming, for the twentieth time, at least. To use his own idealized phraseology, it "just suited his book" to pass for the valued gentleman-visitor of a stylish family, and he not only kept up the assumption in all its required legitimacies, but also elaborated it strikingly, on occasions, with little gratuitous helps to the general comedy of "Laying it on thick."

"Mrs. Fish," said Mr. Stiles, after taking an ottoman, "you're looking remarkably well, as Mr. Fish probably tells you every day. And how is the young President?"

"O Mr. Stiles! I'm sure; he! he! he!"

"I'm happy to hear you say so, Mrs. Fish, if you'll excuse the freedom. Miss Terry, your handkerchief, I believe?"

"Thank you, sir."

"By the way, Miss Hyer, that barouche you wanted papa to buy is not sold yet. The villain will come down to civilized figures before he'll let such a fair offer slip."

"Will he, Mr. Stiles?"

"I'm so sure of it, Miss Meeta, that if *I* were any other barouche in the city I'd die on the spot of jealousy."

"Oh, what a man you are, Mr. Stiles!" and Meeta hung her pretty head in sweet confusion.

"Here's Mr. Fish, now," remarked the mother of the legs, in a tone of complacent importance; and, sure enough, in walked the black-haired and black-whiskered father of the legs, to be greeted and introduced, and made generally uncomfortable on a chair near the suddenly uncurtained teeth of Fleance.

Mr. Fish never could have been strong-minded at any period of his life; for a giant intellect seldom coils its Herculean traits under a perfectly flat head; but the shamefacedness of a young parent sat upon him with a peculiar effect of disordered vacancy, and a cowardly grin did not intensify the intelligence of his profile. He lived under a wretchedly happy certainty that everybody knew about Phineas and wanted to address him publicly on the subject; and when Mr. Stiles whispered something in his ear, he shook hands idiotically with that gentleman and made a futile attempt to pull his chair from under himself without rising from it.

Scarcely had the flutter occasioned by the new arrival subsided, when Miss Terry asked the privilege of retiring from the room, and asked it, too, with such mingled simplicity and dignity of manner that no one considered it a breach of etiquette. Mr.

Stiles opened the door for her, with his most engaging air, and received her slight bow, when she passed him, as though he never could sufficiently appreciate the honor.

"What a charming person!" murmured Mrs. Cornelius O' Doricourt Fish.

"Sister and I could never do without her," simpered Meeta, looking straight at Mr. Fish, as the object least likely to disturb her with any intelligent expression.

Mr. Stiles saw at once how the land lay, and gave one of his most successful touches of art to the comedy.

"Do you know, Miss Hyer," said he to Carrie, with gentle earnestness, "that Miss Terry does not seem to me to be looking as robust as she did?"

"Indeed, Mr. Stiles!"

"I may be mistaken, Miss Hyer, but it struck me when I first came in, that there were traces of secret grief. She did not remember me at all, you saw."

Carrie came near losing her self-possession at such an ultra-ingenious stroke of audacity as that, but managed to say, — "She probably did not look fully at you at first, Mr. Stiles."

Here Mr. Fish writhed complicatedly to the very edge of his chair and chuckled something about heads of large families keeping good hours. This brought the mother to her feet in a full fever of maternal apprehension, and resulted in a leave-taking remarkable for whispering and spasmodic bursts of unmeaning mirth.

As the blissful young parents disappeared, so passed away the smiling, cheerful girlishness of the Misses Hyer, even as though it had never been. Caroline betook herself listlessly to the sofa and bent moodily over the shapeless poodle of her virgin affections, Meeta stood pouting at the piano, and it was the general feminine sentiment of the room that the evening had not been an entire success.

Mr. Stiles, also, as he paused near the door and fingered the bracket of an ormolu "Peace," seemed willing to hear some kind of explanation before bowing himself off the scene. He lingered thus inconsequently for several moments, and finding that woman's tongue forsook its prerogative for once, ventured to speak first himself.

"May I inquire, Miss Hyer, if our remarkably self-possessed friend, Miss Terry, will appear at breakfast? — or has the carriage been ordered to take her home?"

Caroline darted a sharp glance at him, and Meeta struck a chord.

"I'm delighted to hear you say so," observed the unabashed gentleman, "and I hope Miss Terry will not be discontented with her accommodations when she finds that I do not breakfast with you. Now, really, ladies," continued Mr. Stiles, suddenly assuming a tone of considerate kindness, "you must let me speak to you this once as a friend, rather than as a lodger. I'm old enough to be your brother, as you are aware, and you must not mind what I say. This Miss Terry is the new boarder;—*I* know that. Furthermore, as herein aforesaid, nevertheless and notwithstanding, I wouldn't trust her too far. That's the last farewell parting advice, ladies, of one who is old enough to be your brother. Allow me to say good-evening!" and he departed from them in a supernaturally mature and benedictional manner.

"I wish I was dead!" said Carrie to Fleance.

"Always something!" said Meeta to the piano-forte.

It was the privileged custom of Mr. Stiles, when he reached home at a reasonable hour in the evening, to smoke a cigar in the basement before retreating finally upstairs to his own room; and after leaving the parlor he went down for that reflective purpose. Cigar in mouth, therefore, he entered the front basement, expecting to find it vacant; for Mr. Luke Hyer, senior, generally retired early, and the youngest Hyers avoided that part of the house altogether. On this occasion, however, he found the minor salesman of Goodman & Co. still there, with his back toward the door and a worn-looking morning paper on his knee.

"Oh, I wish I was in Rome,
  With the Pope, with the Pope;
Oh, I wish I was in Rome,
  With the Po-ope,"

crooned old Mr. Hyer, dismally, as he weariedly polished his silver-mounted spectacles with a red silk handkerchief, and made various dreamy starts to save the newspaper from falling to the floor. He did not hear the door opening, and had commenced his senile refrain again when Mr. Stiles spoke,—

"Why, governor, you're making a night of it, this time."

"Ye-es, Mr. Stiles," answered he, recognizing the voice and turning toward the speaker. "The fact is, I fell asleep. What time is it?"

Mr. Stiles drew from his vest's upper pocket a wildly staring stop-watch, and, from sheer force of early habit, pressed the stop-spring and said "Go!"

"Eh?" ejaculated Mr. Hyer.

"Beg pardon; I mean half-after ten. Ten; thirty; twenty-one quarter."

"My! Late as that, is it?" said Mr. Hyer, rising slowly from his chair and letting the paper fall; "then I must be getting upstairs. Oh, dear."

"Stop and try a cigar," suggested Mr. Stiles.

"No, thank you, Mr. Stiles. I've given up smoking, as fond as I used to be of it. I can't afford it now. Good-night."

He spoke disconsolately, as he did about everything; and as he took his gray-sprinkled head and sombre form out of the apartment, without so much as a lamp in his hand to make him seem less lost in his own house, Mr. Stiles shook his head and held the wrong end of his regalia to the gas flame.

"Poor old horse, let him die," soliloquized Mr. Stiles, with much poetic feeling.

CHAPTER XIX.

THE DAYS WHEN I WENT GIPSYING.

WHEN once Mr. Reese had introduced me to his strange fellow-travellers in the terms I have repeated, and shared equally with me the crackers, sausage, and strong cheese handed from the wagon by Juan, he seemed to think that the honors were all done and my case definitely settled. The high flavor of the sausage induced me to give nearly all my portion of that delicacy to Mr. Mugses, who ate it with great solemnity, and immediately curled his tail into a tremulous note of interrogation having direct reference to the cheese. The latter, also, I passed to him, as being rather pungent for my own use, and his summary disposition of it called forth a shrill ejaculation from the old woman under the wagon and a laugh from her younger companion.

"Why do you give that to the dog?" asked Reese, looking up from his own lazy meal at the sound. "Old Dolores over there can't stand such extravagance. Don't you like the stuff?"

"No, sir," said I.

"You'll like it better when you get used to it," said he; "won't he, Anita?"

The question was addressed to the young girl, who laughed again, and nodded at me several times with great good-humor.

"Who do you think that lady is?" asked my entertainer, pointing to the girl, and exchanging smiles with her.

I intimated a belief that she was his sister, whereupon the two card-players laughed very boisterously, and the man with the monkey, who, as I afterwards discovered, was her father, looked angry.

"Then you think I'm a gipsy, too?"

His long black hair, which he wore pushed back behind his ears, gave him a half-foreign look; but he had not the dark complexion of the others, and I could not admit that I took him for a gipsy.

"No, I'm no gipsy, Little Breeches; but I may become one some of these days in downright earnest, if things go against me. She's a princess,—you understand?—and would look well in the crown I'd buy for her if I had the money convenient. Not the sort of princess you read of in your story-books, though, but a member of the black-eyed dynasty, queens of the palm. Come here, Anita."

The scowl of the monkey-man grew darker, and the old woman shook her head violently and mumbled something; but the girl unhesitatingly obeyed his summons, and crawled over to us on all-fours.

"Tell this little fellow's fortune," said Reese, clasping his hands across his knees, and motioning toward me with his head.

"He not so small-a," hinted she, in a low, musical voice, and with a laughing look at me.

"Nor big enough to make me jealous, my beauty; so just look into his hand, and see what he's got before him."

Juan and the card-players having come forward to look on, she took the cards from one of the latter, and then pulled one of my hands toward her, and began to trace the lines of the palm with a dexterous forefinger.

"Great-a trouble for him," she said, in a sing-song way; "he go down, down; and then up-a; but I don't know if he marry. Let me see." She shuffled the dirty cards, holding them over her head, and managed to make one shoot out from the pack and fall beside me, face downward.

"You tell-a me, is it black or red?"

"It's got black spots on it," answered I, looking.

"Black-a? Ah, no good," she went on, retaking the card without looking at it, and adding it to the pack. The latter she shuffled over her head again, and then made a fan of it before her, and began talking very fast.

"Black man—dark eyes, dark hair—cross-a you here first. Plenty of money for you; but—but, one red man, two red men, cross you here, and no money. Black man again, and then some one light-a; maybe woman; and you have-a money, and lose-a money. I know no more."

Reese laid back on the grass and laughed a hearty response to the grins of the other men, the latter seeming to view my fortune in an extremely humorous light.

"After that rigmarole for the tailor from Morristown, you'd better shut up shop, my beauty," roared the former. "You've given him more reds and blacks and whites than you gave me. He'll be pretty well tanned if he goes through all the shades."

Anita drew her shawl over her face and went silently back to where the old woman sat; while I rubbed the hand she had examined, as though to discern something of what she had pretended to see there, and was hopelessly confused in my head over the red men, and black men, and money.

"Now go and play with the dog, if you want to, while I take a nap," said Reese; and without more ado he placed his hat over his eyes and paid no further attention to anybody.

The other men resuming their former occupations, and Anita showing no disposition to invite my assistance in the mending of the tambourine, I found no better employment than staring at them and the wagons for a while, and then engaging Mr. Mugses in a series of headlong charges and frantic retreats, in which he displayed a vivacity not always regulated by the most obvious intelligence.

Now that I look back to that day in the woods, and remember how sinister and foreign-looking were the dark faces of those people, I am surprised to think how fearlessly I trusted myself in the uncongenial company of the latter, and how untroubled I was by the timidity so usual to me in the presence of grown persons. It may have been that I had only heard of gipsies in such a fragmentary, indefinite way, that their name as a race suggested no more than the vague romantic difference from common mortals, in which the childish mind takes an unreasoning but sober pleasure. It may have been that the cheerful, familiar manner of the country ox-driver, and the hearty, friendly treatment of Reese, broke down, for the time, my nervous awe of adult mankind and gave me that reactionary boldness which, in dogs and children, is apt to follow closely upon abject fear, at the least encouragement from superiors. Whichever was the reason, I certainly felt at ease with my silent friends from the moment of my introduction to them, and derived no other sensation from their wild appearance than such an agreeable wonder as might have enlivened my mind during the reading of a romantic story. It is possible that the deep black eyes of Anita made me temporarily bashful, and that the snapping gestures and mumbling talk of Old Dolores made me keep my distance from the two for a little while; but as Mr. Mugses grew excited with his sport and ultimately extended his panting retreats to a point beyond them, I finally crawled fairly between the pair in pursuit of my playmate, and was made quite at home by their nods and pretended clutches at me.

Late in the afternoon an old farmer and his wife arrived in a wagon from some place through which the gipsies had passed two or three days before. The man remained in the vehicle where it had stopped on the road, to "mind the horse," he said; but the old woman descended, and, having cast a shrewd look at the vagrants and their gear, walked boldly to where Dolores and Anita were seated and exhibited to the former a finger on which a felon was visible.

As though the whole affair had been arranged beforehand, Dolores drew from a tattered carpet-sack, worn at her waist, a bit of brown paper, a pencil, and a strip of white cloth. Using the tambourine for a desk, she made some marks upon the paper with the pencil, muttered a number of words over the writing, and then carefully bound the enchanted inscription upon the afflicted finger with the cloth. The old woman, after watching the process with some anxiety of countenance, assumed a look of great contentment at its conclusion, and, having paid a quarter of a dollar to Dolores, went confidently back to the wagon and was driven off.

Still later in the day, and when the sun was almost below the horizon, there arrived another great gipsy wagon, containing four more gipsy men, who seemed, by the noisy welcome given them, to have been absent from the main company for some time. They brought a great heap of old rags, bottle corks, broken table-knives, and other trash, in the examination of which Dolores displayed a chattering interest for which I could not account. Anita, observing my puzzled look, said,—"We sell-a them;" and I felt the more confused by the explanation. While these extraordinary treasures were still in discussion, two more gipsies, with hand-organs on their backs, arrived from Newark, as Reese told me, and they seemed to complete the gang.

At twilight, the noisy chattering and swarming about the last wagon having somewhat subsided, Juan built a fire of brush on the grass by the roadside, and Dolores held a long-handled iron skillet over the flames, while Anita sliced and threw into it a number of the strong sausages I have already mentioned. Reclining upon the turf in all directions, the men awaited the completion of the cooking, their dark faces and glistening eyes catching the firelight like the smoky figures of an old, varnish-cracked picture, seen by the insufficient beams of a candle; and had I known anything of banditti by story, the tableau must have suggested the most picturesque chivalry of crime to my attentive gaze. Reese was beside me again on the grass, with Mr. Mugses, vivaciously scenting the cookery at his left hand, and when the sausages were finally ready, and the skillet placed where all could reach it, my new friend asked me if he should help me?

"No, sir," responded I; "they aren't nice; but I'd like some of the cakes."

"That is to say, crackers, Little Breeches," said he; "and I don't know but they are better for young tailors. Here, Juan, some crackers for the boy, and some crackers and cheese for me."

Juan, who had just poured a quantity of crackers upon the grass near the skillet from a coarse bag, went back to his wagon and brought the desired articles on a tin plate; whereupon Reese told me to help myself, if I could see to do so. The gipsies, meanwhile, were plunging crippled knives and forks into the skillet, and claw-like hands into the heap of crackers, and had I been particularly delicate of stomach, their primitive mode of eating might have injured my own appetite. Not being thus delicate, however, the dimly-seen spectacle only amused me, and I ate with a gusto which caused Mr. Mugses to follow each cracker to my mouth with his nose, in repeated disappointment, and finally utter a whine of sheer desperation.

The sausages and crackers being all eaten, and fresh brush thrown upon the fire, Anita and Juan appeared from one of the wagons with a number of small tin pails containing liquor of some sort, and gave one to each couple, to be shared between them. This was a signal for Reese to leave me and take a seat beside the two card-players of the afternoon, and after he had drank from a pail devoted to his exclusive use, he entered into a conversation with the men in their own language, and I was forgotten.

During the drinking, and its accompanying clatter of voices, the fire crackled, flamed, flashed, flickered, and tumbled into broken skeletons of sputtering red; but its light was succeeded by that of a full-orbed moon on high, whose mellow lustre fell in hazy shafts and patches through the tree-tops above, and threw shadows of trunks and twining branches upon the grass and its figures in a gigantic mosaic. Cricket and tree-toad uttered only irregular notes for a while, the loud bursts of laughter and occasional uproar of contention frightening them from persistence, apparently; but soon they appeared to grow accustomed to such dissonant voices, and went lustily to work for the night in full concert all around. A majority of the gipsies lit their clay-pipes before the fire went entirely out, the heaped tops of the bowls glowing, like burning coals, in short parallels and irregular squares and triangles; and as the half-distinct, half-shadowy smokers quickly jerked the pipes from their mouths in the excitement of their talk, and as quickly drove them back between their teeth at each pause, the effect to me was like a curious game with little fiery balls, which the players were fanning to keep above their waists.

With my back against a tree and my feet sprawled out before me I was sleepily amusing myself with this fancy, when one of the organ-men turned to the instrument standing beside him, and, with an exclamation sounding like "Gavota! gavota!" commenced grinding a lively air. A general shout followed, and, as the smokers hastily scrambled apart to leave a space clear between the first wagon and the place where I sat, Reese and Anita sprang to their feet and began dancing toward and from each other in the liveliest manner imaginable. As he approached her, he extended his arms, and she, with the shawl falling back from her glossy black hair, acted as though she would run into them; but when another step or two brought him closer, she turned from him with a graceful motion, looking back at him under an uplifted elbow. Then he turned, too, and came from her with hands upon his hips and his feet flying in all sorts of ways, leaving her to come dancing after him with *her* arms extended and her head very much on one side. Faster came the music, Old Dolores joining it with the tambourine this time, and Anita was almost touching Reese, when he spun swiftly about and caught her around the waist before she could save herself. Tum! went the tambourine, and away they whirled together in a ring on the grass, half in shadow, half in moonlight, until another Tum! from Dolores brought both to a standstill — she leaning back over one of his arms, with a hand on his shoulder and her eyes on his face.

They sank down in their places again

amid a tempest of shouts and laughter; while I, fully aroused by the performance, leaned eagerly forward with the hope that it would be repeated. There was no repetition of the dance, and as the gipsies scrambled together in knots again and renewed their chatter around Reese and the women, I got stealthily up and quietly made my way to the road, where all was light and I could see the bend from whence the wagons had first caught my attention. While I paused there on the road which led, as I believed, to New York, there flashed upon me a sudden thought of flight; an impulse to run with all my speed, and get away from there! I think I should have done so had the thought lasted another moment, though not knowing why; but even while my heart throbbed at its shock I remembered what had driven me there, and a confused vision of Mr. Birch, the rock, the man with the musket, and my father, struck me like a raw blast.

"Boy! little-a boy!" whispered a voice in my ear. The gipsy girl was standing beside me, with her shawl still off her head; and, startled as I was, her hand upon her own lips restrained me, intuitively, from uttering any sound.

"Make-a no noise, or they hear," she said, with a glance over her shoulder. "Where-a you come from?"

I made no answer, but tried to edge shyly away from her.

"No! no!" she whispered, catching my arm; "you tell-a me something. Where you mother?"

"She's in the ground," said I, feeling that I must speak.

"And your father, eh? *He* not your father?"

How it was that I knew she meant Reese I cannot explain. I did know it, however, and positively, if not contemptuously, assured her that he was not my father.

"You know him, eh?" she asked, her eyes glittering upon me and her hold tightening on my arm.

I told her that I had never seen him at all before that day, and unguardedly admitted my having run away from the mad schoolmaster.

The latter part of the speech she gave no heed to, but still clutched my arm and kept her eyes upon me.

"You think he good-a man, eh?"

"Oh, yes!" exclaimed I.

"Now you tell-a me —"

She did not finish that sentence, for some one was coming; and in a moment Reese himself was with us. He had approached from behind, but with no apparent intention of being unheard, and Anita had released me and hidden her face in her shawl when he came up.

"So, so," said he, "you're telling more fortunes are you, my gip? This won't do. You must let this boy alone after this, if you please. For the present he's my exclusive property—you understand? and you mustn't trouble yourself with him at all, my beauty."

She stood like a statue until he had finished speaking, and then turned and glided away toward the wagons, as though dismissed by an authority leaving nothing to say.

"What has she been talking about to you, Little Breeches?"

"Nothing much, sir."

"That's a lawyer's answer; but it don't matter. Come along now; it's time for you to go to bed. Come right after me. Quick's the word."

I wondered where the bed could be, and might have ventured a natural inquiry had he not turned upon his heel immediately and sauntered back to the wagon, leaving me no choice but to run after him in silence and find explanation in the object itself. A majority of the company were still lounging on the grass, with their pipes in their mouths. Dolores and the girl had disappeared, and three or four of the men were dragging what looked like ragged shawls or blankets from one of the wagons, preparatory to making themselves comfortable on the ground for the night. Tied to a tree by a long chain attached to a belt about his body, the monkey sat huddled-up and dozing in a splash of moonlight; and, while I loitered to look at him, Mr. Mugses approached with extended nose and bestowed a friendly lick on the nodding head of the hairy little philosopher. Either the exceeding dampness of the salutation, or its feverish warmth, proved offensive to the exhausted monkey, and, with an irascible squeak, he made a sudden bounce at one of Mr. Mugses' fore-legs and inflicted a bite not to be silently borne. Dismal was the canine yell ensuing, and impatient was the command of Reese that I should cease meddling with the beasts and come to him at once.

He was standing at the back of a wagon, and, without ceremony, swung me into the latter like a bag, and left me sprawling on a deep layer of rags.

"Here's where you are to sleep," he said, "and you might have a worse bed, I can tell you. These are the picked rags, the washed linen ones, and if it weren't so warm that I prefer a blanket on the grass, I'd sleep here myself. Over by the seat in front, are my two trunks,—one full of books and one half full of something else. I'm going to let the dog sleep with you, for company, and if you hear him bark through the night be sure to call for me as loud as you can. I don't want any of these gipsies to be fingering my property—you understand? —and the dog knows 'em."

He whistled for Mugses, who came limping at the summons, and made him leap into the wheeled bedroom and crouch in a front corner against one of the trunks.

"You won't be afraid here, with me just outside?"

"No, sir, not very."

"Then lie down comfortably as soon as

you can, and remember about the dog's barking. Good-night."

"Good-night, sir."

The novelty of sleeping in a wagon in the woods, with a black and yellow hound for a bedfellow and a ready-made dream of gipsies round about, gave me the same luxurious feeling I have experienced in latter years when retiring to rest in some strange and peculiarly pleasant room. The rags were the most comfortable of couches, the canvas arch over my head looked like the roof of a cosey little house which I had all to myself, the moonlit branches and leaves drooping in sight at either opening were lulling pictures; and, to the music of cricket and tree-toad, the murmur of conversation beyond the wagons, and the occasional stamp of a horse, I soon dropped asleep.

It seemed to me, however, that I had only just closed my eyes and commenced to lose consciousness, when two persons began talking very near the side of the wagon. I heard them for a long while, as it appeared to me, though rather as mere monotonous sounds than as intelligible speakers of connected words, and might have lost sense of them altogether in a deeper lethargy had not Mr. Mugses kept my consciousness feebly alive by an occasional uneasy movement in his corner. Even that, though, would not have affected my stupid sense, very long, but for an ultimate growl, which aroused me sufficiently to make me turn over and become vaguely aware that the talking had suddenly ceased.

"Il'sh, Mugses!"

The voice, though suppressed to almost a whisper, was plainly Reese's; and my identification of it restored my dormant faculties enough to make them passively comprehensive of what followed outside.

"You say he came upon you by accident?" some one said, as though in questioning reiteration of a remark previously made.

"Yes,"—it was Reese speaking,—"he nearly stumbled over me as I lay on the grass. I was going ahead to Milton in the afternoon, on one of the nags here, if he hadn't told me such a queer yarn about Birch. I don't know why it was, but, somehow, the story struck me right away as being true. I've felt in my bones that something was going to happen there, and, for all the young sculping had already told me one absurd whopper about himself,—that he was a tailor, or some such chaff,—I cottoned to the thing right off. But what under heaven did the lunatic want to hurt the boy for?"

"Why, don't you know that?"

The last speaker seemed to take a long step toward the wagon, and I could hear the hissing of a rapid whisper.

"By Jove!—no!" exclaimed Reese, and I knew by the sound that he was leaning right against the wagon.

"It's a jolly fact, my boy," responded the strange voice; "and, what's more, the young bird may be worth money to you yet."

"But how did he ever get away?"

"Wolf was the man. He was the identical jolly in-di-vid' who fired the shot I told you about awhile ago. Oh, but wasn't he! It was all a put-up thing between him and that wild-cat before she flew the trap. I was after him up here for weeks, first as one character and then another; and I didn't enjoy sleeping out-doors, or in pig-sheds half the time, if he did. I was on the road at the foot of the cliff when he went up with the musket, and, by some astonishing and jolly accident, I was close on him when he came tearing down with the kid on his back; but I lost him in the storm, somehow. Think he must have struck across lots to shun the village."

"Confound the cracked fool!" muttered Reese, making the whole wagon shake with an involuntary blow upon one of the wheels. "He'll get us all into hot water yet—you understand?—with his infernal gammon about that she one!"

"I thought I'd strike town time enough to catch him, and couldn't have missed him if the governor hadn't told me to let up. I know where he is. One of our up-town 'shadows' saw him yesterday afternoon moving around Union Square, looking like a scarecrow. But we can get him off west for a while now, my boy, by working him up about the shooting."

"I wish he may shake himself to death with Illinois shiver before I lay eyes on him again. It won't be the thing for me to be seen about the Milton mill now, I suppose?"

"The mill!" exclaimed the strange voice, sounding nearer again. "I should think not. If this shooting business gets wind, the Jersey coppers* will be around like hornets, and Sharp will have a jolly time to keep them off the scent. His being postmaster will be a help to him. What a jolly postmaster, too! and all through General Cringer. Have you got any of the stuff with you now, Reese?"

"Yes, some. Not much—you understand?—but more than I want to keep on hand. I'll have to get out of this neighborhood, too, and strike for the crib. But about this young Gilbun, again—what would you do with him? I held on to him, because I didn't know just what might have happened, and didn't care to have him get to Newark and go to blabbing. How about him now?" asked Reese, drumming with his fingers on a panel immediately behind which was my face.

"Take him along with you," was the answer. "If I know the ropes, he's worth money to you. Where's the rest of this gang of beggars?"

"At Hoboken."

"Then you've come by Newark?"

"Yes, of course."

"Well, if you don't hear from me again,

* Police.

I'd advise you to leave them here and go back to town in your old rig. And, now I think of it, I found out, last night, where Wolf and the boy slept. I put up at a farmhouse, and what should I see hanging to the farmer's vest but Wolf's old steel watchchain? I knew it in a minute, and asked the old man what he'd take for it, and where he got it. He said he'd take a pair of braces, worth double the money, and when the bargain was closed he admitted that he had taken the thing in pay from a man and a boy who had slept in his barn and taken bread and milk in the morning."

Though still keeping my eyes closed, I was thoroughly awake when the conversation reached this point, and understood pretty well that part of the discussion relating to myself. It had been growing more surprising to me every moment, that a stranger should arrive in the middle of the night and talk thus curiously to Reese, and when I heard the pair moving away, I raised myself high enough to glance over the trunks and seat. At first I thought the moon was shining, but, as my vision cleared, I saw with astonishment the all-pervading light of early morning, and realized that I had slept soundly through the night without knowing it!

Mr. Mugses was up in a twinkling, with his fore-feet on the trunk he had guarded, and when I squirmed out of the wagon to survey the field he leaped down also, and began making his toilet by twisting round and round after some unattainable point along his backbone.

Several of the gipsies were yet extended on their torn and dirty blankets, here and there, but most of the band stood silently smoking their pipes around and among the wagons beyond mine; and Dolores, Anita, and Juan were engaged about a fire kindled on the bed of the last one. Near these last, and on the edge of the road, was Reese, conversing earnestly with a strange man in a black cloth cap and a linen suit, who sat upon a long, thin box covered with shiny black leather.

It was one of those golden mornings in early autumn, or late summer, when the first rays of the sun seem to evoke from mellowed nature an ethereal kind of yellow dust, and permeate it with such a luminous sentience that your own breathing seems to stir something tremulous in it. Trees, wagons, horses, and human figures took a faint, tawny lustre from the deepening glow of the east; the grass bore a map of a continent of light cut up with a tangle of trunk and branch, rivers and lakes in shade; and the glaring road in front, seen through the trees, sparkled in its sand as though sown with needle-points.

Holding my hat in one hand, and smoothing my hair with the other, I was staring abstractedly at the tied and still drowsy monkey, whose bristling black coat took a reddish burnish from the sun, when Reese called me. I went to where he stood, and as his companion turned to look at me I noted that the latter had dark curly hair, a round face, and eyes yellowish like a cat's.

"So you're up without calling, are you, Little Breeches?" said my protector. "How did you sleep?"

"Very well, sir," replied I.

"I thought you would. Here's a pedler, you see, has come into camp since you went to bed."

"Yes," said the strange voice I had heard by the wagon. "I thought there might be a lad of your size, here, who wanted a new cap."

"I lost mine and a boy gave me this," answered I, willing to be familiar.

"And I shouldn't wonder if you lost one before that still," returned the pedler, comically screwing up one yellow eye. But I didn't understand him and looked inquiringly at Reese.

"Juan," called the latter over my head, "have you brought that second pail of water yet?"

"Yes, seer," responded Juan, looking up from the fire.

"Then, Glibun, you'd better go and wash your face and hands; for we shall have breakfast directly."

CHAPTER XX.

ANITA TELLS ANOTHER FORTUNE.

SOON after the coarse meal had been despatched, the organ-men and the owner of the monkey were called by Reese to the wagon in which I had slept, with strict orders that I should not follow them, and these supplied with handfuls of something that rustled as they thrust it hastily into their breasts. What it could be I did not attempt to guess; but I had an idea that Reese had taken it from one of the trunks; and I was looking toward the group with considerable curiosity, when Anita stepped abruptly before me and held up a finger.

"He tell-a you not to look!" said she, very sharply.

"No, he didn't," I replied, much provoked by her interference; "he told me not to go there; and I haven't gone,—have I?"

"Look here, youngster," sounded the voice of the pedler, from behind me, "didn't your boss say that you wanted a cap?"

I turned, and saw him reclining on the grass, with his great black box opened before him and a gay array of attractive articles displayed therein. Both Anita and I at once gave our attention to the latter, and very soon a number of gipsies, including Old Dolores, stood around us with eyes intently fixed on the treasures of the pack.

"Here's a dry-goods store, perfumer's shop, jeweller's, and Barnum's museum all rolled into one," prated the pedler vivaciously; "and though it don't look as though much had been sold out of it, I wouldn't take a hundred dollars for the profit it's been to me this very trip. Here's your ribbon, — (there's a piece of rose-color for you, my prima donna), — and your glass beads. and your back-combs, and your hooks and eyes. and your braces, and your steel-clasp pocket-books. Here's your toilet soap, and your best double-extract cologne, —(accept this bottle, old lady,) — and your caps packed away like so many figs — (try that one. my lad; I know it'll fit you. because I happen to have your exact measure at home). — and your razor-straps, and your fine combs."

At this point in his enumeration the men with the organs and monkey brushed past us and went briskly down the road, and Reese joined our audience, exchanging a quick look with the pedler.

"Here's your fresh mixed candies, a pound of them," went on the latter, extricating a goodly paper package from beneath some hand-mirrors; "and if you gipsy boys will just divide them up among you, I'll esteem it a favor. They'll melt to a cream in the pack such a hot day as this is, and the children I expected to sell them to at a farm-house where I stopped last night were not there."

If the men did not clearly comprehend his words, they found no difficulty in understanding the meaning of his gesture, and received the gift with broad grins of satisfaction.

"As for you, Signor Reese," continued the liberal trader, again screwing up that yellow eye with humorous effect, "I must make things all square and jolly by presenting you with a watch-chain. It's what you might call a 'Chain of Evidence,' seeing how I came by it;" and he drew from one corner of his box a steel chain, and handed it to Reese with a laugh.

As he did so, I recognized it, and cried, — "That's the man's chain. That's Wolfton's."

"It might have belonged to Wolfton, or Sheepton, or Foxton, once," said the pedler, coolly; "but it's mine since I bought it.

Abashed by his answer, and dimly conscious of having awkwardly committed myself, I sought arduous employment in trying on the new cap, and pretending to find it rather large.

"Little Breeches wants to be a lawyer before his time comes," observed Reese; and both joined in a laugh which made me still less at ease.

Dolores and Anita having retired with the cologne and ribbon to their usual place under the wagon, and the recipients of the candy lounging away to enjoy it by themselves. our only listener now was Mr. Mugses, who had arrived at the pack simultaneously with his master, and was idiotically pricking his ears and wagging his tail at a reflection of himself in one of the hand-mirrors.

"Well, Ketchum," said Reese. as the pedler closed his box, " I've concluded that it's best for us to go down by Newark again this afternoon, and as the women may pick up some more shillings there by fortune-telling, old Hugo agrees to it. I can get off for town then — you understand? — at a moment's warning."

"It's as sensible a thing as you could do," replied the pedler; " and I may as well hold on and go down with you. If the country constables should happen — By-the-by, my lad, you'll miss something if you don't go and look at that bottle the old woman's got."

I was wise enough to take this sudden hint, remembering as I did that I was not supposed to know what they had been talking about at an earlier hour. Accordingly, I promptly went in the direction mentioned, and left them to their own counsel.

Not long after, both men went to the wagon containing the trunks; the pedler placing his pack in it and then starting off with the assertion that he "wanted to try a stroll into the woods," and Reese taking a book from one of the trunks and coming to where the women and I were seated. The latter threw himself down at full length beside the wheels, in pursuance of his latest whim, and opening the volume, which was called Cervantes' Exemplary Tales, made an attempt to read. In a moment, however, he looked up from the page, and smilingly caught the glance of Anita, whose eyes, as I was now pretty well aware, seldom favored anybody else while he was in sight.

"I'll have to read aloud to you. I suppose," he said; " for that's what I do when we don't have company, and I don't take any interest in it any more, when I read to myself. So much for bad habits, my beauty. Would you like to hear a story, Glibun?"

"Yes, sir, very much."

"Oh, yes, yes!" exclaimed the girl with a pleased look, and, as Dolores made no objection, he returned his eyes to the book, and began reading in a sprightly, enjoying way. The story was Rinconete and Cortadillo, and I am bound to say that its titular heroes were not quite as exemplary as the adjective in the name of the volume might have led one to expect they would be. The manner of the reader, however, gave it a charm I had never derived from any other romantic narrative; and although Old Dolores, after several impatient snorts, took herself off to the distant company of the men with the candy, Anita seemed to be as absorbingly interested as myself, and watched every movement of his lips with rapt attention. Notwithstanding his ungraceful position and coarse dress, he looked strikingly handsome then. His twinkling dark eyes, and long, pale face reflected all the varying animation of the story as a native Spaniard's might have done; his long, straight black hair was enough out of the commonplace to help the romantic sentiment of our tableau, and his clear. sonorous voice evoked a sympathy for every emotion described by every intonation of the nicest elocutionary art. Not stopping to consider the incongruity of such abilities with a man of his situation and apparent character, I only felt a new and high respect for him growing within me. In my eyes he had suddenly become a person of distinguished learning.

He was lying flat on the ground, with chin propped up by his hands, and book on the grass under his face, and when the end of the story was reached he caught Anita's look again.

"What do you think of it?" he asked her.

She leaned toward him with her whole countenance full of energetic feeling, and answered, —

"It ees music!"

"Anita," he said, very softly and musically, repeating a verse occurring in the story,

> "'Two lovers dear, fall out and fight,
> But soon, to make their peace, take leisure;
> And all the greater was the row,
> So much the greater is the pleasure.'

You are not angry with me, my beauty, are you?"

"Why you ask-a me that?" she questioned, looking down.

"I thought you acted a little cross with me last night, when you kept your head away so that I couldn't give you a kiss in the gavota."

"You love-a *him* now!" exclaimed the girl violently, and simultaneously flashed her eyes upon me with a passionate quickness that made me start.

"Ho! ho! ho!" laughed Reese; and he was evidently pleased. "Jealous, eh, my beauty? And of a boy, too! I can do better than that with you, my gipsy queen; for I can be jealous of that Newark cavalier who was moping after you last week. We're going back there pretty soon, and then look out for stilettos."

"I hate-a him! Fool!" She ground her teeth and tore a handful of grass from the sod.

"Send him trooping when he comes again, and I'll believe you."

"I do that; I make-a him fool."

Reese contemplated her with laughing eyes, and rompingly snatched away the shawl from her head. How like an untamed, beautiful savage she looked then, her plentiful elf-locks coiling thickly in and out through careless fetters of dingy ribbon, and her olive cheeks mantling with a glow that made them transparent!

"I thought I should find that picture of the booby's hanging on your neck," said he, tossing back the shawl.

"I have-a it," she retorted, holding up the shawl with both hands, and looking under it at him; "but you see how I fix-a it for him. Some girl down there, she ask-a me to see her lover in a pail of water, and I show-a her boo—what you call-a him?—booby."

"Capital!" shouted Reese, sitting up and flourishing the book around his Panama hat. "Let you alone to play a gipsy trick! If a spark was to give you his head you'd manage to turn an honest shilling on it! Halloo! here's the most liberal pedler alive, coming back from his communion with Mother Nature."

The pedler was indeed visible now, on his return through the woods; and as Dolores had crawled back to Anita's side, scolding all the way about something, Reese indolently regained his feet, and sauntered off to meet his friend.

Toward sunset, the miserable horses were hitched to the wagons. Into one of the latter got the pedler, Reese, Mr. Mugses, and I; Dolores, Anita, and two men, into the second one; and the remainder of the gang into the others; and the clumsy vehicles wheeled out to the road and started slowly in a direction contrary to that by which I had come.

"Are we going to Newark, now?" I asked.

"You'll see when we get there, Little Breeches," responded Reese, slapping one of the horses with the ends of the reins. "It'll take six months to get anywhere with these lazy brutes."

In half an hour, however, the spires and outskirting houses of the town were visible from the front of the wagon, and when almost on the first street we turned down a narrow cross-road, which presently brought us to a wayside wood very similar in its character to the one we had left. Here the wagons were all ranged in row again, under the trees, the horses unhitched and turned loose, the passengers debarked and scattered over the shady grass in dozing and card-playing groups; and, but for the jagged line of houses and steeples under a smoky atmosphere across a field before us, and the glimmer of water some distance to the right, the brief process of transit might have seemed like the turgid dream of a siesta.

Soon the organ-men and Old Hugo with his monkey came into camp in a very dusty condition, and, after a lengthy and excited conversation with Reese, to which the pedler listened as though he understood every word, distributed themselves among their companions on the sward and renewed the smoking and clatter of the evening before. A fire was lighted; Dolores and Anita repeated the usual rude cooking; the meal was noisily taken; the liquor went around in the tin pails; the fire went down; the moon and stars shone out; Reese and Anita danced again to organ and tambourine; the pedler danced an overwhelming comic dance all by himself; the blankets were brought out; I went to bed again, very tired, in the wagon with Mr. Mugses and the trunks; and—it was golden morning once more.

Immediately after breakfast, on that same morning to which I have taken such a short cut, Reese gave me strict orders to obey the women until he should return, and then departed for the town in company with the pedler. The latter had his pack strapped on his shoulders, and shook hands with me and everybody else at parting in an affable manner. We all liked him for his good-humor, and when he turned back on the road for a moment to screw up that yellow eye, even Old Dolores uttered a shrill, crowing sound, understood to be a laugh. Hugo and the organ-grinders were the next to depart; then one of the wagons was driven off with a load of rags and junk to be sold somewhere; and the other male gipsies rambled off, singly, and by couples, until finally the women, Juan, I, and the dog were left sole guardians of the scene.

Only the latter good friend showed a disposition to be sociable with me, and while I was endeavoring to make him stand upon his hind-legs thus rendering him languid and expressionless to an incredible degree, the three vagrants gathered loquaciously around a bucket of water, into which Anita, as I could see, threw several handfuls of earth and pebbles. As I could not understand their foreign talk, and saw little to interest in their seemingly childish employment, I kept my distance, nor did they heed me so much as a word.

In an hour or so, however, people from the town began to make their appearance in the grove, and after wandering awkwardly around the wagons and staring obliquely at us, grew bolder and asked questions. It had become known amongst them that the gipsy company of the week before had returned again for some mysterious reason, and hence their visit to the woods. At first the invaders were principally idle young men and rough boys, who gave their chief attention to me as "a stolen child," and were only kept from undue familiarity by the sudden ferocity of Mr. Mugses; but presently a number of women, both young and old, arrived by couples and trios, and eventually managed to have their fortunes told by Anita, or purchase magical cures for their ailings from Dolores. It was amusing to note how they all pretended to be intensely in fun about it, too, and laughed hysterically when the ruder spectators indulged in guffaws; yet nothing was more certain than that they felt a trembling awe of the gipsies and swallowed every word of their broken English with more faith than the simplest common sense should have allowed.

Later in the day there arrived a low, pony-wagon, or phaeton, containing two thickly veiled ladies, one of whom put both her hands upon the nearest arm of the other, who drove, and apparently protested against stopping there. The fair driver, though, seemed very determined in the matter, and turned the well-groomed pony under a tree where he appeared to halt of his own accord. The same lady then pushed her veil slightly aside to take a full look at us and finally beckoned Anita to go to her;

but as Anita only looked steadily in return and did not make the least show of obeying the gesture, the veiled pair held a brief consultation together and at last descended from the phaeton and came to her.

I was standing beside the gipsy girl at the time, as the last stranger had been gone nearly an hour, and I remained to see what was coming.

The lady, who had not wished to stop, and who wore a blue veil and carried her handkerchief in her right hand, surprised me by speaking first.

"Do you pretend to find lost articles?" she hurriedly asked the gipsy, in a clear, young voice.

"I tell-a fortune," responded Anita, standing motionless.

"Does that old woman?"

"She make-a charm for seek ones."

"Pshaw, Allie," exclaimed the other lady, petulantly; "you've no need to ask it in that way. Girl, you're a fortune-teller, are you not? You told fortunes when you were here some days ago."

Anita nodded to the last speaker, but kept her eyes fixed on the first one.

"I've been so foolish," resumed she of the handkerchief, "as to let my mad friend, here, persuade me to consult you about something I've lost. I cannot find a valued miniature of a dead sister, and fear it has been stolen. If you have any way of finding out where it is, tell me, and I will pay."

"Gipsies steal-a not," said Anita, proudly.

"Ah-h!" snarled Dolores, who seemed to understand the word "stolen," and took fire at it. "Ah-h!" and she shook her brown, skinny fists over her muffled head, and summarily retreated to the wagons.

"Let's pay the girl and go," said the offending visitor, in a frightened voice.

"Oh, now we're here, Allie, we may as well have our fortunes told, just for the fun of the thing."

"I wish we'd never come!" exclaimed the other. "It's improper, it's wrong; and if ma only knew —"

"Pooh — pooh!" retorted the lively one; "it's broad daylight; nobody here can know us, and where's the harm? I'm going to have her tell my fortune, at any rate, and you can't go without my driving. Here, girl, tell my fortune."

"Give-a me your hand," said Anita, stolidly.

A green kid glove was quickly withdrawn from a beautiful white hand, and the latter unhesitatingly resigned itself to the gipsy's inspection.

"Long, straight-a line," muttered Anita, stooping over it, and tracing the palm with a finger; "and only two cross-a it. You have plenty good-a, and only two black-a years. You live long-a, too." Dropping the hand she dexterously produced the dirty cards from some part of her dress, spread them before her eyes, and went rapidly on. "Diamonds, diamonds plenty; and hearts. You marry rich—a man with red hair. That's all."

"Red hair!" screamed the lively visitor, with a ringing laugh. "What a charming idea! Only think, Allie, how I should look with such a literal flame as that. Why, I could see to read by him! But let us see, now, what she'll say about you."

"Helen, you ought to be ashamed!" responded the other, reproachfully. "Now let me go."

"You shall show her your hand," persisted the other, in great glee. "I'll make you, if I have to stay here an hour. Come, take off your glove; that's a darling. It's such delightful nonsense!"

The glove was pulled off, as though the act could not be avoided, and another beautiful, but reluctant and trembling hand was extended.

"Nice-a lines here," said Anita, almost touching the snowy palm with her face; "picture here, and no need-a the cards, Aloize Green."

"What! you know my name?" exclaimed the lady, snatching her hand from the grasp of the cunning girl, and quite forgetting that said name had been very prominent, both to Anita and to me, for some moments past, on the handkerchief she carried.

"I show-a you *his* picture," continued Anita, entirely unmoved by action or exclamation. "Look-a in this water," and she stepped backwards a few paces to where the bucket stood, and gravely threw aside a blanket covering it.

"O Helen, *do* come away!" entreated the terrified one, leaning upon her friend, and speaking faintly. The latter had also started at the mention of the name; but either curiosity or infatuation made her stubborn.

"Do let's look at it," she said, eagerly. "Just one glance, Allie, to see ourselves reflected in the water,—that's all it is, you know, dear,—and then we won't stay another minute. Take only one peep with me." She pulled her along toward the bucket, and the two looked down into it for an instant with veils drawn the least bit aside.

It was only for an instant. Whatever they saw there made the timid one turn with a short scream, and actually run away to the wagon, and the other recoil as though she had received a shock. I stole to the pail, and also saw, at the very bottom, set in earth and gravel as it were, a man's miniature!

"Here—you wretch!" ejaculated the future victim of the rich man with red hair, irritably throwing a silver dollar upon the ground; and then she, too, ran to the pony-wagon, which was quickly heard driving away.

"Dolores! Dolores!" called Anita (after picking up the coin, and giving a sign to Juan to go somewhere), clapping her hands and laughing merrily.

The crone came hobbling from her retreat at the cry; and while they were jabbering animatedly in their own tongue, and I was staring amazedly into the bucket, strange footsteps again sounded on the turf, and we all looked road-ward to behold another new-comer.

This last individual was a rakish-looking, short-haired young man, attired flashily in black and white check, and wearing a narrow-rimmed yellow hat with a rounding crown, exactly fitted to the top of his head. Small black eyes, a heavy black mustache, and a large cigar were his characteristic features, and, as he came leaping toward us from the road, Mr. Mugses bounded out to meet him.

"How are you, old black-and-tan?" shouted the invader, just as I discovered, to my infinite amazement, that his was the face pictured in the water. "Know me again, old fellow, do you? How are you, my little gipsy, and respected granny? Heard you were here, from some of the boys in town, and couldn't stay away another minute. All the dons away from home, hey? and a young stolen nobleman on hand. By the way, 'Nita, I passed a couple of stylish ones just now in a pony-wagon, and had to dive behind a fence, for fear they might be friends of mine. Been here, have they?"

As he rattled this off, he came to a halt before the women, with his checkered legs very far apart, and his hands in his checkered pockets.

Anita answered him by pushing me hastily aside from the bucket, plunging an arm into the water, and drawing out the picture, which I saw was a miniature set in some white metal.

"See! see!" she cried, holding up the dripping prize; "I tell-a you something now. Come."

"Ph-h-ew!" whistled he, opening his little eyes as widely as possible.

She glanced aside at me, then at Dolores; and walked away some distance with the picture in her hand, the young man following with alacrity. Having nothing better to do, I joined the old woman in watching them while they talked together, and had little difficulty in comprehending, from the girl's gestures, and the man's frequent pointing to the miniature, that the latter had much to do with their vivacious conversations. They were still engaged thus, and Dolores had once more crawled under her wagon to be nearer them, when Juan reappeared from the road, his perspiring face gray with dust, and his whole aspect that of one who had been running violently. He went directly to where the two were standing, and made some long speech to Anita, frequently pointing up the road; and she in turn made an equally long speech, with similar motions, to the checkered character, who nodded approvingly all through it, and then took a hasty departure from the wood.

The sensations experienced by me in witnessing these varied and rapid doings, were not as acute as they might have been, had I fairly understood what was going on; yet I had an uneasy sense of being partially privy to some disingenuous proceeding, and secretly resolved to reveal all I had seen to Reese, when he should return. Dolores gave me a handful of crackers from the provision wagon; Anita silently brought me a couple of herring from the same storehouse; and, after eating these with Mr. Mugses, I fell asleep at the foot of a tree, and did not awaken until disturbed by the noise of the returning gipsy idlers. They, I am sorry to say, were all intoxicated, and came staggering and bawling up the road in straggling procession. I fled to my bedroom at their approach, peering over the tail-piece at them as they sank down, one by one, upon the grass in drunken slumber, and was greatly relieved when sunset brought Reese, the organ-grinders, and Hugo, who arrived within a few minutes of each other, and appeared to be in excellent spirits. My protector was especially cheerful, saluting Anita, Dolores, Juan, and even Mr. Mugses, with laughing jollity, and following the latter to my refuge, as though certain to find me there. He looked younger and fresher, in some way, than before, and swung himself at once to a seat in the wagon, boy-like.

"Ha, Little Breeches," said he, slapping his knees, "you're in-doors, are you? Well, you ought to be; those drunken brutes are no company for you. I'm half sorry, though, that I didn't take you along with me, for you're sadly in need of a good wash, and I've had a bath that's done me good. How have you contrived to get along? Anything new while I was gone?"

I needed no further encouragement to inform him of all that had transpired; and he heard of the fortune-telling with no particular signs of interest. When I came to the miniature, though, and the arrival and behavior of the last visitor, his face darkened, and he gave me a scowling attention.

"Did the fellow go out of sight of Dolores, or you, with the girl?" he asked moodily.

"Oh, no," replied I; "the old woman and I saw them all the time."

"You say Juan pointed up the road while he was talking to them, and the fellow went that way?"

"Yes, sir."

Reese dropped from the wagon, and I looked out and saw him striding hastily toward where the girl was assisting Dolores to arrange the fire. Upon getting halfway thither, however, he suddenly stopped, turned deliberately about again, and took his way to the company of Hugo and another man, who were smoking their pipes a little distance off.

By the time the rag wagon had returned, without its freight, the meal was ready. The sober ones, and such of the tipplers as could be sufficiently aroused, partook of the latter, and had their usual liquor to end with; but, instead of making himself one of the company upon the introduction of the tin pails, Reese remained by me in my regular outer circle, and scowled across the intermediate Hugo at Anita. She responded with frequent saucy smiles until it became too dark for faces to be distinct, and at last arose from her place and glided out to the road like a flying bird's shadow. He made no attempt to follow her, as I expected he would, but drew his knees up to his chin and muttered something not particularly devout. He had been sitting thus, and I by him, for a quarter of an hour, I should think, when Anita was seen coming back from the road, accompanied by another figure. The latter separated from her at the wagons, and made directly for us, while she slipped into the gipsy ring as before.

The new-comer's face could not be distinguished, but his rounding hat and checkered legs were plain enough in the patches of moonlight he passed through to reveal to me the original of the miniature. Reese did not move at his approach, but muttered something angry again when the self-possessed intruder came confidently up to our very feet and coolly seated himself upon the grass.

"Mr. — your name is Reese, I'm told?"

"Well!" snapped Reese, ominously.

"Mr. Reese, then," said the other, with sangfroid, — "Mr. Reese, I want to explain a little dodge to you, at the particular request of our fashionable young female acquaintance, the Princess Royal of these scarecrows around us."

"Mr. What'syourname," growled Reese, straightening his knees with a jerk, and resting both his hands upon them, "I'll trouble you to seek other company in a jiffy. When I want your society — you understand? — I'll send you my card."

"But in case I should be out then," returned the unruffled visitor, "it's best to settle our little job now. I mightn't take quite so much from you if it wasn't for the sake of that sharp girl over there; but she's got my word to explain the dodge to you, and she's done me too bright a turn to be put out with her friends for it. I saw well enough last week, old man, that you were jealous of me; but you had no need to be. I'm after higher game, you see. Now shall I go on, or shall I pike back to town?"

Reese laid back on the grass with a short, contemptuous laugh, and clasped his hands under his head.

"That means go on, of course," went on the imperturbable checkers, "and now I'll tell you the dodge. I'm on a general lookout for an improvement in my fortune, and when this gipsy crowd was here before, and I happened to see how sharp this girl was about fooling the women with her fortune-telling, it put an idea into my head. I scraped acquaintance with her, and sounded her to see if she could put me in the way of knowing some good-looking miss with more money than brains, and, after thinking over it for a day, she told me, in her rascally

English, to get a small picture of myself for her, and she would try. I got the picture, —a miniature hastily done on ivory when I was out West last spring,—and there you have half the story. I used to notice you around here (though what a chap like you has to do in such company I can't understand. You're a little in my own line, maybe). I used to see by your looks that you felt jealous; but that wasn't my fault. To go on, though, the first thing I knew, you were all gone from here, and I thought I'd been humbugged; but yesterday morning the story was that you'd come back again, and in the afternoon, or about noon, I posted out here to see what was up. As luck would have it, I got here the very minute after the girl had limed a bird with that very picture, and sent one of your men after the bird to see where she lived."

"Skip all that part," interrupted Reese, impatiently; "this boy has told me all that."

"So much valuable breath saved, then. I'll do the rest of the story up as short as possible. After the confab with your gipsy, —yours for all me, old man, and she's the least bit sharper than a Jew,—I made up my mind just how to play my cards, and did it. Off I went to the house the gipsy fellow had seen, and inquired for Miss Green. The servant-girl left me in a handsome parlor—(the house, by the way, isn't fifteen minutes walk from here)—and pretty soon down came as handsome a creature as you'd ask to see, and her mother with her. I advanced with my hand out, but suddenly started back. She started, too, and looked like fainting. 'What does this mean?' says the old lady. 'Who are you, sir?' I put on the confused and tried to blush. 'My dear madam and miss,' says I, 'I find that I have made a mistake. Is this Mr. Green's house,—Mr. John Green's?' (I'd seen the name on the door-plate, you see.) 'Yes, sir,' said she, 'that was my husband's name while he lived.' I was glad to find the old man was out of the way, and says I,—'The Directory, which I lately consulted in a drug-store, has misled me. A cousin of mine, named Miss Green, who comes from the West, where I live myself, is visiting here in Newark at the house of her uncle and mine (by my mother's side), a Mr. John Green. I came here, thinking this must surely be the place, and wishing to see my cousin before returning to the West,—my name is Gamble, ladies,—and am pained to find what a mistake the similarity of names has made me commit. I beg ten thousand pardons.' They both said, 'Oh, certainly, I was very excusable;' and the young one, who was awfully flustered, said something about having seen my picture. That brought her mother up all standing; and the thing ended in the young one bursting out crying and confessing about some harem-scarem girl-friend of hers persuading her to go to the gipsies for news about a lost picture of a dead sister, and their seeing a face like mine in a bucket of

water. There'd have been a scene, then, I can tell you, old man, if I hadn't had my trick all laid out beforehand. 'My picture!' says I, in great surprise. 'Why, I lost a miniature of myself somewhere on Broad Street last week! I was to have given it to my cousin, and you may depend those tramping vagabonds, some of them, have found it, and are using it in their fortune-telling fooleries. To-morrow I shall go to their camp with a constable, and see. Really, ladies, I shall never forgive myself for causing you such extraordinary annoyance.' Then the young one cried, and the old lady didn't know what to say about it; but I did the indignant against you thieving vagrants so well that I finally got them both to talking with me. Fact is, the old lady even asked me to call again; and you can bet high that I'll do it. When I hurried back here this evening, as I promised, to tell our Princess Royal how I'd succeeded, get my picture, and pay her for the job, she let me know that you were angry at her, and asked me to let you into the secret. That's the whole truth of it, old man; and if you'll shake hands I'll be off for town."

Reese sat briskly up; and not only shook hands with the ingenious scamp, but slapped him boisterously on the back.

"You'll do!" said he. "Ha! ha! ha! You're as great a rascal as I am, and a much smarter one! Good-night, Mr. Gamble, and good luck to your wooing."

"Good-night," responded the shadowy figure, springing to his feet; and, with a wave of the hand and a glance toward the gipsies, he walked swiftly out to the road and disappeared.

When I was at rest on the rags that night, and Mr. Mugses coiled against the trunk near my head, I heard Reese singing outside. His serenade was the verse from Rinconete and Cortadillo, to an improvised air,—

"'Two lovers dear, fall out and fight,
    But soon, to make their peace, take leisure;
And all the greater was the row,
    So much the greater is the pleasure!'"

———◆———

CHAPTER XXI.

I HAVE ANOTHER CHANGE OF SCENE.

IF up to this period of my life I had exhibited no marked traits of individual character, it was because the usual demonstrative disposition of a boy had been so repressed in me by the repellant mysteries of my home, and the rapid succession of strange and varied changes away from home, that I was ever kept constrained in my general actions and awkwardly reticent of speech. It seemed to me that I could never become sufficiently acquainted with one person, or one set of persons, to exhibit anything of my true self, before strangers took me in charge, and the incomplete and tedious process familiarizing had to be commenced anew. Affinities, or antagonisms, are no less necessary with the child than with the man, to call his character into action; and as those affinities, or antagonisms, in others, show themselves definitely only after some sort of familiar acquaintance has been established, I never either knew well enough, or was known well enough, to evoke them for myself from anybody. My father and his servants,—Elfie, Mr. Birch, Wolfton, Reese, even the gipsy girl,—all seemed governed in their treatment of me by considerations entirely apart from my own personality. As a sentient and individual being, I had scarcely any recognition; as a kind of little chess-man in a complicated game between alternating pairs of deep players, I was moved here and there in unwitting furtherance of designs altogether unintelligible to me.

If, however, my character, as I have shown, was called into action neither by direct sympathy nor direct antagonism, it nevertheless developed gradually within me as an accumulating force, and took an all the more independent growth from the necessarily arbitrary nature of the silent mental deductions on which it fed. The sudden vigor and partial system given to my thinking faculties, by my brief but arduous studies at school, rendered all that I subsequently observed a continual progress of education. Nothing escaped my sight or memory; what confused me when I first saw it, always resolved itself into some sort of meaning when I subsequently thought it over; and wide of the truth as such final comprehension might be, it yet extended my general understanding and gave fresh impulse to my growth of individual character.

I have already mentioned my sense of superiority at school over the miserable kitchen-boy, and may now add, that a similar sense of superiority to the gipsies was probably the main cause of my fearlessness of them from the very commencement of our association. It remained, however, for the checkered Mr. Gamble to excite in me the maturity of a characteristic feeling first called into existence by Hastings Cutter, a feeling of positive dislike. On his first appearance in the grove and interview with Anita, I felt sure of his evil disposition, and regarded him with a distrust for which I did not attempt to account to myself; but as he rattled off his narrative to Reese, I felt such an instinctive antagonism to the man swelling in my young bosom, that even Reese fell greatly in my esteem for tolerating him as he finally did.

It may be imagined, therefore, that the reappearance of Mr. Gamble at the entrance to the wood, one morning, just as Reese and some of the gipsies were about to follow Old Hugo into the town, did not please me particularly. He came upon a horse which he had hired, he said, for a morning ride, and, without even asking for Anita,

who was busied at one of the wagons with Dolores, called Reese to him as he sat lazily in the saddle, and held a brief conference with him in whispers.

Seated on the grass, with my right arm around the neck of Mr. Mugses, I was frowningly contemplating the horseman, and sincerely hoping that the pretty lady had seen the last of him, when the conversation ended, and my protector called me to him. Upon my obeying the summons, Mr. Mugses saw fit to go also, and my ill-humor softened almost to a laugh when the sagacious animal hastened to seat himself directly under the horse, with an expression of face indicating that he believed himself to be the occupant of a pillared temple of some sort.

"Gilibun," said Reese, carelessly, "this gentleman wants you to carry a note for him to a house that Juan will point out to you. Here, Juan, this way!"

I looked up into the face of Mr. Gamble, who pulled his black mustache with one hand and held a letter toward me with the other.

"I don't want to do it, sir," answered I.

"Ph-h-ew!" whistled Mr. Gamble, returning my stare, with an ugly smile. "Good for the young nobleman! Did he have gold beads and a miniature on when you picked him up, Mr. Reese?"

"Why, Little Breeches, what do you mean?" asked Reese, taking me roughly by the shoulder. "This is something new, you little beggar! Here, take this letter, and do what this gentleman says—you understand?—or there'll be a row."

"Well, sir," said I, "if you tell me to go, I'll go; but I'd rather not."

I took the letter from *him*, and, as he turned to speak to Juan, Mr. Gamble leaned from his saddle and pulled me closer to him.

"Here's half a dollar for you, boy."

"I don't want it."

"Come—come; no foolery. Take it."

"I won't!" exclaimed I, looking him right in the eyes.

He turned very red in the face, but slipped the coin back into a vest-pocket and leaned down to me again.

"You take that letter to the house that gipsy man will show you," he said in an undertone, "and leave it with the servant at the door down under the front stoop. Be sure you go to that door, and say the letter is for Miss Aloize. Can you do that?"

"Yes."

"Well, do it, then. I'll be here again to-morrow. Reese, you'll see that he does it?"

"I've told you I would," answered Reese, moodily.

"Day-day, then. My best respects to the Princess Royal;" and he started off upon a trot so suddenly, that Mr. Mugses had barely time to escape from his temple in safety.

The letter was addressed simply to "A. G.," and, as I stood turning it over in my hands, with a vague determination regarding it taking shape in my brain, Reese curtly ordered me to go with Juan, and himself started over the fields across the road, in the direction of Newark.

I looked after him with very little of the peculiar respect he had once awakened in me. His figure looked meaner than before; his step had not the same confident freedom, to give that idea of fearless self-possession, so impressive to a child; the whole suggestion of his retiring form to me was one of slouching retreat from my former ideal of him; and, immature as I was, I felt in its full force the dissipation of that common illusion in which the imagination appears instinctively to connect moral strength with commanding qualities of mind.

Juan, in his ever dusty and ragged costume, and with his distorted basin of a hat pulled far down over his sharp black eyes, beckoned me to follow him, and trudged silently up the road. Letter in hand I obeyed the gesture, and in that style of companionship we proceeded to the broad turnpike leading into the town. Turning into the former, the gipsy quickened his pace and was, I supposed, going straight to the head of a partially paved street not far beyond us; but, on the very edge of the town, he turned again into a road not unlike the one from whence we had come, and hurried by a number of neat white wooden houses setting back in tasteful little picketed gardens. We had passed some half a dozen of these, when he finally stopped and pointed to a handsome cottage, possessing a much larger garden than any of its neighbors, and standing so much farther back from the road that I had not caught sight of it before.

" That's-a him," said he.

It was a prim, spotless building, with a curved stoop reached by a flight of yellow steps, and a balcony lifted by square pillars above the lowest range of windows. A straight and well-swept gravel-path led to it from the garden gate, through rows of flower-beds and a painted grape-arbor; and up this path I hastened, too full of what I designed accomplishing to note whether Juan waited for me or went back.

Mr. Gamble had told me to leave the letter at the door under the stoop, and hence I was obstinately determined to apply at the higher one. He had told me to give it to the servant, and for that very reason I was resolved to inquire for Miss Aloize herself. In fact, it was my intention to exactly disobey the orders of the man I so strongly disliked, and, with what must have been a remarkable frown on my dingy face, I resolutely mounted the stoop and tapped on one of the panels of the door with a not over-clean set of knuckles. Luckily for my courage, the knob turned very quickly; but in place of the Sirrah-like figure I expected to behold, there stood before me, on the bright oil-cloth of a handsome hall, an elderly lady in cap and gray curls, who surveyed me with no little astonishment.

" What do you wish, my dear? " she asked, mildly.

With instinctive politeness I pulled off my cap, and simultaneously made an abortive effort to hide the letter in the breast of my coat.

" I'd like to see Miss Aloize, ma'am," answered I, somewhat abashed by her questioning look at the crumpled missive. " I've got a letter for her, and want to tell her something about it."

" You can give it to me, then, and I'll give it to her," she said, holding out a hand. " Who is it from? "

" I'd rather give it to her, herself," responded I, looking down. " I want to tell her what a bad man Mr. Gamble is."

" Mr. Gamble! " ejaculated the old lady; " Mr. Gamble! Why, child,—young man, —what do you mean? Here, come in and explain yourself."

Motioning quickly for me to follow her into the hall, she closed the door behind me, and then led the way through another door into a neat little parlor, made cool by the shade of green blinds.

" Sit down there," she said, pointing to a sofa, and taking an adjacent chair herself. " Now tell me what this is about Mr. Gamble. But first give me the letter."

" No, ma'am," returned I, firmly, " I must give it to Miss Aloize, please."

" I'm her mother, child."

In that name — and I knew not why — there was always an appealing sound, to which my nature prompted a wistful obedience.

" There it is, ma'am," I said, handing her the letter without further hesitation. " It was given to me to give to a servant at the door under the stoop; but I thought there must be something wrong in it, because Mr. Gamble is such a bad man. He got our Anita, the gipsy girl, to show his picture to the lady, in a bucket of water, and then found out where you live and told you a story about losing the picture. I heard him telling about it that night in the woods."

" Allie! Allie! " called the old lady, hastening into the hall before the last word had fairly left my lips; " Allie! "

" Well, ma? " returned a clear, sweet voice from some upper region.

" Hurry down, my dear; I want you immediately." And the old lady came back to her chair with a perturbation of manner that put me less at ease than ever. Scarcely was she seated, however, when light footsteps sounded on the stairs near the door, and, in a moment after, a very pretty, brown-haired young lady, in a white breakfast-wrapper, came tripping into the room. At sight of me on the sofa, she started back in surprise, and, slowly turning her head to interrogate her mother, grew instantly pale under the accusing stare of that lady.

" Why, ma! " she cried, sinking upon the nearest chair, " what is the matter? "

" My daughter," answered the old lady, austerely, but trembling as she spoke, " you have been deceiving me. Where is your delicacy, your modesty, that a comparatively unknown visitor to my house dares to address a letter to you clandestinely? This lad, here, has brought this letter for you, — I don't know where he belongs, — from Mr. Gamble, and has been honest enough to tell me what a wicked wretch his employer is."

"He is not my employer. I wouldn't take his money," interposed I, hotly.

"He's the gipsy boy!" exclaimed the young lady, in great agitation. "O ma! don't think I've done anything wrong. I don't know what it means at all."

With a heavy sigh the old lady drew from the pocket of her dress a pair of gold spectacles, and, having put them on, proceeded to tear open the letter I had given her. As she did so, there slipped from the paper to the floor the ivory portrait of Mr. Gamble, relieved of its metal setting. In awful silence, and with her face deeply flushed, she picked up the picture, dropped it into her lap after a single angry glance, and then devoted herself to a perusal of the writing.

"'Send you the picture according to promise,'" she read aloud, "'and hope soon to receive one of your sweet self in return. Not that I need any counterfeit presentment to keep ever before me a face so lovely in nature's tenderest perfection, that art could but prove its own poverty in an attempt to misrepresent what it could not copy.' . . . My daughter, I blush for you!"

Two lovely hands carried the whitest of handkerchiefs to the brownest of eyes, and a voice broken with sobs made answer, —

"It isn't m-my fault, ma. I — I couldn't help it. Oh, dear! He said he would l-like to send his h-hateful picture, and I didn't dare r-r-refuse. Oh-h, dear!"

"My child," said the old lady, turning again to me, "tell my daughter, what you have already told me, about this man."

Addressing myself rather to a figure in the carpet than to either of my agitated auditors, I gave a full account of Mr. Gamble's operations, as I had heard them described by his own lips, and concluded with a tolerably clear explanation of my own reasons for making the revelation. He was a bad man, I said, and I didn't want Miss Aloize to be made a fool of.

Questionable as was the compliment of the last phrase, I felt a quite chivalric glow in uttering it, and probably expressed enough gallantry in my earnest manner to deprive the words of offence.

Upon the conclusion of my story, the matron handed me the despised portrait with a mechanical dignity of gesture indicating a degree of indignation beyond the power of natural expression, and then drew herself up in her chair as though to make what she was about to say the more official.

"Take that picture back to Mr. Gamble," said she, "wherever he may be, and tell him that the mother of this foolish girl understands his character, and will take care that

he has no future opportunity to repeat his impertinence. My daughter's folly — "

"Ma!" interrupted Miss Aloize, rising from her chair, but still holding the handkerchief to her eyes, "it's too bad for you to speak so of me, when I couldn't help what has happened. It's a shame!" And, bursting into a tempest of sobs, she hurried from the room.

Greatly disturbed by this incident, I arose, with the intention of hastily retreating also, but the old lady motioned with her hand for me to remain.

"You said that you were told to give this note to a servant," she said, and slowly tore the missive to pieces with trembling hands; "has there been any particular understanding, that you know of, between my servant and Mr. Gamble?"

"I don't know, ma'am," answered I.

"You have told me *all* you know about it?"

"Yes, ma'am."

"Child!" she exclaimed, appearing to be suddenly struck by something new in my aspect as I stood uneasily before her, nervously fingering my cap, "what are *you* doing with these bad people? You cannot be a gipsy?"

"No, ma'am," I returned, striving to appear manly for a moment, "I am not a gipsy, and only stay with them because Mr. Reese is with them, and he's kind to me. I was running away from school at Milton, because the master wanted to kill me, and Mr. Reese found me and told me to stay with him."

"And have you no father and mother?" asked the old lady.

"Mother is dead," said I, a strange sense of loss coming upon me as I spoke, "and my father don't like me."

"Poor boy!" she murmured, sadly, shaking her head. "Won't you have something to eat?"

Bless the sex! Their first idea for the alleviation of any misfortune is always one of victuals.

"Thank you, ma'am," was my response; "I'm not hungry."

"My child," she resumed, after a thoughtful pause, "you must come to me again to-morrow, and let me talk to you. I am not fit to do so now. You have acted like a good boy in doing as you have done about this wicked note, and I feel interested in you. Will you come here to-morrow?"

"Yes, ma'am, if Mr. Reese will let me."

"Who is he? a gipsy?"

"No, not a gipsy. I don't know who he is."

The latter fact struck me for the first time, as I told her of it, and gave me a queer feeling of confusion.

"Very well," she said, dropping her face upon one of her hands, as though hopeless of understanding more of my situation then. "You may go, now, if you wish."

I awaited no second permission, but said "good-by, ma'am" as I passed into the hall; and made such haste to emerge from the front door that I did not note whether she answered my farewell or not.

Through the pretty garden, and up the road to the turnpike, I was kept tolerably elevated in spirit by a consciousness of having done a rather manly thing and acted the benefactor and mysterious friend to a very handsome young lady; but the thought that Reese might possibly disapprove of the exploit dissipated my romance in a twinkling, and, for a moment, I had an inclination to fly wildly into the town instead of going back to the wood. It occurred to me, though, that my eccentric protector was already in Newark himself, and without further hesitation I walked on to the wood road, and turned into it as resolutely as possible.

Intending to conceal the picture in my coat until Reese should come back to the wagons, and then make a full confession to him of the whole affair, I slipped the artistic treasure into one of my pockets as I neared the encampment, and marched into the latter with a rather longer stride of legs than might have been considered unsuspicious had any one been watching for me.

But no one was lying in wait to criticise the manner of my return; not even Juan, whom I had vaguely supposed to be somewhere just ahead of me all the way back. On the contrary, all the gipsies in the grove seemed, when I came amongst them, to be quite busy enough with some new excitement of their own; for while several were gathered about one of the wagons in very noisy and earnest conversation, others were hurriedly harnessing the horses and making unequivocal preparations for a speedy departure of the whole company. Surprised at the unexpected scene, startled by the fierce, agitated looks of every face I could see, and wondering what had brought some of the gipsies back from Newark at that time of day, I sought for some one to whom I might speak with the hope of being understood, and presently detected Juan at work on one of the animals. After being rudely jostled and pushed several times by those in whose way I came, I reached his side, and was about to ask him what the matter was, when he caught sight of me, pointed impatiently into the wood beyond, and, turning his back upon me, went on with his work. Beholding nothing but trees and undergrowth in the direction indicated, I was making my way to where Dolores was packing something into a wagon, when she, too, saw me before I could speak, and paused in her work just long enough to point exactly as Juan had done. When my eyes followed this gesture a second time, I saw what looked like the head and shoulders of some person, just above the bushes among the trees there, and, hastily concluding that Anita must be the one to whom I was thus speechlessly referred, I wonderingly bent my steps toward where I supposed her to be. The head and shoulders were no longer in sight; but, thinking that the girl had seated herself on the turf, I wound my way amongst the trees to the bushes, and was forcing an opening through the latter, when a new wonder caught my view and held me fixed in astonishment. With his back to me, and one of the trunks from the wagon lying empty on the grass beside him, was a man bending over a spot in the deepest shade of a spreading white oak, beating into its place, with a shovel, a square of turf which had evidently been removed previously for some peculiar purpose. He was dressed in a coarse, dark suit, and wore a black oilskin hat, whose rim extended into a broad flap at the back and completely hid his neck. I could see, however, that he had heavy black whiskers upon his cheeks, and, in considerable astonishment at the spectacle of a stranger thus curiously employed, I had commenced to draw back from the bushes again, when the crackling sound caused him to straighten himself and turn quickly around. I stopped.

"That's you, is it, Little Breeches?"—the voice was Reese's, but the face and form were not his. "Come along, you're just in time."

"S-sir!" stammered I, vastly bewildered.

"Come here, I tell you! what ails you?—Oh, the whiskers, eh?" Seizing the latter with his right hand, he removed them entirely from his face for an instant, and as quickly replaced them; and then I recognized my protector, despite his changed garb and hat.

"O Mr. Reese!" I exclaimed, breaking through the bushes and running to him, "what is the matter? They're all out here hitching up the horses, and you look so queer!"

"It's a queer time," responded he, casting away the shovel, and buttoning his coat as he spoke. "We've got to be out of this place, my boy. Hugo is nabbed, the police will be here on the search before to-morrow morning, and we must be away in an hour."

"But, why?" queried I.

"Ask me no questions," retorted he, "and I'll tell you no lies. It's enough for you to know that I've put on my travelling rig because there's a squall ahead, and you've got to go with me. No more talk, now; come on."

As he ceased speaking, he caught me by the hand, and turned to go around the bushes; but, at the first step, a figure slid noiselessly out from behind a tree, near the one beneath which he had been at work, and stood motionless before him.

"Anita!" exclaimed Reese, releasing me, and pausing irresolutely. "What are you doing here, my girl?"

She made no answer. Her great black eyes gleamed steadfastly upon him from the shadow of the shawl over her head, and, as she held her right hand clenched against her bosom, and the other half-hidden in the folds of her patched dress, there was something in the attitude to make him retreat a step.

"You've been watching me, my beauty," he said, quietly; "you've been playing the spy."

"Where-a you go?"

She spoke quickly, and in a passionate tone, as on the night when she questioned me.

"Where am I going?" repeated Reese, with a short laugh; "why, I'm going to New York — for a while. You don't want me to stay and be taken, — do you?"

"No! no!" she cried, shaking her head petulantly; "you not go. We hide-a you!"

"That won't do, my princess," answered he, going a step nearer to her and apparently recovering his old manner. "I must be entirely out of the way when they come to search the camp, wherever it is. Don't you know, my dear, that they've caught your father? He'll tell them he's a gipsy, and then play the ignorant. That will get him out of the scrape in a few days, if they don't happen to tumble on me. But if they should find me in Old Hugo's camp, there would be trouble. Don't you see? don't— you — see?"

Slowly repeating the last question in a soothing tone, he moved a little closer to her, and then, with the quickness of thought, threw both his strong arms about her and clasped her tightly to him. I was taken by surprise, when the sudden embrace occurred; but how much greater was my astonishment to see Reese give a short, sharp wrench with his right hand at something, and lift that hand aloft with a glittering knife in it, while, with the other, he fiercely pushed her from him.

"Would you? you hell-cat!" he exclaimed, shaking the weapon at her.

Shrinking beyond reach of it, her eyes dilated with terror, and her shawl falling from her head, she moved her lips, but uttered no sound.

"Why do you want to murder me?" he asked, hurling the steel far over her head.

Down went the gipsy girl upon her knees on the grass, and with eyes bent to the ground, and arms hanging nervelessly at her sides, she said, softly and mournfully, —

"I should kill-a myself, too. If you go, I know you come-a not back. I die then."

My capacity for wondering at the vagaries of Reese was exhausted, or I should have been doubly amazed when, instead of either bantering, or leaving the wild creature, he caught her up in his arms and poured forth such a torrent of endearments that some other person than his indifferent self seemed to be speaking. He told her that she was his own princess, and he loved her better than anything else in the world! He didn't think that any woman could ever care enough for him to do what she had done; and he'd come back and marry her yet, if she'd only trust him! He went on in this vein for several moments, giving her

no chance to answer a word, and, finally, with a kiss, released her from his arms, and saw her glide away through the bush like a mocking forest vision.

"Mr. Reese," said I, after waiting patiently for some time to see if he would not notice me of his own accord, — "Mr. Reese, won't the wagons be gone if we don't go back to them soon?"

He turned his head slowly toward me, as though uncertain whether he had been addressed or not.

"Eh?"

"Shan't we go back, sir?"

He stared at me vaguely for a moment, and smiled rather foolishly, I thought.

"Shan't we, sir?"

He caught me by the arm again, and asked me what I had said. I repeated the question in full.

"No, Little Breeches," said he, hilariously. "Our business in camp is all settled, my cherub, and we'll take a cut through the woods, and cross the fields to the part of Newark we're interested in to-day — the stage-house. Now then, lively! — you understand? One, two, three, and — OFF for Cow Bay."

———◆◆◆———

CHAPTER XXII.

THE FIVE POINTS.

MONEY is the root of all evil, and so is bread. From individual possession and general diffusion of the first, come the highest developments of human intelligence, and a consequent aggregate of virtue superior to that which might have existed normally without it. From individual possession and a common plenitude of the second, come the natural physical ease and proportionate clearness of mind which make ordinary good easier to follow than ever-laborious evil. Either money or bread may be profligately wasted, or perverted to unworthy uses; but in both cases the sin is one of perversion purely; the possession is, in itself, a good, and has a sympathy for good alone; it blesses who will be blessed, and is a curse to those only, who, having no sympathetic good in themselves to answer its ennobling magnetism, become the worse, — from lacking unison to be the better, — by it.

To want money, to want bread, is to find each a reflective root of all evil, as the want gives greater or less germination to that root in man himself; and if an eagerness for the former, urged on by poverty, will turn passive honesty into active roguery, a craving for the latter, sharpened by hunger, will work human nature's inoffensive blank into the seething characters of infamy and murder!

Recognize money and bread as blessings, by patiently teaching and helping the poor and the starving to attain them innocently, and the very means of their attainment will make them indeed blessings when attained. Regard them, even in their greatest plenty, as standard evils; teach the poor and the starving that there can be no luxury in them without evil, and your sophistry will make of each a double curse, — a curse in being denied to instinctive necessity; a curse in being gained (despite your admonitions), without appreciation of the beneficent good that is in them.*

Following Reese, who slouched along with none of that free, careless air which had distinguished him in the country, I was going down into the place where bread is the root most iniquitous. Money held the precedence as far as Anthony Street,† in its palaces of trade and sumptuous hotels. It even made an attempt to turn the corner with us, in the shape of a decent building or two down the cross-way to its rival's camp; but there it lost heart very suddenly at a point where Starvation looked out from the shattered windows of a huge tenement-house; and the man and I, and the travel-worn dog panting after us, lost sight of it there.

After crossing Centre Street, Reese paused abruptly upon the curb and fixed his eyes on a great, gray building, some distance down, on the west side, whose heavy pillars and grim solidity of architecture made it loom in the twilight like a huge sepulchre.

"Do you know what place that is?" he asked me, motioning toward it with his head.

"A prison," was my instinctive answer.

"Yes," said he, sullenly; "it's the Tombs. They've got Hugo in there."

"Hugo there!" cried I, in surprise. "Why, what did they put him there for?"

"The same thing that may take me there, yet," he replied, with a quick glance around him; "being too flush with — no matter what. Come on again."

I began to feel certain that something very wicked had been done by the old gipsy, and that my protector was perilously involved in it, to the risk of his very life, perhaps; but of what the offence was I had not the slightest idea. There was such a magnetism of guilt, though, in the man's shuffling, shrinking manner after reaching the city, that I began to contract a sense of some sort of guilt myself, and I even fancied that the dusty and exhausted Mr. Mugses, as he limped droopingly after us, betrayed disreputable signs of an accusing conscience.

A hard and sorry-looking trio were we for any other locality than that to which we were going; but neither fashions nor dignities were exacting in the neighborhoods of Cross and Little Water Streets, nor were the critical spirits of Cow Bay likely to take umbrage at soiled attire and hang-dog looks.

* This, of course, is merely a child's philosophy. As I grow older in my story I shall reason with more sophistry.

† Now "Worth Street."

Immediately after crossing Centre Street, we began to meet these spirits in all their most picturesque pauses and flights; and the rickety, rotting, old barracks of houses, and filthy alley of a street, were frame and perspective to such a figure-piece as art never dreamed of. A new moon was beginning to lengthen out the twilight with such a delicacy of lustre, as would have romanced and softly mystified the most ungainly ruins in the world, or given dramatic pallor to what human shapes might be flitting in the track of time's most grim desolation; but the swarming, crazy tenements of Anthony Street took the tender light, as a dirty pauper face might take the ghastliness of death; and what there was of silver and darkness for the wild and ragged out-door scarecrows of the adjacent Points, suggested a bleary phosphorescence from something noisome walking in rags. On a low wooden stoop running under the sagging half-door, and smeared and shattered window, of one reeking den, lay some creature whose long brown hair was plastered to the boards with the liquid from a broken pitcher still grasped by a soiled and bony hand. Another creature, with monstrous face puffed out like a balloon; with great, filmy eyes, and feet like clods of mire, stepped upon the soaking hair on his way to the half-door. Up rose the prone creature to its elbow, screaming curses in a shrill, wicked voice, and struck at the other with the broken pitcher; and then fell down again like a dead thing. Others, too, must have trodden upon that hair and been cursed for it; for men and women and children were all the time passing through the half-door for the one thing that comforts when bread is scarce; but the owner of the hair might have been milder with them than with her careless old father. She would have natural reason to expect more cautious walking from so near a relative. The claims of relationship, though, were not rigorously honored in that ward; or the tattered brother who was fighting his slattern sister, just off the pavement a little further on, would not have kicked the poor wretch a second time, after she had cried murder. In his case, however, the temptation was great; a number of gentlemen and ladies of the most unquestionable depravity and raggedness were applauding him in a ring, and a young lady in two primitive garments actually came down from a second-story window near by, to hurl a dead cat at the shrieking sister. Public opinion was against the latter, and when public opinion is against any one, you can't kick too often. Seated on a heap of mingled cabbage-leaves and ashes, which swelled away from the curb in odorous fermentation, was a withered hag in a red turban, lustily smoking a pipe, and philosophically observing the tricks of two little vagrant imps with a drunken sailor. The imps were after the jacket and handkerchief hanging across an arm of the reeling mariner, and the pretty game so absorbed her attention, that she had no time for the soiled and tattered bundle rolling out of her arms into the curdled gutter; nor ears, either, or she must have heard the bundle's wheezing cry.

Down that way the traveller had a surprise, too, in coming suddenly upon a three-sided bit of common, with several naked, pauper trees in it, and such suspicious of a green turf as just sufficed to break the hearts of two or three skeleton horses, dimly visible here and there. On lines stretched from trunk to trunk the best washing of the Points hung in patched and dingy profusion, guarded by half a score of just such witches as beset Macbeth on the heath.

"Hubble, bubble, toil and trouble!"

might have been the natural refrain of the laundresses getting up a witches' washing like that; for never did Acheron's caldron yield more distorted shapes, than swung in limp, blotchy ugliness from those lines.

I clung to Reese, and the dog cringed close to our legs, as wild-looking ruffians began to salute us with oaths, and starving curs and pigs yelped and squealed under our feet at every step from the narrow and bemired sidewalk. I tried to make the man tell whither he was taking me, and why he had come to such an awful place; but he was as heedless of my questions as of the salutes of the swarm. A sullen, dogged spirit seemed to have taken possession of him in his very walk.

Along Little Water Street, and the longest side of the common we made our way to where two rows of miserably dilapidated shanties ran jaggedly to an apex some distance on. To speak more definitely, it was a wedge-shaped court of wretched rookeries that we entered, picking our way between yawning mud-holes and sprawling children, and running a steady fire of ribaldry from creatures of all ages and colors, in paneless windows and on tumbling stoops.

Before instinct loses its nicest sensibility under the deprecating encroachments of jealous reason, its intuitions correspond at times to what in reason is known as inspiration; which makes it a question whether reason's inspirations are not mere exceptional demonstrations of instinct alone. This I say, not in my present proper self, but in my identification with the immature self of which I am writing; and the suggestion is drawn from the well-remembered fact, that, without any intellectual process whatever, I instinctively comprehended all the salient meanings of the new and unwholesome scenes around me in the democracy of misery and vice that evening. Hunger was the explanation of everything, and had wrought an unmistakable physiognomy of its own wherever the eye found rest. I seemed to know at once, when I looked upon any face in our way, that its owner had been hungry before he or she had been anything worse. Instinctively, too, I divined the relations of the beings in view; it was instantaneously apparent to me that the fallen creature with the long hair was daughter to him who stepped first upon the profaned tresses; that the boy and girl fighting were brother and sister; that the old crone on the garbage-heap was mother of the creature with long hair, and grandmother of the babe she let fall into the gutter; that several wrecks of women stranded on rickety stoops, with dirty bandages tied about their heads, were the wives of men who got drunk and beat them. To understand all this would have terrified me beyond control, but that I simultaneously understood the first great cause as hunger; and so, in feeling childishly sorry for the furies and scarecrows of the Points, I lost much of that hatred and dread of their malignity which might have been experienced by an older and wiser person.

About half way down the wedge-shaped court, Reese, and I, and the dog went up the hind-legs of a broken step-ladder to what had once been the railed platform of a high wooden stoop, and passed into an entry-way just high and wide enough for two persons abreast.

"Be careful how you step now," said Reese. "If it's too dark for you to see, feel the way carefully with your feet. The floor is full of holes."

The holes were plentiful indeed, as I already knew from stumbling into two or three of them; and sounds in the house we had entered began to distinguish themselves from those of the street as intensifications of the latter. During our momentary pause the noises of singing, swearing, fighting, and every other imaginable source of hideous racket, came to my ears from the different quarters of the den. A conglomeration of tattered caricatures of childhood, who had swarmed up the steps after us, were chattering and peering in through the doorway, and the hoarse snarling of a dog in some lower passage induced Mr. Mugses to contribute several gruff coughs to the general symphony.

"I wish we'd bought a lantern," growled Reese; "it's villanous dark here, and the rats are around. Hallo there! Rumsey!"

In answer to his call there was a movement in a black hole in the wall before us, and a threatening voice cried, —

"Well, wot?"

"Come out and show yourself, or I'll send a dog in after you," said Reese, crossly. "Don't you know my voice? I'm Mr. Reese."

After some indistinct muttering a figure came dimly out of the hole in the wall, and asked, in the cracked voice of an old man, if it — the figure — was a naygur slave? Because, if so, the figure would like to be informed of the fact at once, with a view to the consistent regulation of its unquestioning servility thereafter. Should such however, after profound investigation, prove *not* to be the fact, "why thin, what the divil do ye mane by spakin' parables of sich a characther?"

"I'll tell you what I mean, you old rip," answered Reese, impatiently; "I mean that I want to know where old Mr. Grey is; and I want you to call him, wherever he is; and tell him to bring a candle and my keys. Do you understand? Be off with you now, and I'll give you a quarter, for your gin, when you come back."

"It's th' ould count ye mane," croaked the other. "It's moved to the flure below this he is, boss; in the first room after ye pass the dure under the shtoop. Sure, I'll call him."

He hobbled away into the deeper shadows beyond; the sound of his feet indicating that he wore neither shoes nor stockings; and presently returned, followed by somebody carrying a lighted candle. The feeble rays of the latter revealed him as a short, red-eyed, dirty-faced old man, in a flutter of rags, and also revealed a quite different appearing personage in the candle-bearer, — an apparently old man, much bent, but clean and pallid of face, and attired neatly, though in many patches.

"Grey, how d'ye do?" said Reese, nodding to the new-comer. "Here, Rumsey, take your quarter and be off. I'm under a cloud again, old friend, and shall have to keep dark here in my cage for a while."

"You've got company, I see," remarked the person thus addressed, lifting the candle over his head and surveying me questioningly.

"Oh, yes," responded my protector, shrugging his shoulders; "a stray kid that I'm playing guardian to. This isn't just the place for him —"

"I should think not," interrupted the old man, vehemently; "I should think not!"

"But I had either to bring him along, or cut him adrift, and there's no help for it. Clear away from the door, there, you young brutes! Show us up, Grey, — I want to ask you something."

Going before us with the candle, which was fixed in a large turnip, the stranger led the way up a flight of tottering and creaking stairs to a long hall not more than two feet wide, on either side of which, at short intervals, were low, dirty rooms, swarming with the children of misery. In some of these unclean pens, the passing light of our candle revealed knots of drunken wretches wallowing or sleeping on the filthy floors; while, in others, noisy creatures of both sexes were playing cards, or huddling around benches, bearing the refuse that such beings live upon. Occasional jeers and curses came at us as we passed by. Reese was hailed by name once or twice; and at one of the doors a girl with an old-woman face made a sweeping courtesy to "the count;" but we went on unheeding.

A second hall of the same kind, and still higher up, was next traversed; and I was thinking that we must be at the very top of the house, and expecting to find the very next room our destination, when our conductor paused at the end of the passage, and remarked, "Here is the ladder."

Standing upright and flat against the wall, to which it was secured by a staple, chain, and padlock, was a ladder, some six or eight feet long; and on one side above it, in a square boxed way over the hall-rafters, appeared an unpainted door.

"Been up here lately, Grey?" asked Reese, taking two keys from the other, and applying one to the padlock.

"I've been up to read your books now and then of an evening," was the quiet reply.

"That's right. I've always told and wanted you to do so, you know."

As my protector spoke, he unchained the ladder, and turned it over at a slant, so that its top rested just under the door above the rafters. Then, springing up the rungs, he used the second key, and, in another moment, stood on the threshold of an opened loft.

"Now come up with the candle, my dear count," cried he, gayly; "and you, Glibun, bring up Mr. Mugses in your arms."

With my usual silent obedience, I did as I was bidden, and climbed after Mr. Grey into what I at first took to be a great, desolate garret. When Reese had closed the door, however, and the light of the candle took a wider range, I was able to discern more evidences of habitability than could have been expected in such a locality. Though the rude brown rafters, with their plentiful cobwebs, came down so low that the heads of the men fairly grazed them, the room, or loft, seemed to extend over the whole house, and was large enough for a school. Three glass sashes in the roof were the only windows I could discover. More than one half of the place was entirely bare of furniture; but in the other and further half, several rush-bottomed chairs and a large deal table stood in line against the boarded wall on one side, while a leathern lounge, a clock, and — curious to observe — several long shelves, packed with big and little books, were ranged opposite. There was also a rusty cooking-stove, with its pipe through the roof, a painted pine cupboard standing in a corner, and a rudely-furnished cot-bed and wash-stand against the end wall.

"Here we are again!" cried Reese, rubbing his hands and indulging in another of his quick changes of manner. "I feel at home once more, and as prime as a game-fowl. Make yourself comfortable on one of those chairs, Glibun, if they aren't too dusty. Mr. Mugses knows where he is. See how snug he's making himself on the lounge already. Come, my jolly ancient, leave that candle to take care of itself on the table, and give me a hand in getting up a flash in the stove for supper. It's a trifle chilly up here this evening. I left some kindling-wood over, last time, and here it is, well seasoned, under the cupboard. Fly around, old man; it's a blessing we haven't got a chimney to set on fire."

Pouring out his words like a boisterous youth, he had the bundles of wood out of their hiding-place and into the stove, before his deliberate friend could offer help; and, by the aid of the candle, a lively fire was immediately under way.

"I'll bring the provisions. Back in a moment. You hold on with the youngster, Grey," rattled the rejuvenated proprietor of this unique retreat; and in another moment he was out of the loft and hurrying down the ladder.

The old man, who appeared to be thoroughly dazed by the whirling rapidity of the whole procedure, stared abstractedly at the door for a moment or two, and then turned his pale face slowly upon me.

"Are you here of your own accord?" he asked, pinching his chin nervously, and regarding me attentively.

"Yes, sir," answered I, not knowing what other reply to make without forethought.

"*He* brought you, then, because you wanted to come?"

"He had to leave the gipsies," said I, "because something was the matter about Hugo; and he brought me along because I'd nowhere else to go."

"You're not a gipsy yourself?"

"Oh, no, sir."

"The gipsies didn't steal you?"

"Oh, no! I was running away from —" Here I stopped, conscious that I was going too far with my confidence.

He shook his head thoughtfully several times, as in sympathy with some conjecture not favorable to me.

"Do you know what place you're in?" was his next inquiry.

"Cow Bay, I suppose," returned I, remembering the name Reese had given at starting. "It seems like an awful place. Only hear that screaming and singing down below. Do the people always act so, sir?"

"It *is* an awful place," he moaned, rather than said; "a dreadful place, — a dreadful place. Boy, this is no place for you; you'd better be dead than here, a thousand times. It's starvation, crime, perdition, to be here! It is cruel to bring even that dog here!"

Rising to vehemence, and positively wringing his thin hands, as he spoke the last sentence, he filled me with alarm.

"Why do you stay here, then?" asked I, with involuntary aptness.

"I'm old and you're young," he responded quickly; "I'm ruined already, and you can be saved yet. This is a place for old age, misery, hopelessness, want, ignominy, sorrow; not for youth."

"I saw children down in the street," urged I, scarcely understanding his wild talk, and growing more uneasy at his wild manner.

"God help them!" he exclaimed passionately, clasping his hands and looking upward. "They are children by age, by size, — that's all. But what would you think, or anybody think, to know that their souls are lost already! — to know that they are imps of perdition, doomed by their own parents! Do you hear me, boy," and he came and put a trembling hand upon my shoulder, — "by their own parents! The fathers — they are the accursed ones; the mothers can only follow — the fathers are the soul-killers. By drunkenness, by gaming, by folly, by crime, driven here; and then the innocent, tender, appealing little children must wither into the hideous likenesses of the hell around them, and live only to curse their fathers, in prisons, or under the gallows.— Hear those shouts, and oaths, and sounds of brutish debauch in these houses and on these streets! Fathers howling the requiems of children's lost souls! O Heaven! O Heaven!"— he was pacing to and fro, now utterly regardless of me, and swinging his arms like a maniac, — "that such wretches should live! But they daren't die; the ruin they are working might be even a worse ruin if they should die and leave its finishing to the devils of the Points. No, no, no! Let them live, let them live."

If ever a broken heart wailed its despair in tones haunted with its breaking, there was an unblest ghost in that moan of "Let them live, let them live." I started from my chair as though the voice had come to me from the darkness of an empty room; the miserable candle seemed to flare with the chill that crept over me, and the dog on the lounge uttered a howl like a human cry.

"I'm afraid of you," gasped I, looking fearfully at him.

He fingered his forehead in a confused way, and looked from me to the dog in apparent bewilderment.

"Why do you talk so?" I continued; "I don't understand you at all."

He seated himself upon the lounge, near the dog, and said, with a sigh, —

"O child, the sight of one like you, new to such a place as this, may well make a miserable old man half crazy. Don't mind me; don't mind me."

"I'll try not to, sir," returned I, resuming my chair, "if you won't go on in that strange way."

As I spoke, there was a sound of some one heavily mounting the ladder outside, and when, in obedience to a thumping on the door, I hastened to open the latter, Reese came shuffling in with both hands full. A brown pitcher and a paper parcel occupied either hand, while other parcels were held under his arms or protruded from his pockets.

"You're dull here," said he, vivaciously, as he went to the table with his load; "you ought to see how they're keeping it up below: A light in the front hall; another in one of the second-story rooms; a wake in still another room, and a free dance in a third. That's nearly life enough for one house, I should think. We must keep it up too, though, you know; and here's something to keep it up with. Beer from Crown's corner; ham and bread from Centre Street; cheese from ditto; crackers from ditto; a lot of candles with two empty bottles for candlesticks (light a couple and set them up, Glibun); a lot of herring, and a roll of butter. Now, Mr. Grey, as I'm going to keep you to supper, I'll trouble you to help a little. Stir up the fire, will you, while I hunt up the old skillet."

He had piled his purchases upon the table as they were named, and now skipped to the cupboard like a boy, cast his hat and false beard under it, and brought forth a broken skillet and other cooking and table utensils. Mechanically the old man aided in the preparations; I obeyed the order which had been given to me, and in a very short time there was an array of earthen dishes on the table from the cupboard, and the cooked ham, herring, crackers, cheese, bread, and butter were dished in such a savory atmosphere as that neighborhood could not often have known.

"And now, Mr. Grey," said Reese, as we began eating, "I want to know how you've fared since my last house-keeping in this sky-parlor? I see they call you 'the count' yet."

"Yes, yes," answered the other, "and I let them do it. What started in a sneer has done me some good; for half the poor, ignorant creatures here actually believe now that I used to be an English nobleman of some description, and that keeps them off. I have a comfort now that was not mine before, sir; I can starve without constant insult, at least."

"Starve!" retorted Reese. "pooh! you're not as badly off as that, old friend. I think I've got a little acquaintance who'll see to that."

In a moment the old man dropped his knife and fork and half arose from his chair.

"What do you mean by that?" he exclaimed, glaring furiously at his entertainer. "What do you dare to mean by that?"

"I mean no harm at all, Mr. Grey," returned Reese, more seriously. "You appear to be altogether mad on that point. My idea was, that your little girl would peddle matches, or sell hot-corn, before she'd see you starve; and now I want to know where she is to-night, that I don't find her with you?"

Sinking back upon his chair again, with lips quivering and a look of helpless misery upon him, the poor old creature said,—

"Gone across the river with her accordeon, sir, to try and pick up a few shillings on Long Island. She travels far and wide now, God help her! with no protection but her innocence. Think of such a child brought to such a fate! Away all

this night,—sleeping on the roadside, perhaps. And so hungry! All my work! Oh, if I only dared to die!"

"When will she be back?"

"To-morrow—if she is alive."

"Well then, just mind what I say," cried Reese, impatiently; "we're not going to have our appetites spoiled by your raving, when there's so little cause for it. You can act like a man, if you *are* down in the world; and this eternal kink of yours, about this thing and that thing being all your work, is simply old-womanish. It's sheer drivel—you understand?—and the hardest trial my little acquaintance has to bear. Suppose you were like me—driven here to keep out of jail. There's nothing criminal about *you*, you know; and you've got a child that ought to be the joy of your life even in this hell-hole. That's it! drink the beer and be thankful you're better off than you might be."

I thought this a curious argument for comfort, and hoped that the old man would say something more of his child; but he seemed either cowed or shamed by the rough rebuke, and had indeed applied to the beer with sudden ardor. In fact he drank a considerable quantity of that beverage, and, by degrees, washed away his melancholy with it and allowed himself to be led into general conversation.

From what Reese said, I learned that he considered himself perfectly safe there from whatever danger he had incurred, and did not believe that some "Judge," whom he named, would let the law trouble a man who could control a "thousand votes." I did not understand just what this meant, but I could perceive from the manners of both men that the argument had more than common force.

Finally, Mr. Grey took his departure down the ladder; and, after extinguishing the two extra candles and huddling the contents of the table topsy-turvy into the cupboard, Reese turned his attention to me.

"Are you tired?" he asked.

"Yes, sir."

"Then lie upon that bed yonder, and go to sleep. It has no sheets nor pillow-cases, but the pair of comfortables upon it will do at a pinch. I shall take the lounge, here, and bunk with Mr. Mugses. I'm tired myself, too tired to talk any more to-night. To-morrow we'll have a confab."

I was weary enough from the excitement and exertion I had gone through; and, besides, the small quantity of beer with which my meal was finished made me drowsy. Readily, therefore, I availed myself of the permission given. Dressed as I was, I threw myself upon the cot; and, while yet the candle was burning and the sounds from below came louder, fell dreamlessly asleep.

CHAPTER XXIII.

A LOWER DEEP.

THE best breakfast in Cow Bay, that morning, was ours; and I ate my share without the remotest suspicion that scores of human beings within a few yards of our retreat would not have scrupled to murder us in cold blood, for the sake of just such a meal. There were hungry ones in the house, to whom the fever of last night's gin and whiskey brought an epicurean zest for a crisp and cool breakfast, and a temper to take it, without much regard for trifling obstacles, if they but knew where to find it. Luckily for us, however, there was no odor of cookery to betray our luxury, nor incense of coffee, or tea, to evoke the genius of starving crime from below; so we banqueted undisturbed in our sky-parlor, with the sunlight streaming in upon us through the sash in the roof.

My companion had scarcely noticed the "good-morning" I gave him when first I crawled forth from the cot; nor did he command and direct my assistance in the very primitive arrangement of the meal by more than sharp grunts and imperious gestures. We chose, indeed, to be silent and abstracted until some minutes after the eating was over, when a sudden, and apparently unprovoked howl from the dog on the lounge loosened his tongue.

"Hold your infernal noise, you brute!" he shouted, furiously hurling a billet of wood at the animal. "What do you mean?"

His rage at such a trifle surprised me. I had never before seen him inflict so much as an angry word upon Mr. Mugses.

"The dog," said I, "howled in the same way last night, while you were away and that old man was going on about people's children."

"The old idiot is enough to make any dog howl," replied Reese, scowling at his whining favorite, who had come fawning to his feet; "but I don't want to hear any such noise as that in this place. We'll have enough unearthly sounds in Rack-and-Ruin Row without dog-howls. What a regular groan it was! Ugh! I don't like it. It means something wrong!"

He stared soberly at the creature for a moment, and then began feeding him with the dry remnants of our repast.

"I'd never have brought the old fellow here," continued he, with a gentleness strongly contrasting with his recent anger, "if I had thought less of him. He's the only true friend I ever had. I can love anything — dog, or cat, or bird — that cares for me."

While uttering the last sentence he fondled one of the dog's ears, and looked upon me with a kindness that made my heart swell in my bosom.

"I like you very much, Mr. Reese," said I, strongly emphasizing the personal pronoun; "only I wish you hadn't been such good friends with that bad Mr. Gamble."

He laughed, and leaned back from the table with both hands in his pockets.

"So that offended you, did it, my young Christian? You don't happen to remember, perhaps, that you did him a more friendly turn than I ever did, when you took that note for him! By the way, Little Breeches, you've got to tell me yet how that embassy flourished."

"I gave the note to the lady's mother," responded I, with some spirit; "and she tore it up and scolded the young lady;" and in concise terms, I gave him the whole story.

I expected him to reprimand me savagely for my high-handed perversion of a trust to which he had partly been committed himself. I expected a severe scolding, and was prepared to defend myself; but he only laughed louder than before.

"Good for you!" he cried, in the best of spirits. "Upon my soul, I'm glad of it, and may the rascal be horsewhipped the next time he tries such a villanous business! He had my help for a moment, only because he knew too much about some of the gang's doings to be a safe man to offend. I'm anything but as good as I ought to be — you understand? — but I don't impose on women. I deal with men. This practice on women is too cowardly mean."

It came into my head to say just then, "I think Anita must love you very much, Mr. Reese."

He started, colored, and gave me a suspicious look, for which I could not immediately account.

"What put it into your head to say that, Glibun?" he asked, quickly.

"I thought she acted so," said I.

"Then don't think any more about it," retorted Reese; "you know nothing about such things. You say the old lady, Mrs. Green, asked you to come back to the house again, — do you?"

"Yes, sir."

Bringing down his chair upon its fore-legs again, and crossing his arms upon the table, he fixed his keen black eyes upon me in a searching, speculative gaze.

"That reminds me," he said, "that I must make up my mind what to do with you. Do you want to go back to your father?"

"Oh, no!" And I meant it. Anything but that.

He leaned farther toward me over the table, and asked, as though suddenly possessed of the idea, —

"How should I know anything about your father, boy?"

"That pedler told you about it," was my ingenuous reply. "I was awake in the wagon, that morning, and heard you and him talking."

The man uttered a furious oath and sprang to his feet.

"What else did you hear? Speak quick! Quick!"

I shrank trembling from his reach, and put an arm before my face in anticipation of a blow.

"Nothing but that, sir, upon my word of honor! I couldn't help it!"

His rage was gone in a moment at sight of my distress. In his way he certainly loved me.

"Pshaw!" cried he, smiting the table with an open palm, "there was nothing else to hear. Don't mind my theatricals. The tight place I'm in now makes me nervous as a cat. Well, if you overheard the talk that morning, you know one thing,—you know that I might make something by handing you over to your natural owner. Now, which would you prefer, going to him, or staying with me?"

"Let me stay with you," panted I.

"By G—d, you shall, then!" exclaimed he. I think it really pleased him to find that I clung to him; and I think he was all the better pleased that my choice followed so closely upon his harshest offence against me.

Rising from his chair once more, he came over to where I sat, and looked down upon me with his hands upon my shoulders.

"You shall stay with me," he said, "until I can find some better friend for you. Rack-and-Ruin Row is not a place to improve one of your years, and I don't know how long we may have to stay here; but, if you do as I tell you to, you will come to no harm while I am away. I'm not the best companion for you either, but I'll show you my best side. Read those books over there, keep yourself as clean as you can, and stay in here as much as you can. I'll give you the key of the door, which you can lock after me when I go out, and open for me when I come in. I'll move the ladder, so that none of the wretches downstairs can get at you, and, after to-morrow, I'll fix it so that we can eat in the next house."

"Must you go out much?" I asked, not relishing the idea of being left alone there.

"Yes," was the reply, "I must be out to see what I can do for Old Hugo. Mind, Glibun, that you don't have a word to say about me, or where we come from, to any living soul. I shan't tell you just the trouble that sent me here, but you can be sure of this much: if it gets about that I am here, I shall go to jail, and you will go —to your father! You understand? Now see if you can't get these things back off the table into that cupboard again. There are enough crackers left to make you a dinner, if I'm not here, and there are the books to keep you company. To-morrow we'll be in better working order.

"Won't that old man come up again?"

"Old Grey you mean? Perhaps he will to-night, but not before. Now can you get along?"

"Yes, sir, I think I can."

"That's a good fellow. I'm glad to see you care something for me. I'll help you amuse yourself. I'll teach you book-keeping some evening."

While rattling off this speech he was putting on his hat and false whiskers, and had his hand upon the door when he made me the queer promise. It was the work of an instant for him to toss the key upon the table; and then, with characteristic abruptness, he was out of the loft and springing down the ladder. I had barely comprehended his absence, however, when he was back again, bringing a pail of water and standing it beside the bed.

"There!" said he, out of breath; "you can wash now. I'll be back again before dark."

Thus was I dismissed to stealthy solitude in the very heart of all uncleanness, want, and crime; with but a floor between my yet untainted youth and the swarming of every vice and misery; with but a dog's protection and a child's judgment; yet safer there than in my father's house. This thought came in to me with the sunlight through the sash, as though Heaven would raise for my loneliness a comfort and an assurance from the depth of my greatest misfortune.

After a few minutes of confused reflection, I felt confident enough to clear the table of its rude appointments; and then, with Mr. Mugses standing sentry at my heels, and all sorts of discordant sounds welling up once more from the dens below, I began my acquaintance with the only library in Cow Bay.

Those rickety shelves held a curious array of books for a locality like that. There were translations of Homer, Virgil, Xenophon, Tacitus, Thucydides, and Sallust; Thiers' French Revolution; the Fables of Bidpal; the Koran; Don Quixote; one very old volume of Bayle; Blair's Rhetoric; Roderick Random; a treatise on Book-keeping; two volumes of the Gentleman's Magazine; a Shakespeare; and a score of other books whose titles I forget. All were gray with dust, and some were tumbling to pieces with age and usage.

I happened to take down Roderick Random first; and, having dusted his seedy coat with an ardor that cost Mr. Mugses divers winks and sneezes, I threw myself upon the miserable lounge, and entered upon his career.

Poor indeed is that novel, or even romance, in which some reader cannot find more or less of his or her characteristics and experiences in this or that fictitious personage and incident. No sooner had I begun my intimacy with Roderick, than I discovered a startling similarity between his case and my own. His home was but an uncomfortable place for him; and so was mine for me. He was driven to school, only to be maltreated by a brutal master, and had not my fate been the same? These two points of resemblance were sufficient to perfect my sympathy with the not-over-pious young Random; and when, after a moment's contemplation, I decided that his seafaring uncle's revenge upon the master was not unlike Wolfton's rescue of me from Mr. Birch, I was prepared to accept Dr. Smollett's immoral hero as a glorified ideal of myself, and regard his pictured progress as the natural measure of my own destiny.

There, in that loft in Cow Bay, I had such company as have seldom swarmed forth from between the covers of a book, to make neglected childhood happier than a king. Young Rosa, Tom Bowling, Mr. Syntax, the treacherous Gawky, and the malicious female cousins, were all actual presences to me; and when Roderick demonstrated his poetical and satirical abilities for the benefit of the latter personages, I felt my first definite literary aspirations glow in my breast.

Thus, while I read and enjoyed, — enchanted with all that was good, and innocently ignorant to what was coarse and hurtful, — the hours sped as lightly as my heart could run with them. I forgot who and where I was; I forgot to eat, I forgot to wash myself; and it was twilight when I finally closed the volume, and came unwillingly back to myself.

Discontentedly, and not a little fearfully, realizing my wretched situation again, yet with my brain still full of confused figures, I was beginning to comprehend that Reese had been absent for a long while, when his voice suddenly sounded from the foot of the ladder. Hastening to open the door, I dimly saw him standing below me, and at his side a figure like Mr. Grey.

"Glibun," said my protector, "how have you got on up there?"

"Oh, pretty well, sir," I replied. "I've been reading one of the books."

He uttered some savage ejaculation at the noise made by a herd of half-naked little imps in the doorway of a filthy room near by, and then turned the ladder and bade me come down.

"Shall I bring the dog?" I asked, seeing that Mr. Mugses had turned his head nearly upsidedown in an effort to catch his master's eye from below.

"No," was the answer; "let him stay there and watch our property. Give him some crackers, if there are any, and come on."

I obeyed the command, and, on reaching the foot of the ladder, was saluted by the elder man.

"*Must* he go? You know what a place it is!" I heard him say in undertones to Reese.

"Yes, he must!" retorted the other, quickly. "You know he wouldn't want to be left up there alone all the evening — would he? And I must have some excitement, or I shall get into the dumps. So come along, both of you."

To ask whither, was the farthest from my thoughts; and as, in Indian file, we threaded the narrow passages and descended the tottering stairways, I felt far more curiosity as to where Roderick Random went from Mr. Lavements', than concerning my own destination. So passive to chance had I become.

The rows of dens along the halls were not quite so lively as they had seemed on the evening of our arrival; for two of the choicest spirits in the house, as I afterward learned, had been dragged away to the Tombs that afternoon, by a squad of police, for having carried their facetiousness to the amusing extreme of half-killing somebody on Anthony Street; but several of the rooms had their twilight revelries, for all that; and in one expansive chamber, where two Hibernian families took in colored boarders, they were having a merry time over the vagaries of a lad in delirium tremens.

Like two-and-a-half "fellows of the baser sort," who were excluded from social communion with even such free-and-easy souls as these, we finally skulked into the open air of Cow Bay, and took our silent way toward the base of the triangle. Fathers, brothers, and sons had commenced returning from their daily occupations, — from picking rags, grinding organs, sitting at the corners as blind men and cripples, peddling stolen kindling-wood, collecting cast-away corks, and seeking political appointments from the city fathers, whom they had helped to elect. They were coming home to start a procession of caricature children to Crown's Corner with jugs, cracked teapots, and battered tin cups; to beat such of their wives or sisters, or mothers as chanced to look too much like getting over their last beatings; to flirt for half an hour after supper with such ownerless ladies as happened to prevail at the time on their floors; and then to make a night of it at the hospitable establishments on Crown's Corner and elsewhere about.

These relishable details were not exactly known to me then; yet, as before, I had a vague idea that the numerous scowling and ragged figures we passed were all that too little bread can make of men.

Along Rack-and-Ruin Row we went until arrived at a basement house, so near dissolution that it seemed merely hanging by the eyelids between the sturdier pauper cages on either side of it. Reese turned down the shallow area, which was reached by a descent of three horribly unclean wooden steps; and, through a dingy green door between two red-curtained windows, we entered a room including the whole width and depth of the building.

Two or three candles, inserted in holes cut for the purpose, were dingily burning at intervals down a table extending from the door to the farther wall; but it was some moments before their sickly glare enabled me to discern more of the place than that it was very low, smoky, and damp, and contained other beings beside ourselves. As we advanced toward some of the latter, however, I saw that they were squalid men and women, with eyes and complexions like those of my late gipsy friends. Along the wall, on one side, were ranged a number of hand-organs, around which as many monkeys leaped and chattered; while, upon the table, at which nearly all the men were seated, the women placed tin dishes of coarse and garlicky meat, squares of dark bread, and pewter mugs of — I never could make out what.

Our advent made quite a stir in this musical company. All the men began gesticulating toward us and vociferating at once, while the women ceased work and turned their glittering black eyes upon the intruders.

Casting his hat upon the table, Reese placed both hands on the latter and turned his face in the direction of a burly figure just discernible at the foot of the board.

"You, Brignoli!" he shouted, to make himself heard above the noisy jabbering and chattering; "don't you know me?"

There was a sudden lull in the lingual tempest, during which the burly figure lengthened to its feet and made its way to where we stood. Then Mr. Brignoli was revealed to me as a very stout, gray-haired, dark-skinned, dirty personage, who summarily grasped one of the candles from the table and fairly thrust it into the disguised face of my protector.

"Signor Ricci!" he exclaimed, with uplifted arms; and, with the candle still in his hands, he embraced his long-lost friend. The exclamation and greeting were signals for boisterous cries of recognition from the whole company, Mr. Grey and myself coming in for several rather rude demonstrations of welcome; nor was it until after the host-apparent and Reese had talked rapidly together in a foreign language for nearly ten minutes, that the former returned to his seat in the far shadows, and the object of our visit became manifest.

Hastily saying that we were there for our supper, and assisting Mr. Grey to pull a long bench from under our part of the table, Reese first saw us seated beside himself, and then gave some order which brought two fresh candles and a supply of dishes and knives to our places.

"You'll get all your meals here, after this, Glibun," he said to me; "I'll make arrangements for you; so now's your chance to be broken-in. Help yourself, Grey; *you've* been here before now."

"Yes," replied the old man. "oh, yes;" and looked down at his tin plate to avoid my eye.

"This was my head-quarters at last election, and they remember my stewardship of General Cringer's fund for the incorruptible naturalized!" resumed Reese, replacing his hat to get it out of the way, and turning once more toward the foot of the table.

"Brignoli?"

"Eh?"

Something said again in a foreign language, and some sort of gesture by the old Italian in the direction of two dimly-visible females who were dispensing the eatables in his neighborhood. These females glanced our way, at the sounds of merriment evoked from the assembly by what had passed; and, recognizing my protector and Mr. Grey, came to us without more ado. Both were young, handsome, and dressed in the ordinary costume of organ-women, and both welcomed Reese with great ardor. One, however, who appeared to be the elder, was evidently his favorite, and crowded into a seat beside him when the other women took their seats. The other looked very angry, I thought, at this arrangement, and flirted back to the foot of the table.

Thereafter my protector was in such lively company as left him no inclination to think of anything masculine; so the Italians jabbered, the monkeys chattered, and Mr. Grey sought to entertain me while we ate, with some remarks upon our entertainers. I thus learned from the poor old man (who seemed, in his restless, flighty manner, like one in a fever), that our companions were all organ-grinders with their wives and daughters, and that the basement they occupied had often been the winter retreat of different members of the gipsy band. "*He*," whispered the speaker, pointing cautiously to Reese, "is a great character here. He has worked several local elections in the Points, and these miserable wretches think him some great man. To think I should be in such company! Ah, me! Well. Where can She be?"

Bewildered by the question, I stared at him and uttered my usual half-interrogative "Sir?"

He looked at me without seeing me, his lips twitching, and his right hand nervously clawing the table.

"Who is she, sir?"

He saw me then, and, with a foolish smile, recalled his wandering wits.

"It's all right, boy; it's all right; all right. Don't mind me. I was thinking. Go on eating."

The coarse and noisy meal was soon finished; and, in opposition to an apparent clamor for his staying longer, Reese gave us a signal to arise. Pulling along his laughing female friend by the waist, he, himself, went to, and held a short conversation with, the old Italian, during which I saw myself pointed to more than once; and then, releasing the girl with a kiss, he rejoined us and briskly led the way back to the street again.

He had only time to let me know that I was to go to that basement thereafter for my meals when he was away, before we found ourselves off the broken street once more, and entering what seemed at first like a dilapidated grocery-store.

A dislocated wooden stoop, slippery with every conceivable impurity, and feebly lighted by a suspended transparent ball of dull red, labelled "OYSTERS," led into a shabby store-front. The glass halves of the doors, as well as the wide windows on either side, were pasted over with newspaper cuts of dogs and horses, varied here and there by a printed strip inscribed "SPORTMAN'S HALL;" and, as we passed in, a motley array of hats, caps, and monkeyish heads of hair was visible over a wide screen of green blinds, and a hoarse discord of voices saluted our ears.

Beyond the screen, whither I closely followed my guides with anything but readiness, was a room hung with gaudy fly-paper, ornamented with glass cases containing stuffed dogs, and tarnished gilt frames enclosing cheap dog pictures. A bar occupied one side of the place, divers barrels and a filthy oyster-stand decorated the other; and, through occasional openings in the swarm of customers around a fireless stove in the centre of the room, I could see at the far end an open door to somewhere else.

The company — what a herd it was! Old men, young men, boys, and nondescripts. Men in shiny hats, flashy vestments, and with great seal rings upon their huge hands. Men in battered hats, buttonless and greasy coats, and with their hands stabbed into pockets fit for knife or slung-shot. Half-grown boys, with faces like satyrs, and garments lessened by rags, only, from their original adult sizes. Nondescripts — neither men nor boys — with hair clipped close to the bullet-head, eyes ever darting furtive glances here and there by stealth, and bony, unclean claws, wriggling restlessly toward each other, as though for mutual assurance that the accustomed iron bracelets were indeed off for a while.

"Let us go back! Let the child and me return at any rate!" whispered Mr. Grey, drawing back at sight of this company. "I promised Her I'd never come here again; and now look at me! Let us go, Reese. Don't keep the boy here."

My protector responded to the appeal by roughly seizing one of the old man's arms and dragging him past the throng around the stove to the bar beyond.

"Here, Mr. John Bull," shouted he, to a bloated, short-haired, and coatless personage there presiding, "haven't you got something to put a heart into this countryman of yours?"

"Hi should think so, me 'earty," was the brisk reply; — "hodd if I 'adn't. Why! hit's Reese and the Count! Yer 'ands, me b'ys."

Hands were shaken under the stare of several of the nondescripts, who had shambled bar-ward with us; but Mr. Grey still made feeble attempts to escape from the grasp of Reese.

"What!" cried the latter; "grumpy still, old man? Give him some of your Particular, Jack. That'll steady him. Come, gents, step up and take your drops."

The invitation being a general one, there was an immediate swarming to the bar; and, in the midst of congratulations from old acquaintances who had not recognized him before, my protector enjoyed the proud eminence of paying for such poison as each

chose for himself. It surprised and horrified me, to see the satyr-faced boys toss off *their* doses of the vile stuff, and to hear them laugh over it without smiling. Harsh, rasping noises were those laughs, to which the accompaniment of anything resembling a smile would have been like health blooming from disease.

My friendless situation and look of astonishment, attracted the particular attention of a couple of these promising young gentlemen, both of whom swaggered up to me with tumblers still in hand.

"Don't yer highst?" queried the first, with much patronage of manner.

I answered him with a stare.

Whereupon the second knowing youth came to the rescue, with an explanatory elevation of his glass in the air, and a succeeding conveyance of the same to his mouth. This graceful bit of pantomime, aided as it was by an instinctive wink, enabled me to understand that "highst" meant "hoist," and was intended to poetically describe the act of drinking.

Thus enlightened, I politely answered my new friend's question in the negative, and was conscious of an immediate fall in his esteem.

"Come to see the ki-yi's, I s'pose?" remarked he, with a sneer which might have been a success on a cleaner face.

Here, again, I was all in the dark, and again the second gentleman took pity on my ignorance.

"Don't you hear that ar' cuyoodling down cellar?" he asked, compassionately.

Above the uproar of voices and jingling of glasses, I certainly had heard divers moaning and whining sounds, which suggested nothing definite to me, until this abstruse question was propounded. Then a hint of the truth suddenly flashed upon me, and I replied, with some alacrity, — "Why, they must be dogs!"

"You bet yer," observed number One, "Ki-yi's is dogs, me covey."

My progress in an ornamental branch of education was cut short at this critical point, by a boisterous rush of the company for the farther door, to which I before alluded, and Reese's hand upon my shoulder. As I moved forward in obedience to the action, I asked where Mr. Grey was.

"On ahead with a couple of custom-house fellows," replied Reese, " and as lively as a cricket. Because he's a Britisher, they think he knows more than all the rest of creation about dogs. As though that made any difference!"

I should have inquired concerning those mysterious dogs but for the crowd in which we again found ourselves; for, on passing through the aforesaid door into a narrow passage-way, or hall, the limited space checked the movement of the herd and compelled a more deliberate progression. Instead of going straightforward, however, we turned down a flight of stairs, preceded by a swearing ruffian with a very large lantern, and saluted at the first steps by an uproar of barks and snarls frightful to hear.

The cellar to which we descended seemed to extend under the whole building; and, in the broad glare of the lantern, was a spectacle at once unique and appalling. Secured by short chains to rings in the walls and staples in the floor, ranged about the sides and standing in the middle in all possible arcs and angles of position, were dogs of every size, character and species. There were bull-dogs, terriers, curs, whiffets, mongrels, mastiffs, hounds, and St. Bernards. There were white dogs and black, brown dogs and yellow, streaked dogs and speckled, shaggy dogs and smooth. A thousand coals of fire, alternately lurid and glassy, seemed blazing at us from amid a gloomy wilderness of writhing monsters; and the fiendish yells, howls, groans, growls, and muffled thunders smiting our ears made complete the infernal illusion of the next world to Cow Bay.

Through a lane between these bloodthirsty creatures, several of whom had lost parts of their jaws while the heads of others still dripped blood from recent wounds, I was dragged with the ribald and excited crowd to a vault under the sidewalk, where an enormous black bear growled through his muzzle, a dozen coons snapped at the fingers of the spectators, and a mastiff as large as a Shetland pony howled over his own degradation to such human company. From this vault, the wretch with the lantern produced a pailful of reeking brute entrails, wherewith to feed the raging beasts for our entertainment; and then, heartsick with such devilish scenes, I found myself once more carried upstairs by the rushing crew, and into a third haunt of brutality.

The new place was a room about thirty feet square, with board seats ascending in all directions from the edge of an enclosed ring in the centre. The latter was, as nearly as I can recollect, some nine feet in diameter with a clean floor, and a clumsy chandelier suspended above it. From the chandelier waved several political posters bearing such inscriptions as "Vote for the Hon. Mealy O'Murphy;" "Regular Demolition Ticket;" "The Workingman's Champion;" "Honest Labor *versus* British Gold;" and so on.

As, with many oaths and wild cries, the fierce company scrambled to the seats, their number being continually augmented by fresh arrivals from the bar-room, Reese pushed me along to where Mr. Grey and half a dozen of the more flashy visitors had placed themselves. The old man no longer exhibited anything like repugnance to the scene. His eyes flashed in a kind of frenzy; he stood erect as any young man while pouring out a torrent of dog-talk, and paid no heed whatever either to my protector or to me.

"It takes but few drops to make the old man merry," said Reese, as though he had read my thoughts; and then he turned from me and commenced conversation with a stylish-looking gentleman whom I had not before seen, and whom he addressed as "Mr. Stiles."

The seats were all occupied and a throng of grinning tatterdemalions crowded the passage-way, when Mr. John Bull entered the ring, wherein a large box with a wire cover had already been placed. Bowing his acknowledgment of certain choice salutations volunteered by the friends around him, he proceeded to cautiously raise the cover of the box, drew forth six live rats by their tails, and threw them upon the floor. The box was then removed, and a terrier, about as large as 'an ordinary cat, was handed into the arena. No sooner did the little monster behold his prey than he uttered a shrill yelp and sprang for the nearest victim. The poor rats could not climb the smooth sides of the ring, and were, therefore, obliged to run for it. Terror-stricken, yet furious, the unhappy animals sprang convulsively into the air, jumped at their foe in sheer despair, or endeavored to hide; but all was in vain, for the terrier had killed them all in a few seconds.

Then were brought up from the cellar a pair of Russian terriers belonging to the two custom-house officers, who began betting noisily at the appearance of their favorites. Nothing could exceed the fury of these little animals when confronting each other. Their eyes turned green with rage and they shrieked with concentrated passion. For a moment they were held within a few feet of contact, and then, when the word was given and the men loosened their holds, the creatures flew together in conflict dire. The noise was terrific, and both animals were torn out of all canine semblance; but, from what I could understand of the violent conversation about me, the combat was not considered satisfactory. Nor, indeed, were two others, between additional terriers, which followed; but popular disappointment was to be atoned for at last.

The great mastiff from the vault was brought up, and opposed to him was a huge and ferocious white bull-dog. Four muscular ruffians were required to hold each brute; and it was while all heads were stretched forward to survey these fierce beasts, that the person whom I had heard addressed as "Mr. Stiles" suddenly stood upright on his seat and called general attention to himself by a loud "Ahem!"

"Fellow-citizens!" called this gentleman, graciously removing his rakish slouched hat and revealing a head of hair dressed with particular reference to a knowing curl over the middle of the forehead, — "Fellow-citizens, I am here this evening to represent that tried and trusty friend of honest labor, General Cringer."

The enunciation of this last name occasioned a tremendous uproar of savage shouts, and a gentleman whose laundress was evidently unreliable was heard to consign General Cringer to eternal torment as a — something — "old Ebullitionist."

"Ebullitionist!" exclaimed Mr. Stiles, turning in the direction of the voice and caressing a goatee on his chin with a hand rendered noticeable by an enormous ring, — "is my honorable friend off his feed, that he speaks thus? Fellow-citizens, General Cringer is proud to be a member of the glorious old Demolition Party (great cheering), and prouder still to be a friend of our illustrious champion and candidate, the Honorable Mealy O'Murphy. (Overwhelming applause.) This mastiff, here, is Gen. Cringer's, while the bull belongs to that noble and exalted spurner of British Ebullition gold, the Honorable Mealy O'Murphy. (Wild enthusiasm.) Whichever side wins the stakes in the approaching battle will immediately turn them over to our mutual friend, here, John Bull, to furnish free beverages in honor of the workingman's defender."

A tempest of terrific yells greeted this announcement; but one of the nondescripts across the ring made some sort of discontented interrogatory about what I understood to be "Macginnis."

"Ah! very true my amiable jockey," proceeded Mr. Stiles, smiling benignantly. "I nearly forgot that. The truth is, though, that General Cringer, on behalf of that stanch Demolitionist, the Honorable Mealy O'Murphy, has requested Mr. Macginnis to send him, at once, twenty baskets of the best Champagne. Money paid down at once, and wine to be sent when convenient. 'The Mealy O'Murphy Club' are hereby invited to call upon Mr. Macginnis and make sure that the amount has *not* been paid in British gold."

Then followed three tremendous cheers for MacGinnis; and three for General Cringer, and three more for the Honorable Mealy O'Murphy, who would certainly be elected, Reese said, "by a ripping majority."

During this interlude, the nobler brutes in the ring had been struggling like giants with their holders, and defying each other until their eyes looked like clots of glazed blood, and the foam boiled from their cavernous jaws like scum from seething caldrons. The word was given as Mr. Stiles took his seat, and, in an instant, the gnashing gladiators were clinched in a rolling globe of bristling hair. Round and round they flew, howling, yelling, and sending up clouds of hot dust to sparkle in the chandelier, — sometimes both springing clear of the ground in one huge mass, and, again, both dashing against the side of the ring in desperate plunges. Excited to frenzy by the spectacle, the inhuman wretches on the seats stamped, clapped their claw-like hands, and shrieked encouragement to the maddened animals. Quitting his hold on the throat of his adversary, the bull-dog made a ferocious snap at one of the fore-legs of the latter. It was a fatal mistake for him. The dripping fangs of the mastiff sank into his head with a hideous crunching noise, and he folded his exposed fore-leg under him, beyond the teeth of his foe. At this point, the eight men sprang again into the ring, and, seizing each animal by the tail, beat them apart with clubs.

Under the spell of a horrible fascination, and with all the clamor of Pandemonium bursting around me, I was gazing fearfully at the dogs. — their heads shapeless masses of raw flesh, from which their eyes glared with devilish fierceness. — when something brushed quickly between Reese and me, and passed forward through the crowd about Mr. Grey.

"Father! Father!"

Of all sounds in the world, that was the strangest to be heard in such a place. There, where man's deepest degradation found congeniality in the degradation of the last fidelity such fallen humanity can know; where hardihood in wickedness was the only virtue credited, and timidity in crime the only vice avoided. — there, in that amphitheatre of bleeding brutes and viler shapes of men, rang the tenderest sound of home.

At its utterance, every rude tongue about us was instantaneously hushed; and, in a moment more, the silence of the whole room was broken only by the low growling of the dogs. The creatures on the other side of the ring came crawling stealthily as cats toward the spot whence the words had come; and, as those immediately about that spot fell instinctively aside, I wonderingly saw what had occurred.

With head drooping, shoulders bent, and every limb visibly trembling, stood the elder companion of my wretched experiences that night, — a miserable object indeed. Before him, with one little hand upon his nearer arm, and the other holding a bruised and faded accordeon, was a girl, apparently about nine years old, whose young face, upturned to look at him, wore such a look of grieved and loving innocence, as might well give a touch of brute awe to the sinister and misshapen countenances, that had never before, perhaps, been moved to expression, by aught of pure affection.

She was dressed in poor, patched garments; and the discolored straw bonnet on her head was starving poverty's last broken thatch of shelter; yet in the clear dark eyes' fondly reproachful look, from beneath the smooth bands of chestnut hair, and in the pallid face just quivering to the birth of a tear, there was that inward purity made an outward show, which to childhood — and to that alone — gives counterfeit of the angel.

"Father! Father!" Again that word of love and prayer, in accents of childish dismay. She saw only him and the place. "Oh, why are you here? I couldn't, couldn't believe it when they told me. To think you should come, after promising me never to come again to this dreadful place. O father! father!"

He only trembled the more, and seemed to grow older, and shabbier, and more broken down.

"I came home so tired, father. Not hungry, you know,"—she could even spare him there,—"but *so* tired; and you wasn't there. Then I went to Brignoli, and he told me to look for you in this awful, awful place."

A cropped head was thrust forward at her from the crowd, like a snake's, and a grinning, wicked face approached hers. "Give him a tune for his supper," it said, mockingly.

A dozen blows descended upon it in a second, from hands unaccustomed to championing the defenceless; and, with fierce oaths, a score of his fellows hurled him to the ground, bleeding and insensible.

The clear, sad eyes never moved their glance from the bowed gray hairs.

"Come with me, father! I know you'll come. Don't be afraid. I'm not a bit hungry. Come!"

They all stood silently aside to let them pass; the child leading the tottering old man, and Reese and I as silently following.

We watched, and went near them, until, in the same speechless tenderness and stricken dependence, they disappeared through the low door, beneath the tumbling stoop; and then my protector and I climbed the broken ladder, and went on up to our loft, while yet the drunken revelries and crimes of Rack-and-Ruin Row made the night's blackness darker to the stars.

<hr>

CHAPTER XXIV.

APRIL GREY.

FEELING like one who had awakened unrefreshed from a wild and feverish dream, I moped so abstractedly next morning that my companion took me to task for it with some temper.

"Glibun, are you sick, or what ails you?" he asked, after various attempts to draw me into frivolous conversation. "You're as dull to-day as a Sunday in Lent. What are you thinking about?"

"I am sorry I went with you last night," I replied, defiantly. "It was no place for a boy like me, and I'll never go again."

"That's the gratitude I get for not leaving you here alone with the rats all the evening," said Reese.

"I'm not half as much afraid of the rats as I was of those horrid men and dogs," returned I, very earnestly; "and I shouldn't think you'd want to go there yourself."

"I went because I didn't know what else to do," he answered, vehemently. "I'd have cut my throat if I hadn't gone where I couldn't think; for I was that blue,—you understand?—last night, that I wanted something rough and noisy to keep me up.

Old Hugo is having a harder time of it than I thought he would, and will be tried in a day or two. The police are after the other gipsies, and if they get any witnesses I may have to stay in this hole for months and months. That's bad luck enough to make a better man want to see a dog-fight! I'm sorry I took you, though, and I wish I'd left the old man behind."

"Mr. Reese, what has Hugo done?"

"Done?" muttered he, sullenly; "why, he offered a bad ten-dollar bill in mistake for a good one, and he got the bill of me. Now you know."

Yes, I vaguely knew that there must have been something wrong in the act, though not comprehending its criminality.

"Is that all?" I inquired, with all innocence.

The man laughed. "That was ALL, Little Breeches; and quite enough, too, as you'll find out when you're older. Hugo is Anita's father, you know. Poor Anita!"

He sighed heavily as he named her, and leaned back in his chair. "What'll become of her, and me, and all my acquaintances, Heaven only knows."

It came into my head to say, "Why don't you run away,—away off, somewhere? I'll go with you."

"I believe you would," exclaimed Reese, with the kindest smile he had ever given me. "You're a good fellow, Glibun. You, and the girl, and the dog, are the only creatures I've cared for in many a year. I wish I'd been as innocent as you when I was at your age; but I was a young scamp. I ran away from my father and little sister, and went to sea as a cabin-boy on one of Astor's ships. The voyage was a long one, and when I got to the other side of the ocean I shipped in another vessel for China. When I reached home at last, my father, who was a very stern man, refused to either see me, or have me at home, but offered, through an uncle of mine, with whom I stopped, to send me to boarding-school and college. Uncle persuaded me to accept, and for four years I stuck to my education, and never once saw home. Finally, the old man wrote me his forgiveness, and I was making ready to go back to him, when I fell into the company of some wild fellows, who persuaded me to gamble for just one evening. I lost everything, of course, and got awfully in debt. I didn't know what to do then; and while I was thinking how to get the money from my father, without telling him what it was for, news came that he had died suddenly of apoplexy. . . . I never saw home again. Somehow it came into my head that I had in some way hastened the old man's end, and that idea made a reckless scamp of me. My sister and uncle both wrote to me, but I never answered them. I was bewildered with an exaggerated sense of guilt, though I never really comprehended what I had done to deserve such a hard name as that. . . . The gambling debt had to be paid, so I started off suddenly to

New York, assumed false hair, whiskers, and a false name, and gambled again. I paid my debt, and then struck for the West. How I did drift about there!—A gambler, clerk on a steamboat, book-keeper in a counting-house, gambler again, beggar!—Back here again, and croupier in a gambling-house. My uncle and sister probably thought I had gone off to sea again in some wild freak, for some one of my name was reported in the papers as having fled from New Haven on account of a gambling difficulty, and shipped from Boston for Hamburg. It's quite as well they never tried to hunt me up, for the perverse devil that took possession of me in my very infancy made me of a different stuff from them. . . . A still worse devil, and a handsome one, gained the sympathy of my familiar demon at last, and led me into the very fine art of making money without labor, and blessing mankind with it through the medium of a gang of vagabond gipsies. Well, here I am."

He said all this in a monotonous, hurrying way, as though rehearsing it by rote; with his hands clasped behind his head and his eyes staring vaguely across the loft at nothing.

The average man of any class, as my maturer observations have taught me to believe, is always either better, or worse, than he appears to others. Vice, whether much, or little, invariably exaggerates itself in the language and actions of life; while virtue as invariably has a tendency, in its every degree, to conceal its greater proportions from the merely passive senses.

Instinct (which is God and nature) has a far keener eye than reason (which is man and civilization) for the true moral condition in either case; and I, by my childish instinct, finally accepted the changeable being in whose charge I so strangely found myself, as one not so entirely vicious as he appeared.

If I did not respect, I certainly felt a kind of affection for him; and enough of his hurried and evidently imperfect story suited my comprehension to give my feelings toward him a warmer glow of kindness.

"Where was your mother, Mr. Reese?" I asked, after a brief silence.

"In heaven," said he, passing a hand over his forehead with an air of weariness. "She died soon after I was born."

"So did mine," I said, less mindful of grammatical construction than of a new bond of sympathy.

"So I've understood,"—and he eyed me intently; "we're alike that far. You've had a queer time of it, too; and that may account for the sort of elder-brother feeling which has all along been mysteriously prompting me to tell you all about myself. With all your rough usage, Glibun, haven't you ever felt a sort of castaway inclination to do bad things, just because you didn't have any one to praise you for doing good?"

"Oh, no! I never did," was my ready answer. The reason he gave for evil-doing had never even occurred to me.

"Well," he went on, "that has been the way with me, I think. To tell the truth, though, I don't know much about myself. I must be a hard case; and yet, whatever I've done has always seemed as though set for the express purpose of catching me."

He got up from the seat, sighed, stared at the floor for a moment, and then tossed his hat upon his head with an entire change of manner.

"Come down and scrape an acquaintance with Grey's little girl," he said, briskly.— "Toss the scraps to Mr. Mugses, and never mind putting the things into the cupboard now. I'm going to Old Brignoli's, and I'll leave you on the way. Lively's the word. Hurry up."

To see more of that little girl was what I greatly desired, and the mention of her drove everything else from my mind. With alacrity I donned my cap, and we went down the ladder in closer accord than ever.

Followed by a retinue of grotesque children, who swarmed on our trail by twos and threes from nearly every foul nest of each story, my protector and I reached the main hall, at the head of such an inconvenient procession, that hard words and threatened blows were necessary to drive it back. As the ragged and screaming little parodies of childhood went scattering up the creaking staircase, or scrambled into the nearest doorways, Reese guided me down a flight of steps leading, as I supposed, to a cellar. My supposition, however, was inaccurate, for we presently stood in another hall, darker and more dangerous than the one above it. Advancing toward the end, where a door with a broken light over it was dimly observable, we found another door near it, in the right-hand wall, and this my protector pushed open without ceremony.

The room thus revealed to me was defined by the light from two quite clean windows, the latter being curtained with two old newspapers, beneath the bottoms of which could be seen the naked, or fearfully slip-shod feet of such Cow Bayites as passed upon the street. The interior looked fairly spacious after the rows of small dens upstairs, and in opposite corners were straw-mattresses spread upon the bare floor. There were also two clumsy wooden chairs, a pine table, a wash-tub, and a curtain of pinned newspapers to partly conceal one of the bed-places; but what especially caught my attention was that one of the mattresses on which appeared the prostrate figure of Mr. Grey.

"Is he dead?" whispered I, drawing back.

"Nonsense! Of course not," was my companion's answer, in a repressed voice; "don't you hear him breathing?"

Yes; I could hear that, then; and I also heard a rustling of the paper curtain across the opposite corner.

"Good-morning, little woman; I've brought

you a beau," said Reese, in a higher tone; and, as I looked in the direction to which the salutation was addressed, I saw the little accordeon-player coming tranquilly out from behind the suspended journals. With a quick glance toward her father, as though to make sure that he had not been aroused, she came noiselessly to us.

"Miss Grey," whispered Reese, humoring her evident wish for proper quiet, and at the same time assuming a mock-ceremonious air, "permit me to present my friend, Mr. Avery. I want to leave him here for a short time, while I call on Brignoli."

Notwithstanding the awe inspired in me by the little girl on the preceding night, I had expected to at least feel toward her a modification of that complacent, if not contemptuous, superiority with which I had thus far regarded all the children of the Points; but when she quietly shook one of my hands and gave me an inquiring look with those precociously-thoughtful eyes of hers, I was back again in Mrs. Le Mons' parlor, with Nettie Beeton as my terror.

"You'll get along, I see," said Reese, playfully pushing our heads together; and with that he left us, and I heard him opening the door which led to the street.

Red-hot with a fever of unexpected bashfulness, I stood for several minutes in a sightless and paralyzed state, ready to perspire coldly at the first sound of a voice; but, finding that no such sound came, I took courage to steal a side-look at my new acquaintance. Instead of admiring me, she was gazing earnestly upon the sleeper. Now that she wore no bonnet, her smooth and glossy brown hair, curling at the edges, gave her colorless little face an effect almost ghastly, and her patched frock hung upon her slender figure with a limpness caught from the tomb-like dampness of the room.

Turning my look from her to her father, with a sort of chilled sensation, I was conscious that *she* had turned to observe *me* again, and my desperate effort thereupon to appear gravely unconcerned, probably gave my countenance an expression of sinister scepticism.

"He *isn't!*" she said.

I shuffled my feet, smiled feebly, and squinted in a futile attempt to meet her eye boldly.

"He is NOT!" she repeated, stamping angrily with one of her bare feet; "and you ought to be ashamed to think so, too!"

Her manner was so injurious that despair gave me strength to speak at last.

"Isn't what?" I asked.

"My father *isn't* drunk!" she said, with sharper vehemence than before.

"I know that," returned I, forgetting diffidence in my haste to clear myself; "I know that. He's only asleep, because he's tired."

I looked straight at her then, and could tell, from the lessening sparkle of her eyes, and the relaxing of her arms, how excited she must have been while speaking.

"Does father know you?" asked she, looking from me to him, very sorrowfully, I thought.

"Oh, yes, indeed; he's been up in our room."

I was becoming quite confident again, and spoke more loudly than was prudent.

"Hush-h!" was her quick reproof. "Come over here and sit on these chairs, where we won't wake him."

We went on tiptoe to the chairs, which stood along the wall near the farther window, and took our respective seats like a couple of stealthy and diminished lovers; the proceeding giving me a feeling of subtle importance as though I were assisting in some momentous work of meritorious secrecy.

"How did *you* come to the Bay?" was the first question put to me in my new position.

To which I replied that I had come with Reese; and further explained that we had both come from a gipsy camp.

"This is such an awful place for children!" moralized my companion, with an air of having, possibly, at some remote age, been a child herself. Whereat my assurance went down again, and I couldn't help wriggling in my chair like a very little boy.

"My name's Avery," chattered I, with a hysterical consciousness that I was talking like a baby. "What's your name?"

"April Grey."

Of course I grinned at the idea of a girl being named after a month; but her surprised look restored me to gravity in a moment.

"Who gave you that name?" I inquired.

"Father, I b'lieve."

"Why, where's your mother?"

"Dead."

I had been playing with one of her hands, in my infantile infatuation; rubbing mine over it and twisting the soft, dingy fingers across each other; but, as she spoke that word, I looked into her eyes with a full restoration of my oldest self, and put an arm about her, just as naturally as I had before acted the babe.

"My mother's dead, too," were the words of mine which instantly ended her first and last attempt to get free.

"Haven't you got no father?"

I hesitated. Miserable thoughts thronged thick upon me. I had been warned to say nothing of him.

"I've got a father," I said, vaguely unhappy for the moment; "but I mustn't talk about him."

"Why, how queer that is!" exclaimed the little girl, picking at the sleeve of my coat, and smiling animatedly. "I love to talk about *my* father, ever so much. Only, I can't often find any one to talk to. They're such dreadful people here! They say father gets drunk; when he don't! But sometimes they call him 'the Count,' —that's a great name, you know,—and treat him real good, because he's English. Ah, there was one man, though, that used to live here when we lived upstairs, and he'd talk real nice to me about father. He used to write for Sunday papers; and he gave me that accordeon, now, too, and showed me how to play on it — he did. He was a real nice man and used to read us his stories. Oh, they were so beautiful! Me and father were near being so sorry, too, when he, now, died. We didn't see him for a week; and he starved to death right in this room."

The smile with which she related this catastrophe struck me aghast.

"'Near being sorry?'" echoed I, with a start.

"Oh, yes," continued April Grey, with the same bright air; "we came so near being sorry; but then father said, now, that it was happy for him to be dead out of here, and if it was happy, you know, we ought to feel glad. Me and father's all the time wanting to die, so bad."

I stared at her in earnest this time, and half withdrew my arm. To hear her talk in that way, as though she had been speaking pleasantly of some inclination of the most ordinary kind, was too unnatural. The pretty light in her eyes made me replace my arm quickly enough, but I involuntarily exclaimed, —

"You must be crazy!"

"I aint, neither," she retorted, with the utmost composure. "Father often says that he only wants to die, and I want to do what he does. Sometimes, now, we're so hungry; and sometimes so cold; and oh, they're such dreadful people here! Besides, mother died."

Utterly unable to comprehend this state of things, and feeling decidedly uncomfortable thereat, I made a bold push for a change of argument.

"What makes him sleep in the daytime?"

With the sorrowful expression coming back to her face again, she looked down and spoke slowly, —

"He's so tired. We sat and talked almost all night. He asked me where I'd been, and who I'd seen, and if anybody had been ugly to me; and when I showed him how much I'd made, he cried right out and wished he was dead. He always does that when I come home. Aint it strange?"

"Yes." I knew not what else to say.

"Why does he?"

I gave it as my deliberate opinion, that it must be "because something hurt him."

"He puts his hand here when he says it," said April Grey, placing one of her own hands against her heart. "I'm afraid it hurts him there. He used to like me to play the accordeon before I commenced, now, to go out; but he hates it now, and I have to go and hide it away as soon as I come home. Aint it strange?"

Her repetition of this question, and the half-eager look with which she accompanied it, made me fancy that she hoped for some answer more sympathetic than a mere affirmative.

"I don't believe he likes to have you go out and play," said I, very sagely, "and I shouldn't think you'd do it."

"Why, we'd starve if I didn't, you know!" exclaimed the little girl, releasing herself from my arm by standing up. "Father used to make a little by cutting kindling-wood for some Irishmen in Little Water Street; but he got sick one day, and they hired somebody else. He used to help the man in this room, sometimes, to write his stories, and he had something for that; but it was only a little. My father can write — oh! like anything. He's got a whole lot of paper written on, put away in a cigar-box under his bed over there."

"Is it a story?" asked I, with intense interest.

"Oh, no!" returned she, decisively.

I was disappointed, and wished to be informed what it was, then.

"I don't know," she replied, shaking her head; "but I know that it aint, now, a story. When the man wrote stories, he'd always scratch his head a good deal, and look up to the wall as if he felt sick; and I saw father when he was writing that in the box, and he only groaned sometimes."

Something in this description put it into my head, — I know not why, — that his work must have been poetry, and I said so.

She seemed to think there might be something in this suggestion, and was apparently turning it over in her mind preparatory to remarking upon it, when a noise in the direction of the sleeper made both of us look that way; and I had barely time to notice that the old man was staring broadly at us, before the little girl was at his side and bending listfully over him.

"He! What's he doing here?"

Propping himself upon an elbow, he fixed his eyes intently on me and spoke in a quick, startled way.

"It's Avery, father, — Mr. Reese's boy. Mr. Reese left him here while he, now, went out."

"Yes, yes, I recollect," murmured he, turning his gaze from me to her. "Another child brought here to be — Well, no matter, no matter."

"Father, don't you want something to eat?"

"No, dear, not now. Wait awhile. That boy was with me last night, wasn't he?"

"Yes, Mr. Grey," said I, going to April's side, and willing to make myself agreeable; "I was with you and Mr. Reese to see the dogs. I wish I hadn't gone, though, and I'm never going again."

He had wearily gained his feet, and looked, with his hair and dress disordered, more haggard and shabby than ever.

"Never going again?" he said after me, though with his eyes still on his child. "I've said that fifty times, — fifty times; and where was I again last night! Ah, I'm an old man, though; — but" — turning quickly upon me, in sudden excitement —

"but he'll be old, yet, in the same way that I'm old; and then what will he do to forget what he is, but go there again! and again! and again!"

"O father!" exclaimed the little girl, bursting into tears, "I thought you wasn't going to be unhappy any more."

That was enough. In a moment he was dragging her after him in a wild and grotesque dance about the room, to my unspeakable astonishment and dismay.

"All a joke, my lass," he sang. "My heart is as light as a feather; I hope it may never be sad. I'm going to be married to-morrow, and won't you have me, pretty lad? Come, boy, fly around, fly a-r-oun-d!"

Striking against one of the chairs in his last crazy whirl, he staggered, swung half-round, and fell panting into the seat, with his child's flushed face pressed close to his breast.

"There, there, there;" and one trembling hand patted her head; "I'm all right now, and ready for that breakfast."

"You aint angry at me, father?" came in smothered tones from the lips hidden in his ragged waistcoat.

He was not angry, — no, not he; and to prove his perfect amiability, he seized a lock of her hair with his teeth (which were perfectly sound and handsome) and pretended to pull it. Not satisfied with that proof of incorrigible cheerfulness, he briskly swayed himself, and her with him, from side to side, and broke hoarsely forth with the song, —

> "Giles Scroggins courted Molly Brown,
>   Right fol de iddle dol de da;
> The fairest maid in all the town,
>   Right fol de iddle dol de da;
> The day they were to have been wed,
> Fate's scissors cut poor Giles's thread,
> And they could not be mar-ri-ed,
>   Right fol de iddle dol de da."

The execution of this melody in husky, cracked tones, the while its singer wore a smile frightful to behold, and turned eyes, yet bloodshot with recent sleep, in every direction, decided me to get out of such perplexing company as soon as possible. I had an indistinct idea that Mr. Grey was acting a part; but, as I was not mature enough to grasp its purpose, my faint enlightenment only served to make my departure the more willing. In a manner which could not have been strikingly graceful, I edged away to the door, and was about to make a precipitate retreat therefrom into the hall, when a patter of feet caused me to pause, and look back over my shoulder. April Grey had escaped from her father, who, with face still smiling, and eyes rolling, was half-humming, half-singing another verse, evidently unconscious of anything save his own hysterical self-delusion. With a scared flush on her cheeks, she came to where I stood, and pushed me into the hall with both her hands.

"He must be happy when he does in that way," she whispered; "but you'd better go 'way, because it worries him to see people in the room. — Yes, father, I'm coming" — he had called her — "in a minute! Come again, Avery."

Before her hurried words had fairly entered into my comprehension, she was back in the room and had shut me out in the dark entry. Simultaneously I heard the harsh singing again, as though the miserable father could not sufficiently mock the choking protests of his own breaking heart.

Eager to reach the open air and sunlight, I tried the door with the broken sash over it; and, as it yielded, I emerged upon a trodden ash-heap directly under the old wooden stoop of the house. A few steps farther took me to the pavement; and here, as I paused to look about me before going up the hind-legs of the step-ladder, I saw standing upon the opposite curb, with back toward me, a figure that seemed familiar. It was that of a man, carrying in one hand an iron pot filled with corn, and in the other a portable furnace ablaze with charcoal. As I looked, and tried to recollect, he turned, caught sight of me, and was out of sight down an adjacent alley-way in less time than it takes to tell of it.

Old Yaller!

I stood rooted to the spot, staring helplessly at the alley entrance, and unmindful of the remarks my appearance had begun to excite among the street and window population of Rack-and-Ruin Row. I was thus standing when Reese found me.

"Why, Glibun, how come you here? I thought you were to stay in Grey's room."

"I've seen Old Yaller — from Mr. Birch's," was all I could answer.

"And I," said Reese, moodily, "have seen that spy, Juan, skulking out of Brignoli's, like a smoked ghost. There's mischief in the wind."

<hr>

CHAPTER XXV.

SOCRATES AND CHARMIDAS.

THE aristocracy of trade, no less than that of society, requires a certain politic pomp of outward circumstance to command such continual deference and support from serviceable inferiors as mere intrinsical superiority might not always be overpowering enough to secure. The genius of mercantile progression, with a sharp eye to the more artful uses of ostentation and domiciliary display in private life, demands of the rising American merchant an ambitious "Establishment" at the earliest possible day after he has fairly graduated in business above the primitive shop and secondary store. To this demand he must accede with shrewd alacrity, or forfeit a goodly share of profitable consequence before trading mankind; for a towering front of marble, or brown-stone, will draw throngs of obsequious customers to the counters of yesterday's humble shopman, while the stateliest old patrician of fifty years' fame in dynastic dry-good operations, finds comparatively few to do him remunerative reverence in the ancient, one-story warehouse.

The ponderous firm of Goodman & Co., wisely appreciating and adopting this brilliant principle in the philosophy of money-making, had formed of their Establishment an imposing temple of Mercury, wherein the simple-minded children of Retail could not sufficiently offer auriferous sacrifice to imperious and pompous Wholesale. Though built of bricks, those bricks were of that intensely red, fresh hue which unanswerably assert the very highest aristocracy of special kilns. Furthermore, the windows were of plate glass all the way up, and beamed in the sun like the spectacles of some princely middle-aged gentleman, conspicuous for the severely simple elegance of his general attire. In short, the Establishment was imposing; an Establishment conferring unmistakable honor upon him who, with a proper sense of his own unworthiness, left his "orders" there; an Establishment where salesmen could be solemnly supercilious without lacking the justification of princely surroundings.

At least one member of the mighty firm, however, was thus ostentatious only as a tradesman. Beyond the impressive outward state of his counting-room, the grave senior depended solely upon the personal magnetism of the innate and hereditary Gentleman, to maintain for him the social ascendancy belonging of right to his private station.

Only in point of locality was there anything of current fashion in the home of Mr. Goodman. It stood on Broadway, opposite Union Park, where it was, at that time, considered fashionable to reside; nor were its external appointments substantially inferior to those of its neighbors; but the plain stone stoop had simple iron railings where other mercantile stepping-stones were flanked with lions, or dogs in metal; its knob, bell-pull, and door-plate were of polished brass, unglorified with the prevalent silver-plate; its three tiers of windows were plain in their copings as those of a prison; and the barouche which made its appearance before the door at three o'clock on every clear afternoon was distinguishable from a hack only in perfection of varnish, neatness of upholstery, and the scrupulous polish of horses and driver.

Two handsome elms on the edge of the sidewalk, and a square patch of lawn grass between the area railings and the basement windows, subdued the house to a retiring look almost rural; yet, withal, the place had a substantial, hereditary air, from which the philosophical beholder would argue something like a pride above the tawdry, architectural freaks of vulgar Yesterday.

Nor was the interior of the building more ostentatious than its sober front. The doors were of dark mahogany, as was most of the furniture, also; the mantles of black marble bore no fanciful sculpture; the chandeliers held their glass lustres in the simplest shapes consistent with requisite reflection of light; carpets and curtains carried ornament no farther than the extent of use; and throughout rooms and halls reigned such studied modulation of toning as might have been dedicated to the spirit of ancestors regal in the quieter dignities.

The master of the scene was worthy of it in all the essentials of unassuming refinement; and an impressive exemplar was he of the American merchant-gentleman. as he stood in his library, with one hand resting upon a heavy, vellum-covered writing-table, and the other tipping an imaginary hat in a passive bow of assent. The venerable house-keeper, Mrs. Keyes, might well experience a pleasant complacency on receiving approval, thus courteously signified, from an employer so unexceptionable in bearing; for, with his fine, bold features, his graying dark hair, his portly form, his speckless black attire, and his neatly-ruffled bosom and wristbands, Mr. Goodman was honor itself.

The noble name of gentleman is often but a concession of courtesy; more frequently an imperious assumption by virtue of the higher social usages; and, in rare instances, an honest right, founded upon personal possession of those natural, as well as those acquired, qualities which, only, can fully justify it. Each class of mankind has its own ideal of the perfect gentleman, who, to each, is a supposititious embodiment of certain refined characteristics, and refining advantages of worldly circumstances, which it knows itself, in the aggregate, not to possess. All these ideals, however, varied and even fantastical as they may be regarding the details of superficial manner and domiciliation, have at least two or three points in common, when the especial and exceptional traits of natural character associated with the name are considered. By all — boors and scholars alike — the gentleman is gifted with an understanding and use of money, neither profligate nor sordid; with such a perpetual and chivalrous respect for women as remains, like some continuative incense, from the holiest intensity of mother-love; and with that subtle, indescribable air of individual superiority which seems an involuntary radiation of a lofty instinct, rather than a result of any process in reasoning.*

In his use of wealth, respect for women, and commanding aspect, Mr. Goodman was a gentleman according to any ideal. His ancestors, the colonial Goetmans, who held all Terrapin Island by grant from the Dutch, were possessors of the genuine *sangre azul;* and their last descendant in a direct line (the Von Rumsellers being somewhat *off* the direct line) could not well be otherwise than a model of unquestionable gentility.

* Be it remembered that the term "Gentleman," as a title, belongs especially to merchants.

"Yes, Mrs. Keyes," said he, to the admiring house-keeper, "I give my consent with pleasure. Your son has been so faithful to all his duties in my Establishment, that he will carry with him, to his new station, the respect of his fellow-clerks, no less than the commendation of his recent employers. The offer of this chief-clerkship comes to him, if I understand you, from Havana?"

"From Havana, sir; from an English merchant there," replied the old lady, earnestly. "My cousin, the packet captain, heard of the place, on his last trip, sir, and applied for it for my son. You know Storrs is delicate, Mr. Goodman, and Havana might do him good. I was only afraid, sir, that you might think it ungrateful in him to change."

"By no means, madam," said Mr. Goodman, with a pleasant smile. "Both for your sake and his own I am glad that he has such a favorable opportunity to try the effect of a tropical climate. Storrs Keyes has conducted himself uniformly well in my employ, and my partner and I will see to it that he is suitably provided for his departure."

"I thank you, sir, a thousand times, I'm sure. I do, indeed, Mr. Goodman."

Another bow, wave of the hand, and smile, from the senior of the firm.

"You will be good enough to see that I am not disturbed, Mrs. Keyes, in my interview with the gentleman whom I am momentarily expecting. Let him be shown up here, if you please, and tell William that he is to take any other visitor into the parlor."

"Yes, Mr. Goodman," replied the idolatrous house-keeper; and, in a state of unutterable gratification, she reverentially withdrew from the room.

As the merchant resumed his comfortable arm-chair, the indulgent smile faded from his face into a gravity which might have been either a reminiscence of the stately gloom of the Broadway Establishment, or of a shadow brooding nearer home. With hands clasped before him, and forefingers pressed against his lips, he travelled slowly with his eyes along the great rows of shelved volumes on the walls, as though seeking temporary company in their familiar forms and titles.

Many another lonely man, unable to enjoy that strangely soothing companionship for the solitary which nature gives in the murmuring and music of the woods, has found in his library a forest as tranquillizing to the fevered mind, and discovered between its unfading leaves the birds that make tenderest music for the soul.

But the merchant sought other company in that same forest of the mind; and, in reaching it by a circuit of its lesser rivals, he followed the example of one who should involuntarily torment his own eagerness to look again upon the thing he best loved, by lingering mechanically over every object on the way. Right before him, in an interval between two of the polished mahogany bookcases, hung a full-length portrait of a graceful woman, framed in gilt and ebony.

There she stood, in the nearest approximation to bodily reproduction that art could achieve; her golden hair hanging in negligent curls about a head moulded to the most delicate type of the feminine oval; her mild hazel eyes and regular features expressing that intelligent gentleness which is the divinest intellectuality of woman; and her plain dress of ashen silk, clothing a form stately with all dignity, and ripe in every womanly charm.

Her life, her monument, her resurrection, were all in that silent picture for the merchant's eye; and if the gravity of his countenance grew profounder as he finally fixed his glance full upon what only He could see, it also took the transparency of a shadow with untroubled waters for its resting-place. The time was past when his heart would wildly throb, and his breath come brokenly as he gazed there; the finite of mortality's concentrate storm had lulled into the infinite of immortality's reflective calm; and, as the ruddy sunlight of that hazy October afternoon fell across the portrait on the wall, he saw in the radiance death's symbol when the point and not the hilt was toward his vision, and was touched with the night only as it verged most closely and tranquilly upon the eternal morning wherein — beyond the peaceful glory of the dawn between — he knew his wife again.

This world — the poor relation of the other — is ever treading upon the heels of the world to come, for patronage or alms; and the beautiful death some men may die in silent communings with eternity has a damnable resurrection in the first reactionary contact with beggar earth. While yet the merchant lingered with his earliest love in her other home, a knock at a door turned heaven into a library and an angel into an oil painting. What further celestial illusion remained was dispelled summarily by the entrance of a servant attired like a sexton, who announced, —

"General Cringer!"

The face of Mr. Goodman lost its serenity at the sound, and was occupied for an instant by a look of resentment; but, before the visitor had entered the room, the merchant was his every-day self again and arose to the greeting with a countenance expressive of naught but dignified hospitality.

"General Cringer," he said, extending his hand, while the servant placed a chair, "allow me to acknowledge my obligations for your politeness in giving me this interview informally and in my own house. I am aware that such accommodation is scarcely in accordance with high political usage."

"Say no more on that point, my dear sir," responded the great man, vigorously shaking the extended hand, and affably accepting the chair. "I take pleasure, sir, I assure you, in meeting Mr. Goodman wherever and whenever he may appoint."

The merchant bowed. "I trust, General

Cringer, that you are well, and find the current of public events congenial to your views and interests."

The General sat very upright and coughed an important cough behind the glove which he had not yet taken off. "Ill health, Mr. Goodman," he remarked with dignity, "is what I seldom have to complain of,—permit me to lay my cane aside, and excuse my forgetfulness in bringing it into the room,—and public events can hardly be expected to exactly follow the wishes of an humble private citizen like myself."

"Still, General, it is to be hoped that the events mentioned indicate nothing seriously averse to the ultimate official elevation of a private citizen who has so long and arduously furthered the political aspirations of others."

The merchant said this with a gracious suavity of manner, putting it beyond suspicion of being the question a vulgarly curious person might have made it.

"It is the usual lot of the citizen thus philanthropical"—and here the General smiled benignantly—"to be the last man thought of when rewards are being distributed; and could I credit myself with the importance you are good enough to describe, my dear sir, I should expect little more than my labor for my pains."

"It is evident, General Cringer, that you have not taken public opinion for your mirror, or you would not so far under-estimate yourself."

"Mr. Goodman, you flatter me. 'Praise from Sir Hubert Stanley!'"

All this was very courtly and subserved politeness to the last degree. It was a fitting prelude to the decanters of generous Burgundy now brought into the room by a second unexceptionable servitor and symmetrically arranged with glasses upon the table.

"General Cringer, you will join me in a toast to a gentleman whose abilities can influence senates and cabinets, even if not possessed by them." And Mr. Goodman indicated the freedom of the wine with a wave of the hand.

"Provided, my dear sir, that it may be followed by a similar pledge to the success of one whose honorable name and numberless noble charities shed a lustre upon the commerce of our republic." And the General bowed impressively over his glass.

This, again, was a neat exchange, strongly suggestive of those affectionate flourishes with which a couple of European potentates greet each other preparatory to seeing which can outwit his well-beloved brother.

Mr. Goodman duly acknowledged the return-compliment, and then, setting aside his glass, assumed a graver look.

"It is some years, General," he said, reflectively, "since you and I met for the last time in a political atmosphere. You may be able to recall the day when you addressed me in the cloak room of the senate chamber, at Albany, in reference to a bill then before the lower house. The bill, as you may remember, provided for the purchase by the State of certain marsh lands as a site for a State Observatory."

"Hem! Well, a—yes, Mr. Goodman. I have some recollection of it," replied the great man, in momentary perturbation. Indeed, he remembered having addressed several other members of the legislature on the same subject; nor had he forgotten what peculiar arguments he used with some of them. "Yes, Mr. Goodman," said he, with a sharp look at the merchant, "I think I do recall the time."

"The bill did not pass," proceeded Mr. Goodman, "owing to certain premature developments of some of the outside means being used in its favor, and the owner of the land remained poor as before. From conscientious motives (I think they were explained to you that day in the cloak room) I voted against the bill, and even spoke against it. What specially reminds me of the circumstance is, that the son of the man who was to have been enriched by that bill, called upon me only yesterday in relation to a mercantile transaction. You know, I presume, that I allude to young Mr. ——, who, by his energy and felicitous manners, has gained for himself a fortune and an enviable social position."

"My dear sir," returned General Cringer, completely restored to his sage and assured self again by the safe turn the topic had taken, "that also reminds me of a circumstance affecting the same brilliant young member of society. I know him,—we all know him,—by name, at least, and he chanced to be named by a lady the other evening at a select social gathering in which I had the pleasure to participate. Different persons made different remarks of friendly eulogy concerning Mr. ——, until it became, as it were, the turn of Mr. Stiles, my secretary, who was also present, to contribute his views. I was surprised, my dear sir"—and, as he spoke, the illustrious man leaned confidentially across the table, and lowered his tone almost to a whisper,—"I was surprised, my dear sir, to see Mr. Stiles shake his head regretfully several times. I was astounded to hear him draw a heavy sigh; and I was deeply pained to hear the words, 'It's a pity he drinks.'"

"Is that unhappy fact so public, then?" exclaimed the merchant, with a look of grieved astonishment. "But, tell me," he added, with some interest, "who is this Mr. Stiles? He must be very familiar with private matters in the higher walks of life, to know what his remark could intimate. I fancied that but few persons besides myself were cognizant of Mr. ——'s unfortunate failing. You are to be congratulated, General, on having a secretary who must, apparently, be remarkably well connected; though I can scarcely approve his publication of another's error, in company."

"I have every reason to believe," returned the General, blandly, "that Mr.

Stiles formerly moved in the highest circles of our metropolis, and that he was, at one time, distinguished for the completeness of his equipage. Reverses of some kind have befallen him, as they might befall any man. I must observe, in his justification, too, my dear sir, that those to whom his words were addressed, are people with whom a secret of the kind may be safely trusted." ·

"I am pleased to hear you say so, General, and shall be happy to know your secretary, Mr. Stiles, on some future occasion. And now, if you please, we will proceed to business."

The General bowed a magnanimous assent, moved his chair nearer, and assumed an expression of mingled importance and beneficence.

"Having been informed," continued Mr. Goodman, "that my partner would not be unwilling to accept the honorable office of Naval Officer, you have been good enough to make him a definite proposition in relation thereto. In the kindest manner you have undertaken to assist — facilitate is your word, if I mistake not — his attainment of the position, by exercise of your personal influence at Washington."

Another bow from the maker of political destinies, — a bow saying more plainly than words, "A mere trifle for me to undertake."

"My partner, General Cringer, authorizes me to say, that he must peremptorily decline being a candidate for political preferment of any description. He sincerely regrets that you should have been misled concerning himself, by the newspapers and popular gossip, and hopes you will credit him with an ample appreciation of your kindness in the matter. His determination, however, is irrevocable."

"Then, sir, there is nothing more to be said about it," observed the General, stiffly. But in the twinkling of an eye he was all affability again, and added, that he could not find it in his heart to be disappointed with anything which should yield him the honor of his present interview.

"You are complimentary, sir." was the response, tinged with as much impatience as good-breeding would allow. "Do not neglect the wine, General, if it is agreeable to you."

"Thank you, thank you, Mr. Goodman; and perhaps I shall do no violence to your political preferences, sir, if I drink to the success of the glorious Ebullition cause?"

"Ebullition!" ejaculated the merchant. "Excuse me, General Cringer, — but I have inferred from the papers that you were acting, generally, with the Demolition party, this fall!"

That same speech, from a less dignified and opulent citizen, would have filled the great soul of Cringer with compassion, and charged his countenance with pity for the speaker's unsophisticated ignorance; but, as it came from the senior of Goodman &

Co., he merely smiled amiably, and took pains to explain.

"Although but an humble citizen, my dear sir, whose political views are of the least possible consequence to the public, I am not unfrequently subjected to gross misconstruction, by partisans, and the popular prints. Engaging, as I do, occasionally, from motives of friendship, or — allow me to say it — patriotism, in an unostentatious facilitation of certain nominations, appointments, or measures, I sometimes find it necessary to consider expediency. To get the right man into office, or to secure the enactment immediately needed by the country, it is at times advisable to seemingly side with former opponents. If to do this is inconsistent and trimming, then I am inconsistent and a trimmer."

"Misconstruction and aspersion are the sure attendants of political eminence, you know, General," said the merchant; "and common minds can seldom grasp the true principle behind the apparently equivocal action. To aspire to anything above the elective franchise is to become the sport of calumny on every vulgar lip, in every ribald newspaper column. For myself, I shun politics, from the polls to the White House, and trouble myself with neither the broils of the cotton farmers of the South, nor the schemes of the iron, corn, and woollen factors of the North. By moral, not political, principle I am an Ebullitionist; and when I say that, I sum up my whole character as a citizen interested in the elections."

"Sir," answered General Cringer, in a surprising glow of sincerity, "you astonish me! Am I to understand that your distaste for party strife extends to an abstinence from voting?"

"I have not visited the polls, sir, in years."

This was said with a coldness of manner indicating that the merchant's distaste also extended to everything in the way of political catechism; but the novelty of a thoroughly-honest emotion, made the General aggressive beyond his wont.

"Then, Mr. Goodman," said he, turning red in the face, — or, perhaps it would be accurate to say, redder in the face, — "Then, Mr. Goodman, you must pardon my freedom of expression when I ask you, upon what possible grounds you can justify your neglect of what is not only the right, but the positive duty, of every American citizen?"

"General Cringer," — and the speaker drew himself up with an air of seriously offended dignity, "it is not my custom to give detailed reasons for any course I may see fit to pursue; nor can I allow myself to answer a question put in those terms."

"I beg your pardon, Mr. Goodman; but your eminence, sir, as a citizen, is the inspiration of whatever extra warmth may have offended you in my language. It seems incredible to me, that the famous and honored senior of Goodman & Co. can esteem it consistent with the duties of his high social, and mercantile position before the community, to neglect the ballot. With all due respect for you, my dear sir, I must still express my surprise."

Gravely, if not sternly, the merchant received this courteous reiteration; yet it was plain to perceive that nothing of contempt mingled with his apparent displeasure.

"Your warmth, sir," said he, "is excusable, for reasons more creditable to your own independence than you allow yourself to state. I must persist, however, in retaining my own conceptions of duty, and exercising my own judgment in their reduction to practice. Your courtesy demands the concession, that, in the abstract, citizenship under a government ostensibly of the whole people, like ours, involves the duty to govern infinitessimally,—that is, to vote; but, sir, when a visit to the polls compels even a temporary sacrifice of all self-respect; when it demands of a gentleman not only a hypocritical pretence that he reposes faith in the integrity of the American ballot-box, but also a voluntary surrender of himself to a political equality with the refuse of the bar-room and the vilest drainings from the ignorance and crime of foreign countries, I can only look upon it as, at best, a countenancing of notorious frauds upon the nation; and, at worst, as a mercenary concession to the most turbulent agrarianism of the hydra-headed mob. What Thucydides has said of the old factions in Greece is equally true of our own corrupt political tribes; the baser sort advance their schemes with such unscrupulous violence and intimidating appeals to mob passion, that it is only left for the intelligent and self-respecting few to abstain altogether from the defilement of contact in a hopeless battle."

At mention of the Athenian historian, General Cringer wagged his head profoundly, as though seriously baffled by such testimony from the disciple of Anaxagoras. There was in his expression of face, however, a certain hurried vagueness, calculated to cast some suspicion upon his classical knowledge. The merchant noticed this; at first with gentlemanly compunction for having availed himself of an assistance not common to his guest; and then with a sense of the ludicrous, which at once restored him to his usual kindly serenity. In fact, he was inclined to be the milder once more, from observing that the great man before him betrayed a decidedly nervous uneasiness under his denunciation of corrupt political customs.

But if General Cringer recoiled from Thucydides and the imputation upon the ballot-box and on Demolitionism, he was still sufficiently in possession of his ordinary acuteness to perceive that there was more decision of manner than of meaning in what was being said. Quick to improve this perception, and nettled at his own momentary discomposure, he returned to the attack with spirit.

"Mr. Goodman, you have been plain with me, and I shall take the liberty of being as straightforward with you. Your reasoning is, perhaps, satisfactory to yourself; but to me it sounds like a compromise with duty for the sake of personal comfort. If the political condition is what you suppose it to be, the commonest patriotic instinct should induce you, and all men of your high and influential position, to give the full weight and force of the highest respectability in society to the practical reformation of the abuses you so contemptuously name. I say their *practical* reformation, meaning that you should work in the only practical way. It is because you and your class refuse to protect the ballot-box with your ballots, that its integrity is violated. If it contains only the votes of human cattle too ignorant or too mercenary to vote otherwise than as they are misled, or bribed, what abuse *can* there be of it in contravention of any pure intent? It is because you and your class refuse to appear at the polls on election day, that groggeries and European exportation have it all their own way. I regret to differ so widely from a gentleman of your eminence and high character, Mr. Goodman, but I cannot, honestly, do otherwise."

He was preparing to arise from his chair, expecting such lofty resentment of his plain-speaking as would compel him to withdraw with what ceremonious politeness he might. Great, then, was his surprise, when the merchant reached across the table and shook him cordially by the hand.

"General Cringer," cried Mr. Goodman, "I honor you for your sentiments. To hear you utter them with such unmistakable earnestness is the strongest proof I could have of the hasty injustice of *some* of my prejudices, at least. The theory of our government is surpassingly noble. In the idea of a vast people appealed to, to govern themselves, to submit only to such restraints of law and office as their own intelligence and moral sense may choose to impose, there is a majesty far above that of kings. Believe me, General, I devoutly admire the simple grandeur of the system, and appreciate the real nobility of being an enfranchised citizen under it,—*but*, I fear that the theory is in advance of civilization; that the idea is too refined for the still-prevailing grossness of mankind; that the system is based upon a too-exalted estimate of humanity's aggregate truth to its own best interests. This view of the matter, however, is no key to my avoidance of politics during a few past years; for the latter I have a reason less flavored with sophistry than the argument you have already heard. Shall I give it to you?"

"My dear sir," responded General Cringer, in his blandest manner, "I shall feel honored by any confidence you may repose in me."

For the first time during the interview, Mr. Goodman turned his eyes to the portrait. There he let them rest a moment, and then, with perfect quietness of demeanor, proceeded,—

"On returning with Mrs. Goodman from our first visit to Europe, where we had near friends, I found political excitement running high by reason of an impending presidential election, and, for the first time in my life, allowed myself to be drawn into the ranks of party. Shortly afterwards, partly to please my beloved wife and friends, and partly because the common infatuation of politics was beginning to take hold on me, I accepted a nomination for the legislature. I was elected, sir, and went to Albany, where, as you may remember, I had the pleasure of meeting you for the first time."

The general bowed and scratched his nose.

"Mrs. Goodman, as I have already intimated, had been eager for my election. Her affectionate pride in me took the form"—and here the merchant smiled sadly toward the picture—"of an implicit faith in my capacities for distinguished public office; and, in her tender solicitude for my success, she thought not of herself. I had been in Albany but a short time when I learned, through a friend from the city, that my wife was ailing; and, although she had carefully refrained from any mention of it in her letters, I was seized with the idea that some serious peril menaced her, and hastened back to the city with all possible speed. She was surprised, almost provoked, at my return, for she knew that an important bill was before the legislature, and had been gleefully anticipating a sounding speech from me. She laughed at my apprehensions, assured me that she was in no danger of any other peril than such as good wives love to bear, and insisted that my immediate return to Albany, and that alone, would secure to her the satisfied state of mind most needful for her safety. A lady across the street, she informed me, was likely to become a mother at about the same time with herself, and they had together agreed to keep their husbands out of the way until men's nervousness could no longer drive nurses to distraction. With such badinage, sustained by her physician, she finally made me think my fears imaginary, and ultimately persuaded me to go back to Albany. I went, sir, full of fair hopes for the future, and pleasant dreams of what I was to thank Heaven for when coming home again. Our first-born had died, and if the recollection of it came upon me in moments like an omen, I remembered my wife's clear laugh and healthful bloom again, and was at peace. The bill was delayed for alterations and amendments, but finally came up for decisive action. I was speaking upon it with all the ardor of a political novice, when a page handed me a paper. One glance, and my political career was finished! The paper said: 'Return home at once,' and was signed by the physician. General Cringer, my wife was dead! My boy was dead!"

Again the eyes rested on the portrait, and the politician looked thither, too, with a new comprehension.

"I returned to a home desolate indeed. But for politics she might have gone to sleep in my arms. I thought only of her. When they showed me the poor little marble child I could only look at it in a cold, unemotional way. I was surprised at myself for it, but could not change the feeling. I heard that the lady across the way was dying also, but that *her* child was likely to live. Strange as it may sound, I envied the father that child, while I scarcely thought about my own; so confused were my sensibilities by the blow I had endured. After following my home to the grave,—for the soul of my house had gone out of it forever,—I came hither to live,—here, where you find me. And such, sir, beyond all sophism, is the true explanation of my own death in politics."

General Cringer arose to his feet with something that sounded like a sigh; and, as the widowed and childless father did the same, there appeared to be that sympathy between the unlike men which would oftener awake charity in the upright and better aspirations in the tortuous, could it be oftener evoked by a touch of simple nature.

"Mr. Goodman," said the great politician, extending his hand, "I never had wife or child, but I have the most devoted and single-hearted of sisters. If, as the papers say, I have no soul, I have a heart; and you, my dear sir, have reached it."

The man spoke there. It was seldom he did speak from those tutored lips, and the instance was worth recording.

"In a few months hence I shall go to Europe," said Mr. Goodman, "to be gone for two years, at least. Until then, General, I shall be happy to see you here at any time."

"Sir," said General Cringer, "I shall do myself the honor of profiting by your politeness."

And so they parted. The man of primary meetings, conventions, and lobbies, to be escorted to the street by a monument of a servant, and go forth thence to the great civic duties of Facilitation.

The man of bales, exchange, and princely charities, to sink back into his chair, press his hands against his lips, and gaze steadfastly upon the picture on the wall.

———◆———

CHAPTER XXVI.

ARCHERY MEETING AT MR. SPANYEL'S.

SCANDAL is woman's politics. Give her a grievance to inspire it, a set to be rallied with it, or a rival to be crushed by it, and you shall hear her manipulate that serpent of the tongue with an art known only to the wiliest diplomatists of the other sex.

"Rose," said Miss Flora Spanyel, who was arranging a bouquet, to her sister, who was donning kid gloves before a mirror, "has Miss Terry gone down yet?"

"Yes! yes!—oh, how hideously hateful of these gloves, to be so small at the wrist!" And Rose tried her pretty teeth upon the obdurate Alexandres.

"Well, I *do* think!" exclaimed Miss Flora, petulantly. "If pa will be so utterly absurd with that woman I should think he'd just make her a present of the whole house, and be done with it. She was only Lil's governess when she first came, and had her place; but now she's the fine lady of the house, and ma and I are nobodies. It's too perfectly ridiculous for anything."

"Why, Flo," murmured Rose, still nibbling at the glove, "she's always polite enough to ma; and if she always goes down when there's company, it's because pa insists upon it, you know."

"Pa is the absurdest creature!" continued Flora, with increasing impatience. "To think of his bringing her here without even knowing where she came from last. Who knows but she may be a murderess, or some other ridiculous thing?"

"Don't get mad, Flo,—oh! these abominably horrible gloves!—you know pa thought it was a good sign in her to refuse to say anything about her history. He said that she must have been in different circumstances and had too much pride to speak of them. And Mr. Stiles, too, you know, says he's seen her somewhere in good society."

"Oh, yes," snapped the queen of flowers, "it's very well to quote Mr. Stiles. He may have seen Miss Terry before, but Miss Terry don't trouble herself to show much recollection of him. It's perfectly ridiculous to see her snub him."

That was the speech to make Rose show her thorns. "How utterly absurd! Snub Mr. Stiles! Why, she's only a servant!" And the fair speaker tossed her head in that intense way peculiar to the ladies when they desire an unutterable "Indeed!" to be distinctly understood.

Flora smiled contentedly at this evidence of her dear young sister's conversion, and gave particular attention to an obstinate violet as she resumed the strain,—

"Pa'll go on treating her like a countess, or some other utterly absurd thing, until she *snubs him*, if she *is* a servant. You'll see! She's too good to even look at anybody but Mr. Wynne. I don't believe it would take so very much coaxing to make her give him her two eyes. It's perfectly disgusting!"

"Oh, well; you know, if pa will bow down and worship people that answer advertisements for governesses and won't say anything about themselves, we must expect to be trampled upon. I'm sure Mr. Stiles thinks she's horrid!"

With which tender remark the budding Rose hung a little green wreath upon her back-hair, and could not help simpering to find that it became her so well.

Beautiful flowers in the parterre of the Spanyels! With such soft communings did they put on the last rustling leaves of their toilets, preparatory to blossoming in the full sunshine of one of those graceful festivals of suburban fashion for which we are indebted to the refined example of England's castellated nobility.

For there was an archery meeting at Todeville, in compliment to the British sea-officer, Mr. Lord, and his friend, Mr. Seaman. An innocent and healthy observance in graceful memory of the historical times when the great, great lord's sturdy tenantry followed him to battle as an archer-train.

The spring-time radiance of that afternoon was favorable to the hardy out-door sport, and also exhibited to great advantage the Spanyel "place" and surroundings. Prompted by a taste for the impressive in architecture, Mr. Spanyel had added a cupola to the roof of his house, that the latter might wear a more distinguished air as seen from the road; and he had also placed over his front door, on the sign of the "Spanyel arms," and in various other appropriate places, the escutcheon and crest of the family. Sable, three dogs' heads erased argent were the features of the coat-of-arms, and the crest bore another canine head argent.

"My cousin writes," Mr. Spanyel had remarked to Mrs. Spanyel one day at dinner, "that he has made researches in London, my dear, and obtained our arms. The Spanyels, he says, undoubtedly came over with King Charles."

Where they "came over" from, and with what particular royal "Charles," did not appear; but those unimportant details did not trouble the aristocrat of Todeville, whose first step after receiving the upholsterer's letter was to have his crest immediately engraved upon the head of his cane, on the side of his silver-plated coffee-urn, and upon some hundreds of visiting cards.

In the spring-time radiance, then, the archery guests first noticed the coat-of-arms sign at Hucklebury-on-Harlem, as they came along; next, the cupola; and, finally, the escutcheon. Whereupon, old phrases of admiration were reiterated, old sneers were rewhispered, and the general commentary was of a piece with what high-bred and fashionable people fondly delight to say of each other.

As on the memorable occasion of the *conversazione*, Mr. Spanyel stood before a mantel, and Mrs. Spanyel sat upon a sofa to receive the company; advancing to the centre of the room only upon the arrival of Messieurs Lord and Seaman, in whose especial honor, as before stated, the festival was given. With more or less of the motion of the stanch "John Thomas" still visible in their gait, those naval Britons regarded the brilliant assemblage with marked approval, and were, in turn, surveyed reverently by enough feminine grace and beauty to make even Neptune forget Amphitrite.

Smiling pensively, as in mildly sportive memory of their recent sisterly confidences upstairs, appeared the Misses Flora and Rose, with bouquet and gloves made satisfactory at last. Fashionably languid, yet duly appreciative withal, shone the fair Misses Ilyer, under escort of Luke, junior. Innocently enthusiastic beamed Mrs. Cornelius O'Doricourt Fish, newly introduced to the Spanyels by those dear girls, Carrie and Meeta, who, on their part, had known the Todeville family but a few delicious weeks. Graciously complacent loomed the dowager, Mrs. Purser, from Queen's Place, with the thin, pale, and interesting Reverend Harry Lewyer, lately ordained, to sustain her. Admiringly ecstatic quivered the two Misses Titterly and their indulgent ma, from one of the first families of Hucklebury-on-Harlem. Likewise Miss Keeter, Miss Peller, and Mrs. Heroldun, widow, from the other leading houses of Todeville. To whom might be added, Miss Lily Spanyel, who admired her sisters; Mrs. Barlow Wapples, who came with her husband on the strength of a Spanyel debt for family groceries; and Miss Terry, the governess, whose presence was generally overlooked by a company willing to deport itself after the supposed best *apres-midi* assemblages of Europe.

The gentlemen present, besides those already named, were Mr. Benton Stiles, Mr. Barlow Wapples, and about a dozen young or middle-aged dry goods persons of Mr. Spanyel's acquaintance; all of whom did circulate conversationally among the ladies after the introduction of the Europeans was over, and agreeably assisted the passage of time until lunch should be served.

It could not be denied that the guests were rather numerous for the dimensions of the Spanyel parlor, but there was something of fashionable dissipation in being crowded by well-dressed figures; and the affable head of the family was pleased to experience a certain emphasized sense of social popularity as he complacently surveyed the rustling throng.

From his position of hospitable state before the mantel-piece, he smiled into the ox-like face of the Britanic sea-officer, and lost no time in making that gentleman feel as much at home as he could in this country.

"Your last voyage, I hope, Mr. Lord, was free from the gales we have along the coast in March and April?"

"'Ead winds 'arf the way, Mr. Spanyel, I .assho' yo', hand a 'eavy swell until we parsed the 'ook," was the nautical reply of Mr. Lord, who had rashly undertaken to feel easy in kid gloves, and was quite delirious about the wrists and elbows in consequence.

"Ah, I perceive," observed Mr. Spanyel, gracefully adjusting his eyeglass with the thumb and forefinger of his right hand; "the sort of weather that makes the inner man a trifle quarrelsome with the outer.

Ha! ha! That's where we drylanders have the advantage of you. I think, though, that my family have enough hereditary English in them to stand the sea as well as most people."

"Were your people Hinglish, then?" queried the other, with some signs of respect for his host.

"The Spanyels came over with King Charles, I believe," returned Mr. Spanyel, trying to speak like an ordinary mortal.

"Good gracious, sir!" exclaimed Mr. Lord, greatly excited; "I always thought, ye know, that Miss Spanyel, ye know, and 'er sisters, seemed like my country folks, ye know. I say, Seaman! our friend Spanyel's one of ours, ye know; 'e's just told me."

The brother-officer thus appealed to, had been gazing with an utterly blank countenance at the profile of Miss Keeter, and responded to his superior's call with a lifeless glare from his corner of the mantel.

"Don't you 'ear, me b'y?" continued the other, "the Spanyels that came over with King Charles, ye know, and all that sort of thing."

Which piece of genealogical information so touched Mr. Seaman's English heart of oak, that he promptly starboarded and bore down upon Mr. Spanyel, for the particular purpose of saluting him as a fellow-countryman. This he was accomplishing by wringing the nearest hand of the gentleman with a protracted affection not unsuggestive of incipient inebriety, when the lovely Flora, fresh from an exquisite filial grouping with her mamma on the sofa, came gliding up.

"You're not persuading pa to cross the ridiculous ocean with you, Mr. Lud?" insinuated the melting creature, leaning a blooming cheek upon her bouquet.

Whereupon Mr. Lord's gloves nervously sought to crawl off the fingers of the sea-officer, and were only reduced to resignation by a lively working of the digits, and an apparently disconnected jerk of first one leg and then the other.

"Nothing of the kind, I assho' yo,' replied Flo's foreign admirer, after this brief spasm. "But on me honor, Miss Spanyel, I'm delighted, I assho' yo, to learn that your family came over with King Charles."

"And do you know, Mr. Lud," added the coquettish fair, accepting his arm for a joint expedition into the throng, "my friends tell me I'm more English than American. Isn't it perfectly absurd?"

Mr. Seaman witnessed the capture of his superior officer, as one who felt himself thereby dismissed to cruise on his own responsibility, and at once ceased pumping his host's arm, as suddenly as he had commenced the operation. From the mantel to the first sofa was but a short distance, and, with seamanlike hardihood, he went instantly tacking to the latter, through breakers of silk and broadcloth, and had Mrs. Spanyel by the hand before that lady could finish her last sentence to the Reverend Harry

Lewyer. Staring stonily at her he swayed her hand up and down in his own, as though abstractedly ascertaining its exact weight, and was believed by observers to be on the point of shedding tears. At the moment, however, when his swimming eyes seemed on the point of slopping over, a beaming smile came aboard his countenance, but was immediately chased below by a heavy sou'-west frown.

"Sir," said the Reverend Harry Lewyer, in a deep bass voice, "you seem indisposed."

Mr. Seaman unceremoniously dropped the lady's hand and fixed his melancholy eyes upon the young disciple.

"Muff!" was his stern remark, — "you're a muff!"

"Really, my good friend" — began the astonished clergyman.

"Go for'ard!" commanded Mr. Seaman, thrusting a blunt forefinger into Mr. Benton Stiles' left ear, in an attempt to point imperiously toward an imaginary foremast. "Go for'ard, sir!"

"Sir-r-r?" — in tremulous barytone.

"Go for'ard!" was the awful reiteration, followed by a sound not unlike a hiccough.

Instantly an arm of the ever-ready Mr. Stiles was hooked around the eccentric gentleman's elbow, and the said eccentric gentleman was led softly and dexterously away, with a stationary smile on his countenance, to a chair in a corner.

"It's all right, Spanyel," roared Mr. Barlow Wapples to the master of the house, who was hurriedly approaching to learn the cause of the excitement, — "nothing but one of your English friends with congestion of the hat. He'll be all right in a little while. Hor! hor! hor!"

"Mr. Seaman sends his excuses, ladies and gentlemen," cried Mr. Benton Stiles, reappearing, "and hopes you won't mind his recent remarks. He's subject to mental aberrations, from a late attack of brain fever, and is now eating a pickle, with a view to the restoration of his faculties."

"Hor! hor! hor!" roared Mr. Barlow Wapples; "I had brain fever, once, when I was a young spark, and stood for two hours on the stoop, trying to find the key-hole in the door-plate."

An immediate murmur of disgust ran through the whole company, at this vulgar plebeian parallel to an English gentleman's innocent vertigo; and Mrs. Heroldun said to Miss Peller, on the spot, that she wondered how some people *could* invite some people, when they knew that other people were to be present.

"Now, Mr. Stiles," said Mrs. Cornelius O'Doricourt Fish, archly poking that skilful diplomatist with her fan, "you don't mean to say that pickles are good for insanity?"

"Madam," returned the former top-sawyer, "I have known pickles, *or* soda-water, to cure a person who not only believed, like the rest of us, in two worlds, but could actually see both of them together."

"Well, I do declare! He! he! he!"

"My dear, darling Mrs. Fish," exclaimed Miss Carrie Hyer, about whose bewitching waist circled one lovely arm of the fond Rose Spanyel; "you haven't told me yet about little Phinny."

"Nor me," added the amiable Meeta, with Miss Lily's arm over *her* shoulder.

"Oh, he's the preciousest! and" — in a whisper — "such legs!"

It was inexpressibly beautiful, by the way, to note how those tender young creatures continually fondled each other, and also how the sisters, of each set, exchanged loving glances between themselves, at every opportunity. It was as though their hearts said, "Turn your eyes this way, eligible young men, if you want to find souls that *can* melt in the least atmosphere of affection!"

"Carrie," questioned Meeta, cooingly, "have you noticed that heavenly pastel, over there, of the Pigs and Cabbage?"

"Yes; isn't it exquisitely divine?"

"And that engraving, love, of Signing the Declaration of Independence. Isn't it perfectly sweet?"

"Oh, it's utterly exquisite."

Mr. Benton Stiles fingered his horse-head breastpin, and sighed, heavily; then looked hastily around, and betrayed signs of painful confusion.

"Mr. Stiles," murmured Miss Rose Spanyel, appealingly, "you don't care for pictures?"

As she spoke, he suffered his fingers to rest on the horse-head breastpin in such a manner as to bring the locket-ring to bear full upon her.

"For one picture — yes," responded Mr. Benton Stiles, sadly and softly; "but she's gone!"

Rose pouted.

Mr. Stiles motioned as though to open the locket-ring; but changed his mind, and contented himself with breathing upon the rich bauble, and polishing it on his coat-sleeve.

"Why, Carrie!" cried Mrs. Cornelius O'Doricourt Fish, "that very quiet person who stays away over by that window there, must be the Miss Terry I met at your house one night! I thought I'd seen her somewhere before."

For a second, the eldest Miss Hyer lost her color. It immediately returned, however, sufficiently deepened to atone for its desertion, and brought with it that touch of anger, which, like fever in sickness, often gives superficial strength to essential weakness.

"It is the same lady," she replied, stiffly, conscious that the Misses Spanyel were staring at her in wonderment, and her sister and Mr. Stiles in dismay. "Miss Terry proved to be a peculiar character. She chose, for some reason known only to herself, to leave us, and become a governess. I was not aware, though, that she had come here."

"How absurd!" ejaculated Rose Spanyel.

"It's perfectly ridiculous," said Lily.

And so it was, indeed!

What time the swarm of dry-goods persons, — who, from business habits of meek subservience to snubbing customers, did not despond at being neglected by the more distinguished members of the family and company, — politely snubbed the Misses Titterly, Keeter, and Peller, and discussed the latest fashions in dress-goods, with more or less of the vivacity of the counter. Though of different complexions, statures, and cuts of beard, they were, as a general thing, monotonously alike in style and effect; but one amongst them, with a smoky head of light hair, and an intrusively high forehead, rather dwarfed the others by his Byronic aspect of ill health and chronic melancholy.

"Now, really, Mr. Coffin," Miss Keeter was saying to this blighted being, "you must be quizzing me. I always thought that you gentlemen preferred gentlemen to lady customers, because the ladies beat you down so."

"It may be so with others, Miss Keeter," returned Mr. Coffin, with the air of one who offered mourning goods at a great reduction; "but I am peculiar. Some have called me strange. Woman can always appreciate sincerity; and when I say that the lowest price is ten shillings a yard, no lady ever asks if I can't say nine. I try to be sincere; I try to say ten shillings as a true, unselfish friend would say it, and a well-bred woman seldom cheapens me."

"Perhaps you are never too dear?" lisped the younger Miss Titterly.

"Coffin was too dear for one lady," hinted a cheerful young glove-clerk, who kept his hands on his hips after the engaging manner of one who should say, "I think that pair will fit you, madam."

"Tomkins," said Mr. Coffin, turning pale and glancing reproachfully at the last speaker, "there are some things that may as well be forgotten. You will oblige me, Tomkins, by saying no more about it."

There was a mercantile legend that Mr. Coffin had once contracted a passion for a lady in high life, who bought her laces at his counter, and who so deeply reciprocated his attachment, that she suffered a broken heart shortly after being forced to marry a rich man with a glass eye.

Conversation was thus engaging the whole assemblage, save Mr. Seaman, who presented an attitude of general dislocation in the corner, and Miss Terry, who stood motionless by her window, looking out toward the road, — when lunch was announced and a procession at once began a march from the parlor to the dining-room.

After seeing that Mr. Lord and Miss Flora headed the advance, and the Reverend Harry Lewyer, in arms with Mesdames Spanyel and Purser, came next, Mr. Charles Spanyel went mincingly around by the flank to the rear, and approached the silent and neglected governess.

"My dear Miss Terry," said he, with a thumb thrust under the right lappet of his coat, "I am afraid you have not been enjoying yourself. Be good enough to accept my arm to lunch."

Without the slightest indication of offended pride, or conscious neglect; in fact, with the pleasantest smile in the world, Miss Terry at once obeyed the gesture and went gracefully with him in the track of the others.

"You must not think, Mr. Spanyel," she quietly remarked, "that I do not enjoy myself because I am less demonstrative than others. The view from the windows at this time of year is so charming, that I am apt to forget everything else in the world while attracted by it."

Opportunity was not given for a reply to this pretty little speech; for a few steps took them into that part of the hall where a supplementary table was spread, and the sharp gaze of Miss Rose Spanyel reminded her father that too much politeness to the governess might — and not for the first time — subject him to a temporary coolness with his family.

Those who could not get into the dining-room, contented themselves with hot-house fruit, sandwiches and coffee in the hall; Mr. Benton Stiles, Mr. Luke Hyer, junior, and Mr. Coffin being notable for their exertions in behalf of Miss Rose, Miss Lily, and Miss Keeter.

"Miss Terry," said Mr. Spanyel, "let me ask you to try these Malagas."

"Certainly, Mr. Spanyel, if you will take half the bunch."

Which proposition was overheard by Miss Flora, as she passed by on the arm of the British sea-officer, and caused her to favor her sire with a look of anything but filial affection.

In the dining-room all went merrily until some commendation of the raisins, by Mrs. Purser, induced Mr. Barlow Wapples to name the exact price per box at which he had furnished them; when Mrs. Spanyel gave signs of feeling quite faint, and such a sense of outrage came over the others as vulgarity can inflict upon the high-strung alone.

Whether gay or grave, however, the lunching was soon finished; and, at the opening of the rear door of the hall by the stable boy in an eccentric livery of green flannel jacket and corduroys, the butterflies of fashion fluttered gayly forth into the open air.

A gentle slope of about one hundred yards, between the rear piazza and the slowly moving river, was covered with a tender growth of short, velvety grass, over which certain stray cloud-sheep, wandering from a shepherd shower in some distant part of the azure plain, threw their sluggish shadows. On the water's edge, and some distance to the right of the house, stood a pretty little grove of newly-clothed trees, apparently shivering for an additional depth of drapery; while on the opposite bank of the stream, arose that delicate veil of haze, with which spring Nature, like a modest virgin, sometimes affects to confuse the sight of man as she puts on her dimity of daisies.

Near the trees stood three targets, each surmounted by the Spanyel crest; and when they, and the throng of ladies in green merino and gipsy-flats, and the seasoning of gentlemen in semi-sporting suits, and the liveried stable-boy with arms full of bows and arrows, — were all added to the landscape, the effect was creditably suggestive of the step-mother country, merrie England.

"A charming day this, Spanyel," said Mr. Stiles, dealing the first of the "scoring cards" to that gentleman. "I never saw Todeville —"

"Toe-der-veal!" syllabled Mr. Spanyel, impressively.

— "look more like good keep," went on the unabashed secretary of Gen. Cringer. "Good grooming will do wonders for a place."

"It's just like 'ome, this is, ye know," put in Mr. Lord. "Just like the harchery field at the seat of the Duke of 'ardupshire."

"It must be so ridiculously lovely in England," simpered Flora, looking archly sideways at her bouquet.

Possibly the British sea-officer might have responded rather gallantly, but for suddenly catching the eye of Miss Terry. There was so much of mingled amusement and perfect understanding in that eye, that Mr. Lord paused and lost his inspiration. Miss Spanyel saw the eye, too, even if it did not trouble itself to be caught by her, and she mentally marked the governess for another private conversation with Rose.

But all was now in readiness for the shooting, and the new excitement merged every topic in one. Cavaliers handed bows and shafts to their allotted fairs, the serf in livery took his station near the targets. Mr. Spanyel produced a case of pretty trinkets to serve as prizes, and Mr. Lord and Flora stood forth to inaugurate the imported sport.

Mr. Lord did not wish to make the first shot, because that belonged to the ladies, you know. In England the ladies always shot first, you know, and all that sort of thing. But the ladies would have it that he must show them how; that he must lead them in their humble imitation of the archery so familiar to him at the seat of the Duke of Hardupshire; and, after many painful slips by reason of his gloves, he finally despatched an arrow.

That he did not also despatch the menial in livery was a wonder, for the darting missile just grazed the carroty head of that devoted slave, causing him to rub one ear in great terror, and immediately refuse to continue longer on the field of carnage. He had an "aged parient," he said, who depended on him for support, and he couldn't think of dooming her to a childless sojourn in the county-house for the brief remnant of her days.

Mr. Lord explained the accident by admitting that he had not allowed for the deflection, you know; which statement, like the showing of great men, generally, when they blunder, was received with great bewilderment and satisfaction by everybody.

Messieurs Tomkins and Luke Hyer, junior, volunteering to collect the arrows, however, the shooting went gayly on as though nothing deadly had occurred; and the Reverend Harry Lewyer was just remarking, in a terrible voice, that he didn't know but he would try a shot himself, for the credit of the cloth, when all ears were surprised by the sound of one lamentably singing, and a remarkable figure made its appearance, as by magic, right before the targets. The apparition was that of a man with one sleeve of his coat disengaged from the arm, his Wellington stock elevated some inches above the edge of his collar, and his gigantic silver watch dangling wildly by its polished steel chain. In the midst of a profound dancing effort, which proceeded no farther than a shaky balance on one leg, the eccentric intruder dolefully chanted, —

"One night it blew a 'urricane,
    The waves were mountains r'holling
When Barney Buntline turned aside,
    And said to Billy Bowline, —
'A strong north-wester bl'howing, Bill,
    Don't y' hear it roar, now ?' " —

at which point in the ditty the singer suddenly cut it short and executed a lively prance.

"Good gracious !" ejaculated Mr. Lord.

"Oh, let's run," chorused half-a-dozen female voices.

"Hor! hor! hor!" roared the coarse Mr. Barlow Wapples; "I'm blest if it isn't that 'ere nobleman with the brain fever."

"Mr. Seaman!" exclaimed Mr. Spanyel, instantly dropping prizes and "scoring card," and running hastily toward the musical invalid, followed by Mr. Stiles.

Then swarmed the whole astonished company, bows in hand, to the same new centre of attraction.

"My dear sir," was the anxious salutation of Mr. Spanyel, "you are ill and excited. Our climate does not agree with you."

"Have a little Kissengen," urged Mr. Stiles.

Mr. Seaman surveyed his friends with a haughty smile, and performed a stately hop toward his superior officer. That superior falling back from his proximity, he frowned with much severity, as though wounded by such very palpable desertion, and deliberately picked a large artificial rose from the head-dress of Mrs. Heroldin. Upon this flower he smiled. After which he winked a great deal and seemed about to slumber.

"Ladies and gentlemen," said Mr. Benton Stiles, with his usual diplomatic aptness for a difficult situation, "I see how it is. Our friend is not in a fit condition to bear the giddy whirl of this gay and festive scene. Return, if you please, to the track, — I mean, to your shooting, and I will take our friend to where he can lave his burning brow. This way, my boy, —

> "'Turn thou thine eyes above,
> There's rest for thee in heaven.'"

And, with such comforting quotations, did Mr. Stiles lead the eccentric invalid unresistingly and gloomily away to a shady spot near the house, while the archers straggled talkatively back to their places, almost persuaded that some Englishmen were vulgar.

The arrows were flying again, and all going briskly as before, when a horseman turned into the semi-circular sweep in front of the house, from the Harlem road, and leisurely walked his shining sorrel thoroughbred through a maze of standing vehicles to the very edge of the piazza. He was a gentleman with very black eyes and beard, very glossy black silk hat, and very brilliant single diamonds on his scarf. and the little finger of his ungloved right hand. His broadcloth coat, and the lustrous coat of his steed displayed not a speck of dust, the lemon-colored riding-glove on his left hand was cleanly delicate to view as the white kid straps of his bridle. and but for the mature manliness of the rider's watchful eyes and flowing whiskers, there would have been something of the fop in the spotless handkerchief showing a negligent corner from the pocket on his breast.

The gentleman glanced quietly around him for a moment, for the purpose, apparently, of ascertaining if any hostler was in view. No such personage appearing, he dismounted from the saddle to the piazza without the slightest sign of impatience at the deficiency, fastened his horse to one of the square pillars, and then passed, with hat removed, into the hall.

Divers colored waiters from a city restaurateur's were busily spreading tables in the hall and dining-room, and them he passed as though they had not been. Out upon the rear piazza, in the open air again, he resumed his hat and paused to contemplate the scene. The archers, fair and masculine, were at the sport in a living tableau not altogether beneath the admiration of an admirer of the picturesque, but his look wandered over and amongst them with a quickness of review not indicative of any great interest. From them it glanced to the targets, and from thence to the little grove beyond, coming back again indifferent as before. Finally the look went off at a tangent to where Mrs. Purser. Mrs. Heroldim, and Mrs. Spanyel formed a side-group by themselves. to look on, merely, and taking a straight line from them to the water's edge, rested intently at last on a slender figure with a parasol, walking slowly back and forth there. The black eyes lighted with something like a smile when they found that object, and turned from it only when their possessor descended the steps to the lawn and leisurely paced toward the company with bows.

"Mr. Wynne!" cried Mr. Spanyel, "I'm delighted to see you, sir; we'd almost given you up. You see, we're at it in earnest."

Mr. Wynne bowed lightly to the ladies and escort generally, and, while declining to accept a weapon for himself, expressed his admiration of the feminine portion of the scene in a few easy and complimentary phrases.

"You must excuse me to your fair guests, Mr. Spanyel. for not joining them in a sport which so well becomes their many graces. I prefer to admire the scene from afar, rather than mar it by my own amateur awkwardness. Permit me to pay my respects to Mrs. Spanyel."

He turned to accomplish this courteous desire, and confronted Mr. Benton Stiles.

"The humblest servant of your throne!" declaimed Mr. Stiles, with an elaborate salaam, greatly to the surprise of Mr. Spanyel.

Waving the least possible recognition with his jewelled right hand, the imperturbable owner of the beard passed the secretary in silence, and was presently bending over the plump fingers of the Spanyel dame. To her and her attendant matrons he said so many elegant things, that they were quite lost, temporarily, in a soft confusion, nor noted his one quick glance toward the river-side, and momentary contraction of brow at the solitude thereof.

Leaving the ladies, and casting one more sweeping look in the direction of the water, the chevalier strolled at his ease along the edge of the "meeting," touching lips and hat to acquaintances here and there, and taking such glimpses of the archery as courtesy required. Strolling thus sunnily, and with such fine effect that Carrie Ilyer confidentially characterized him to Mrs. Cornelius O'Doricourt Fish as "perfectly splendid," he once more came upon Mr. Stiles.

For some inexplicable reason, the latter personage could *not* become aware of Mr. Wynne's presence in polite society, at any time, without thereupon becoming curiously overpowered and absurdly grandiloquent. "Your Majesty's most obsequious," he said, mechanically, and yet with an air of irrepressible dramatic deference.

His sovereign returned the compliment with a flash of the eye just one degree sharper than the gleam of a smile.

"Mr. Stiles, may I trouble you to walk a few steps with me?"

"Command my life, most mighty liege!"

Side by side they moved lazily riverward, like any two gentlemen who would while away an interval of conversation in joint contemplation of a quiet stream.

Arrived at the verge of the bank Mr. Wynne turned sharply upon the former top-sawyer, with a countenance sternly different from that of a moment before.

"Mr. Stiles, I must request you to abstain in future from such conspicuous demonstrations as you have, on several occasions, seen fit to subject me to in the presence of third parties. When I tell you that they annoy me, your good sense as a gentleman will prevent their repetition."

The secretary of the great man was momentarily taken aback by this unequivocal warning, but regained self-possession in time to reply, rather defiantly, —

"I am quite capable of sustaining the character of a gentleman, your — Mr. Wynne, without suggestions from other parties on the road."

"And for that reason, Mr. Stiles, I have offered you a reminder, rather than a suggestion. We may rejoin our friends, now, I think."

Still side by side they returned to the archers, betraying no other signs of peculiar emotion than a look of vague mystification on the face of the one, and a tranquil calmness in the black eyes of the other.

The sun was far down in the west when bows and arrows were finally relinquished to the liveried minion, and the guests of the day marched back to the house to partake of *the dinatoire* before separating. General was the surprise and admiration of the company, on regaining the mansion, to find not only a table spread in the most showy manner, but also a band from town getting itself into order on the front piazza.

"Isn't it celestial?" asked Meeta Ilyer, so loudly that the Spanyels were sure to hear.

"Oh, it's divinely splendid!" returned her enthusiastic elder sister; and several other young ladies murmured "Exquisitely enchanting!"

Barely had the brilliant throng gathered about the groaning board, when all three of the fascinating Spanyels marvellously disappeared, to the distraction of Messieurs Lord, Stiles, and Ilyer, junior. As marvellously, though, they immediately reappeared to their adorers, again, wiping their ruby lips; for they had been taking their mixtures.

"I was in despair, Miss Spanyel, I assho' yo," said Mr. Lord, assisting Flora to a chair. "I thought you'd vanished, like an angel, ye know."

"O you absurd creature!"

"I did, I assho' yo. Allow me — some of this 'am? Madam (to Mrs. Cornelius O'Doricourt Fish, across the table), — let me 'elp *you* to some of this 'am."

"*Merci vous.*"

Those who heard it told the others; from every direction eyes full of new interest were turned upon Mrs. Cornelius O'Doricourt Fish. "She speaks French!" was the universal murmur; and even the British sea-officer gazed with awe upon the accomplished mother of the legs.

"She's been to Europe, you may depend!" whispered Miss Titterly the elder to Miss Keeter.

"Gifted woman!" soliloquized Mr. Coffin.

From that moment the lovely linguist was queen of the banquet, and assumed the gently pensive air of one with dreamy memories of Parisian salons.

"My dear madam," — from Mr. Spanyel at the head of the table, — "permit me to send you some olives."

"*Merci vous.*"

"Mrs. Fish," — from Rose, — "you will try some of this guava, just to oblige me."

"*Merci vous, cheri.*"

That was the finishing touch. Mrs. Cornelius O'Doricourt Fish ruled supreme indeed; for the only member of her sex in Todeville who could have lessened her triumph by correcting her French, was at that moment pacing solitary and alone in the shade of the grove by the river.

While there was lighting of many wax candles within doors, to render more conspicuous Mr. Spanyel's new epergne and add a stronger air of fashionable dissipation to the protracted feast, a clear, roseate twilight bathed house, lawn, and river in a hushed beauty that had been fashionable since the first sunset on a grander Eden, and revealed amongst the trees an Eve as ripe for the tempter as the first.

Heeding not the tranquil glory of the scene around her, deaf to the sounds of merriment wafted thither ever and anon, alive only to her own fierce thoughts, the governess, with her hat swinging from her arm, and her colorless hair rippling in the breeze, walked to and fro under the branches as though willing to find congenially bitter company in hurrying from herself to herself.

When a woman walks thus, he is generally unwise for himself that intrudes; for, in the duality of tortured self which she so instinctively strives to realize, there is peril of a hasty resolve only half human, by which an inhuman half, alone, of herself, falls prize to the intruder.

Yet he was no tyro in woman's ways, who, at the moment when sounds of music first began to steal from the house to the air, strode down the lawn and unerringly approached the place where such danger threatened intrusion. He was no amateur in woman's moods who came suddenly face to face with one in her darkest mood, and pressed her hand to his lips with a confidence bred of no recent acquaintance.

She started, and stood rooted to the spot, but made no resistance.

"Well," she said, "you have found me."

He released the hand, and, leaning easily against a tree before her, made his reply, —

"Yes, I have found you. I should do that, if you hid yourself in a cloak of invisibility."

"Then I should feel flattered, I suppose," she said, with a listless look toward the water.

"And how should I feel, after being deliberately avoided by you for hours?"

"You should feel," she answered, laughing lightly, "that I only fled to make you come here after me. That would be feeling very like a man."

"You are an amiable, merry soul, to-night."

"Well, what would you have me be?"

He leaned toward her and again took her hand, speaking in a low, intense tone,—

"Be an angel,—be a devil,—be anything but commonplace!"

She threw off his grasp and clasped her hands before her, but looked him steadily in the face.

"I might have been an angel," she said, measuredly, "with more of an angelic atmosphere around me in my life; and I might be a fiend situated just as I am here; but you seem to think me commonplace, after all."

"And I," he responded, "should be nearer the angelic mood here than in any other place on earth. For in that house I first met the only angel upon earth,—a true wife; under these very trees we took our first look forth upon a married future,—man's earliest heaven."

"Hypocrite!"

She uttered the word with a mingled impatience and fury not to be described.

"If that is the meaning implied by my words, I regret that they so misrepresent me."

"Plato Wynne!" exclaimed the governess, becoming more impassioned at his coolness, "your words are not—never were—any index of what you really do mean. If you come here to mock me with them, let a sense of the mockery already inflicted on me by these fools, here,—these friends of yours,—preserve me from further contumely. Go and talk of your angels and your heaven to the senseless girls who may believe you."

A third time he took her hand, and again carried it to his lips. He knew the power of his touch.

"I need not go from you, most queenly of governesses, to find belief for the only words to which I myself attach any vital import."

"And what are they?" she asked, indifferently, as at first.

"I love you!"

She started back from him with a half-pleading look; but he had her imprisoned in his arms in a second, and held her to his breast as in a vice.

"You do believe that, woman!"—he spoke rapidly, but very clearly,—"and you love me as my love deserves. Do not struggle,—it is useless. Between a woman like you and a man like me there need be no waste of words. I know that your heart is mine, and you know it. You are an object of scorn, here, and the longer you remain, the lower you will sink in your own estimation—and mine. These people neglect and insult you. Let me raise you above them."

"Will you remove your arms?" She spoke very quietly and without an effort to release herself.

"Do you wish it?"

"I do."

He left her free at once, and leaned against the tree as before.

"As you have said," was her answer: "there is no need of superfluous words between you and me. I am in your power. What are your commands?"

Mr. Wynne's face was in shadow and its expression could not be clearly noted, but a hidden listener would have inferred, from his manner of speaking, that he intended an effect from his look no less than from his words,—

"You have me far more in your power, now, than you ever were in mine. You have already obeyed all the commands I shall ever give you; and while I now ask you to become my wife, I claim no more right than your own feelings may freely concede, to control your answer. Is that answer, freely given, yes, or no?"

The music came to their ears in a prolonged cadence, and the leaves overhead rustled fitfully in the breeze. The first, in its cheeriness, reminded her of the world from which she was excluded; the last, in their desolate whispering, told her of the world to which she was condemned. Her answer was ready,—

"Yes."

He pressed his lips to her extended hand, and then upon her forehead.

"To-morrow, at noon, a carriage will be here to receive you. Provided, of course, that you agree with me in the conclusion that you cannot leave this place too soon."

"Yes! yes!" she replied, hurriedly, "Please leave me now."

A curious change had occurred in her manner and voice, and the bold wooer hesitated.

"Leave me now!" she repeated, vehemently, and with a nervousness that would have seemed more natural in a timid school-girl; "anything, anything to-morrow!"

The elegant gentleman was himself again, and bowed the only answer a gentleman could give to a request thus peremptory. No sensitive, suspicious swain was he, to dispute the mode of his dismissal. Satisfied with the point gained, he could bear a woman's subsequent caprices philosophically, and without a care to fathom their mystery. So, with exemplary quietude, Plato Wynne emerged leisurely from the grove and sauntered up the lawn.

He left his betrothed to cast one swift glance after his retreating figure, and then fixed a wild, frightened stare upon an opening in the branches of the tree beneath which he had stood. For, even in the last moment of his standing there, she had seen, right above his head, in an interval of the dark foliage, the sharp, black outline of another human face. There it was, with the clear gray sky behind it, as distinct and unmistakable as the tree itself.

While she looked, fascinated by the weird terror of the sight,—her lips apart and her hands clutching each other across her throbbing heart,—the spectral head seemed to fade slowly into a cluster of leaves, and Something slid swiftly down the trunk and stood before her.

"To be *his* wife!"

There was enough light to reveal a great beard, and long, tangled hair, and a form clothed in coarse, unshapely habiliments. There was enough light to show an arm and hand pointing in the direction of the fine gentleman's departure.

"You?" came like a husky shriek from the woman.

"To be his wife!" was repeated, in a voice weak and low, but full of sorrowful meaning.

The governess neither fled, nor called for aid. One moment of bated breath, and then her arms were about the neck of the prowler and her hair mingled with his.

"Oh, you have come back to me again, at last!" burst from her lips like a great sob. "What shall I do? Oh, what shall I do?"

His claw-like hands trembled upon her shoulders, as though fearful to meet about her waist, and he spoke again in the same weary, sorrowing way,—

"After what I have heard, there is nothing to do but part again. I did not come to reproach you, child. I have been wandering about here all day to see you; and when I climbed this tree, at last, it was because I saw you coming this way, and wanted to look upon you for a while before we spoke. I would have made myself known when that man was here, but I was afraid for you."

"Poor soul!" she murmured, softly stroking his tangled locks; "how much you have suffered! Come, sit down here with me and tell me where you have been."

She led him like a child to a rustic settee under one of the trees nearer the water, and made him sit beside her. The last lingering radiance of the dying day fell not upon another such strangely mated pair.

The man's voice scarcely rose above a whisper as he said,—"I have wandered far and wide, trying to forget you, him, myself,—everything. But I can't do it. Day and night I can think of nothing but that which has made me what I am. It will be so until I die; and it is selfish in me to be forever coming upon you, as I do; but I can't help that, either. Perhaps, though, I might have gone away to-night without speaking to you,—satisfied with only looking at you,—if I had not heard what I did between you and that man. Child! child! what have you done?"

She sank down upon the dewy turf beside his knees, and clasped her hands upon the latter, in an attitude half of deprecation, half of appeal.

"I have done," she replied, calmly, "all that was left for me to do. My destiny is stronger than my will, and has been ever since I first saw Plato Wynne. If you, who are a man,—God help us both!—have come to what you are, because of him, how could I, a woman, escape? Think of what I

have done; think of my present situation. I am miserable! I am almost desperate. To see you, as you are, to know of you what I do know, would alone be enough to make me reckless of myself. As you say, we must part again; we must talk together stealthily, like two thieves, and then fly from each other. Yes, yes, I know it well enough;" and she bowed her face upon her hands and moaned.

"Well, well," muttered the weaker unfortunate; "we are both on the high road to madness, I believe. I'm sorry I came here at all. Get up, and let me go."

The governess rose mechanically to her feet, and saw him rise, also, and prepare to go, without sign of further emotion. Once more the sound of the music came over the lawn to mock her; once more the leaves rustled to tell her she was outcast. It was in the power of the broken scarecrow there to have saved her even then. One word of strong, protecting human love; one touch of a firm, caressing hand; one look of inspiring sympathy and daring,—would have done it. But he offered no one of them. There was not enough of his stronger manhood left in him to recognize and rescue what there *was* left of her gentler womanhood.

"Good-by," he said, in a feeble, hesitating, hopeless tone.

"You have heard for yourself where to find me next," was her cold, hard answer. "Good-by."

With heavy, dragging steps he left her, as a sullen beggar might have left the unlighted shrine of Uncharity; and the first stars of the evening had been justified in thinking him a murderer, too, when they looked down upon where he had stood, and saw there a woman prone upon her face on the grass.

Yet still the music rose and fell while the archery guests danced gayly in tune; the leaves sighed and rustled in the freshening air of night, and the sharp click of a horse's feet on the road told that the King of Diamonds went riding to the city.

CHAPTER XXVII.

OLDEN GREY'S LEGACY.

I DID not see Old Yaller again, and the train of miserable memories awakened in me by his goblin-like appearance and disappearance in Cow Bay soon reverted to the ever-ready slumber of boyish forgetfulness. But the gipsy goblin of my protector, the dark and stealthy Juan, did not allow such laying of ghosts in the breast of his old friend; for, from time to time, both Reese and I caught sight of him flitting out of wretched Italian dens, or around corners, like a guilty genius of the sinister; and Reese never failed, on such occasions, to become momentarily uneasy and moody, and predict "mischief."

I shrink from confessing how many, many months of my life were passed in Rack-and-Ruin Row. It has been a forced task to describe in detail even its earlier days, and I cannot but fear that some of my auditors will have their nicer moral sensibilities offended by my introduction of scenes and characters from a line of human existence much below the lowest level to which the fastidious permit their refined personal cognizance to sink. Yet have I a hope, that the merely curious observation of that younger self with which I am mentally identical while writing of such scenes and characters, will prove a sufficiently innocent medium to convey the whole picture as innocently as the original was observed and wondered at.

With season succeeding season, and our virtual imprisonment still remaining unrelieved, I gradually became thoroughly accustomed to the nightmare kind of life, and scarcely wished for a change. In fact, those books in the loft were such a continual and absorbing delight to me, and April Grey such an all-sufficient companion, that my particular world poised in the atmosphere of sin and misery around it like a pleasant dream in a deadly fever, and while its spell lasted I was asleep to aught else than the mere physical entity of things beyond.

Two or three times a day Mr. Grey would come up and read with me, often explaining those knotty sentences which fascinated me in proportion to my difficulty in comprehending them, and occasionally interrupting my studies with outbursts of raving over his own and his child's misfortunes. At first I was greatly surprised to find that, notwithstanding the merciless blame he gave himself for that child's unfortunate situation, he still permitted her to support him with the scant proceeds of her musical journeys; but, as his mental condition became more familiar to me, I formed a tolerably correct estimate of the utter wreck he was, and no longer regarded him as enough superior to myself to command any strong interest. A child's judgment of a man, like a woman's when unswayed by passion, is pitiless as acute. I speak, of course, of a child at the maturity of childhood, when, in point of perception and judgment, it is what a woman remains all her life.

As for April, her few hours of rest from work were divided between her father, the books, and me. Being left my own master after the memorable night at "Sportman's Hall," it was my custom to slip some favorite volume under my jacket when I supposed the little girl to be at home, and then slip down through the intervening floors of squalid wretchedness and noise to the dreary basement, there to enjoy the treasure with my old-womanly sweetheart. If this happened after dark, each could take turn in holding a cheap and dismal candle while the other read aloud (for April could read, though with many superfluous "nows"), Mr. Grey sitting in a dark corner and dolefully watching us, or stretching himself upon his comfortless mattress and staring blankly for hours at the webbed and broken ceiling. On Sundays, as neither of us dreamed of church, April would pass half the day in the loft with me and the dog, talking; for we in some way adopted the notion that it was wrong to read for pleasure on the Sabbath, but quite proper to speak and think as we pleased. Our conversations upon the wickedness of other people in the house were particularly earnest. I remember, and strike me, when recurring to them now, as having been singularly coincident with Sunday practice in larger and more aristocratic circles.

Poor Mr. Mugses! He never took kindly to that life. From the night of our arrival a change came over the animal. He lost his spirits, became mopish, and would follow me to and from the Italian's, where I took my meals, with a drooping sluggishness very different from his former activity. Twenty times a day would he rise to his feet with a sigh, walk innumerable circles of undecided measurement, and then go down with a thump, his countenance for some minutes thereafter exhibiting an expression of grieving imbecility exasperating to behold. Between him and his master there was an unwilling coolness, owing to the plaintive howl with which, at the most unexpected times, he startled and enraged the superstitious man; and, although I soon discovered that this demonstration of his was made only when the somewhat similar noise of some drunken revellers' singing came up from the rooms below, Reese never could hear it without showing mingled fear and anger.

Reese I mention last in my summary, because, from the time when he gave me that broken sketch of his history, he was less my companion than either of the others. Natures not naturally strong can never voluntarily reveal much of themselves, privately and individually, to their neighbors, without experiencing a subsequent fear of having thereby put themselves to that extent in the power of the latter. They feel the less independent for having confided in others; a vague sense of lessened importance and suspicion of a disposition to take advantage, torment them; and, after giving the last spontaneous proof of friendship the most free and actual, they cease to be friendly, save by imaginary compulsion. Thus, Reese, from the day of making me his scarcely comprehending confidant, seemed to regard me with a certain awkward shyness not devoid of irritable distrust; and, although I could see that he struggled to suppress the feeling, he was never quite the same with me again. For days, and even weeks, he would be away, I knew not where; and, again, he would spend day after day at Brignoli's, apparently infatuated with the Italian girls. He said no more of leaving the Points; so far as I could see, he cared no more about it; but then he no longer gave me his private thoughts.

On occasions, however, it was his fancy to assume something of his old manner toward me, and chancing to notice the "Treatise on Book-keeping," during one of these spells, he reminded me of his promise to teach me the art of keeping mercantile accounts.

"Would you like to learn?" he asked.

"Oh, yes!" cried I with my usual alacrity for education.

Accordingly, on that and other following nights he gave me his company and services as teacher of book-keeping by double entry.

An odd-looking pair were we as we sat upon the bare floor of that sin-and-hunger-crowning loft, with two lighted tallow candles properly arranged on the table, and the book upon the ground between us. The floor was also "Journal" and "Ledger," the columns for dates, dollars, and cents being drawn thereon with a bit of chalk, and the entries made with the same primitive instrument.

Quite as deeply interested as myself, Reese would explain to me a lesson in theory, and then hand me the chalk and proceed to practice, —

"Now, Gilbun," he would say, "suppose you buy forty pounds of sugar, and pay ready money for it, what entry do you make?"

To which I would laboriously reply, chalking away as I did so, — "Why, I Deb-it mer-chan-dise. and Cred-it cash."

"Suppose I buy the sugar of you and give you my note for it?"

"I Deb-it bills receivable and Cred-it mer-chan-dise."

Could any one of our dissipated Irish friends downstairs have looked in upon us as we sat thus, with our candles, our book, and our cabalistic chalkings on the floor, he would have taken us for magical heretics working diabolical sorceries.

I had brought Roderick Random tremendously in debt to Don Quixote for "merchandise," and was well under way with the former's account current from the latter, when my vacillating tutor wearied of the work and began to leave me alone again for days and weeks. Then, one night the dog awoke me with one of his longest howls, and I heard, coming up from the rooms beneath, a roaring and singing, so hoarse and shrill, alternately, that the vocalist might have emitted the unearthly sounds under some instrument of torture. The din was unusual, even for that foul temple of tumult; and, while I listened with no little dread, the singing was changed to wild shouts, intermingled with the cries of women; and a rushing noise, as of some furious beast tearing through the hall, brought the clamor right under the door of the loft. Springing to the floor, I cautiously opened the door just widely enough to permit a view of the scene beneath, and beheld a sight more frightful than any that had gone before it. Struggling furiously with four cursing and screaming women at the foot of the ladder, was a half-dressed man, whose starting eyes, disordered hair, and hideous yells made me think at first that he was drunk. The hall beyond appeared to be swarming with wretches of both sexes, some of whom held bits of candles in their claws, while all joined in the general uproar; and. as the man's struggles grew fiercer, two or three tattered members of his own sex threw themselves suddenly upon him and bore him to the ground. After the crash came a lull for an instant, but this was quickly broken by a howling outburst of grief from one of the women, of whose words I could gather little more than a repeated "Och, hone! och, hone!"

Then the fallen man renewed his struggles, as the others dragged him toward one of the rooms, and the woman howled afresh.

"Sure, Mag, he's wild wid the poteen this time," I heard one of the miserable creatures say.

"Poteen is it?" screamed the howler. "Isn't it the fayvar that's on him and 'll kill him? Didn't he bate me down wid his two fishts and come flyin from his blessed bed wid the tormints of it. Och, hone! och, hone!"

"The fever!"

A score of harsh voices snarled the dread word; and. with imprecations and inhuman cries, the whole satanic crew crowded and tumbled over each other toward the nearest stairway.

Yes, the fever — bred of hunger, intemperance, and all uncleanness — had fallen upon Rack-and-Ruin Row like the last delirious excess of an orgie, when besotted creatures sing, rave, reel, and fall. It had come to give sin and misery the one dignity that no height of station can exalt, that no depth of degradation can lower — the awful dignity of death. It had come, like a hot breath from the furnace of which Cow Bay was the caldron, to set the scum seething in frantic torments of heat, and burst a thousand bubbles of impure life into as many noisome exhalations of corruption. It had come like the last blow from offended Deity, to make the scarred face of lowest crime white with the only whiteness it could know; and, perhaps, to find, in falling, more than one poor, starved heart never breaking until then, and so, in its helplessness, finding a mercy unknown to the justice of man.

For, before another night closed upon Cow Bay, scores of the distorted, bruised, and dishonored images of God were turning to sullied marble in Rack-and-Ruin Row, with hags, harpies, and monstrous satyrs wailing and blaspheming at the awful change. The midnight murderer; the thief of the highway; the blear-eyed, rag-hung daughter of Want and Wickedness; the shambling, shapeless goblin of Rum; the elf-haired, impish, claw-handed grotesque of Childhood;—all staggered, stumbled, and fell, under the fierce pestilence. In one doorless, reeking den of a room, a broken effigy of a mother and two brawling witch's children crawled about the heap of straw whereon lay the dead husband and father. In another, somebody's wife, or daughter, or sister was dying, without one friend near to say, "It is better so." In another, two children raved and struggled together on the slippery and rat-eaten floor, the while their parents sat upon the straw in the corner and turned their red eyes on each other in maudlin abstraction. Even in the narrow halls, and on the broken stairs, creatures were delirious with the fever, or dragging themselves along with pitiable cries for air.

Through such scenes I wandered to and from the street, unnoticed by any one, and staring at all in alternate curiosity and horror. A few policemen and Catholic priests appeared here and there on the third day, the former seeming to have direction of several shabby workmen who bore coffins of pine up and down stairs. Once I attempted to descend to the basement to find April Grey; but a priest who was following a coffin down, requested a policeman to prevent my following, saying that it was no place for me. I discovered, afterwards, that they carried the dead down there, previously to conveying them to burial vans outside, to avoid the tottering front stoop.

At the Italian's I found Reese, Brignoli, the two daughters of the latter, and an old woman,—the other organ gangs having fled at the first outbreak of the fever. All save the first were gloomy and sullen; but Reese laughed at their fears, and spoke of the impending elections as a certain cure for any sickness that the Five Points could harbor. He also made a display of considerable money, which he said was for the voters of the "straight-out Demolition Ticket;" and, when I bitterly reproached him for deserting me at such a time, he angrily told me to "go home," or he would indeed leave me for good.

Heartsick, and not daring to attempt sleep, I sat up all that night, with my arm about the dog, and my confused head resting against the door of the loft. Dreadful enough were the human sounds reaching my ears there,—wails, and groans, and ravings, mingled with drunken yells; but worst of all were the startling noises made by the *rats*. There seemed to be millions of the latter, among the rafters over my head, in the floor under me, between the laths of the hall-walls, and even on the ladder. Their shrill squeaks, sudden rushes, and sounding falls were like ghostly counterfeits of the other miserable sounds, and I fancied that, at times, I could hear human whispers in their racket.

Near morning I slept from exhaustion, and was roused, again, soon after daybreak, by the whining of the dog and the voice of some one at the door. Upon open-

ing the latter, I found Reese standing on the ladder, and was shocked at the pallor of his face.

"Grey is down with the fever," he said, in a suppressed voice, "and one of the priests has sent word that he wants me. You had better come down with me."

"You're afraid to go alone," I peevishly exclaimed.

"I don't choose to, at any rate," he replied, roughly; "so do as I tell you."

Without further words we went down through the plague-stricken rookery as stealthily as cats, hurrying by doors and doorless rooms, whence low, moaning sounds spoke of inner horrors, and gliding past silent men who were burning coffee and other disinfectants along the lower halls. At the top of the basement stairway Reese spoke to one of these men,—

"Are there any people down here?"

"Nobody but the people in the front basement," was the answer. "The last of the coffins was carried away last night; but they gave the well ones a scare, and you're the first that's offered to go down this morning. Are you the man the priest sent for?"

"Yes."

"Then you'd better travel," said the man, "for they're in a hurry for you, I should think. I was down, just now, to open the windows, and the old man looked near gone."

Down the dirty, cracking stairs we went; and as Reese, after a moment's hesitation, pushed open the well-known door and entered Mr. Grey's room, I noticed that his hand trembled very much and his steps were hurriedly irregular.

What a scene was there! Stretched on his poor mattress, a mere spectre of what was wan enough before, lay the unhappy master of that wretched retreat, his head pillowed upon a roll of old clothing and his form barely covered by a tattered blanket. The colorless lips, sunken cheeks, and hair matted to the temples with the chill moisture of approaching dissolution, would have been dreadful to sight, but for the strong, peaceful light which shone in his eyes as he turned them alternately from the sobbing child on one side of him to the tall, black-vestured man on the other. In the light thus shining on life's last scene, he looked younger and manlier, and more like his child; and she, with her face hidden from us on his breast, and arms clinging about his neck, looked more like the bowed, despairing creature he had been.

Seated on a chair beside the mattress, was the sad-looking priest, holding in his right hand a roll of paper and in his left a prayer-book.

"Old friend," cried Reese, tremulously, as he bent over the sick man and took one of his nerveless hands, "I'm sorry to see you down."

A glance of recognition, and a feeble motion of the hand, were his reply.

"Your name is Reese, I presume," said the priest, touching his arm.

"That is my name, sir."

"And this lad is your son?"

"No."

The priest turned to the sufferer, while pointing to me, and asked, "Shall he remain, my son?"

The answering look appeared to be one of acquiescence; for the questioner noticed me no more, but spoke again to Reese, in a low, clear tone.

"I have been with this sick man for some hours, and it is his request that I should read, in your presence, a paper he has given me. He has told me that you are his only friend here; and, on that account, he would have you and his child hear what he has written."

With arms folded, and brows contracted almost to a frown, Reese stood gazing fixedly upon father and daughter, as though he heard not; and, after regarding him questioningly for a moment, the priest softly unrolled the paper in his hand, and deliberately read, as follows, —

"I, Olden Grey, pauper and outcast, of the Five Points, mindful that my days of want and woe cannot be long protracted in this miserable place, and that I have a child, to whom her father's wretched history may yet bring the friends he has not known, — do here pen this sketch of my life, — my only legacy to April Grey.

" What else can I give to her before I go? What other testimonial of me would appeal for her so strongly to the charity and protection of any mortal with a human heart? I trust God to lead her, when she reads it, or hears it, from this black haunt of the despairing and lost, to some ear of pity, some soul of charity, — anywhere, to any one, than here, and to those like her father. Heaven help me! I scarcely know what I write; I scarcely know what I hope. I only know that, for weeks, months, more than a year, I have been impelled, night and day, to pen this confession for my child."

The reader paused. The same strong, tranquil light beamed from the eyes of Olden Grey; the same fixed stare was upon him from the man with folded arms. I, with heart full of awe and dread, stood fearfully beside the priest; but the child shook in her agony of grief, and "Father! Father!" broke, like a drowning call in the night, from her smothered lips.

The priest read on.

· "These gray hairs, this bowed form, these premature wrinkles, come of evil-doing and remorse, not of lengthened years. Old as I look, my age is barely forty-one. I was born not many miles from Liverpool, on the estate of my father, an Honorable Captain in the Royal Navy; and, being an only child, enjoyed much more indulgence and luxury than were good for me, either mentally or morally. The death of my mother, when I was about six years old, drove my grief-stricken father nearly to distraction, and induced him thereafter to obtain orders for a foreign station from the Admiralty; so that, while he sought solace for his sorrow by sailing across the world in his frigate, I was left in complete orphanage, to find comforters and associates in menials and toadies. Naturally imperious in disposition, and prone to headstrong extremes in everything, I was not long in making myself the young tyrant of the estate. Nor did the arrival, shortly after the captain's departure, of my aunt and her son, prove any material check to my capricious assumptions. This aunt, Mrs. Keene by name, was the widow of a poor Scotch army officer, whom she had married, in defiance of the most strenuous opposition from her family. Owing to this marriage, she and her sister, my mother, had been totally alienated from each other, until just before the death of the latter, when the decease of Colonel Keene produced a reconciliation, and the widow attended my poor mother's funeral, as third mourner. From this sad duty she had returned immediately to her small property in southern Scotland; but was scarcely there, before a hasty letter from my father notified her of his intention to go immediately abroad, and invited her to assume control of his son and establishment during his absence. For reasons best known to herself, she promptly accepted this invitation, bringing her son with her; and thus was I threatened with subjection in the very hour when I fancied myself safe from any species of authority. But, as I have said, the advent of my aunt and cousin did not really put any restriction upon my dangerous freedom. Mrs. Keene was a tall, stately, quiet lady, of about thirty-eight, with regular features, fine eyes, and plentiful brown hair; and I quickly discovered that she could be nothing but gracious mildness to me, however austere to others. Indeed, she humored my boyish pride and follies in a way to make them greater than ever; and, upon my having a quarrel and fight with her son, Brighton, she not only bestowed all her resentment upon the latter, but actually packed him off to a collegiate boarding-school, near Southampton, there to remain, as she told him in my presence, ' until he had learned how to treat his superiors in life.' I felt sorry for the fatherless boy when he went crying away; but his mother's argument too well suited my self-appreciation, to lessen her in my regard; and, from thenceforth, I looked upon her as a sort of accomplice in all my mischievous doings, and gave her as much affection as could exist without positive respect. When my father returned, he found matters working so smoothly with us, apparently, that he requested Mrs. Keene to continue her guardianship, and then went off again, on another cruise, with his ship. Still another such return and departure occurred, before the Honorable Captain Grey finally came home to stay, and to help his friends of the Ministry with his vote in the House of Commons. By that time, I was thirteen years old, with a face and figure as prepossessing as my youthful character was perverse. Upon resuming his authority over me, my father held a long conversation, respecting my future, with Mrs. Keene, the result of which was, that Brighton was to leave school, and teach me what he had learned there, and then we were to repair to Oxford together. My aunt evinced considerable gratitude, on her son's behalf, at this arrangement, and only waited to see him duly installed, as my amateur tutor, before returning to her home in Scotland. The young man, who was some three years my senior, came back from his studies, a fine, manly illustration of his mother's quiet beauty; and would have won my heart, at once, in any other position than one apparently giving dominion over me. I was inclined to rebel boisterously against any tutorship whatever, and treated the student, at first, with systematic defiance; but, in a few days, he abashed me by boldly taking my part, when my father reprimanded me for my conduct, and, finally, won me over completely by soundly threshing the son of a neighboring squire, who undertook to punish me for writing love-letters to his sweetheart. Having thus made me his own, my worthy tutor next gave me to understand, by insinuation rather than in direct terms, that if I would attend enough to the superficialities of study to satisfy my father, he, Brighton Keene, would be accommodatingly blind to any freedom of conduct in which I might choose to indulge beyond the library limits. Only too ready to join in this sinister compact, I forthwith acquired knowledge and evil in about equal proportions, and laid the foundation of all my future woes, by practising deliberate deceit against the fondest and most indulgent of parents. When, at length, Keene and I were about to start for college, intending to stop in London, on the way, for our outfits, my father took us both by the hand. 'Young men,' said he, showing great emotion, 'I trust you to each other, relying upon your principles of duty toward mother and father, no less than upon your gentlemanly ambition, to keep you true to yourselves and to the purpose for which you go from home. You, Olden, will give me cause of genuine pride as a father; and you, Brighton, will reflect honor upon that admirable lady, your mother.'

"I was touched by his manner, and remorsefully meant what I said when I gave my promise. Keene, too, seemed deeply moved; but I could not help noticing that all *he* promised was, to stand by me. He had a letter from my aunt in his pocket at the time, and, perhaps, acted according to maternal direction.

"At any rate, we had no sooner reached London than he at once threw aside all pretence of scholastic propriety, and became my willing companion in the opening career of dissipation to which I speedily committed myself. Indeed, he became my leader in the most dangerous of follies,—gaming,—though simulating violent sorrow thereat, when compelled to draw upon my purse. He did not tell me, in so many words, to write falsehoods in response to my parent's letters of affectionate inquiry; but he managed to hint that too much filial honesty might lessen the monthly drafts from home; so I told my father that I was trying to honor his wishes, and promised to confide, as he desired, in the judgment of my adopted brother! Yet, how frequently did I feel tempted to confess my unworthiness of so much love, and open my father's eyes to the true character of my companion! Alas! that I did not. Let me hasten over my wild life at college; my graduation as Master of Arts, with Keene, at the end of our last term; and our second visit to London. In the latter metropolis I had the paternal consent to remain for some months before going home. The high connexions of our family there, and the repute I had gained for intellectual parts, procured me a fashionable status at once, and invitations to assemblies, routs, and elegant entertainments of all descriptions, soon loaded my dressing-table. With Keene ever at my heels, to echo each bit of flattery and augment each vanity, I plunged recklessly into the vortex of stylish folly. I was courted by male and female adventurers for my supposed fortune, praised by elegant women for my good looks and impudence, and rallied by lady-mothers on my dashing disrespect for their sex. All this I might have borne without serious contamination, for, with all my foolishness, I was not dishonorable; but Keene's blandishments and wily temptations made me a persistent and reckless gambler, and, as a consequence, a continual liar to my still-unsuspicious father. It was during the recess of parliament, else had that father been there to see for himself. Oh, if he only had been there, what a different destiny were mine! Deceiving him, and accustoming myself to so doing, were the sins by which I ceased to be a gentleman, and lost that moral pride of caste on which alone my salvation hung.

"One morning, after a night of excitement and heavy loss at the roulette-table, Keene proposed a trip to Ramsgate. My aching head and guilty conscience made me ready for any change, and I sullenly accepted the suggestion, little dreaming how great a change its adoption was to bring me. On her way down the river, the Ramsgate steamer caught fire in some of the woodwork over the boiler, and although the flames were extinguished without even necessitating a stoppage, the panic they momentarily occasioned was sufficient to dissipate my vapors like magic, and consign a fainting girl to my arms. Angela Evans was the name of the young lady thus strangely cast upon my protection; and, although her terrified parents quickly relieved me of my lovely charge, her remarkable beauty had already worked my destiny. She was the only child of a well-to-do London tradesman, but an early knowledge of this fact failed to cool my impetuous passion. Upon being formally introduced to her just before reaching the pier, I spared no pains to let her realize the impression she had made, and left Keene to give such an account of me to the tradesman as would secure the complacency of the latter. What my cousin thought of my conduct I could not tell; indeed, I scarcely thought of him for a fortnight, so absorbed was I in my new pursuit; but when, after gaining Angela's too-hasty consent to become mine, I gleefully imparted my good fortune to him, he surprised me by exhibiting the bitterest indignation, and threatening to acquaint my honorable father with my intended *mésalliance*. I, in turn, grew furious, passionately accusing him of hypocrisy, and reminding him that he had ever encouraged me to deceive the father and uncle upon whose bounty he was living. Exasperated as I was, his sudden coolness at my words did not lessen my rage, and he well knew that it would not. Instead of resenting my fiery attack, he apologized for what he had said, in the humblest manner, begged me to forget his 'hasty misconception of my purpose,' and demurely hoped that 'the affair might be so arranged' as to prevent any knowledge of it ever reaching my father's ears. The insinuation was too plain to be misunderstood. I loaded the scoundrel with every epithet of scorn at my command, and, maddened by the smiling sneer with which he listened, I struck him! The blow seemed to carry a devil with it into his face and leave it there; for, in an instant, the man's countenance glowed with an unutterable malignity, and the hatred of an eternity burned in his great eyes. We had been standing face to face in my own apartment, and, as he retired toward the door, he pointed to me with a finger that traced some sentence in the air.

" 'Cowardly fool!' he said, in a tone lowered from my ears to my heart, 'you have wantonly struck the only friend between you and destruction. Now take your own way, self-deluding libertine! Marry a shopman's daughter — heir-presumptive of a title! You have rewarded me for not ruining you a year ago, and I owe you more thanks for what you have done than if you had handed this wench over to me for my own. Pah! strike me again, if you wish to. You have given me an argument, at last, wherewith to justify myself for what it has always been my purpose to do, justly or not. You have given me *good cause* — mark me! a perfect justification in any man's eyes — for hurling you to the dogs. And I will do it, — you and your shop-girl!'

"Despising his threats as I did, there was yet a calculating intensity in them to have occasioned serious thoughts in any other mortal than a headlong lover. Between my contempt for him and my love for Angela, his peculiar words lost their immediate force, and, as he did not wait long enough to let me kick him into the street, I soon had no other feelings than pleasure at having got rid of him, and eagerness to salute my enchantress again. Common prudence would have sent me home immediately, to be first with my own story before my ever-indulgent father; but there was no prudence in me. I flew to Angela, and implored her to be mine at once, before fate could separate us. Bursting into tears, she told me that her father refused to permit our marriage until he should be assured that my parent consented. In her tears she was weak, and when I raved over the mercenary vacillations of old heads, and bitterly reproached the young heart that could temporize with its own truth for them, she cast her arms about me in affright, and consented to my desire. We were secretly married that same day, and departed as secretly for London, — Angela leaving a letter of confession in her mother's room, and I posting one to my father.

"Angela's parents followed us straightway to the city, and her father sought the first opportunity to let me know that he should punish our disrespect of his wishes by giving her no marriage portion. Although this decision did not give me much anxiety, — for I had no thought of failure in my own monetary supplies, — it yet touched my pride sufficiently to influence my demeanor toward the tradesman, and our relations had more of abstract politeness than geniality in them. It surprised me to receive no answer to my first letter home; but inasmuch as the generous sum deposited to my credit with my father's London banker, on my second visit to the metropolis, was not yet entirely exhausted, I did not think as much as I should have thought of my father's ominous silence. In truth my love for my wife was so extravagant and iconoclastic, that, for a time, it left no other image than hers in my mind, and measured days only as the lengthening or shortening shadows of that one image. It was a love to regenerate me; my graver follies were extinguished by it; and had my preceding life constituted any sort of basis for its legitimate moral fruition I had been changed by its influence into a new creature. Strange to say, I passed two whole years in this love-life with scarcely a troubled thought of my parent. Then, the death of our infant gave me enough of a father's deeper feelings to call vividly to my mind the father to whom my duty was due, and, with a keen mingling of penitence and apprehension, I sent another letter home. This time there came a reply from my father's own hand. It denounced me, in the severest terms, for having brought lasting shame upon an old and honorable family, exiled me peremptorily and forever from the paternal presence, and enclosed a cheque for £500, as the last cent I must expect to receive from an insulted and injured father! I could hardly credit my senses when they interpreted these words to me; but soon the reality of my situation grew plainer and I cowered under the blow. It was not, however, until Angela persuaded me to show her the letter, and, in her great love for me, wept at its cruelty, that I became passionately rebellious against the paternal decree, and indignantly resolved to see my offended sire at once. Taking my wife with me to Liverpool, and leaving her there, I proceeded in furious haste to the home of my undisciplined childhood, and burst unannounced into the presence of my father. He was seated in his library, reading; and, though changing color at my rude entrance and disordered appearance, gave me not the least sign of welcome. 'Well, sir,' he said, very coldly, 'what do you mean by this uninvited and unmannerly intrusion? Are you mad, or have you forgotten my express commands?' His careworn look spoke louder than his tongue. Panting with emotion I fell upon my knees and strove to take his hand. 'Father!' I cried, 'what has turned you so bitterly against me, your only child? What unpardonable crime have I committed, to be treated in this manner? In all that I am conscious of having done to offend you, dear sir, the thoughtlessness of misguided youth has been my greatest sin. Will you not at least shake hands with me, my father?'

"Snatching away the hand I sought to seize, he arose from his chair and spurned me pitilessly.

"'Call me anything but father!' he exclaimed, hastily; 'I am your father no longer. Go back to your new kindred, unworthy young man, and, in their appropriate society, learn the arts and sciences of barter. Throw aside the honorable name you have disgraced, and, upon that condition, only, I will see that you never starve.'

"'Sir,' I cried, starting indignantly to my feet, 'something more than my marriage with a woman to honor any estate is accountable for this treatment from you. No longer as a son will I address you, since you discard me so arbitrarily; but, as a gentleman, I demand to know who it is that has poisoned your whole nature against me?'

"The proud old captain gave me a smile to which a frown would have been caressing, and replied, —

"'Brighton Keene.'

"He evidently expected to strike me dumb with the name, and I did indeed reel and catch my breath. Let the fact plead for me; let it palliate some of my waywardness with the key it affords to my natural character; — I had never, for one instant, thought of attributing my calamity to my cousin.

"'Brighton Keene?' I gasped, a flood of light breaking upon me in a moment.

"'Yes,' was his harsh reply; and with something of triumph in it, too; for he mistook my horrified astonishment for the confusion of guilt surprised; 'yes, presuming gentleman! He who would have kept you upright when you persisted in falling into every dissipation; he who would have restrained you when you squandered fortune and honor at the gaming-table; he who warned you of my displeasure when you sought a wife from the rabble; he whom you struck in the face for his fidelity to my trust in him; he whom I have taken to the heart and place no longer yours. You have your answer, gentleman!'

"I rushed headlong from his presence with brain on fire and a thousand murderous impulses flashing across the stormy blackness of my despair. Coming upon a servant in the garden, I asked for my cousin, and was told that he had gone to a neighboring village, but would be back presently. The man gave me a look of recognition in a double sense, as he said it, and I knew that he would not betray me. Procuring a pair of pistols, I took my place at the park gate, and there awaited Brighton Keene. Presently he came riding up, mounted upon a favorite horse formerly ridden by me and wearing a suit I had given him in London. The horse was right abreast of the steward's lodge when I bounded from the hedge and swiftly dragged my maligner from the saddle, checking his instinctive call for help with my hand on his white throat. 'Treacherous scoundrel!' I hissed in his ear, 'you well know why I am here. I have pistols with me. Will you fight me like a man, on this very spot, and now; or must I strangle you like a dog?'

"Pale as a ghost, and making no attempt to speak, he reached toward the weapons in my breast. One of these I permitted him to take; but no sooner had I released his throat, than he suddenly presented the pistol and snapped it in my face. The coward had no opportunity to repeat his treachery; for, in another moment, he was gasping on the sod with a ball through him. Giving a hysterical laugh, I threw down my pistol and fled from the accursed scene. Rejoining my agonized wife in Liverpool, I told her, in a few hurried words, what I had done, and expressed my determination to embark for America in a vessel sailing within the hour. She, with no other preparation than a hasty and guarded letter to her parents, was ready to go with me to the world's end, if need be, and before the sun went down we were homeless fugitives upon the trackless sea. We arrived in New York early in June, and, after stopping for a week at a hotel in Greenwich Street, under assumed names, the advice of a kind-hearted Commissioner of Emigration decided us to go westward in search of a living. After pawning some of our clothing to raise the means of travel, we repaired to Illinois, (near Jacksonville), where a wealthy farmer readily found a place for my wife as an upper house servant, and for me as a driver of stock. Unaccustomed as I was to trace God's just hand in all human mutations, I looked upon myself as the hapless victim of evil in others, not of my own folly; and the agony of seeing my patient wife reduced to servitude, added thereto, not only excluded me from the blessing of penitential resignation, but rendered me still less worthy of any relieving mercy from the Lord and Saviour I had forgotten. A year rolled around, and with the next spring came a daughter to our arms, and the intelligence that my wife's father had died, leaving her the possessor of £20,000 in drafts on New York. Thus were we suddenly lifted from disgrace and want to prosperity again, and we called our darling April, from the month of clouds and sunshine in which she was born. Taking leave at once of our western refuge and our assumed name, we came back to this city and resumed our proper mode of living. No one cared to inquire of our precedents; we were rich, we were Europeans, and the trading aristocracy of the shopkeeper's metropolis asked nothing more to make our home its shrine of fashion. I might have commenced a new and better life then, had not my restoration to something of my old rank brought with it a spectre unknown to my adversity on the prairies. I began to think of Keene's pale, twitching face upturned from the grass; day and night a relentless ghost stood between me and all else, and my peace was gone forever. As in life, so in death it led me toward destruction. It led me again from home and love; it taught me to deceive love again; it led me to the gaming-table for relief; and one night it led me back, home, a beggar!

"Yes, Brighton Keene! you did this; and I saw that moving finger of yours pointing to my wife, when I reeled into the dimly-lighted room on that early morning, and beheld her sleeping on her knees beside the bed of our child, with her tired head resting on the tear-wet pillow. I saw your finger there; and I read in your eyes that your lost soul hoped she would not forgive me!

"She awoke to learn, from my self-accusing lips, that beggary had followed neglect; that the reckless gamester had finished what the graceless husband had begun. She awoke, to hang upon my neck in the face of that ghost, and say, 'We have God, our child, and each other, left!'

"Keene disappeared at the words. He did not return when we sank with our home to abject poverty in one of the poorest parts of the city; he kept under the grass while I toiled daily as a common laborer, and Angela sewed for a weekly pittance. One night, as we sat over our poor meal, the woman who had borne every wrong from me without murmuring rebuked me sharply for spilling my tea upon the patched table-cloth. I answered, with some bitterness, that such a cloth was past injury;

she retorted with the words, 'You have made it what it is!' and met my stare with a fixed frown. Aghast I looked at her, and then, like the riving of every heartstring came the discovery, that my wife was homely!

"It went to my heart a very death to the last fair hope of my life; and, as I drew my tortured eyes away from the changed face, and groaned under the shock, they rested on Brighton Keene. He stood near the door, pointing at her. Uttering a wild oath, I sprang from the table, hastened madly forth with the ghost; and was from that hour a drunkard. . . . .
. . . . Once more he was with us; standing between Her comfortless pallet and the low cot of our child; whilst I, shivering in my rags, stood on Her other side, watching Her — and Him. He pointed *then* to the child, with that writing forefinger, and looked intently at Her, — not at me.

"'My poor little one!' murmured the sufferer.

"I knelt beside the pallet with a stony calmness bred of the awful instant when my immortal soul seemed already lost.

"'Angela,' I whispered, 'there is another than ourselves and April in this room.'

"'Who will take care of my poor little one?' she moaned, starting up in bed and looking toward the cot of the sleeper.

"Still possessed with that awful calmness, not of myself, I folded my ragged arms about her.

"'My wife, heed Him not. My darling, heed Him not. Don't let Him make our child a witness against her father and your husband in such an hour as this. We are all starving, — my heart is breaking. O God! give me Her forgiveness in thine!'

"She turned to me without a frown on her face; her eyes deadened for an instant, and then flashed full of her earliest love; she was beautiful to me again: 'Dear husband, forgive —' Her arms raised to circle my neck as of old; then slipped away from me as her head fell upon my shoulder.

"She was dead; — and Brighton Keene had left me forever!

"I can write more calmly of this than of any other event in my married life; for I know that Heaven was more than merciful in sparing that matchless woman the sight of what I am now, — of what I have made our child. To have seen this natural and fearful end of my folly and madness, would have been *not* to forgive.

"Here, in a damp, miserable cellar of the Five Points, a half-crazed pauper writes his story for a begging accordeon girl! Is this indeed the end of all? . . . I must cease wishing for death in her presence; I must make her think me happy; and so keep from her childish mind the sense of her position that might, from its very hopelessness, make her feel the more of the contagious curse of the place. I must let Reese read this confession, sometime, and make him promise to take her away from here when I am gone. I must —

"O thou long-offended Deity! *what* must I do? What can I really do, but delicate this legacy of April Grey's to the protector of the innocent, no less than the deserter of the guilty, and seal it with an unworthy father's tear?"

The voice of the reader trembled with irrepressible emotion as he enunciated the last words; and, while the child of Angela's husband moaned upon her father's breast, and I hung down my head and wept in sympathy, he solemnly knelt beside the dying man, and said, —

"My son, your sins have been great; but it may please a merciful Creator to weigh your sufferings against them. I find that you are not of my faith; but in this, your full and free confession, I see hope that the Holy Mother of God may absolve you through the last office of the only true church. Your child I will take with me to a place where good sisters will keep her safe from harm until the right friends for her shall be found. This I promise you."

I looked at Olden Grey, because I dared look at no one else, and saw the peaceful face brighten for an instant, and then begin to change awfully.

"Look at the child!" cried a voice that was almost fierce in its sharpness; "is she dying, too?"

The priest and I both raised our eyes involuntarily to where Reese stood.

"She has fainted," said the priest, "and her father is too far gone to know it." Adding, with a touch of awe in his grave manner, "It is a mercy to both."

Reese turned a haggard face upon the speaker, and dropped his arms to his side as though hopelessly resigning his heart to something against which he had striven to guard it by his first attitude. "You are a good man," he quietly remarked, "if you *are* a Catholic. You are a better man, too, a far better man, to take the girl, than I am. Poor Grey"—his tones sank to a hoarse whisper—"is dying, then? I always thought that man had a ghost in his face; I always thought he had a ghost in his face."

Saying these last words audibly, but apparently to himself, he turned his gaze to the bed again, shook his head regretfully, and walked slowly from the room.

I stole away after him in a couple of moments, and found him standing under the stoop, with his arms folded again, his face even paler than before, and his eyes staring dilatedly at vacancy across the street. I touched him, and he smiled foolishly, and said that he must have been dreaming.

— ◦◦◦ —

CHAPTER XXVIII.

THE LAST DAY.

I CERTAINLY felt a kind of frightened pity for Mr. Grey, and a hearty sympathy for poor little April; but, upon regaining the loft, I found myself thinking more of the strange story read by the priest than of the suffering I had witnessed. To hear such a tale right from the very paper on which it had been written, and in the presence also of two of its actors, was an actuality of romance producing a stranger effect upon my imagination than even Roderick Random had done; and in the solitude of that queer Cow Bay library of mine, I sat and speculated upon Brighton Keene and his victims until the dying father and fainting child downstairs were as the inconsistent figures of a dream to me. After such a close acquaintance with the stuff that books are made of, I felt no inclination to resort to the staler stuff on the shelves; but was seized with a misty sort of desire to write something for myself. A stubby wooden pencil belonging to Reese was on one of the shelves, and simultaneously with my wish for paper came the recollection that the "Treatise on Book-keeping" contained quite a number of nearly blank leaves. In no little flurry I got down that least romantic of volumes, opened it upon the table, and could scarcely contain myself until I had written that standard imprimis, "There was once a man."

That assertion, at once definite and non-committal, being fairly inscribed, time and trouble fled away, and I plunged excitedly into an imaginary world of astonishing occurrences. I played Providence to that world with just the same lack of logic and coherency that mistaken piety too often attributes to the Providence of this; and the way I shaped the extraordinary destiny of the "man" who "was once," is to this day one of my most amusing recollections. I made that man's short and eventful life an ingenious combination of Mrs. Fry's Sunday literature, Mr. Grey's pistolling work, and Roderick Random's general exploits; I attired him in a gorgeous costume, whereof each piece must have belonged to a different century, and I charged him with so much slaughter for the attainment of a wife, that he might have had a separate ghost for every hour of the day.

Not until nightfall did I give a moment's rest to this preternaturally active and incoherent adventurer; and I only relinquished him then because his last murder (of a couple of singularly timid robbers) brought him right against a column of figures in "Profit and Loss Account," and because hunger began to render me too malignant with my other characters. I found myself writing of the "hellish designs" of somebody; and then it was time for me to go to supper.

The journey down through those ranges of fever-stricken dens again, and the moans sounding here and there above the chattering of half-intoxicated women, drew my thoughts back to the scene of the morning; and my heart beat quickly as I went down the ladder from the stoop, and hurried past the basement window without courage to look in. I expected to find Reese at Brignoli's; but he was not there, and neither the lowering old Italian nor his daughters could tell anything of his whereabouts. On my return from my combined dinner and supper, however, I found him at the foot of the stoop ladder, and was sententiously informed that he designed ascertaining how Mr. Grey did before going upstairs. So, up to the loft I repaired once more alone, noticing — not for the first time, either — that nearly all the ragged, goblin children who formerly swarmed in the passages and on the stairs, had disappeared. Now and then one would sprawl in a doorway; but the swarm was gone; the miserable old tenement missed the yells of children, and was much the drearier therefrom.

Wretchedly depressed in spirits I regained the society of the lethargic Mr. Mugses; and, after feeding him with sea-biscuit and sausage from Brignoli's, I lighted a candle and sat desperately down to read. I cared not to write then.

When Reese came up, some two hours subsequently, I threw aside the book, and asked how Mr. Grey was doing.

"He needs less sympathy than we do," was the evasive reply, the speaker throwing himself heavily upon the settee and wearing an expression of countenance anything but happy. "What an infernal fate there is in my being kept cooped-up here in the Points so long! I feel like suicide every time I come up those stairs. But day after to-morrow's election day, and if I can only buy enough Irishmen to give Judge O'Toole's son the votes he wants for the legislature from this ward, — you understand? — O'Toole has promised to make it all right for me to clear from here in another week."

His face grew quite animated at this prospect, but clouded again immediately with a new thought. —

"Who do you think I saw across the way this morning, — watching me, too?"

"Juan?"

"No. I've seen him dogging around the Bay often enough; but it wasn't him. Upon the whole, youngster, I don't think I'll tell you who I thought it was."

I was too familiar with his caprices to mind this one. In fact I did not care to know whom he had seen, though I was determined not to be put off with his unsatisfactory reply to my first question.

"You have not told me yet, Mr. Reese," said I, "how poor Mr. Grey gets along."

"Dead!" he exclaimed. "If you must know everything, he's dead! dead! dead as a door-nail! Now I don't want to talk to you any more to-night. I'm blue enough without thinking of dead men. Go on with your book, or go to bed. I'm going to sleep."

Dead! I had no wish to talk more. The word had an awful sound to me, though I realized very little of its full meaning. I went to bed softly, and thought sorrowfully of April until I slumbered.

Early in the morning, while my unstable companion yet lay sleeping, I slipped down the ladder and stairways to the basement, drawn thither by an irresistible curiosity. At the door of the room I paused and listened; and, as no sound came from within, I turned the battered knob and timidly entered. No one was there. The mattresses, the paper curtains, the chairs, all were in their old places; but no one was there. Surprised at the lonely and desolate look of the apartment, I retreated to the entry with some precipitation, and met a woman coming down the stairs with a sick child in her arms.

"Can you tell me, ma'am," I asked, "where the little girl, that used to live in that room, has gone to?"

Yes, she could tell me something about her. The old man was carried away in a coffin last night, and the girl went away at the same time with a priest. The doctor from the Almshouse, who was attending the sick on the first floor, made them bury their dead almost before the breath was out of them. She — the woman — was going into that very room to see if she couldn't get some air for her child.

I let the poor creature pass me, and then I sat down upon a step and cried heartily for my lost sweetheart. I could scarcely appreciate the highest value of a father, yet I was sure that April must have loved hers much more than I loved mine; and, besides, like me, she had no mother. I am glad to remember how bitterly I cried for another's troubles in that dark, damp cavern of an entry; for the very refinement of my feeling was a proof of how far God had preserved my young heart from the contagion of wickedness in that terrible place.

Reese was pacing the floor when I returned to him, and immediately noticed my red eyes and trembling lips. He, too, looked downcast and disordered, and when I related what had happened, he pressed a hand to his forehead and stared gloomily at the floor.

"I feel very unwell myself," said he; "my head feels ready to split and I have had crazy dreams. Rumsey died yesterday, too. They have a headache, first, I believe." Then, resuming his walk, he added. — "I'd about as soon die outright as be worried to death with the nervousness that's hung about me these three or four days. But let's go down to Brignoli's and get some breakfast," he continued, tossing his hat upon his head and pretending to shake off his presentiments of evil; "we're worth a dozen dead men yet; and as to-morrow's election, and to-night's a mass meeting out here by the Park, there's a prospect of something lively at last."

I was afraid that he felt really sick, and, at the thought, what affection he permitted me to feel for him came to the surface again.

"If you have the fever, I'll take care of you," was my impulsive remark.

It seemed to put him into a better humor immediately. He held me by the hand all the way to our dingy eating-house, and paid more attention to me than to the girls during the meal.

I left him on the sidewalk paying election money to half-a-dozen sinister-looking denizens of the Bay when I went back to the loft, and did not see him again until nearly noon, when he came boisterously up the ladder greatly excited, followed closely by another man. The dog barked, I stared from my book in unspeakable amazement, and the pedler whose sudden visit to the gipsy camp afforded me such entertainment, and perplexity at the time, stood grinning familiarly in my face. A coat of mixed gray stuff buttoned to the neck, and a jockey cap aslant over his keen eyes, changed his aspect somewhat, and vaguely reminded me of somebody I had seen elsewhere than with the gipsies; but he was unmistakably the pedler, for all, and I answered his nod of recognition with one of like kind.

"Well, this sky-parlor *is* jolly!" exclaimed he, drawing up his shoulders and taking in every object with one sweeping glance. "It's precisely the apartment in a private house, neatly furnished, for a bachelor with one child. Access to a good library if desired, and windows commanding a fine view of the sky. Reese, my boy, you're better off than I thought you. Only, if I was you, I'd take a dollar or so for myself from O'Murphy's allowance for voters and buy an extra bedstead."

"Oh, confound the bedstead!" cried Reese, pushing a chair toward the pedler, and taking a seat himself on the table. "I'll turn the whole establishment over to you to-morrow, if what you tell me is true. Come, Ketchum, stop skylarking with that dog and just give me the story over again."

My protector was evidently under the influence of some very strong feeling; for his eyes sparkled with it, and he pinched his chin and cheeks as though trying to make sure of being awake.

"All true as gospel," returned the other, twirling the chair about on one leg. "The old governor is dead, his lawyer, who is executor, too, has got the will, and he sent me to hunt you up. I don't know just what the sum is, but it's something jolly. You're in a ticklish fix, though, about that business with Hugo, you know."

"Bah!" exclaimed Reese, snapping his fingers, "I'm working up the election down here for a man who'll see that any indictment against me is put out of the way in less than a week. But this thing takes away my breath, fairly. I can hardly believe it yet! I hardly know as much about my family as you do; and as for the old man remembering me, — why, I'd as soon expect a testimonial, — you understand? — from the Tract Society."

After some further talk of this kind, Reese persistently questioning the truth of the story, and Mr. Ketchum as persistently reaffirming its truth, the two men finally went down from the loft together, leaving me to make what I could of their conversation. I did try to draw some definite idea from it; but, failing in this, I was about reverting to my book again, when Reese came leaping up the ladder once more, without the pedler, and began dancing around the place like a maniac.

"What ails you?" questioned I, in alarm.

"Good luck ails me; good luck!" shouted he, bringing up against the cupboard, and leaning there while he panted for breath. "I'm a made man, my dear fellow, and you never could guess what a good thing it may be for you, too. I shall be able to live like an honest Christian once more, — you understand? — for there's money left to me by an uncle I haven't heard from this many a year."

"I'm glad of that," said I; "but he isn't my uncle, too, — is he?"

Reese gave me a sharp look.

"Not ex-actly. Don't you mind who he was, Glibun. It's enough for you to know at present that this is our last day here. I wouldn't be here for another hour if it was not for the election. Doesn't it sound like a miracle to talk about this being our last day, after what we've gone through in this death-hole?—It does to me, my dear fellow."

"Poor April Grey! I wonder where she is?"

"We'll find her and take care of her for her folks in England. I'll have money enough."

"And you won't make me go back to father?"

"If I'd had that in my mind, youngster, I'd have done it before this."

"Was Mr. Ketchum the one you thought you saw across the street, yesterday?"

Reese's countenance fell at the question, and he hesitated awhile before answering.

"N-n-no. But don't let's talk about that."

I was still without any very definite idea of just what had happened, yet the exhilaration of my companion cheered me considerably. Until the breaking-out of the pestilence in Rack-and-Ruin Row I had not been positively unhappy there; I was at least free from ill-treatment and fear of my father; yet the idea of escaping from thence gave me a thrill of pleasure not unlike what a prisoner might have felt on finding his dungeon doors unlocked.

At various times during the day Reese came to me, to see, as he said, how I was getting along, and displayed altogether so much affection and high spirits that one would scarcely have taken him for the same being as his yesterday's self. He promised me that I should take the books when we went away on the morrow, predicted for me a great treat in the mass-meeting to be held that night, and even declared that Mr. Mugses should also be present at the same meeting as a regular Demolition dog.

Downstairs, too, such people as were not dead or dying gave noisy indications of reviving cheerfulness; all the liquor shops of the Points being free to them for twelve hours by order of the Honorable Mealy O'Murphy.

As night approached, the uproar in the houses and street waxed more furious under the gratuitous flow of raw spirits. Two or three times when I ventured down the ladder I found desperate fights going on in the passages and rooms, between negroes and Irishmen crazed with drink; only some squalid apartment here and there being comparatively quiet because creatures were dying in it. The liquor, the money paid for votes, and the impending Election Day, all tended to produce a howling and murderous saturnalia, in which the ghastly presence of Death was forgotten, and the fiends of Crime and starving Debauchery held the revels of wild beasts.

It was shortly after dark that Reese called me to go with him to the Italian's to supper. He advised me to carry down the dog, as it would be some protection to have the latter with me at the meeting; "for," said he, laughingly, "I'm going to another sort of show myself, and shan't be on hand to look out for you. As this is the Last Day, I propose to wind it up with a little glorification."

I inferred from this that he intended remaining at Brignoli's; nor was I mistaken. When we had finished eating, and the half-dozen organ-grinders at the table began to light their pipes, he told me that I had better go up to the Park at once, and see what there was to be seen; adding, that he would try to find me there on the way to his "glorification." I unquestioningly obeyed him, as usual, taking the dog with me, and if his arrangement of separate amusements for himself and me had any significance beyond his ordinary oddity, I did not trouble myself to think about it.

Along one edge of the withered little mockery of a park, lying just out of the Cow Bay triangle, a rickety platform of rough boards had been hastily constructed, with dingy lanterns hanging at each corner of the rude railing surmounting it, and when I joined the throng of ragged men and women already gathering before it on Little Water Street, it was swarming with the filthy and half-naked children of the Points, who climbed the props and swung on the rails like frantic monkeys. Presently, however, a tar-barrel was fired in the Park itself, throwing the whole wild scene into a flashing, yellowish glare; and then the platform was deserted for the new attraction, and the impish crew fled screaming to the blaze. In the ghastly illumination, which extended high into the vaporous night above, like a sallow, pestilential day turned upside down, the blighted Park, with its dying trees, starving, rag-cart horses, lines of drying rags and fire-surrounding ring of young furies, was centre to an irregular circle of such tottering rows of wooden purgatories as Death himself might shrink from entering. A hundred yawning windows, many of them all askew with the sinking of the rotten tenements, were filled with the swollen faces and bony arms of hags and harpies, who gesticulated and hooted at the snarling mob below. The light from the fire seemed to rouse a kind of frenzy in the whole concourse; so that when the Poorhouse hearse came up from Cross Street, to bear away some new load of departed Demolition votes, in long, heavy boxes, from Cow Bay, the driver was saluted with jeers, curses, and missiles, and could scarcely guide his stumbling old black horse through the excited crowd. By the time the tumult and the light had drawn the more sluggish of the Pointers from their holes in the alleys and cellars, a fife and drum sounded at hand, and a procession with torches and printed canvas transparencies was seen turning the corner of Anthony Street. It was the "O'Murphy Club," as several of the transparencies affirmed in large black letters; and, although its members worked their way to the platform by the rather summary device of thrusting their lighted brands into the ingenuous faces of all who stood in their path, the populace of the Points received it with a fearful roar of approval. Right upon the heels of the club, the "O'Murphy Invincibles," similarly equipped, came pouring in from Pearl Street, and were welcomed in the same way; the fact that nearly all of them were but half-grown boys making no difference in the fine political enthusiasm of the multitude. The sputtering torches and a second tar-barrel had given an even greater distinctness than before to the wild forms and faces of the lost and their surrounding dens of misery, when about a dozen men appeared upon the platform amid a tempest of unearthly howls, and bowed in all directions to their admirers. Then, after a couple of torch-bearers and several transparency-holders ("Vote for O'Murphy, the Workingman's Friend!") had climbed up, also, one of the men stepped forward to the front railing, with his hat in one hand and a paper in the other, and proposed that "our noble candidate for Alderman, Mr. John Bull, be appointed President of this triumphant gathering of freemen."

Frightful applause having confirmed this nomination, the speaker thoughtfully stroked his yellow whiskers, and proceeded to remark, that this was a sight to stir the patriot heart with glorious emotions, and bind America and Ireland together in a brotherhood too strong for British gold (sarcastically) to sever. (Dreadful noises, intended for cheers.) The eyes of the whole world were upon that assemblage, which sternly and boldly and defiantly represented the dignity of American labor. The tyrants of besotted Europe would tremble on their ill-gotten thrones, when they heard how that assemblage had arisen in its majesty, and proclaimed that the Honorable Mealy O'Murphy should vindicate the true grandeur of honest toil in Congress, and do something for poor old Ireland.

Terrific bellowings of delight crowned this eloquent little speech with success, and broke out afresh when Mr. John Bull, of "Sportman's Hall," came modestly to the front and addressed his esteemed fellow-citizens. He had not, he said, surveyed such a scene before, since he left Seven Dials, and 'oped the b'ys would excuse 'im hif 'e felt 'imself overcome by the sight; 'e, 'imself, 'ad been called a 'ated Saxon by the great Hamerican people after the latter 'ad been drinking; but ever since the day when he sailed from Liverpool (and away from a warrant), for this free and heasy country, 'e 'ad put 'is 'and upon 'is bosom and declared that 'e would never go back! Hit was not for 'im to say what qualifications 'e 'ad for the hoffice of halderman; nor what merits 'ad been recognized in 'is appointment as president of the meetin' then before 'im. Per'aps 'e 'ad some dorgs that were credits to their speeshes and a source of hinnocent hamusement to the Hamerican people. (Cheers.) 'e only knew that 'e preferred a one-eyed poodle to an Ebullitionist, and would cast a freeman's wote for Mealy O'Murphy and Liberty.

Mr. Bull retired under a prolonged roar of popular delight, which renewed itself with ingenious variations upon the sudden appearance, from Anthony Street, of the "Mealy O'Murphy Guard," bearing colored paper lanterns and fireworks. The drum and fife enlivening the march of this military pageant remorselessly delayed the oratory of a third speaker on the platform, he being compelled to await their conclusion of an elaborate Irish jig; and, to make the din greater, the drums and fifes of the "Club" and the "Invincibles" now joined in the concert. By way of rendering themselves the more attractive as a fiery spectacle, the Guards wound tortuously into the surging heart of the meeting, like an endless serpent, under a shower of green, red, white, and blue transparencies; and this device, added to the scattered constellations of torches, the murky glow of fresh tar-barrels in the Park, the hissing flight of rockets, and the curdling, festering sea of shapeless hats and caps and bull-dog heads, completed a lurid pit worthy to be walled-in by the flame-whitened dens of the Five Points.

From what I saw and heard I was deriving much instruction for my youthful mind, and a precocious insight of my country's very free institutions, when the "Mealy O'Murphy Guard" came curling past where I stood, and, in one who marshalled them, with a particularly large lantern, I thought that I recognized an old friend. In a moment he was hidden by the mob again, and, while I was straining to tiptoe for another glimpse of him, my jacket was sharply twitched from behind. I turned, and confronted Reese and the elder Brignoli girl, arm in arm, the former in his false whiskers and sailor dress, and the latter in tawdry attire.

"I thought I'd find you somewhere about here," said Reese, with a rattling, boyish air; "you're always on the edge of things, instead of in the middle. We're going to a select family party at that big rookery, with a Dutch roof, over there by Cross Street. You stay here until you've seen enough of this, and then you and Mr. Mugses go up to the loft. I'll be there by midnight. I wouldn't leave you now if I didn't feel so much like one parting celebration of our good luck. It's the Last Day, you know." And he turned back, after going a few steps, to repeat, gleefully, "It's the Last Day, Glibun!"

Not altogether pleased with the arrangement, yet sufficiently accustomed to the man's freaks to see nothing strange in it, I gave my attention once more to the meeting, hoping presently to catch another glimpse of the man with the big lantern. Either he was my rescuer from the burning House that Jack built, or my first glance had been curiously delusive. But for the dog, who crouched affrightedly against my feet, I should have followed through the ruffian throng, and endeavored to satisfy my doubts. Not wishing, however, to lose the poor animal, I remained quiet, and presently heard the speaker on the platform saluted by a name not altogether strange to my ears, — Mr. Stiles.

"Men of America!" shouted he, supremely indifferent to certain facetious remarks of the populace upon the rakish style of his costume, "the national melody having ceased, I will proceed to return thanks that I am permitted to live to see this evening, when the noble working-man stands here under the blue dome of the empyrean, to protest against all richness whatsoever. The rich man rides in his luxurious carriage, drinks his rare wines, and counts his millions in Wall Street. Would a poor man do this, think you? (Earnest cries of 'Niver a bit.') No! the honest poor man, the noble working-man, scorns to assume the pomp of foreign lordlings. I, myself, once threaded the glittering ranks of haughty fashion and took my place in the gaudy throng; but shortly after losing my property I became the friend of the poor man, and am to this day in favor of either the abolishment of riches, or their equitable division among all men, without further confusion." Here Mr. Stiles took advantage of much applause and several spirited single combats among his auditors, to pause until he had inserted a thumb in either armhole of his flowered waistcoat. "I am not ashamed, fellow-citizens," continued he, "to own that I am now a poor but honest shaft-horse where I was formerly a prancing leader. I am proud to range myself with that glorious old Demolition party on whose outpourings even lovely woman looks smilingly down. (Animated shrieks of approval from the nearest windowful of furies.) I am doubly proud to be of the same political denomination with one whose earnest facilitation of every public good has justly established him as the friend of humanity and of down-trodden Ireland. I allude to General Cringer."

A tremendous yell, and a wild rush for the platform took place at this announcement, several hoarse voices howling, "He's a black-sowled Eb'litionist!"

Mr. Stiles pensively cracked and ate peanuts until the tempest softened down; and then went calmly on, —

"The revered name I have uttered belongs to one who may have been an Ebullitionist yesterday; but who is now, from honest conviction, a Demolitionist and a Mealy O'Murphy man! (Frightful cheers.) General Cringer's dog has fought for the O'Murphy (great enthusiasm, and an exhibition of deep emotion on the platform by Mr. Bull); General Cringer's parlor has been the home of O'Murphy target warriors; and General Cringer has *seen* — Macginnis."

Then roared the ruffian mob again, as it surged back and forth with half a dozen hand-to-hand fights; and the roar took the form of one deafening, half-menacing question, —

"How much for Macginnis?"

"Gentlemen of the Five Points," answered the courtly orator, blandly, " I will answer satisfactorily, if you will. but hold your horses a moment. During the many months of our extraordinary campaign for the O'Murphy, our mutual friend Macginnis has been preserved from want, despite his unparalleled generosity to the noble working-man; but this very morning he was heard to ask a noble working-man, ' Will ten dollars a day, for two days, pay you for staying home from rag-picking and laboring for the glorious old Demolition ticket? If so, have you not a hundred friends, or so, whom you could persuade to also give two days to their country at a similar sacrifice?' Such, fellow-citizens, were the inspired words of Macginnis. (Ecstatic hurrahs!) But let us return to our thorough-bred standard-bearer, Mealy O'Murphy; let us contemplate his virtues and repel the insinuation of the insidious Ebullitionists. It is objected that his nose is broken; it is objected that he once met that enemy of Ireland, the ' Hunky Boy,' in a twenty-foot ring, and defeated him gorgeously after twenty rounds. (Cries of ' shame!' from the other gentlemen on the platform.) Yes! Shame indeed! That nose is a red badge of the patriotism which does not shrink from violent personal collision with the foes of our country, —

"'Such hue our Yankee banner wears,
    And shall until the world is done,
  To show the sacred stain it bears
  Where freedom's martyrs bled thereon.'

"That defeat of the ' Hunky Boy,' and the victor's subsequent election to the legislature by the votes of this ward, —

"'How light the ballots fall,
    Like snow-flakes on the sod, —
  And execute the Freeman's will,
    As lightning does the will of God.' —

"That defeat and that election, were at once the patriot's trial and the patriot's reward. (Applause of wild beasts.) They are the record which the Honorable Mealy O'Murphy presents in justification of his claim for your ballots now. Arise, then, noble working-men of America, and vote for the man whose nose has bled for poor old Ireland, and to whom a bloated aristocracy furthermore object, because the present green baize-covered tables (Ireland's own color), from which he derives a frugal livelihood, are free for an occasional innocent game of cards. (Prolonged snarls of indignation.) And who are the accursed Ebullitionists running against him? Who but one Mr. Knickerbocker? (Howls.) Yes, Knickerbocker! A pretty name to be thrust before the voters of New York! A man with such a name has no business to even ask a vote in this city. Mealy O'Murphy is our man; *he* will never insult you by calling you the equals of the depraved negro. No, no! Cheer for him, then, until the very skies tremble

"'As though the fiends from heaven that fell
  Had pealed the banner-cry of hell!'"

Up rose again that frightful mixture of roar, howl, groan, and shrieked imprecation. The torches danced and swirled like phosphoric death-beacons on an ocean of the lost; the rookeries of the Points frothed at the windows with all that was hideous in hopeless womanhood; the rockets went up in lurid streaks through the glare from the hags' washing-ground; and several black men in the mob were promptly beaten half to death by the noble working-men.

Mr. Bull introduced the next speaker as Judge O'Toole. The latter was a short, stout man, with high cheek-bones, red face, and a head of red hair resembling a bushy fur cap.

"F'hat's that?" exclaimed the judge, rather nervously, as a low, black-covered wagon, drawn by a pale and weary horse, was seen working its slow way past, and nearly against, the platform.

"It's the bone-wagon, sure," yelled a voice.

"The grace of the saints be wid it!" cried Judge O'Toole, striving to appear vigorously self-possessed. "It's the living that I'm talking to when I say, that me countrymen haven't eshcaped from the tyranny and ohprayshun of Saxon rule, to be made aiquals of the dirty naygur. If it was the lasht day I ever had to live; if it was the lasht day — "

There *was* something wrong down there

by the corner of Cross Street. I thought there was when the crowd in that direction murmured so, just after his first sentence. A sudden, unaccountable fear flashed a chill through my very heart, and I darted instinctively toward the house with the Dutch roof. Simultaneously, a hundred gaunt and ragged forms crowded wildly thitherward, too, and swept me and the yelping dog along faster than we could run. Something was the matter in that house. Men and women, with pale faces and unintelligible tongues, were hurrying frantically up the broken cellar-steps as we were tumbled down past them, and two policemen with pistols in their hands struggled just behind me in the thickest of the eager swarm. Down we went, scarcely touching a step; out of the light into darkness, through a dilapidated half-glass door, and down another flight, into light again. The light of fifty tallow candles stuck upon a cross of wood suspended horizontally from the rafters overhead by ropes. The light of half a dozen battered tin lamps against the moist and filthy walls of the noisome dance-cellar.

The rush of the multitude carried me far into the midst of a paralyzed company of sailors, negroes, rag-pickers, thieves, and white and black spectres of women in gaudy turbans and dresses. They were all packed in motionless pressure toward a rude bar on one side of the cellar, and there it was that something was wrong. Before I could pause for breath I was dashed mercilessly against shoulders, elbows, and limbs, as though the barrier were but a thicket. A moment I was hurled back upon my tormentors by a man who went bursting through their dense mass like a shot. A moment I pushed and struggled through the last line of the barrier, with a startled sense of having recognized Juan in the resistless fugitive. In a moment I was in the light again, and saw an amphitheatre of villanous faces, a man lying on his back upon the sawdust of the floor, a woman prone beside him, with her arms around his neck, and another woman standing like a Fate over the two, with a shawl covering her head.

The whole scene reeled about me, and I should have fallen had I not been caught by a policeman, — for there, before me, on the ground, was Reese, stark and dead!

With a great gasp I recovered myself sufficiently to stand, and turned in wild unbelief to glare upon something that should show me the unreality of the horror. I saw fierce, wicked faces, and a background of torches and lanterns, and heard the curses of the human wolves outside who leaped and fought to get in.

A burly negro was standing upon the bar, and his voice made me turn again.

"She done it!" he cried, addressing the officer and pointing vindictively at the shawled figure. "She stole up right thar, and stabbed him while he was dancing with that gal."

A sharp, shrill howl followed his last word; something sprang past me into the air, and the dog was at the throat of the murderess before an arm could be raised to seize her.

Quick as thought the officer drove the butt of his pistol, full force, upon the skull of the animal, and brained him; but at the first touch of the creature the motionless figure had swayed sideways in rigid fall, and now dropped to the floor, like an unbalanced statue, with her face at my feet.

"Poisoned!" said the officer.

The face was Anita's.

END OF VOLUME I.

AVERY GLIBUN;

OR,

BETWEEN TWO FIRES.

VOLUME II.

CHAPTER XXIX.

ANOTHER WORLD.

AT the word of the policeman, whose quick eye had read the fate of the gipsy girl in her distorted countenance. several other stout men. with clubs in their hands and brass stars on their breasts, roughly forced a way through the dense mass of horror-stricken voters and revellers, to the side of their comrade, and, after exchanging hurried whispers with him, at once began the work of clearing the cellar. Requests, or even commands, would have been unavailing with such an assemblage, fascinated by such a spectacle; so the officers sprang at their old enemies with elbows pointed and clubs uplifted. and began driving them back from the dead like cowed hyenas. The spell of silence broke with the onset; savage curses and yells of rage burst from a hundred hot throats, and more than one long knife was stealthily drawn by the raving wretches amongst whom I was once more hustled and dragged along. But the flight before the determined and merciless guardians of the law was still that of brutish fear, and presently I was being pushed and borne up the steps to the open air again in a surging and irresistible welling-up of the foulest scum from underground.

Bruised, blinded, and beside myself with horror, I gained the broken and slippery sidewalk. only to be dashed against a barrel of garbage and left to roll in the gutter; while the maddened tide which had wrecked me thus, and upon whose waters no man threw bread, poured on to lose itself in the wicked ocean of the streets. Half-stunned and wholly miserable. I was rising to my feet, when a man with a great red paper lantern over his right shoulder came leaping up the cellar-steps with such headlong speed that he ran against the barrel before he could stop himself, and nearly fell over me in the effort to retain his balance. I knew him, by the light of the lantern, as I had before known him by the glare from the Park.

"O Mr. Waters!" I cried, piteously, grasping one of his arms, "don't you remember me?"

Mr. Hosea Waters — for he was the man — had commenced a lively address to the offending barrel; but, at my salutation, he ceased his remarks with a jerk, and swung his lantern around my head several times. as though looking into some deep excavation.

"Hamlet," said he, "I'm your father's ghost!"

"O Mr. Waters!" I repeated. "don't you remember me? I'm the boy you saved from the fire that night!"

He thrust the lantern close to my face, so that its red glow made us distinctly visible to each other, and stared at me for a moment in lurid wonderment.

"You don't say you're that same tarrier?"

"Yes, sir, I'm the same one, upon my honor."

"Why, where's the fire this time?" he queried, staring over my head in evident expectation of witnessing some new conflagration to account for me.

"It's worse than a fire," replied I. miserably. "Oh, if you would only take me home with you again; only take me away from here! The man I came here with is the one they have murdered down there. He and the dog were all the friends I've got in the world. My heart feels like bursting. Oh, dear, what am I to do?" I fairly wrung my hands in helpless grief.

"There, there," murmured Mr. Waters," tapping me soothingly on the head with his lantern, "try to be cam. Let's get away from this cellar before they bring the coroner and lug you in for a witness."

I but faintly grasped his meaning, yet comprehended enough to perceive that it touched the possibility of my being compelled to look upon that awful scene again. The dancers were crowding back to the place, accompanied by the torch-bearers and others from the disordered mass-meeting, and I shuddered at the thought that some of them might know me as having lived with the dead man. I was unhappy, despairing, and distracted enough, Heaven knew, at what had so frightfully occurred; but it filled me with unspeakable terror to think of ever going down again into that vault of horror.

"Take me away from here!" I entreated, grasping the muscular arm of the fireman-politician. "Take me away before they notice me."

"All right, my cherub," was the response, in a tone of relief; "you can't do a dustier thing than come right along home with me. It kind of flashed on me that you was to do it, the minute I knew who you was. Now, vamose!"

The hordes of the Points were pressing around us, clamorous to re-enter the fatal house, and no time was allowed me for further explanation until Hosea had resigned his lantern to another member of the "Guard," and I found myself walking up Centre Street beside him. As on other occasions of bewildering misfortune in my unfortunate life, I felt like a sick creature in a miserable dream; yet I managed, as we walked on, to give my old friend some idea of how I got to Cow Bay, though refraining from telling him what ended my schooling, or under what circumstances I became acquainted with Reese.

In truth, my story, told hastily and with many sighs, would have been far from satisfactory, even if intelligible, to a more critical or curious listener. Mr. Waters, however, applauded it throughout with startling whistles and concise apostrophes to his favorite eye; and through Marion Street to Prince, and through Prince to near the corner of Crosby, these vivacious commentaries of his alternated very briskly.

Too much absorbed in my wretchedness to heed particularly which way we had come, I stopped when he did, without at first noticing that we stood before a door belonging, apparently, to a small store of some description. The door and single show-window of the establishment were arrayed in movable shutters, and closed for the night; but a huge brass key from Hosea's pocket was in the lock, and he and I were in the store in less time than it took me to comprehend the fact of the situation.

"Why, what place is this?" asked I, peering around into the darkness, while he closed and relocked the door.

Before undertaking to respond, the fireman struck a match, and lighted a swinging oil lamp, whose feeble rays presently revealed a small, square, dingy room, with shelves, along the walls, for cheap toys, jars of candy, and a confused assortment of thread-and-needle ware; not to mention a short, painted counter, bearing a little show-case on one end.

"This is my crib," explained Mr. Waters, in subdued tones. "We moved, you see, from that other place when we found this one was to let; and my old woman's mother came to live with us, and set me up in this dusty little shop. But you don't want to hear about that now. What you want is to go to sleep till morning, and then see what's best to do. Hold on here till I see if Milly's awake."

He disappeared through a half-glass door behind the counter, but quickly returned, on tiptoe, to say that his wife was asleep. It was evident from his manner of giving me this information, that, under the circumstances, he hardly knew what to do with me; so I at once insisted upon making my bed on the counter until morning, assuring him of my familiarity with couches not much softer, and scarcely so quiet. In short, I declared, rather impatiently, that I would either sleep in the store, or return to the street; and, after many whispered regrets at his "pickle," as he called it, and several hopeless efforts to explain the altogether discomfited state of mind he found himself in, Mr. Waters finally withdrew, under his first apparent realization of the curious thing he had done in bringing me home with him.

There was no slumber for me that night. Seated upon the counter, with my back against the show-case, and my knees drawn up to my chin, I watched the swinging lamp until it exhausted its small store of oil and flickered out. The darkness was an awakening shock to me, and the background against which the confused trials and bewilderments of my perverted life took visible form and hurrying action. The last frightful act in the unwholesome drama was still all a suffocating blur in my mind. I could not grasp it yet, and gave it only the physical recognition of a heart throbbing like an instinct frantically striving to run away from it; but oh, how distinctly and succinctly came the train of all that had gone before! The scene of Elfie's dismissal; the conversation overheard in that back parlor at home; my return to the custody of the school-master, and my father's significant glance at the latter when they parted; the madman's words on the Summit; the rescue by Wolfton; the gipsies; the pedler; the flight; the Five Points; the fever; the death; the last day; the ——! What a whirl of woe and wickedness was here for a boy's thoughts; what an unblest confusion of all that was worst in human weakness, degradation, and crime! As I sat there in the darkness, with such crowding disorders all alive in my brain, there gradually grew out of the latter two distinct and energetic mental results: a settled feeling of bitter resentment and defiance against my father, and a resolve — reckless enough — to be no longer dependent upon any other than myself. I had turned a second corner in my life, and become prematurely a man in the precocity bred of persecuting adversity.

Milly Waters came down to me in the morning, carrying a little babe in her arms, and made me go with her into a neat little room behind the store, where I recognized the picture of the military firemen, the trumpet and fire-cap, and the same stove and table which had been associated with my first breakfast from home. As on the former occasion, Mr. Waters had told his wife all that he knew of me, before my eyes fell upon her, and she greeted me with no greater signs of surprise, than if but a week had elapsed since the morning after the fire. In her old, soothing, gentle way, but with something more sisterly in her manner, she stroked my tangled hair, said she was glad to see me, and asked me if I would not like to hold the baby while she prepared breakfast? In all this there was a tender delicacy toward misfortune, which women only can show effectively; which makes their very footsteps soothing to pain, either of body or soul, and defines their true and holy sphere, with a power far beyond the cavils of all unsexed intellect. It cooled and quieted me at once; and when Hosea appeared, I was even trying to play with the child.

There was another, and a, to me, new member of this little family circle, though, whose greeting and subsequent proceedings were not so tender to my sensitive nerves. This was Milly's mother, a severe and wrinkled old lady, in shawl and cap, named Mrs. Hurstiches, who had to be led into an adjoining room, by her daughter, and there favored with a partially fabulous account of my character and adventures, before she would be persuaded to sit down at the same table with me.

Milly was coaxing me to eat, and, at the same time, striving, by nods and winks, to restrain Mr. Waters from talking about the events of the night before, when the old lady burst upon me with the question,—

" Are you a Roman Ketholic, Av'ry?"

"No, ma'am, I am not," responded I.

" Why, of course he aint, mother," put in Hosea, willing to relieve me, and to talk on some subject not forbidden; " he's no more Irish than I am, and how can he be a Catholic?"

" I've always told you, Hosea," said Mrs. Hurstiches, grimly and oracularly, " that the Roman Ketholics ruled this country, and they'll be a-killin' and a-burnin' us all in our beds, yet, if the Pope tells them to."

"Oh, they will, will they?" cried Mr. Waters, moving his head in quick little jerks from side to side, and drawing up his nose in supercilious scorn. " Well, then, Sixty's boy-y-s would jest like to see 'em try-y it ou-u-u! Say-y, mother, why don't yer try another sleeve-button?"

That being the poetical name for a fish-ball, the venerable matron held out her plate to be helped again, and started afresh.

"The Roman Ketholics, Hosea,—"

"Try a little West Broadway," urged the fireman, passing the hash; and Mrs. Hurstiches gave up the argument, in high dudgeon.

In consequence of a solemn compact with Macginnis, Mr. Waters was engaged, as he informed me, to spend that day at the polls, as a particular friend of the O'Murphy cause; but, before departing, he took down the shutters of the store, and installed me as temporary clerk, explaining that the price of each article was marked upon it in plain figures.

" Try to rush off some of that ere m'lasses candy, before there's more ants than peanuts in it," said he, sagaciously: " and don't go to worrying about yourself. My old woman will come in and talk to you for a while, after she's got the cherub asleep. She looks about the same as old times, don't she?"

" She's just as handsome," I said, — and I did think her beautiful, — "but she didn't have those marks like wrinkles on her forehead, before."

"Wrinkles!" exclaimed he, vehemently; " why, them aint wrinkles! What are you cackling about? Them's my troubles, and wouldn't 'a' been there if I hadn't been down, sick enough, about six months ago. They came then, and they aint no more wrinkles than I am!"

" She's so good," was my commentary.

In an hour thereafter, the kind and meek-eyed subject of our conjoint eulogy was taking advantage of a lull in business, and her babe's morning nap, to hear from me as much concerning myself as I would voluntarily repeat, and give such kind, judicious counsel as her womanly wisdom dictated in the case.

" I can see plainly, my poor child," were her words, " that your father wants to get rid of you in some way; though, I can't, of course, tell what for. He cannot be a good man, I am afraid, or he would not treat any helpless child as he did you; but then, we can't tell how he may be deceived about you by other people. At any rate, I would not let myself feel too angry at him, if I was in your place; for he is your father, after all. That morning, in our other house, when he found you with me and took you away, I could make out easily enough that he didn't feel kind to you, and that there was something strange and unnatural about the whole affair in some way. If I was you I'd try to support myself by any honest employment I could get, and keep clear of that man until God changes his heart. You might get a place in some store, after I've fixed your clothes a little; or I should think you could earn a living at a trade. Whatever you do, though, Avery, must be good and decent, like a gentleman's son; and you ought to forget all about such people as gipsies and Five Points' creatures. That murder was dreadful, and maybe the man they killed had been kind to you; but you had no business with such people at all, and it's better for you never to think of any of them again. Just stay quiet here for a day or two until I can make your dress look fit to be seen; and then try to get yourself a place. Hosey and I would like to give you a home right-out; —for Hosey's bringing you home twice, so, looks as though it was meant that we should help you; — but, Avery, we're too poor. All we have is Mr. Waters' wages and the little I can take in here in the store. The rent of three little rooms, besides the store, and the cost of living, make it hard work for us to get along at all, sometimes. Still, you shall share with us; and if you don't mind sleeping on a mattress in the store you may stay here at night until better times come."

The rugged common-sense, honesty and practical kindness thus expressed by this good and clear-headed woman nerved me to look my apparent destiny in the face and become stronger in my resolution to depend no longer upon others. Absurd as it may seem to those who would fain have human nature accordant with the stereotyped rules of precedent, I found my regret for Reese sensibly lessening under the idea of my own superiority to him and his gipsy crew. Shocked as I was at the manner of his death, and sorry as I was for him, there was yet no definite sense of bereavement in the feeling with which I contemplated the last awful scene in his misspent life. I had not respected him; he was no proper friend for a "gentleman's son!"

"Mrs. Waters," said I, "if you'll let me sleep in the store until I can get something to do, I'll be as little trouble to you as I can. I'd sooner go and beg cold victuals than ever go back to my father again; and I'd rather die than live as I have lived. You haven't heard half the story."

"All that I ought to hear, or care to hear," replied she, quickly. "If you take my advice you'll never tell any more of it to any one, if you can help it. I don't know much about such things, but I'm sure there's some queer family trouble at the bottom of it all, and that it shouldn't be talked about to strangers. Now I must go and see to baby."

If she hurried away through fear that I would insist upon telling her all, she was mistaken in me; for it was not in my natural disposition to be more communicative than circumstances made absolutely necessary. I was, in fact, ashamed of my vagabond experiences; and, aside from my fear of further persecutions from my father, should he again find me and learn that I had been talking of him, his conduct and the school-master's was so far from explicable to myself that I dreaded relating it to others lest they should infer some deserving, on my part, of such unnatural treatment.

It was quite late in the evening, and long after I had gone clumsily through the business of putting up the shutters, when Mr. Waters returned home, greatly exhilarated by the ascertained success of the Regular Demolition Ticket and Mr. O'Murphy. At breakfast next morning, too, he proposed three cheers through his fire-trumpet for the same Honorable Gentleman, and nearly threw Mrs. Hurstiches into a fit by sounding a hideous blast in response to her insinua-

tion of Catholicism against the new congressman; but Milly quieted him at last by suggesting perils to the baby from such unearthly noises, and then he listened to her relation of what she had planned for me to do.

Anything suggested by her was sure to be entirely approved by him; so thoroughly did he believe in her; and, consequently, the proposition that I should seek honorable employment seemed to him the perfection of wisdom. With both elbows resting on the table and either hand supporting a closely-shaven cheek, he fixed his dancing little black eyes upon my anxious face, and exhorted me to make a man of myself.

"You've been used rough, my cherub," were his words, "and that dad of yours must be as bad as one of these here stepmothers. But you're clear of him now, and you're out of Five Points' company, and you can't do a better thing than my old woman here tells about. Let Milly slick you up a bit, and then start out and try to hunt up a place. Suppose, now, you was to get in with some blacksmith?"

"I'll never be a blacksmith!" exclaimed I, indignantly. "I'm a gentleman's son!"

Mr. Waters was decidedly discomfited by my snappish resentment of his idea, and scratched his chin for a new thought.

"You wouldn't like to drive a coach, neither, I suppose? I know a chap that drives for the King of Diamonds, and he's the deepest cuss! He slung himself into that business when he was about your size, and now he owns the kerridge and buckskin horses — both."

"I'll never drive a coach!" was my second indignant retort. "I know how to keep books; and I'm going to go round to the stores and ask for a place. Other boys get places in stores; and they don't understand book-keeping, either, as I do."

The announcement of my clerkly proficiency made a visible impression on him.

"If that's your figure, old fellow," said he, in great admiration, "me and Milly may live to see you turn out a regular, fancy drygoods snob one of these days. I'd give you a letter of introduction to Goodman & Co. themselves," added the fireman, jocosely, "if it was not for my rule, never to put my name on anything short of bankcheques. But I'll tell you what I *will* do for you, my cherub. I'll introduce you into the Fire Department, when the right time comes."

Not to indulge further prolixity over my frequent consultations with these staunch friends, suffice it to say that a few days more made me ready to start forth in quest of employment. The ingenuity and industry of Milly, hindered as they were by much unnecessary and irrelevant advice from her mother, proved equal to the redemption of my well-worn attire into something like proper shape and decency; but it was as a rather tall, slim, poor-looking lad, with luxuriant chestnut curls, colorless face, and downcast eyes, that I took my first step toward independence.

Various arbitrary criticisms of my personal appearance were volunteered by the boys of the street; but I felt myself too much above such vagabonds to be seriously wounded by their vulgar freedom of speech! With characteristic quasi-forgetfulness of my last degradation and misery, I began to experience a premonitory gentleman-feeling the very moment I started for the stores, and already saw myself rising to mercantile eminence and opulence, with a quill pen of the largest size sticking out, like a wing, behind my ear.

Only in youth do we know that fair, unmercenary Hope which is bright to us in its own light and asks not the hire of favoring circumstance to make it stay. Free in the freedom to be ever with us then; buoyant on the unguided pinions that permit not its sensitive feet to once touch the retarding edges of earth, — it leads the young spirit aimlessly onward in space, with no object to rest upon, because with no capacity for tiring.

Half the rebuffs encountered by me in my round of the Broadway stores between Prince and Bleecker Streets would have discouraged any grown person. Entering a place where small laces, buttons, and embroidering worsteds formed an alternately ghostly and sanguinary effect for the eye, I addressed a marvellously spruce young clerk who, with his legs very far apart, was thoughtfully admiring his reflection in the glass of the door, and who looked thin enough to have been half-sliced from a man of ordinary size, in some economical exigency when two clerks were demanded at the price of one.

"Do you want a boy, sir?" I modestly inquired.

"No; I've got three boys already," responded the slice, with considerable clerkly humor. "I think I'd prefer a girl next."

"Oh!" said I, densely confused; and, as he immediately returned to the contemplation of himself in the glass, I withdrew to the street again.

In another store, where they sold razors, brushes, knives, and a flashing armory of cutlery, a stout little man in green spectacles, and with only a few wisps of hair on his head, made a pass at me over his desk with a ruler.

"Clear out! clear out!" he shouted, irascibly. "I *don't* want any matches, nor any blacking, nor any lozenges, nor any combs. Get out!"

"If you please, sir," I commenced, "do you want —"

"No! no! no!" cried he, waving the ruler and stamping passionately, "I *don't* want any steel pens, nor any soap, nor any cigars. I *aint* going to be tormented out of my life to buy apples, and peanuts, and gumdrops, when I don't want 'em. Get out!"

He was actually climbing over the desk to assault me, when I retreated precipitately to the sidewalk once more, bitterly indignant at such imputations and treatment.

In a third establishment I innocently and seriously answered a series of questions, from a boy not much older than myself, touching my command of capital and supposed inclination to take a partnership in the firm, only to be heartlessly laughed at by a circle of older hirelings, and directed to send my card to the president of an adjoining bank.

Not far from Bleecker Street was the goodly retail dry-goods house of Cummin & Tryon. The two broad show-windows, with their silken mountains and delaine cascades, seen prismatically through a transfixed snow-storm of lace collars and handkerchiefs; the double plate-glass doors, revealing an endless perspective of counters, shelves, and straggling ladies and gentlemen, — were splendors to make me hesitate before entering therein, upon such an errand as mine. But, while I stood in doubt, looking through one of the doors, I saw a boy taking some direction from a clerk; and if that boy works here, thought I, there can scarcely be anything wrong in another boy's solicitation of work in the same store. So, in I walked, desperately determined to try my fortune, come what might. At the counters on either side were many ladies, in the very deepest reflective moods of the sex, listening, half infatuated, half incredulous, to the mercenary blandishments of as many foppish holders aloft of dress-patterns, fanciful shawls, spotless cambrics, and other costly plumage for piano-birds.

Everybody was too busy to notice me, and I was getting well toward the farther end of the store, where a red-faced man at a standing desk seemed the most appropriate person to address, when I trod upon something which grated and chinked under my foot. It proved to be a purse worked in steel beads, and, as I raised it from the floor, its weight and protrusions indicated contents of no small value. Easily enough could I have carried off the prize, for my finding of it had been unobserved; but the thought instantly flashed upon me that it must belong to some one of the many ladies gathered just there along a counter covered with laces; and, by the most natural of impulses, I wedged my way to where a tall, thin, large-featured, flaxen-haired man was sentimentally recommending a honiton collar, and thrust the purse directly under his nose.

"I found it on the floor just now, sir," I said. "Some lady must have dropped it."

The words had not more than left my lips, when a richly dressed young lady came pushing excitedly toward me, exclaiming, —

"It's mine, sir."

"Then let me have the pleasure of returning it to you," said the lace-man, taking it from my hand and passing it to hers.

This little scene had drawn the attention of all the ladies at that counter to me, and the lace-man felt justified in addressing me on their behalf.

"You are an honest young man," said he, approvingly. "and have gained what many a man would almost die for — the admiration of the ladies." Here he paused long enough to enjoy a flutter of applause, and then asked, "What can we do for you?"

"I wanted to get a place, sir."

"What kind of a place, foolish boy?"

(It was *so* evident, from his sentimental manner, that he only said "foolish boy" because it had a melancholy sound.)

I stared at his hair, which was thin and wavy, like yellow smoke, and answered, rapidly. —

"Any kind of place that's fit for a gentleman's son. I understand book-keeping, and I'd like to have a place to write."

"You'll find the Firm in the private office, back there. I believe we want an assistant entry-clerk." He pointed toward a square enclosure, partitioned off from the rear of the store; and I had started to go thither, when the young lady whose purse I had found arrested me with a touch of her parasol.

"Perhaps, sir," she said, addressing the smoky-headed salesman, "if you would go with him and tell the gentlemen of his honesty, they might be more willing to employ him." And seeing that he hesitated, she impetuously added, "I shall go myself, if you don't!"

Looking gratefully up at her handsome, flushed face, from which she had thrown aside the veil, I recognized Miss Aloize Green. She did not know me, however; for my colorless cheeks, taller figure, and combed hair, were not vivid reminders of the embrowned and tangle-headed gipsy boy she had once seen.

The sentimental salesman blushed, and gave sign of confusion, at the lady's very decided championship of me, and stammered something about not being able to leave his counter without permission from the other ladies.

"Oh, we'll excuse you. Do go!" chimed half a dozen pleasant voices; and, without more ado, he came out from amongst the laces and hurried me along to the private office, where Messieurs Cummin & Tryon were writing at handsome rose-wood desks.

"Mr. Cummin," said the salesman, to a short, stout, sandy-haired gentleman, who looked up from his paper at our approach, "this young man found a purse near my counter just now, and restored it to the lady who had lost it. He is looking for a place, and the lady insisted that I should at once tell you of his honesty."

"Do we need any one just now, Mr. Coffin?" inquired the partner, looking at him over my head.

"Mr. Terky, the entry-clerk, wants an assistant, I believe, Mr. Cummin, and this young man understands book-keeping."

"Does the applicant live with his parents, Mr. Coffin?" asked Mr. Cummin, mechanically.

"No. sir," replied I, for myself; "I'm living with Mr. Waters, in Prince Street, until I can find another place."

"From the country, I presume," commented the tradesman, still ignoring my personality altogether, and addressing himself exclusively to his salesman. "Well, if he's honest, as you say. Mr. Coffin, and will suit Mr. Terky, we will take him on trial, at four-fifty a week."

After which concise settlement of the case, Mr. Cummin turned inexorably to his writing again, and I was led past the desk of the equally imperturbable Mr. Tryon into the open store.

"Would you like to try it?" queried Mr. Coffin, pausing and surveying me doubtfully.

"Yes, sir. if you please."

He beckoned a passing porter, charged him to take me down-stairs to Mr. Terky, and hastened away to his counter, as though unwilling to trust himself with me another moment.

Taciturnly enough the porter led me still farther back to where a steep flight of iron stairs led to a lower floor, and down those we went, into a dreary twilight lane, between drearier ranges of dry-goods boxes and shelves with feeble gas lights glimmering at irregular intervals, like phosphorescent fungi in a dustless catacomb.

At a tall, long desk, lumbered with huge books and sprouting all over with iron wires impaling written sheets of paper, stood a thin, sallow man of middle height, writing for dear life. He had black, curly, dry-looking hair, a sickly mustache, and a countenance too languid to express either age or youth.

"Mr. Terky," said the porter, pushing me toward this doleful figure, "Mr. Coffin towld me, would I bring this lad to you." And, believing that he had properly fulfilled his mission, the porter turned upon his heel and left us alone together.

"Well, what do you want of me?" inquired Mr. Terky, looking as though the very sight of me tired him more than ever.

"I believe I'm engaged to help you, sir," was my answer. "One of the gentlemen in the office upstairs said that he would take me."

"Oh. I understand. What's your name?"

"Avery Glibun."

He took a paper from one of the wires, and asked me if I could copy that bill into one of the books on the desk.

Yes, I thought so.

"Try it, then," said he, "and let's see how you'll do."

Not recognizing much responsibility in such a task as that, I readily accepted a pen, heeded the few sententious directions he gave me, and carefully copied the bill, or invoice, into the book.

I am afraid that my handwriting was not as handsome as it might have been, but Mr.

Terky seemed tolerably satisfied with the performance, and gave me several other bills to enter. I noticed that he, himself, never looked me straight in the face, but made all his remarks as though afraid to take his eyes from his own book longer than a minute at a time. Concluding from this that he had a great deal to do, I did not expect to be favored with much talk; but it soon became evident that he could converse and figure simultaneously; and presently I was answering a series of mechanical questions about myself. Mr. Terky, like his employer, jumped at the conclusion that I was "from the country," and did not appear to feel very deeply interested in that fact; but upon my saying that I only stopped with Mr. Waters until I could find another home, he abruptly paused in his writing and asked, with some animation, if I would not like to board at his house.

"I should like that very much, Mr. Terky," said I. "How much will it cost me a week?"

"We'll board you for two dollars," he responded, drawing a large 2 upon the desk with his pen.

"That will leave me two dollars and a half to buy clothes?"

"Yes."

"Then I'll do it, sir."

Immediately upon the settlement of this unceremonious treaty between us, the jaded entry-clerk took me into his confidence with a freedom proportioned to his earlier languor, and informed me that he received only nine dollars a week wherewith to support his wife and himself. It was elaborate starvation, he said, to live on such a miserable salary; but he didn't dare to ask for more, lest he should be discharged, and he could not afford to run the risk. Cummin & Tryon passed for benevolent prodigies, and had just contributed several hundred dollars to the fund for the starving poor of Ireland, but they didn't give their clerks the wages of day-laborers. The salesmen did well enough, because they commanded trades of their own and got commissions on what they sold; but as for the poor wretches of clerks — well, I saw one of them trying to keep his family out of the poor-house by taking a subordinate to board with him!

Mr. Terky was too low-spirited altogether to speak with energy of anything, but there was enough bitterness in his tone to indicate mortification, hopelessness, and life-long disappointment.

When I returned to Prince Street and vaingloriously related what I deemed my good fortune, Hosea and Milly helped along my vanity with a score of flattering conjectures touching a distinguished mercantile future, and even Mrs. Hurstiches expressed the comforting belief that I might have gone farther and fared worse.

Next morning I said good-by; for I was to go home in the evening with Mr. Terky.

Milly, with her child in her arms, went to the doorway of the little store to see me off, and when I turned at the corner, for a last glance, she still stood there looking after me.

In that sensitive tenderness of early motherhood which so refines in woman the beautiful instinct of sympathy with all that is neglected and unloved, she felt a kindness scarcely less than motherly for the motherless boy going from her; and if the faint lines upon her fair forehead were a husband's troubles, no less were they the impress of the unseen crown God gives to unselfish goodness, when they deepened with womanly pity for the outcast child of the stranger.

CHAPTER XXX.

EZEKIEL REED.

UPON that ambitious section or segment of the Fourth Avenue which skirts Union Park to the eastward, and vaingloriously styles itself Union Square, stood a house wherein the readers of this narrative are expected to feel more or less interest from henceforth. It was one of a uniform block of brick residences, and stolidly bore its share of the brown wooden cornice, first-floor iron balcony, and black area railings, which capped and strapped the entire range; but, being a corner building, and having no immediate neighbor's pattern to consult on its right side, it ventured a little dash of originality toward that side, in the shape of white marble steps instead of sober brown ones. From the foot, too, of the solid marble scrolls flanking said steps on either hand, sprang a tall, black lamp-post, bearing its octagon glass cage for the ever-ready blossom of fire; and at the edge of the curb stood another mark of distinction, — a slender iron hitching-post, surmounted by a horse's head, and a marble carriage-block considerably worn and discolored.

The original proprietor and occupant of this edifice had been a ship-chandler of eminence, and signalized the advent of his family therein by such a ball as very few ship-chandlers ever dreamed of in their tarry and tallowy philosophy. It was an unprecedented triumph of splendor and bad taste; the best society came to scoff and remained to prey, and a young English stocking-maker, who was visiting this country on business for his firm, allowed himself to be utterly captivated on that occasion by the ship-chandler's only daughter. Six months thereafter a marriage ensued; nine months thereafter a lady arrived in great haste from England, to assert prior marital claim to the husband; twelve months thereafter a sale of house and furniture took place, and the ship-chandler, with his wife and heart-broken daughter, retired to rural privacy in another State.

Then the house had passed through a

variety of occupancies, all terminating unluckily, until it finally became the habitation of persons concerning whom the genteel neighbors could as yet tell nothing.

The difference between positive fame and negative fame is this: that, in the former, you attract general attention and varying respect because people know much about you; and, in the latter, you attract general attention and great respect because no one knows anything at all about you.

The people last tenanting the house just described were negatively famous; and, as a consequence, whatever seemed related to them excited the liveliest interest and mystification throughout the block. When, on a certain morning. a tall, slender, delicately clerical figure walked up the white marble steps and apparently shot a nervous bell into some remote depth of the building, at least half a score of robustious Irish maidens simultaneously ceased their sweeping upon as many adjacent sections of sidewalk, and stared at the slender gentleman with all their eyes. In truth, some of them even exchanged husky speculations as to the gentleman's business, the prevailing impression being that he was a doctor suddenly called to attend a very mysterious lady known to be in that uncommunicative house.

Quite regardless of the flattering emotion he had excited in the ample bosoms of the curious fair, the gentleman put some question to a prim young colored man who answered his ring, and was at once favored with a nod, an induction to an elegant front parlor, and a gliding reception of his card for transmission to her whom he sought.

The newly and sumptuously furnished apartment contained only such enfeebled indications of the radiant outer morning as could strain themselves through the strangling shutters of the tall windows; but a brighter atmosphere might not have been so favorable to the careworn face of the young visitor when he first removed his soft round hat; nor to the threadbare elbows, knees, and salient edges of his well-brushed suit of black. In the full glare of day, indeed, the refined poverty of his dress would have contrasted too strongly for good taste with the luxurious plush-covered sofa upon which he had seated himself; yet, in the thoughtful, preoccupied look of the large and concentrative blue eyes under a sweeping curve of careless golden curls, there was an intellectual indifference to surroundings which destroyed all relative character in the latter.

The smooth, pale face, and fine, regular features, looked prematurely careworn in the loneliness of that dim parlor, but a still more anxious expression came over them when the sound of approaching footsteps promised company.

With a precision of face and rigidity of bearing which argued defiant reaction from irresolution rather than normal arrogance, a lady, richly attired in light-purple silk, and with a white crape shawl thrown over her shoulders, entered the parlor and approached its thoughtful occupant.

Her hair, doubly parted to a point over her forehead, and hanging curled on either side the face, in the fashion of the day, was almost colorless in its flaxen delicacy; and her steady hazel eyes looked an intensification of the cold repulsion of her face. From the moment of entrance she gazed unflinchingly at the visitor who arose to greet her, and did not relax the almost insulting stare even when frigidly acknowledging his agitated bow.

"Mr. Reed," she said, with something in the tone to restrain him from offering his hand, "you are unexpected; · but I am happy to see you."

Though all the color was gone from the lips of her guest, their momentary quiver ceased at the sound of her voice. An instant he caught her eye, as though willing to be certain of her mood before showing his own; and then, with an air of mingled constraint and embarrassment, wheeled a chair to where she stood.

Here, again, the uncertain light of the parlor was in favor of Ezekiel Reed, and did not betray the awkward changes of color on his cheeks, nor make prominent the contrast between his manner and hers.

"Excuse me," he said, hurriedly, "for calling upon you without invitation."

"You need make no apology."

"I heard that you were living here —"

"Who told you that?" She put the question rudely and imperiously.

"Mr. Allyn Vane."

That name made her start and flush crimson, imperturbable as she would have been. Anger at her own weakness succeeded, and shone in her eyes with a revengeful glitter. Still, she spoke quietly and with a very evident effort to appear tranquil, —

"Then you have seen that man, — I mean Mr. Vane, of course, — in the city?"

"Yes, madam, I met him on Broadway; or rather, he was about to pass me, when I stopped him, for the particular purpose of inquiring for you."

There was sharp suspicion in her look now; she was eagerly scanning the strong, yet girlish, face, to detect there some lurking taunt of the past relations between Allyn Vane and the school-master's wife, — some excuse of covert insolence upon which she might seize to rise contemptuously upon the school-master's son, and leave him to skulk from the house, like a whipped dog. But in that face there was nothing but sorrowful gravity, tempered by an almost childish singleness of thought; and she dared not interpret his meaning beyond his actual words.

"You thought, then," — she played with the fringe upon her shawl with seeming unconcern, — "you thought, then, that Mr. Vane could not fail to know all about me?"

"I thought that he might know something of you; that is, he might know from others."

"And you did not suppose that he would know positively, himself?"

"No, madam, I did not."

Ezekiel Reed said this very firmly, and with a steadfast, answering glance.

"Why?"

This was a question open to several responses; amongst others, to one questioning in its turn; but the school-master's son understood it exactly, and replied, —

"Because I knew that you never liked Mr. Vane."

At the words, frankly and earnestly uttered, a better, more womanly expression dawned in the face of the lady. She found irresistible comfort in the idea of being rightly understood, in, at least, one matter. Like many other people in this world, who attribute all their faults and troubles to the failure of others to justly comprehend them, she never gave those others the slightest clue by which they might reconcile her character and doings with any rule of reason; yet, like all of her irrational and wayward kind, again, there was a magic for her in that arbitrary comprehension of herself which came spontaneously from the intuitive instinct of another; and, for an instant, —despite past scenes,—she felt a sympathetic attraction toward the mere youth before her, such as she had never felt toward any matured man.

Only for an instant, though, did she permit this better feeling to influence thought or face. Then it was gone, and she once more toyed with her shawl and questioned, —

"I am obliged to you, sir, for doing me that justice; but am I to understand that you, yourself, can forgive and like the man who —"

Ezekiel Reed hastily raised his hand to stop the ungenerous words, —doubly ungenerous as coming from her, —and commanded her with a look not to be disobeyed.

"No! don't speak in that way," he exclaimed, reproachfully; "don't make me believe far worse of you than of him."

"Of me!" she cried, her eyes flashing wickedly again. "What do I care for what you think of me!"

He pressed a hand to his white, boyish brow, in apparent pain, while his pale cheeks took a hue such as they had worn on the night when she struck him. She remembered it, and, in spite of her scorn and passion, was ashamed.

"Ezekiel Reed, I beg your pardon! I spoke very rudely, and will take back what I said."

He removed the hand from his head, let it drop upon his knee, and turned upon her a look all gentle and earnest again.

"Perhaps I spoke rudely myself, madam," he said.

"No; you were right."

"If I do speak hastily, or from anger," he went on, lips trembling, but his voice clear and low, "I do a great wrong to the cause which brought me here. I have not come here, madam, on my own account, but for the sake of an unfortunate parent. I come to ask for him what no human heart can be hard enough to refuse the helpless and unfortunate, —forgiveness."

She had given him a dark look when he began; but now her head was bent to the shadow and support of one hand, while, with the other, she drew the shawl-fringe through and through her compressed lips. Thus far she had no reply to make; and, in the same clear, low voice, he continued, —

"I am but young to judge between man and wife now, and I was still younger when you and my father were together; yet I think that I could, and do, see where some of the wrong was. My father's nature was warped and disordered by the evil influences of wicked, unscrupulous men. He was a kind, good husband to my poor, dear mother, ... and when she died, ... she blessed him for it. I think he would have been good and kind to you, too, if he had been himself. But he was not himself! Oh, nothing, nothing like himself. He did wrong —"

"And I did wrong!" came passionately from behind the hand whose white fingers moved like sightless snakes in the flaxen hair, but which, yet, did not tremble.

There was something sterner in the young man's manner, as he proceeded, —

"Your account is with God. I speak only of my father. He was not himself while you were with him, and, whatever other reasons may have existed, he acted unwisely, wrongly, toward you. As his son (for he was my mother's husband), I feel this deeply. As a Christian, I come to offer for him all the reparation in my power,—to say to you that I repent for him, and to ask that you forgive him."

He paused for a word, or a look, or a gesture from her; but the face was still hidden, and neither lip nor hand encouraged him.

"When you left my father —"

The woman raised her head with an abruptness that made him pause again, and her altered look indicated one of her impetuous and characteristic caprices.

"Are you living in New York now?" she asked, sharply, her whole manner full of resistance to his.

"I am, madam," he patiently answered.

"Where?"

"I am boarding at present in Fourth Street, with Mrs. Le Mons, a widow."

"Have you any other address?"

"I am engaged in a law-office in Nassau Street."

"Then leave me your number, and perhaps I will write to you."

Again the color came to the wan cheeks of the school-master's son; for the rebuff was heartless.

"If that is intended for my dismissal, madam," he said, looking intently at her, "I can only pray that the Almighty may deal more graciously with you when you appeal to him in your own behalf. Look at me! Do you see how thin I am, how worn my face looks? I have striven not to spare myself in taking care of him who was good to my mother, and who might have deserved better of you, madam, but for the disorders of that reason which has since deserted him. If it was your wish to be further avenged, after leaving him a broken and disgraced man, with a servant's ignoble blow upon him, with a murderer tracking him to the last refuge of blind despair, and there at once saving him from a crime, and inflicting the wound destined to work worse than murder; if you wish for more than this, be satisfied with knowing that the man who abused you, neglected you, struck you! is a hopeless maniac. O madam, bestow your resentment upon me if I speak unworthily of my mission; but harbor no anger against him!"

Springing from her chair, with every perverse devil fighting the angel in her eye, she muttered, chokingly, through her set teeth,—

"I could KILL you for daring to talk so to me! What do you mean by it? Great Heavens! what have I done? O me! O me!"

Paler, but still erect and resolute, Ezekiel Reed encountered her wild, tigerish stare with a look half remonstrative, half pitying, and all steadfast. She cowered under it, hurried past him to where a noble portrait of herself looked out from a rich frame on the wall, and, with head thrown back, and hands uplifted and clasped, gazed upon the picture like one entranced.

"Those eyes!" she murmured, in a soft, rich, appealing voice. "Are they the eyes of a wretch, an outcast, a murderess? Is that a bad woman,—a wicked, wretched, lost woman? Oh, no, no, no!"

The pleading, melodious wail might have drawn pity from a heart of stone, and yet there was something unnatural, unwomanly, and terrible in it.

If Ezekiel Reed had understood her before by intuition, he also understood her now by a perception still more subtle and difficult to explain; by the promptings of an inner nature which gave no reason for its awe-stricken shrinking from what to the outer nature seemed all but divinely touching and beautiful.

"May God have mercy upon you!" he said, in tones which were like those of paralyzing fright; and arose to leave her.

She turned slowly toward him, her whole face beaming with an ecstasy that saintliest martyrs might envy.

"You talk of God!" she murmured, clearly and trancingly as before. "He understands me. I am not afraid to be with him."

"May he lead your heart aright," said Ezekiel Reed, solemnly. "Good-by."

"Good-by," she answered, nodding and smiling to herself, rather than to him; "Good-by."

So they parted,—never again to meet in a world too wide for what we would recall, too narrow for what we would forget.

That night when Ezekiel Reed returned, from a day's weary toil and study, to the house he called his home, bright black eyes noted the deepened sadness of his look, and a gentle little heart beat the faster for the sigh which he unconsciously breathed, after a vain attempt to read an evening paper at the parlor-table.

Constance Le Mons — grown nearly to womanhood, and with quite a woman's dignity in the confident poise of her curly head, the penetrating glance of her eyes, and the almost rigid stateliness of her form — took no small interest in her faded lady-mother's lodger. There was just enough mystery about him to fascinate her as an ordinary member of her sex, and just enough moral individuality in his character to attract her as a very peculiar member of that sex.

Her mother had gone out to call upon a neighbor, and she improved the opportunity to apologize for that parent's latest breach of delicacy.

"I hope, Mr. Reed, that ma did not annoy you too much just now, by her remarks upon your low-spirits. She did not mean to, I am sure."

"Not at all," was the lodger's answer. "She is always kindly thoughtful of me, and I take it as a compliment that either she or you should be affected by my moods."

Inasmuch as the latter portion of this reply had an affectation and constraint very unlike the usual boyish simplicity of the speaker, Miss Le Mons was a little disconcerted by it. So it was with the faintest touch of asperity that she said, —

"We don't treat you exactly as we would a stranger. There was something about your being at the same school with poor little Avery Glibun, that made both ma and me feel well acquainted with you; though I'm sure I don't know why it should."

Ezekiel noticed the covert petulance of the young lady's terms, and made an effort to banish its cause from his own manner.

"The kindness I have met with here," he rejoined, with a conciliating smile, "is so pleasant to me that I can't bear to hear you try to explain it. It was quite by accident that I said the few words I did about Avery, when your mother surprised me by mentioning his name; and, besides, you both had been very kind to me before that. And now that we are on the subject, Miss Constance, I must tell you that your old playmate might not speak favorably of me if he could be found now. There were circumstances"—here the young man colored, and seemed embarrassed, — "there were circumstances, attending our mutual school-experience, which were not happy. Some day I may tell you more about this."

Constance did not like the reservation, though it certainly added to the delightful mystery and romance which she solemnly insisted upon attributing to this most prosaic of young men.

"Have you any idea of where Avery Gliban is now?" she relentlessly asked.

"I have not."

Seeing that his brief reply had again wounded the exacting and sensitive little girl-woman, he impulsively drew his chair around to her side of the table, and took one of her hands in his own, as a repentant brother might have done.

"My dear Miss Constance," he said, looking affectionately into her great dark eyes, "don't be provoked at me. I know you think there is something strange about me, and, were you older, you might think still more strangely of it." She withdrew her hand quite gently, but also quite decisively. He placed his own disengaged hand on the back of her chair, and went on. "I wish you, though, to have the satisfaction of knowing that I have done nothing disgraceful, and that I try to be a Christian. My life has not been a happy one. I do not complain of this, for it is the will of the Almighty, and is intended for some divine end; but it accounts for all that may seem strange to you in me. A trying incident, related to my past life, occurred to me this morning, and so your mother has noticed my depression this evening. If God spares my life, and I can do so without involving others, I will tell you more about myself some day when you are older. Now you won't feel vexed with me, Miss Constance, will you?"

If any proof were needed to show what a very boy Ezekiel Reed still was, it might have been found at once in his innocent unconsciousness of the great blunder he was committing in imputing youthful immaturity to his companion. Woman, old or young, can forgive anything in a man sooner than a want of tact, especially where the latter calls into question her fitness for implicit confidence from everybody. The least bit of experience with the sex is generally sufficient to save a man from disturbing this feminine idiosyncrasy, — at least, until after marriage; but the simple-hearted school-master's son was a pitiable novice in tact of any kind; and the girl just out of school resented the imputation of being too young for wholesale confidence, with as much indignation as though she had been the maturest of women.

"I hope," was her remark, as she bent stiffly to a piece of sewing on her knee, and turned a very rosy cheek to the offender, "I have not been so ill-mannered as to make you suppose that I want to know what doesn't concern me. I am not quite such a child as that, if I *am* very young!"

"You *are* vexed with me," cried the puzzled Ezekiel, resting his face upon his arm on the table, and anxiously trying to catch her eye.

"Oh, pshaw! no, I'm not," came petulantly from the fastidious little beauty; "only, if you want to be a Christian, Mr.

Reed, and expect God to help you bear the troubles you speak of, why don't you join the church, and give your heart to the Saviour?"

This sudden and arbitrary turn of the subject was intensely characteristic of the girl's nature. She, too, like the school-master's son, had been warped in the natural spirit of her youth by family trial, and, as in his case again, the spiritual deformity had evinced itself in a precocious religious sentiment; yet it was at this very point of apparent harmony that the characters of the twain least assimilated.

From the manner in which the young man drew himself back in his chair and wearily dropped his eyes, it was plain that the substance of the same intolerant question had been at least hinted to him before.

"Miss Constance," he slowly said, "we should all bestow our hearts in that way. Perhaps you are right as to the necessity of a public profession in serving the Almighty; but when you are a little older you may realize that there are peremptory individualities of character which dictate, if they do not justify, different methods of following the right faith."

Constance looked up at him with a glance rendering it questionable whether she had comprehended his idea, but leaving no room to doubt that she understood his reference to her immaturity again. Her only response, however, was a dissatisfied "Well;" and from thenceforth, until Mrs. Le Mons returned from her call, there was silence between them.

Later in the night, when at respective bedsides each earnest young soul knelt, as before altars the most innocent in the world, the woman's heart prayed that it might never waver from its own standard of right, and the man's mind petitioned for light to see what the true standard should be. They differed only as heart from mind, as instinct from reason, as woman from man.

CHAPTER XXXI.

THE MILLER AND HIS MEN.

THE most artful illusions of light are but innocent child's tricks in comparison with the commonest deceptions of the disingenuous and humbug republic of darkness. Despite all its world-old associations of pitfall, thievery, murder, and ghost, there is a restful, gentle, protecting assumption about darkness, which curiously imposes upon the weak-minded and timid for their comfort. Darkness, genuine and profound, revenges itself against the mildest bit of moonlight, candle-light, or will-o'-the-wisp, with all sorts of ghosts, spectral draughts, and imaginary goblins; but, in its uninvaded opacity, suggests an utter vacancy and security by which at least one great human sense is incapacitated from transmitting fear to the coward heart.

An acceptable philosophy will discover that all our actuating emotions are incited —possibly created—by material objects. What we see in form is what we are in spirit; and were this world a flat, unbroken blank, with but one self-sustaining man upon it, we may question whether that man could attain enough emotional character in a lifetime to move one step beyond the spot on which Deity had first placed him. Curiosity, the true key-note and beginning of all natural emotion, owes its primal awakening in the infant to material shapes, — toys, forbidden food, the human face. Imagination, the leaven and luxury of sentient existence, takes its first start from some material reality, however fantastically it may thereafter swim in space and distort the likeness of its practical origin into fifty vague unlikenesses. And both curiosity and imagination can have no original action in the apparently objectless blank of a perfect darkness.

Hence the vast amount of illusive humbug there is about atmospheric opacity, — which is only an egregious sham upon reason, and (through instinct) inclines the latter to temporarily die in sleep that its living weakness may not be exposed by the swindle! Hence the entire unsuspicion of any objects at all — much less of any living and sinister objects — with which an unprejudiced stranger, on a certain night, might have surveyed a certain pretended blank of this kind, until, —

Well, until a quick scraping sound and perpendicular streak of phosphorescent fire were heard and seen simultaneously; when, of course, light had commenced to overthrow the artful deception and give the imagined observer objects for his emotions. The scraping sound and streak of fire came from a lucifer match (to give the striker time to find which the foregoing overture has been ingeniously improvised), and when said match terminated its fiery little trip down the invisible upright post in a snapping explosion of minutely spiteful flame, it partially explained its own action by vaguely revealing a long, bony hand, and part of a yellow cloth arm. Still borne by this lank and sallow human member, it went sputtering to a point of rest but a few inches distant, and there called up a second, stronger, and whiter flame, in which its own was swallowed and lost. A tallow candle was the burning revelation this time, and further quarried from the insensate gloom a hand and arm to match the other, and a face and figure to match the whole. Additionally thereto, divers dingy rafters, tumbling wooden props, splintered posts and rusty iron axles were also brought into murky view; and — strangest of all — the yellow figure was seen to be confronted by a frightful female shape hung by the neck.

The large-featured face of the yellow personage, as illuminated by the candle, expressed none of that amazement and horror which such criminal and ghastly company might pardon. Indeed, its expression was incipiently humorous to the extent of a grotesque twist of the small gray eyes and widely-slashed mouth.

"Easy, now, old girl," was the irreverent remark of the yellow mystic while he carefully erected the candle in what appeared to be an extended hand of the hanging lady; and as the highly-colored shining face and curiously unsymmetrical white robes of the latter took the light, there appeared some excuse for the covert levity of her executioner.

The old girl had that dissipated, slinky aspect which might have overcome the most chivalrous instinct of respect for her sex; and when the jaundiced hangman stepped back a pace and began drawing her up through an opening in the rafters above, by means of a second rope, her demoralization was complete in the passive slovenliness of the ascent.

The dreary squealing of an unamiable wooden wheel somewhere overhead was the solitary sound that accompanied the first two or three pulls of the rope; but its further requiem was temporarily checked by the noise of a fall and an imprecation close at hand.

"What's the matter, Gamble?" queried the yellow man, suspending his labors and staring into the gloom of the nearest corner.

"I've barked my shins in this cursed rat-hole. That's what's the matter!" growled a voice from the obscurity. "You're a polite one, Sharp, to invite a man into such a precious old shebang as this, and then leave him to come after you without so much as a match!"

"Don't bawl so!" was Mr. Sharp's hasty caution. "Didn't you have the dark-lantern?"

"Yes, — with your orders to keep the slide shut!" sounded in a deeply-injured tone, as a pair of small, glassy black eyes, a heavy mustache, and a slim, sombre figure came limping into the dim light. — "Here! I say! What are you up to?"

"Just pick up that lantern again, and pull up the slide, and I'll tell you, my son," returned the other, paternally. "I've lighted the ghost's-candle, and I'm hoisting up the fair victim of parental pig-headedness."

"Explain the dodge," urged Mr. Gamble, making a desperate attempt to appear as though he had not turned pale at first.

"Human credulity is the game," moralized Mr. Sharp, in the same piquant phraseology, as he resumed his exercises with the rope. "When once the old girl is swinging —(nothing but a false face, old gown, and stick to hold the light, you see) —in the story above, her candle gives a kind of frightful look to the dusty old windows of the mill, and if anybody should look in, he'd see the ghost of the miller's daughter. Milton is a good half-mile away from here; but there isn't a soul in it that don't think this a haunted institution."

With the upward disappearance of the candle and ghost, Mr. Gamble had turned the full glare of the dark lantern into his own face to keep himself in countenance. Emboldened by this glorification of his beauty, he jauntily asked, —

"Was there ever a Maid of the Mill, who, if she wasn't dead, would live here still?"

Mr. Sharp, having tied his rope to a post, produced another match and candle from one of his yellow pockets, as he replied, —

"There was such a maid, my roaring blade. She was only daughter to a sanguine old widower, with a green patch over his left eye, who ran this mill when I was but a sunny youth Down-East, and you was but a freckled little cuss in your native Sixth Ward. She fell in love with the butcher, who served from Milton, and the courtship was getting as tender as a prime cutlet, when, suddenly, the butcher had a call from the constables for sheep-stealing. In this chopfallen situation, he sent word, by a friend, to the miller's daughter, that she must get her pa to bail him out; for he was too full to say more. She made the request of her parent, and that sarcastic old sinner led her to a back door of the mill. 'You want me to go bail for the butcher?' says he. 'Yes, please,' says she. 'What's that I'm pointing at?' says he, extending a forefinger down the pond. 'It's the dam,' says she. 'Well,' says the miller; 'I'll see the butcher *that-ed* before I'll bail him!' This was a fresh cut to the miller's daughter, who felt that all her hope of matrimony was at stake. That night, after the old man had gone to sleep, she came down into the mill, with a candle in her hand. If she could not be a help-meet to the butcher, she would not live to be any other man's rib; so she hung herself, and was found next morning, just as you see her up there now."

Mr. Gamble stood under the opening in the rafters, and gazed critically upward at the ghost.

"Was she holding out the candle in that way, when they found her?" asked he, sceptically.

The yellow man's face was now very visible in the light of his second tallow-dip, and displayed a momentary contraction of thought.

"Ye-e-es," returned he, with some caution.

"It's against nature," urged the critic. "It aint in nature for anybody to be hung dead, and still hold a candle out in that broomsticky way."

"Of course it's against nature," rejoined Mr. Sharp, brightening up. "It's supernatural. That's the mystery of it."

This happy solution of a knotty point left the yellow worthy at liberty to heed other matters. In a spirit of communicative hospitality, he explained to his friend that they were then under the mill; and that the slanting bank of earth, sloping down from the far ends of the rafters to their feet, was a part of the descent from the road on which the rickety old building stood. From the bottom of this bank, however, the ground had been rudely floored with boards, which extended to a broad, low window, and narrow door, looking over the neglected mill-pond, and under the ruined mill-wheel. Aided by such light as they had, the two prowlers succeeded in stumbling upon a goodly pine table, around which several clumsy wooden chairs were standing and lying, and on which Mr. Sharp stuck his candle after having first closed the window, near by, with a hinged wooden shutter.

"Take a seat, close that lantern-slide, and make yourself at home," directed Mr. Sharp, with no little gayety of manner, as he established himself on one of the chairs. "Hallo, there, Old Dolly!"

The startling summons — for such it was — called a new figure to the scene. Out of the shadow to the right of the table came a stooping, ragged, and brown-faced old woman, her sunken eyes shining like those of a cat as she approached the light.

"Bottles and candles, mother!" cried the yellow man, while she was yet coming; and, at the sound, she wheeled silently about, and went into retirement again.

"What's that?" ejaculated Mr. Gamble, rubbing his eyes. "Another ghost?"

"Like enough she's made ghosts in her day," chuckled the wizard, vastly enjoying his comrade's surprise. "She's anything but a spook, herself, though. She's the Witch of the Mill, as they call her in Milton, and helps the ghost to keep the bumpkins away from this old chateau of ours. She's Old Gipsy Dolores; and the governor has kept her here ever since a daughter of hers got poisoned, somewhere down in the Five Points. Her gang is in with us."

"Is there anything else to appear?" asked Mr. Gamble, querulously, — "any living skeleton, or chap with his throat cut? Because I'd like to know it beforehand, and not have my hair flying up every five minutes."

"No, my son, you've seen the whole show," returned the friendly Mr. Sharp.

"If that's so, all right. Come to think of it, Sharp, I've seen the old lady before."

The reappearance of the crone, with bottles, cracked tumblers, and candles, prevented an immediate rejoinder from the other; for he at once devoted himself to the attainment of increased illumination and spirituous refreshment. With the second retreat of Dolores, however, he resumed the conversation, his bristling sandy hair and yellow attire coming out cheerfully in the imperfect light.

"Help yourself, — old Jamaica and sherry," quoth he, looking from the bottles to his companion, and leaning comfortably back in his chair, glass in hand. "I'll give you a toast."

"Done!" assented Mr. Gamble, patronizing the nearest bottle.

"The Miller and his Men."

"Here's to 'em. Thus we toss the ruby wine."

Both gentlemen drained their glasses in honor of the vague sentiment, and then the leading spirit of the revel plunged his spade-like hands into his pockets and reflectingly surveyed the new miller.

"You say," remarked he, "that you've seen Old Dolly before?"

"I'm certain," was the reply, "that she's the identical old one of a gipsy crew, that I fell in with in Newark, quite a spell ago. I put a girl of hers up to a little woman-game for me, there; and a nice mess it got me into. An airy customer named Rice or Reese, or something like that, was travelling with them, and a queer sort of boy of his went and upset my whole game, instead of giving a note to the lady he was sent to. When I called at the house again, I'm blest if the door wasn't slammed in my face!"

"Reese!" exclaimed Mr. Sharp, drawing his huge feet together with a jerk. "As sure as my name is Easton Sharp, that very fellow has been in this mill often enough. He was one of us before he got killed in some sort of dance-house row in town, and a live genius he was! Why, Gamble, my boy, when Reese wasn't in New York attending to primaries and elections for the governor and General Cringer, he was tramping with our gipsy boys to 'shove the queer.'"

"I suppose that means passing counterfeit money," said Mr. Gamble, captiously. "Well, I know who he was, then; and I'd like to be sure that his infernal young imp died with him."

"Who was the boy?"

"I don't know; some young thief."

Easton Sharp sprawled out his feet again, and resumed his former pensive air.

"It's curious how things work," was his audible reflection. "When I think how nearly every man of us has wound himself up and gone off, I wonder that we don't have real, original genuine ghosts in the old mill. There's poor Birch. He used to be school-master over beyond the village, and had his hands full to blind a perfect cat of a young wife and a regular parson of a step-son, when he slipped off to Milton of a night and sneaked down here after the rest of us. Well, he got shot in the head by somebody for something about a boy, and now he's a raving lunatic. That's the end of him!"

"Cheerful," was Mr. Gamble's commentary.

"And Wolfton! A man that could do any bank signature — right off-hand — so that its own writer would swear to it. What has he been for the few last years? If what I've heard is true he's an idiotic dock-rat!"

Mr. Gamble began to show signs of depression, though frequently snuffing the candles and applying to his bottle for diversion.

"Cheerful again," grunted he, looking nervously about him.

"There was Reese, too," continued Easton Sharp, in the same retrospective vein. "There was a fortune and a Presidency in that genius, if he hadn't always been such a queer, demoralized sort of play-actor. He had an eye for a bank-note that was next door to magic, and if one of our plates had a hair-line difference from the true bill, he'd see it at a glance. And, then, in politics, too! Why, that man could do more in the Sixty-sixth Ward with five hundred dollars, than — well, more than Macginnis himself could! He used to have a mysterious friend named Mr. Mugses, and when it came to squaring things with the governor and General Cringer after an election, he would always say, — 'Mugses must have a berth in the custom house, too, you know;' or, 'My particular friend, Mr. Mugses, must have his name in this new railroad bill, as well as mine;' or, 'M. was along with me in doctoring those ballots for Comptroller, and he's got to have his clerkship if I have one.' Well, sir, the name of Mugses went into more than one prime bill at Albany, and the same name was drawing a salary of twelve hundred for a custom-house clerkship: — the very clerkship that General Cringer has just given to a wide-awake chap named Stiles. The mystery of it was, that this Mr. Mugses could never be seen by anybody. His share in a railroad bill was always sold (at a round figure, sometimes), and his salary was always drawn by some second party. Now who do you suppose he was? As sure as my name is Easton Sharp, he was *a dog* — a black and yellow hound! Yes, sir! There was genius for you! And yet Reese had to go and get his head turned by a gipsy wench, — the very one you've got cause to remember, I'm thinking, — and she knifed him for jealousy while he was dancing, like a fool, with another girl. What a blow it was to the Regular Demolition Ticket! The governor and General Cringer have never worked together half as slickly since then."

"I 've got into a neat little business," snarled Mr. Gamble, sullenly eying a candle, "if all the partners go to blazes in a string."

"Then, Old Hugo came near a bad slip-up; though he was only one of the gipsies. He was caught 'shoving the queer' in Newark and New York. The charge was made in New York, and they took him from Newark. Reese was with the gang in camp at the time, just outside the town, — you seem to know where, — and had to bury a stack of the stuff and make tracks for his congressional district in the city. An indictment was found against Hugo, and if the governor, and his friend, the city council, hadn't just managed to get him before one of our judges, he'd have gone to Sing-Sing as sure as fate. It was touch and go with him, I tell you! He, and another gipsy named Juan, work here now when it's safe."

The auditor of these lively biographical sketches folded his arms very tightly across his closely-buttoned coat, and looked forlornly across the table at his entertainer.

"I suppose you know how the governor, as you call him, roped me into this arrangement?" he uneasily observed.

"I can guess at it," answered the yellow man, refilling his tumbler and speaking in a light and engaging way; "he first ruined you, as he did all the others, — except me, — and then, seeing that you had sharp points, and were in a bad pickle, he made a gentlemanly proposition to you, and gave you my address at Milton. You came to the Milton post-office, introduced yourself to me, had a little talk about the business, and here you are."

"True as gospel!" cried the ruined innocent, greatly surprised at the accuracy of the statement. "I'm in for it now, and shan't back out. But you say that he didn't ruin you?"

Mr. Sharp wagged a denial with his egg-shaped, sandy head, and gave a chip of a laugh through his spacious nose. -

"I was ruined before I ever saw him, my son. I edited a country newspaper," — there was a touch of sadness in the tone, — "and took unwholesome vegetables for subscriptions until my compositors and pressman refused to take any further salary in seed-cucumbers and frosted turnips. Then I suspended payment and went to New York. I was seeing the elephant there, prior to looking up some travelling agency, when I came across the governor. He happened to want a sharp Yankee to superintend his mill out of town, and I happened to want something livelier than starvation. So, through poor Birch, who knew me before, he offered me the position; and got me the Milton post-office, through General Cringer, to keep me near the spot and help draw the wool over the eyes of the Miltonians."

"You must be fond of it."

"While it pays," was the judicious reply. "I think I'm going to lose the post-office, because the governor and Cringer seem likely to have a split. If it's true that Cringer is over with the Ebullitionists again, there's a split already, and my head's as good as off. When it does come off, I'm done with Milton. The thing that I want to do then is to start a political organ in New York, and wax the Ebullitionists until they — advertise with me."

The subtle, journalistical instinct, the natural genius for the press, evidenced by the postmaster's concluding phrase, did not kindle in the massive brain of Mr. Gamble that appreciation which it eminently deserved. Indeed, the later annals of the haunted mill, as quoted by the yellow philosopher, and the gloomy, half-buried tone of the place in which they sat, had precipitated upon Mr. Gamble a corroding melancholy; and his intellectual powers wilted into silence.

Noting the mood thus commended to his forbearance, Mr. Sharp also lapsed into reticence for a time; the only indications of his continued mental activity being the alternate stropping of his soles and paring of his nails with one of those huge jackknives which eternally assist the abstraction of the philosophical Connecticut mind.

A yawn simultaneous with a noisy shutting of the weapon was finally the postmaster's signal of returning sociability; when he furthermore reminded the opposite dreamer of his presence by pushing one of the candles into scorching proximity to the Gambletonian mustache.

"It's about time for the governor to put in an appearance now," said he. "Suppose we look out for him."

"I'm agreed," returned Gamble, jumping to his feet. "Anything but moping in this dead-man's corner."

Mr. Sharp produced a pair of caps from where they had been deposited earlier in the evening, and the two miller's-men donned them and left the table.

"I don't see your dies, and presses, and other stock," remarked the observant Gamble.

"They're all safe enough in boxes under the floor," explained the postmaster. "Now slip out of this door after me as quick as you can, for I don't want the light to shine out."

The narrow threshold was cleared with prompt dexterity, and the unhallowed twain came out upon the sandy edge of a small, stagnant pond, and close to the verge of a huge, mutilated water-wheel. Across the slimy depths ran a slippery footway of single planks, eked out on the other side by the trunk of a fallen tree; and, save where the dark shadow of the mill fell upon it, the surface of the pond looked rank enough with weed to pass for marsh-land. High over all hung the full August moon, — a heaven-ringed lantern in the starry dome of silence and of night, — showing mill, pond, swelling field, and clustering wood, in that cool, subduing light which makes the night like a day reflected in still water.

"Look there!" cried Sharp, pointing excitedly across the pond.

From that side the verdant land sloped by scarcely perceptible degrees to what was a wide stretch of champaign, rather than valley, though groves and separate trees darkened here and there, and a blue line of hills faintly cut the distant east. Down somewhere near the sedgy heart of this luxuriant expanse, where countless watery antennæ twined insidiously among dank bogs, and snaky pools slept treacherously under coverts of beaten grass, a fog had welled up like a ghost of the sea that once might have lain there, and filled the vale with spectral waters. Groves laving in it half-way to their motionless tops, their lower branches and foliage showing dimly through the mist; scattered oaks and apple-trees, lifting a green cone, or an indented dome, above the milky level, — were fairy continents and islands sleeping on their shadows in a waveless and illimitable ocean. And out — away out — far beyond the last green shore, and seemingly given egress through a sinking gateway in the remote hills of blue, the unmoving waste stretched without a sail to the twinkling lights of infinity.

"Look there!" cried Sharp.

"Hanged if I didn't think it *was* water, at first!" exclaimed Gamble, half in admiration, half in fear.

"I've seen it before, on moonlight nights," said Mr. Sharp, gazing fixedly at the lovely illusion; "but it's always new to me. It's a sight to make a man wish himself something better than he is, and — there's the governor and his friend, by jingo!"

"Where? Where?"

"Don't you see? Over the pond, there."

Two figures were indeed visible, coming, like languid swimmers, through the fog on the field across the pond, and resembling human heads and shoulders on ghosts of bodies and legs.

"Why, how the mischief did they get there? Isn't there a road just up beyond the mill, here?" asked Mr. Gamble, with a bewildered air.

"The governor drives up from Jersey City to a snuggery he's got down below there, in what used to be a saw-mill," returned the postmaster, "and comes across lots. Did you think he came through the village and told all hands where to find him?"

Not encouraged to a further pursuit of knowledge by this inquisitive bit of sarcasm, the novice contented himself with silently watching the approach of the miller and his friend.

The former was tall, and the latter short and stout; but as each had a handkerchief tied over mouth and nose to guard against malaria, and a hat drawn over the eyes to prevent recognition by any possible straggler in the fields, not much could be told of their respective aspects until they had, with difficulty, passed the narrow bridge of planks and were at the door of the mill. Then they removed the handkerchiefs, and the splendid black beard of the miller, and red beard and hair of his round-faced companion were disclosed to view.

"So, gentlemen, you are waiting for us," was the miller's gracious salute. "Mr. Trackum, these are the friends I mentioned, — Mr. Sharp, and Mr. Gamble."

"Sirs, to you! Happy to know you," said Mr. Trackum, bestowing a jerky nod and a very sharp look upon the gentlemen named.

"That's a fine effect over there — that fog," remarked the miller.

"Yes," said Mr. Trackum. "Very curious indeed."

"Have you got lights inside, Sharp?"

"Yes, governor."

"Then, gentlemen, we'll go in-doors and try to wash some of this fog out of our throats."

Upon entering (or, rather, going under) the mill, Mr. Trackum took pains to be the last of the party, and, while their backs were still turned upon him, he swept all that was visible of the place in one curious and searching look.

The four were quickly seated at the table, Old Dolores appeared, like a superannuated bacchante, with fresh candles (spermaceti, this time), bottles, water, and glasses, and the convivial miller pledged his merry men in a bumper.

"Our friend Trackum," said he, flourishing a hand, on which sparkled a large diamond, toward the plump gentleman with red hair, "is determined to be one of us, and you will remember, Mr. Sharp, and Mr. Gamble, that we are to have no secrets from him."

"You do me proud," cried the newcomer, raising his tumbler with great alacrity. "I know good company when I see it, and you really do me proud."

"Yours respectfully," answered Mr. Sharp, drinking.

"Ruin for four," growled Mr. Gamble, who was very low-spirited again, already.

"You'd better not drink any more, Mr. Gamble," said the miller, transfixing that individual with an uncomfortable smile. "Mr. Trackum will not understand a joke of that description, for he's not yet 'up' in the free-masonry of our club."

"Club!" ejaculated the stout man, with an inquiring look, — "Club? Oh, I see; to be sure. The 'Queer' club, I suppose you call it."

"Queer?" queried the miller, raising his eyebrows.

"Ha! ha!" laughed Mr. Trackum, in great animation. — "Yes, thankee, Mr. Sharp, I *will* try another swallow of that Bourbon. — Ha! ha! you keep it up well, gov'nor."

The miller looked hopelessly at Mr. Sharp, as who should say, What is the man talking about? and Mr. Sharp sent back the expression of one who wanted to look unspeakably wise, but was not quite sure enough of his own sanity to make it out.

"Club, hey?" added the humorist, with another burst of laughter. "Well, club it is. You gents would make your fortunes in a theayter, — you carry it off so well."

"Ha! ha! ha!" bellowed Mr. Gamble, his countenance writhing with saturnine bitterness.

"Gamble," said Mr. Sharp, anxious to be sure by the sound of his own voice that he was himself, — "Gamble, you're acting like a beast."

"Mr. Trackum," observed the miller, adopting an air of mild but firm remonstrance, "if you have finished your laugh and your glass, I should like to ask you what you are pleased to mean by the term 'Queer,' — as you emphasize it? and what you wish us to understand by the phrase of 'carrying it off well?' I am afraid that my friends, here,—one of whom appears to be in a condition not entirely gentlemanly"—here a contemptuous movement of the eye toward Mr. Gamble—"will be at a loss to account for your apparently extraordinary views of our 'Governor's Club.'"

Both Trackum and Sharp watched him closely while he spoke, and the shrewd, smooth face of the latter suddenly flashed with a new intelligence. The former, too, evidently experienced an emotion of mingled surprise and impatience.

"Guv'nor," said Mr. Trackum, leaning firmly upon his elbows and changing his manner at once to the severest gravity, "I'm only a poor, ruined devil, but I won't be fooled too far! I threw myself in your way like a man. I told you that I was a starving engraver and was ready to go into your line of business. You sounded me for two or three days, and then asked me if I wanted to join a 'Club.' I twigged what you meant, and said yes. You've brought me out here,—and now you're trying to rig me. What's the use?"

The miller's wicked eyes darted something like menace, but his demeanor was still quietly forbearing.

"My good fellow, you are losing your temper. If you chose to twist my words into some abstruse species of slang, it is your own business. I have my eccentricities; Mr. Sharp has his; Mr. Gamble, his; other gentlemen, not now present, theirs. If it is our pleasure to meet in this old mill, at certain times of year, as a club, that is our own business. You came out here to join the club—having eccentricities of your own—"

"Club be cursed!" interrupted the man, furiously. "What has clubs and eccentricities got to do with a chap that don't know where he's going to get his breakfast to-morrow? I came here to look at your dies. Where are they?"

"He's going to dye his whiskers," ventured Mr. Sharp, with a fine touch of original pleasantry.

"He's going to die on the gallows," moaned Mr. Gamble, who sat all in a heap and seemed to be shedding tears.

"Your ideas about some things appear to be tolerably true ones," said the imperturbable miller. "About as truthful as my idea of you would be if I took you for anything else than—a traitor in camp!"

Trackum started to his feet; but not more quickly than the Milton postmaster lugged, from some mysterious depth below his waistband, a huge pistol and pointed it at his head.

The miller also arose to his feet, but in a quite leisurely manner, and looked steadily into the unflinching eyes of the spy at bay.

"Sharp, don't be excited. Trackum, if you move another step, or put that hand near your breast again, I'll blow your brains out myself. Remain perfectly still, and you are as safe as you would be at home. I know you, my good fellow. You are a Boston detective, employed by the Ormolu Bank, of Quadunck, to discover where certain promising counterfeit tens and fifties on that institution have come from. Some political opponent of mine—courteous gentleman as he undoubtedly is—put into your head the preposterous idea of playing the shadow to me! Why, Trackum, my man, I knew all about your absurd purpose the very first night you entered my house. You were being looked after by a useful and experienced friend of mine; a member of your own fraternity; perhaps you know him,—Mr. Ketchum?"

The florid countenance of the detective had turned white at first, but now wore its natural hue, and his voice was only gruffer than before, as he undauntedly replied,—

"I see that my game's up."

"I humored your 'game,' as you epigrammatically call it," continued the miller, blandly; "because, being a student of human nature, I wanted to see if you would really have the courage to come here alone and at midnight with me—you supposing me, of course, to be the head of an adroit and desperate gang of counterfeiters. You are one of the bravest men I ever met. You know, undoubtedly, that it would be the easiest thing in the world for Mr. Sharp and I to put you into that pond outside and leave you at the bottom, if either he or I had any possible object to gain by doing so?"

"I suppose you could."

"Mr. Sharp, be good enough to put up that pistol."

The postmaster unhesitatingly returned the weapon to its hiding-place, and leaped to a seat on the table, like a grotesque yellow goblin.

"Now, Trackum, I've got a few words more for you. Whatever your ideas of the 'Governor's Club' may be, you have not seen the first thing to justify you in annoying me further relative to this outrageous business. But let me tell you that, had I brought you to a workshop full of counterfeiters indeed, you would have been but little better off. You must have preferred your charge in New York, for it was from there, as Mr. Ketchum tells me, that the Ormolu counterfeits are supposed to have commenced circulation. And what chance—I speak very frankly—what chance would you have in New York with a charge against me? Who are the two most powerful men in New York City and State, respectively, to-day? General Cringer and—I. From elections of governor and senator, down to those of aldermen, the men who *make* the men are Cringer and—I. You are a sensible man, and I'm talking the plainest sense to you. I could shoot you dead on Broadway, to-morrow, my Boston friend, and be undisturbedly hobnobbing with my legislative friends at Albany in a week after. You must see, then, that it will be a neither safe nor paying business to even remember your visit here."

"I never go beyond my business," returned the detective, bluntly. "You've managed to do me badly, somehow, and there's the end of it."

"Sensibly said, my good fellow. Now, if you'll follow me up to the next floor (where, by-the-by, you shall see a little ghostly contrivance we have to keep countrymen away from our club-room), I will take you to the front of the mill and put you upon your road to the village. Milton is not far off, and you can get a room there, at the tavern, until morning, when a stage leaves for Newark. Mr. Sharp, here,—whom you probably took for one of the Ormolu party!—is the postmaster at Milton, and will undoubtedly see you off in the morning. Of course you will say nothing about us in the village, as we do not wish to be annoyed in our occasional convivial meetings by rustic curiosity."

"Guv'nor," said Trackum, breathing freely, and putting on his hat, "if you was a detective, you wouldn't care to talk to anybody about them that got the better of you, after you'd worked-up the job to the point of risking your throat."

"Come with me, then," cried the evergentlemanly miller, taking the dark-lantern from the end of the table, and directing its rays to a ladder leading up through a trap. "Mr. Sharp, I shall come down again before I go."

As the two disappeared through the aforesaid trap, Easton Sharp slapped, first one of his yellow legs, and then the other, in a manner indicative of some excitement.

"Gamble, my son!"

A faint snore came from between Mr. Gamble's arms on the table, where Mr. Gamble's head was resting.

"Gamble," repeated the postmaster, quite oblivious in his ecstasy to the present inattention of that sensitive gentleman, "if that isn't a ruined detective, I wouldn't say so! The way that chap was done to a turn! I must be mistaken about the governor not ruining me. I must be mistaken," said Mr. Easton Sharp, gazing pensively in the direction of the ladder. "It *must* be that he ruined me, for he's the ruin of everybody."

———◆———

CHAPTER XXXII.

If the style in which I am writing this narrative is progressive, as I endeavor to make it; if the successive ideas, sentiments, and views of character have kept due pace toward practicality with the advance in years of my recorded self, the reader will tacitly understand that Avery Glibun has now got fairly beyond the chronic indecision and crudities of boyhood (as the latter is limited in this country), and begins to have opinions and theories of a riper cast.

After the excitements and vicissitudes of my previous years, the monotony of an obscure clerkship at Cummin & Tryon's wearied me sadly at first. To be confined to a tall, ink-stained, subterranean desk all day, and, sometimes, nearly all night, beside a sallow, sententious man who sighed more frequently than he spoke; to have my existence completely ignored by the firm, and feel myself the meanest kind of small wheel in a machine owned by somebody else,—were circumstances not calculated to quicken the blood of youth. They served, however, by their plodding reality, to make my past seem more and more to me like a dream, fit only to be forgotten; and, as time passed on, and the magnetism of surrounding examples worked upon me, I gradually adapted myself to the stereotyped, clerkly world, and was content to have neither thoughts in my head nor money in my pocket, if a gorgeous necktie and an imitation sporting-suit but adorned my gallant person.

In the home of Mr. Job Terky, where I boarded, there was an element of discord to at least vary my emotions as a spectator, though not engaging me as a participant. Mrs. Terky, a buxom and lethargic lady about three years younger than her husband, was surely an affectionate wife and (when the time came) an idolatrous mother. Residing in a snug little two-story cottage on Banks Street, under trifling rent, with their rooms decently furnished, and their infant not necessarily a great pecuniary burden, the couple might have lived without either distress or boarders (in those times), even upon the small salary of the entry-clerk. But this they were far from doing, and I was not long in discovering the reason therefor.

Mrs. Terky was too much like her husband, in as far as a woman's radical nature can be like a man's, and but multiplied all his natural deficiences by two, instead of helping him by contrast to lessen them. He lacked energy, judgment, and practical management,—so did she. He did not know how to be prudent, self-denying, or consistent with circumstances,—nor did she. Consequently, the two together amounted to twice the weakness of either, though each possessed certain strong qualities which might have been developed with noble effect by an appropriate mate.

Mrs. Terky loved her husband dearly, but it was with that utterly unintelligent affection which a husband could as well obtain from his dog. An affection full of fascination for any ordinary man before marriage, and as full of inanity and weariness for him thereafter. In sluggish resignation to nonentity as distinguished from personal energy, she moved but as he moved, thought but as he thought, desponded when he was despondent, was frivolous when he was frivolous, and displayed not one whit of that mental individuality which should have made him trust to her, for counsel in his perplexity, and intellectual companionship in his argumentative needs.

There is a nice line to mark where the first perfect unity of husband and wife must begin to have the qualifications of an intelligent and wholesome difference, or degenerate into a supine mockery of all that is most ennobling and livingly harmonious in human intercourse. To ignore this line at the point where it rightfully reveals and explains itself to a practically unselfish intelligence, is scarcely less an assurance of unhappiness in the marital relation, than to draw the same line across the very threshold of marriage. She who knows when to combat her husband's intents, only that, when he has seen and admitted the accuracy of her intuitions, she may find the less cause to hold her judgment separate from his thereafter; he who knows when to firmly command his wife, only that the profit of obedience may render her the safer repository for his subsequent implicit trust, — are the wife and husband who give to human love its purest and wisest illustration, and render marriage a divine assimilation of strength and beauty.

Mrs. Terky's disregard, or, perhaps, ignorance, of this essential principle of harmony, made all her indiscriminating affection for poor, weak Job insufficient to preserve tranquillity for either of them. She eternally followed him about like his shadow at home, and called him "my precious fellow;" she heartily joined him in deploring his low salary, and despondently agreed with him in his hopelessness of ever doing better; but she also persisted in an extravagance which kept him continually in debt, and made the slavish drudgery of his desk a relief from the carking pressure of home.

I think I see her now, as she sat at the little dinner-table in the front room with Job and me, one Sunday, and petted the fantastically-dressed child on her lap. It was some comfort to Job, that she was quite pretty, and had smooth brown hair and sleepy blue eyes; though it certainly struck him often enough that her beauty would have been as creditable to a husband of his means had it been attired less showily.

"Tooty-ootsy-pootsy!" sang she, dancing the baby on the edge of the table for a moment, and then squeezing it deliriously to her silken Pompadour waist. "Tootsy must have a newy cloaky with cety yibbons before another Sunday, if mamma lives, — so he must."

"Why, Etta," cried Job, nervously dropping the apple he was peeling, "what's become of the cloak he had this spring?"

"Oh, you forgetful creature!" said Mrs. Terky, with girlish animation, "don't you remember how Bridget tore it on the railing that day when I let her take Tootsy out walking?"

"That Bridget costs us more than her wages every week," exclaimed Mr. Terky,

"and it's as much as I can do to pay them. Can't you mend the cloak, Etta? Where am I going to raise the money for a new one?"

"My precious fellow, you're so unreasonable. No you aren't unreasonable, either, — I didn't mean that. But you don't understand. Avery's board, you know, just pays Bridget's wages; so *she's* no expense. I can't mend the cloak, because my eyes hurt me so when I try to thread a needle; and it never would look fit to be seen, at any rate. A new one will only cost nine dollars, and it'll please Tootsy so!"

"A whole week's salary," sighed the entry-clerk, staring vacantly over his wife's head.

"Well, but he *must* have it," said Mrs. Terky, quite sharply.

"All right, my dear," replied Job, with desperation in his look and tone, "he shall have it. I only hope, though, that the grocer won't come here again with that bill of his for a month; nor the baker for a year. *I* can't pay them."

"I'm sure I try to save all *I* can," murmured the wife, her eyes filling with tears.

"I'm not finding fault with you, my dear. I didn't mean to hurt your feelings. Only, we must both try to be as prudent as we can. If you'd just, for instance, have our washing done at home, instead of paying for it outside. I should think Bridget might — "

"Oh, I couldn't think of it, Job!" interrupted Mrs. Terky, precipitately. "I can't breathe in the steam; and it hurts Tootsy's eyes so. I couldn't possibly, you know!"

"All r-i-ght, my dear," repeated the husband, reduced to resignation and despair again. "I wish somebody would get Cummin & Tryon to have a little soul for their clerks, — that's all! I wonder some of them don't steal, if they're as hard up as I am."

"It's SHAMEFUL they don't give you more!" cried Mrs. Terky, in the fulness of her love and admiration for him. "Isn't it shameful, Avery, that they treat my husband so, when he does half their business for them? It's so ungrateful!"

It rather surprised me to hear that so much of Cummin & Tryon's prosperity was due to the entry-clerk; but I politely assented to the lady's idea, and said that it was shameful indeed. A sickly and peculiar smile passed over the sallow countenance of Mr. Terky when she magnified him thus, as though it were a hopeless task to explain anything of business to women; and I saw that smile more than once again during the afternoon while she sat as closely to his chair as she could get, and used Tootsy to illustrate the pattern of his own new cloak.

There were other Sundays, though, when Mr. Coffin sentimentally came to dine with us; and then we had no little romance and covert merriment to drive away the skeleton from the board. In the lace-salesman's smoky yellow hair, long, solemn face, and round shoulders, there was a ludicrous commentary upon his Byronic tone of mind and willingness to be accused of an incorrigibly rakish past. Mr. Terky, it seemed, had made a friend of him for life, by pretending, on one occasion, that he recognized his exact style in a dissipated poem signed "Don Juan," in one of the Sunday papers. From that time he took the entry-clerk to his heart, as one whose sympathetic penetration had discovered that of which the thoughtless world little dreamed, and sought his abode when inclined to enjoy the sweet confidence of appreciative friendship. With me, too, he held a mysterious bond of sympathy, by virtue of my having been originally and strikingly commended to his good offices with the firm by one whose beauty dwelt with him like a dream, as he observed. It was tacitly understood that this bond, like the other, should have only a vague and distant existence in the insensate mart of mercenary trade, where iron custom obliged salesmen to disregard the finer ties and sensibilities of humanity by universally failing to recognize low-priced clerks; but around the private altar of our friend Terky intellect alone was to be the gauge of equality.

"It is strange, Mrs. Terky, how few intellectual people we meet in real life," was a thoughtful observation of Mr. Coffin's at a meal dispensed on the aforesaid altar. "Our people grow more and more absorbed in gross realism; we have not enough ideality, not enough mind-play."

"Yes, indeed," was the safe and not remarkably relevant reply of Mrs. Terky.

"I feel, myself, sometimes," continued Mr. Coffin, "like an island in the desert — I should say ocean. Except at the intelligent family hearthstone, like this, a man of mind, a man with a history, finds few congenial souls to mingle with."

Mr. Terky was always in a strong reactionary flow of spirits when the lace-salesman dined with us, and he now winked facetiously at me before going to the rescue of the inanely-smiling lady.

"Society, Mr. Coffin," said he, crossing his knife and fork, "thinks too much of money, and too little of brains. Your Goodmans, and your Cummins and Tryons are the men that get all the honors."

"Too true, Terky, too true; though I have heard that Mr. Goodman is as eminent for his mental calibre as for his rank in the Temple of Mammon. The last time I ever went into the Circean circle of society for pleasure's sake," pursued Mr. Coffin, slowly buttering his bread, and looking back through half-closed eyes to that remote period, "was at an archery meeting in Toe-der-veal, or, rather, at the tasteful seat of my old friend, Charles Spanyel. (By the way, my friend Spanyel, as I am informed, is descended from the Spanyels who came over with King Charles.) The company was select, stylish, socially brilliant; but I found no mind-play, no ideality, no salient intellectuality. It suggested to me, I recollect, an

idea for a poor verse or two, on the superiority of intellect over mere beauty in woman."

"You must read those verses, sir, to us," cried I, sure that he had them with him, by his manner. "You've mentioned them, and now it is only fair to let your friends hear them."

"Oh, yes, Mr. Coffin," said Mrs. Terky, coquettishly; "we ladies, you know, are always partial to poets. Do!"

"We're all friends, too," added Job.

"The poem is but a wretched trifle," returned the lace-salesman, drawing a folded sheet from his coat-pocket with seeming reluctance. "As I happen to have it with me, though, and the criticism of friendship is merciful, I will let you hear the stuff."

Thereupon Mr. Coffin solemnly unfolded the paper, cleared the butter from his fingers by abstractedly running the latter through his smoky hair, and, in doleful tones, read to us as follows, —

"Though white be the spell as a bosom divine,
  No conquering charm it discloses
To woo to the lilies' inodorous shrine
  The heart that has worshipped the roses;
And worthy the heart to be buried in snows,
  Where nature is frozen and stilly,
That dreams, though it catch but a breath from the Rose,
  Of paying its court to the Lily!

"'Tis not in the Temple of Beauty alone,
  If shineth no Fire at its portal,
To draw the true soul to an altar of Stone
  From one where the Flame is immortal;
And turns the true soul to the beauties that warm,
  Nor stops to bestow e'en a sigh on
The statelier Fane, whose fair votaries swarm,
  For dry goods, to Cummin & Tryon!"

"How lovely!" simpered Mrs. Terky.

"Something like Wordsworth," was my innocent comment.

"Don't you wish, Etta," asked the hypocritical entry-clerk, addressing his wife, "that I could write like that?"

"Well, I've no doubt that you could write as well as anybody, if you ever tried," returned the doting partner of his bosom, with a positive and confident look.

The sickly smile appeared on Mr. Terky's face again, and with some expression of mortification this time; but it quickly gave place to a quizzical stare when the lace-salesman coughed for attention.

"Glibun's remark about Wordsworth," observed Mr. Coffin, in a wrapt and musing way, "may be true in one sense. I love simplicity; I love the simplicity of nature and human feeling. In these little verses, — which, you may as well know, will be extensively published by Our Firm about the holiday season, — I have crudely tried to entirely idealize a literal fact. The poem is founded on fact. If I must confess the truth to the unbetraying ear of friendship, it derives the melancholy cast you may have noticed from my memory of One who had Intellect and Beauty."

"It refers to the Lady, does it?" inquired Job, his countenance showing deep interest.

Seized with sudden agitation, the poet could barely stammer the incoherent question, "which of them?"

"The one who married the nabob with a glass eye."

I positively thought Mr. Coffin would have a fit, and Mrs. Terky thought he would wake the baby,—he ground his teeth and drew the air between them to that extent.

"Terky, this is too much!" he cried, frenziedly plunging all his fingers into his hair, and springing half-way up the back of his chair. "It's unmanly! It's cruel! It is maddening! Must a man's heart be wrung like this, even at that intelligent family hearthstone where its bitter memory should be held inviolably sacred?"

"He didn't mean it!" pleaded both Mrs. Terky and I, in a breath.

"Upon my soul, I didn't!" exclaimed the repentant offender, seeing that he had pressed the broken reed too rudely. "My dear, good-hearted friend, you must excuse my thoughtlessness; let me help you to some pie."

Heaving that exhaustive and supernaturally muscular sigh wherewith the more debilitated lovers in dramas are wont to assure the audience that they have dismissed a harrowing remembrance for the time being, Mr. Coffin suffered his hands to fall slowly in a rigid clasp upon the table, and fixed his eyes dreamily upon the pie.

"Is it apple?" he gloomily asked.

"Dried apple," responded the voice of sympathy.

"I'll try some," was his unalterable resolve; after the model of the same lovers when they accept poison before dishonor.

Wishing to give the conversation a livelier turn, I poured out beer for all around and vivaciously inquired of Mrs. Terky whether she had finished the smoking-cap I saw her working on the previous morning.

"Oh, I do declare! if you aint provoking," cried she, making a pretty show of vexation. "Now you've let Job know, and I can't surprise with it as I wanted to. Since you've let the cat out of the bag, though, I may as well tell the whole story. You needn't look at me in that way, either, Job dear, for I haven't been extravagant! You know I told you the other day that we must have a new china coffee-pot, because the handle of the old one was so loose. You gave me the money—"

—Mr. Terky's face twitched nervously.

—"but instead of buying a new one, I mended the old pot with some patent cement (Here it is, you see, good as new)"—

—"Mr. Terky brightened.

—"and took the money to get worsteds and lining for a nice smoking-cap. Now, Mr. Coffin, I'll leave it to you if that wasn't being something like a good, economical little wife."

Job looked really gratified, under the wild momentary conviction that a miracle of self-sacrificing parsimony had been enacted for his pecuniary relief; and Mr. Coffin was undoubtedly in the first intellectual pangs of a speech destined to place woman's domestic virtues in a new poetical light, when Mrs. Terky started half-way from her chair, with raised forefinger.

"Hark! . . . Yes! I thought so! Tootsy's crying."

As she sprang from the table to fly to the bedroom where Tootsy was lamenting, her dress caught in the wired edge of a japanned tray containing the whole coffee-service, and dragged all to the floor with a crash.

Madly regardless of polite company, the entry-clerk sprang up, tearing his hair.

"Another twenty gone to smash!" burst from him like a shriek. "Now let the grocer and the butcher and the baker come on and finish me!"

"Oh, plague on my dress, I wish it was in Guinea!" sympathized the devoted mother. "I've been expecting to do that ever since I got it. I must run to Tootsy, or he'll scream himself into fits."

During her absence from the apartment, I endeavored to console and instruct the delirious man with a series of desperate fictions concerning the peculiar tendency of broken china to regain more than its pristine firmness and beauty by being mended with a certain unpronounceable cement. Driven to frenzy by his glassy stare at the carving-knife, I even cited fabulous instances of my own unheard-of ingenuity in repairing the fractures of invaluable Sevres punch bowls. The while Mr. Coffin, upon whom the crash and outburst had produced an unspeakable dazing effect, solemnly picked up the fragments from the floor, one by one, and carefully slid them into his various pockets like so many fragile gifts for a friend's children.

But when Mrs. Terky brought Tootsy into the room with the unfinished smoking-cap upon his head, showing how becoming it was going to be for anybody when it had the tassel on it, we all grew calmed; and when Mrs. Terky explained how thankful we ought to be that Tootsy-ootsy-pootsy was not on her lap when the tray fell, and so, didn't need an expensive doctor to dress the awful scald that might have been his death, we unanimously drifted to the happy conclusion that a providential escape had occurred, and took high ground with Bridget for her apparent inclination to view the breakage as an unprofitable affair.

My flattering appreciation of his literary efforts finally produced such a profound impression upon the Wordsworth of the lace counter, that he was tempted to confide to another fashionable salesman, popularly known as "Gloves," his high opinion of my brilliant intellectual gifts. Thereupon Mr. Gloves sought an early opportunity of inviting me to lunch with him at a tawdry restaurant; where, over a feast consisting chiefly of a small island of tenderloin in a desolate ocean of white plate, he unfolded to me his desire that I should lend him my supposed muse for a few amatory stanzas.

"You may as well know, Glibun," said he, with abrupt candor, "that I want the stuff for a certain lady, and that I want her to see the lines in one of the Sunday papers over my own signature. Couldn't you let fly three or four verses,—about music, say? Talk about there being music everywhere, and especially in the lady addressed. That's my idea."

In default of a better one, it was mine, too, and, with a scowl of superhuman thoughtfulness upon my countenance, I promised to write the poem.

I did write that poem:—There was music in the mountain, there was music in the plain; there was music in the desert, there was music in the main; there was music in the streamlet, there was music in the air; there was music in the tempest, there was music everywhere. After which it followed, of course that,—There was music in HER glances, there was music in her nose; there was music in her mantle, there was music in her shoes; there was music in her laughter, there was music in her hair; there was music in her manner, there was music everywhere.

I saw this reckless piece of "music" reduced to blurred print on the following Sunday, and with an editorial introduction attributing to it "more or less of that poetical perception of things which renders it an ornament to our advertising columns, and a significant contrast to the disgusting platitudes starvingly inserted, at reduced rates, by our debilitated and green-eyed cotemporaries." I also learned that the line about the "nose" was not felicitously understood at first by the fair subject of the poem; she having a bad cold in her head at the time; but upon the arrival of her brother at Cummin & Tryon's, on Monday morning, to inflict personal chastisement upon the offender, an explanation took place, and Mr. Gloves and the brother went out and drank themselves into a tearful and nearly speechless stage of inseparable fraternity.

The new friend gained for me by the whole affair was not my most important acquisition. I also gained a sudden confidence in my own literary abilities, and was tempted to compose, stealthily, another short poem, which I addressed to the same paper and signed "M. T. Head." It was published; and, in his "Answers to Correspondents" the editor was kind enough to say that,—"Gratuitous contributions in prose from this source will always be acceptable when our columns are not otherwise occupied."

The moment bringing that assurance to my notice was the proudest of my life. That one moment of enjoyed immortality! —Sublime and Ridiculous are but vague terms to him who has not lived it. To fold the paper in such a way that my piece seemed its leading attraction, and then retire from it with a studied air of long familiarity with such intoxicating fame, was my delight until the dinner hour on Sunday. To take my little mirror down from its nail, stand it at a proper angle on my table, and practice in it such attitudes and melancholy smiles as denote lofty intellectual abstraction, was the solemn joy of several succeeding mornings. A curious and complacent sense of impressive stoutness, too, came upon me when I walked, and gave to my steps a firmness and confidence quite elephantine.

While this inward glory lasted (and it made me indifferent to dinner, until after I had secretly contributed for some months to the *Sunday Tap*), Mrs. Terky seemed disposed to suspect me of drinking, and even left upon the mantel in my room an exciting tract, entitled "The Dissipated Young Man." Mr. Terky, however, whose depression had increased of late, under a humiliating sidewalk dun from his milkman, and the present of a costly watch-case from his wife, openly accused me of trouble with my tailor. I smiled in mournful pity over both misconceptions, and carried so many copies of the *Tap* in all my pockets, that I seemed the victim of the most complicated dislocations and deformities.

Having thus sufficiently specified the new circumstances and interests tending to make my clerkship with Cummin & Tryon a change of life, indeed, let me pass on to the evening which brought me the first reminder of my unhappy earlier days. Mr. Terky had just said to me,—

"The new assistant-cashier, from upstairs, was speaking to me about you this morning, Glibun, and thinks he used to know you. He's coming down again, tonight, before he goes home."

"Who is he?"

"I don't know his name yet."

Wondering who it could be, I resumed my work upon the bill I was copying, and did not look up again until I was attracted by the sound of some one stumbling through the gloom, beyond the circle of our gaslight.

"There's your friend," said Mr. Terky.

The person so indicated was a slender, neatly-dressed young man, apparently but little older than myself; and, at the first meeting of our eyes, I was sure that I had seen him before.

"Your name is Glibun, I believe," he remarked, frankly offering his hand.

"That is my name," responded I; "and yours is Trust."

"To be sure; I'm Noah Trust. How are you?"

I had not loved the grocer's son when he was my playmate, and the events recalled by his presence were anything but cheerful; yet I was really glad to see Noah in his new character, and eagerly drew him away from the desk, for a hurried talk about old times. Greatly improved was Noah over the selfish, disagreeable school-boy of former days; and I was pleasantly surprised at the amiable manner in which he spoke of all our old associates. Gwin Le Mons, he said, had turned newspaper correspondent, and gone to Europe, somewhere. His mother and Conny had moved to a house in Fourth Street, and were reported as taking boarders. Upton Knox had gone to college. Luke Ilyer was with Goodman & Co., where his father also had a position. Ben Poore was in a bank; and Ben Beeton had gone West, to a Methodist university.

"The old boys are pretty well scattered about." concluded Noah; "and you and I have changed as much as any of them, probably. You've grown so tall, and put on so much style, that I shouldn't have known you if I hadn't seen your name on the books upstairs."

"And you," returned I, greatly relieved to find that he did not question me about myself, "are very much altered, too; but I knew you, for all."

"I suppose you couldn't get off, to-night?" he asked, with a glance toward the desk.

"I'm afraid not. We've got several long bills to make out yet."

"Too bad, Glibun! You remember Nettie Beeton, Ben's sister? I'm engaged to call on her this evening, and would like to have you along. She's a pretty girl."

I remembered her vividly enough; for she it was that threw me into such a state at Gwin Le Mons' party.

"I'd go if I could," was my answer.

"You *can* go, if you choose, Glibun," came unexpectedly from Mr. Terky, who had overheard my last words. "I can manage what work there is for to-night, if your friend wants you to go with him." He looked at his watch, and continued, — "It's not eight yet. I'll be home as soon as you are."

"I hate to leave you with so much —"

"Nonsense!"

"Well, at any rate I'll finish that bill I was —"

"Glibun," interrupted the entry-clerk again, with an unaccountable display of irritation, "I wish you'd clear out as quickly as you can! I want to figure these bills myself, and should have let you off, any way. Don't stop to talk; but go, for Heaven's sake!"

Surprised and indignant at his snappish manner of speaking, I donned hat and gloves in a great glow of resentment, and followed Noah upstairs without another word on the subject.

"That entry-clerk seems to be a curious fellow," remarked Noah, as we emerged upon Broadway.

"He's a perfect old granny," was my impatient comment.

On the way to our destination, which was on Grand Street, my companion and I amused ourselves with an interchange of boyish reminiscences; nor did the grocer's son shrink from recalling his unpopularity as a playmate. Laughingly he referred to the corruption fund of suspicious almonds and raisins wherewith he was wont to procure surreptitious aid in his school compositions and sums; at the same time affirming that shame in the recollection of those days had gone far to disgust him with his father's business and incline him to another branch of trade.

Positive genius seems to be the only possession that can carry the primitive character of childhood into manhood, whether for better or worse. Without that energetic, imperious, and unabsorbing antiseptic, the minds and dispositions of men appear to undergo some kind of fermentation between youth and maturity, changing from sweet to sour, or from sour to sweet, according as the original condition may have been.

Noah Trust seemed to have turned, or be turning, from sour to sweet; and, by the time we reached the Reverend Mr. Beeton's house, I liked him better than any other young man of my acquaintance. I liked him so well that I fairly clung to him as we entered the tasteful room where the clergyman, his wife, and daughter arose from their reading to receive us; and Miss Nettie saw me at first to not much better advantage than on the incredible evening when I struggled against her kiss.

It is due to myself, however, that I should not confess more awkwardness than was mine on the occasion. With an ease of manner possible only to well-bred people, Mr. and Mrs. Beeton received me, through Noah's introduction, as though my call were the most natural occurrence in the world; and Nettie so freely shook hands with me, in honor of our earlier acquaintance, that all embarrassment left me in a moment. I may say, indeed, that I felt quite at home when, after a few general remarks, the silver hair and gold spectacles of the elders concentred upon Noah, leaving the young lady and me to properly renew our acquaintance.

In five minutes I loved Nettie Beeton; in ten minutes I had madly confided to her the secret of my connection with the press; at the expiration of a quarter of an hour, I was assiduously seeking torture for my jealousy in every glance she cast toward the grocer's son. She had lovely blue eyes, shining auburn braids over her head, distracting shoulders, and a miraculous little foot, — and she knew it.

"It seems so odd, Mr. Glibun, that you should meet Noah in such a way. Don't you think he has improved?"

"More so than any person I ever knew, except One."

Here I languished.

"Pa and ma think there's no one like him."

This sounded like taking advantage of my last magnanimous admission, and I was betrayed into the most mercenary of questions. —

"Do you buy your groceries of his father?"

"No, sir, we do not!" returned Miss Beeton, with an unfavorable blush; and it stung me into an inflated attempt to cover my rudeness with sophistry.

"Noah is a splendid fellow," said I, hastily, "and will be a rich man one of these days. That is the great thing in this world, after all. It opens the door to preferment, fame, and love; it wins the throne for a plaything, and the palace for a home; while intellect in rags kneels at the footstool, and shivers at the gate."

This surprising bit of rhetoric was quoted from my last contribution to the *Top;* but I must confess that it sounded in my own ears provokingly like one of Mrs. Fry's speeches.

"Don't you think Noah has intellect?" asked Miss Beeton, evidently awe-stricken.

"If he has, so much the worse for him!" The sentence struck me as being so manfully bitter and misanthropical, that I repeated it in a hoarse whisper, — "If he has, so much the worse for him! To be intellectual nowadays is to be crushed by men, and scorned by women." To give this sentiment due weight, I poetically ran my fingers through my hair, and had commenced a hollow laugh, when a sudden thought that the frightful sound might attract some attention from Noah and the parents, caused me to disguise the imperfect performance in a scrape of my chair on the carpet.

"You're not fair, Mr. Glibun, in saying that women scorn intellectual people," said the clergyman's daughter, with all the thoughtfulness of mature years and unspeakable experience. "At least, I know that I do not scorn them; and I often tell pa and ma that they don't understand me at all. I do not pretend to be particularly intellectual myself, but I do like to meet with people who can sympathize in something besides dress and new music. It seems to me that the hardest thing in the world to find is true sympathy."

"That's exactly the way with me!" sighed I.

"My brother Ben understands me better than any one else, and while he's away I hardly know how to talk with any one else. It seems to me that woman must have some mission. At least, I'm sure that if people only understood me better, — if I could only find more true sympathy, — I should not cry *quite* so often over my crochet."

"Yes!" murmured I, insanely; "that's exactly the way with me!"

"Pa and ma, over there, are as good as they can be; but they don't understand me any more than if I were an entire stranger."

I nodded my head, and smiled sadly. For a moment I even contemplated the propriety of pointing impressively upward with a forefinger, by way of indicating the place where true sympathy can always be found at last. But, as the Reverend Mr. Beeton happened to look my way just then, I thought better of it.

"They say it's dyspepsia," continued Nettie, looking timidly, and almost tearfully, at me.

"It's attributed to drink, in me," hissed I.

"Because one is young," pursued the intellectual girl, "people think there can be no shadows nor crosses in one's life."

"That's exactly the way with me!" I broke out again, lost to all prudence.

"You have had shadows, then, Mr. Glibun?"

I eyed her with a frowning intensity, which, from the corrugation of brow and contraction of pupil of which I was sensible, must have approximated to an acute squint.

"My life, Miss Beeton," said I, in my deepest bass, "has been all in shadow, — a mystery, — a terrible secret, — darkens my existence; and you are the first human being to whom I have ever confided the fact that I do not know what that secret is!"

In this unpremeditated confidence, — this passionate revelation of a blighted inner life, — there was something so appalling that we both remained silent after it for some moments. Then, with that eagerness to do something for the afflicted, which is so natural to woman, Nettie gazed wistfully at me, and spoke again, —

"Won't you eat something?"

Her kind intention to comfort me went, rather than her words, to my heart.

"No, Miss Beeton," I responded. "Thank you; but I had a plate of fishballs early in the evening."

How pretty she looked in profile, with her long lashes cast down under my refusal! I should have proposed marriage to her on the spot, had not the remainder of the party moved their chairs toward us at that juncture, and persecuted us with worldly conversation.

When Noah and I finally took our leave, it was my crowning happiness to be included with him in an informal, but hearty, invitation from the whole family to attend a little social gathering there on the fifth of the following month; and my last vision as we left the house was of the divine Nettie, grouping affectionately with her father, as though she would say, — "I can never leave him, whoever I marry." From that moment I resolved to support the old man.

Noah Trust would not have disappointed my guilty expectations had he improved the opportunity of our homeward walk by calling me to account for what he might have deemed my flagrant flirtation with Miss Beeton; but, instead of so doing, he only gossiped pleasantly of the family, until we parted at Bleecker Street; and I paused to look after him, as he crossed Broadway, with a feeling of amazement at the change in him.

Arriving at home, in Banks Street, and using my night-key with as little noise as possible, I let myself in, and had gained my room, as I thought, without waking any one, when, to my surprise, Mr. Terky made his appearance at my door, candle in hand.

"You're home, I see," said he.

"Yes," responded I, nervously. "Is anything the matter?"

"No! But I wanted to ask you, Glibun, to overlook my snappishness with you this evening. I was miserable, and couldn't bear to talk. I'd been applying to the firm, for the fiftieth time, for a little more salary (that was what I was after when your friend asked me about you); and Cummin as much as told me to give up the situation, if the present terms didn't suit me. That was what ailed me to-night."

"Why, Mr. Terky," I answered, going to him and taking his hand. "I didn't think of it five minutes afterward. It's a shame for those old snobs to grind you so. You do the work of half a dozen men for them."

"That sounds like my wife," said he, with a sickly smile. "But I'm glad you don't feel hurt. Did you have a good time to-night?"

"Splendid."

"Then you've got something to dream about. Good-night."

I heard him wearily dragging his slippered feet through the hall to his own room, like one whose nerveless step followed that which led he knew not, cared not, whither; and, in the sleep that should else have brought me pictures of loveliness and true sympathy, I fancied myself Mr Coffin, flying from an unpaid bill in the hands of one who had a glass eye and was disguised as a milkman.

CHAPTER XXXIII.

My spirits were buoyant for breakfast, and I sat down to that meal with the liveliest inclination to banish everything serious from conversation and thought, by all the humorous conceits known to a young noodle in love. It was soon evident, however, that I had literally reckoned without my host; for the entry-clerk received my opening sally concerning the weather with a countenance of inflexible gravity. His wife, also, resented the vivacity of my looks and manner with the information that little Tootsy was quite unwell; and presently I was eating my mackerel in silent exasperation at having been too familiar with inferiors!

But silence would not have been long endurable to Mrs. Terky under any pitch of gloom, and after the inspiration of two or three sips of coffee, she brightened up and addressed me characteristically.

"Only think of it, Avery! my precious fellow has been breaking his watch. He talks about my being careless, and not saving; and now he'll have to spend several dollars, I dare say, for mending."

Remembering that Mr. Terky had told the time from his watch only last night, I looked toward him for further explanation, and noticed, simultaneously, that his chain and key were gone from his vest, and that he was frowning and shaking his head to stop my intended question.

"I shan't go after the watch until I'm able to pay for it," exclaimed he, hastening to prevent any words from me, "if it takes ten years."

"Well, dear," returned Mrs. Terky, soothingly, "I hope it'll make you a little more charitable to me when I break things. Just think! my watch has only been to the jeweller's once, and I've had it ever since we were married."

"That 'once' cost me twenty dollars, though," said Mr. Terky, turning irritably to me. "She was looking out of a window upstairs to see what company were going into a house across the street, and dropped her watch clear to the sidewalk."

I thought that a laugh was allowable here, but qualified it with a sage comment upon the inconvenient delicacy of watches in general.

Mrs. Terky, though, seemed to take her husband's sharp tone very much to heart, and his next words were obviously intended to comfort her, —

"No matter, Etta, we're both careless enough to break a bank. Here! take this and pay off some of our debts with it."

To our unspeakable amazement he carelessly flirted two ten-dollar bank notes across his wife's plate.

"Why, Job! Where did you get it?"

"I borrowed it of my uncle."

I had never heard this liberal relative mentioned before; but he seemed to be known to the lady, for she folded the notes with a satisfied "H'm — h'm!" and looked very much pleased.

"There! haven't I always told you that things would be sure to come out all right, in some way?" she asked triumphantly, — "haven't I always told you so? Now I can pay the milkman and the grocer, after all our worry. Tootsy ought to have a pair of red morocco shoes; but then — well, no matter. I suppose you know, Job dear, that Mr. House sent here, again, yesterday for last quarter's rent?"

The last feeble ray of light went out of the entry-clerk's sallow face at the word, and he seemed to collapse with a groan into an older and thinner man.

"I know what you're going to say now!" she continued, with a change of manner equally quick and forlorn. "You're going to remind me that you gave me the rent-money two weeks ago, and that I lost my pocket-book on the counter in some of the stores where I was shopping. I know you think I'm your ruin!"

"The meanness of Cummin & Tryon is to blame for it," cried I, roused to the rescue by her look and tone of distress. "If the firm would half pay either Mr. Terky or me, there would be no trouble."

"You're right, Glibun," said Mr. Terky, speaking like a man utterly tired out; "a starvation salary is my ruin. Cummin & Tryon can't afford to pay their clerks decently; but they could afford, the other day, to send their check for a thousand to Plato Wynne in aid of the Demolition Ticket for next week's election. I remember when they used to give as much to General Cringer, for the Ebullition side (generally); but then they hadn't any Demolition Southern customers to toady, and Tryon hadn't been to Europe. Isn't it a nice thing for an American to know, that when old Tryon got back from London and reported that all the English nobs were hot for Demolition here, our firm wheeled right around for Demolition, too? I wish from my heart that I was an Irishman! There'd be some chance for me, then, in America!"

He was somewhat excited by his theme, or the last two sentences, absurd and inexplicable as any one must know them to be, would not have escaped him.

On our way to the store, I asked him what he had done with his watch.

"Took it to my Uncle Simpson's as soon as I got you out of the way last night," he answered, with a reckless air.

"You don't mean to say you pawned it?"

"Yes, I did; and I'd pawn my soul if it would bring anything, and wasn't worn out! It was my father's watch, and it isn't long since I pawned another legacy — a breastpin. Simpson is the uncle I tell Etta about; and she thinks he is a genuine relative who's too proud to associate with me. You know how women are."

Yes, I had a very profound knowledge of women, of course, and laughed in a knowing way.

Noah Trust came down to our den of entry soon after the first bills of the day had been "called off," and managed a brief conversation with me to such friendly implication, that I felt assured by it of his comparative indifference to the charms of Miss Beeton. As I grew bolder in praising the latter he became more eloquent in certain obscure references to some young lady unknown to me; and his final declaration that Nettie seemed "like a sister" to him certainly made me feel more like his own brother. As a consequence of this tranquil understanding between us, I began at once to be more practical in my views of the inevitable, and dwelt thoughtfully upon such items in the entries as represented the feminine wardrobe. In case of an early marriage, I presumed that I could avail myself of a clerkly privilege not yet abolished in the larger dry-goods houses, and obtain dress-patterns, handkerchiefs, gloves, etc., at cost; but this cost, even, was rather staggering in some cases, and I was reluctantly brought to the conclusion that silk dresses would be out of the question until after several increases of salary.

"Mr. Terky," asked I, at the very climax of my calculations, "how many yards of stuff does it take to make a dress for Mrs. Terky?"

The entry-clerk turned slowly from his column of figures, and answered half-mechanically, though with some feeble signs of wonder, —

"She generally wants a whole piece, I believe; so that if one of the breadths, she says, gets torn, or burnt, it can be replaced without costing anything. But what in the world do you want to know that for?"

"Oh, nothing," said I, affecting carelessness; "only curiosity."

"It's dangerous ground," he muttered, returning to his drudgery.

On pretence of failing appetite, I did not accompany him, at noon, to the cheap eating-house where we were wont to lunch inexpensively together, but took advantage of his brief absence to pen an alarming epistle to Nettie! There was some appearance of a flagrant outrage on etiquette in the proceeding, for ladies are not accustomed to hear by mail from gentlemen of last evening's acquaintance; yet Miss Beeton might possibly award some indulgence to our early intimacy in society; and, besides, had I not revealed to her the awful mystery of my life? Conscious of the rectitude of my intentions, I commenced my letter with that elaborate multiplicity of excuse which, curious to relate, is peculiarly characteristic of all persons conscious of the rectitude of *their* intentions. Having exhausted my apologetic power so completely that I was left in the middle of a frightfully-involved sentence, with no alternative but to close it with unexpected precipitation, I had barely room on the small note-sheet to assure the maiden of my madness and wickedness, in darkening her young existence with the knowledge of a fatal secret, and to implore her to keep that secret inviolate for the sake of her desolate friend. In my agitation, as I afterwards discovered, I wrote the word desolate with one more "s" than strict orthography sanctions, and also left the first "e" without a loop, and the "a" without a roof. Hence, in the earliest reading, I was supposed to have confessed myself *dissolute* — which accounted for Miss Beeton's delay in answering me.

The directing and sealing of my letter were but just accomplished when Mr. Terky returned, with toothpick in full play, — not being exempt from our horrible national habit of gracing conversational abstraction and post-prandial reverie with the manual of the table-quill. To hide from him the flutter of spirits into which the surreptitious purpose of my fast had thrown me, I endeavored to display renewed energy in the afternoon's work, and as evening came on my labors amounted to a goodly array of completed invoices. These he revised, as was his custom, and then briefly informed me that I need not remain to assist him that night.

As the "busy season" had commenced, and many of the salesmen, even, were compelled to stay until near midnight, I knew not how to understand my good fortune. Indeed, I felt quite guilty at leaving my superior to do all the work of the desk for two nights in succession, and should have persisted in keeping him company had he not received my protest with positive anger.

"Now, see here, Glibun!" he impatiently exclaimed. "I know what I am about. It's a pity if I can't have my own way in some things. When I really want you to stay at night, I'll tell you; but, for a while, now, I can do all the night-work myself, and your being here only makes me nervous. For Heaven's sake, clear out and let me alone!"

"You'll know it when I offer to stay again!" snapped I, out of all patience, in my turn, with his inexplicable perversity. "You'll know it, I can tell you!" And away I bounced for fresh air and freedom, resolved to think less of other people's comfort next time.

After depositing my secret missive in the nearest box of the penny-post, the first impulse was to repair at once to my own room in Banks Street, and devote the evening to a mysterious tale of high life for the *Sunday Tap.* Happening, however, to be rendered suddenly inane by a cheap but plentiful supper of hash at an obscure chop-house in a cross-street, I permitted myself to be seduced by a glaring theatrical poster, announcing a new comedy from London, and presently found my way into the dramatic temple where that original delicacy was being dispensed.

Incredible as the assertion may seem to the present generation, the play was enjoying the hearty approval of a large audience, although its character-list included neither an Irishman plotting England's ruin, nor a semi-nude heroine standing on one toe. But the period was anterior to that in which we see mince-pie and apples audibly eaten in the dress-circle between acts, and have our chambermaid and hostler for next-door neighbors in the reserved orchestra-seats.

With an unsophistication proper to that comparatively ingenuous age, I was deriving entertainment from the performance; with that keen appreciation of true wit and humor which is an American peculiarity, I was roaring laughter in chorus with everybody else, over inimitable and entirely incomprehensible hits at local London politics, when a twisted programme smote me sharply on the cheek and fell into my lap. Looking quickly in the direction from which the assault must have come, I at first saw only a number of smiling faces expressing no particular meaning, nor was it until the carved ivory handle of a black switch-cane had been thrust after my gaze several times from the last row of boxes, that I distinguished and recognized the author of the rudeness. To do this was to lose indignation in surprise, and the latter emotion still prevailed when I got beyond the final range of seats and saw the owner of the cane awaiting me.

"Mr. Vane!" I exclaimed, in a suppressed voice.

Hair puffed out in curls until it looked like a huge fur cap under his jaunty silk hat, and a fine broadcloth suit of the most stylish description, did not for a moment confuse my identification of the former teacher of the classics at Oxford Institute. The old indolent look of his handsome face was still in the eyes that questioned my opinion, as their possessor hesitatingly took me by the hand.

"You seem to know me as readily as I knew you," he said, in a half-laughing undertone. "Excuse me — will you? — for attracting your attention as I did. You would not notice my several previous attempts to catch your eye, and I was too anxious for recognition to neglect any means of making myself known."

While he spoke, the whole distempered panorama of my school-days passed rapidly before my mind, and became a troubled, questioning thing of yesterday.

"I have wished to see you, sir," I replied, drawing him back beyond the hearing of others, "quite as much as you can want to see me. I cannot tell just how far I have to thank you for what came near putting an end to my — "

"Wait a moment," interrupted he. "Do you care to see any more of the play?"

"No. I've had enough of it."

"Then suppose we step into a private supper-room some where near by, and have our talk over a bottle of wine?"

I nodded acquiescence, and suffered him to link arms with me; but on reaching the street a new consideration made me hastily propose an amendment.

"Wouldn't it be as well to go into the reading-room of some hotel?" asked I. "Probably we could have a corner to ourselves at this time of night."

"Reading-room!" ejaculated Vane, contemptuously. "I don't know how much public interest there may be in what you have to say to me, Glibun; but I don't care to share *my* confidence with a herd of dry-goods drummers and Southern blacklegs. That's about the style of company you'll find in a reading-room at this time of day."

"To be frank with you, Mr. Vane," was my candid remark, "I am not in circumstances to warrant wine suppers."

He deliberately withdrew his arm from mine, assumed an attitude favorable to an easy contemplation of a curious object, and alternately bent and relaxed his switch-cane against a lamp-post near us.

"Glibun," said he, "you must not take it too hard if I tell you that your manners are heathenish."

Unable to decide from the tone whether he spoke in jest or earnest, I only looked at him.

"That speech of yours," continued he, "was insulting. When I ask gentlemen to take wine with me, they do not generally think it necessary to consult their own pockets. You're only a boy, however."

"Gentlemanly deportment was one of the branches taught by you, I believe, at Milton," sneered I, thoroughly aroused by his supercilious air and words. "Good-night, sir."

He caught me as I turned to leave him, and again linked arms with me by main strength.

"Come along," he cried, "and let us stop advertising that play-house with a farce before the door;" continuing, as I yielded somewhat reluctantly to his impulse and walked with him, "I see that you have some of your old simplicity left."

In one of the small but luxurious private rooms of a fashionable temple of refreshment we presently confronted each other across an elegant little table set out with the appointments of a mild revel. There, with his hat removed and the light full in his face, Allyn Vane looked not the same man as before, and I watched him, while he gave his order to the waiter, in no small wonder at the swaggering arrogance of his manner. Indolence still looked incredulously at all exertion through his eyes, and vain assurance still discredited humility in the curves of his nose, lips, and chin; but the indolence had darkened into a glamour of insidious sensuality, and the assurance had coarsened into the defiant audacity of incipient licentiousness. As I gazed upon him, leaning back in his chair and abusing the servant for some trifling misapprehension, there came a regret that I had met him again, and a sense of humiliation at being taken by the servant for one like him.

Until the arrival of the wine and salads, he boisterously rallied me upon my growth and sober air, interspersing sundry incidental pleasantries the while concerning our old relation of teacher and scholar, as though the events of Oxford Institute had been no more than the ordinary school-story. When the bottle was with us, however, and the final retirement of the waiter made our privacy secure, he lapsed abruptly into a silence which, in some way, made me feel obliged to ask the first question.

"Mr. Vane, where is Elfie, — Mrs. Birch?"

Pointing to the glass he had filled for me, and clasping both hands about his own, he looked unflinchingly at me, and replied in a word, —

"Married."

I understood enough of his meaning to start at the sound.

"What do you mean, Mr. Vane? Mr. Birch —"

"Is not dead," said Allyn Vane.

I looked at him in hopeless bewilderment.

"But Mr. Birch is dead to her," he added, with an evil smile, "for she got a Western divorce. Nothing easier to get, my young friend. 'Absolute decrees. Good everywhere, and obtained for any cause. No charge until decree is gained. No publicity.' That's the style of the advertisement. You go to the lawyer, — formerly a detective, probably, — and say that you want a divorce. That's enough. Call again in

three weeks. The thing is done, and you pay your fifty dollars."

I hoped he was practising a rude joke on me; but one more glance was enough to detect that he relished not what he said, and only assumed a light manner to hide the real feeling.

"Do you mean to tell me," cried I, aghast, "that Mrs. Birch has married again, after such an infamous fraud as that?"

My earnestness (and I was near crying) seemed to amuse him for a moment, and he laughed as he replied, "Why, bless your innocent heart, Glibun, the thing is common enough." Then becoming serious again, and even changing color, he added,— "I may as well tell you the whole truth. She had at least one *bonâ fide* witness that I know of, who testified by affidavit as to the brutality of Birch. I was that witness."

"You!" ejaculated I, in still greater amazement. "Why, you ran away with her!"

"Or she with me," he retorted, sharply. "But that made no particular difference. The bill of divorce, duly signed by the court, was obtained. Mr. Birch, branded with criminality and brutality, was sentenced to permanent celibacy for his sins; and Mrs. Birch went free. *Vive la bagatelle!*"

He had taken but a few sips of his wine, or I should have attributed to the latter a continual variation of manner, not at all suited to the miserable subject of our conversation.

"Mr. Vane," I remarked, with a feeling of real sorrow, "the woman you speak about was the best friend of my neglected infancy. I have neither seen nor heard of her since my school-days until to-night; and it was solely to learn something about her that I met you so cordially at the theatre, and agreed to come here with you. I knew, of course, that she had acted very imprudently; but, until now, I have treated every recollection, that could accuse her of worse than that, as a dream."

"And may still do so," returned Allyn Vane; "for she has, at any rate, committed no crime that I am aware of. Everybody at Oxford Institute knew of Birch's brutality, or, at least, of his drunkenness. And as for his criminality, there were such good reasons to believe in some sort of connection between him and a political gang of counterfeiters, that he never would have dared to contest the charge. This fact I have learned lately, and you may take it for gospel. Finally, Mrs. Birch might have gained an open divorce from him had she chosen to try, and I can hardly blame her for preferring the secret method, when it virtually served as well. Let me do her justice so far."

I had been upon the point of asking where Elfie then was, when he began speaking; but his specification of the crime charged against the school-master paralyzed my tongue. Another sinister circumstance was thus added to the dark complications which already made my own history a hopeless enigma to me, and I could only stare blankly at the table, and draw a heavy breath. Noting my mood, Mr. Vane also fell into a fit of sullen musing. From this he roused himself after some moments by draining his glass with a sudden air of bravado.

"Here's death to the blue devils!" exclaimed he, filling again. "Why don't you drink, my boy? I can't see what *you've* got to make you blue."

"I was only thinking," said I, mechanically. "I wonder what has become of Mr. Birch? I thought he was dead."

"Dead!" ejaculated Vane. "Why, what are you talking about! He's a raving maniac in one of the asylums out of town. By the way," added he, changing his manner again, "there was something curious about that business. The first boys back to school, after the vacation that year, were packed off home again, with a strange story, by that fellow Reed. They were told that old Birch had been severely injured while exploring the Summit. That was the saintly monitor's half of the story. But in the village, when the boys took stage for Newark, they had a different sort of rumor for the other half. Birch, they said, had a frightful gunshot wound in the head when he was found, at the top of the hill, and it was hardly dressed in the school-house by Dr. Pilgrim, before he commenced raving about a murder, or a murderer, or something of the sort. To tell the rest in a few words,— the school was at an end; the affair was hushed up, and poor old 'Rufus,' as the boys called him, went to a mad-house. And now I want to ask you a question, Glibun. Who fired that shot?"

Perhaps he intended to surprise me into an answer before I could recover from the abruptness of the query. If so, it was a miscalculation.

"It was fired to save my neck," I responded, coolly. "Mr. Birch was already crazy,—made so chiefly by your exploit, sir!—and would have carried me with him in an awful flight from the Summit, if that shot had not been fired. I did not fire it. No matter who did."

He colored at my parenthetical allusion to his share in the last wild scenes of the Institute, and at once discharged from his demeanor whatever signs of carelessness it had thus far retained. He was intensely in earnest at last.

"Whether you like to be reminded of it, or not," were his words, "you were continually mixed-up and concerned in my affairs, at that infernal school. At the request, or, rather, the command, of Elfie— I'll call her that, or devil!—I looked out for you as though you had been my brother, and fussed around you like some old woman. Why? To this moment I haven't the first sane idea. I only know that she told me to do it, and with about as much mildness and explanation as she would have given to Old Yaller. She had been a kind of nurse to you,—that much I ascertained from Mr. Bond; but beyond that I was all in the dark. Besides this, too, she always selected times when you were by to treat me most like a dog! You remember? And I put up with everything, because— well, because I was just the fool that such infatuation always makes a man. You saw for yourself, Glibun; any boy could understand what you saw, and should not want me to explain why I ask questions of you now. I feel that I have a right to know what actual relationship there was between you and Elfie Birch. Will you tell me?"

"You seem to know as much of it as I do," was my answer. "I knew her only as my nurse; but I loved her as a sister."—I might have said "mother."

"Very satisfactory, that! Have you any idea of who the vagabond was that haunted the place after dark, and played the ghost at your window that night?"

"I can only guess."

"Who?"

"I shall not tell you," said I, meeting his searching look with one as determined. "I can't see that you have any right at all to question me about either myself or other people."

"Why what, in Heaven's name, do you suppose I wanted to see you for, then?" he asked, flushing angrily.

"To pry into what don't concern you!" I answered, passionately. "But you shall see me no longer;" and I was rising from my seat to quit the place, when he reached quickly across the narrow table and pushed me down again. My impulse of resentment vanished as I marked the agitation of his whole aspect, and the expression of entreaty which had succeeded the angry flash of his eyes.

"Don't go yet," he said; "you're the only living being to whom I can talk of my troubles, for you are the only one who knows anything of their rights and wrongs. You saw how that tigress played with me,—boy as you were, and I was not much more! She treated me with intolerable caprice and insolence, only to make maddened pride an additional motive of my infatuation; and, then, when I thought myself finally a victor, it was but to find that I had been used as the despised tool of a furious woman's revenge upon her husband. Used, and then contemptuously cast into the dirt without another thought."

He smote his clenched hands together as though he could dash himself to the earth for having calculated so falsely, and I listened with increasing astonishment to words strangely contradictory of that which I had not questioned in my own mind for a moment.

"She fled with me from that accursed den, forcing me into the parting mockery of apparently stealing the miserable horse and wagon of the drunken husband, no less than his wife. She spared me no circumstance of flaunting publicity to make the disgrace and ruin all the keener to the poor wretch whose blow still tingled on her cheek. And yet, through all, she bore herself to me as to some barely-tolerated footman, and, upon our arrival in this city, imperiously dismissed me until I should be needed again! First in a hotel, and then as a boarder in a private house, she passed for a Miss Terry, and graciously permitted me to supervise those proceedings for divorce of which you have already heard. Fool, as she ever found me, I thought that I worked no less for myself than for her, and looked patiently forward to the time when the tigress should have me to hold her chain and bear all her untamed ferocities. Dolt that I was in my maudlin adoration, she won her freedom by my slavery, and then spurned me from her in a letter 'enclosing money for my past services!' Glibun," shouted Allyn Vane, dashing his fist upon the table, and glaring at me like a wild beast, "I was a vain, unscrupulous coxcomb before; a worse enemy to myself than to anybody else; but that devilish wrong made a sworn murderer of me. I swore, from the bottom of my heart and soul, that the love for which I had so degraded myself should be the death-warrant of any other living thing she gave it to; and, by the heaven above us, there shall be an awful reckoning yet between Allyn Vane and him she calls her husband!"

"Her husband!" I exclaimed, scarcely less excited than he.

"Yes," said Vane, savagely; "Plato Wynne."

The King of Diamonds! The courtly gamester, the arch politician, whose flirtations with his neighbors' fortunes were the spice of a hundred romances, and whose mysterious power in the councils of Demolition already contested the proprietorship of the Empire State with the great Cringer; of whom everybody believed more and knew less than of their own national Constitution! — Ellie *his* wife?

"How could it have happened?" I incredulously exclaimed; "what could have thrown her into the path of such a man as that?"

"From what I can learn," answered Vane, moodily, "she met him in the house of a Mr. Spanyel, where she was playing governess at the time. An acquaintance of mine, named Stiles, has told me this. He saw both of them there, and also saw that the family (who must be blind snobs, indeed) were not aware of Wynne's regal identity. Did you ever see him, Glibun?"

"No. I have heard him mentioned hundreds of times; but—and the fact is a little curious, by-the-by—I have yet to know the first person who ever *has* really seen him."

"*I* have seen him more than once; and shall see him again,—the glittering scoundrel! Could it have been that man who hung about the school-house?"

The question was put awkwardly and hesitatingly.

"Of course not," was my reply. "Didn't you say, just now, that the acquaintance was formed after that?"

"To think!" he went on, vengefully clutching the table-cover, and addressing his own pride,—"to think! that, perhaps, I—I—was used as much to help the new husband as to punish the old! By all the gods, I'd sell my soul to bring that woman to the gutter!"

By such vaporing, by such angry pertinacity for double degradation in his martyrdom, did Allyn Vane show me how the cross of love may be made the crown of self-love. Forgetting, even, that the object of his unprincipled infatuation had been the wife of another, I must still have seen, with a sensation scarcely congenial enough for compassion, the half-complacent character of his rage under disappointment. His was one of those clogged, unhealthy natures, wherein a turgid selfishness not only limits the impressions of all generous emotions to the most superficial depths, but even throws them back undigested to the surface at the first shock of that sensitive vanity by which alone it has its capricious ebb and flow. He found, without knowing it, the first settled aim and purpose of his life in a morbid embitterment upon the surface of that which, though vain, had been sweet in the depths; and with such aim and purpose, unworthy as they were, came a novel sense of strength — of individuality — to make self-love exultant at its own unnatural power of perversion.

Not being able to enter into all the illogical ingenuities by which my vengeful companion petted each of his wrongs into an arbitrary plurality with its thinnest shadow, and believing that he had told me all in which I was concerned, I suddenly took upon myself an air of philosophical gayety, and both checked and surprised him with another phase of his own disposition.

"Oh, well," observed I, with a defiant snap of my fingers, "women are curious creatures, and it's scarcely worth while to be broken-hearted about them, whatever they do. There was Ezekiel Reed, you may remember, who took a blow from Ellie without even losing his angelic temper. I wonder what has become of Reed?"

"He's in the city," answered Vane, after a glance at his watch. "You'd not expect him to feel very affectionately toward me; and yet, by all that's hypocritical, when we happened to meet, once, on Broadway, the saint spoke as mildly to me as though nothing had happened, and coolly asked for the address of the former Mrs. Birch!"

"His Christian manner of reproaching you," suggested I.

"That may be. By the way, Glibun, there's another of your old friends gone to the bad besides me,"—he thus characterized himself with a half boastful, half rakish air, — "the fellow you tried to eat, once, — Hastings Cutter. Like a true Carolinian he has joined the chivalry of the green cloth."

"I'm not surprised at that," remarked I, with angry recollections of my old enemy. "He always was a scamp."

"You may be right, there, Glibun; but he and I are thrown together occasionally, now, and I won't pass judgment on a comrade."

This equivocal speech made me think it possible that Vane was a gambler, too. As he had not said so directly, however, I felt justified only in adopting a rather presumptuous moral tone in my next observation.

"Mr. Vane, it seems a great pity that a man like you should go to the bad, as you call it. I'm sure if I had your education — "

"Education!" exclaimed he, jumping at the word and fuming again. "That reminds me of what a boy you are. The very education you talk about has been a curse to me from the hour of its commencement! My poor, widowed mother meant well, meant nobly, when she undertook to give me advantages, as she called them, which had never been her own; but oh, what a mistake it was! If she had only sent me out to work on a farm, or to drudge in a store, or to learn some plodding trade, I might have grown up to comfort and protect her old age, and be a man suited to my origin. It is an abuse of education, a miserable perversion and abuse of it, to simply gain and hoard it without regard to position in life and the leading mental inclination to be fostered and worked into effective execution by it. In some cases the stereotyped education of colleges and books is either a suffocation, a paralysis, or a poison. In mine it was all three: it suffocated my first natural and inherited inclinations for the active life and practical pursuits of my father and forefathers; it paralyzed the peculiar energies born in me for the career to which I was adapted, and which would have gathered its own sufficient education from men and things according to its own real wants; it poisoned my best and tenderest instincts by warping them to the deformities of an artificial reason and a monstrous intellectual pride. Monstrous is the right term! I returned from college a monster, — an unnatural distortion of what I should and might have been. My mother praised my looks and words; and because her grammar in so doing was defective, I heard her with contemptuous impatience. She exhibited me proudly to her old friends and my father's; and because those good and worthy people were not nicely intellectual, I insulted them with my superciliousness. She had a fond pride and delight in welcoming such of my fine college friends as called upon me; and I was miserable in the belief that they were amazed to find so illiterate a mother for so

learned a son! She boisterously scolded the kitchen servant, and I writhed at her coarseness. She, in her ignorance, was proud of me; I, in my education, was ashamed of her! Do you understand me, you motherless boy? — I was ashamed of the mother that bore me! and I speak as truly and frankly when I say that I despised myself for it. I tried to overcome the educated devil within me; I felt myself a monster of folly and ingratitude and strove like a giant to put down the eternal mocker of my conscience; but it would *not* be put down. Finally, when I saw my mother's eyes opened to the miserable truth; when I found — God have mercy on me! — something akin to actual *dislike* of her mingling slowly and irrevocably with the guilt I felt in her presence, the awful conviction of my hopeless condition blotted out every remaining aspiration for a worthy life within me, and I became reckless, with a sense of God's utter desertion. Could I have any self-respect, knowing as I did that it was no longer in me to give else than the blackest ingratitude to the best friend man has on earth? Could I live a self-respecting manhood after those insulted gray hairs went down in sorrow to the grave? What better can be expected of me than you, yourself, saw in that school-room? What higher can be expected of me than you see now? A curse upon the education that made me ashamed of my mother, as German philosophy makes Germans and Bostonians ashamed of their God! With the miserable possession fast slipping away from me, — its terrible work being wrought; with but a remnant left of my heritage from the parent it drove me to condemn; what fate is there before me!" He clasped his hands, looked wildly at me, and panted through his trembling lips, "Only revenge and a grave."

I had listened to him, during this unpremeditated and startling confession, with varying sensations. The fierce intensity of his manner, as he arraigned himself impetuously, to avoid reproaching the memory of his mother, alarmed me with vague suspicions of lunacy; and a certain touch of the theatrical in his peroration prevented the full sympathy due to such curious misfortune. But if I had touched the major keynote of the man's character by mere accident; so, also, he had touched the minor of mine by the least important of his admissions. In fact, my sole comment upon his story was, —

"Then you're *not* a gentleman's son!"

It was most natural that such an inconsequent reception of his confidence should act as an abrupt damper upon the victim of education, involving, as it did, the very last idea he had expected to evoke; and it was only after a lengthened stare, in which mortification and impatience had equal expression, that he deigned to reply, —

"You're a sympathetic youth, I must say!"

It flashed upon me that I had indulged my idiosyncrasy in a flagrantly unmannerly way, and, somewhat abashed, I hastened to apologize for the rudeness. But for that, we might have parted pretty good friends. As it was, my blundering apology only made me very hot about the ears, and Mr. Vane very sullenly dissatisfied. We left the place side by side, and walked in company for a couple of blocks; but the difference in our years seemed to vindicate itself at last in the constrained demeanor of each, and we finally separated without much affectation of a desire to meet again.

My head ached, a dull weight pressed upon my heart; and I hurried homeward, with no care but to find oblivion, in sleep, from miserable recollection of disordered and unwholesome things. The house of the entry-clerk had a new meaning of rest and refuge to me that night, as I looked up at it while mounting the stoop; the very door gave me a gentle thrill of relief as I noiselessly opened it; and the cool air of the hall touched my hot cheeks like the fanning of a loving hand.

CHAPTER XXXIV.

THE COARSE OF TRUE LOVE.

THE depression, pain, and, I may say, discouragement, brought to me by the conversation related in the last chapter, found slow mitigation and even temporary cure — according to homœopathic principle — by contact with the same affections in Mr. Terky. His chronic melancholy, already deepened to morose misgivings by a defiance to single combat from the brother of an unpaid Bridget, and a present of a pair of embroidered slippers from his wife, had sunk to nerveless despair under the continued ill-health of Tootsy. Curiously enough, he seemed to derive no observable comfort from sudden and spasmodic supplies of extra cash, that made me suspect him of having gained more salary, after all. From being moody with Mrs. Terky, and working up into hair-tearing frenzy at her tireless pertinacity in affrightedly accusing him of consumption, he at length became apparently prejudiced against me, and preferred to go to business before me in the morning, as well as to remain after me at night. I am glad to remember that I took no offence at this, but sincerely pitied the broken man with all my heart; and in that pity found blessed abstraction from my own troubles.

And besides, — pity being akin to love, — had I not also my first portentous affair of the heart on hand, to make luxuries of all the low spirits I could justify myself for entertaining, and condense them to that awful air of fixed melancholy which is so Byronic and impressive in the eyes of woman? If I could not be unhealthy, and thus render myself irresistible to all maidens, I could, at least, find gloom enough in honest retrospection to play a very passable Hamlet for the conquest of one soft young woman's heart.

The huge letter-box at Cummin & Tryon's was a glorified Pandora's box to me on that memorable day, when — some scores of "immediate" country orders having been first set free for the distraction of as many clerks — hope was found at the bottom, in the shape of an epistle from Nettie to my excited self. I received the missive from the hands of the mail-clerk with a guilty blush, not altogether untinged by an insane suspicion that the mail-clerk recognized the writing. As he ventured no impudent remark, however (and thereby escaped the fury of a desperate man), I hastened away with my treasure to a perpetually damp spot under the front-cellar light, and there tore it open in a great state of nervousness. A painting in water-colors of what I at first took to be a strawberry on lettuce, but subsequently discovered to be a moss-rosebud with leaves, bloomed at the top of the adorable page. I kissed it.

SWEET HOME — Tuesday Eve —
MR. GLIBUN —
Your note — believe me — shall be held sacred, though a temporary mistake of a word in its concluding sentiment has so long delayed my answer — the word was Desolate — both pa and ma thought it was dissolute, but I knew it never could be —

[Then she's shown my letter to them! thought I, growing very cold in my feet and hands; but I read on], —

even when we were children together — how sweet is childhood — I always thought there was something weird in your look, as though some cloudy sorrow cast a shadow o'er your brow, — it seems to me that some natures have a misty affinity for sorrow rather than joy, and shrink from the mirth of natures that are less weird — what is your opinion — I may not be understood by some persons, and mustard seed has been recommended for my sadness; but I can give you True Sympathy in the weird Secret that obscures your young ray, and I hope you may yet be able to say He doeth all Things well — as I look out at the sky before finishing this letter — which you will excuse — heaven's lamps seem to twinkle with a weird light — look up, dear friend, and you will feel that He doeth all Things well — I've always thought so and hope you will too — pray overlook all errors, and believe me —

— your sincere friend —
NETTIE B.

The plenitude of feminine punctuation and remarkable economy of capital letters in this touching messenger of True Sympathy did not lessen my unspeakable transports over it, and I felt, as I still held it open before me and dreamily luxuriated in my possession, that I must be callous indeed if I did not thenceforth believe that all things were done well. Indeed, it was when raising my eyes, I think, in impulsive gratitude for the beautiful moral lesson thus conveyed, that I discerned upon the street-grating, above my head, the crouching figure of an execrable boy, who, with eyes horribly twisted to make his view the clearer, was lost in admiration of the moss-rosebud.

Roused from his artistic abstraction by my hasty concealment of the letter, and, smiling agreeably down at me as I glared darkly up at him, this depraved boy remarked, with an approach to pleasantry quite characteristic of infant crime, that it was probably a "wollytine!" After which he stuck a copper cent in one eye, by way of indicating, with a touch of playful satire, the manner in which clerks generally mounted their eyeglasses when wishing to be particularly engaging with the ladies, and swaggered off the grating, thus adorned, as bent upon the immediate conquest of an heiress.

The incident occasioned me some bitterness of feeling, and originated my earliest inception of that sarcastic and incredulous view of police efficiency which is apt to become chronic with men after a first street experience of All-Fools Day. It also reduced my inflation of spirits sufficiently to make me think seriously for a moment of what might result from the showing of *my* letter to the Reverend Mr. Beeton and wife. But, thought I, they must know all about me when they become my parents-in-law; and this sage second thought sent me to my desk in a tolerably placid state of mind.

The little party, or sociable, at the home of my charmer, which Noah Trust and I were to attend, being only three days off, I concluded to delay writing again until after a preliminary interview should have given me a little more audacity. I did not fail, however, to ponder a significant speech, wherein moss-rosebuds were to be poetically touched upon, for the ears of my future wife; and while my eyes and hands were busy with invoices, my mind pictured all sorts of romantic occurrences in the shade of Beetonian window-curtains.

No other foolery in life is half so delightful as first love, excepting, perhaps, the amateur hunter's first deer. The two, indeed, are somewhat alike, not only in sound, but also in character; for, in either case, the hero labors under a deliciously crazy sense of having incredibly done something too much for himself, and cannot for some time get rid of imbecile doubts as to the game being his own.

All my confidence sank into tremulous misgivings on the night of the party. From impetuously regarding the game as my own, I suddenly fell into doleful cowardice about it, and my journey to Grand Street was a progress in affliction to which corns were a trifle. Suppose Nettie should be only flirting with me. Suppose she should regard my letter as a sign of pitiable weakness, and be instigated solely by compassion in her friendly demeanor toward me. Suppose — anything but supposability.

Additionally aggravated by a firm belief that my hair never clustered so unbecomingly before, I followed the servant's obtrusive shoulders to the parlor door, and then bolted feverishly into the middle of a company whose chairs, sofas, ottomans, and attitudes against tables and mantels seemed

ordered, especially for the best view of my entire performance. This idea put me upon my mettle, I think; for, although the scene wore a confusing blur to me at the first shock, I inclined my head in general salute with some degree of style, and advanced without either stumble or collision to where Miss Beeton and another young lady sat examining some engravings.

It would have been an awkward task for any fresh guest to cross a roomful of strangers and only find his welcome when he had found one of the remotest corners of the apartment; and I was just enough irritated by it to feel rather stronger in mind than I had expected to.

"Allow me to offer my compliments, Miss Beeton," said I, bowing, as she arose to receive me.

"Thank you, Mr. Glibun," she replied, returning my courtesy rather coldly, I thought; "I am happy to see you, sir."

"You are perfectly well, I hope," said I, questioning her with my eyes. Then adding, in a lower tone and with much expression, "You are looking charmingly."

"Thank you," she returned, stiffly; "I am quite well. Excuse me, please; ma is beckoning to me."

Good gracious! What was the meaning of this? Did it comport with the ordinary usage of parsonage parties, or was I being purposely regaled with cold shoulder where others enjoyed warm tongue? I followed Nettie with my eyes as she wound leisurely and chattily through the company to her mother in a distant arm-chair; and I saw her mother glance over at me through her spectacles, and then into her daughter's face, with a significance of pre-understanding that brought the blood hotly to my cheeks. Others had certainly noticed the peculiarity of my reception, though they were generally too well-bred to show it in any marked manner; and my position was fast growing unendurable, when Noah Trust made his way to where I was standing and shook hands with me as heartily as though we had not seen each other for some years.

"Well, Glibun," said he, cheerily, "how do you find yourself? Quite a lively scene, isn't it? Let me initiate you." And before I could either reply or resist, he had introduced me to half a dozen people and established me in a seat near the young lady at the engravings.

"Miss Green," he remarked, vivaciously, "my friend Glibun is a little bashful, and you must oblige me by showing him some pretty pictures, while I go and help the Reverend Mr. B. to get up the lemonade."

Neither Miss Green nor I knew how to escape from an arrangement forced upon us with such good-humor; and, for my part, I was too much dazed by what had passed, and by my recognition of the unsuspecting damsel, to take the departing step at first dictated by offended dignity.

There, looking timidly at me over the engravings, which rested on a small quartette-table, was the adored of Mr. Gamble and the joint patroness of Mr. Coffin and me; yet she gave not the least sign of remembering either the gipsy boy or the finder of her purse. One sharp look at her pretty but not very reflective face quieted all my anxiety on that score. She did not flatter me with any place whatever in her recollection, and I was willing enough to disguise the real perturbation of my feelings by sharing with her the engravings.

Comprehending only enough of the situation to know that I had been subjected to a public and pointed slight, and waxing both wretched and reckless under the inexplicable outrage, I no longer experienced either diffidence or sentimentalism. I'll let her see, thought I, that I am not to be crushed by any such snubbing as this! and, with an air that was positively rakish, I devoted myself exclusively to Miss Aloize Green. A volubility not far removed from the hysterical characterized my criticism of the pictures, to some of which I loudly attributed so many unheard-of defects, that quite a throng of admiring listeners were involuntarily attracted to our table; and by dint of unparalleled presumption I gained an amount of consideration for which modesty might have striven in vain. My edifying dissertation upon crude art was attaining a climax over an engraved copy of Paul Potter's "Shooting Ponies" (which I innocently took for an American picture and, consequently, thought perfectly safe to hold lightly), when Nettie came hastily to her friend again, with a request that she would "play something" on the piano. "Mr. Glibun will excuse you, Allie," concluded she, with a rather scornful toss of her head toward me.

"I could excuse you for anything, Miss Green," said I, affectedly, — "for anything but a refusal to do just what Miss Beeton has asked. Let me escort you to the instrument. Allow me," and, with all the neatness and dispatch of a policeman arresting a civil offender, I literally took the alarmed Miss Green into custody and guarded her to the piano-forte. My imperious style of excuting the manœuvre admitted no practical protest, and the startled captive could only sink mechanically upon the music-stool and endeavor to regain composure by practising bits of the scale; the while I ostentatiously opened the notes upon the desk of the old-fashioned Guyb, and darted defiant glances around the company in hostile assertion of my resolve to pass for somebody. It is but fair to say, that a portion of said company rather resented such highhanded assurance on my part by audible tittering, being instigated thereto, undoubtedly, by a bristle-headed young man in green spectacles, who had been to the Holy Land, and was not disposed to be overshadowed by violence. Nettie, too, as I saw in a passing glimpse, regarded me with disdainful wonder; and Mrs. Beeton stared through her glasses with a severity too intense for speech. All this stir and indignity only lashed my bravado into something still more like insolence (for a youth of my years), and poor Miss Green's scared look gave her the rather ludicrous aspect of being just on the verge of a gape or a sneeze.

"Oh, really, Mr. Glibun," she faltered, in a low tone, "I won't trouble you any farther."

"I'll turn the leaves for you," said I.

My arm was extended to put the intention into effect, when she placed one of her hands upon it, and said, firmly and audibly, "I *beg* that you will not, sir. I beg that you will not longer insist upon making me so unpleasantly conspicuous."

The rebuke brought me to my senses. In a flash I became conscious of the rude impropriety of my conduct, and, after a clumsy apology, I retreated from the piano-forte under the very palpable disfavor of the whole company.

My impulse was to plunge directly at the fair, false, fickle Nettie, — knocking down the bristle-headed Holy Land-er on the way, — pathetically upbraid her for goading me into insanity by unprovoked contumely; inform her that the worm turns when trodden upon, and fly forever from a house where hospitality compared unfavorably with persecution. I was deterred, however, from this dramatic demonstration by the timely arrival of Noah, who re-entered the room in company with Mr. Beeton, and looked very gravely about until he caught my eye. Not pausing to hear even one verse of "Rose of Lucerne," he came directly to me in my pillory, and unceremoniously asked me to "step into the hall" with him for a moment.

"Why should I do that?" I asked.

"I've something very particular and important to say to you, Glibun," he replied, in a hurried whisper; "and we can be private there."

"All right," said I, carelessly; "I've got beyond being surprised at anything tonight;" and with a parting glance of reproach at Nettie, — which she acknowledged by looking another way, — I followed the grocer's son from the room.

After an irresolute pause of a moment under the swinging-lamp in the hall, Noah suggested that we should have our talk on the stoop; and as moonlight and mild weather prevailed out there, I urged no objection, and out we went.

"And now that we are here, Trust," said I, donning my hat, which I had brought out with me, "what great secret have you got to tell me? Has the reverend gentleman desired you to draw me gradually away from his premises, while he bolts the door?"

"Ah, that's it, Glibun, that's it!" ejaculated Noah, who was either very much at a loss for introductory ideas, or very nervous about something. "Have you noticed anything peculiar here this evening, — anything not usual at a party, you know?"

My previous knowledge of fashionable "party" usages had been chiefly derived from novel-reading; but no lesson of practical experience was needed to teach me that there *had* been something decidedly peculiar in the manner of my reception and treatment that evening.

"Peculiar!" I echoed, in a rage; "why, Trust, I've been used like a pickpocket! And I'm bound to know what it all means before I stir one step from this house. I am invited to come, the party is given by an old playmate; and then, when I am here, no snub is too outrageous for me. Who are these Beetons, I should like to know! I never was treated so before in my life!"

"Have you no idea of a reason for it, Glibun?"

I stared at him, under the impression that he was disposed to quiz me; but his face was too grave, and even troubled, in the moonlight, for that.

"What reason should there be?" asked I, with vague apprehensions from his look. "You, yourself, heard me invited to come; and yet I've been received exactly as though I had bolted in without even the privilege of acquaintance. If you can explain it, I wish you would. Perhaps you've had something to do with it yourself," added I, in sudden suspicion.

"Now, Glibun, that's nonsense," he retorted. "I've stood up like a Trojan for you this very evening. I saw that something was wrong the moment you came in, and went up to the old gentleman's room on purpose to ask him about it. If I had known and thought what they did, do you suppose I would have introduced you to the lady I brought here myself?"

"Known and thought what they did!" I repeated, staring at him again. "What on earth are you talking about? Is everybody crazy, or am I a lunatic myself? What in the world have I done?"

"Well, Glibun," replied Noah, working his hands together on the railing, and looking down at them in manifest embarrassment, "if you really *don't* guess the secret, and *will* have the truth, I'm afraid that letter of yours to Nettie has made all the trouble."

"What!" cried I, aghast; "has she shown it to you?"

"No. But her father told —"

"That's enough, Mr. Trust!" I struck in, furious at the betrayal of my confidence. "If you've managed to sneak into my private business that far, you can make the most of it with your friends, and keep clear of me hereafter. I'll have nothing more to do with either you or them."

Thus speaking, and almost choked with rage, I motioned as though I would have descended at once to the street; when, by a quick movement, he placed himself directly in my way, and kept me back.

"Just hear me fairly out, Glibun," he entreated, "and then you may do as you please. When I saw how Nettie acted with you, and her mother looked at you, I knew, as I said before, that something was wrong. It would not do to make a fuss about it with so many strangers about, so I took pains to put you as much at your ease as I could, and then made an excuse to slip off and find Mr. Beeton. To cut the story short, he was sorry to hear you had come; said that Nettie and her mother were acting as he himself had told them to act, and blamed me for bringing you to the house in the first place."

"Let me go!" shouted I, attempting to pass him.

"No, not yet," holding out his arms; "I took your part like a good one, and asked him what he could possibly have against you. Then he told me that you had written a very odd letter, or note, to Nettie; — something about a great 'mystery' in your life, and all that. The little goose handed it right over to him, on account of some word that puzzled her, and he read it through. Then, you see, he wanted to know something about you before the correspondence went too far, — you can't blame him for that, you know, — and got Nettie to tell him where your family lived." My heart began to throb wildly, and I listened fearfully. "He went to the place where you *used* to live, and found that you had moved away. This afternoon, though, he was there again (I don't know what made him so curious, — he didn't say), and found out, — I'm sorry to have to say it, Glibun, — all about your father."

What was it that I dreaded with a dread like that of death? Why did my right hand go instinctively up to my mouth, and twitch nervously there, as though to plead with *his* mouth, in poor, dumb show, against the utterance of — I knew not what?

"My father?" I tremulously said; the silence of the street seeming to deepen at the same instant and take the word into its whole space.

"Yes. I thought you'd sooner hear this from an old playmate than from Mr. Beeton, and I told him I would speak to you myself. The people in the house, or the neighbors, I don't know which, told him. He feels sorry for you, Glibun, and would have kept you from coming to-night, if there had been time and he'd known how to do it. It's pretty hard for you; but you know he's a very strict man, himself, and — well, I hardly know how to express it, Glibun, but he has to look out for Nettie. I hope you're not mad at me. *I* don't think any the worse of you for what I know is no fault of yours. They think at the store that your folks live in the country, and *I* have never contradicted them."

"What was it about my father?" I asked the question under a kind of nerveless fascination. It expressed every thought, feeling, and remembrance of the moment.

Noah stepped aside to let the moonlight strike fully upon my whole face, as though expecting to find some qualification of my words in my look.

"Why! don't you *know?*"

"What is he,—what *is* my father?" I could not have prevented the jerking distortion of my mouth into a smile if I had been dying. I could not have kept my fingers from working on my chin if their touch had been ruin.

"Glibun, I really don't know what to make of you!" exclaimed Noah Trust, moving uneasily about. "If *you* don't *know* anything about your own father, I'm sure *I've* got no right to pretend to know. Mr. Beeton says that *they say* he's a—a—"

"Well?"

"A—counterfeiter!"

If I could have told him then and there—whether from my perfect ignorance, or my imagined knowledge of the truth—that he lied; if I could have flown from him to the reverend tale-bearer in-doors, and honestly (as regarded myself) told *him* that he lied;—there had been no other imputation or humiliation which I could not have borne with a laugh as merry as any that came out from the parlor that night. But neither the impulse nor the word would come. Never had I so much as dreamed of what, in its very first enunciation to my ears, paralyzed and silenced me with the all-revealing flash of elemental truth. I had not a word to say. I could trace and count every line of demarcation between the gray slabs of the walk; every ring, oval, grotesque profile, and sunken egg in the cobble mosaic of the street; every brick, jalousy-slat, iron rail, and lower window-pane of the opposite house; and had not one word to answer.

"You're not mad at me, I hope, for letting you hear it quietly?" urged Noah, full of sympathy still, although he must have doubted that I had dealt ingenuously with him.

"Oh, you're all right, you're all right," I assured him, in a forced, absent, parrot-like way. "That's all right, you're all right," I continued, moving down the steps, with an arm over the rail, like a boy.

"Plague on it! I hate to have you go off in that way," he cried, following me because he knew not what else to do. "I'd go with you if I hadn't Allie on my hands. Give us a good shake, old fellow, to make sure that it's all right between *us*, anyhow."

I shook his extended hand with both of mine, just as I would have shaken any other hand that had been offered me then; and, again declaring, in a high key, that he was "all right," left him.

Looking back over the whole treacherous time of my betrayed youth, I can remember no other hour so darkly blank, so ghostlessly dead, with the stunning shock of fatal misfortune, as that in which I moved mechanically away from the house in Grand Street toward the one I called my home.

Man knows not how deeply his wildest, most arbitrary hope can sink, until the inexorable disappointment follows, like a harsh word after a kind one, to sound and harrow the placid depths which held it unaware. He knows not how that vain and unsubstantial hope can insensibly assimilate and grow in sentiency with his whole nature, until the stern, relentless ending comes, and, like the traitorous sword which stabs the heart that looked to it for generous vindication, brings more than death to what was more than life.

Such a hope of mine had gone out that night. I had been living upon it without knowing it to be my own; it had been my higher self, to keep me in protecting and ennobling company, even when I deemed myself most lonely, dishonored, and unsustained; it had been a star above my head to give me unwittingly an eternal motive for an upward look and thought, whatever depth I sank to in transitional adversity. And I knew it not for itself,—I knew it not for itself,—until I read its epitaph in this: that I was not the son of a gentleman!

<hr>

CHAPTER XXXV.

WHITE SLAVERY.

LAMP in hand Mrs. Terky met me at the door. My night-key was scarcely in the lock when she turned the latch from the inside and brought me face to face with herself. Had my condition of mind been in the slightest degree normal, I must have been greatly surprised at her appearance in such an action, especially as she wore her night-robe and looked pale and flurried. As it was, I paused in the doorway, and stared blankly at her, with but a dull, inconclusive sense of something unusual.

"O Avery!" she hurriedly said, "won't you run for the doctor? Tootsy's very sick and I haven't a soul to send! Oh! oh! *what has happened to Job?*"

She staggered against the wall, as from a blow, when almost shrieking the last sentence, and fairly stopped the beating of my heart by the wild and sudden terror of her look.

"Job?" I echoed.

"I see it in your face!" she groaned, ghastly as a corse. "O God, have mercy! have mercy!"

She would have dropped the lamp had I not caught it, and the action recalled my stunned senses to life.

"Nothing is the matter with your husband, Mrs. Terky," stammered I, in nervous haste. "He's at the store, of course."

Having, by my assistance, gained a chair which stood in the hall, she sank into it and put both hands to her head.

"Your look—gave me—such a shock," she panted. "I'm so nervous. Bridget left—this afternoon. Here I've been, all—alone, and the child—so sick."

"Don't worry, don't worry," entreated I. "It will not take me three minutes to fetch the doctor, and Mr. Terky will soon be home."

Only waiting to see her safely on her way upstairs, I hastened after the family physician, whose residence I knew to be only a few blocks off, and was presently holding gruff conference through a speaking-tube, with one whom I at first supposed to be the doctor himself.

"What's wanted?" came through the tube, in answer to my jerk upon the bell-pull directly under its street-end.

"Mr. Terky's child is very sick. Please come at once."

"Doctor's out. I'll tell him when he returns," grumbled the voice in the darkness; and the tube immediately became closed, at its remote end, against me.

A something told me that there was peril in delay, and, without a moment's hesitation, I darted down from the stoop and hurried across the street to a policeman pacing there.

"Officer, where can I find another doctor?" said I. "The one over the way is out, and I want one this instant."

"Second door around the first corner. Doctor Knight."

I was off with a flying "thank you," and quickly had Doctor Knight underway at a speed suited to his mistaken idea of the infantile purpose for which I had called him. He and I were bounding up the steps, when a third figure abruptly joined us from the street, and Mr. Terky's voice arrested us in the doorway, —

"Here, Glibun! You, sir! What's the trouble?"

"Go on upstairs, doctor," whispered I. "The baby seems to be a little worse, Mr. Terky, and I've called the doctor."

"That wasn't Doctor Dunn," was the captious reply. "Why didn't you get him?"

"I did go after him, but he's out."

"Out!" repeated the entry-clerk, with an oath. "Yes! he's out because his confounded bill isn't paid. I'll go and pay the old scoundrel this minute, by Heaven! I'll see that he isn't 'out' by me, at all events." He sprang down the steps again at a full run, and was away before my remonstrance could get breath.

Leaving the door ajar, I went slowly upstairs; the perspiration bursting coldly out upon my forehead at a convulsive sobbing which had suddenly followed the low murmur of voices in a room I was nearing. Another moment found me in that room, where a night-lamp on the hearth revealed the white figure of the young mother with a motionless little form across her knees, and the gray-haired physician bending over both, watch in hand.

A board in the floor creaked as I entered, and the sobs gave place to a moaning, desolate cry, —

"O Job! Job! Job!"

"He'll be here in a moment, Mrs. Terky," I tremulously said, standing appalled beside the vacant little crib.

Again the sobs broke out; the doctor stood speechless and watchful; and the whole silent house seemed to have resolved itself into one awful and prophetic ear. Then the hall-door slammed with a sound that went through me like a knife, rude steps counted the merciless stairs, and the husband and father — flushed and impious — stalked heavily into the room.

My eyes were on his face when he heard the scream and saw the sight. I could not have taken them off to save my soul; and I cannot now!

"Etta — Doctor — not DEAD?"

The doctor turned his head, and spoke the words of fate too solemnly to leave a hope.

"Medical aid should have been summoned long ago in this case. The disease has reached the brain. I am afraid that I can do nothing."

The man's heart was broken already and could not heave a sigh; but it must have fluttered enough in its dry ruin to half strangle him; for his face changed from pallor to a sickly gray. He went to his now-stupefied wife and leaned over her chair, with his elbow upon the mantel-piece, —

"Doctor, how soon?"

"Very soon, Mr. Terky. It will be painless."

"Doctor, there is your fee. I'll put it on the mantel here, and you can take it when you go."

The doctor stood erect, and stared.

"I mean no disrespect to you, doctor; but this life must be the last that goes for my poverty. A man of your profession has killed this baby of mine, because I have been too poor to do for him what I've just done for you. Two minutes ago I left him returning to bed with my debt paid, and with my baby's life paid with it. He could have saved the little one a week ago, if he'd been willing to wait until now for his money. But he wasn't. I mean no disrespect to you; but I've made my rule."

He spoke measuredly and monotonously as though rehearsing something written; yet with a determined emphasis, too, which betokened full activity in all his thinking faculties.

"This is extraordinary, Mr. Terky," said the doctor, looking sternly at him; "but I will do as you wish. Madam, I must warn you that your little one is dying now, — painlessly."

The mother neither raised her head nor uttered a sound. The doctor bowed to the father, took the money, and softly retired.

Watching there in the lifeless glimmer from their desolate hearth to see the first-born die: she, with hands clutched against the forgotten breast, — the mother-heart, — and eyes seeing only frozen disbelief; he, with wrinkled brow on rigid palm, and darkened eyes that through the angelic palingenesia right beneath them saw no God. so I left them. So they haunted me through all the livelong night, until the world and life came back with unbelieving morning.

The door of their chamber was closed at the hour when I finally summoned composure enough to go downstairs again; but I found Mr. Terky pacing the floor of the dining-room, and learned from him that all was over. Older and thinner he certainly looked; but his manner was calm, his hair and dress were orderly as usual, and his voice sounded no more despondent than it had for weeks past.

"I've been to let the neighbors know," he said, gazing moodily out of the window, "and some of the ladies will be in directly. Poor Etta takes it very hard. I couldn't ask her to get breakfast for us this morning, and perhaps you won't mind getting what you want at one of the saloons."

"I want no breakfast. Let me stay here and help you," I said.

"Ah, Avy, there's no help for me now," replied he, looking at me with a strange and bitter smile in his tired eyes. "The kind people next door will be with Etta all day, in case the firm refuse to excuse me."

"Mr. Terky!" exclaimed I, hardly believing my ears, "you don't mean to tell me that you think of going to the store to-day!"

"Can I afford to lose the place, Glibun?" he asked, bitterly. "How am I to bury my child, if I haven't even an employment to get credit from the undertaker with?"

"But, my dear Mr. Terky, if *I* go, and tell Mr. Cummin himself—"

"No use, poor fellow; no use," he interrupted, shaking his head and wearing that bitter, despairing look again. "Mr. Cummin—or Mr. Tryon, either—would tell you that he was very sorry, but those bills *must* be ready. You've been a clerk long enough to know that we're nothing but salaries—we're not men! What right has a low salary with a dead baby in the middle of the busy season? Cummin & Tryon can't keep their southern customers waiting for invoices because a low salary wants to lay out its only child. There aint trouble enough in debt, death, and damnation, together, to make me forget *that* common truth!"

The approach to positive ribaldry in this extraordinary speech, and the short, unnatural laugh with which the speaker turned to the window again, left me too much amazed and shocked to venture an immediate reply. It seemed incredible that our employers would be guilty of such barbarous inhumanity to a faithful servant, and I began to have a dread that Mr. Terky's mind had become diseased by his troubles. Recollecting, too, that all through his recent extraordinary depression he had seemed to shrink from meeting the full gaze of any eye, — even his wife's, — and recalling his peculiar excitement in regard to the doctor, the idea of his mental disorder grew still stronger, and vague apprehension of some new and more terrible disaster turned me sick at heart. I was in no condition, myself, to attempt the part of adviser, or comforter; yet I felt that some one should do something to change the unnatural and ominous atmosphere of our unhappy household. Thus reflecting, I was about to remonstrate once more with the bereaved father against his going to the store that day, when the bell rang and he went past me to open the street door.

"Upstairs," I heard him say, in apparent response to a murmur of feminine voices; and, while the rustling of dresses sounded on the flight, he came back to the dining-room. "Come on, Glibun. We may as well go first as last."

"Then you are really going?"

"Heaven and earth! haven't I told you I must? Do you want to make me shoot myself?"

Without further remark I put on my hat, and we went out together into the sunshine, — the warm, glad sunshine, which should make charitable and humane those hearts, at least, whose gains and hopes are all inward reflectors of its inspiring brightness. And yet, many a possessor of an untroubled soul whom we unoffendingly passed that morning must have visited flippant verdict upon the deadly chill and shadow which gave our mourning one letter more than theirs. Many a gay heart, so richly blessed in the glorious light that some of it were easily spared to thought of anything human, must have carelessly fancied truculence in the pleading misery of a childless father's eye, and wanton recklessness in the desolate neglect of a fatherless child.

Mr. Coffin and Noah Trust came to him and me at our dreary desk, having noticed our altered countenances as we passed through the long retail salesroom to the iron stairs which led to the basement. Both were surprised and grieved at the special cause; for each had imagined a far different one; and while the romantic lace-salesman condoled stammeringly with Mr. Terky, the kindly grocer's son soothed me with a delicate commiseration which generously ignored the wound best borne when shared the least.

Noah joined with me in thinking that the firm could not possibly expect the bereaved parent to remain at business with death in his family; but Mr. Coffin sadly shook his smoky head and doubted.

"I'm afraid, I'm afraid," sighed he, in the lowest possible spirits. "Those whose hearts and intellects are all given over to the insenate mart of mercenary trade, recognize no human joy or woe but in the gaining or losing of a dollar. Tell them that the Shadow of the Destroyer has fallen over the intelligent family hearthstone, and their mind-play will rise to nothing higher than a certain wild astonishment at such an unbusiness-like occurrence. You might ask, though, my poor Terky; you might ask."

"I shall ask," said the entry-clerk; and, turning abruptly to his books, he grasped his right wrist, to check the pitiable shaking of that hand, and endeavored to write.

At least, he made a pretence of writing until about half an hour after our friends had left us, when he suddenly drove the pen into the desk, and dragged his hat down from its nail.

"I must have a glass of brandy," he muttered, in answer to my inquiring look. "I see too much besides words and figures on that book, and I must have something to keep the devil out of me."

He was gone but a few moments, and then came back to his pitiless drudgery with a hard and desperate air of blind determination. After two or three more attempts, however, he again dashed the pen violently aside, clasped his hands clutchingly across the invoice book, and dropped his head upon them with a long, low groan.

I could only stand and watch him, in the silent helplessness of a wretchedness unnerving as his own. I could only stand there beside him in that gloomy, unwholesome slave-pen and pray speechlessly for him and myself in the broken petitions of bewildered despair.

As suddenly as before he turned a second time from the desk, dragged down his hat, and answered my mute appeal.

"I'm going to see Cummin now. He must be in by this time. If he ever had a child of his own he'll let me off. I can't stand it!"

It was a real relief to hear this; for it sounded like right and natural feeling. I wanted him to leave his work with me, and go home; and I had not doubted, from the first, that the firm would unhesitatingly tell him to do it. So, I beheld him going up the iron staircase as though he carried up with him at least one of my torturing apprehensions to disperse to the four winds above, and resumed my work in calmer mind and more courageous mood.

Fifteen minutes passed, and the entry-clerk was coming toward the desk at a sharp, quick walk. Without a word, he threw his hat from him, brushed by me to his place of toil, and, pressing his handkerchief to his eyes, wept aloud like a boy!

But one interpretation could be given to that final breaking-down of an overwrought excitement. Kindness had come, as the west wind across a false sky of fervent brass, and brought the gentle rain at last. I cried, too, but in a kind of triumph over the truth of my own obstinate intuitions. Cummin & Tryon *had* human hearts, even for an entry-clerk; and where he had expected nothing but the callous inhumanity against which he had hardened himself, the voice of fraternal sympathy met him like the rod of Moses, and drew melting waters from the arid rock.

"Didn't I tell you how it would be?" quavered I, gently trying to pull down his hands. "It'll do you good to give way to your feelings like that, dear old friend; but do go home now, — won't you?"

With a passionate gesture he uncovered his face, and I involuntarily recoiled from the expression glaring in every swollen feature. An awful oath burst from his lips, and he turned upon me as though he could tear me to pieces.

"Go home? you — idiot!" he snarled. "Didn't I let your baby-talk fool me into believing that I was something more than Cummin & Tryon's cart-horse?"

My blood boiled. Not because the poor, tortured creature struck at me in his agony; but in sympathetic rage at a hardness of heart beyond belief.

"What did they say?" I managed to ask.

"That they felt very sorry. That it was unfortunate. That *I had better go home earlier — to-night!* — That was all."

"But, did you tell them that your child was actually dead? You couldn't have done so!"

"I did. There! let us say no more about it. A cheap clerk has no business to be a father; but I thought I'd have one good cry before I went to work to earn the burial expenses."

His tears seemed to have washed out all the remaining good from his worn face, leaving it darkly wicked; and I turned from him with a shudder.*

The salesmen who came down to "call off" bills that afternoon were all as kind and forbearing as they could be toward the frequent mistakes of the entry-clerk and his assistant; for they had heard, upstairs, of the sorrow in our house. Such of them as prospered sufficiently to reach large stores of their own, would then, of course, hold all minor clerks to be very common cattle; but, in the interim, they had some fellow-feeling for the hirelings below them, and were willing to make allowances for domestic afflictions.

It must have been somewhere near four o'clock, when a porter brought me word that my presence was desired immediately in the private office of the firm. He was *not* mistaken, he said: "If my name was Glibnn I was the one Mr. Cummin had told him to call."

The circumstance was so unusual that I would fain have consulted my companion before obeying the summons; but seeing that he did not even raise his eyes from the invoice book, I refrained from troubling him about it.

Leaving him thus, apparently absorbed in his work, I quietly repaired to the partitioned room of the partners, where Mr. Cummin and Mr. Coffin appeared to be in close consultation, while the night-porter of the store stood before them, cap in hand. All three looked intently at me as I entered, and I thought the lace-salesman seemed greatly agitated.

* There is no exaggeration in this incident. I have known a firm to exact business services from a clerk on a day when his wife laid dead in the house.

"Young man," said Mr. Cummin, motioning toward a chair with his forefinger, "just sit down there, if you please; I wish to ask you a few questions."

Unable to form the slightest conjecture of what was coming, I took the seat indicated, and glanced inquiringly from the chief to his subordinates.

"You have not remained here at night recently, I understand from the porter."

"No, sir," I replied, readily enough; "Mr. Terky has preferred to stay alone."

"Yes, I see. Have you any idea of the reason *why* Mr. Terky has been so indulgent?"

"Because he thought there was not work enough for two, I suppose, sir." (I felt, however, as I gave this answer, that it was not a very clear or consistent one. But what was all this questioning for?)

"Well, we'll let that pass," went on the merchant, with a dissatisfied glance at Mr. Coffin. "You live in the same house with Mr. Terky, I believe?"

"I do, Mr. Cummin."

"Board with him?"

I bowed.

"Has he seemed, within the last few weeks, to have any more money than usual? — given presents to his wife? — bought things? — or anything of that kind?"

The look of wonder in my face gave way to a hot flush, and a new and vague anxiety for my friend made me violently alive to the insulting character of this last strange interrogation.

"I mind my own business, sir!" I said, indignantly. "If you wish to know anything of Mr. Terky's private affairs you must ask him himself."

The tradesman eyed me suspiciously for a moment, and then turned to the porter, — "John, you say that you have seen the entry-clerk hanging about Mr. Coffin's counter, on several occasions, after all the other clerks had gone for the night? You're sure about it?"

"It's no harm I'd be afther shpaykin' of any man, sur," returned the inevitable Irishman; "but it's Mr. Terky was in it, sur, afther ev'ry wan lavein'; an' I saw him, whin me back was turruned, lanein' right over fornint the shelves convaynient to Misther Coffin's counter. Fair and aisy goes far in a day, sur, an' I only tell ye the truth."

The man spoke honestly; there could be no doubt of that; and his words made clear the object of Mr. Cummin in questioning me. The miserable clerk was suspected of ROBBERY. The terrible word no sooner took shape in my mind than it recalled to memory the several recent occasions when my unhappy friend had seemed mysteriously possessed of money; his late avoidance of my company, too, and obvious uneasiness under the mildest eye. Alas! instead of defending him from a foul aspersion, my impulse was to feel almost guilty myself, and look to the floor in silence.

"Mr. Coffin, you hear what John says," observed the sandy-haired inquisitor. "It will be as well, I think, to call the man himself, now."

"Mr. Cummin!" cried the salesman, pale and excited, "my intellect tells me that there's a cruel mistake here, somewhere, sir. I'd sooner pay for the missing lace myself, than have Mr. Terky accused of such a thing, when he already has the Destroyer across his Desolate Hearth. I'm amazed, my mind-play is utterly confounded, by the turn this thing has taken. I could swear that Terky is as innocent of such guile as any woman of the higher classes. I'll stand the loss, myself, sir, though it should reduce me to penury!"

"If the man is innocent, he can say so," returned Mr. Cummin, coldly. — "John, go and call the entry-clerk."

The porter obeyed the order so hastily, that Mr. Terky was in the presence before either the salesman or I could say another word for him. In he came; neither respectfully nor defiantly, but with the step and air of one who was stolidly indifferent to anything more that could happen to him.

"Entry-clerk," began his proprietor, in a hard, dry voice, "I am sorry to say, that—"

"I'm a thief!" broke in the white slave; not shrinking from *his* eye. "You're sorry to say that entry-clerk — or block of wood, or whatever else I am — has stolen lace from you. Well, I have. I've taken two hundred dollars' worth, and got fifty for it. Here are the pawn-tickets" (deliberately drawing them from a vest-pocket and placing them on the desk) — "all of them. I've never taken anything else than lace; and I should have taken another piece of that, to-night, if you hadn't found me out to-day. I wanted it to bury my dead baby with."

He spoke clearly, calmly, and monotonously; looking straight into the sharp little eyes of his astounded judge all the time.

"Then you confess it?" gasped the latter. "You are not ashamed to—"

"No!" — catching him up again. "I've no more business to have shame than to have manhood, or human feeling. Do you and your partner treat such as I with any regard to our shame, or our manhood, or our human feelings? Don't you drive and drudge us down, as boys, until we haven't the soul, mind, or body, for anything different; and then drudge and drive us as burlesques of men for any miserable pittance that we don't dare to lose? Ten years ago I came into this store of yours, a poor orphan boy, glad enough to work like a scullion, and be abused and slaved by every whipper-snapper of a salesman in the place, because I hoped to make my way up in the business some day, and get decently paid for my labor. I've done the work of six men ever since; I've toiled for you day and night like a slave, and you've made a thief of me for it!"

"*I* made a thief of you!" sputtered Mr. Cummin, turning purple with rage. "You scoundrel! how dare you?"

"Yes; you and your partner," continued the victim at bay; "you and your sharer in the profits of unrequited toil. You have grown rich on such sufferings as have made a criminal of me, and many another poor counting-house drudge before me. You can afford, Mr. Cummin,—you and your partner,—to give hundreds to the starving poor of Ireland; you can afford to give hundreds more to buy Irish votes here, at the bidding of your brother slave-drivers from the South; you can afford to subscribe thousands for a new church; but you *can't* afford to pay your own overworked clerks enough to keep them from want, from the scorn of every well-paid hod-carrier, or from disbelief in the pity of God himself!"

"Upon my word!" ejaculated the rich man.

"I say again, YOU have made a thief of me!" His clenched fists, heaving chest, and burning eyes, began to show how the inner tempest lashed him, now that the smothering repression of years had forced to vent. "I have asked you, I have servilely begged you, to save me from ruin by paying me some living part of my just earnings; and you have dismissed me like a dog, with permission to look for another bone if I didn't like yours, because you knew that other rich merchants like you gave no better bones to poor, hungry dogs like me. Starve a dog, and he'll steal from your table, and you've made a thief of him!"

There was something so stupefying in the fierce audacity of this mere low-priced clerk, that the Majesty of Wholesale and Retail could only stare dumfoundered.

"I'm glad to be found out," went on the presumptuous hireling, looking round upon Mr. Coffin and me for the first time, but quickly facing his owner again. "It's a relief to have it all over, and not go crazy waiting for it and expecting it every moment. I'd sooner go to prison than go home to-night, a thousand times over. I'd sooner go to prison, than not be such an example to this poor young fellow you've given me as an assistant,—about all you ever did give me,—as will warn him (not against theft, but) against clerking in a princely dry-goods house! He'd better go and saw wood, if he wants to be treated, at least, like a human vote. I'll ask the policeman to let me have one last look at my dead child; and then I'll go willingly enough with him to less of a prison than the one I've been in for the past ten years."

I went and stood beside him, grasping his hand, as he undauntedly welcomed his fate; and Mr. Cummin turned stiffly to his salesman.

"Mr. Coffin, will you be kind enough to step out and call an officer?"

"No, sir! no, sir! I will not, sir!" was the startling reply, as Mr. Coffin bounced from his chair as though he had been shot out of it, and rumpled the smoky hair with both hands. "I'll see you d—d first, if you'll attribute the remark to unusual intellectual excitement! Mr. Cummin, the quality of mercy is not strained, sir; 'tis mightiest in the mightiest; and it has might in it *because* it is not strained. I only sell lace in your Mart of Trade, Mr. Cummin; but, as Man to Man, sir, I have a right to advise you not to strain yourself in this matter. I will take those tickets, and redeem the laces myself! I will see that this bereaved robber has means to convey his child to the insatiate grave without stealing any more of our best point appliqué! I will give security, sir, to the full extent of twelve hundred in bank, for his future good conduct out West somewhere! I will get you another entry-clerk, Mr. Cummin, from one of the orphan asylums, to do twice as much work for a third of the money! I will—"

"Coffin, my dear, good friend!—"

"Not another word, Job Terky, or I'll commit a dastardly assault on you!" squeaked the exploding laureate, his voice growing very thin and wheezy with such unwonted declamation. "I don't want to hear anything more from you. Mr. Cummin, remember the withered bud in this burglar's blighted garden, and do not insist upon embittering the last drop of dew that bud can know—a father's tear!"

Thanks to a God whose loving hand leaves some of its own deathless light and tenderness in everything it fashions, I have never yet, in all my wandering and varied life, beheld a soul so base that no immortal warmth from the creating palm lingered somewhere within it, to flush an innate divinity at times through crime's own chilling climax; nor one so ridiculous that no grand impulse lightened by chances through all its shallow vagaries of folly, to thrill the senses with a touch sublime.

The mingled absurdity and pathos of the salesman's vehement appeal seemed to soften the tradesman's feelings a little. At least, his heavy features relaxed somewhat in their severity, and his answer, though very gravely spoken, was not contemptuous.

"Entry-clerk," said he, "in consideration of your domestic affliction and Mr. Coffin's offer of reparation, I shall merely discharge you. The language you have used makes it doubtful whether any parting admonitions from me would do you any good. You may go."

Silently, and without even a bow of acknowledgment, Mr. Terky turned upon his heel and left the private office, and I noticed, as I followed him back to our dreary floor of servitude, that he cast a half-threatening look on all who looked at him, as though he presumed that they knew all about his disgrace, and would sneer if they dared. At the desk, where he and I had been such close companions for so long, he mechanically closed his invoice-book, made a bundle of an old linen coat which he sometimes wore during business hours, and gazed slowly around at all the familiar features of the old place.

"This is the end of it, then!" he said, slowly and bitterly. "This is the end of the best years of my life. Debt and death at home, disgrace and discharge here. Well, well, well."

I could not speak, but held out my hand. He shook it for some moments, and then continued.—

"You must have seen, Glibun, from affairs at home, what I was being driven to. I don't ask you to forgive my crime, but I hope you will remember what made me commit it. They'll give you my place here, I think, and you'd better keep it until you can find another place."

"I will," said I, firmly, "on one condition."

"Well?"

"That you shall accept nine dollars a week in board from me, until *you* can find another place."

He shook my hand again, and shook his head.

"It is strange," he muttered, "that the first real kindness I have known for years should be given to me just when I deserve it less than I ever did before in my life. There's Coffin, whom I always took for a fool, pleads for me like a father, and saves me from jail. I can never pay my debt of gratitude to him any more than I can pay my other debts. But I can't let you do what you ask; and I may as well tell you at once, that it will not do for you to live with me any longer. Even if you could continue to stay with me without ruining your own prospects, I shall not attempt to keep house after this week. I don't know what I shall do, but I shan't do that."

Here some one tumbled down the iron staircase with a crash, and, amidst a chorus of laughter from upstairs, the lace-salesman came limping to join us.

"Ah, I'm glad you're not gone yet," he cried, addressing the entry-clerk with a haste which was obviously intended to prevent any thanks. "I wanted to tell you, Job, that I didn't express my own sentiments, at all, when I called you a robber and burglar. I only did that, you see, because it was policy to humor Mammon's rage against you, a little, while, at the same time, I insinuated the intercession of friendship."

"Don't speak of it, dear Coffin," returned Mr. Terky, breaking down. "I hope God will bless you for what you've done. That's all I can say. You know all I mean. God bless you! God bless you! You shall be paid—"

"Mr. Terky," said Mr. Coffin, with sudden violence, "if you finish that sentence I'll hand you over to the police."

"Then let it be complete as it stands, for I mean it. I leave this store now, forever, Mr. Coffin. You have learned this afternoon what I have suffered here, if you did not know before; but, in spite of it all, I shall always look back to this place and day with a better feeling than I often have, because they have shown me the noblest heart a man ever had! Coffin, Coffin, I never thought it would make me cry to look at you, but it does now."

There were tears in his eyes indeed, and the lace-salesman gave them multiplied reflection on his own lantern-cheeks.

They went upstairs together, after Mr. Terky had persuaded me to let him go home alone; and I remained at work in that gloomy dungeon—more lonely and chill now than ever—until the last bill was entered and invoice "made out."

At a late hour of the night I stood once more in the desolate house in Banks Street, and the chill air of the shadowy and deserted hall seemed to have lost all that beautiful freshness of home which had so soothed me after a very different evening. My steps sounded harshly loud, as though every room and passage within the walls had a sullen emptiness to resent the wounds of brooding silence. Yet that hall was not solitary to me; for I saw again the white-robed, fearful woman on the chair, the gray-haired doctor going spectrally up the staircase, the furious debtor springing down the steps.

On the way to my own chamber, I paused an instant before the closed door beyond which *they*, I knew, held awful communion with darkness and with death. Only a low, fitful moaning, like the wind when the summer's last flower lies withered, and the young trees stretch torn and bleeding arms in mute appeal to heaven.

———◆———

CHAPTER XXXVI.

A CERTAIN amount of permanent confidence in self is, of course, the primary requisite of a good conversationist; but to this must be added a judicious moderation in reading, or study. Great readers are never good general talkers, though they may be voluble enough on one or two special topics. Reading abstracts the mind to an ideal world so different in many respects from the real, that the intellectual faculties gradually become adapted almost exclusively to the former, and proportionately lose aptitude for the latter. In the aggregate, women are much better talkers than men, because they usually read much less profoundly, and do most of their thinking in conversation. Their daily occupations, too, require far less meditative study than do the business pursuits of the other sex; and hence a woman's mind is almost always in rapport with living actualities, and prepared to express in ready words whatever their instantaneous suggestions may be.

Whether from too little confidence, too much law-reading, or an excess of daily meditation, Ezekiel Reed prospered not in the earlier part of an evening's conversation with Miss Le Mons, though that straight and self-possessed young lady discoursed fluently enough upon a dozen passing themes to encourage freedom in the most timorous tongue. The cosey little Fourth-Street parlor never looked more like perfect comfort for two; the pictured shade of the tall astral lamp on the centre-table could not have thrown down a brighter little round world of light for the exclusive habitation of "two souls with but a single thought;" yet the pale, slender law-student, for nearly an hour, gave no sustained proof that *he* possessed that single thought. Although he certainly made several creditable exertions to do better, Miss Le Mons found that talking with him on ordinary subjects, that night, was like teaching a child to read, when the teacher, after divers jerky pauses at simple words, to give the backward pupil opportunity to join in, if so disposed, should finally be compelled to finish the lesson herself, or give up the task in despair. Good and patient little girl as she generally was, the fair Constance became slightly provoked at last, and ventured a mild snap in the following terms, —

"If you feel at all sleepy, Ezekiel, you must not let me detain you."

"I may be dull company for you, Conny," returned Ezekiel, blushing for himself, "but I'm not in the least degree sleepy, nor even tired. And if I don't talk much, Conny, it's because I like so well to hear those earnest little sermons which you preach about nearly everything. It is pleasant to watch you while you are preaching them."

She was pretty to watch; with the long dark curls down her back, the short tangled ones crowning her brow under a band of pink ribbon, and the great, deep eyes forever changing. The compliment, honest and plain enough to be a child's, seemed to stir in her virgin bosom a sensation more grave than gratifying, and she responded to it reprovingly, —

"I am sorry to have made you say something at last, if you are going to ridicule sacred things. In sermons and preaching there may be good for others, if not for you."

"Dear Conny," answered Ezekiel Reed, turning his strong, yet gentle eyes upon hers, with a look of patient entreaty, "I would give anything in the world to make you understand that I despise irreverence as much as you do. Can't you distinguish between intentional scoffing and a mere innocent pleasantry? The people I meet in business every day think I am a religious fanatic; and yet you, knowing me as well and long, will have it that I am hardly more than an infidel."

"No," cried Constance, with great earnestness, "I know that you are not an infidel. But how can you, Ezekiel, with so much that is great and noble in your nature, refuse to be a servant of Christ? It is not enough to believe in him. You must pro-fess him openly and become one of his people."

With the light of a strong purpose in his peculiarly sensitive face, — a purpose to be maintained in spite of all sacrifice and suffering, — the young man returned the earnest gaze of the girl, and spoke very firmly, —

"I believe in the religion that is lived for a life, and held sacred from all common uses of the lips. In the beautiful life and sublime death of the Saviour of men, I see an example of purity, charity, love to all men, and self-sacrifice for the meanest, by following which in spirit and in truth we may secure peace on earth and acceptance in heaven. To me, the Sermon on the Mount is, in itself, sufficient to intellectually prove the divinity of the preacher. How wonderful is it in its perfect intelligibility for all ages and minds; its complete presentment of human nature's noblest possibilities; its touching and perfectly practicable lesson of charity, tenderness, and a religion to be silently lived; its marvellous prayer, which, in a few simple lines, holds every want, weakness, circumstance, and emotion of the human soul! Human genius in its grandest immortalities never approached the ever-living divinity of that Sermon and Prayer. Oh! if *I* could but live them as I know they might be lived! If I could but live such a life, and crown it, as He did, with a matchless sacrifice!"

Involuntarily clasping his hands as the subject glowed more intensely through his whole nature, the enthusiast poured forth his words at last in a kind of frenzied soliloquy, to which every feature lent tremulous fervor. Character innate awoke within him at the touch of its affinity, and arose in his apostrophe with a resistless energy before which the girl grew weaker than her cause.

"If I could only speak as I should," she replied, quietly, but with a strong feeling, "you would see, Ezekiel, that God requires us to renounce the world and join the communion of his disciples, if we would give proof before men of our belief in his Son!"

"The world is God's," said Reed, solemnly, "and the poorest creature in it has his love and image. I will not insult a benignant Maker by turning from the triumph of his hands as though the fiend had torn it from him. I will not fly from his likeness because it has fallen from that high expression to which I, perhaps, as a stronger brother, may lift it again. Let me keep my religion fresh and active out in the world, not seek to horde it all in a pew. Let me feel love and charity for all created things, and study to conquer selfishness by making self mean others, — all whom I can reach and joy or suffer with. Let me see good in all creeds, — the right principle in all, intentional impiety in none. — too little simplicity and spontaneity in many."

Conny had gradually drooped her eloquent eyes to the floor while he thus addressed her, and on lifting them again showed tears on their reddened lids.

"You remind me so much of my poor brother," said she, tremulously. "When I write seriously to him, he always tells me that we church-people are mere religious politicians, only moral as we are superstitious. It is so terrible to think that he is not a Christian. Dear Gwin!"

The loving sister did not intend that the parallel should be a cutting one; but Ezekiel Reed knew that the brother he recalled was a wild, dissipated, reckless young scapegrace, with scarcely a higher aim than self-indulgence.

"Your own goodness and prayers, dear Conny," he remarked, gently, "will save your brother, yet."

"But I am not good, Ezekiel. I am a very weak, sinful girl."

"My second sister! If it can be any consolation for you — any hope of final success with your brother — to know that your example has made me wiser, better, and more earnest than I could have been without it, take my assurance without a doubt of its plain truth. I know what a trial your only brother's alienation from his home has been to you; and I have seen you bear it with an uncomplaining patience, a hopeful trust in God, from which I have learned better how to be cheerful under my own peculiar lot. A good, Christian woman is the best earthly friend a man can have."

Like sunshine through a shower came the bright look of unmistakable pleasure into Conny's swimming eyes, as she asked, rather archly, "Do you think, then, that female Christians live more of their religion than masculine ones can?"

"I know so little, practically, of either," returned Ezekiel, with a smile, "that I do not like to give a hasty opinion. Indeed, Conny," he added, after a pause, "it is strange how few people of any kind I have known since I came to this city, several years ago. My poor, sick sister, at her home in Greenwich; you and your mother here; and the people at the office are really all whom I can call acquaintances. Without caring for what is called company, I still have the feelings of a social being, and am so oppressed with a sense of loneliness, sometimes, that a dog would comfort me. I do not know that I have an enemy in the world; I try to treat every one with courteous kindness; yet none seem attracted to me as to other people."

"You are over-sensitive, I think," said the young lady, thoughtfully, "and shrink from those who would be friendly with you."

"That may be," he answered, a careworn look suddenly clouding his peaceful face. "I am never without the remembrance that my unhappy father is under the ban of men, as well as under the Almighty's; and when strangers approach me, I do feel that they should know *that* before being allowed to know me."

The words came hesitatingly. He evidently wished to make them carry a meaning as ordinary as possible. His fair companion, however, found something in them to rouse again her spirit of reproof.

"You show a very morbid, worldly pride, then," she said, with her old air of pious antagonism, "and are not resigned to your cross in the spirit of Christ. I never could see, either, how you can be disgraced by the misfortunes of one who is only your step-father, after all."

"He was good to my mother, Conny. She loved him to the last, and I know no difference between him and a father. He never wronged me nor my sister; he never did anything that should make my interests separate from his; and now, when he is dishonored, forgotten, and worse than helpless, I do take a kind of defiant pride in feeling no higher than he. When I go to that asylum each week, and find that I and a poor black servant are all whom he remembers of the many who brought him good, or evil, in the past, I vow anew to myself that I will know him only as a father; that his sins shall be mine to repair, or endlessly repent; that God shall find in my reason the eagerness to do life-long penance and suffer all just humiliation, by which his reason might have partially atoned, had it been spared to him, for multiplied transgressions."

"I can't understand it," she said, leaning her dimpled chin upon the palm of her right hand, and eying him both curiously and affectionately. "Never, since you first confided your step-father's condition to me, and said that he had committed great errors, have I been able to comprehend why you should darken and sacrifice your whole life from a strained and unnatural idea of the Scripture command to bear one another's burdens. Just see what such mistaken feeling has done for you already! You look coldly upon the church of Christ, in which, as you have told me, you found every joy of your childhood. You wrap yourself up in a forced, unnatural martyrdom because it is a kind of insane pleasure to you; and so fetter yourself from the wide good you might do to many others, — to hundreds, perhaps, — by a life of practical, devout, happy Christianity. The heathen make sacrifices like yours, Ezekiel. They burn themselves alive for the sake of their dead."

She was inspired to speak thus by that just perception of falsehood in truth's extreme which so often invests earnest women and children with a character for startling penetration, though it comes rather from the instinctive protest of the heart against what seems to transcend natural feeling, than from any peculiar understanding of a fine intellectual energy indulged to inordinate excess.

Ezekiel Reed felt, as he had often felt before, that this grave and unsparing young natural critic could both see and recognize the morbid fallacy he would fain adopt as the noblest principle of a true Christian life. At least, her words gave him a torturing dread of something fallacious in the darling purpose of his whole moral nature, and the despair of momentary self-distrust, no less than a passionate sense of injustice, gave vehemence to his answer, —

"I could bear misjudgment better from any one else in the world than from you," he cried, returning her troubled gaze with one full of unutterable pain. "I can be patient with any misconstruction but yours. Why will you so intolerantly refuse to perceive that my belief, my principles, my religious intentions are the same as yours? Conny, it is the wish, the great hope of my life, to save, at least, one human soul. To do that, I would sacrifice every earthly good of my own, — life itself, if necessary. I feel that my poor father must die in the wrath of an offended God if some mortal's reasoning power does not take the place of that which he has lost to beseech pardon for him, to deserve mercy for him by due humiliation, penance, and self-abnegation. As I have told you before, a miserable black servant — who is bound to him by no natural ties, who even struck him once because *he*, in a moment of frenzy, struck another — comes from his wretched refuge in some squalid haunt of the city's poor, to hover around the place of his old master's captivity, and lament and pray over him when he can. How much more, then, is it my charge — mine, because that poor maniac was blessed by my mother's dying lips — to exceed that ignorant servant's devotion, as my duty exceeds his."

Drawing a deep sigh, the young girl bowed her head and was silent. Whether from hopelessness of bringing him to her views of duty by any argument that could be advanced, or from conscious lack of capacity to combat in mere words such an arrogation of God's own prerogative as his purpose seemed to her to be, she looked down and remained silent. Long and intently did Ezekiel Reed watch her as she thus gave to his avowal a comment harder than all others to bear from one we love. And while he watched, the resolute, rapt, almost defiant expression faded from his delicate face, leaving it gentle and plaintive as a woman's. Moving impulsively from his chair to the sofa, or settee, on which she sat, he seized both her hands and boyishly pulled her toward him, so that she could not help meeting his questioning eyes.

"Conny, if I am mistaken in my ideas of paramount duty, my eyes will be cleared before it is too late. I am very honest in those ideas. I hold them because they seem to be the only ones suited to my own conception of the best and least selfish use of life. If they involve a wrong view of God's intent for me; if I ought to content myself with preserving my stricken father from mere bodily harm, and devote my religious energies to ordinary uses, I shall be checked in time. Do not doubt that I want to do my whole duty rightly. Do not doubt that I would joyfully suffer everything for the sake of being truly right."

Without exactly yielding entirely to his ingenuously affectionate manner, Constance shrank not from him when he placed an arm about her neck and caressingly smoothed her luxuriant tresses with its conciliating hand. She neither shrank nor yielded; but sat calmly still in his brotherly half-embrace, thoughtfully scrutinizing his countenance.

"I do not doubt your unselfishness, Ezekiel," she said, in a low, feeling tone. "I believe you to be capable of any grand sacrifice for what you deemed a noble object. You couldn't have another friend in the whole world to honor and admire more than I do your devotion to principle and moral duty. You seem to me so much purer and more generous than any other person I ever knew, that my very appreciation makes me talk to you, as I never could to any other person, of the one thing needed to make you perfect!"

In the fervor of her willingness to do him full justice, she had involuntarily betrayed a stronger sentiment of admiration than she was aware of; and, with a bright smile, her companion drew her closer to him, and confidingly rested his cheek upon her shoulder. It was so naturally done, so innocently and boyishly done, that an older and more prudish woman could have found in it no definite offence to her dignity.

"Help me, then, to what I need, dear little girl," whispered the voice at her ear. "Pray for me; and pray, also, that you may be the instrument selected to work my full salvation. We are both very young yet; we have been thrown together in a strange kind of confidence, and perhaps Providence intends some great result from our association. Don't you feel that this may be so?"

A just perceptible pressure upon the hand within his own, answered him.

"You cannot imagine, Conny, how lonely all my life has been since my mother died. At school the boys seemed to dread me because I liked study better than play, and shrank from their rude games. I was monitor of the school, and they might have been repelled on that account; but, then, I spared them all I could, and why should they prefer every teacher else to me? Even your old playfellow, Avery Glibun, treated me with dislike. Since then, though, when grown men and women have turned coldly from me, even when repaid good for evil by me, I have not blamed the school-boys so much for their antagonism, — though I never wilfully deserved it, I am sure. Excepting my poor, sick sister, whose affection is greater than I deserve, you, Conny, are the only one who seems to understand that I have a heart. The years I have spent in this house are like a dream to me, in the peace, trust, and affection which have been mine under all my trials."

"They have been happy years for me, too," murmured Constance, still speaking calmly and steadily. "You have been like a son to mother, and like a brother to me. We both wish that poor Gwin could have had a brother like you."

The hand on her head patted softly, and the voice from her shoulder went on, —

"Possibly your grief for your brother made you and me sympathize at first; but ever since then we have been even more harmonious than own brother and sister, — except in one matter."

"Yes; that has been the only exception, Ezekiel."

"You have thought me lacking in correct religious belief, because I have refrained from professing religion in the usual way."

"Yes," very sadly.

"Do not persist in that hopeless tone, Conny. I have long been aware of a something wanting to satisfy myself in the good life I strive to lead. It has not seemed, to my own conscience, to be an implicit dependence upon any set creed —"

"Don't talk in that wicked way!" she interrupted, making a quick attempt to move away from him."

"No, no, don't do that. Hear me out," he remonstrated, raising his head, but still detaining her with his arm. "I was going to say, that my restless want had not *yet* defined itself to my conscience as that. But if that be really it, Conny, grace will be given me, I hope, to see it in time. Only have patience and help me."

"Ezekiel Reed!" exclaimed Constance, with the emphasis of her whole soul, "I should think that I deserved to have every prayer for my brother granted, if I could help you to gain that grace."

The young man instantly drew his hands to himself, and confronted her with a look and demeanor all dignified and manly.

"Dear Constance! Let us no longer be children disputing over different paths to the same goal, but man and woman working lovingly, prayerfully, and in life-long unison, for a harmonious attainment of a common end. Where I am self-deceived and erring, you, in the clear light of affection, shall point out to me those guides of wholesome humanity and mutual well-doing which have thus far had no place in my life, and, which, when commended to me by your constant example, shall become mine through you."

"I scarcely understand you," she said, hurriedly; "I hardly know what you would have me do."

"I would have you teach me the right way," he answered, appearing agitated, also, but speaking very distinctly and fervently. "Already in the new feelings your words have given me I can see some possibility of different purposes, different aspirations, from those you have called mistaken. Love me, Conny; give me a fresh world to learn and live in, and we will find the true cross together."

"I do love you, very dearly, Ezekiel," she tremulously returned, fixing upon him a startled look.

"But can you not love me still more, dear Constance? Could you not find your happiness in making our whole future lives a near, closer, and more sacred continuation of the past few years?"

"Oh, what do you ask me?" she cried, alternately pale and flushed; the while her eyes grew luminous with a half-divination of what kindled in his. "What more can I do for you, than pray God to make both of us wiser?"

"Give me a hope," he returned, impetuously, — "give me a hope, that when I shall have made for myself an honorable position and name; when I shall have lived down a heritage of humiliation and ignominy; I may come to you for the inspiration to still nobler endeavor, and the companionship destined to make that endeavor the joy and salvation of two loving hearts! Until to-night, Conny, I have never realized all that you have become to me; and to-night I ask you to become still more; to promise —"

"Ezekiel, — please!" she entreated, involuntarily stretching both hands toward him.

"Conny! This from you!" he exclaimed, catching his breath. "Didn't you say that you loved me?"

"Ezekiel, I do love you — very dearly — as a friend — but not in that way." She spoke very nervously, and with lips that quivered almost to crying.

Alas! Saint and sinner alike have the one question for such a case.

"Is another more favored?"

"I am only a mere child, yet, Ezekiel," she pleaded, piteously, striving to soothe the wound she had given. "I have acted very foolishly and presumptuously, and hope you will forgive me."

"I have confided the story of my misfortunes, to you," he said, bitterly; "I have told you how disgraced, poor, and friendless I am; and, like all the rest, you turn me off."

In an instant the girl was rigid as a statue, and spoke coldly and monotonously. "Mr. Reed, I will never marry any man who is not a professing Christian!"

Pliant and relenting as she should have been by her youth, there was a hard, mature determination in that frigid utterance which left no chance for appeal. That the suitor understood it, was evidenced by the shocked, ghastly look overspreading his St. John face, and the disordered air with which he left the sofa and mutely paced the room.

Yet, she loved him dearly; loved with a love protesting against his descent from her high ideal of him to sue and fume, like any common mortal, for what her natural womanhood deemed a gift utterly unworthy so noble a suitor! If she sacrificed him to a pitiless and inexorable religious sentiment, she also sacrificed herself. Thus, as he strode back and forth past her, with lips compressed, brow contracted, and arms tightly folded, she followed him with eyes swiftly losing all expression of self-assertion and gaining only an eloquent depth of regret.

"Ezekiel," she softly said, frenzied to see him suffer so, and fairly beside herself to lessen his distress, — "Ezekiel, won't you eat something?"

He was near the door, and seemed about to depart abruptly without another word, when, by an impulse natural to her years, she hastened to his side and stopped him with a touch.

"Ezekiel, I couldn't help it." Then sank into a chair and gave way to a hearty fit of crying.

"Poor little Conny!" he whispered, and touched the bowed head with his lips.

"I am so sorry to pain you, Ezekiel."

"I have deserved it, Conny, — richly deserved it."

"Oh, no, you haven't."

"God has justly punished me," began Ezekiel Reed, in a tone so full of some great emotion that the girl looked up at him in sorrowful bewilderment. "God has justly punished me," he repeated, "for my selfishness, and I despise myself for what I have said to-night. How could I dare prove so false to my own sacred purpose, and seek my own selfish good, regardless of every holy duty in the life of denial and sacrifice appointed me to lead! Yes, I am punished as I deserve," he continued, with the old, rapt, intense look upon him, "and may God preserve me from further temptation."

"You do not blame me?" asked Constance, in a faltering voice.

"No!" exclaimed he, regarding her tenderly. "I thank and honor you, Conny, for teaching me how to be true to myself and the mission that is mine. I ask you to forgive my ungenerous words of reproach, and think that I was not myself when they were spoken. I must go away from here; I must not peril my poor father's soul again by remaining where selfish thoughts and schemes may drive me to forget myself a second time; but I would still retain your affection."

"You shall always have that," was the earnest answer. "I am proud of winning the confidence and affection of a man like you, — so much my superior in everything; so much nobler and better than I can ever be. Oh, if you would but — "

"Do not tempt me again!" He spoke quickly and checked her with uplifted hand. "I cannot change; I cannot think as you do. I was weak a moment ago, but I am firm now."

He stood upon the threshold of the opened door, and, as Constance arose to give him parting answer, his face looked a clearer white than ever against the dark background of the hall.

"You will not always feel so, dear brother," said Constance Le Mons, mournfully shaking her head. "You will not always

neglect the true sacrifice, to make one which God does not require."

Like one thrilled with a despairing ecstasy, Ezekiel Reed threw back his head, raised his hands clasped as in prayer, and — while his blue eyes beamed with a kind of fanatical triumph — replied, — "The sacrifices of God are a broken spirit: A broken and a contrite heart, O God, thou wilt not despise!"

CHAPTER XXXVII.

PLATO WYNNE.

Her Equivocal Majesty, the Queen of Diamonds, was hard to please. Sister women, consider her case. She had a fine house, a fine carriage, fine acquaintances, a fine Mystery to make her interesting enough for any woman's vanity, a fine freedom to do precisely as she pleased, and, above all, a fine husband, who remained exactly as fine after, as he had been before, their fine marriage. What more could mortal woman ask, to realize the highest boarding-school ideal of the hymeneal consummation? Yet was the Queen of Diamonds incorrigibly displeased with some imaginary imperfection of her lot; and sorely did she try the serene patience of His Glittering Majesty with her inexplicable murmuring.

It seemed, too, as though her unreasonable discontent became most importunate on occasions when every outward accessory of personal gratification appeared in climacteric combination for her especial glory. For instance: when, like the true queen of gems colorless, she was becomingly set in a luxurious sky-blue velvet cushion of a chair; the flaming blossoms of an inverted golden gas-tree giving a charming finish of light and shade to her enamel-relief of silken robe and ermine cloak; a wreath of gilded wheat modestly crowning her royalty of the hueless; and the more darkly lustrous king in obedient waiting.

What could there possibly be in a jewel of a situation like that, to trouble the female heart? If such an abstruse conundrum is susceptible of any answer at all, let us seek its development by giving action to the bright charade.

"My dear," remarked the appreciative King of Diamonds, smoothing gracefully with his fingers that portion of an immaculate black hat which extended above a neat band of crape, and gazing admiringly at his treasure, "you look remarkably well to-night. You will do more than usual credit to my taste at Mrs. Cornelius O' Doricourt Fish's reception. It is quite a sacrifice not to be able to go with you."

"You never go anywhere with me," returned the royal lady, languidly, "and must be resigned to that species of sacrifice by this time."

A tinge of refined melancholy was in the answer, "I cannot deny the imputation. Merely going after you to escort you home is an imperfect satisfaction; and it may not be in my power to do even that, to-night."

"Other men can find time to wait upon their wives, occasionally, Mr. Wynne."

"Try not to talk commonplace, my dear. Other men are less enslaved by business. Other men do not trust a wife so implicitly as I do mine."

He smiled graciously as he spoke; thereby expressing, in a quiet and pleasing manner, his gentlemanly satisfaction in possessing such a particularly trustworthy mate.

"And must this go on for ever?" asked Mrs. Wynne, her despondent tone and troubled look contrasting oddly with the courteous vein and placid demeanor of her lord.

"I am afraid not, my dear. If I could hope so, my happiness would be complete. A forever of such mutual confidence and smooth agreement would be delightful indeed."

The Effie of former days would scarcely have taken such a foil as that with mildness; but the Queen of Diamonds, in all her state, offered no sharper retort than a meek plea for better interpretation: "I mean, am I never to expect from you any more show of heart, any more sign of familiar regard? Must we always go on in this way, like two people acting cold, elaborate parts in some public play?"

"Why, what would you have, my dear?" queried Plato Wynne, in gentle surprise; the while he carelessly rested an elbow on the mantel and drummed softly upon the craped hat. "Doesn't it satisfy you to be treated like a princess, trusted like a saint, and honored like a goddess? This house yours, the carriage at the door yours, the servants yours, and myself ever yours devotedly."

"I want to be treated like a woman," she replied, with spirit, — "like a wife! Your confidence and liberality might as well be given to a costly horse, for all the human sensibility you recognize in me. Pride keeps me silent to it generally, but sometimes the unnatural mockery of your conduct makes even the pride of common self-respect in me a mockery, too."

Removing his arm from the mantel, Mr. Plato Wynne extended it at length, so that the single gem upon the little finger beamed and flashed again. "Did you ever notice," said he, as he mused upon it, "how this ring of mine catches fire in some oblique lights? Mr. Stiles, an imaginative young man whom I sometimes meet, calls it the midnight sun."

Ordinarily, the conversation would have ended here, with a cold request from Mrs. Wynne to be handed to her carriage, and a prompt and courtly obedience on the part of hers devotedly. To-night, however, she seemed to be meekly firm beyond all precedent.

"If there is anything, past or present, in my record with you, Plato, to justify your manner of treating me, let me know what it is. I have a right to ask that, at least; and I do ask it, here, to-night. I will not go out again amongst the contented wives of other men, until I know what I have done to be denied everything that is dear to a wife's heart."

"Madam," said the King of Diamonds, appearing to be in earnest for once, "you should be intelligent enough to know that the most intense love loses strength and refinement, both, by too much familiarity. It is the bane of ordinary domestic life, that husband and wife lose respect for each other by degrading affection into indignity, and love into mere license. Be wise for yourself, as you have been for several years, and permit me to apply the results of my own experience and observation in the manner best fitted to keep *our* mutual affection from any degeneration."

"Is this the language of affection, or, of contempt?" she asked; and her yearning gaze sought to read the truth in his imperturbable face.

"It is the language of true philosophy, Mrs. Wynne."

"Philosophy!" Bitterly. "Yes. A philosophy for ice, or marble, but not for creatures with hearts. If you yourself had ever felt one spark of human affection, Plato Wynne, you could not stand there and coldly tell a woman, that love lessens and dies by the very essential of its birth."

"The same wind that augments a spark into a flame may blow out the flame," said Plato Wynne.

Passionately the importunate wife threw back the ermine cloak from her shoulders, as though to breathe more freely; and cruelly bit her lips before suffering them to shape the rebellious answer, — "Your words to me, like your actions, are all unfeelingly studied. You cannot even speak passingly to me, without making me feel how unloved I am!"

"What a true Woman you are! Always preferring the chevalier to the sage; the foe who flatters to the friend who foils," said Plato Wynne.

"If your heart had ever been filled with love for any living thing, sir, you would know better what a true Woman is."

"To speak of filling the heart with love is paradoxically inaccurate; for love is the creation of the heart," said Plato Wynne.

Then, as though her hungry, beseeching look were intended to plead for another, he went on, — "Pardon me, though, my dear, for not remembering how well satisfied the first partner of my name and home was to have our married life one long, chivalrous courtship. That I treat you, my dear, precisely as I treated her, is the strongest proof of my admiration and comprehension of the nobler woman in you."

"Say at once that you have never felt anything for me but contemptuous pity," she cried, with the vehemence of mingled resentment and despair. "Say that you cared only to tame me, to break my spirit, and then use me as a living trophy of your triumph! Act the falsehood no longer, unless you would have me doubt that even the poor mercy of honest hatred will ever be mine."

"Doubt," said Plato Wynne, "is expectation in excess of probability."

"Not one honest, feeling word for me! Only the coolest sarcasm in return for the humblest entreaty. God knows how I have changed with circumstances; but you never change."

"Woman assimilates with all around her, is a component part of all about her. Man is a unit, complete in himself," said Plato Wynne.

As he stood there petting his hat before her in that luxurious room, the inclination of his gentlemanly head almost deferential, and the nice modulations of his soothing voice giving musical finish to each airy epigram, he looked handsomely wicked enough to have won the eternal adoration of any woman. He looked the incarnation of all that cows, commands, and universally infatuates women. He was an embodied jeer, insult, and stealthy lash, to his wife; yet that once proud, imperious, and tigerish woman loved him with all the invincible fidelity of a spaniel.

"Plato," she entreated, in a voice full of plaintive propitiation, "do not let us separate to-night without hope. To show my love for you, I have forgotten God, nature, and all the pride that makes a woman more than a slave. You are the only man I ever loved —"

"Except one Mr. Glibun," he interposed, smilingly.

"You are the only man I ever loved," she repeated, wildly. "I have sacrificed kindred, conscience, and my soul's salvation for you; yet you refuse me even the knowledge of that further crime for which I am so pitilessly condemned. O my husband!" she moaned, sinking from the chair to her knees, in an irrepressible agony of supplication, "give me some little kindness to save my heart from breaking! Have pity, have pity, upon the worst and most miserable of women!"

"Madam!" exclaimed her scandalized master; "are you a lady, — are you my wife, — or an actress! Rise instantly, and prepare to go with me to your carriage."

She silently obeyed; and the pale misery of her face seemed to touch suddenly some long-forgotten, tender emotion in him; for he added, in softer tones, —

"My dear, you should believe me when I tell you that I know of no possible difference between us. I know how unalterably true you are, and always have been, to me; and it is because I value you the more, that I am jealous of the least vulgar love-making which should put our relations in jeopardy, for one moment, of the coarse vicissi-

tudes of common passion. Now draw on your hood, my dear, and let me escort you down."

She threw a rigolette hood over her flaxen hair, and softly insinuated her hand under his arm, as though she would coax him by that action to melt still more. Looking over his shoulder at her, he seemed to encourage the notion with his eyes, and inclined his head to speak again.

"You have been very free with me to-night, my dear; and although our delay has left me scarcely a moment to spare, I think I must return the compliment before resigning you to Mrs. Fish. Would you really like to know who I love best of all the world?"

No spoken reply could have been so expressive as that pressure of her cheek against his shoulder.

"Let me show you, then."

He led her, willingly and wonderingly, to the front of a large mirror on the farther wall, and paused where both their figures found full reflection on the polished glass. For an instant she stared vacantly at the picture; but quickly the light and color of an exultant anticipation came to eye and cheek.

"The one whom I love best of all the world," said Plato Wynne, very deliberately, evidently bent on dallying with the sweet confession as long as possible, and affectionately trying the nerves of her whose beating heart became more riotous every second, "*the one* (her eyes were upon the mirror) *whom I love best* (his right hand, on which gleamed the Midnight Sun, had commenced moving toward her in a slow sweep) *of all the world is*" — his eyes sought hers in the glass, and the hand touched — HIMSELF!

The heartless, cold-blooded mockery of the thing would have fired the soul of the most pusillanimous slave; but hers it apparently froze. She mechanically withdrew her hand from his arm, looked him full in the face, with an expression in which some new feeling and resolve grew to icy maturity in an instant, and left him in the midst of his most charming smile.

At the street-door, however, he had overtaken her; and to lead her by the lily-white hand from thence to an elegant carriage at the curb, hand her into the vehicle with every suggestion of the most exquisite fragility, and dismiss lady, coach, and all, with a kiss and waft of the hand, were the parting devoirs of the King of Diamonds.

So, the queen being gone and the palace desolate, what better could his most philosophical majesty do than at once proceed, himself, to the important cabinet business in order for that evening? Unto this high duty, then, he promptly turned his steps, and was presently leisuring elegantly down Broadway, at that easy, medium pace between hastening and lounging, which none but your true New Yorker can artistically achieve. In the brilliant lights of the retail

26

and drug stores, he was a figure fit for a ball. — In the shadows of wholesale stores and dwellings, he was an unexceptionable gentleman out for an evening walk. Many of the other strollers of the street mused upon him respectfully, as tacitly according him distinguished position in society, and vaguely conjecturing where they could have seen, or figured to themselves, somebody looking like him; but the few more fortunate passers who had, like himself, a certain fresh, elastic air about them, as though night were their proper season of rejuvenation, indicated by nods their clearer knowledge of his illustrious identity. Thus, the admired of all, — the recognized of a select few, — did the King pass on, rich in the quiet enjoyment of that refined privacy of person which is so seldom allowed to eminence. Thus could he appear in public, on the most public street of his dominions, without suffering the rude stare and criticism of the vulgar multitude. For it only needed the announcement, this is Plato Wynne! to have brought scores of thousands out, like magic, to wittingly behold but once a celebrity of whom every man, woman, and child in the great city had heard and read countless mysterious things. Had he not developed, from the standard hero of midnight Fortune's every romantic legend, into the great Demolition rival of the mighty Cringer? Was it not common for the most matter-of-fact knowing ones to say that Plato Wynne carried New York City in his breeches' pocket, and would carry the State there, too, after the next senatorial election! Yet, was it the anomalous and inexpressible blessing of this master of pecunious and political destinies to enjoy wonderful immunity from the recognition of the street rabble, and be able to come and go as he chose without being pointed or gaped at.

Serenely conscious, then, of his inestimable advantage over other popular lions, Mr. Wynne complacently pursued his way to where the temptations of a certain genteel cross-street successfully protested against any further concession of the royal progress to Broadway. Turning the corner thereat, he went dimly down several stately blocks of domiciliary gloom, and finally rang the bell at the door of a residence beautifully respectable and private. Scarcely did his gloved hand relinquish the pull, when the door opened noiselessly into the most respectable of vestibules, and an aged African, soberly attired, bowed-in the coming guest. "I always know your ring, Mr. Wynne," observed the venerable black, as in explanation of some ignored formality; to which Mr. Wynne airily responded by slipping a piece of silver into the man's hand, and striding leisurely past him to the hall.

Several rooms seemed to open from either side of this hall, which, from its width and double staircase, evidently represented a consolidation of two houses in one; and, after resigning his hat to the servant, the guest passed into one on the left, where some six or eight gentlemen in flashing attire were enjoying the delights of conversation and wine. Panelled walls, frescoed ceiling, and gaudy furniture matched well with these elegant creatures, through the midst of whom Mr. Wynne passed, with slight bows of recognition, to an apartment similarly garnished beyond. Here there was but one occupant, — an indolent young exquisite with a tremendous head of black curls, — who no sooner caught sight of the intruder than he lazily raised himself from his sprawling attitude on a divan, and came forward.

"How are you, Vane?" said Mr. Wynne, carelessly.

"Oh, I'm well enough," returned the dandy, rather sullenly, and then added; "you're after Cringer, I suppose."

"I am one of a party to meet General Cringer here to-night; if that's what you mean."

"Yes, of course, that's it. You take stock in the bank?"

"I bank with Mr. O'Murphy."

"Then good-by, General, with two such old heads against you! You'll be plucked to the last pin-feather; and then the Senate for the O'Murphy, and a new set of pearls for the Queen of Diamonds!" Mr. Vane, who seemed slightly flushed with drink, said this quite boisterously and impudently.

"Your champagne wit improves, Vane," answered Mr. Wynne, with the contemptuous toleration of one who never allowed himself to be ruffled by a drunken man. "And now, if you'll stand away from that door a moment, I'll try to find my party."

"Here they are, for you!" cried Vane, unceremoniously throwing said door open, and facing the company beyond it. "Gentlemen, the King of Diamonds approaches!"

The announcement was not quite so obsequious as it sounded; in fact, there was more or less ostentatious irony in the exaggerated court-etiquette of the self-appointed usher; but Mr. Wynne tolerated the unfortunate's infirmity as before, and passed through the door with a countenance supremely tranquil, as usual.

The apartment thus entered might have appeared to an unaccustomed eye like the directors' room of some flourishing bank or insurance company; for down the centre extended a long, narrow table, covered with green cloth, on either side of which, in easy postures, sat a small party of well-dressed men. A beaufet at the remote end of the scene bristled with glasses, bottles in ice, and two colored attendants; but if this looked unbusiness-like, it was balanced by a huge iron safe, all silver-plate and bronze-relief, which stood against the wall, near a fireplace. General Cringer, too, would have passed for the most benignant of bank-presidents; Judge O'Toole, despite his bushy, red hair and high-boned, red face, realized the average pigheaded director; and Mr. Benton Stiles, with soap-locks, forehead-curl, and locket-ring, typified the promising young cashier. When, however, the aforesaid unaccustomed eye reached the Honorable Mealy O'Murphy, who sat opposite the General, it might have winked undecidedly. Indeed, the honorable gentleman's bullet-head, slightly flattened at the top; short, wiry, yellow hair; wedge-shaped, corrugated nose; scrubby, yellow mustache, and squinting, blue eyes, did not — would not — suggest anything more bank-like than that species of bank visitor against whom private watchmen and unpickable locks are ingeniously employed. There were present, also, two other gentlemen, named respectively Dodge and Bilk, who were too blinking about the eyes and friezy about their costumes to set a heavy depositor or insurer entirely at ease. Still, the room and occupants had a suggestion of accumulated capital, and a kind of corporation air of "Company."

"Glad to see you, Wynne, me dairlin'," cried Mr. O'Murphy, whose speech was touched with the brogue of the governing class. "Vane, my rayspicts."

The other gentlemen were equally polite; bottles and glasses were summoned from the beaufet, and the whole party became promptly convivial: that is to say, they all sipped champagne as though the world had no other business for them; and the congressional host proposed a toast.

"Gents," said the O'Murphy, grasping his glass very much as another man might have grasped a knife, "we're not all exactly agrade in politics, — worse luck to it! and meself, the judge, and Mr. Wynne will shortly have the misfortune to tayche General Cringer and the black naygur party that the man who slathered the 'Hunky Boy' aint to be baiten aisy for senator. But there's wan toast we can all drink without pretince, and it's that I'm about to offer, — Here's to Ould Ireland!"

The sentiment was honored with all the enthusiasm consistent with refined breeding, Judge O'Toole and Mr. Bilk actually shaking hands across the table.

"You hit it there, exactly, O'Murphy," observed General Cringer, in a benignant burst of congeniality. "It is to Old Ireland that we all look for more or less aid in the facilitation of good government; and I have no hesitation in admitting that a proper amount judiciously invested in Irishmen, about election time, will often materially assist a man to that political elevation for which his genius and incorruptibility make him eligible. Mr. Stiles, you may be able to recall that passage from my recent editorial in the *Morning Dog*, which refers to the eminent services of our adopted citizens."

"That passage, sir," said Mr. Stiles, in deep tones, "has rung in my ears ever since I first wrote — I mean, read it. If the Demolition party would indeed show us where their great strength — their whole strength — in this city lies, let them frankly call the roll of every tenement house, rum shop, and gambling hell —"

"No, sir! No, sir! That's not the — that's not it!" blurted the General, in great haste.

"Oh! I know now," returned Mr. Stiles, with perfect composure. "You mean the other one. The inexhaustible pertinacity with which the noble-hearted fellow-countrymen of Emmet and O'Connell have combated for freedom in their own down-trodden island is an earnest of what we may expect from them when the impending election for alderman of the Sixty-sixth ward calls upon them to choose between the staunch champion of freedom to all men, and the miserable parasite of human slavery. Richly manured with Irishmen, the glorious tree of liberty will yet —"

"Yes, yes. That'll do. Thank you, Mr. Stiles," struck in the General, rather nervously. "I only wished to remind you, gentlemen, that I have always spoken well of Old Ireland; and have, in fact, been upon the point of joining the Catholic Church, myself, on several occasions when elections have looked a little shaky for us."

"Sure, Cringer," remarked Judge O'Toole, who had just changed off from champagne to something stronger, "it's but little more manuring there'll be for *your* three of liberty, if it's Ebullitionist you've turned. Didn't you facilitate our frind Mealy, here, all the way from a twinty-fut ring to Congress? And now ye're opposin' him for the Sinate wid a naygur-worshipping crayture named Crow!"

"My dear judge." returned the great Cringer, meekly, "I'm but a humble individual, and must really decline to be invested with so much importance as my friends and the journals like to give me in politics. If I do occasionally lend the best efforts of a strictly private citizen to facilitate the political success of a valued friend, I do no more than any other private citizen might do under similar circumstances. If, on the score of honest conviction, — you see I am perfectly frank with you and O'Murphy, — if, on the score of honest (and, let me add, recent) conviction, I feel bound to side with my friend, the Honorable James Crow, in the next contest at Albany, I do no more than Mr. Wynne, also an old friend, is pledged to do for my equally good friend, Mr. O'Murphy. And, by the way," he added, turning affably to the last-named gentleman, whose squint had begun to sharpen somewhat malignantly, and who evidently needed a little soothing, "I can hardly understand what temptation there can be in further political turmoil for our friend Mealy, when he is already in Congress, and owns such a sumptuous home as this."

"Well, then, I'll tell yez," exclaimed Mr. O'Murphy, quickly taking him up. "I want to get joost as high as I can, and become as great as I can, for two raisons: First, because I want to show that I'm nayther a

Yankee nor a naygur; and, second, because I want to lave the purest and most illoostrious name I can to— my — kid." Here the honorable gentleman's voice became tremulous with emotion; and, as he went on, his corrugated nose worked like a dog's. "Belave me or not, gintlemen, it's not at all for me own sake that I'd put up me hands against any cove, even for the Presidency. I'd sooner go out again with that baste, the 'llunky boy,' than be referee of all Ameriky. But people be's saying that my past life wasn't good enough; that a game man in the ring is but a blackguard out of it; and I want to be Mr. Senator O'Murphy joost for the sake of my kid, gintlemen, my poor, innocent little kid. that's upstairs this minute with his own mother."

Who could help being moved by this exquisite touch of paternal love and self-abnegation? General Cringer surveyed the backs of his hands with watery eyes, Messieurs Dodge and Bilk exchanged glances of the deepest pathos with Judge O'Toole, and Mr. Stiles was heard to murmur softly, —

" Men the most infamous are fond of fame,
　And those who fear not guilt, yet start at shame."

Throughout the conversation Mr. Wynne had been very reserved and quiet, nor did he betray visible agitation now. Perhaps a galling consciousness of his American birth left him not enough confidence to join verbally in Irish affairs of state; or, perhaps he was thinking of other things altogether. At any rate, Mr. Allyn Vane, who was none the better for recent draughts, seemed disposed to treat his abstraction at last with a direct personal appeal.

"I say, Wynne," said he, "you ought to appreciate O'Murphy's feelings as a father, if any one could. You've worn crape for a child of yours ever since I first knew you. That's something like the feelings of a parent."

The ribald tone and offensive manner of the speaker could not have been lost upon their object; but, with no other sign of anger, or even attention, than a certain fiery flash in his cloudy black eyes, the King of Diamonds turned unheedingly to Mr. Benton Stiles with a sprightly question, —

"Have you ever found out anything more, Mr. Stiles, about that mysterious Mr. Mugses, who was so kind as to die and leave you such an easy berth in the custom house?"

"Nothing that I can fairly hitch to, your maj—I mean Mr. Wynne," responded Mr. Stiles, in manifest confusion; for the identity and antecedents of his immediate predecessor in the customs were really the great puzzle of his life. "I've been told that Mugses had something to do with a bark; and I've thought, from that, he might have been in the seafaring line before he got the office."

"A fair inference," said Plato Wynne, smiling.

And so the talk went on until midnight, wine flowing, political arguments intensifying, buzzing and exclamatory sounds coming more frequently from other rooms, and distant stony detonations indicating that occasional carriages were arriving with new guests at the street door. When midnight came, there came, also. to this particular room, a gorgeous youth with kinky black hair, heavy lips, and flat nose, who swaggered in without removing his slouched black hat, and looked around upon the company with eyes dull and bloodshot.

"Faith, here's Cutter," cried Mr. O'Murphy, recognizing this hopeful, and rising suddenly from a profound disquisition on some State topic with General Cringer and Judge O"Toole. "Now, gintlemen, let's have a little diversion after so much gab. Hastings, me darlin', joost be sated here at the lay-out, and deal for the boys until I'm ready to relave you."

"Nothing easier, I reckon." replied Hastings Cutter, tossing his hat to a waiter, and proceeding to the central seat just vacated by the host.

With this new advent and movement the tone of the whole scene changed, and lost every suggestion of banking, save such as might nominally refer to a famous royal house of Egypt. With wonderful celerity the thirteen cards constituting the suite of clubs, were distributed on the long green table, — six at intervals down either side, and one at the head, — by Messieurs Dodge and Bilk, who unexpectedly came out as a couple of croupiers. With equal rapidity Mr. Cutter presented a full pack of cards in full shuffle, while a great heap of ivory cheques appeared on the table at his right hand, and a bright silver card-box before him. Buy your cheques, gentlemen. — one dollar up to a thousand. Shuffle and cut the pack. Put it into the box. Put your stake upon your card on the table. Deal. — one right, one left, etc., and — the bank wins a hundred at the start!

There was magic for you! and executed in about the time it takes to tell of it. Alas, for the morality of an humble individual, a private citizen, a friendly facilitator, the great General Cringer was the first man in that glaring room to put a cheque upon a card; and, of course, the first to lose; while even the King of Diamonds and Congressman O'Murphy stood apart together in apparently hesitating consultation, though ever with an eye upon the table.

"Judge," — exclaimed General Cringer, pushing one of the croupiers aside with no gentle hand, that he might get at the chief ornament of the bench, — "Judge, you must lend me a thousand! I'll make, or break somebody before I give it up this time!"

"Sure I will," was the prompt answer.

"Make it twenty-five hundred!"

"Here's the stuff."

That some desired point had been gained here was at once evident; for Mr. O'Murphy and Plato Wynne now advanced with alacrity to the table; the former unceremoniously taking the dealer's place, and the latter standing close beside him.

"Wynne takes twenty-five per cent. of the bank, gentlemen," announced the host, hoarsely. "Is that agreeable?"

No objections were heard from those appealed to; and then the "diversion" was in full tide.

More than the vicissitudes of money infatuated those men. Supremacy in the rich and powerful Empire State was involved, if not staked, at that table; and each side, with its principal and satellites, dared everything to win the final triumph. Wine was drank and cigars smoked, with no more sensibility on the part of drinker and smoker than an engine feels when water and coal are added to its heat and fume; but the eyes and cheeks of the players radiated a subtle excitement which, as the small hours passed away, seemed to permeate all the other rooms of the house, and, from thence, the very streets. Games elsewhere languished, and ended, and the gamesters came gliding, one by one, to the table of State. In places all over the town, where lights never went out from evening until morning, men whispered vague rumors of the great game, without being able to tell where they had heard them, or why they should be so. Dawn came, and slowly lightened into day; and when the full sunlight stole warmer and warmer into the chamber of fate, it found the gilt chandeliers still ablaze, wine and smoke still coming, and General Cringer and his friends still mad with the entertainment of O'Murphy and his partners. Then the story started afresh outside; flying in and out of the newspaper offices; through the courts of justice, and about the corners of Wall Street. Cringer was ruined, said one; the bank was broken, said another; and still all was unreliable, contradictory rumor.

Noon. Afternoon. Evening. Midnight again. General Cringer the winner of one hundred thousand dollars!

"That's the ind of it!" shouted the O'Murphy, thundering a frightful oath, and sweeping cards and cheques to the floor.

"One hour more," pleaded the great Cringer, his stock all awry, his iron-gray wreath of hair in damp spikes, his eyes swollen and red, and his entire appearance that of a scarecrow.

"Not another minute!" roared the equally disordered banker. "Bad luck to it if I don't throw up the sponge dead bate!"

They were a hard-looking set of beings, with their bleared eyes, streaked faces, soiled dresses, and twitching hands; a ghastly and terrible crew to be seen through a tobacco cloud, — all save Plato Wynne.

For the King of Diamonds, like a sleek, imperturbable creature from some other sphere, looked cold and glossy, as though he had but just come in and found the scene not very interesting. To be sure, his faultless beard appeared blacker from the barely apparent fading of his face; but there was perfect composure in his voice, as in his manner, when he addressed the importunate victor.

"General Cringer," said he, and drew a lilac kid over the Midnight Sun, "be satisfied with crippling Mr. O'Murphy's bank and winning from me about all that I had to lose."

"Pooh! pooh!" was the reply.

"And let me add, sir, that the simulated good-will between you and me, as politicians, may as well end at once. This is not the last time we shall oppose each other, and I purpose, in future, to tolerate no pretence with you."

"Meet me at Albany!" returned General Cringer, after the style of a celebrated Roman ghost.

Deigning no retort to this significant summons, the King of Diamonds was turning to leave the room, when Vane, looking reckless and wild as any sickening reveller, literally thrust himself upon him, from the crowd at the table, and said, with an oath, "Here, I want a word with you, Wynne. I want to remind you that you've still got at least one piece of property to lose."

"What do you mean, Mr. Vane?"

"I mean your wife!"

In an instant Allyn Vane was senseless on his back upon the floor, his face terribly gashed, from eye to lip, with a glass goblet.

The occurrence was the more remarkable, because Plato Wynne, like any other perfect gentleman, had never been known to lose his temper — away from home.

CHAPTER XXXVIII.

I BECOME AN EDITOR.

WHETHER Mr. Terky did, or did not, confide to his wife the whole truth respecting his crime, I could never discover. Mrs. Terky's unbounded violence of grief at the funeral of their poor little child seemed, at first, to indicate that a still harsher pang than that of bereavement augmented her sorrow into frenzy; but when, in response to Mr. Coffin's condolence, she suspended her transports long enough to complain bitterly against Cummin & Tryon for discharging her husband at such a time, there was much reason to doubt her knowledge of the immediate cause of the discharge. Positive as this latter circumstance would superficially appear in proof of a negative, it actually amounted to barely more than a chance for diversity of conclusions in the case of Mrs. Terky. From past experience of her curious incapacity for any really intelligent construction of her husband's acts, or necessities, I was prepared to find her indiscriminately justifying his miserable offence against honesty, and, thereby, aggravating a remorse which might have been soothed by a more regretful sympathy. Rarely do our warmest friends, of either sex, appreciate the inestimable blessings of that frank common sense, which openly enters with us into a just estimate of our errors, before softening into the practical sympathy of co-operative schemes for their repair. Mrs. Terky possessed not such appreciation; and, of course, if her husband had really imparted to her the full extent of his misfortune, she had not proved capable of yielding him the only true consolation for the erring. If, on the other hand, he had simply acquainted her with his loss of employment, it was equally sure that her wholesale denunciation of his late employers had given him anything but solace. So, from the frenzied anguish of the bereaved mother, and the settled gloom of the dishonored father, I could infer no satisfactory decision in the matter.

The most absurd and generous of lace-salesmen not only redeemed the stolen goods from pawn and restored them to their shelves, but also went around amongst his business-acquaintances and procured subscriptions of enough money to carry the entry-clerk and his wife to a far-western city.

"I shall miss your intelligent family hearth," said he, shaking the limp hand of his despondent friend; "I shall be as lonely as a word without a rhyme; but I want you to get west by the fastest train. Go there; commence at the foot of the ladder again; and don't bother about my little loan until you're strongly on your feet once more."

"That will never be," returned Mr. Terky, without a ray of hope in look or tone. "I've sunk too far for that. I'll take any work I can find; I'll do the best I can; but I've no more heart for anything."

"And I've no heart, either!" rejoined Mr. Coffin, with energetic melancholy. "My heart was withered and lost years ago, Job Terky, under circumstances which had better not be recalled! But, have I given up? Have I tamely sunk from an intellectual being to the dark depths of inanition and despair? No, sir! I have borne up against circumstances; and that's what you must do. Be a man. Exercise mind-play; look your errors and troubles in the face, and swear to yourself that you'll deal in better property hereafter."

The fine manliness showing through all Mr. Coffin's sentimental self-consciousness would have been some inspiration to a nature possessing one nerve of strength; and even Job Terky took at least a momentary hope from its contact. Very quickly, however, the dark spell deepened again; and it was with the air of a man lost to every manly emotion that the fallen clerk called upon me for final aid.

It was on the night prior to his departure for the west, and my removal to lodgings in Warren Street, that he entered my old room and sat down upon the edge of the small trunk I was packing.

"Glibun," he said, biting his nails, "they're giving you the same salary they gave me, I suppose, now that you've got my place."

"Yes," I answered, "but I shan't stay there after you leave here."

"It's considerable more for you than it was for me."

Evidently he did not care to have me look at him, so I kept my eyes upon my packing while making the remark he apparently desired to hear, —

"It certainly is more for me than it was for you. Mr. Terky; and I still wish that you would let me hand it over to you, for this one week, at least."

"Can you spare it?"

"Easily as not. I don't feel comfortable at all in keeping it, and wish you would take it."

"Not all?"

"Yes, all of it, Mr. Terky. It won't cost me much to live, where I'm going; and what I get each week, after you go, until I find some other place, will pay my way well enough."

"Avery," said he, in a low, tremulous tone, "I'm ashamed to tell you that I have come upstairs to ask for the money. I know how mean, how contemptible I must appear in your eyes, to take advantage, as I do, of your generosity; but after a man has done what I have, he may as well give up everything like self-respect. I've begged and borrowed of everybody I know, and here I find myself without five dollars beyond what our railroad tickets will cost us to-morrow. Lend me what you can spare, and I'll send it back to you as soon as I can earn as much."

I tried not to think it mean; I tried to regard it as only the bitter compulsion of his necessity; but, try as I would, contempt got the better of my every charitable feeling toward him. I had drawn my week's allowance that day, and now handed the whole to him, save one dollar, which last I felt it but prudent to retain. And this money, as I afterwards learned, was expended in mourning handkerchiefs, mourning note-paper, mourning collars, and such other little elegancies of grief as the mother of lost Tootsy said that she *must* have before going amongst strangers.

In reckless defiance of store rules, Mr. Coffin and I left business at an early hour on the following afternoon to accompany the luckless pair to the Albany boat, and were deeply affected by the terms of gratitude lavished on us by both husband and wife. The former told us that he would never forget our kindness to a ruined drudge, and the latter pressed us to come and see them as soon as they were settled in a house of their own.

We stood talking with them, as cheerfully as we could, until the last bell warned those who were not passengers to leave the boat.

Then came a hasty farewell and a precipitate flight of Mr. Coffin and me to the pier. The latter movement had to be executed across a sort of extemporized bridge, in the very middle of which we ran blindly against a belated couple who were as blindly rushing on board. There was no time for apologies, but, as we made way for the tardy arrivals, I noticed that the gentleman was very fat and had an odd appearance about the eyes, and that Mr. Coffin reeled away from him and his fair companion like a very sick inebriate.

"What is the matter, sir?" I cried, in some alarm, when the lace-salesman came to a full stop on the very edge of the pier, and grasped one of my arms with a grip that made the bones ache.

"That was the — the fiend in human form!" he gasped, staring fixedly into the crowd on the now moving boat.

"You don't mean that fat gentleman with the lady?"

"Yes-s-s. Him-m-m!" came with a hiss and a groan from his colorless lips.

"What ails his eyes?" asked I, awkwardly.

"One of them is a glass one!" moaned the lace-salesman, spasmodically grasping either lappel of my coat, and commencing to choke me with my own garment; the while his face worked convulsively, and his inflamed eyes followed the receding steamer.

Then I remembered the terrible romance of this man's life — the rejection of Intellect for Mammon. I also remembered, however, that I was being slowly suffocated; and, with an indignant jerk, I freed myself from his hold and started to leave him. Recalled to his sober senses by my action, he came after me at once, and it was only after we had left the river several blocks behind us, that he summoned sufficient composure to speak again, —

"Excuse my conduct just now, Glibun. I was excited. Did you notice how She looked?"

"You mean the lady with that gentleman?"

"Yes. Did she seem happy? Was she much agitated? Don't be afraid to tell me, Glibun; I can bear it now."

"Why," said I, "if I'm not mistaken, she looked remarkably well, and was sucking an orange."

With a wheezing sigh Mr. Coffin relapsed into silence, and where our ways parted he wrung my hand in token of his heart's deep anguish.

Life in lodgings is, at best, but little more than rank vegetation; and, for an untrained youth like me, just about to undergo compound reaction from the strongest excitement, it was scarcely less unwholesome to the mind than solitary imprisonment. The last illusion of a home — poor as it was — vanished with the Terkys, in whose departure I not only lost my sole familiar companionship, but also that active sympathy for the trials of others which is the best

possible opiate for our own. Thrown back upon myself again, and with nought but self to care for, I reverted to what Allyn Vane and Noah Trust had told me.

What an unhappy fate is mine, thought I, to have nothing to look back upon but desertion and degradation, and nothing to look forward to but drudgery and disgrace! My father a criminal, and, probably, an inmate of some prison by this time; she who stood to me in place of a mother, the confederate of a notorious gamester and politician. To remember the only home I have ever known, is but to recall scenes fraught with everything dark, unkind, and unnatural. To contemplate the future is but to anticipate a life's hardest toils crowned with a heritage of infamy. For whose unparalleled sin was my infancy made an exile from all parental affection; my school-days a preparation for murder; my boyhood a hunted existence with vagabonds and felons; my youth a time to drudge for shopkeepers, and to hear that the one solitary hope of my life was the most miserable of mistakes? Now I could understand the full meaning of Vane's story of himself; the loss of self-respect following a loss of filial reverence, and the loss of all incentive to good following a loss of self-respect.

Thus did I soliloquize over my condition, until all honorable energy seemed to die within me, and I became recklessly demoralized. After returning from the store one evening, in a very paroxysm of sullen discontent, I endeavored to find savage comfort in penning for the lately-neglected *Sunday Tap* a sketch of the most malevolently tragic description. Had I succeeded in that intent, the more or less thousands of tapsters would have revelled in such a triumphant combination of blood and thunder as seldom emanates from the most sanguinary quill; but, to my great surprise, the very first sentence insisted upon taking a grotesque turn, and, in five minutes, I was fluently spinning out rollicking nonsense by the yard! Absurdities crowded into my brain so fast that the words to express them were as snails to lightning. My mind took on a tempest of incongruous perceptions and conceptions; my brow and cheeks glowed with the fiercest fever of composition; I shook with laughter over the thick-crowding, ludicrous conceits, before my teeming pen could be delivered of them; and when I finally turned the concluding paragraph with an amazing joke, and sat back in my chair to take breath, my ecstasy was that of the angels!

Ah, dear, dear, what an incomprehensible fit it was! What an inconsistency and a discovery it was! To think that I must be so miserable, before I could be so merry! To think that I must be the forlornest of young wretches, before I could know myself to be the most promising of jesters! Hamlet, with the skull of Yorick in his hand!

My prelude to sleep, on that glorified night, was a hot delirium over the question of what leading journal, or magazine, should have that miracle of humor; for the *Tap* sank as the sketch rose in my estimation; and, in suffocating dreams, I subsequently beheld myself on horseback, leading an acclaiming populace, under a triumphal arch bearing the name of " M. T. HEAD;" the while fair women leaned from a thousand windows and balconies, each languishing for such a lord as myself.

It was a blank and stunning thing, to be thrown by such a thoroughbred nightmare as that. It was dreadful to emerge from that triumphal arch into the narrowest and most tumbled of cot-beds. But more disgusting than all was the waking to a recollection of what I had written, as so much intolerable silliness, and to a degrading doubt whether even the *Sunday Tap* would gratuitously accept such puerile trash.

Yes; with the dawn came, first a chilling renewal of all previous discontent, and then so sharp a heartsickness with my " humorous production," that I was actually ashamed and afraid to read over a single line of the manuscript. Desperation alone nerved me to enclose the latter in a wrapper, and address it to the *Tap*.

Leaving the explanation of this intellectual phenomenon to those who are dexterous in mental philosophy, let me pass over my disconsolate breakfast at a retired ordinary, and present myself at the desk of entry, on Cummin & Tryon's cellar floor. Without opposition, I had succeeded to poor Job's ancient position, and even underwent the astounding sensation of having fifty cents added to the standard weekly yield of that clerkship; but from the day of my predecessor's fall I had been resolved to stay there only so long as no other means of support should offer. I hated the place with all the more unction, because I no longer knew any tangible justification for an instinct above it; and, with the thought that any Irish porter on the premises might take rank above me on the score of social antecedents, came a general angry defiance of the whole concern, from which I did not exclude even Mr. Collin, nor Noah Trust. The two latter did not fail to make friendly advances for several days; but my surly rebuffs finally took natural effect, and I was left without a friend in the store, at last. Having gained the unenviable result, it proved so far from satisfactory, that I grew the more morose upon it; and, in the end, my bad temper brought a crisis. One afternoon, about a week after my last literary freak, one of the salesmen came down to " call off" a bill, and ventured some impatient remark about my tantalizing deliberation in selecting a pen for the entry.

" I shall take as much time as I please," said I; " and if you don't like my style you can enter for yourself."

Accustomed as he was to finding the most servile obedience at that desk, the salesman opened his eyes very widely and flushed scarlet.

" I don't want any of your impertinence!" he returned in angry surprise. " Attend to your business."

"And I won't take any of *your* impertinence," was my rejoinder, so fiercely given that the man took a quick backward step as though anticipating a blow. " You can make your own entry, now, for I won't write a line of it."

" I'll report to the firm!" he cried, aghast.

" And just report my resignation with it," cried I, hurling away the pen and snatching my hat from its hook. " I've taken orders from a parcel of counter-jumpers long enough."

In the full whirl of my wrath I brushed past him so violently that he nearly lost his feet, and was upstairs through the salesroom, and into the street, before he could have fairly realized what had happened. I recall the event, myself, with no little shame; but, with the dissipation of the hope that my father was a Gentleman had disappeared nearly all my own qualification for that title.

I had not premeditated such an abrupt conclusion of my clerkship, and experienced considerable embarrassment, after my rage died away, in finding myself thus suddenly upon the town, as it were. Curiously enough, though, the very magnitude of my mishaps was their redeeming characteristic. In the consciousness that one's troubles, however produced, have got to the worst at last, there is unmistakable relief. And if to this can be added a good, hearty belief that no other human being was ever so frightfully afflicted, the first principle of consolation is already at work. Intense realization of an extreme, and earnest conviction of being isolated to some degree in that extreme, are necessary elements of all real power, whether over ourselves, or mankind in general; so, in the fancied extreme of my misfortunes, and my belief in their lack of all parallel, I found a cool and novel ability to face and handle the worst.

Nerved with a bold resolution to try a new field, I devoted a whole evening to the composition of the most humorous paper my melancholy could devise, and an early hour of the morrow found me on my way to the office of the *Weekly Earthquake*.

This spirited " periodical," be it known, had been enlivening the advertising columns of the *Daily Bread*, the *Morning Dog* and the *Morning Cat*, for several weeks past, with exclamatory announcements of its varied improvements under the new proprietorship of one Easton Sharp, Esq. " While it will be our special aim," said the print, " to blend literature with news, and adapt our columns to the illustration of the whole world's choicest reading, we shall not fail to invite the occasional co-operation of native talent in making a truly national newspaper. Young American Writers, of genius, who may desire opportunities of communicating with the public, with a view to gaining compensation for their efforts at some future time, will find the *Weekly Earthquake* an efficient aid to eminence." Encouraged by these words to try my fortune, and being anxious to rise, if possible, above the general literary level of the *Tap*, I proceeded audaciously to the editorial rooms of Mr. Easton Sharp, prepared to substitute unlimited assurance for my past humility.

The last refuge of native talent was located in the narrowest and dirtiest of downtown streets, and up the shakiest possible Parnassus of slippery stairs; but too sturdy was I, in my new mood, to be repelled by outward trifles, and there was none of Dante's sensitiveness about my strides up the stranger steps of Mr. Sharp's palace of genius. Guided by a battered tin sign, on a door too old to remember when it was last painted, I entered a dreary den on the third floor and found myself close upon a small and very rickety counter, whereon a well-inked youth of direful aspect was giving edges of paste to some hundreds of newspaper-wrappers for the mail. Behind this youth, the office was divided into small compartments by means of unpainted boards reaching to the ceiling, and through the narrow doorway of each I detected portions of a desk with a pair of human legs beneath. My request to see the editor attracted a brilliant smile, quickly succeeded by a dense frown, from the paster; and it was only after several curious sliding movements along his side of the counter that he thickly enunciated the following question, —

"Yeditor?"

"That's what I said, sir."

"Oh! you mean th' yeditor? Yes. Ver' well. In there."

An unsteady wave of the paste-brush over his shoulder left me at liberty to select either compartment I chose, and, passing around the counter and through a strong whiff of gin, I bolted unceremoniously into the nearest one. The occupant looked up from his writing, and electrified me with the sharp black eyes, furzy black head, and laughing mouth of my old school-mate, Will Dewitt.

"Willie, how are you?" exclaimed I, impetuously grasping his hand. "What on earth are you doing here?"

"I'm pretty well," said he, eying me in great confusion, "and I'm wondering where I've seen you before."

"You've seen me in the neighborhood of a shell-house," said I, "where it was the custom for the curtain to drop when the play was done, and to roll punctually up again when another play begun."

"Avery Glibun!" ejaculated Dewitt, jumping up and throwing both arms around my neck. "Why, old boy, I didn't know just what to take you for at first. Sit down on that pile of papers, and let's have a good look at you. How did you happen to find me?"

"I've stumbled upon you accidentally," I answered, seating myself on a pile of old papers beside the desk. "Are you editor here?"

"Only dramatic editor. I've done the theatrical since Sharp bought the paper. I did some of the other departments, too, under the old management; but Sharp wants to make a feature of theatricals now, so I attend to them alone."

"Who'd have thought, Dewitt, when you and I were at Oxford Institute, that we should ever meet again in such a place as this!"

"I say, old boy," cried Dewitt, with renewed vivacity, "what was the row between you and old 'Rufus' in that vacation? You managed to break up the school, we heard, and Rufus shot himself, they told us."

I satisfied his curiosity, so far as I could do so without telling too much about myself; and took the first opportunity, after his wonder and speculations had sufficiently expended themselves, to change the subject.

"I'm heartily glad to meet you again, Willie," I said; "but never dreamed of doing so when I came in here. The fact is, I've got a sketch to sell, and I thought it might suit the *Earthquake.*"

Dewitt's countenance fell at the announcement, and his reply was anything but inspiring.

"You might see Mr. Sharp," said he; "but I'm afraid you'll be disappointed. He believes in encouraging native talent to write — gratuitously; but when it comes to paying, the case is altered."

"If that is Mr. Sharp's style," retorted I, cavalierly, "he needn't enjoy the pleasure of my acquaintance. I'll step around to the *Tap* office, where I'm known, and see what can be done there."

"Then this is not your first literary attempt?" queried Dewitt.

"Not quite. I've written a number of things over the assumed name of 'M. T. Head.'"

"You don't say so!" cried my old mate, brightening up again in his whole aspect. "Why, Glibun, old boy, I had no idea of that. Why didn't you tell me at first? That last thing of yours — 'Sir Single's Bridal' — has made a regular hit, and is copied into two-thirds of our exchanges. And you're 'M. T. Head!'"

The news that I was so famous, and his amazed admiration of me, almost took away my breath. My first adored and then despised bit of burlesque had been a success, then, without my knowledge. I pretended however, to appear unconcerned.

"I'm nobody else, Willie."

"But how comes the *Tap* to let you go?"

"I haven't asked it."

"Well, then, I'll tell you what it is, Ave Glibun, just know when you're in luck, and let me introduce you to Mr. Sharp, right off. He's on the lookout for an assistant-editor of the whole paper, and its my opinion that 'M. T. Head' can have the position if he wants it."

27

"Done!" said I, with a will.

The dramatic censor lost no time in conducting me to the second compartment of the office, and there introduced me, by both my names, to the great benefactor of native talent.

The smallest, shrewdest gray eyes, and largest nose and mouth I had ever seen, adorned the egg-shaped head of Mr. Easton Sharp; and his lank figure, spade-like hands, and long feet, gave one a whimsical impression of something decidedly monkeyfied.

"Mr. Glibun is an old friend of mine, Mr. Sharp," continued Dewitt, after we had shaken hands, "and I thought he'd be just the man for us."

"Yes, I see," remarked Mr. Sharp, affably. "I appreciate Mr. Glibun's abilities, and find nothing in his humor to offend the most fastidious."

I bowed; and my friend, who had seated himself beside me on the same pile of papers, appeared to regard the observation as entirely satisfactory.

Sliding himself into an attitude of incipient syncope, for a moment, that he might the more easily abstract an enormous jack-knife from one of his pockets, and sliding himself erect again with the weapon in his hand, Mr. Sharp drove the blade into the right arm of his chair and thus trained his Connecticut mind upon me.

"You propose, then," said he, with an odd mixture of cunning and suavity in his look, "to become a journalist, Mr. Glibun?"

"That is my inclination, sir."

"And about what is your idea as to compensation?"

"Whatever I can make myself worth to a paper."

"Yes, I see. Do you think, though, that you would feel willing to do all that there is to be done on a paper like ours?"

My bold assurance, growing bolder every moment, was astonishing to myself; but I enjoyed it to the utmost, and assumed a tone of patronizing consideration. In fact, I may as well admit that I was fairly intoxicated with my own new power of sheer impudence.

"Mr. Sharp," said I, "a permanent position on a paper is a greater object to me, at present, than maximum of compensation, or leisure (!) I have no doubt that I shall be able to give you satisfaction in any kind of writing, or quantity of writing, suited to my abilities. But I should like to know, of course, beforehand, what you will expect me to do."

"Ex-actly," remarked he, twirling the knife upon its point. "Well, in the first place, we should expect you to give us a fortnightly letter from Europe."

This took me all aback, and I could only scratch my ear and smile feebly.

"That's done easily enough, Glibun," said Dewitt, noticing my bewilderment. "You needn't go out of this office to do it."

"Certainly not," added Mr. Sharp, grinning comically. "You've only to copy the style of such letters in the dailies, and make out that everything is *more so* in Europe — especially in England — than it is here. If you've read much of the foreign correspondence of the dailies, you'll know what I mean."

A light broke in upon my benighted understanding as he spoke, and I grasped the idea at once.

"Oh, yes," said I, winking vivaciously, "I can do that, I think."

"You must humor public sentiment," he went on, "by continually insinuating, rather than asserting, the superiority of European society and literature over our own; and avoiding all that might offend the most fastidious."

"Of course; I understand."

"We should also expect you to write up our department headed 'The Shooting Season.' Looking over the exchanges, — particularly those from the South and California, — you would have to pick out all the liveliest pistoling incidents, and work them over in humorous style; though, of course, in such a way as not to offend the most fastidious."

I thought I could do justice to that, also, and told him so.

"We should expect you to furnish such stories, poems, and minor essays as might be required to fill the literary columns of the paper each week."

Here I shrank, appalled, again; for how was I to find time — not to speak of versatility — for such a book-like job as that? But once more my old school-mate came to the rescue.

"You're to do it with scissors, you know," he explained.

"Ex-actly," assented Mr. Sharp. "What don't come in gratuitously from native talent, you must scissor from English magazines; being always very careful, of course, to select nothing that could offend the most fastidious."

"Oh, certainly, certainly!"

"Then, on the editorial page proper, we should want one editorial a week, all the year round, on the certainty of a universal war in Europe, overturning effete despotisms, and resulting in universal republicanism. Also, one on British oppression in Ireland; also, a leader (until further orders) pitching into Mealy O'Murphy and Plato Wynne."

I felt the color flying out of my face at that name, and was saved from an awkward scene only by Mr. Sharp's complete misapprehension of the cause of my discomposure.

"You're thinking of libel, I see," he continued, with another comical grin; "but we avoid that by the Cringerial Method. If you're to come here," he added, strapping his knife upon the sole of one boot, and surveying me with grotesque gravity, "I may as well tell you at once that General

Cringer is really a half-owner in our concern. If it wasn't for that, we should support O'Murphy for the Senate. Wynne, as everybody knows, is to lobby for him; and, as Wynne and I have been the best of friends in private, for several years, I hope he'll gain the day. That's between ourselves, you understand. But, as I was saying, General Cringer owns half of us, and we are obliged to support his candidate, Mr. Crow. So, until the election at Albany, you would have to make your leaders dead against Wynne. Cringer is too busy now to write them himself, as usual; but you could easily follow the Cringerial Method, and write as savagely as you pleased, with perfect safety."

With enthusiasm materially abated, I asked for some tuition in the Cringerial Method.

"I'll give you an illustration," he replied, pulling a written sheet from a hook above his desk. "Here, for instance, is an article against Senator Home, for opposing a grant of half a million of dollars to the Hibernian Catholic College. Just listen: —

"'True to the most infamous political an-
'tecedents that ever covered a shameless
'intriguer with fathomless dishonor, Mr.
'Senator Home has outraged every prin-
'ciple of intelligence and humanity by op-
'posing a reasonable grant of national aid
'to one of the noblest institutions of our
'land. Making a pretended respect for
'public economy his hypocritical plea, he
'insidiously throws himself across the path
'of that national generosity which would
'sustain the institution dearest to the
'adopted citizen of the republic, and crowns
'the wiles of a scoundrel with the frenzy
'of an intolerant bigot. Fitting is such a
'deed from one whose whole public career
'has been but a succession of iniquitous
'follies and imbecilities. In private life,
'however, Mr. Senator Home is the honored
'and revered epitome of every domestic
'and social virtue. Noted no less for his
'courtly ease in polished society, than for
'his benignity as a husband and parent, he
'thoroughly realizes in his person and at-
'tributes that gentleman of the old school
'whose refined presence is at once a com-
'mentary and a sarcasm upon modern man-
'ners. The Hon. Mr. Senator Home is fifty-
'three years old, but looks to be scarcely
'thirty-five.'

"That's the Cringerial Method of doing it," concluded Mr. Sharp, as he replaced the paper on the hook; "and it never draws a libel suit. The second part, you see, takes back, as it were, all that you've said in the first part, and leaves nothing to offend the most fastidious."

"I think," returned I, in great admiration, "that the Method would reconcile a man to any number of attacks. I will take the position and its responsibilities at once, sir, provided we can agree upon terms. What is the salary?"

"Six hundred," was the answer.

"I'll take it."

"You shall have it."

Thus did I fall upon my feet. Thus did reckless assurance promptly gain for me what modest merit might have pleaded for in vain. A raw, untrained young dabbler in ink, I went, without half trying, into position and power, while scores of professional veterans knew not where to look for the next meal. But then, those veterans *would* drink!

After handing the sketch I had brought with me to my new employer, and seeing it passed, without reading, through a square hole in the wall to the printers in an adjoining room, I returned with Dewitt to his own compartment, and freely gave way to the exhilaration I felt. What mattered it now who I was, or what my antecedents were?

"Glibun, take that chair of mine at the desk," exclaimed Dewitt, pushing me into it, "and let me sit on the papers. By George! you're the coolest, oldest hand I've seen in an age. You've walked into an editorship as though it were a public house soliciting your patronage! Such luck I never saw. Why, I thought I'd have to speak for you, at least; but I might as well have been out of sight altogether."

"I confess myself surprised," answered I, in a glow; "but you won't envy me, Willie, when you hear that it's the first good luck of my life. There's certainly an amazing amount of impudence in my undertaking to edit a paper without one hour's previous practice; but I'll do it, as sure as you live! I feel it in me. Can you spare one of those sheets of foolscap and a pen for half an hour?"

"Help yourself," said he, evidently at a loss to know what to make of me.

"I'm going to try my hand at once on that foreign letter," rattled I, dipping into the ink; and, like one possessed, I fell briskly to work.

It was a moment of true inspiration, superinduced by a fit of extravagant self-satisfaction; and, as the letter subsequently made quite a sensation in print, and assured my success in the new vocation, it is entitled to record here. Behold, then, the first of my European essays: —

"(From our Special Correspondent.)
   "LONDON, —— 18—.
"The sunlighted days and dark nights
"under which we are now passing in this
"part of the world make us realize that
"autumn follows summer, and that a man
"grows twelve months older with each ad-
"ditional year of his life. Whether one
"sails upon the damp waters of the Thames,
"or navigates the moist current of the
"Hudson, he is still pitiably sensitive to
"the degrees of heat and cold, — still draws
"his robes closer round him in October
"than in July, and still prefers comfort to
"discomfort.
"It is characteristic of Englishmen, how-
"ever, that they never experience intense

"chilliness in midsummer, and invariably
"find a glowing stove warmer in proportion
"to its quantity of ignited fuel. Not only
"are they habituated to these sensations,
"but they assiduously teach them to their
"children, whom they educate to believe
"that a too great degree of either heat or
"cold is unpleasant to the more exposed
"portions of the system. Hence, I have
"seen boys and girls in Devonshire shiver
"violently on first arising from their beds
"on January mornings, and complain of
"over-warmth when playing 'tag' in June.

"And, speaking of English children, it
"may not be out of the way to give you a
"few carefully observed facts of their gen-
"eral early training; than which I can con-
"ceive nothing more judicious and improv-
"ing. After the lapse of a proper period
"from birth, the child of English parents is
"carefully weaned; or, in other words, its
"gastric impulses are directed to other
"sources of internal nourishment than the
"lacteal fount of nature. Its nose is wiped,
"and face washed as often as necessary;
"water being used for the latter purpose,
"and a handkerchief for the former. In-
"stead of waiting until old age has set in,
"the English parent sends his offspring to
"school while it is yet a child; the object
"being to let the little one acquire the
"primary elements of education, such as
"reading pot-hooks, and simple addition.
"As the child grows up, consequently, he
"becomes larger in size, presents more
"surface for merited chastisement, eats
"more apples, and has more stomach-ache.
"In the mean time, however, the parent
"grows older; so that when an English lad
"is twenty years of age, his father is
"just twenty years older than he-was at the
"birth of the boy. This is invariably the
"case in England, so far as I can observe,
"and accounts for the difference of years
"between parents and children, so often
"noticed in Europe.

"English daughters, unlike English sons,
"are kept in frocks until maturity; after
"which they also continue to wear frocks
"of various materials. Those of the poorer
"classes never wear expensive silks or vel-
"vets when engaged in toil; but on Sun-
"days and holidays they don dresses of
"fresher appearance, and often look quite
"clean. On the other hand, the daughters
"of the aristocratic classes never wear de-
"fective shoes, or patched calico dresses;
"but are attired in robes without rips in
"them, and often purchase new bonnets
"and gloves. In fact, the whole domestic
"and social system of England is superior
"to our own; and what I have written of
"it may be perused with advantage by
"American parents and children alike.

"No other news occurs to me as worthy
"of chronicling for this steamer; but if
"anything fresh has happened, you will find
"full details of it, undoubtedly, in your
"foreign files."

CHAPTER XXXIX.

BOHEMIAN GLASS.

AND now, my dear Redundant Adjectives
and Conjunctions, must I indeed begin to
prune you? Must I ruthlessly cut you off
and cast you from me, because you would
never be tolerated in a professional writer?
Must I suppress all the long-respired enthusiasm of nature for the measured prac-
ticalities of literary art, or submit to be
called "vealy" and "fresh" by my new
associates and critics? Even as a rustic
nymph, who has lavishly adorned her locks
with wild flowers for her first visit to a ball
at the great house, turns chilled and dismayed when told that such floral extravagance will never do for fashionable society, — so do I turn dampened and abashed
at thought of sacrificing to approved style
that florid diffusion so long the pride of my
heart. Even as a young swimmer, who
would joyously dive and dive again in the
untiring wave, reluctantly obeys the professional bather ashore to be content with
but so many submersions, lest they should
perilously weaken him, — so do I unwillingly heed the stereotyped journalistic rule
to take only so many conjunctive plunges in
an exhilarative idea, or come out of it hopelessly debilitated.

But Dewitt said that I really must do it,
or the Bohemians of the other papers would
make life a burden to me. He said that I
must forever drop Isocrates and exaggerate
Aristotle, unless I wished to be a standing
joke with the Sunday papers, particularly;
and counselled me to write concisely what
I knew, or thought I knew, rather than
what I felt, or ought to feel. Only in mal-
edictory leaders, according to the Cringerial
Method, was any degree of enthusiasm ad-
missible. To display it in any other kind
of writing was to lower one's self to the
level of war correspondents and Harvard
graduates. For his own part, he — Dewitt
— found it good policy to affect a used-up,
rather insolent style in his dramatic criticisms, cutting any little irrepressible burst
of natural feeling into so many fragmentary
paragraphs, that it was like a full breath
chopped into coughs.

So instructed by my former school-mate,
and occasionally reminded of the exactions
of the most fastidious by Mr. Sharp, I did
not long work *invitâ Minervâ*. Indeed, the
practice of a fortnight enabled me to take
pretty fair rank in "the mob of gentlemen
who write with ease," and the *Earthquake*
waxed lively with the most complicated
shocks I could devise. Our "Shooting
Season" grew into a marvel of humorous
chronicles, graphically delineative of Southern life; our Foreign Correspondence was
a continual revelation of court secrets and
European progress; and our articles on the
impending Continental explosion kept con-
sular circles in a perpetual fever. The
British magazines were generally equal to

the task of furnishing such romance of fashionable life abroad as our literary columns required; but when they now and then were scant in that description of reading, I encouraged native talent to come out stronger than usual for nothing, and threw additional severity into the editorial on English tyranny in Ireland. In the Cringerial Method of consigning political opponents to public wrath and social admiration, I achieved such honors that the General himself was moved to visit the office late one afternoon and make my acquaintance.

This remarkable man had been shown to me on the public street, where, with measured step, eyes thoughtfully downcast, and right hand buried in the drapery of his broad chest, it was his custom to invite popular investigation at times. Never before, however, had the great victor in politics and faro come so near to me, and when, after Mr. Sharp's introduction, he gave me a paternal shake of the hand, I esteemed his broad-brimmed hat and benignant countenance the very head and front of disinterested greatness.

A desk for me had been added to the simple furniture of Dewitt's compartment, and upon this I seated myself, somewhat flurried, while the General and Mr. Sharp took the chair and the paper pile. In what particular army the celebrated man commanded I have still to discover; but the military authority of his shoulders was beyond all question, and, like everybody else, I felt myself to be a very raw recruit in his presence.

"I have been telling Mr. Sharp," said he, with a blandness quite indescribable, "that your articles upon the approaching senatorial contest, Mr. Glibun, are eminently satisfactory to me, — eminently so."

"I write them to order, sir," said I, cautiously.

"That is," observed General Cringer, smiling very sweetly, "you square them to the policy of the journal with which you are connected. In doing that, however, I hope that you do no great violence to your own honest convictions; for I shall be very sorry to be the occasion, in my political relations, of anything at war with frankness and openness in the censorship of the press."

"Or anything offensive to the most fastidious," added Mr. Sharp, who was gracefully cleaning his nails.

"Precisely so, Mr. Sharp," pursued the General. "I want to impress it upon my young friend here (I have stolen a few moments from pressing engagements for no other purpose) that the style of argument which my editorial friends are pleased to denominate my 'Method,' is always in keeping with the amenities of private life, and, in the present instance, particularly, severe only as a wholesome public sentiment dictates. Political differences should never, in any case, be allowed to embitter private relations, nor violate the sanctities of private life. Hence, I counsel final justice to the domestic virtues of the most virulent political opponent, however uncompromising may be our simultaneous denunciation of his political tortuosities." Here General Cringer paused a moment to beam gratuitous justice to all men; and then added, "Besides, it prevents the bother of libel suits."

This last sentence startled me from a beautiful dream of Utopian magnanimity into which I was falling; but the great man lulled me again with a fatherly pat upon the knee, and went on, —

"The Honorable Mealy O'Murphy may be as honest with his packs of cards up-town, as any Wall Street magnate is with his list of stocks down-town. Therefore we say of Mr. O'Murphy, in his private capacity, that he is the soul of honor and the friend of Ireland. But, in the same breath, we as justly remark, that Mr. O'Murphy is coarse, ignorant, and ruffianly, to an extent utterly disqualifying him for a seat in the august senate, and that he is an unmitigated scoundrel for pretending to it. Of his great supporter and manager, Plato Wynne, we first hazard the opinion that bribery and corruption are the sole means he employs as leader of the depraved Demolition party in this great city; and wind up with the candid admission, that no more fascinating *arbiter elegantiarum*, or courtlier gentleman, than Mr. Plato Wynne, is known to the most select circles of metropolitan society."

The perfect enjoyment of his own even-handed justice with which General Cringer said this, made me almost ashamed to follow it with a petty objection. It was upon my tongue, however, and I gave it vent. —

"To be frank with you, sir, I shall not be sorry when Mr. Wynne can be left unmentioned. His wife is a lady whom I once thought a great deal of; and, though I know what he is, it comes awkward for me to write attacks upon him for print."

"Young man, the feeling does you credit," said the General, patting me on the knee once more; "but, in journalism and politics, private inclinations must be held secondary to public interests. Why, my dear young friend, Mr. Wynne has been the particular associate of Mr. Sharp and myself for years; and were not a great national principle at stake in the coming contest, Mr. Sharp and I would sustain Mr. Wynne against all odds."

"I would back him, single-handed!" struck in Mr. Easton Sharp, with tempestuous animation. "I'd guarantee him to be the ruin of any man!"

This fine tribute to the merits of an absent friend caused the faces of both gentlemen to light with an expression of the liveliest approbation, and led me to imagine that a superior capacity for spreading ruin must involve some subtle element of virtue.

Dewitt happening to arrive just then, General Cringer patronized him with a protecting nod, and arose to go.

"You two young men have eminence before you," was the parting blessing heaped upon us. "Be honest, be fearless, be studious. I said that to a young friend named Stiles, a few years ago, and now he holds an honorable office in the service of his country. Good-day, gen-tle-men."

As he passed affably into the outer office, attended by the proprietor of the *Earthquake*, Dewitt rolled up his eyes and shrugged his shoulders, like one who acknowledged a remarkable dispensation and despaired of doing justice to the benefaction intended.

"The old man knows how to soft-soap all hands," said he, "and there's something in it, too. He's carried the State half a dozen times by sheer force of soft-soap; but things look squally for him this time."

"Has his candidate got the worst of it, as matters rest now?" asked I.

"I should think so. The legislature is about evenly balanced as to parties; but O'Murphy will spend money, and Crow won't. O'Murphy will pledge himself to anything, and Crow is all highmindedness. Besides, Wynne can control the whole delegation from this city at the start; and Cringer will not only have to get his majority out of the country members, but also to take the risk of paying something out of his own pocket."

"He'll be able to do the last," remarked I. "if the story of that great game at O'Murphy's is true."

"Some people think that game was a turning point for Wynne," rejoined Dewitt, thoughtfully, "and Cringer will make a desperate fight. It's my own opinion, however, that the cards will be too much for the old man this time. But bother politics!" he exclaimed, impatiently. "If you're through for the day, let's go up and see the boys at Solon Tick's. There'll be quite a party of them, for they expect those two fellows who are just home from Europe."

This proposition was agreeable to me; for I had already seen enough of Bohemianism to feel an anticipating relish of its free-and-easy customs. I did not bother myself to care who the two expected fellows were, taking it for granted that their foreign experiences had not made them widely different from such of their supposed kind as sauntered into the *Earthquake* office now and then with manuscripts to be refused. So, I briskly acquiesced in the dramatic editor's suggestion, and we started off in the early twilight for Mr. Tick's hospitable halls.

"Now, Glibun, I want to ask you one question," said Dewitt, as we lounged along Broadway,—"How are you off for soap, to-day?" *

To which I answered, that my purse was decently lined. But why did he ask? Could I oblige him with a temporary loan?

"No, thank you," returned he; "I don't want to borrow just now. But the company we're going to will expect you to stand a little treat as a new-comer. I thought I'd post you."

Appreciating his friendly forethought, I assured him that I was quite ready to do the proper thing; and, with the full confidence of men not unprepared for any emergency, we turned into the cross-street where Solon Tick possessed his local habitation.

That the latter had originally been a private abode only, was evident from the modest and homelike style of the house; but Mr. Tick's genius had turned the front parlor into a snug bar and chop-room, wherein divers little oak tables, dining-chairs, a large clock, several fruit-pictures, and a liquor counter not unlike a coffin in its tone, invited persons of a retiring disposition to refresh themselves in quiet. A bald-headed gentleman of irascible aspect at one of the tables was the only customer in sight; but sounds of talking and laughter were audible from beyond the folding-doors, and suggested that the back parlor might be more thickly inhabited. Presiding at the funereal bar was a fleshy, florid, coatless little man, whom Dewitt straightway addressed, —

"How are you, Tick?"

"As well as could be expected," replied Mr. Tick, as though speaking of Mrs. Tick under interesting circumstances,— "as well as could be expected, Mr. Dewitt. Your servants, gents."

"School's in already, isn't it, Tick?" queried the dramatic editor, looking toward the folding-doors.

"Some of them are on hand,—Mr. Church, Mr. Gushington, Mr. Steele, Mr. Scribner, and one or two others, I believe," answered the proprietor, nodding in the same direction.

"All right, then," returned Dewitt. "If Hardley Church is here, the rest won't be far behind. This way, Glibun."

"Step in, gents," concluded Mr. Tick, hospitably, "and knock on the table when you want the waiter."

Returning to the hall, and passing farther toward the rear of the house, we entered the back parlor and found ourselves in the presence of the incipient symposium. Seated on either side of a long, oak dining-table, with mugs of ale before them and wooden pipes between their teeth, were half a dozen heavily-clouded gentlemen of various ages, whose unstudied attire and spacious foreheads were intrusively literary. All were talking and gesticulating at once when we appeared; but, at sight of my companion, a tall, thin, round-shouldered, sharp-eyed elder, with a nose like an eagle's beak and beard and hair streaked with gray, rapped on the table for order, and directed attention to us. Then everybody greeted Dewitt, who promptly introduced me; and in less time than it takes to tell it I was seated amongst the economical revellers, and knocking magnificently for the waiter. A fine literary instinct told me that I could

---

* The use of the term "soap" in this sense is classical. When Demetrius Pollorcetes sent a purse of two hundred and fifty talents to the luxurious Lamia, he delicately informed her that it was merely "for soap." Hence the modern saponism.

not distinguish myself in that way too soon for my own credit. The young man who is not prepared to drink deep himself, and offer others facilities for inexpensively doing the same, has no kind of business with the Pierian spring.

In short, I ordered ale for all, thereby bringing myself into immediate favor with popular gentlemen, of whom the following notes may as well be made at once: —

Mr. Hardley Church, as before stated, was long, stooping, and gray, with a perpetual twinkle of kindness in the sharpness of his eyes, and an odd mixture of discontent and philosophy in the many nervous lines of his face. His *forte* in letters was a kind of atheistical sophistry, which made pungent reading, but did not return much income.

Mr. Gushington, aged about thirty, wore his black hair down to his shoulders, like a converted Indian, and was chronically affected with an incredulous smile. He believed all men and women to be virtuous only as they missed opportunities to be otherwise; and wrote sarcastic poems and criticisms for the weekly press.

Mr. Steele's face and head were so closely cropped that none could tell how old a boy he was, but rumor made him about twenty-one. Adapting plays from the French for the theatres, he was kind enough to put his own name to them, and passed amongst Sunday critics and provincial stars for a tremendous genius.

Mr. Scribner was a short, frail youth, of tender years apparently, and wore his yellow hair tumbled into as many radiating spikes as plentiful sprinklings of water would develop, it being his idiosyncrasy to esteem it luxuriantly curly. He did books and the opera for an æsthetical weekly.

Next to him sat little Mr. Bird, with dusty brown hair and the foggiest little blue eyes ever known to wakefulness. His weaknesses were poetical comparisons of different imaginary magazine ladies with different kinds of wine; and as he was known to be a favorite with the young fairies of a Centre Street bookbindery, and had been seen to drink several glasses of elderberry cordial, there were suspicions of truth in some of his verses.

Dewitt's left-hand neighbor, Mr. Fox, was an athletic, sandy-haired writer of anything that would pay, from an attack on an opposition dictionary down to a spurious telegraphic market report. He translated from the Greek and German, too (by the aid of a cheap and broken-down school-master who drank), and acquired some grace of bearing from an honest conviction that half a dozen theatrical ladies fought for him.

In such company (having learned their peculiarities before seeing them) did I sit down to my first dissipation in Bohemia, and right willing was I to be accepted by them as a comrade. They were free, reckless fellows, whose past histories were nobody's business; and what material dif-

ference, or superiority, could be claimed for me, now?

"Do you know, gentlemen," cried I, when the waiter brought my ale order, "it strikes me that we ought to do something for the house in the way of eatables? Dewitt and I have touched no supper yet, and if you'll join us we'll practise a little in the knife and fork manual."

"A genuine inspiration, per Jovem!" exclaimed Church. "I don't mind admitting that the subscriber breakfasted with Democritus to-day, and kept an appointment for dinner with Duke Humphrey. Mr. 'M. T. Head,' the humor of your 'Sir Single's Bridal' is simply inimitable, and I'll take a ham omelet myself!"

"Sirloin and celery for me," said Dewitt.

"Poached eggs on toast," ordered Mr. Gushington; and he had barely uttered the words when the other gentlemen were chorusing the whole bill of fare at the agitated waiter with a vehemence eloquent of recent fasting. There was, indeed, a positive frenzy about this part of the performance which made me secretly rejoice that Mr. Tick's establishment did not deal heavily in the fancy-game line. From the devouring expression of Mr. Fox's eye, it was plain that he would have been equal to any number of woodcocks, had those nourishing birds been attainable at my expense.

The compliments lavished upon me as a humorist and an editor, by these hungry wits, were spiced with no more irony than was absolutely requisite to save my modesty; and when Mr. Scribner fraternally asserted, over his half-dozen roast, that my paragraphing was really much less coarse and trashy than some he had seen, my delight in the tribute made me hot in the face. As for Mr. Gushington, he, indeed, seasoned his poached eggs with the audible reflection that certain persons thought they could buy the press, at any time, with a glass of beer; but this was manifestly intended as an arch pleasantry, for he privately requested from me the loan of a dollar before the evening was out. It is but just to admit, however, that I was chiefly indebted for the favor in which I found myself to the open-handed approval of Church, whom the rest seemed to regard as a kind of leader. Nothing could be franker than that philosopher's expressed determination to remain my bosom friend so long as I had a shilling, and he called Steele and Fox to witness the contract.

But our party was far from complete then; for when the door presently opened, and I expected to behold the two returned travellers, there entered, instead, a gentleman and a lady. The former in flowing yellow hair, Byron collar, and spectacles, was Mr. Nemo, city-editor of the *Morning Dog*, who excused himself (mere literary mechanic as he was) for coming into such intellectual company, by serving as cavalier to the brilliant and erratic Miss Iona Hart. Of course, being a newspaper man, I was familiar with the stories, verses, and transcendental dramatic criticisms of the saucy Iona, but never before had I known her by sight.

"Ah! here's our own queen," cried Church, springing to his feet; and we all arose to render homage.

Putting the now superfluous Nemo behind her, as though he were Satan, Miss Hart accepted a hearty kiss from Church, shook hands with all the rest, including me, and permitted the philosopher to conduct her to the head of the table. Then, when we were all seated again, not excluding Mr. Nemo, she tossed bonnet and shawl away, and asked where "Wild and Baby" were.

"Haven't come yet, my enslaver," answered Church, whom I began to envy.

She was handsome. Luxuriant tresses of jet, sparkling black eyes, dimpled chin, and an English form of the healthiest type, constitute the loveliest angels of gas-light; and Miss Hart knew how to give such charms all the piquant finish of tropical hues in dress. There was, to speak freely, a touch of the actress in her semi-masculine basque-coat of purple, trimmed with pink binding and steel buttons; but then her air and remarks were informed with a girlish simplicity not to be associated with the theatres.

Hardly was she instated, though, when the popular light comedian, Mr. Drinkard, came in, escorting the equally popular Miss Leggett, — both of King's Theatre. The popular light comedian was a bleachy blossom of fat features and kinky black hair, on a parent trunk not unlike the dummy of a fashionable tailor's shop; and his plump demoiselle looked as though she might be his blonde sister, in her regular stage costume of singing chambermaid.

Fresh enthusiasm marked the welcoming and chairing of this second couple, — Miss Leggett carrying her flaxen ringlets and bare white arms to a seat next Miss Hart.

Then, for the third time, the door opened again, to admit Acton Wild, late foreign correspondent of the *Daily Bread*, and his boon comrade, Gwin Le Mons.

I knew my old playmate the moment I laid eyes on him. He was no other than "the Baby" I had heard of more than once in Bohemia. There he was, indeed, going around the table with Wild, to shake the two outstretched hands of each boisterous friend in turn. The healthy bloom of boyhood had gone from his cheeks, leaving them tinged with hectic spots instead; the riotous brown locks had civilized into the coils and partings of the hair-dresser; the laughing eye had quieted to a look almost moody; and the green jacket with pearl buttons gave way to a rakish sporting-coat of claret hue; but Gwin Le Mons was not to be mistaken by Avery Glibun. I waited silently for him to reach me, noting, meanwhile, that everybody seemed to pet him, and that Acton Wild was a rather dissipated-looking, black-eyed youth, much given to mustache, frilled bosom, and profanity. I expected my old playmate to be as pleased

at the meeting as I was, and, when he finally got to me, I sprang up, regardless of observers, and fairly clasped him in my arms.

"My goodness!" he exclaimed, pushing me rudely off, amidst the laughter of the whole crew. "What ails *you*?"

"Gwin!" cried I, amazed and mortified.

"Hal-loo!" he drawled; "I believe I do know you, now. How are you, Glibun? Haven't seen you for some time. Wild, let me introduce you to Mr. Glibun. Knew him when he was a boy!"

I shook hands with Mr. Wild very heartily, to hide my confusion, and gained him an opportunity to be quite humorous about the meeting of two life-long friends, who hadn't heard of each other since infancy.

"You're looking well, Ave," said Gwin, carelessly.

"And you are not," returned I, shortly.

"No; I'm half dead with 'Coughs, Colds, Consumption,' as the advertisements say," he answered, and went around to a seat beside Church.

It needed not the satirical nods and laughter of the table to teach me that I had been badly snubbed, and, for a moment or two, I was inclined to make a scene of it by rushing indignantly from the room. Being encouraged, however, by a look of sympathy from Miss Hart, and a whispered "Take it coolly," from Dewitt, I suddenly assumed an exaggerated, don't-care demeanor, and loudly insisted upon calling for refreshments.

Need I say to those who understand the thirsty literary character, that this proposition brought me into favor again? Need I say that the clamor and laughter of those reckless souls gave way at once, and for a time, to serious consideration of what should be imbibed next? The ladies thought they would try milk punches, — very weak; the gentlemen agreed to toast "M. T. Head," in beverages varying from brandy to soda-cocktail; and all said "Ay" to my princely suggestion of almonds and raisins to complete. The waiter came and went, and came again, until the banquet was served. I led a toast to "the ladies," with my eyes particularly directed to Miss Iona Hart; and the conversation began to be characteristic of a high-toned literary company.

"Now, Mr. Wild," cried Miss Iona, addressing Gwin's adopted brother, and tossing her curls back of her shoulder to give me full view of a maddening cheek, "I want to know if there's any chance in Europe for me. *Does* the London Times want a Fashion-editress; or *is* Blackwood looking for a sharp writer on American society?"

"And *does* Drury Lane want an 'unrivalled delineator of female Yankee characters'?" chirped Miss Leggett.

"No hope over there for any of us," answered Acton Wild, with a languid travelled air. "Baby and I had hard work to make the English Bohemians believe that we Americans ever did anything more in literature, on this side, than pirate their books, and appropriate their newspaper and magazine articles. Why, they won't give us credit even for understanding the language, you know. And as for American actresses! —well, the most of them could get to court more easily than into a decent theatre. Professional jealousy is simply infernal there."

"It's crushing, you see," added Mr. Drinkard, who had once gone first-cabin across the Atlantic, in pursuit of an engagement, and returned in the steerage, with an unpaid board-bill for baggage.

"Then you and I, Hart, had better stay at home, still, and keep Mr. Church steady," giggled Miss Leggett.

"Churchy, you incorrigible old beau!" said Le Mons, slapping the philosopher on the shoulder, "are you never going to let any one else have a chance with the women of America? Why, you're as old as Hesiod's crow, and ought to be thinking of your latter end."

"Ah, Baby," retorted Church, affectionately squeezing Gwin's arm, "the subscriber will outlast you, if you don't do something for that cough of yours."

I noticed then, and afterwards, that they all seemed to adopt a particularly kind, petting manner toward Gwin, as though none of their literary jealousies could include him; and Church and Wild, especially, explained by their actions the unanimous sentiment that had procured for him the caressing and protecting title of "Baby." I noticed, too, that he frequently coughed in a low, hacking way, and that his voice became weak very quickly.

"By the way, Baby," cried Dewitt, winking at Church, "did you finish that novel of yours while you were across the water?"

"No, Will; I hadn't time," replied Gwin, looking vexed. "But you needn't laugh so, you Archilochus, you! I'm going to go right at it next week."

"Will Dewitt, you shan't tease him so about that book!" exclaimed Iona Hart, as she threw a handful of almond shells at the offender. "He's promised me to finish it this year, and I won't have him teased about it any more."

"Are you writing a book, Gwin?" asked I.

"Oh, yes, of course I am. That is, I've got the plot all laid out, and as soon as I have a fair chance—oh, bother the book! I'll finish it yet!"

He seemed to be half amused, half impatient, under the question, and I had a shrewd suspicion that the novel in question was that stereotyped "Book" by everybody which is never, never finished in Bohemia.

"He's talked about it, and planned it, and dwelt upon it, for three years,—poor Baby! —but I don't believe he's written the first line yet," whispered Dewitt.

Wild now ended a noisy conference on late English comedies with Steele, Gushington, and Fox, to turn his attention once more toward our end of the board. "Church," he inquired, pulling his mustache, "is your fortune nearly made yet?

Steele tells me that you've been trying your hand at a play for Maggie Dalen. That looks like a pretty severe case of hard-up,—don't it?"

Hardley Church turned very grave of countenance at this remark, and spoke earnestly in reply,—

"Yes, young man, that's what it really is. It was a toss-up whether I should go to the almshouse, or write a play, and the play won it. Whether Maggie will keep it or not is yet to be seen. If she don't, the subscriber is sorry for his landlord and laundress,—that's all. If you happen to know anybody who believes in an overruling Providence" (here I saw Gwin look very intently at Church), "just point me out to him as a particular victim of that celestial agency. Everything turns unlucky for me. But then it's the same with all but some half a dozen native writers in New York. The newspaper offices are all packed full of foreigners,—Englishmen, Irishmen, Scotchmen. And nice specimens they are! The literary critic of one daily is an Irishman who ran away from home with another man's wife and purse; the dramatic critic of another left Dublin under such constabular circumstances, that, even now, he don't dare to wear his own name; the Englishman who does the European articles for another was a porter in a warehouse three years ago. And the papers and departments not personally run by all sorts of foreign ragamuffins are filled up with stealings from the first English periodical that comes along. Look at Nemo over there, for instance,—an Irishman!"

Finding himself thus tremendously dragged from obscurity, the luckless city editor made a feeble effort to show some spirit.

"I'm as good a man as you, any day," he retorted. "I've got a clear record myself, and my father was in a bank."

"To be sure he was," rejoined Church, "and they nabbed him before he could get out again."

Mr. Nemo took this as personal, and was apparently about to rise, when the laughter of the company and the request from Miss Hart that he would "not make a perfect goose of himself," induced him to retire out of notice again with a ghastly smile.

"The Yankees," I ventured to say, "ought to teach us New Yorkers a lesson. See how those New England writers manage to keep their ground against cheap, or stolen, foreign competition, by sticking to each other."

"That's it!" cried Fox, suddenly coming into the conversation. "Instead of picking at each other, as we New York Bohemians do, those eastern fellows puff and puff each other at every turn, until they're actually leading the literature of the whole country. That, too, when their best things are rehashes of the English poets, or of Comte, and Carlyle."

"The Yankees," proclaimed the philosophical Church, "are the Bacons of this continent; 'the wisest, brightest, meanest' of American-kind. They do everything by machinery, those fellows, from chopping wood and starting a train of cars, to chopping logic and starting a train of thought. In the words of a popular work, 'They have hands, but they handle not; feet have they, but they walk not; neither speak they through their throats,'—but through their noses."

"You seem to forget, Mr. Church," I observed, "that our greatest of modern transcendental philosophers is a Yankee."

(I was really distinguishing myself just then, for the ale affected my head.)

"That same philosopher's philosophy amounts to just this," returned Church, filling a pipe from his tobacco-pouch; "he goes out to sea in the language, touches irresolutely at two or three scattered islands of meaning, and then goes down with all standing. That's what transcendentalism amounts to."

At this juncture the ladies protested that they were heartily tired of hearing old Churchy "publishing;" whereupon the talk went off into nonsense of the liveliest sort, running chiefly on theatrical events and personages. It came out that Church's new play was called "Tomyrus," and that it was founded upon the chronicles of the Amazonian Massagetæ, as given by Herodotus. Steele and Miss Leggett had never heard of Tomyrus before; but that did not prevent their jokes at the philosopher on his selection of what they called "Heathen heavy-weight" for a melo-drame; and the philosopher was finally led into promising the actress a copy of the First Act next day, if she would get upon the table and give us a singing jig for which she was famous. Taking him at his word the fair Leggett ordered everybody save Miss Hart to retire from the table to the farthest limits of the room; and then, mounting by a chair to the proposed stage, she actually went through au Irish song and shuffling dance over the confused array of dishes, almond shells, and empty glasses.

Great applause greeted this performance, from everybody save Iona Hart; who, in fact, scarcely looked at the actress at all during the dance. But when Mr. Drinkard, the popular light comedian, subsequently mounted the same boards and sang a comic song, her loudly expressed approval made Mr. Nemo turn purple with jealousy.

There was not much of the Parisian Bohéme in the curious scene; there was little in it to remind a traveller, or literary student, of that dauntless intellectual democracy which first heartily rallied in the France of Louis Philippe, when the amalgamated Faubourg and Chaussée d'Antin constituted an aristocracy too thoroughly snobbish to associate any social value with genius; yet was it truly "Bohemian" in the cosmopolitan sense of the term. Free and careless mortals were these in Mr. Tick's back parlor; living by their wits; dining with no less zest to-day because not knowing where the morrow's meal was to come from; fraternizing with actor, singer, and politician, alike; worshipping the brother who had risen from the ranks, and keeping close fellowship with him whose mediocrity, or demoralization, doomed him to remain Bohemian forever; jolly good fellows; claqueurs but one degree removed from loafers; — all life, love, and carelessness, — no money!

The withdrawal of chairs from the table and lighting of pipes giving more freedom for general intercourse, I improved the opportunity to saunter about from one group to another and become better acquainted with my new friends; but it was not long before Hardley Church privately suggested to me, that, as a novice in the ways of that particular world, I might like to accompany him to the front room and be formally introduced to Solon Tick. Promptly understanding this as a delicate method of saying that I might as well pay my score at once, I went with him like a lamb, and had the honor of knowing the proprietor more intimately.

"Tick," said the philosopher, vivaciously, "this is Mr. Glibun, of the *Earthquake*, and one of us. I authorize you to give him whatever he pays for."

"Ha! ha!" laughed Mr. Tick, cheerily; for he saw that I held a pocket-book; "I'm always happy to oblige your friends, Mr. Church;" and he obliged me by taking the money I tendered. He took it, too, with a feverish nervousness, as though not quite accustomed to such prompt payment from men of genius, and perceptibly trembled when rubbing my score from a slate under the bar.

"There's a little something against the subscriber, too, for the early part of the evening, I think," observed Mr. Church, with two fingers in his near vest-pocket.

"Ha! ha! ha!" laughed the proprietor, rubbing his hands like one thrilled with unexpected good luck, and gazing at the fingers with sparkling eyes, "I don't know but there is, Mr. Church."

Out flew the fingers from the pocket with — a tooth-pick between them; and Hardley Church addressed Mr. Tick in the following concise and poetical phrase, —

"*Trust* me, Clara Vere de Vere, — as usual."

Something like a groan disguised in a cough accompanied the host's effort to make the words "with pleasure" sound hopefully, and the philosopher and I returned in haste to our friends.

Said friends, however, were then preparing to separate for the night. The ladies had resumed their bonnets, the gentlemen were refilling their pipes for the street, and both ladies and gentlemen were saying the most witty and humorous things they could think of by way of leaving good impressions. The procession to the sidewalk had plenty of laughter and parting phrases for music, and from the foot of Mr. Tick's stoop our company broke away in affinitive divisions. Church and Nemo escorted Miss Iona Hart away; Fox and Drinkard protected Miss Leggett on her homeward journey, and Messieurs Scribner and Bird fluttered congenially off together toward their lodgings in a Bowery boarding-house. The rest of us marched conjointly as far as Broadway, in close and measured Indian file; but there Dewitt and I felt impelled to part with our companions.

Not that we should have experienced anything else than true enjoyment in going farther with them; for Messieurs Gushington, Steele, and Scribner had that day discovered a particular block of nobby residences where ash-barrels might be overturned and door-mats exchanged with fine, humorous effect, —and would have had us proceed with them, before retiring, to their intended consummation of those practical witticisms.

--------◇--------

CHAPTER XL.

RACK-AND-RUIN ROW.

Gwin Le Mons's manner of greeting me had given my best feelings a deeper cut than I chose to admit even to myself; and, of course, I had no inclination to let others speculate upon the wound which Iona Hart's quick eyes had so soon discerned and pitied. His vagabondizing abroad has made a snob of him! was my first indignant thought; but the gentler emotion of regret inspired me when I noted how ill he looked, and how all humored and petted him. Nevertheless, he had pointedly repulsed me under the most humiliating circumstances, and if we were to have any association in future, the advances must come from his side. Upon that I was determined; and, in rigid observance of it, I not only saluted my old playmate very distantly when next we chanced to be in the same company, but also refrained from mentioning his name to any of our mutual literary acquaintances. Certainly no one took the trouble to mention him to me until a week after our little dissipation at Tick's, when Church — who had visited the *Earthquake* office, to either sell a manuscript or borrow three dollars from me — happened to mention him as a fellow-lodger. Rendered particularly genial by my gracious concession of the desired loan, the grisly philosopher exhibited a deep interest in my domestic welfare, and wished to know my home address. On hearing that I lodged in Warren Street, he spoke slightingly of that part of the town, and urged me to make a sociable move.

"Come up to Benedick Place," said he, persuasively, "and take a room in the same house with Fox and Le Mons, and Steele, and me. Iona Hart boards in the second block above us, Gushington lives just around the corner, and the climate is salubrious. The house is all let out in lodgings, to literary fellows, young lawyers, and Dr. Mitchell's medical students, and the terms are easy. What do you say to it?"

"Will Dewitt advises me to try a second-class hotel for a while," responded I, turning uneasy under his very quizzical look.

"Because then you won't be in the middle of a continual panic in the money market," quoth Church, poking me in the ribs. "So Dewitt has been posting you about Bohemia, eh? He's been putting you up to his own old-fogy style of Miss Nancyism."

Dewitt had unquestionably advised me to avoid a too great intimacy with the impecunious fraternity, unless I wished to start a Disinterested Loan and Trust Company, for the benefit of general mankind, and I blushed guiltily when the philosopher stated it thus.

"I knew that was it!" pursued he, poking me again; "and, to speak frankly, Dewitt has acted like your friend. But I've taken a liking to you, myself, and I'll tell you how it shall be. You come to our house, and *I'll* see that nobody sponges on you — but myself. You're luckier than most of us poor devils, — in having a regular salary, I mean, —and you ought not to be unaccommodating to your friends. What do you say now?"

There was something about this old philosopher that drew me to him, despite all good counsel; and, as I looked upon his gray hairs and wrinkled face, and reflected that he must often go hungry to bed, there arose within me such an excuse for his borrowing that I could no longer refuse.

"I think I'll try Benedick Place, for a while, at any rate," said I, with a laugh; "for you Bohemians would be down here with your manuscripts, if I wasn't up there with my trunk."

"O wise young judge!" cried the philosopher, in profound mock admiration of my penetration. "How much more elder art thou than thy looks!"

In this style was I persuaded, against my better judgment, to become housemate to the most improvident fellows in the world. I may add, however, that my room in Benedick Place (near what is now called University Place) was much pleasanter than any I had previously occupied, and that Hardley Church did indeed protect my pocket from all hands but his own. Homelessness is the first condition of Bohemianism. Dewitt had a proper home, and, by the stable attraction of that noblest centre of gravity, was withheld from going farther than the verge of Bohemia. I had required less than a month of life in New York lodgings to make me a vagabond at heart, and more willing than I was myself aware, perhaps, to fraternize indiscriminately.

Despite my own vagabondage, however, I was not without a certain lazy wonderment at the adoption of that kind of life by Gwin Le Mons. I thought, indeed, with some earnestness, of him in that connection, on the moment of entering the public door of the great brick house in Benedick Place, to occupy my new room upon the third floor thereof for the first time. That he lived there was the immediate suggestion of both street and house to me that evening, and speculations upon the whereabouts of his mother and sister abstracted me more and more as I plodded up the long stairways and through the long passages. So pondering, and taking little heed to my steps, a lap in the matting on the second-floor hall proved a snare to my feet. Tripping full force upon it, I went plunging awry against the nearest door; and that door, being only half latched, gave me a treacherous fall into the room it belonged to.

Wild flourishes with my arms saved me from complete prostration on the occasion; but, as the door flew open, I was revealed kneeling upon the mat at its threshold, after the manner of some frantic monarchical subject who had eluded all the guards of the palace and now urged his petition in the very bed-chamber of royalty itself.

The speedy operation of regaining my feet gave me just time enough to note a seated figure, with its head apparently resting upon its arms on a table. Standing erect, I had further opportunity to see the head raised, and recognize the features. There was no mistaking that St. John face and golden hair, though, like their owner's dress, they were notably disordered; but, beholding them in that place was somewhat akin, in my mind, to beholding a supernatural apparition. Owing, however, to a tolerable familiarity with odd occurrences, I was not compelled thereby to either start or gape, but evinced my high breeding in a prolonged whistle.

"This is a rather unexpected meeting, Avery Glibun," observed the former monitor of Oxford Institute arising and giving me his hand. He was as calm and collected about it as though he had indirectly appointed to meet me there.

"It certainly is," returned I, stiffly; "and I have to apologize for the clumsy accident. I tripped on the matting out there and was thrown against your door."

"If you are not hurt, the accident was fortunate, for me, at least. I am glad to see you."

"Thank you," I rejoined, ugly memories and my old antagonism rising within me; "but I will not take further advantage of the accident than to excuse myself and bid you good-evening."

"Then you regret our meeting," he quickly remarked, before I could turn upon my heel.

"I can think of no particular reason for being gratified with it," said I, nettled at the placidity which was so characteristic of the former young apostle. "It is a long time since I saw you last; but I can still remember the good turn I owe to a prominent member of your family. I have no especial grudge against you, personally,

Mr. Reed; yet you—are associated with scenes not pleasant to recall."

"Please sit down for a few moments," he requested, drawing a chair for me.

"You are very polite, Mr. Reed, but—"

"Do it to oblige me, Avery. I ask it as a favor."

I noticed his worn, disordered appearance more particularly now, and might have melted toward him, in his seeming trouble, but for that old, instinctive antagonism.

"If you persist in taking advantage of my unlucky accident," was my ungracious answer, "I will do as you desire." And I sat down.

He then resumed his own chair beside the table, leaned his head wearily upon his hand, and regarded me with thoughtful and—I thought—troubled look.

"If I can make any reparation to you for my father's errors," he said, very earnestly, "let me do so. I will do anything you ask."

"Look here, Ezekiel Reed!" I exclaimed, with rude passion; "the errors that come under the head of Attempted Murder are not to be preached away. Of you I want nothing but avoidance. I never liked you, and I tell you so frankly."

It was not in human nature, however saintly, to keep the flush of indignation from those milky cheeks, or the fire of wounded pride from those womanish blue eyes; but both were gone again in a moment.

"Do you know how my father has suffered since then? For years?"

"I have heard that your step-father did not die on the Summit, as he deserved; and that he went mad. I am sorry to speak about him in this way to you, but you drag it out of me."

"Avery," said Reed, without change of tone, position, or look, "you are able to use a man's reason now, if your passion permits, and should be able to exercise a man's judgment over the things you so bitterly remember. I ask you, then, whether you, as a just and thinking man, can still regard my unhappy father as the principal of a wrong in which he was only a helpless tool?"

"What do you mean?" cried I, angry, but impressed strangely.

"This," responded he; and he raised his head and spoke sternly; "that the unfortunate man, whose misery finds so little mercy with you and others, was made what he was, and is, by your own father!" He did not stop to give me time to fiercely deny what I felt to be a miserable truth. "But we will leave that with God. I am sorry that you have forced me to say it at all. I wish to speak with you of an entirely different matter. You thought it strange that I did not express more surprise at your appearance here."

"That's of no consequence now, sir," I replied, twirling my hat. "Just be good enough to state your business as briefly as possible."

. "I have been inquiring and looking for you some time," he went on, resting his head again; "and learned this morning, from an acquaintance upstairs, that you were coming here to lodge. I saw by a paragraph in one of the papers that a person-bearing your assumed name had obtained an editorship, and I had before heard, from the casual remarks of the acquaintance I have mentioned, that Avery Glibun was your true name. So, you see, I was not altogether unprepared for your appearance, accidental as it was."

"Your interest in me and my affairs is very flattering," was my ironical response. But I couldn't help wondering, though, what he could so particularly want of me.

"I wished to talk with you about an old friend of yours, Gwin Le Mous."

Surprised out of all anger in a moment, I leaned back in my chair, and gave my whole attention to the speaker.

"For a long time," pursued he, distinctly and steadily as though he read, "for a long time I boarded with your friend's excellent mother, in Fourth Street, and was so kindly treated, so generously confided in, by that lady and Miss Le Mous, that all their affections, feelings, and interests, became, as it were, my own. I found that they had a great sorrow; their only son and brother—an old playmate of yours, as they told me—had become alienated from them by dissipated associates,—especially by one unprincipled young man named Wild,—and had finally gone off to Europe without even bidding them good-by. Some unnatural disagreement with his mother seemed to have been one reason alleged by the young man for his conduct; but his sister, apparently, retained a strong hold upon his affections through all, even though her exemplary piety could not influence his misguided mind. He has lately returned, I hear, to New York; is in this house, in fact; and still neglects his home. The already bleeding hearts of his mother and sister will be broken if this continues; and, as I have reason to believe that any personal effort on my part would be angrily received by him, I have sought for *you*, in the hope that you would exert your influence with him."

Curiosity and surprise were equally excited in me by this statement, to the exclusion of all previous emotions. A loving pity for Gwin accompanied a better feeling toward Reed, and I answered the latter in a kinder tone than my past language could have led him to expect.

"Gwin has made no effort, since his return, to renew our boyish friendship; but I shall not hesitate, Ezekiel, to be at him about this at once. Poor Gwin! I thought he seemed unnatural in some way. He is certainly ill, too. Are his mother and Conny well?"

"They were when I left them,—in all but that."

"Conny makes quite a handsome girl, I suppose."

"She is beautiful as she is good."

"Phew!" said I, beginning to feel quite good-natured, and wishing that he would not shade his face quite so much with his hand. "Perhaps you have a particular reason for taking such an interest in Gwin, Mr. Reed?"

"No; you are mistaken," returned he, quietly. "I did forget God's purpose for me so far as to love Constance, and tell her of it; but she was truer to her duty than I to mine."

The simplicity of the confession, in that calm, uncomplaining tone, made it pathos to me. Taken, too, in connection with the dejected attitude in which I had found him, and the repressed melancholy of his whole appearance, it sounded like an echo from some solitude of suffering.

"Reed," said I, moving nearer to him, and touching his disengaged hand, "I'm afraid that I've been unjust to you, old fellow. You were not to blame for what your step-father did, and you were perfectly right about my own father's inhumanity. To be honest with you, I'm soured against everybody connected with my boyhood, because I never knew what it was to be treated like a child. I've had an outcast, despised, dog's life of it ever since I was a baby. If you can take that as an excuse for my snarling just now, here's my hand."

He shook it warmly, but without raising his head, and I then noticed, for the first time, that a felt hat on a chair near him had crape upon it.

"You have lost some near relative, lately," I added, quickly and remorsefully.

"Yes," said he, retaining my hand; "my sister died last week."

"Why didn't you tell me that, before I insulted your grief with my ruffianism?"

"She had been an invalid long, and was glad and prepared to die," he answered. "I should be selfish and ungrateful to grieve for my dear sister."

"Can it be, then, that Conny's—"

"No!" he exclaimed, in sudden vehemence, at the same time throwing back his head and giving me a wild look. "Do you feel kindly enough toward me to really care what my trouble is?"

"Try me, and see."

"Well, then, you shall know it," he cried, with trembling lips and a manner singularly changed. "I am distracted, Glibun, with a new and awful trouble. My poor father has escaped raving mad from the asylum, and can nowhere be found. My God! my God! why hast thou forsaken me!"

"You shock me!" I exclaimed, grasping both his feverish hands. "When did this happen?"

"Yesterday."

"How?"

"They can only say that an old colored man, who had long haunted the outside of the asylum, was there yesterday morning about the time my father escaped, and must have helped him away."

"An old colored man?"

"Yes. Old Yaller. Long ago the black saw me in the street, questioned me about my father, and has been hanging about the asylum ever since. He told me at the time, in a confused way, that he was living in some wretched quarter of the city; but who can say where? My father may be sick — dying — at this moment, in some miserable den, like a wild beast!"

"I know where Old Yaller is!" cried I, scarcely less frenzied than he. "In Cow Bay, at the Five Points."

He shrank from me for a moment, and then hastily asked how I knew.

"I once saw him there."

Up sprang Reed, nearly overturning me in the act, and snatched his hat from the chair.

"I must let the police know of this instantly," were his hurried words; "they have been looking for him on the west side of the city."

"But," said I, recovering my scattered senses, "it was several years ago when I saw him there."

"He's there! he's there! I can feel that he's there! You'll excuse me. I must not lose a moment," and the inexplicable mortal was gone.

Left again in one of those odd situations which had so often made me their sport, I rubbed my eyes, rubbed my hands, and sat gazing at the gas flare for some moments before I could make anything probable of what had occurred. My own momentary excitement by sympathy with Reed's startling outburst made me the more confused in thinking of it, and it was with an uneasy sense of having in some way contributed to a great trouble, that I finally turned down the light, slipped from the room, and repaired in haste to my own chamber above.

In the morning I went down there again, and found the gas still burning, — everything as I had left it. He had not returned. At night it was the same. And when I inquired for Gwin, amongst the Bohemians of my floor, intending to remonstrate with him at once on his cruelty and folly toward mother and sister, they told me that he had just been hurried off to Washington on special business for some paper.

In truth, it seemed as though the unpremeditated interview was fated to have no sequel whatever; and, after being haunted by recollections of it for three days, I determined to think no more about it. But on the fourth evening Reed entered my room almost as abruptly as I had entered his, and stood before me like a ghost.

"Have you found him?" I asked, instinctively.

"Yes."

"Where?"

"Where you directed me to look. I want you to go there with me immediately. I have come from my father's death-bed to call you."

The ghastliness of his face, the solemn light in his eyes, and the awful character of the summons, paralyzed my will and tongue. I felt that I must go with him. Every faculty expressed that, and that alone; and, without another word, I arose, took my hat, and followed him from the room. That his look, though, rather than his language, produced this peremptory effect upon me was soon to appear likely; for when we had taken seats in a hack in waiting, and his face no longer caught the light on it, my wits returned, bringing a sharp spirit of rebellion with them.

"I believe you've bewitched me," I said, as the vehicle started. "What does all this mean?"

"I have told you," he answered, drawing a deep sigh. "My father is dying, and wishes to see you. I believed that you could not refuse the request of a dying man, even though he had injured you."

Then, with his hand on my knee, and his voice weak with repressed misery, he told me how he had gone with the police to the darkest haunts of crime and starvation, and, after days and nights of relentless search, had found the poor maniac in the garret of the old negro. Escaping from the asylum, whose authorities had been deceived into temporary laxity of discipline by his simulated fitness for such indulgence, the crazed school-master had been joined outside the walls by his former slave, and conveyed swiftly away to the den of the latter at the Points. There, a terrible fever had seized him, and, when discovered by his step-son, he was too ill to be removed. The fever itself was leaving him then, and carrying his life with it; but, in the last hours of mortal existence, reason had returned once more, bringing remorse for its past abuses. The dying man had plaintively called for his wife and for me, imploring our forgiveness. The wife was his no longer, but the old pupil might be summoned.

"But why," I asked, "should the black play such a part?"

"Because, in his ignorance, he attached an exaggerated idea of wrong and persecution to what he considered the forcible imprisonment of his master. Added to this was an affrighted and remorseful consciousness of having once struck that master, and a yearning to atone for the deed by some act of devotion. Poor father! all have not been unfaithful to you because of your sins."

Feeling quite incapable of even an attempt to console my companion, I expressed the incapacity by a sigh, and gave a half-listless attention to objects outside the hack. We were jolting down Leonard Street at the moment, already crossing the scummy outer circle of the foul maelstrom of iniquity once hiding me in its pestilential heart. Rags, rum, and ruin began to lap me in again on every side, and sights and sounds of despair without God to revisit my shrinking senses like taunts of past horror. The same reeking kennels and cellars still blotched the noisome gloom of those tottering coffins of the soul with their bleary lights, streaming in and out with the poor lost creatures who drank madness and crime from their polluted springs. At sashless windows and on tumbling stoops appeared shadowy slatterns and sots, shrieking coarse salutes, or howling ribald songs; and as the carriage plunged from one swamp of filth to another, in passing an end of the blighted "Park," the impish progeny of the Points swarmed under and around it like the very corruption of life stirred up from teeming decay. But for the officer of police who rode on the box with the driver and held his club ever ready to beat down the first matted head that came too near, more than one knot of jeering ruffians would have revenged the intrusion of such a vehicle by dragging us out by the throats. As it was, yells and oaths greeted us from every groggery and cellar-way, and when we turned into Cow Bay, one creature, — a half-naked woman, — tried to thrust her screaming babe through the sash at which my face appeared.

And when the hack stopped, and I followed Ezekiel Reed from it, what a climax came through sight to feeling as I found myself standing before that very tenement in Rack-and-Ruin Row, where Reese and I had lived and Olden Grey had died! In a kind of incredulous stupefaction I stared up at the looming ruin of a house, which seemed to shiver in the wind like a freezing beggar, and fight convulsively with it for its miserable tatters of shutters.

"Here?" I ejaculated.

"Yes," was the whispered answer. "You need not be afraid. This way. The hack will wait for you."

Shame at being suspected of cowardice prevented any farther questioning on my part, and I bade him lead the way.

Up the half of a step-ladder to the high stoop again, and along halls and stairways thronging with ghosts for me. Along and up, past the old dens and scenes, to the ladder trained to the old loft. Up the ladder, and —

There, on a pallet under the window in the roof, laid the man with whom I had once before been in company on the verge of death. Ghastly and frightful he was then, in all the frantic despair of wrong avenging wrong; and doubly frightful to me, in that I read my own death in his storm-lighted face; but now, in his gaunt hideousness and whiteness, he looked like his former self and me revenged to death upon himself — like the retribution of murder too merciless to exact life for life and become in itself an awful existence. The shaved head, the bloodless face, seamed and drawn into an appalling mask, the skeleton outline of the bedclothes, — were an awful transfiguration of Roderick Birch.

Seeing this, I felt, rather than saw, also, that a figure like a large ape sat on the floor near the bed's head, with its knees drawn up to its chin; and that a stern-looking man, with the air of a physician, stood motionless on the opposite side of the dying.

The standing figure whispered something to Ezekiel Reed, who bent for a moment over the dreadful spectre on the pallet, and then motioned for me to draw nearer. Mechanically I obeyed, my heart rising in my throat when the glazing eyes of the school-master slowly opened, and stiffened upon me.

"Say to him," said Ezekiel Reed, in the tone of one praying, — "say to him what God bids you say."

Forcing my fascinated gaze from the bed to the floor, I falteringly uttered words which seemed to come to me by rote, —

"Mr. Birch, I am very sorry for you. I truly forgive you for any harm you tried to do me when I was a boy at your school. I am satisfied that you were driven to do what you did by the wickedness of those connected with me. In that sense, I need forgiveness from you, perhaps."

Spasmodically raising my look to that terrible face again, I had perception enough in my horror to fancy that the sunken eyes were gentler, but, alas! it was the leaden dulness of the last cold sleep coming into them. Ezekiel Reed, too, had marked the change, and threw up his arms in a frenzy of grief.

"Too late!" he wailed. "My father! my father! you have not heard!"

Sinking upon his knees beside the pallet, and pressing his clasped hands against his breast, he watched in mute and rigid agony.

And the ape-like figure, too, — the old negro who, in his servile devotion, had brought the poor maniac hither as to a sure refuge from all persecutors, — arose to his knees and stared in trembling affright. He had found this deserted garret one day in his search for a hiding-place where the minions of the prison would not think to look for their rescued victim, and held it thenceforth against all comers, like a snarling wolf, until he had brought his master there. In the dull, yellow light of the two candles on the table against the wall, his wrinkled, black face, dripping with the damps of abject terror, was like the first vision of the lost in another world.

"Mr. Reed," said the physician, "it is a mercy that your father has lost consciousness. He will now die without pain. Your affliction seems to be a peculiar and terrible one, but it is the Almighty who sends it, and you should try to resign yourself to his will. From what I have seen of your conduct in this extraordinary and fearful trial, I feel that I need not remind you of that hope, through Christ, which should be a support to you as a Christian son."

At the words, Ezekiel slowly arose to his feet, and turned to the speaker a countenance in which fanatical resolve struggled convulsively with outraged nature.

"Yes, doctor, you are right," he answered, in a husky, unnatural voice. "I must be resigned. I must even take strength from what I see here, to make my own life an expiation, by sacrifice, of the sins my father cannot repent for himself. How soon will he die?"

"Very soon, Mr. Reed."

"You can do no more?"

"I cannot."

"O my mother!" cried the young man, raising eyes and hands to heaven in a kind of hysterical transport, "bear witness that I have been true to him you loved, and that I will be true to him still!" Then, looking mournfully from the doctor to me, and pointing to the negro, he added, — "We two will do the rest."

Moved by a common instinct, the doctor and I exchanged glances for a moment, and then proceeded noiselessly together toward the door. Gaining which, I turned for a last look, and saw that Ezekiel Reed was on his knees again, with hands clasped against his breast.

In silence we descended through the teeming abode of want and misery, passing two policemen who seemed to be stationed in the halls to enforce quiet, and reaching the street without encountering aught to disturb the gloomy current of our thoughts. A second hack had arrived for the doctor, but we exchanged a few words before parting.

"This is a very strange case," observed the kindly man of medicine. "I do not know what to make of it. Are you at liberty to enlighten me?"

"I fear not, doctor."

"Pardon me, then, for asking you, sir. My interest in a very singular young man overcame my professional discretion. As you appear to have a hack of your own, I will bid you good-night, sir."

He sprang into his vehicle without more ado, and I into mine. The drivers, and the very horses, seemed eager to get out of Cow Bay as soon as possible, and the clatter of hoofs and wheels was like the quickening sounds of departure from a funeral and a newly-filled grave.

————◆◆◆————

CHAPTER XLI.

EZEKIEL REED never returned to Benedick Place. When my wits were sufficiently concerted again to reconsider calmly the distempered events last described, I experienced a temporary yearning toward the only familiar of my younger days who was not intolerably disreputable; but still calmer second thought made me doubt whether, after all, I could find anything more congenial than tacit sanctimonious reproach in his companionship. In the end, therefore, I was content to think no more about him, save as I had pledged myself at his request to expostulate with Le Mons. For a week my newspaper work was oppressive in its tone of jaded mentality, and Dewitt plainly imparted to me his belief that I was "going it strong" with the Benedicktines. For a few nights I was afflicted with ghastly dreams. But the impressions created in my mind by the miserable death of the ex-school-master soon grew faint, and blended with my general passive sense of unblessedness.

Church, Steele, and Fox lost no time in adopting my room as a common lounging-place, where they might smoke their pipes and freely criticise absent friends. Thither, too, they occasionally brought divers vagrant artists, players, and knowing gentlemen about town, who were pleased to consider it a friendly thing in me to send out for crackers and beer, and not unfrequently repaid my hospitality with pencil caricatures of myself, gallery tickets, and solicitations for memorial locks of my hair. There were moments when I had irritable qualms about being identified with such "shiftless" society; but quick would come the recollection that I had no business to feel any pride in myself; and then I would riot with them to their own eclipse. The three worthies first named seemed proper sources of the preparatory information I had resolved to obtain before addressing Le Mons on the subject of his truancy from home, and to them I appealed, passingly, one evening, after the theatre, for what were their knowledge and views of "Baby." Each had a separate opinion, of course, of his literary incapacities, but in affection for him personally their unanimity was complete. He was a prime fellow; he was always ready for anything; he travelled with Wild; and he'd been talking about writing a book ever since he began to scribble for the papers. His family were all blue presbyterians, and he'd cut clear of them. He had a good education and some talent, but not enough energy to make anything of himself. In any other kind of company this last deficiency would have been reprobated as almost a crime, but these poor fellows were just enough, from their own experiences, to mention it tenderly.

A lack of that concentrative force of character which is requisite for the creation of all honorable and distinguishing success in life, too often meets reproof and contempt as a voluntary fault, when it should really be tolerantly regarded as an involuntary misfortune. Energy is one degree of genius, nor can it, any more than the latter exceptional power, be a common possession. It is not synonymous with industry, or perseverance, though necessary to render them greatly successful; and if it has not been born in a man, all the cultivation in the world will not develop it within him. Its deficiency is a misfortune in this sense, that, whosoever feels it not to be his, has proof thereby that nature inexorably designs him for those humbler grades and occupations of life which lead to neither fame nor fortune, and that all his efforts to escape such predestination must be futile. Energy, or want of energy, is simply Nature's imperative predilection for greatness, or humbleness.

I had suspected, from my own observations, that Le Mons lacked energy, without which a literary life is particularly hopeless. No other kind of life makes more demand upon that quality, and, at the same time, no other life tends so insidiously to undermine it through early physical deterioration; and to undertake it without energy was to insure disappointment, failure, and slow torture unto death!

Gwin returned from Washington in disgrace. Report in our circle said that he was recalled for drunkenness. Knowing which room he occupied, I went to it early on the morning after his arrival, determined to "catch him in." He was still abed, and, on seeing me enter, after I had mercilessly knocked him into bidding me do so, turned scarlet with vexation.

"Well!" said he, rising upon his elbow, "what is the row?"

"The row is, that I'm determined to have a talk with you, Le Mons," I said. "Shake hands with me."

He did so with bad grace, and petulantly desired to know if my own room was in flames.

"Now, don't be ill-natured, old man," said I, drawing up a chair. "I've resolved not to let another day pass without inquiring what grudge you hold against me? When we were boys together we were close cronies, and even at this distance of time I have enough of the old love left to feel hurt at a snub from you. If I have accidentally offended you in any way, tell me how."

"Your grandmother! I've never said anything about having a grudge against you, Glibun."

"Am I to understand, then, that it was nothing but wanton whim made you cut me in that style at Tick's?"

"You can understand just exactly what you—" He caught himself, broke into a frank smile, and impetuously added,—"Oh, bother all this highfalutin! The fact is, Glibun, I was afraid of what you might say to me if I didn't put on airs. I didn't know, yet, that you were one of us, and thought you might want to preach."

"Preach! What about?"

"Why," rejoined he, coloring, "about mother and Conny. You've found out, of course, that I don't go home?"

"Yes," said I, cautiously, "I could tell that much from finding you in Benedick Place."

"You think the blame's on my side, of course; I can see that in your looks. Mother and Conny have been giving me a character, I suppose."

"There you're mistaken, Le Mons. I have never seen either of them since I was a boy. But I must say that I'm sorry to see you acting such an unnatural part."

"There it goes again!" groaned Gwin, throwing himself back upon his pillow in

boyish despair. "A fellow must always keep tied to his mammy's apron strings, or every old granny has to interfere."

"That's complimentary," said I, laughing.

"I do declare!" he went on, clasping his hands over his head, "there's no end to the sermons I catch from everybody. Even Iona Hart had to bore me about the same thing before I'd been home from London a week. Leggett will be lecturing me about filial duty next, and then Maggie Dalen, and then old Church himself! As for you, Glibun, I wonder you don't turn Methodist parson—"

Here the poor fellow was seized with a violent fit of coughing, which left him too much exhausted to complete the sentence.

"O Gwin!" I cried, in a sudden terror, "that cough of yours goes right through me. Can't something be done for it? How can you abuse yourself as you do, with your wild life, when a little care might do so much good?"

"Don't let's talk about it," returned he, pressing a hand against his racked lungs. "It's only a cold. I've been going it too fast, lately, but now I'm going to be respectable for a while."

"And go home," I added, pleadingly.

"To be scolded and preached to death!" he exclaimed, in a tone of peevish irritation. "Glibun, *you* should have some fair idea of the trouble between mother and me; for you must remember how she used to thump and pound me in the old days. It was scold and whip from morning till night; and Conny had her share of slaps, too. *Flagelletur frequenter et fortiter* was the prescription for me, until my temper was ruined, and my spirit broken. Slaps made a Methodist of Conny, and whippings made me a *coward*! It's a fact, and you needn't stare," he continued, lashing himself into a passion; "my beatings when I was a boy made me a coward for life. Any bully can cow me now; and all because I was lashed like a thieving cur, when I was trying to grow into a man! After I'd finished my education I was too old for blows; but then mother scolded the more. I was always bringing disgrace upon her, and going to ruin; all my friends were dissipated; and, one evening, when I had Wild home to tea with me, neither mother nor Conny would sit at the table with him. Finally, I couldn't stand it any longer, and left in a huff. Then, when I went across the water with Wild, what does mother do but open a boarding-house,—just to mortify me, I do believe, Glibun! —and one of her boarders, some canting fellow named Reed, had the impudence, after a while, to write me a whining, puritanical letter about a broken-hearted parent, and a devoted sister pining with grief! He even had the confounded insolence to say something about my unhappy subjection to evil associates! Mother and Conny can have him, if they want him, and do without me."

"Well, well, what is this world made of?" retorted I. "You're the second one of my

29

acquaintances to blame a mother for his ruin! And your sister, too!"

"Oh, she's a good little girl enough," said he uneasily, "if it wasn't for her eternal religion."

"That does sound like cowardice, Gwin. Conny's religion is a reproof to your vices."

"Oh, of course! A fellow must live on psalms, or be an incorrigible reprobate. As old Churchy says, religion is nothing but a parcel of dismal sophistry, to make old women believe that they're not afraid of death."

"Gwin Le Mons," cried I, horrified by his words, — and he with the fatal hectic flush on his thin cheeks, — "Gwin Le Mons, you do not mean what you are saying! Such men as Wild and Church have been using you as a plaything, to your own destruction. Be advised now by me, and go home. If anything should happen to your mother or sister, while you have this feeling, you could never forgive yourself. The way you have acted is the strongest possible proof that your mother's severity was needful and deserved. Don't spurn the truest and best love in the world, for the sake of a set of reckless, dissipated vagabonds, who think as much of any common player that can ' treat' them, as they do of you. I tell you, you are very sick, and must go home!"

I spoke strongly, as I felt, and the wayward "Baby" could not answer rebelliously enough to entirely disguise the serious effect of my words upon him.

"You're a nice one to preach home-doctrine to a fellow, Glibun, I *don't* think," he remarked, with an attempt to appear unmoved. "What are you doing here, yourself? Why don't *you* live at home?"

"Because," returned I, with swelling heart, "I have no home. Because I never knew what it was to have a mother; and only knew a father's power long enough to be driven out homeless by it into the world, in fear of my life! That is why your ingratitude to your mother and carelessness of home seem so monstrous to me."

Mere spoiled child that he was, his eyes moistened in a moment, and he leaped out of bed and gave me a deliberate hug.

"You're right, Ave Glibun," said he, beginning to dress with great expedition. "I've been ashamed of myself ever since I cut and run the first time. It's as well to own up at once, you know. I'd have made up with the old lady and Con, long ago, only I was ashamed; and the longer it has gone, the worse it has become. You mustn't lay it to Wild, though; for he has been like a brother to me."

"You *will* go home, then, Gwin?"

"Yes; honor bright. By the way, Glibun, couldn't you go with me, just to make it less awkward?"

"Willingly. But when?"

"Oh, before very long," said he, hesitating.

"Why not at once?" I asked.

"Well, to be honest about it," responded he, in some confusion, "I want to have two or three good Bohemian weeks of it, before I turn respectable. After I'm once at home again, I must try to conciliate mother by being steady as an old clock for at least a year, — in fact, my health requires that much; so I must get through with all the engagements on hand before going. I've promised to take Leggett to a race; I've promised to be at a little supper at Maggie Dalen's; I've promised to go with Wild to a masquerade ball, for a lark; and I've got half a dozen other appointments to keep. Think of the row mother and Conny would make, if I took leave of them about noon, on a fine day, to escort Miss Fatima Leggett to the Fashion Course!"

That seemed highly probable; but was the female player worthy to be humored at the expense of his mother's and sister's happiness?

"That's not a fair way to put it," he retorted. "Whatever these people may be, — worthy or worthless, — they've always treated me well, and I will not insult them for anybody. That's just the long and short of it."

It was useless to urge him farther. Greatly complacent at having finally determined to end his folly some time or other, he made sufficient merit of it, in his own volatile mind, to counterbalance any amount of present wilfulness. Ending all delay at once, and promptly restoring himself to home and ease of conscience, would have required what he did not possess, — energy.

"Do you know, Old Glibun," he said, pausing long enough in the operation of brushing his hair to give my chestnut locks a fanciful touch, — "it's as good as breakfast in bed to see you on pleasant terms again? I felt wolfish when you first came in, so policeman-like; but that was only a part of the bad-conscience feeling about home. Now, though, that we're all square once more, I don't mind telling you that you've turned out a good-looking fellow. Had any breakfast yet?"

"No."

"Of course I haven't, either; and my head will not be right from last night until I have a cup of coffee. We'll breakfast at Tick's together."

"Agreed."

"And after that I'd like you to go down with me to King's Theatre for a few minutes. Steele has got an adaptation of an English comedy rehearsing there to-day, and I promised to meet him there. Church is to be back from Brooklyn this morning, and he's likely to be there, too. Dalen's playing there now, you know, and we'll give you an introduction. What do you say?"

"Agreed, again."

I went to my own chamber for hat and top-coat, and a brisk walk of a few blocks took us to the familiar banquet-hall of the much-trusting Solon, where we found Gushington and Fox already revelling in too many dishes to leave the ghost of a probability that they intended to pay cash that day. Those varied and sumptuous breakfasts said plainly, that when deserving men of intellect had to eat on credit, anyway, it was part of a correct philosophy to be as extravagant as possible.

My recovered friend and I were fraternally greeted by these millionnaires, and unanimously advised by them to try quails that morning, and have cognac with our coffee. It would be as well for us, however, to commence with fresh salmon and cresses, — the latter combination being admirably calculated to exasperate the appetite to the highest degree, and provoke a breakfast sure to look gentlemanly on the private slate. But it happened that neither Gwin nor I proposed to go upon the slate on that occasion; so we took only coffee and cutlets.

Need I say that the general conversation refining our meal was worthy a party so intellectual? Need I record that either Apicius of the more luxurious tables regaled Le Mons and your chronicler with frequent filtration of wit and wisdom through divers eatables in process of deglutition, and that your chronicler and Le Mons vivaciously responded with the intellectual flavors of cutlet? Much proper scepticism as to the existence of disinterested virtue in the world was to be learned from Mr. Gushington's playful remark, that paying all you owed (whether for past meals or waistcoats) was destructive of the only earthly bond strong enough to make your dearest friends remember your full initials. A judicious comprehension of the delicacy of the softer sex was the natural consequence of hearing Mr. Fox assign, as his reason for not lately patronizing the green-room of a certain playhouse, the liability of the soubrette and first walking lady to come to blows at any imagined partiality of his attentions to either. Useful European knowledge flowed into the mind from Le Mons's animated exposition of the art of living upon credit and pawn-tickets in the literary quarters of London and Paris. And the pleasures of quaint humor were afforded by a cheerful disquisition of mine upon the prevalence of delirium tremens and consumption among the livelier young journalists of our age.

It was past ten o'clock when we finally arose from this lingering feast of reason; and then it became a question whether Gwin and I were to leave the other two.

"Where are you two giant minds going to now?" queried Gushington, combing his Indian locks with his fingers.

"To King's Theatre; rehearsal of Steele's latest appropriation from the foreign stage, you know," said Gwin. "Won't you two go along?"

"Of course I'll go," answered Gushington. "I'd forgotten all about the thing. Steele has only asked us because Maggie Dalen hires him to work up the press for her, personally; but then, we can go, and pitch into Maggie and the piece just the same. I'm with you."

But Fox (who by-the-by, stuttered interestingly) was otherwise inclined, and gave his reason. "I b-b'lieve I'll not go with you, gents. That L-l-leggett would make c-capital out of it if I went to a rehearsal where she was on. I'll go on down-town."

Consequently, there were but three of us for the expedition to King's Theatre, whither we proceeded at once.

Mr. King's popular dramatic shop was located on Broadway, not too far from the City Hall, and presented that brownish front of yawning vestibule and never-occupied windows which seems to be the one idea of all theatrical architects. On either side the main entrance were huge bill-boards, glorifying, in mammoth type, that "beautiful and accomplished artiste," Miss Margaret Dalen; strung along at irregular intervals between said bill-boards stood some four or five gentlemen, with their feet very far apart, their gloved hands on their hips or in the side-pockets of their picturesque talmas, and a general air about them of having just donned full dress for an evening, and forgotten to wash and shave; the sidewalk in front of the establishment being sprinkled with admiring apple-women and hackney-coachmen on call, who gaped in mute awe at the supper-party gentlemen aforesaid.

Exchanging light salutes with these gentlemen, who were all players, and well known in Bohemia, we passed through the vestibule to a couple of muffled green doors, and by these into the auditorium of the theatre. Single figures and groups of two were sitting here and there in the twilight gloom of the parquet; but they were principally the unworthy fathers or brothers (and sometimes, alas! husbands) of the younger women on the stage; and not our fellows. *They* were to be looked for somewhere on the stage itself; for, in those days, the remotest connection with the press was a genuine "free pass" to any part of a metropolitan playhouse at any hour, generally speaking, and a manager was but too happy to have all gentlemen of the connection make themselves perfectly at home on his premises. To the stage, then, we climbed, by help of the orchestra railings, in search of our friends; the dim lights and number of people thereon not allowing us to distinguish faces until we stood under the uplifted curtain.

In the prompter's corner, just beyond the right-hand proscenium box, were Steele, Church, Scribner, and Wild, all smoking pipes, and bandying pleasantries with a knot of ballet girls. An airy, *petite*, fashionably-dressed fairy, with a profusion of "frizzled" golden hair, walked or tripped back and forth along the line of footlights, dropping a word here and there to other members of the frail sisterhood standing about. Masculine players, of the same style with those in the vestibule, strolled in all directions, humming, or reciting to themselves. Beside a table near the centre of the stage stood little Mr. Speck, the stage-manager; and beside *him* loomed the tall figure of the curled and mustached manager, King himself.

I had barely joined the literary group, and caught the principal features of the scene, when Mr. King came magnificently forward to welcome us, and was at pains to lift his irreproachable silk hat and display the glossy dressing of his (dyed) sable hair.

"Good-morning, gen-til-men," he said, with all the complacent stateliness of another elder Vestris; "I'm glad to see you join your friends here, and regret that the present business of the stage will not allow me to offer you chairs. Mr. Glibun, I never had the pleasure of meeting you before, I believe; but I may say that I have *heard* of 'M. T. Head' occasionally." This with an insinuating smile.

"Honored, I'm sure," said I.

"I say, King," observed the dramatist; "that set scene in the second act ought to have a carpet. It's an extra drawing-room, and the green floor will spoil it."

"I think not, Mr. Steele."

"But I do."

"Mr. Steele," exclaimed the regal manager, mildly, but firmly, "I desire to meet your views in every reasonable detail; but I must remind you that *I* am the Manager of this Establishment." You could imagine, from his superb manner, that the elder Vestris actually stood in his irreproachable boots, and was saying again, "*Moi et le Roi de Prusse nous sommes les plus grands hommes en Europe!*"

"Have it your own way, then," growled Steele.

"No offence, I hope; no offence," added the politest of powers. "You see, gentlemen, there *must* be a Head. Excuse me now, while I attend to a little business with Mr. Speck."

"Well!" ejaculated I, as he left us; "that fellow knows how to oil his words."

"And he can use them without oil, when he chooses," grunted Church.

"Yes, indeed!" assented Wild and Le Mons.

"No mistake about it," chorused the ballet girls, behind us.

In fact, the mighty manager was even then illustrating his ability in that line. Instigated, apparently, by some whispered observation from the stage-manager, he loudly snapped his fingers, as for some truant dog, and, without turning his head, called, "Bulger!"

Thereupon a slender, sallow, over-dressed Hamlet of private life advanced sternly from the rear of a castle, and stood haughtily beside his chief.

"Bulger," remarked the latter, passingly, "there's a comic servant in this piece, who falls down with a tray of glasses, and gets kicked by the Leading Juvenile. Mr.

Speck didn't know who to give the part to. You'll take it."

"Sahr-r-r!" uttered Mr. Bulger, in a sepulchral tone.

"I say you'll take it, Bulger."

"Sahr-r-r," gurgled the other, clutching his cloak and setting his teeth. "I am an artist; not a — ha! ha! — a scrub, sahr-r."

"He'll take it, Mr. Speck."

"Never-r-r! never-r! I'll none of it!" hissed the insulted First Utility, who believed himself to be a wrongfully suppressed tragedian.

With a movement like lightning the manager grasped him by the back of the neck, and shook him until his talma appeared to be the sport of a hurricane. Then his face was drawn close to that of his proprietor, his biography was related to him in one short sentence, and a fist plentifully garnished with rings was advanced to the very edge of his nose.

"If you want that pretty face of yours spoiled, you just put on airs again," roared his majesty. "I'll let you know that *I* am the Manager of this Establishment!"

Stung to the very soul by such public humiliation, Mr. Bulger could only retire grinding his teeth. Nor did the amiable Miss Leggett contribute greatly to his happiness by calling out, as he passed through the giggling mob of players, — "So much for putting on too many frills at a time, Bulgy."

"I call that simple ruffianism!" said I, indignantly.

"It's the only way to manage these cattle," returned Wild.

Perhaps so; but it would have rejoiced my heart at that moment to see the gifted Bulger knock the chief drover down.

Le Mons and Gushington here came back to our nook, from exchanging a few words with the prominent little lady of the golden locks, and asked me why I had not followed them for an introduction to the "star"?

"Because," put in Wild, answering for me, "he's got enough pride in his profession to let the 'star' come to him. We literary fellows in this country are too ready by half to run after these player folks, and the consequence is, they think no more of an editor or a critic, than of one of their own kind. On the other side of the water a newspaper man is Somebody in a green-room, because he keeps the crew down, but here, — well, we're nothing but call-boys."

"What are you growling about now, Mr. Acton Wild?" cried Miss Fatima Leggett, striking at him from the next *coulisses* with her parasol.

"About your failure to take notice of me, darling," replied the travelled censor, with true *esprit de théâtre*, and at once went with Le Mons and Church to join her.

Then Steele repaired to the stage-manager's table for business, Gushington fell back amongst the ballet girls at the doors of the dressing-rooms, and I was left in comparative loneliness to watch the rehearsal.

The play in hand was a comedy called "A Trip to Devonshire," and had been "adapted," in an original and masterly manner, by the substitution of "New Hampshire" for "Devonshire" wherever the latter name occurred. Of all Steele's numerous dramatic works it was said to be the most elaborate in its fidelity to the text he took it from, and did the most credit to his lively capacity for realizing dramatic copyright without severe mental labor. The scenes in "Wellington Hall" in "New Hampshire;" the conquest of Lord Saykesalive, a rusticating nobleman (from Canada!), by a wild country girl; the concluding tableau of the nobleman and his bride presiding at a floral fête of the tenantry of Wellington Hall,—were all likely to charm the public, and delight such newspapers as had a sufficient number of front seats and private boxes distributed among them for the first night. The rehearsal, however, interested me only as it involved that dainty, willowy little blonde, who, unlike the other female players on the stage with her, gave the closest attention to it.

Margaret Dalen seemed to be scarcely more than eighteen, and, with her shining cloud of hair, large limpid blue eyes, and laughing mouth, suggested, at first sight, a childish freshness and simplicity which it was heart-breaking to associate permanently with such a scene. Longer observation, however, developed maturities of the form, and coquettish turns of eye and voice, not so juvenile; and an occasional careless display of the prettiest little gaiter boots in the world, went, as far as trifles in that case surely do, to indicate the absence of that finer delicacy of women which, like the tint of a butterfly's wing, becomes sullied forever at a familiar touch from the gentlest hand. For instants, too, when petty mistakes were made by those with whom she was rehearsing a scene, the sharp fire in her eyes, and rude passion in her ejaculations, were scarcely above her profession. In truth, had no previous jar disturbed the momentary dream in which I would fain have separated this soiled dove from her surroundings, the illusion must have vanished, with a shock all the harsher, when I saw her, at the conclusion of her work, hang over the huge gothic "throne chair," which Mr. King had caused to be placed for himself, and fondle the face of the managerial aristocrat with a freedom the more guileful from its failure as a counterfeit of trustful innocence. Still, there was something singularly winning in the fairy figure, bright looks, and merry laugh of Margaret Dalen; something to make me fancy that she must be like those belles of the mimic world who had kings for their subjects in the olden times.

This woman had gone upon the stage in another city, as a dancing girl, when she was but fourteen years old. Her ambition to become an actress soon procured for her an opportunity to appear in a third-rate character; and, making an unexpected mark in that, the higher steps came as rapidly. Confident at once that her abilities were adequate for success anywhere, and not waiting to finish her first apprenticeship, even, she "set up for a star," and went to a larger city in search of engagements. These however, she could not obtain, for managers did not care to develop new genius at a risk, while they could secure plenty of the old at a profit. Reduced to despair, ashamed to return whence she came, and not owning the means to do so had she desired to, the young girl was finally glad to sail for England as "dresser" to a veteran actress going thither. This actress proved to be a kind friend, and obtained for her maid a professional opening in the London company by which she was herself supported. The girl succeeded greatly, again, in a petty part; was promptly promoted to higher ones; and, at the end of the first year, sent an old play and a fifty-pound note to a great English critic, with the request that the former might be "adapted" for her possible use. The play was "adapted," sent back, and burned; the critic and his friends hailed the genius of the new American actress in all their papers, and she became famous. Returning to her own country again, she found every theatre open to her, every manager eager to secure the fortunate possessor of an English reputation. That was the theatrical history of Margaret Dalen.

A scenery-rehearsal of the "tenantry" tableau concluded the business of the morning, and, immediately thereafter, a procession was called for the green-room, where a little lunch had been prepared, under managerial auspices, in compliment to a well-known weakness of the literary gentlemen present. Dalen, escorted on either side by Mr. Steele and Mr. King, led the moving pageant. Then came Miss Leggett, in charge of Wild and Le Mons. Following whom were Scribner, Gushington, and myself, abreast. The players came indiscriminately in our wake, and we all hastened to the extemporized spread of sandwiches, chicken salad, and champagne, like creatures who had not breakfasted.

Steele and Le Mons favored me, as a *nouveau*, with an introduction to Miss Dalen immediately upon our arrival in the green-room, and I had the pleasure of being at once told by her that she had wanted to meet me for ever so long.

"And how is Mr. Dewitt?" she inquired, after coyly touching my glass with her lips. "He always speaks kindly of me in the *Earthquake;* but he won't be sociable."

"He is one of your practical men, Miss Dalen," was my response, "and not more than half a Bohemian. I think, though, that he will regret not having been here to-day, when I tell him that my presence, as representative of the paper, only emphasized to you his absence."

"Now don't be severe, Mr. Glibun," she laughed, "or I shall actually wish that a more merciful critic had been here to keep me in countenance. Do you think I shall fail very frightfully in this new character?"

"Well, to be frank with you," said I, "I did not pay much attention to that part of the rehearsal."

"You ungallant creature!"

"Excuse me, I meant to be particularly the reverse. My eyes and ears were all for you in your own character."

"Really?"

"On my honor."

"Then I'll forgive you, unless you are going to say something severe again. What do you think of me, then, Mr. Glibun, in my own character?"

"You wish me to speak honestly?"

"Ye-es," she replied, with a graver and questioning look, "that is, I —— yes! speak out."

My answer was sober and earnest enough to sound almost like lunacy in a place and company like those, —

"I think it a pity, Miss Dalen, that a woman of your appearance and genius should be a player."

A momentary expression of mingled surprise and (what I took for) pain, was succeeded by one of plaintive thoughtfulness on her changing face; and, in a still lower tone than that in which we had exchanged the last few words, she hurriedly said, —

"Suppose I cannot help it?"

"Then I pity you all the more, Miss Dalen. You must excuse me for talking to you in this style, but I can't help it."

"You speak like a friend, and I want you to be one to me," she whispered, quickly and earnestly. "You must come to a *petit souper* of mine, with your friends. Now let us laugh and joke, or we shall be noticed."

We had already been noticed very suspiciously, and Miss Leggett came romping to our settee, with Drinkard and Le Mons behind her.

"Law! Dalen," cried the singing chamber-maid, "some people are very thick on short acquaintance, I should think! Come over here, Mr. Church!" she added, calling that venerable philosopher from a chat with the walking lady of the company. "Your friend, Mr. Glibun, wants looking after. He and Dalen have been whispering for the last three minutes, by my watch."

"If that's the case," returned Church, "he's a fiend in human form; for everybody knows that Maggie and the subscriber are to be married on the One Hundredth night of the run of 'Tomyrus.' Scoundrel! away from my bride!"

"I'll hold your hat, Churchy," laughed Le Mons.

Greatly abashed, I stammered some nonsense about pistols and coffee, and was thankful to Miss Dalen for diverting attention from my confusion by a question

in another direction, — "How is darling Iona, Churchy? I haven't seen nor heard from her since last Sunday."

"Iona Hart would be in a celestial state of mind and health," answered the philosopher, "but for one thing. She's jealous as a French poodle."

"Of who, *mon ami?*"

"Of you, *mon ange!* She can no longer blind herself to the fact that you adore me."

Snatching Miss Leggett's parasol from her, the "*ange*" sprang gleefully at the "subscriber;" and a desperate chase had just commenced, when a new object of interest appeared upon the scene. That object was the crushed Mr. Bulger, who, with his hat very much over the left eye, and his step wildly geometrical, came recklessly into the green-room. By a series of narrowing circles, in the nature of a fierce "walk-around," the wronged artist finally reached a central position, where, with folded arms, right leg thrown forward, and talma piled chiefly upon the left shoulder, he favored the entire assembly with a dark smile.

"Ladies and gentle-lemons," said he, in tones husky with tragic genius. "Hear me — h'm me — for me cause; and be ssilent that . . . youmayhear!" He swayed gently to and fro for a moment, the motion causing his hat to slip still farther down over his eye; smiled, scowled, and proceeded. "Youwav seen me, a man, — a *man*, by the gar-r-ds! — ssspit upon by a — ha! ha! ha! — a Thhinggg!"

"He's been indulging in fluent crockery," murmured Gushington, alluding to the flowing bowl.

"Noshir!" exclaimed Mr. Bulger, thickly; patting his breast, and lurching forward with closed eyes, — "Noshir! I'm norabit so."

"*I* am the Manager of this Establishment," observed Mr. King, confronting his victim. "If you don't stop drinking, Bulger, I'll discharge you."

To which aggravation Mr. Bulger responded by awaking from a brief doze, and laughing scornfully in those three sepulchral syllables wherewith the infernal hosts behind the scenes in Bowery dramas are wont to respond to the cue, "Demons of hell, rejoice!"

"Then out you go, Bulger," said the despot, closing an outstretched hand upon the collar of the talma. And out Mr. Bulger was led, or lifted, presenting in the process a curious likeness to those limp and irresponsible figures which quiver eternally on wires before the tailor-shops in Chatham Street.

Upon the conclusion of this episode the laughing and jeering lunch party broke up in admired disorder, Church and I following Miss Dalen, Mr. King, and Wild, to Broadway; Le Mons disappearing through the stage door with Miss Leggett, whom he proposed to see safely to her boarding-house ; and Steele, Scribner, and Gushington adjourning with Drinkard and other players to a neighboring saloon.

At the steps of a hack which was waiting to convey her to her hotel, the "star" shook hands with us, —

"You will not forget our little supper, Churchy?"

"Never fear, sweetheart."

"Nor you, Mr. Glibun?"

"Oh, no."

"Then day-day, cavaliers. I shall look for you both in the front row to-night." And, amidst a general tipping of hats and kissing of fingers, she drove merrily away.

"You ought to have a four-horse turnout, King, for such a card as she is," remarked Church, as he and I turned to go down-town.

"Thanks for your suggestion, Mr. Church; but *I* am the Manager of this Establishment!"

CHAPTER XLII.

A BIRTHDAY BALL.

THERE had been a notable flutter in fashionable circles over early semi-official news, that the sixteenth birthday of Mr. Goodman's adopted daughter was to be celebrated with a masquerade ball. Not that festivities of the character were either strange or rare in those same distinguished social rings, but because the gatherings of the élite at the hospitable residence of the princely merchant had hitherto been limited to select dinner-parties, informal evening receptions, and other assemblies below concert-pitch. The more or less blasé oracles of the Old Families, being appealed to for a solution of the phenomenon, had gone sagely upon the tripod of past aristocratic experiences and explained the thing in Delphic utterances. There was a mystery about that 'adopted daughter — or ward, properly speaking — of Mr. Goodman. Upon returning, some years ago, from one of his several voyages to Europe, the courtly merchant was suddenly found to be the guardian, as he briefly styled it, of an unknown, thoughtful little girl, who dressed in deep mourning and gave precocious replies to guests at her guardian's table. Before it got fairly established in society that this little girl was certainly no relation of Mr. Goodman's, though evidently of no common connexion, she was whisked off to a famous seminary near Philadelphia, and there subjected to luxurious educational treatment for the approved term. Returning from thence, an elegant and undemonstrative young creature, she had quietly assumed an only daughter's position in the sober house opposite Union Park. At table, at receptions, and in society elsewhere, the grave merchant had tacitly conceded, and she had filled that position ever since. Well, and who does she turn out to be? Ah! who, indeed? That was still the mystery. Frank and genial as her guardian was in all his associations, those very qualities were the fine sunshine of a commanding dignity which forbade question, or even conjecture, beyond what he chose to divulge, of anything concerning himself. In this case he had not chosen to do more than introduce the young lady as his adopted daughter, as though it were a matter of course; and no one could tell from whence came the vague, but persistent story, that she was English, an orphan, and entitled to an estate in England on coming of age. Given, these particulars; and given, the further item that the nominal Miss Goodman had thus far figured only in the milder dissipations of fashionable life; what was the proper meaning of this birthday masquerade? Why, of course, it was to be the formal inaugural of Miss Goodman's First Season in full society.

Thus spake the oracles ; and thus believed, as in duty bound, the seekers after such supernatural knowledge. The Old Families felt sure of invitations to the ball; for the descendant of the illustrious colonial Goetmans was not likely to think twice before putting *them* on the list. But it was otherwise with the New Families. Those who, from ancestry and heritage in Washington market, the soap-boiling line, etc., etc., had violently driven into social distinction with race-horses, steamed into it with railroad stock, and (last and most piratical) sailed into it with schooner-yachts. *They* were not quite so sure of enamelled and engraved recognition, in a body; and as all pretence of indifference to Goodman recognition would have been *too* transparent for anybody, these jockeys, steamers, and riggers were sensible enough to attempt no concealment of their anxiety in the matter.

For invited and uninvited, however, the night of the ball came in due time; and, by ten o'clock, the street in front of the great merchant's ordinarily sedate mansion began to show symptoms of unusual travel. Huge, glossy coaches, with immaculate coachmen and footmen, and hammer-cloths; fantastical little calashes, with red and yellow pigmy wheels; in fact, vehicles in every type of stylish heaviness and deformity, commenced streaming around either end of the Park opposite, and forming an irregular, moving wall along that whole block. As each of these varnished and padded vans came before the door of the brass plate, and within the glow of window-curtains illuminated to the roof, the immaculate coachman brought his champing steeds to a stand with one imperceptible suggestion of his broadcloth elbows, the dapper footman did his duty with the dexterity of a harlequin, and two or four picturesque figures, like those in historical engravings, flitted across the walk and up the stoop in palpable terror of the admiring populace. But, rapidly as the moving wall jerked forward to this point, broke off, and either went to pieces around corners or reformed along the Park across the way, it still lengthened faster than it shortened, and a plethoric gentleman-usher, in white kids and cravat, who served as guide from the curb to the hall, seemed to have interminable miles before him, however hard he strove to be over with the hottest of it. Now and then a cloaked Romeo, or Crusader, bearing a muffled Queen Mary of Scots, or Italian peasant girl, upon his arm, would rashly leave the carriage some doors below the festive mansion, and save time by a short cut through the throng of motley citizens on the pavement; but the evident and critical delight humorously expressed thereat by said citizens did not encourage any formidable number of other dramatic and historical celebrities to follow the daring example. By eleven o'clock the block was blockaded strictly enough to have satisfied even an English Minister of Foreign Affairs; the plethoric gentleman-usher put on the fourth fresh pair of gloves, with the air of a man who would not allow himself to think longer of what was before him; and certain coachmen of the highest respectability and political influence, so far forgot the well-bred virtue of patience as to cut with their whips at the occasional Irish gentlemen who casually asked them what circuses they drove for?

Within the building, upon which concentrated all this jam and bustle, a corps of experienced assistants to the outside gentleman-usher danced attendance upon fresh arrivals, and led the way to the second floor, where some six or eight brilliantly-lighted chambers were luxuriously appointed for dressing-rooms. Into some of these latter retired the princes, monks, knights, warriors, and cavaliers,—into others the queens, nuns, shepherdesses, and fairies,—to cast off cloaks and wrappers, and adjust masks, wigs, swords, and other romantic paraphernalia. These, again, streamed down the staircase in full feather, to give place to other illustrissimi just going up; the latter, in their cloaks and wrappers, being unto the former as grubs unto butterflies. There was also a third, and much smaller class of guests, who were more or less past the bloom and frivolities of youth, and disguised their identities with black, pink, and white masks, only; and a fourth, and still smaller one, who, being parental and serious of mind, were ordinary evening party figures. Such severely simple apparitions, however, were made in a degree unique by their very contrast with the plays, romances, and histories hustling them genteelly on every side; as the much duplicated "Portrait of a Gentleman" is popularly supposed to attract a peculiar interest from staring at intervals in a public gallery amongst landscapes and fancy pieces.

Through the main hall the varied tide flowed into the spacious ballroom, which, after being long unused, was now thoroughly renovated in its delicate frescos and gilt panelling, and glared with the light from one immense glass chandelier in the centre. Near the orchestra stood Mr. Goodman and his lovely ward to receive their guests; the rich merchant, courtly and hospitable as usual, in full evening dress; and the young lady, modest and graceful, in white satin and ermine. To them, and past them, with bow, greeting, and courtesy, moved a continual procession of maskers; personal recognitions now and then occasioning as much mirth at the expense of the recognized as was decorous, and more than one plumed knight and powdered lady wishing that certain eyes and ears were not quite so sharp. As a general thing, however, incognitos were well preserved, and the first march from the band found scarcely one heart to distract from any grave emotion. Too many had been called to the carnival: that was the only fault. They overflowed from the ballroom into the hall and parlors; and when dancing commenced in the former, the well-chalked floor had not surface enough for all the saltatory maskers, scores of whom were impelled to pursue their diversions in hall and parlors aforesaid.

After seeing his ward masked, and temporarily resigning her to a courtly cavalier for the first quadrille, Mr. Goodman repaired to the parlor next the street, where a small group of his elder friends were withdrawn from the younger people to exchange such political and mercantile thoughts as must always have vent when such seniors come together under the same roof.

"Gentlemen, I hope that you are enjoying yourselves," observed the host, in his easy, welcoming way. "I see that you have my partner, Mr. Coe, with you, and infer from the circumstance that the Firm, at least, is exempted from any charge of neglect."

Mr. Coe, a smiling, fleshy old gentleman, with pink face and snowy hair, laughingly asserted that he regretted having not appeared in the character of Falstaff, with the remaining elders as that hero's renowned army; for then he and they would not feel quite so much like a party of venerable clergymen unexpectedly dropped into a dramatic convention.

"If that is the case," rejoined Mr. Goodman, "I must apologize for my own bad taste in rendering such incongruities possible. But, to be frank with you, gentlemen, this masking and costuming business is a young lady's idea—not mine; and I assented to it only in accordance with the most amiable precedents of indulgent guardianship. To be still more frank," he continued, in a graver tone, "these masquerades are so frequent in society nowadays— amounting to a spasmodic mania, I may say—that young people can scarcely avoid having some participation in them; and I preferred that my ward should have her first experience under my own roof."

"For my part," piped a short, sandy-haired member of the group, "I can see no good reason at all for any serious objection to an occasional entertainment like this. Young folks will be young folks, with unconquerable tastes for romance and mystery; and if we now and then countenance their enjoyment of those natural tastes by select private masquerades, where is the harm?"

"I agree with you, Mr. Cummin," murmured a thin, timid-looking little man. "We must not sacrifice the natural tastes of our young folks, because we old ones prefer rest and quiet,—must we?"

"I should say not, Mr. Hyer!" returned the opulent retail tradesman, magnificently patronizing. He was astonished, too, that a mere salesman should abuse the privilege of being in such company by presuming to speak before he was spoken to. Possibly this supercilious manner of Mr. Cummin's had something to do with the marked cordiality of tone with which Mr. Goodman now addressed himself to the poor little salesman in question,—

"Mr. Hyer, I hope your young ladies are all well? Are they here to-night?"

"Luke and Meeta are, sir. My oldest and youngest daughters are out of town."

"Why, you must be quite lonely without Miss Caroline?"

"Ye-e-es," returned Mr. Hyer, slowly, rubbing his hands, "it does make me a little lonely."

"Goodman, my old friend, accept my compliments," sounded a sonorous voice, the owner of which was a tall, pompous, black-bearded gentleman, who had just entered the room. "This is dissipation, Mr. Goodman; this is dissipation, sir!" and the dignified ex-congressman, the Honorable James Crow, nodded aslant toward the ballroom.

"My dear sir," returned the merchant, shaking hands with him, "you are quite right; we are rather dissipated to-night; but, as I have just been informing some old acquaintances, young ladies of sixteen are satisfied with nothing less in these days. Am I to congratulate you on your prospects senatorial?"

"By all means: that is, if you can enter into my own actual feelings,—as I believe you can,—in reference to those prospects. There is virtually no possibility of my election at Albany next week, and I am positively glad of it."

"Indeed! You surprise me. I pay very little heed to current political matters myself; but my impression has been that parties were pretty evenly balanced in the legislature."

"And such is the case, sir," said Mr. Crow, linking his hands behind him; "but the Demolitionists are united upon one candidate, while our side divides between my friend Judge Black and myself. I would peremptorily withdraw my name at once, but for Cringer's positive assurance that, in such an event, at least two or three Ebullition members would vote for O'Murphy,

rather than for Black. It is only upon patriotic principle that I allow my name to remain."

"Can it be possible, then, that this notorious person, O'Murphy, has a chance of election to the United States Senate?" asked Mr. Goodman, in blank astonishment.

"A chance!" ejaculated the other. "Sir, it is a certainty. He has the sole nomination of the Demolition party, and will spend, through Plato Wynne, any amount of money for the election. I have the support of but one wing of our party, and have refused to give Cringer one dollar for the lobby. So the case stands. I resigned my seat in the house four years ago when this O'Murphy was so corruptly re-elected to a seat there; and I should not be in politics now, at all, but for the importunities of some old political friends in the Ebullition Central Committee. Cringer will work for me like a giant; his own political salvation depends upon it; but the pugilist must win."

"I am shocked and grieved inexpressibly to hear it," said Mr. Goodman; and his contracted brow told as plainly that he was. "That man in the United States Senate— next to a cabinet minister! Truly after this we may say with Antony,—'O judgment, thou art fled to brutish beasts, and men have lost their reason'!"

While thus the elders talked platitudes and politics, the younger spirits devoted themselves to the dance with all the ardor imaginable. Although a larger proportion of guests wore dominos than might have been expected from the general character-costuming of the earliest arrivals, a sufficient number of rich military and court suits were in view to make the scene in the ball-room very brilliant to the eye. Jewelled caps and feathers; powdered wigs, French, Italian, and Spanish head-dresses, and wreaths of every classical description, were continually rising and falling on that kaleidoscopic sea of decorous revelry, as the modulated tempest of music swept over it; and the non-dancing civilians who occupied the numerous crimson sofas and settees ranged along the walls beheld a spectacle picturesque and animated enough to make them less impatient about the room's overcrowding. With all the apparent gayety of the maskers, there was, however, a certain feeling of constraint which fairly prevented the especial enjoyments of a masquerade. Ever conscious that they were guests in a house no less renowned for its gravely decorous proprieties than for its princely hospitalities, and that the present entertainment was rather an exceptional indulgence than a cultivated usage, even the liveliest of the partakers in the scene hesitated to avail themselves of the most trifling privileges of the mask, and actually felt less freedom than an ordinary evening party would have permitted. Dancing, then, and promenading, and conversation with acquaintances whose identities were scarcely in doubt, constituted the only amusements open to perfect liberty of action before supper; and to these the merchant's guests devoted themselves with what might be termed a fantastical solemnity.

The first novelty of the event being over, Miss Goodman herself was one of the earliest to realize that some element of incongruity gave a monotonous, unsatisfactory character to the scene, varied as the latter superficially was. She had no need to complain of any lack of homage to herself; for, inasmuch as her identity was known to every guest, all congratulated and courted her by turns with flattering *empressement;* but this very concentration upon herself was embarrassing, and only made her the more observant of the stiff reserve involuntarily practised by the maskers toward each other. Weary of the labored nothings of a gentleman with whom she had just danced, the discontented young heiress excused herself, and was hastening to another part of the ballroom, when a figure in a close black domino and mask placed a hand gently upon one of her wrists, and so detained her.

"May I ask you to tell me where Mr. Goodman is?" inquired a low feminine voice.

Regarding the questioner with some surprise, Miss Goodman rather haughtily responded that the gentleman was probably upon the floor somewhere, and prepared to pass on.

"Pardon me for troubling you," said the domino, softly as before; "but will you not be so obliging as to indicate him to me in some way, — so that I may know him?"

"He is not masked," was the brief answer.

"Still I should not know him," continued the domino, mildly yet earnestly. "I have particular reasons for wishing to speak with him. Please oblige me, I entreat!"

Women, young or old, are a natural moral police over each other. Instinctive dislike and suspicion were in the sentiment with which Miss Goodman regarded this gently-speaking incognito, and for a moment it was her impulse to turn disdainfully away without answering the appeal. Reflecting, however, that such ungracious action would be ill-bred, especially if the disguised lady should chance to be some person entitled to a courtesy beyond that of mere ballroom acquaintanceship, she threw a hurried glance over the brilliant throng, and, by a slight but intelligible movement of her fan, indicated where her guardian stood.

"That gentleman is Mr. Goodman," she said.

"Thank you," returned the domino; and, without another word, disappeared amongst the dancers.

Shortly thereafter the same muffled figure accosted the foster-father, as he turned from a passing conversation with some old friend.

"Mr. Goodman looks lonely this evening, and has my compassion."

"Madam, you honor me. I cannot sufficiently regret the concealment of eyes bright enough to discern that of which I was not myself aware."

For the dignified merchant at once suspected that some lively young lady was about to favor him with a witty thrust at his wifeless condition, and was on his guard to at once encourage and caution the daring mask.

"The eyes, Mr. Goodman, need not be so very bright that can discern what not only exists in itself but is even contagious," observed the domino, in an easy conversational tone, as though passing some ordinary comment upon the company.

"Why, madam, as to that," returned Mr. Goodman, feeling his way, "I must admit that I do not exactly understand you."

"Then you have no suspicion that this room contains at least one other person as lonely to-night as yourself?"

"Meaning *yourself?*"

"Meaning Miss Goodman."

Quite startled by this unexpected reply, — which was given in an intense, earnest tone, and accompanied, as he fancied, by a peculiarly searching glance from the eyes behind the mask, — Mr. Goodman hesitated an instant and then gravely offered his arm. The domino took it, promptly but undemonstratively, and they walked on.

"Why should Miss Goodman be lonely, madam?"

"Ah! why are you the same?"

"The assertion was yours, not mine."

"True. You are lonely because you call her daughter, and are yet childless. She is lonely because she calls you father, and is yet fatherless. In all this company there is kindred for neither father nor child."

"Whoever you may be, madam, your words surprise and pain me. I am not yet certain, indeed, that I fully understand you."

"I do mean more than I can express in words — *here,*" said the domino, lowering her voice almost to a whisper, and closing her hand upon his arm.

"Pardon me; but I am still unenlightened."

Whatever response followed this remark, it was observed by those who were casually noticing the merchant at the moment, that his countenance and manner underwent an instant change, becoming agitated and interested to a degree seldom exhibited by men of far inferior self-command. This, and his subsequent disappearance with the domino in the direction of a hitherto uninvaded conservatory, would have provoked flippant criticism upon any other masculine member of society than him whose immaculate repute as a gentleman of the old school was an ægis against which naught of disrespect dared to turn its point.

It was not until long after supper had been summoned, and all masks removed, that the master of the house reappeared amongst his guests and greeted them in their proper personalities. Then his more observant, older friends, noted that the calm of his face was colder than it had been, and that his eyes were more solemn with the shadow of some great preoccupation; but to the superficial and younger majority he was the same urbane, genial, and courtly gentleman as ever, only worn a little with the late hour.

Still later toward dawn, after the last of the company had departed and the last carriage driven away, he stood in the parlor still disarranged from the crowding gayeties of the night, and looked down into the fair young face of his adopted daughter with an affection which strove in vain to appear wholly cheerful.

"Are you very tired, my dear?" he asked, as she laid a little gloved hand on his shoulder and bent her head to the caressing touch of his own hand. It was a head lustrous with locks so darkly brown that they seemed black in the gas-light.

"No, pa; only a little tired," she said.

"Has your enjoyment to-night been equal to your anticipations?"

"Almost, but not quite."

"And why 'not quite'?"

"Oh, I don't know, pa." Then looking up at him more frankly, she exclaimed, "I am sorry it was a masquerade!"

"It was your own wish, dear."

"Yes, I know; and it was very gay and pleasant to look at; but I was disappointed. Besides," she added, after a thoughtful pause, "I can't help believing that there were utter strangers here to-night."

A moment Mr. Goodman scrutinized her countenance with unwonted sharpness; but, detecting no hidden thought in the clear gaze returned, he smiled as he replied, "If your belief is correct, the 'utter strangers' were not obtrusive in their strangeness, and we may pardon them for coming.

As those soft and deep brown eyes began to return his own recent scrutiny with a timidly questioning expression, he regarded her more gravely again, and spoke more seriously, —

"My dear girl, it was my selfish wish that you should not be too greatly charmed with the giddy social pleasures that too often become a young woman's whole world of fancy and thought. The wish was selfish because it contemplated my own interest, as well; for, if the opening of your first season in society should fascinate you with a successful rival to the quiet of home, I could not expect to find you the same demure, domestic little girl toward me thereafter. As a young belle of the highest fashion you could no longer be content with an old man's company and an old man's friends."

"I'll never ask, or want any other!" she interrupted, ingenuously kissing his hand.

"Don't be too sure of that, my dear," said the merchant, smiling, and tapping her dimpled chin. "The son of a certain old and wealthy friend of mine was the most devoted of cavaliers not many hours ago."

"Now, pa, it's a shame for you to tease me any more about *him*," returned the young lady, with a pretty attempt to pout. "I really dislike him."

"My dear, I am sorry to hear you speak so strongly."

"But, pa, he is so tiresome; and, besides, he's — he's —" and she broke down there, and was pitiably confused.

"Well, my dear, go on."

"He's — oh, dear! — he's dissipated."

"My darling girl!" exclaimed the astonished gentleman, "what ever put such a sweeping, such an indecorous idea into your little head?"

"Don't be offended, pa," pleaded the adopted daughter, bending her head to avoid his look. "Meeta Hyer says that she was told so by a gentleman named Mr. Stiles. Mr. Stiles's words were that it was a pity he drank."

"Mr. Stiles!" murmured the merchant, abstractedly. "Spanyel tells me, too, that he was once in my employ. Yet he seems to know every secret of Society's prison-house. Strange! strange!" Catching the surprised look fixed upon him, he roused himself from the temporary reverie, and affectionately took her hands in his.

"My child!" he said, resuming the graver vein, "when it becomes your womanly destiny to leave me for a nearer and dearer protector, you shall carry with you no bitter memory of my dictation to the impulses of your heart. Until then, however, it shall be my aim, so far as I may, to spare you the loneliness of feeling neglected in your orphanage. And I would have you remember always, my dear," he added, solemnly, "that in causing you to bear my name, calling you daughter, and teaching you to call me father, I have been actuated rather by a desire to emphasize to you your possession of a second father than to make you forget the first. In the memory of the beloved dead there is no loneliness, my child, no loneliness. Living in such memory myself, for many years, I have not been lonely."

Deeply touched by the affectionate solemnity of his voice and manner, the young beauty stole an arm about his neck and rested a flushed cheek against his shoulder.

"My dear second father!" she softly said.

They were a fine picture as they stood thus: he in his grave and gentle humanity, and she in her fervid gratitude and confidence; he in the dignity of honorable years, and she in the simplicity of trustful youth. A grand old gentleman he was, and she a lovely debtor to his Christian chivalry.

"I have been childless as you have been fatherless," spoke the merchant, gently pressing back the graceful head and gazing tenderly down into the fair young face. "Who knows but that in giving you some day to one nearer than a father, I may find a son? Who knows?"

Here was no chance for any girlish pretti-
ness of talk, and she only blushed in reply.

"And now, dear, I have preached sufficiently to banish any giddiness the ball
might have produced in you, and you must
go and take the rest you need. It is morning, but I will say good-night."

He kissed her lightly on the forehead, and
she turned to go. In an instant, however,
she was beside him again, looking anxiously
into his face.

"You are not troubled about anything,
pa?"

"I am afraid your head will ache to-morrow, my dear."

"But you are not worried? You are not
troubled because you consented to my foolish wish for this childish masquerade, —
are you?"

"My dear child," replied the merchant,
with singular earnestness, "do not imagine
such a thing. I would not have failed to do
so for all I possess!"

The seeming extravagance of this answer
took her by surprise, and she could only
say, —

"I thought you looked careworn. I was
afraid something disagreeable might have
occurred."

"Why, my dear," answered the foster-
father, eying her steadily, "I did hear one
disagreeable piece of news during the evening. Mr. Crow gave me assurance of
coming political events, which makes me,
although no politician, despair for my country. Now, good-night again."

He could not foresee the future, terrible
and sublime, when all that was vitally false
in his country should rise, like a night of
eclipse to the sun, against all that was loyal
and true; when, from the judgment chaos,—
throbbing with the thunder of falling fetters
and quickened with the lightning of the
sword that struck them off, — should come
the second creation of Man; when, in the
first calm of the new genesis, there should
whiten into immortality, like a star into
morning, the one soul of a century, simple
and grand enough to take the highest embassy of a regenerate nation.

<hr>

CHAPTER XLIII.

THE FINE ART OF FACILITATION.

DEMOCRACY will not wash. So long as
it remains the Great Unwashed, individual
wealth and assumptions have no peace for
it, and the scheme of universal Equality
("excepting persons of African descent")
meets its heartiest support; but with the
very first washing come aristocratic aspirations for clean collars; then for a separation
of the home-parlor from the pig-pen; then
for the dignities of office; and finally for
recognition as a lofty species of post-
nobility.

Generally, this statement applies to im-

ported democracy; particularly, to the
mighty Demolition party; and personally,
to the Honorable Mealy O'Murphy. As lives
of great men all remind us that it is at our
option to make our own existences sublime,
and, deceasing, bequeath to admiring pos-
terity the impressions of spiked shoes on
the sands where we came to time; and, furthermore, as such impressions, when finally
beheld by some forlorn and fistianically ship-
wrecked brother borne against the ropes
amain, are calculated to make him still hope
for the prize-belt and Congress, and pugi-
listically go in again; — why, such being the
case, the "lives" (numerous as a cat's) of
the Honorable M. O'Murphy were an edifying study for aspiring youth. A native of
Killmurraymacmahon, County Clare, the incipient statesman came as a Demolition del-
egate to this country at an early age, and
carefully refrained from washing himself for
several years. At length, however, there
arose in his path that enemy of Old Ireland,
known as the "Hunky Boy," and him the
O'Murphy resolved to fight. Now it chanced
that daily ablutions were a necessary part
of the artistic training for this noble encounter, and no sooner had the fierce young
Mealy tried the first of these insidious nov-
elties than his colors began to run and his
radical democracy to fade. Washing number two inspired him to give a haughty
order to his "trainer" for a ruffled shirt,
and inflict condign corporeal punishment on
that negligent inferior because the garment
he procured had not a "French yoke."
After washings three, four, and five, he
ceased recognizing the Mac Tulligans and
O'Flynns, who were *not* descendants of King
Brian Boroihme, and spent as many daily
hours over newspapers as though he could
read. In the great battle he beat the Hunky
infant past all semblance to himself, and received an immediate proposition to run for
the legislature, with all the dignity becoming a clean countenance and spotless collar.
Is not the rest of his story recorded in that
excellent volume of Pye, Rait, & Co.'s
Youth's Library, entitled "The Bully Boy;
or, How a Poor and Friendless Lad became
a Congressman"? Lives there an American man with soul so dead that he remembers not how the Honorable Mr. O'Murphy
washed himself into Congress for two
terms?

But now the cleansed statesman, in a very
frenzy of washing, proposed a still higher
wash to Washington. Not contented with
a mere membership of the house; not satisfied with social eminence as a prosperous
banker of the royal Egyptian order, the
O'Murphy would fain be a senator; and,
having Plato Wynne to act as his prime
minister of manipulation at Albany, who
could doubt this last triumph of palm soap?

To come to the point at once, the prospect was unmistakably "blue" for the leading Ebullition candidate, the Honorable
James Crow, and upon the day preceding
that on which the State legislators, at the

State capital, were to vote upon the respective caucus nominations in joint session, A. Cringer sat glumly in a certain room of a certain New York hotel, with such a drooping air in his very knees and elbows that his chair seemed to be all that resisted his utter collapse upon the floor. For a whole week he had been at Albany, — had A. Cringer, — expostulating most fervidly and generously with those obdurate Ebullition Solons who persisted in preferring Mr. Black to Mr. Crow; persisted in dividing the Ebullition camp in the face of a united enemy, and thereby assuring to the complacent King of Diamonds a certain majority for his enterprising client. Vainly had he vied with his darkly-glittering majesty in lavishing hospitalities, blandishments, and beautiful arguments upon these amazing recreants, who, under the direction of two hard-headed country members, met each primary Cringerial temptation with polite disregard, and mysteriously chose the defeat of their party under Mr. Black to its triumph under Mr. Crow. So it was that General Cringer had returned hastily to the metropolis on the day before the election; had secretly sought the hotel where, on other occasions, he had so often distributed scores of profitable offices to throngs of the faithful, and had given strict orders at the desk that none should be allowed to intrude upon his despondent privacy save the few local dignitaries whom he had notified to meet him there in hasty consultation.

And while thus the great man pined under his cloud in his old official mill, there entered the building a party of four gentlemen of eccentric aspect, who, by their shuffling gait, questionable linen, and bad hats, seemed to be members of a social class not usually residing at first-rate hotels. A casual observer, noting their arrival and the apparent confidence with which they started upstairs, would have taken them, say, for the workmen of some stove manufactory, on their way to bring down one of the hotel stoves, or ranges, which might be out of repair. Or, they were not unlike tinmen, summoned to mend a leak in the roof; or plumbers; or hod-carriers, to ascertain how much mortar would be needed for the repair of the chimneys. So prone is the misguided human mind to associate humble station with unfashionable attire, that common perception would have done these four shambling gentlemen the gross injustice of taking them for mere workmen in the dirtier trades, when, in reality, they were illustrious and powerful members of the city government, elected to honorable office by the suffrages of their enlightened fellow-citizens. He who led the way, and spat most frequently upon the Brussels carpets of the stairway and hall, was Mr. John Bull, President of the Board of Councilmen, and particularly famous just then for having recently fought two councilmen, and survived a shower of inkstands, in a spirited combat in the Council Chamber over a resolution to declare St. Patrick's Day a national holiday. The three dignitaries following him were, respectively, Alderman O'Grocery, and Councilmen Ockhone and O'Mecyi, the last named having been one of the civic statesmen engaged in the memorable fight with the President. The party, therefore, were entitled to peculiar reverence, instead of ignorant depreciation, for their unostentatious attire and bearing; true dignity, like beauty, being adorned the most when unadorned; and the lounging transitory guests of the hotel who thoughtlessly set them down for vulgar laborers, should have been slavish Saxons rather than free-born American citizens.

Arriving at the door of General Cringer's well-known reception-room, President Bull and staff dispensed with the useless aristocratic ceremony of knocking, and marched into the presence like gentlemen who despised all petty affectations of humility. In the same simple republican spirit they neglected to remove their hats after entering; but that piece of servile sycophancy was not requisite to reveal the fact that they all had heads closely cropped, very low foreheads, and tremendous necks. Messieurs O'Grocery, Ockhone and O'Mecyi exhibited cheek-bones which projected into actual shelves at their upper extremities, — while Mr. Bull's round and fiery countenance was diagonally bandaged across one eye in remembrance of the last inkstand opposed to him in debate; but what their combined faces lacked of unmeaning beauty was amply supplied in those sharp retreating angles of brow and chin which denote inexpressible force of character.

"Gud marnin' to ye, Gineral, and 'oping that meself and frinds find ye in health," observed Mr. Bull, who, although a Briton by birth, deemed it politically advisable to affect the brogue of the governing class.

"Good-morning, gentlemen, good-morning. You are prompt," answered the General, without rising. "Be good enough to take seats. I will detain you but a moment."

The strong originality natural to all great characters developed itself once more, after this greeting, in the peculiar methods adopted by the committee (for such they were) to seat themselves. Mr. Bull gravely twitched two-thirds of himself upon a small writing-table; Alderman O'Grocery dexterously balanced his sturdy form upon the back of a chair by a single upward swing of his right leg; and Councilmen Ockhone and O'Mecyi hoisted themselves on either arm of an old-fashioned sofa. In the Spartan severity of their early training, these gentlemen had beguiled their sedentary hours so exclusively on barrels and hydrants, that mere force of habit impelled them to avoid any aid to a sitting posture which would deny the accustomed pendulous freedom to their nether limbs.

"Well, Gineral, and how's the sinatorial row comin' on at Albany?" inquired Mr.

O'Grocery. "It's that naygur-worshipper, Crow, that's likely to be bate so his mother won't know him, I'm thinkin'."

"Hurroo for O'Murphy!" exclaimed the impulsive Mr. Ockhone.

"Aisy, aisy, gintlemen," interrupted Mr. Bull, whose fine sense of delicacy was shocked by such rude humor toward the friend of Mr. Crow; "aisy, if ye plaze, and don't hact like 'ogs in a nouse."

A something sharp in the expression of General Cringer's attentive eyes indicated that he took ample cognizance of the touch of indignity conveyed in the speeches rebuked by Mr. Bull; but his manner continued drooping, and he spoke without vim, —

"You all know, I suppose, gentleman, how matters stand at Albany."

"Av coorse," chuckled Mr. O'Meeyi.

"Thank you, Mr. Councilman. And you all know that I would not be here just now, in your esteemed company, but for some very momentous cause. I am compelled to admit that the cause *is* momentous. I am compelled to admit that the various nominal members of my own party in the legislature who choose to split off on Mr. Black, seem more inclined to be confirmed in their perversity — for so I must term it — by the liberal inducements of Mr. O'Murphy and Mr. Wynne, than converted from it by the limited personal resources of the humble citizen who now addresses you. I am compelled to admit that Mr. Wynne is as unscrupulous in his lobbying as he is truly gentlemanly and high-toned in his private associations; and that the financial pressure he, in particular, has brought to bear against me in my friendly efforts to facilitate the success of the Honorable James Crow, obliges me to ask a little assistance from you, gentlemen."

"Is it from us ye mane?" cried Mr. O'Grocery, with some fervor. "Sure, and aint we mimbers of the ould Demolition party? It's little we'll do, be gorra, but take our poteen in honor of M'aly O'Murphy!"

"I think you'll do a little more than that, my friends," returned the General, in a softly conciliating manner. "The suicidal clique of Mr. Black is led by a member from Mr. Bull's own district, and the rural member from Cattawampus. We all know, between ourselves, that the member from Mr. Bull's own district is really a member of your ring, gentlemen, although nominally an Ebullitionist. Very well! I beg that you will at once telegraph him, over your combined signatures, to stop his nonsense, and support the candidate whose election I am striving to facilitate."

Down from their perches came the whole committee, as though hurled therefrom by a tremendous electric shock, and notably distorted were the ingenuous countenances of Mr. Bull and his friends with mingled astonishment and wrath.

"Wot?" ejaculated the President of the councilmen.

"F'hat?" panted Alderman O'Grocery.

"— support the candidate whose election I am striving to facilitate," repeated the humble citizen, smoothly.

"If that don't bate the Rooshians!" exclaimed Mr. Ockhone. "Is it thraitors ye'd have us to ould Tammany, Gineral, and bastes to our party? It must be mad ye are to ask it."

"I merely ask it as a little friendly accommodation, my dear friends," returned General Cringer, sadly yet genially. "I merely ask it as a lift for myself. I will not promise anything positively in return for such a favor, gentlemen; but I *may* have an early opportunity to facilitate the passage by the legislature of certain little bills affecting the city government."

"Bad luck to it all," muttered Mr. Ockhone, exchanging scowls with his friends.

"Mr. Bull, here, hopes to be our next comptroller," pursued the frank diplomatist, twiddling his thumbs before him and gazing abstractedly at them; "Mr. O'Grocery expects to be a police justice; Mr. Ockhone and Mr. O'Meeyi have reasons to believe that their admirable services to the Demolition party will yet be rewarded with the honorable offices of sheriff and street-inspector. Their nomination for these positions, however, will all virtually depend upon the appointment of Judge O'Toole's brother to the postmastership of this city. That appointment comes from Washington, and will be controlled by — ME."

A just perceptible jump went through the whole committee, and Mr. Bull's sudden pallor made the carnation at the end of his nose display new inflammation.

"And now I'll tell you what I propose to do," continued the General, abruptly jerking himself to a rigidly upright position in his chair, raising his voice to a higher pitch, and favoring his friends with an ominous stare; "I propose, when I return to Albany, in a few hours, to buy the member from Mr. Bull's own district! There is not time now to convince him by friendly argument, and I must have him instructed to do without that on this occasion — to drop into my hands, as it were, for the sake of you, his friends. Query: will you telegraph, gentlemen? Yes, or no?"

"Sure, Gineral, there's no resistin' ye," answered Mr. O'Grocery, who now, in common with the other gentlemen, wore a decidedly cowed air.

"Thrue for you, me darlin'," murmured Mr. Ockhone.

"We'll do it," muttered Mr. Bull, sourly.

"Of course you will, my dear friends, or why do we have a 'Ring?' What *is* a 'Ring?'" asked General Cringer, as though exercising an interesting class at school in Hazen's Definer. "A Ring is a private and magnanimous understanding and association between certain prominent gentlemen of opposite parties, whereby the triumph of either party, in city or state, is conducive to the common welfare and emolument of those gentlemen. It is a humane device for the mitigation of those acerbities and violences which would naturally rage between those gentlemen after each election, but for such understanding and association. You, my dear friends, are the Demolition members of a Ring, whilst I am, temporarily, an Ebullition member. You help me to facilitate the election of my friend to the senate, and I help you to facilitate the appointment of your friend to the post-office. There is something generous and brotherly about such an arrangement; something nobly mollient of party bitterness. I don't know but I ought really to call it a progress in Christianity."

The committee were but men,—only men, although co-rulers of a great city; and the moral beauty of the fraternal scheme thus set forth had an irresistible effect upon the finer sensibilities of their natures. The eyes of Mr. Bull moistened, Messieurs O'Grocery and Ockhone were seized with troublesome coughs, and Mr. O'Meeyi gave vent to an audible sigh as he abstractedly raised a large bottle from the writing-table.

"Excuse me, Mr. Councilman," cried the General, rather hastily, "but that bottle contains ink. You will find a more agreeable beverage on the mantel, yonder. I must ask of you gentlemen, however, to use the ink in a proper way. Mr. O'Grocery, allow me to tender you the friendly office of penning the telegraphic dispatch we have been talking about. There are pens and paper on the table."

The worthy alderman, with that humility which ever accompanies and adorns true merit, advanced bashfully to the table, fumbled laboriously at the stationery, and paused.

"Do you prefer quills to steel pens?" inquired General Cringer, kindly.

"Why, Gineral," returned Mr. O'Grocery, in marked confusion, "it's half killed I am with the rumattizzum in me right arrum, and it's the same with me friuds. We cotcht it, I'm afther thinkin', in debatin' a hospital bill lasht wake."

"I'm 'arf dead wid it meself," added Mr. Bull. "It was called 'ygiene in the bill, Misther O'Grocery."

"Av coorse it was," said that gentleman, brightening up at the friendly reminder, "it's Hygiayne that we've all got in our right arrums."

"Ah, I see," observed the General, pleasantly; "none of you can write,—a mere book-keeper's trade, by the way,—and you wish me to pen the despatch for you. I shall take pleasure in obliging you."

Whereupon that most courteous of men promptly drew his chair to the writing-table, penned the brief telegram desired, read it aloud to his friends, invited them to affix such signatures as their severe hygienic affliction permitted, made a copy, and sent the latter to the telegraph office by a servant of the hotel. This little business having been transacted, he dismissed the committee with a truly paternal benediction,

stood at a window, softly rubbing his hands, for five full minutes, and then made swift preparations for a return to Albany. In fact, he was on the point of ringing for a porter to carry down his valise, when the door reopened, and Mr. Bull came shambling back into the room, with an air of having forgotten something.

"How much for Macginnis?" asked Mr. Bull, in a hoarse whisper.

"Ah, to be sure," returned the General, affably. "My cheque for a thousand."

Whereupon the taciturn President of Councilmen retreated once more, and General Cringer rang for the porter. . . . .

If the city of Albany possesses one distinction over any other habitable locality on the peel of this terrestrial orange of ours, it is that of demanding the very highest development of especial social genius to render tolerable to familiar guest or stranger one hour's sojourn within its corporate dulness. Such being the case, the hapless State legislators, compelled to assemble there at certain times of year, need all the ingenious social devices their many friends can extemporize, to save them from a melancholy madness by which the great legislative interests of the Commonwealth might disastrously suffer. To the eternal credit of those many friends be it said, they have ever rallied most nobly around their favorite representatives in Albanian session; and so varied and cheered with lavish conviviality the process of legislation, that the latter has generally been far more farcical than morbidly serious; but whoever of the present day can remember the time of the great O'Murphy-Black-Crow contest, will readily admit that the financial and social delights devised and administered at that period by Mr. Wynne, for and to the particular friends of the Honorable Mr. O'Murphy, surpassed all later lustra quite as greatly as all preceding experiences. Commanding no less than four luxurious private parlors, and as many smaller rooms, in the fashionable Lobby Hotel, the elegant and sparkling chieftain of City Demolitionism dispensed such splendid and unique hospitalities therein and therefrom to the true friends of the O'Murphy, that those faithful statesmen would scarcely have exchanged Albany for Paris; while the indomitable Black faction of the opposing camp were so positively overwhelmed with courtesies from the same quarter, that their own proper friends had but little to do for their entertainment. Beautiful and improving was the spectacle when the hospitable King of Diamonds stood in his finest parlor to receive some timid country member in the Black interest, introduced by this or that friendly O'Murphyite, and at once put that timid country member perfectly at ease by the gentlemanly cordiality of his manner. Pleasant it was to see him sauntering familiarly, yet undemonstratively, with his latest callers, from one parlor to another. In this handsome apartment a huge sideboard loaded with the rarest wines, brandies, and aromatic Havanas, all free to every comer; in the next a gorgeous supper-table, ravishing with fifty delicacies for anybody who would eat, and attended by half a score of waiters eager to serve up fifty more; in the next, three nice little card-tables, whereat the merest rural tyro in dominos could confidently sit down with Mr. Cutter, Mr. Dodge, or Mr. Bilk, and win quite a decent fortune from that victim of sudden and unaccountable ill-luck, without half trying. Or, supposing some stern Presbyterian Black member, from the more truly rural districts, absolutely refused to either eat, drink, smoke, or play dominos, how thoughtful was it in Mr. Wynne to accompany that old-fashioned gentleman quite away from the bustling hotel for a quiet evening call at the stately residence of some estimable private family, where the young ladies would make quite a pet of the old worthy on account of his striking resemblance to a favorite uncle of theirs!

But let it not be supposed that the adherents of that impracticable man, the Honorable James Crow, were suffered to pine in utter neglect and natural Albanianism. Although Mr. Crow had, from the first, inhumanly refused to do anything whatsoever toward dissipating the intolerable *ennui* of legislative existence, the more tender feelings of General Cringer came partially to the rescue. Like his great rival, the General had a fine suite of hospitable apartments for his friends, in the Lobby Hotel, and was equally magnanimous in rendering the most polite attentions to the Black gentry; but, despite his generosity in this respect, the latter recreants had thus far returned his advances rather coldly; and, without their countenance, all the Cringerial amenities must prove unavailing.

Thus stood the lines of battle on the morning of that momentous day when a majority of one hundred and sixty votes in the State Congress was to decide the mighty senatorial war. That morning found the heroic Cringer in his private room in the Lobby Hotel, holding earnest converse with his first-lieutenant, Mr. Benton Stiles.

"So these misguided minions of Black would not come to our rooms, even while I was gone?" murmured the General, in a forced, mechanical way.

"They steadfastly refused to haul-up under our shed," returned Mr. Stiles, with much equine fancy; "and gave me the dust every time I tried to hail one of them on the road. That McCracken is the sharpest nag of the stud, General Cringer."

(Now McCracken was the celebrated member from Mr. Bull's own district.)

"Very true, Mr. Stiles. He and his fellows prefer the allurements of a pair of profligate gamesters, — as a strict moralist might severely term our friends O'Murphy and Wynne, — to the humble attractions of our unpretentious apartments. Hem!"

"They won't eat hay, when they can get oats and hot mashes in the next stall," suggested Mr. Stiles, polishing his locket-ring with the curtain of the street-window near which they stood.

"Very true again, Mr. Stiles. Mr. Crow has left a hard battle to me. I have fought it faithfully thus far; but it has been, as I may say, the always unequal struggle of Labor against Capital, Labor against Capital. Did Phelan O'Digit secure this McCracken's pocket-book for us, Mr. Stiles?"

"He did, me lord. He had it in less than ten minutes after I'd pointed out McCracken to him in the cloak room of the House. I made the addition to its contents as you directed, and there it is in your desk yonder. Ah!" exclaimed Mr. Stiles, caressing his goatee, and indulging in a smile of meditative admiration; "that brilliant young Irishman will make his mark yet. He says he'll never pick another pocket after you've got him that place in the Tax-Commissioner's office. He wants to reform, you see, and spoke quite affectingly. I told him to get the pocket-book, and never despair of being somebody yet."

"That was right, Mr. Stiles," said General Cringer, nodding gravely; "we can all of us do some little work toward moral reform, even for the most erring of our instruments."

"I told Phelan O'Digit," rejoined Benton Stiles, with fresh animation, "that the race is not always to the thorough-bred. I recalled to his mind the fact that Flora Temple was originally a cart-horse, and can now do her mile under the twenties."

There is little doubt that General Cringer would have been suitably moved to express his approval and admiration of this apt argument for youthful perseverance, but for the abrupt entrance into the room of a brisk, cross-eyed, red-nosed gentleman, with high cheek-bones and spacious standing-collar, who wore an excited look, and carried a slip of paper in his hand.

"Good-day, gentlemen," was the hurried greeting of the unceremonious intruder. "What does this telegram from the committee mean, Gin'ral Cringer?"

"This is what it means, Mr. McCracken," answered the General, not at all startled or ruffled; "it means that you and the colleagues you control are to quietly drop Mr. Black, and give your votes for the worthy and able citizen whose election I am striving to facilitate. It means that you must either do that, or give up all hope of ever being returned from New York again, on either ticket."

"Bad 'cess to it!" snarled the member from Mr. Bull's own district, grinding his teeth and crumpling the paper.

"Oh, this partisan prejudice, this partisan prejudice!" exclaimed General Cringer, shaking his head and smiling mournfully. "See how it weds a man to the most worthless idols! Look at me, Mr. McCracken.

I sent Mr. O'Murphy to Congress; but when patriotism, when principle, bade me perceive that same good friend's unfitness for a higher post, I dropped him instantly. You have erred in your choice for a time, sir; but your friends set you right."

"It'll be the ruination of me fortune," muttered Mr. McCracken, sullenly; "afther me giving me wurrud to Mr. Black's frinds, and to Mr. Wynne besides. Me pocket picked, too!"

"Mr. Stiles," said General Cringer, "just be kind enough to hand me that article from my desk."

The official successor of the mysterious Mr. Mugses executed the mild request with alacrity, and conveyed a bulky pocket-book to the grasp of his beloved commander.

"There's your lost property again," continued the benignant man, handing it to the astonished legislator. "Stricken with remorse for his wicked deed, and attracted, possibly, by my gray hairs and friendly look, the penitent thief returned it to me, with the request that I would find its owner and restore it. If you should find it to contain anything more than it did when you lost it, — *if* you should, — we may conclude that the unhappy robber wished to make some special amends for having put you to temporary inconvenience."

A broad, peculiar smile broke slowly over the honest face of the member from Mr. Bull's own district as he dexterously slipped the recovered treasure into his pocket and favored Mr. Stiles with a presumptuous wink.

"The thing's as clare as daylight, ould man," quoth he, with much ironical humor, "and you're the missionary that could convert the divil himself! I'll do as I'm tould in the telegram; and I'll be mum about it to all but me colleagues, as you call them, until it's over; but I tell ye, your man won't be elected. There's that mimber from Cattawampus and his wan frind, that's neither to be bought, sold, nor scared into voting for your Jim Crow; and with thim two holdin' out, it's O'Murphy will carry the day by one majority. So I and me frinds can affoord to make belave help ye, anyway. That's what thim fellows in New York must mane."

"It seems but too likely, my friend; too likely!" sighed the General, drooping at the sound. "Well, be the consequences on the head of the member from Cattawampus. I shall have done my humble duty. Good-morning, friend."

For some moments after the departure of Mr. McCracken, the fine old Roman stood with folded arms by the window, apparently watching the people below as they crowded through the street toward the capitol, but really communing with his own great soul. Then, stepping first to the table for his well-known broad-brimmed hat, he advanced sturdily to the door.

"Whither? Oh, whither?" cried Mr. Stiles, too much awed by the solemn manner of the great man to say more.

"To the cloak room!" was the stern, emphatic answer; and Mr. Stiles was alone.

The great moment was at hand in the capitol. The galleries of the national chamber were packed with a motley array of fair women and brave men, eager to witness an event "big with the fate of Cato and of Rome." The lobbies swarmed with editors, lawyers, railroad officials, and general lobbyites, who, having diplomatized untiringly for a week with the great minds now about to assert the free senatorial choice of the Empire State, were watching for the end with the feelings that such men, only, under such circumstances, can know. The members were all in their places, the usual preliminary business was nearly concluded, and all seemed preparing for the tremendous business of the day, when a page came hurrying to the desk of the stony-hearted member from Cattawampus, and whispered a brief message. The member stared, looked surprised, but arose at once from his seat, and proceeded sternly to the cloak room of the Senate Chamber, where he who had sent the message stood, waiting to receive him.

"General Cringer," said the veteran country statesman, before the other had time to address him, "I consent to see you here for a moment only as a matter of courtesy. To prevent a useless multiplicity of words between us, I tell you at once that I, and those whom I can influence, will give no vote for Mr. Crow. I tell you plainly that the mere fact of your advocacy of Mr. Crow would make me vote against him, though he were my own brother. I know you to be an impure man; I choose to support Mr. Black because I prefer him; and I will not forego my own honest convictions for the sake of any party, or any individual in the world."

"Sir," said General Cringer, drawing a paper from the bosom of his coat, "you may choose to believe calumnies against me; but I shall never cease to respect and admire the unimpeached integrity of a man whose moral principles I know to be beyond all personal interests. Allow me to read you the contents of this paper:—

"'A. Cringer, Albany, N. Y.,— Dear Sir: Yielding to your singularly pertinacious importunities, I consent to receive a complimentary vote. After which, however, my name must positively be withdrawn in favor of Mr. Black. Yours truly,

'JAMES CROW.'

"That note reached me at a late hour last night."

"Well, sir?"

"You will perceive from it that Mr. Crow virtually gives up the battle. You are the only person to whom I have confided this fact. To be concise and frank, — as you have been yourself, my dear sir, —let me beg of you to record your name for Mr. Crow in the complimentary vote."

"And suppose that should *elect him*," observed the member from Cattawampus, with a look of suspicion.

"My dear sir! will not McCracken and his followers prevent that?"

"General Cringer," returned the other, coldly, "I'd prefer not doing it; not even to insure Black's election, sir."

Shade of Brutus! what was A. Cringer doing? His form seemed to sink as though some enormous weight were slowly and irresistibly pressing him down by the shoulders. He was upon his knees!!

"My dear sir, on my knees I entreat, I *beg* you, to yield to me in this matter! When Mr. Crow and I were young men he once saved me from ruin and dishonor by an act of friendship which I may not name, but shall never forget. I would lay down my life to repay him now, by succeeding in my efforts to facilitate his elevation to a higher official dignity than he has yet known; but, since that is impossible, I wish to make the vote of compliment to him a compliment indeed. I wish it to include every name of particular honor in the legislature; and with yours withheld it will be a mockery. My very heart bleeds—"

"Get up, sir!" thundered the man from Cattawampus, fairly goaded into compliance by his own indignation at the awkwardness of the situation. "I'll do it."

Up rose General Cringer, with every feature eloquent of humiliation and despondency, and his knees white with the sordid dust of the floor.

"God bless you," he said tremulously. "It will be merely a matter of form; but God bless you!" And the member went back to his desk.

In his reception-parlor at the Lobby Hotel sat the imperturbable King of Diamonds, smoking an unexceptionable cigar, and regarding the reflection of himself in an opposite mirror with careless complacency. Having punctiliously discharged every polite duty to official society, and given the highest social eclat to the cause of his client, Mr. O'Murphy, this immaculate gentleman had committed the brief remainder of the business to that client himself, and was now awaiting news of the final result with all that high-bred superiority to emotion which restrains the years from leaving superfluous lines upon a lofty countenance. As he sat thus, giving gracious audience to the assimilative courtier of the mirror, and occasionally withholding the cigar for a moment in the hand on which gleamed the Midnight Sun, that, with an aspect less like "cloud-compelling Jove," he might bestow a keener glance upon his silent familiar, there was a justifiable self-sufficiency about the whole man, — a warranted assumption of despotic superiority, — to exact a tribute of involuntary admiration from the most penetrative intelligence. Self-command was such an exact science and consummate art with him, that it amounted to a full abnormal faculty, — a faculty of creating a special well-balanced self to suit any contingency. In the event then transpiring at the capitol there was a Damoclesian sword for him, which, if it should chance to divide its thread and fall, would wound him mortally; yet, in full consciousness of the peril, he sat there tacitly approving himself in unruffled serenity, while men with far less at stake in the great game playing were sick with uncertainty and apprehension.

Three raps on the door of the room called the solitary occupant to his feet, and when he answered the sound there entered a man with iron-gray hair and a broad-brimmed hat, who seemed to have grown ten years older since last night. A man with downcast look, drooping shoulders, coat buttoned awry and coat-collar twisted out of shape under one ear, — a shabby ghost of the great Facilitator.

"Excuse my intrusion, Mr. Wynne," said this lamentable apparition; "I am too nervous just now to remain in public, and have taken the liberty of giving you a quiet call."

The least perceptible elevation of Mr. Wynne's black eyebrows accompanied the address, but the gentleman's general manner and answer were without indications of surprise.

"You are quite excusable, sir. Allow me to offer you a chair."

"Thank you, Mr. Wynne."

"Will you try a glass of wine?"

"No. I'm obliged to you."

"You do not smoke now, I believe. Will you excuse my indulgence?"

"My dear sir, don't mention it."

"The New York papers of this morning are on the table near you. Be good enough to amuse yourself."

This was a polite way of saying that further conversation was hardly called for on that occasion, and sounded rather abruptly for the *arbiter elegantiarum;* but before the latter could resume his chair again, and leave his uninvited guest to amuse himself according to permission, the door was thrown open with a single blow, and Mr. Bilk made a sensational appearance.

"Sold!" ejaculated the new-comer, sinking upon the nearest chair, and exhibiting a countenance lively with dismay.

Mr. Wynne received the monosyllable without changing the cold stare which he had fixed upon Mr. Bilk, on the instant of his rude entrance. General Cringer's shoulders straightened.

"Sold!" repeated the panting Bilk. "The American voted for Crow, after all!"

"Honor to Cattawampus!" intoned A. Cringer, like some good Episcopalian, responding at church.

"It was an outrageous sell!" exclaimed Mr. Bilk, violently. "It was intended to be only a complimentary vote; but, by some confounded! infernal! dishonorable! hocus-pocus, it gave Crow every Ebullition vote, and *elected him! !*"

The bearer of this astounding news

looked at Mr. Wynne almost fearfully, as he spoke, and received this return for his enterprise, —

"When you come again to a room occupied by me, sir, you will be good enough to knock before entering."

But the effect upon General Cringer was not quite so subdued. His head became stiffly erect; his eyes sparkled; his chest swelled out in a military manner, and his voice was like a trumpet.

"King of Diamonds, I have won another game. Two and the rubber!"

"And I have lost," said Plato Wynne.

Flash the news to all your papers, good reporters! Let it be known, far and wide, that the free will of the people, freely expressed by their incorruptible representatives, has elected to the toga of the laticlave him whom a true majority of his fellow-citizens the most delight to honor. *Senatus Populúsque Romanus.*

--------♦--------

CHAPTER XLIV.

PIQUANT notes, beginning "*Cher ami,*" and boldly written on perfumed and tinted paper, informed Hardley Church and me that we were to hold ourselves engaged for a little supper with Miss Margaret Dalen, at nine P. M., on the second evening after the termination of her own engagement at King's Theatre. We were to send no regrets; but come like dear good boys, and meet a select party of literary friends. R. S. V. P.

The most superficial traveller through Bohemia must be aware, that the intellectual dwellers in that æsthetical province make it a matter of principle to decline no invitation of that kind. So Church, and I, and all the remainder of the wealthy fraternity, favored with the rather theatrical *mot d'ordre*, returned prompt answers of acceptance; said answers being further flavored with as much *galanterie* as the occasion seemed to justify.

When the night came, the philosopher proposed to me that we should go somewhat earlier than the appointed hour, as he desired to have a little private chat with the fair player about his drama, before the others arrived. To this I assented, and, after a short sojourn in the establishment of a friendly hair-dresser around the block, who had literary tastes, we proceeded arm-in-arm to the fashionable hotel where the angel of the foot-lights had her suite of apartments. On gaining that populous locality, it would have been the ordinary etiquette to send up our cards, and wait for permission to follow them; but as it was not the practice of our caste to adopt the affectations of unintellectual people, we went straightway to the actress' rooms, without troubling the servants, and knocked at the proper door with distinguished ease of manner. Over this door was a movable glass light, which, being partly open at the time, permitted us to note that our knocking had put a sudden period to some conversation within. From this we concluded that the dressing-maid was with her mistress, and would, probably, admit us. But instead of that, the mistress presently opened the door herself, and received us with such a fluttering air of discomposure, that we involuntarily looked beyond her for the cause. That cause was quickly made evident, to my mind, at least, by the appearance of a slender, light-haired gentleman, dressed in deep mourning, who held a hat in his hand, and had, apparently, been in the act of taking his leave, when our arrival interrupted his parting words. My first glimpse of the figure told me that it was Ezekiel Reed; nor should I have been more disconcerted myself had it been unquestionably his ghost. The utter incongruity of his presence there, the incomprehensible solecism of it, flashed upon me to my complete unbalancing, for the moment; and I am sure that the mere expression of my countenance must, in itself, have been enough to produce the embarrassment mirrored in his. Church, too, seemed stricken with a kind of paralyzing wonder at beholding him, and it needed a conventional remark from somebody to break the awkward spell.

"Mr. Church, and Mr. Glibun, this is Mr. Reed," said the actress, in a voice anything but assured.

"I have the pleasure of knowing both gentlemen, already," said Ezekiel, blushing crimson as he spoke, but shaking hands with Church and myself. "You scarcely expected to meet me here, I presume, and I"—here he threw a quick glance at the actress, — "scarcely anticipated seeing you here."

My wonder reached a climax at his apparent recognition of my Bohemian companion as an old acquaintance; and my point-blank stare did not help him to regain his natural ease at once.

"But now that we have met, as you say, Mr. Reed," responded Church, with a desperate effort to be himself, "you're not going to run away from us, I hope? You ought to wait and take sup—"

"Mr. Reed has already declined prolonging his call," interrupted the actress, with strangely rude haste.

"I was indeed on the point of departure, when you and Mr. Glibun knocked," added Ezekiel, "and have barely time now to bid you good-evening."

"Well, if it must be so, good-evening, Mr. Reed," said Church. I inclined my head mechanically, and, after two or three low-spoken words from the actress, the school-master's step-son left the room.

Hardly was he beyond hearing in the hall, when Church threw himself upon a chair, and indulged in a loud laugh.

"By all that's dramatic!" exclaimed he, "but this *is* a good one! Why, Maggie, my enchantress, how, in the name of all that's sanctimonious, did you ever get that handsome apostle in your train?"

"He was here in relation to some law business," returned Miss Dalen, very coldly. "He never was here before, and may never be again. Mr. Glibun, won't you take a chair?"

"Thank you," said I, and took one.

"Why, what ails you, to-night, Mag.?" continued Church, moving to the sofa on which she had unsmilingly seated herself. "You're as cross as two sticks. Instead of meeting me — your fine-looking, chosen suitor — with the usual kiss, you positively act as though we had broken up a surreptitious lovers' meeting."

She tried to look at him resentfully, but quickly softened into a half-provoked smile, under his aspect of serio-comical anxiety.

"What brought you here so early, you plague?" said she. "I haven't even dressed yet."

She was very neatly and becomingly attired in a dress of pale-blue material, and certainly looked more like the modest pride and beauty of some refined and quiet home, than like a popular player awaiting company to supper.

"Then you have one costume for us, and another for our pious young friend, Reed," insinuated Church, whose native impudence had all returned to him.

"Hardley Church, I wish you wouldn't speak in that way!" answered the actress, her eyes sparkling rebelliously. "Mr. Reed is a gentleman very much above people like me, — or like you, either, you bad old creature! He is in the office with the lawyer who drew up my contract with Mr. King, and that's the way I happen to know him. I only wish I was fit to have such a man for a friend; but I'm not. That's the whole story for you." And she sighed in proof of the real feeling with which she spoke.

"Well, then Maggie," rejoined the philosopher, more soberly, "I'll run you no more on that subject. If Mr. Reed had given me time to get over my surprise at finding him here, I'd have shown him that I don't forget how he proved himself a good friend to me, once."

"If Miss Dalen will excuse me, Churchy," said I, no longer able to restrain my curiosity, "I should like to know how in the world you ever came to know him."

"I'll tell you," replied he, with remarkable earnestness. "He had a room in our house, in Benedick Place, for a while; and when I was sick with typhus fever, and everybody else fought shy enough of my room, that young man heard of it from the doctor, and came to my bedside like a brother. Many a night he sat and read to me for hours, and then kept the ice on my head until morning. I won't deny that he preached an occasional sermon, and gave me more or less gospel while I was down; but I could stand it from such a noble fellow as that. If he'd been my own brother, he could not have been kinder to the subscriber.

He kept away from me when I got well enough to go about again, and I haven't seen him since, until to-night. I'd as soon have expected to meet St. Paul at an opera ball as to see him here. You know him, too, it seems!"

"Yes. I went to a boarding-school kept by his step-father, when I was a boy," was my guarded reply.

"Was he always psalm-cracked?"

"He was very religious as a boy."

"What I saw of him puzzled me," said Church, musingly. "By-the-by, I think I remember his asking me something about you one night. Do you know much about him?"

"Not much more than I have told you."

"There's something peculiar in the expression of his eyes, — a kind of unutterable loneliness, I should call it; but God bless him, whatever he is!"

Margaret Dalen had given close attention to this short conversation, so unusually grave for Hardley Church; and now turned to me with the same troubled, doubting look she had worn during my brief private talk with her in the green-room.

"And *you* thought it very strange that your friend, Mr. Reed, should call on me?" she said, questioningly.

I could not deny what my face had so flagrantly betrayed, but made an effort to explain it on commonplace grounds. Mr. Reed and I had seen very little of each other during late years, I observed, and a sudden meeting with him anywhere would have caused me momentary surprise.

"Yes, I suppose it would," said she, leaning her head upon her hand. A clock on the mantel-piece striking the half-hour at that moment, caused her to look quickly up again, and as quickly rise to her feet and pull a bell-rope.

"Half-past nine, and I not dressed yet!" she cried, petulantly. "You must excuse me for half an hour, gentlemen, and amuse yourselves as well as you can."

"Why, Mag.!" urged Church, "the subscriber came early for the particular purpose of talking to you about that play before the others were here. Must you leave us?"

"I'm sorry, Churchy; but I haven't a moment to spare now. Do excuse me."

The entrance of her dressing-maid, in obedience to the bell, left nothing more to be said; and, with a coquettish demeanor so exaggerated that it betrayed its own purpose of disguise, the lovely little blonde followed her attendant into a room, through whose half-opened door several immense trunks had been visible ever since our arrival. Looking after her, and scratching his venerable head in a lively manner, Mr. Church gave vent to his emotions in the following style, —

"Not one French word in fifteen minutes, and as prim and demure as any rustic prude! Glibun, my child, when a woman like that commences to study for the character of

Caia Cœcilia, it's high time for fellows like you and me to admit the possibility of that Bohemian mentioned in the Metamorphosis of Apuleius. He, you know, as the old Platonist humorously observes, was a young man of great literary ability, and, *on that account*, was consequently remarkable for his piety and modesty! The subscriber hereby nominates Mr. Reed Chaplain to Bohemia, as a reward for his conversion of Miss Arsparsyar* Dalen from the error of her ways."

He plainly attributed no other than a sanctimonious purpose to Ezekiel's odd acquaintance with the actress, though such a conclusion would have seemed at least arbitrary to nine men of ten. It was not strange, however, that I should tacitly agree with him; for, in my estimation, every natural feeling of the former "monitor" of Oxford Institute was merged and lost in a species of religious insanity that could not be inconsistent with its own diseased abnegation of self.

"All joking aside," observed I, "it seems to me, Church, that Miss Dalen has some pretty serious inclinations for something better than a theatrical life. I judge so from what we have seen to-night — night-mareish as it was in some respects — and from something she said to me when I first met her."

"Ah, what a refreshing specimen of verdancy you are!" rejoined the philosopher, stretching his legs to the laziest extent, and surveying me with a sardonic grin. "Mag. is a good little creature, and will be still better if she buys my 'Tomyrus;' but as for 'serious inclinations' — gammon! She's an actress, heart and soul, and will be while she lives. It's a part of her cleverest acting to counterfeit simplicity; and that simplicity might take a young parson in; but a Bohemian ought to be awake to the trick. I'm too old a bird to be caught with such stale chaff.

' If women were little as they are good,
    A peascod would make them a gown and a hood.'

Iona Hart is good enough for me."

After which Byronic disposal of the question, Mr. Church gave me to understand, by a yawn, that he felt himself to be slightly bored, and wandered away to a table where some theatrical engravings promised better entertainment.

Improving the opportunity to take more particular notice of the room in which we were, I found it to be a large and handsome parlor, furnished in the choicest hotel style, and communicating at either end with a dressing-room and a breakfast-room. The door of the latter stood open, revealing a table "set" with silver-plate, china, and bouquets, and apparently all in order for the eatables and drinkables of the impending "little supper." On the walls of the

* Aspasia pronounced according to the "Continental Method," which Church had unfortunately contracted.

parlor hung a number of lithographs, representing the actress in varied characters, — from Hamlet down to Jack Sheppard; on the marble mantel-piece stood a gilded French clock, a cigarette case, and a miniature liquor-stand; and upon an *etagère* of elaborate rosewood appeared various silver cups, music boxes, sumptuous books, etc., which had been presented by admirers in different cities. Two chandeliers, three or four immense mirrors, heavy red curtains at the windows, a piano-forte with pearl keys, and a carpet of white and crimson velvet on the floor, made a glare and glow quite in keeping with the leading theatrical idea; and as the flaring, midnightish spirit of the scene impressed itself more fully upon me, I began to lose my anti-theatrical suspicions of Margaret.

That American Shakespeare, Mr. Steele, made his appearance in advance of the general company; his office of temporary business-agent and local literary man to our invisible hostess involving the duty of performing as her associate in the evening's entertainment. Shortly thereafter he opened the door to Scribner and Dewitt, who were quickly followed by Gushington and Bird. The evening toilets of all these talented gentlemen, like ours, ran very much to highly odorous hair-dressing; Mr. Scribner's poetical locks being even more spikey than usual with oleaginous perfumery, and Gushington's ebon ones gleaming down his back with a lustre both rich and fragrant. Then came Mr. Nemo and Miss Hart; the latter a Juno in the colors of Iris, and the former an incumbrance to be deserted and neglected from the moment of reaching the parlor. Mr. Fox appeared next, introducing a weakly little strip of a man named Mr. Little, whose affectation of a crimson necktie gave an effect of recent suicide to his aspect. Mr. Little was not exactly a literary man; but then he was separated from his wife, which was all the same.

The brilliant company thus gathered were exchanging strokes of wit in scattered groups and couples, and several colored waiters had made their appearance in the breakfast-room with trays of viands and liquors for the table, when Steele was seen escorting Miss Dalen from the threshold of her dressing-chamber to the society of her literary friends in waiting. With her crisp flaxen curls running riot over a coronet of theatrical pearls, her complexion heightened to the regulation bloom of a court-lady's, her petite form attired in a blue silk dress *à la Maintenon*, and her neck, arms, and fingers encrusted with a full retail stock of jewelry, the *cara* of the playhouse looked like something between a German princess and a French *précieuse*. With her simpler attire she had also thrown off her former subdued manner, and now laughed and equivocated with her guests so boisterously that Iona Hart was tempted to reprove her.

"And suppose we *do* disturb some of the other people in the hotel," cried she, in response thereto; "what harm will that do, my love? Is there to be no *gaieté du cœur* because some folks want to sleep as soon as it's dark? But you're only severe with me, my darling, because you're afraid I shall rob you of Churchy."

"Just let the subscriber put in a word for himself before you come to blows about him," interposed the philosoper, in his usual vein. "I know I'm a prize for any woman of taste; but why can't you two graces appreciate my exquisite discrimination between you. As Dumas says, *la brune c'est la passion*," bowing absurdly to Iona, "*mais la blonde, c'est l'amour!*"

"Oh, you may leave me out of the question altogether, Mr. Hardley Church," laughed the brunette.

"She'd like you better if you had a little of Mr. Nemo's retiring modesty," said the actress.

Mr. Nemo seemed to look pleased through his spectacles at this reference to himself, and bowed vivaciously to the fair flatterer.

"Why, that may be so, Maggie," replied Church; "for I've often thought, that if Nemo and I could be combined into one personage, perfection would be the result. I possess all the great qualities that he lacks, and he lacks all the great qualities that I possess."

This speech produced a general laugh at the expense of the luckless city-editor of the *Morning Dog*, who made a ghastly effort to join in the mirth and seemed heartily glad of the diversion afforded by Steele's announcement that the table was ready.

To the manifest disgust of several inspired intellects, Margaret Dalen selected me to lead her to the board, and whispered, as she laid a hand upon my arm, "Just remember, Mr. Glibun, that I'm acting now."

Indicating my comprehension of her meaning by a slight nod and an intelligent look, I performed my office with what grace I could, and handed her to the head of the table under a fire of jealousy from every masculine eye in the company.

All being seated, and the waiters dismissed to the hall, Mr. Steele noticed that the party was incomplete, and appealed for an explanation, —

"Wild and Le Mons are not here, yet, are they? What can keep them?"

"Their European in-manners, I sup-p-pose," stammered Fox, who was slightly out of humor because Miss Hart preferred Scribner to him as a neighbor at the table.

"I've been in Europe, Mr. Fox," said the actress, "and I never noticed anything of the kind in European manners. Had we better wait?"

"Not a moment, Maggie," answered Church. "The late Mr. Wild and the late Mr. Le Mons would be too vain if we did. When the subscriber realizes that hundred thousand dollars from 'Tomyrus,' he intends to make it a rule that no one shall be admitted to his suppers after the first joke."

"Have you taken his 'Tomyrus,' Maggie?" asked Iona Hart.

"I'll take it if I can only get Churchy to do what I want him to," returned Miss Dalen, glancing at the venerable dramatist. "If he would only let it pass for the work of some London writer it would do so much better. He'd make more and I'd make more. You can't get people to come and see an American play."

"They think it hasn't got the style, you know," observed Mr. Little, with marked profundity.

"Take it, and pay me for it, and do what you please with it, my adorable," exclaimed the philosopher, striving not to show irritation. "That's the fate of pretty much everything American. If you take an article to a New York paper, the editor will tell you that it will not pay him to buy original matter when he can get plenty of better stuff from any English magazine for nothing. If you take a book to Pye, Rait, & Company, they'll pleasantly inform you that it's a losing business to pay copyright to a native when they can have Thackeray and Dickens and Tennyson for the taking. When I did manage to get my 'Whims in Verse' published ten years ago (where are they now!), nobody on the New York press would speak a good word for the book until after some London weekly had said that it wasn't so bad. Irving had to be appreciated in England before we provincial snobs found out that he was the 'American Addison.'"

"I never could see much in Irving," observed Mr. Bird, whose foggy little eyes were not calculated for any great optical penetration.

"For my part," said Miss Hart, after tasting a glass of wine with me, "my one attempt to write a novel ended all my ambition for book-making. Mr. Scribner remembers how I got as far as page one hundred after working three months, and then gave it up because he said that it didn't have enough plot to make a good sketch of ten pages."

Scribner looked up from his plate to smile assent, and Church took the lead again.

"It's no joke to write a book, let me tell you," grumbled he, "though every fool thinks he can do it. I tried a novel in my green and salad days, and suffered more over it than any amount of adversity has made me suffer since. One day away up to the skies about it; full of pride and confidence; fairly bursting with good ideas, and half crazy with anticipations of fame and money. The next day heart-sick of the whole thing; disgusted with what you've written; so broken down that you can't drivel three pages in twelve hours, and ready to curse yourself for not having learned some good, honest trade. All this, too, supposing that you've really got the brains to write a book at all. I wrote five hundred pages in eight months, and — threw them into the fire."

"I'll tell you what your trouble is, Church," remarked the malicious Mr. Gushington; "you won't consent to write like a Christian, but must always be aping the pert, choppy sentences of Jules Janin, Berlioz, or some other foreigner."

"You think so," sneered Church, "because you know nothing about style of any kind. My model is good old Seneca. Read him, if you can, and you'll see what can be done with short sentences, my boy!"

"I never could see much in Seneca," carolled little Mr. Bird, with his mouth full of chicken salad.

But here the discussion was interrupted by the mistress of the revel, who, being greatly enlivened by the champagne she pretty steadily sipped, had leaned across the table to where Mr. Scribner sat, and snatched a folded paper from the breast-pocket of that gentleman's coat.

"That's not fair, Maggie," cried the victim, holding the paper by one end and striving to draw it back.

"Ah, let me see it," pleaded the actress.

"But you will not return it?"

"Oh, yes — *parole d'honneur!*"

Scribner relinquished his hold, and the actress tore open the sheet in great glee.

"It's poetry!" she ejaculated.

"Read it! Read!" cried everybody.

"May I, Mr. Scribner?"

"If you think it worth while. I scribbled it off in a hurry for my own paper and don't think much of it myself."

"*Voici!*" exclaimed the actress, holding up one hand theatrically, and at once read aloud the following: —

"A BRIDAL GIFT.

The mother saw her only one
  Before the parson stand,
To seal another love than hers
  With willing heart and hand;
And down her wrinkled cheek there rolled
  A fond, regretful tear,
For, though she gained a tender son,
  She lost a daughter dear.

That daughter marked the sign of grief, —
  And turned a paler hue,
As back to childhood's helpless years
  Her thoughts reminded flew, —
And, bending from her lover's side,
  She kissed the hand that e'en
Had gently ministered to her
  In all the years between.

'Dear mother, do not weep,' she said,
  'Though going far away,
In two short months we both return
  To be your double stay.
And if your thoughtless daughter fails
  In duty to be done,
Look up, dear mother, for the help
  That's stronger from a son!'

Then smiled the mother on her child,
  Such loving words to hear,
And pressed upon her glowing cheek
  The sequel of the tear;
And, raising up her trembling hands,
  When plighted was the troth,
She whispered, through her quivering lips,
  'God bless ye, darlings, both!'

A moment did she disappear,
  And then returned again,
With something by her fingers clasped
  And dragged along amain.
Then fixed her idolizing eyes
  Upon the youthful pair,
Where, silent in a sweet surprise,
  They stood to meet her there.

''Tis little I can spare,' she said,
  ' For scanty is my store;
Yet here accept a bridal gift,
  Before ye leave my door.
Though o'er-familiar to the sight,
  And homely, it may be,
It ever nurtured peace between
  My dear old man and me.

' Then take it, daughter, at the start
  Of this, thy married life,
And give thy promise as a bride,
  To use it as a wife;
Nor ever in thy darkest hour
  A friend more potent crave;
For, 'tis the very broomstick, girl,
  That made thy sire behave!'"

"Ah, *que c'est beau!*" ejaculated the fair reader, with mock sentimentality.

"I don't believe it would be possible for a man to be funny without some slur upon women," exclaimed Iona Hart, who seemed to have been disagreeably surprised by the turn of the last verse.

Mr. Gushington did not enjoy the general attention given to Scribner on account of the poetry, and felt that it was time to say something remarkable.

"Women," observed this profound misanthropist, "are living illustrations of Hegel's postulate, that everything is at once that which it is, and the contrary of that which it is. Women are at once angels and — the contrary of angels.

"I'll give you a better illustration of that kind of logic," rejoined Church. "That's so — so's that. There's not another such perfect phrase in metaphysics to be found or made in the language."

"Churchy, you're intoxicated," said De Witt, while the others laughed. "Let us get back to books again, if you can't talk about anything else without running into metaphysics. What sort of a hero do you think Plato Wynne would make for a novel?"

"He would have made a good melo-dramatic figure," answered the philosopher, good-naturedly, "but he's down now. That was a tremendous *coup* of Cringer's, at Albany."

"It was outrageous!" exclaimed Mr. Little, who was a Demolitionist. "It's time for the people to act, when that sort of thing is ventured."

"Mob law would'nt be much improvement," said Church. "I don't believe in the virtue of mobsmen. Give them an ynch and they'll take an L — they'll lynch."

"Oh-h-h — what a pun!" groaned the whole company.

With inflexible gravity the philosopher stared around the table, and sagely added, —

"There's too much freedom in this country. That's the trouble. Rome had her Metellus and we have our Cringer. As old Colley Cibber says, when liberty boils over, such is the scum of it."

This led to a sharp debate between the last speaker and Mr. Little, during which the other gentlemen, excepting myself, stole away from the table, one by one, in a mysterious manner, leaving me to entertain the ladies. This I did to the best of my nonsensical ability, noticing, by the way, that Margaret Dalen drank far too much wine, and occasionally used terms so exceptionable that Iona Hart felt impelled to stop her mouth with a restraining hand. While we sat thus, there was a cry from the parlor that Dewitt had gone home. Then followed a burst of laughter; and in another moment there trooped into the supper-room a company fantastical enough to have served for illustrations of the different moods of madness. In fact, the wild Bohemian crew had been plundering the actress's great trunks of their theatrical wardrobe, and now came pouring in upon us with the spoils on their persons. Fox wore a red cavalier hat with white plume, Dick Turpin's gorgeous dress-coat, and was armed with a foil. Little Bird was disreputable in Jack Sheppard's cropped wig and cocked hat, and Romeo's domino. Gushington mounted the spangled turban of the French Spy and was wrapped in an ermined cloak of some stage-queen. Scribner wore nearly the whole gay attire of the page in Don Cæsar de Bazan. Steele was adorned with the feathered cap of Maffio Orsini, and the curls, mask and cloak of some Elizabethan character. Nemo's spectacles and yellow hair were ghastly between Lady Gay Spanker's riding-hat and the gold-laced mantle of some character in burlesque. The five of us who had remained at the table could not help laughing at these incongruous metamorphoses, though the actress soon found breath to scold the exhilarated wags for taking such liberties with her property. It was enough, she said, affectedly, to destroy *une patience d'ange*, and she did not wonder that Mr. Dewitt had gone home from such a company of foolish children. Mr. Church also remarked severely upon the indiscretion of allowing minors to drink too much wine; but the offenders responded to all sarcasms with such bursts of wit as came handiest to their lips, and sat down to their wine again in the highest spirits.

The humor of the thoroughly Bohemian scene was waxing furious, and Mr. Fox had begun a French song to the accompaniment of musical glasses, — or glasses tapped to the measure with knife-blades, — when a rapping at the parlor door called Steele thither, and quickly resulted in his reappearance amongst us with Acton Wild.

A burst of badinage at the lateness of the latter was suddenly checked by the strangely serious look and bearing of that foppish gentleman, who, drawing the chair offered him to a distance from the disordered table, threw himself upon it with an air of weariness and dissatisfaction.

"What is the matter? Where is Baby?" asked half a dozen voices, in sharp discord.

"Le Mons has gone home at last," said Wild, half sullenly.

"Gone home!" echoed I, with a start.

"Yes," returned he, "gone home. Baby came down to the *Daily Bread* office, about an hour and a half ago, to come up here with me. He'd scarcely said three words to me when one of his coughing-fits came on, and, the next thing I knew, he was leaning over a chair with the blood streaming from his mouth."

Every cheek paled at the sound, and the fantastical revellers of a moment before sat mute and affrighted under a chilling apprehension.

"He isn't — dead?" exclaimed Church, in a suffocated tone, scarcely above a whisper.

"No, you raven!" retorted Wild, nervously. "He had as bad a hemorrhage while we were in London, and got over it. I sent to the Park, as quickly as I could, for a hack, and was directing the driver to Benedick Place, when Le Mons pulled me by the coat, and whispered, 'Take me home, to Fourth Street. My own home.'"

"The poor soul!" ejaculated Iona Hart, her eyes filled with tears.

"He was a little frightened, — naturally. And there *is* something frightful about such a thing!" continued Wild, his own face growing paler as he spoke. "I did as he wished, and took him straight to his mother's, though I'd sooner have died, almost, than gone to that house again. It was a dreadful scene there, — a dreadful scene," he repeated, passing a hand across his brow. "Le Mons's mother and sister would not speak a word to me after we'd made the poor fellow comfortable; but they looked at me as though *I* had been the cause of Baby's sickness! I came away feeling as though I'd been killing somebody. That's my pay for standing by a fellow like a brother!"

He tried to say it carelessly, and added, in a lighter tone and with a straightening of his shoulders, that Gwin was very comfortable and would be about again in a day or two; but neither he nor the rest of us could really brighten after such a shock, and it was not in wine, wit, nor philosophy to banish the skeleton that had suddenly arisen to the one vacant chair at the table.

Church did not attempt to even smile again; and when the wearers of the theatrical dresses stole away, in very shame, to get rid of their tawdry shreds and patches, he and Iona Hart took leave of the actress and us, on pretence that it was later than they had thought, and hurried away together. Seeing Wild arise to follow their example, I declared that I would walk with him; nor did Margaret Dalen show any disposition to detain us. She accompanied us to the parlor door, however, and once more whispered; as I bade her good-by, "Remember, Mr. Glibun, I have been acting to-night."

Wild was a but a moody companion for the distance we had together, and seemed disinclined for free conversation on any topic. He did not feel at all uneasy about Gwin Le Mons, he said, for the hemorrhage had ceased with his first swallow of salt and water after reaching home; but it was hard for a fellow to be scowled at like an assassin by the mother and sister of the friend he loved best in the world. He didn't feel much like talking after that.

To divert his mind, and my own, too, from the subject, I repeated what Church had said at the table about having published a book once, and asked whether he had ever seen a copy.

"Yes, — some time ago," he replied.

"And what did it amount to?"

"It was a dull book, with some redeeming pages; a volume of smoke, with occasional sheets of flame."

And with this question and answer, Acton Wild and I parted for the night, — or morning.

CHAPTER XLV.

IXION AND THE CLOUD.

THE mingled regret and satisfaction felt by me, in the knowledge that my misguided, but dear, old playmate was ill and in his old home, had a peculiar turn of ultimate self-reproach given to them by the conviction that I, by my present associations, was rendered scarcely more worthy the esteem and welcome of his mother and sister than Wild had found himself to be. Willingly would I have repaired to the house in Fourth Street, and shown my solicitude for the early recovery of poor Gwin, but for the vague, half-guilty shyness of so doing, with which, in common with my brother-scribes, I had been infected by the representations of Wild. Had not Ezekiel Reed, on the memorable evening of our sudden meeting in Benedick Place, said enough of my first sweetheart, Constance, to teach me that she would scarcely be rejoiced to recognize a former friend in a present Bohemian? Had not Gwin's own confession shown me the characters of his mother and sister in aspects of such stern moral severity that even a son and brother could not be literary in our grade without guilt to them? If relentless accusation was the award of the afflicted little household to Wild, the fellow-Bohemians of the latter had reason to expect no hearty welcome should they go to that house where no trouble might have entered but for the wayward invalid's brothership with them, as with him. Church, Fox, Bird, — all of us, were thus deterred from at once carrying such hope and cheer as we could to the sick-bed of poor Baby; but, late one afternoon, not many days after Dalen's supper, while several of the brotherhood were enjoying one of their frequent lounges and smokes in my devoted room, the philosopher waxed particularly rebellious at the situation, and suggested a bold movement.

"Iona Hart," said he, puffing a vindictive cloud of smoke, "has sent three bouquets to Baby, in as many days, 'with the compliments of a literary friend;' and they've all been taken in at the door. Which proves that his blue-presbyterian folks are not too godly to allow the poor fellow an occasional touch of sunshine in his cell. Now I propose that three or four of us go there in a sort of surprise-party to-morrow afternoon, and give the old chap a good rousing-up, in spite of his women. It'll do him more good than all the dosing and coddling in the world. We know what a merry soul he is; we know how he'd enjoy a select little spree, if he *is* sick; and I say, let us go, and let each of us carry something or other to cheer him up. I'll take him all the unchristian weekly papers. Glibun might carry along a basket of fruit — "

"I'll tell you what I'll take," interrupted Gushington, in high glee. "You know what a fellow Baby always is for sporting-dogs. I'll get an acquaintance of mine to lend me his fancy-terrier, — so small I can carry it in a pocket. I'll take that!"

"And I'll carry a pack of cards, — for a quiet game of euchre on the bed, you know!" added Bird, rubbing his hands.

"I'll take my f-f-fiddle," stuttered Fox, "and g-give him a tune!"

I never saw old Church enjoy anything quite so much as the immediate success of this amiably vandalish idea of his; nor could I find it in my heart to oppose a scheme grounded in such thoroughly good feeling. He laughed, choked with smoke, shed tears over his pipe, and gave me a slap between the shoulders that sent my pipe sparkling to the floor.

"We must let Wild and Scribner into it, too," said he. "The more the merrier. We must go in couples, though, ten or fifteen minutes apart, or the ladies will faint at seeing so many sinners all in a row."

"But suppose the ladies should refuse us admission," urged I, compunctiously.

"Then we'll take the liberty of passing the act over their gentle veto, and apologize to them afterwards," laughed the venerable hyena. "But I'm not afraid of that."

"Well," returned I, plucking up courage, "as Mrs. Le Mons and her daughter were very good friends of mine when I was a boy, and have received no offence from me since, I don't see why I should fear it much, either."

In fact, the audacious expedient was just what we needed, to overcome our hesitation at facing the two best earthly friends of our sick comrade. It was not rigorously in keeping with the more punctilious usages of polite society, and might be open to a suspicion of positive impudence; but if superior literary minds shrink from showing true independence, why might we not as well be all slaves at once, and have done with it?

The great and subtle spirit of progressive civilization depends upon the free and soaring intellects of an age for a gradual but sure emancipation of our race from those degrading fetters of Form and Usage which are forever compelling the mighty human soul to Conform, Conform; and it is due to the mental giants of the New York Bohemia of my time to state that they would *not* conform. No, sir.

When my friends had decided, then, upon said expedient for restoring the health and spirits of Gwin Le Mons, they knocked the ashes from their brierwoods into a hat of mine which stood upon the bureau, nominated Mr. Church to solicit a temporary accommodation of two dollars from me for evening refreshments, and departed in a vivacious body for the green-room of King's Theatre. Not being in a mood to join this latter expedition, nor yet disposed to rely upon solitude for those charms that sages have seen in its face, I suffered those free spirits to get fairly clear of the building, and then sallied forth, myself, to make a friendly call.

Directing my steps to a neat brick house just two blocks westward of Benedick Place, and affably stating my business to the servant who answered my ring, I was conducted to a sitting-room on the second floor, where Miss Iona Hart did make her scriptorium and cosey home. A knock at the door was responded to by that literary Juno in person; and, encouraged by a graceful and easy welcome, I deposited hat and gloves upon an ottoman, drew a chair into sociable proximity with that which the goddess adopted for her own occupation, and at once plunged into those absorbing observations on health and weather so necessary to the inauguration of every well-ordered chat.

The room was large and airy, and had plenty of substantial furniture in mahogany and hair-cloth; but two opened trunks against the wall, with half of their contents boiling over the sides, lent no improvement to the general effect; nor did a shawl on the floor, a bonnet on the sofa, and a veil caught in the joint of a gas-jet, convey the most tasteful idea of a boudoir. Furthermore, a table heaped with writing-paper, ink-bottles, scrap-books, and newspapers, was demoralizing to behold; and a tumbler, containing egg and spoon, failed to render the mantelshelf picturesque, even though assisted in the effort by a pair of curling-tongs and a handful of curl-papers. But, if these disorderly surroundings were repugnant to the fairest ideal of womanly domesticity, there was an ever-varying intelligence in the animated face of Juno; an arch literary grace in her flowing black curls, ink-tipped fingers, and studiously-negligent delaine gown, confined at the waist by cord and tassels; to make the critic appreciate something higher in woman than mere housewifery, something more intellectual than a mere feminine capacity for vulgar, mechanical home-duties.

My own unparalleled experience as critic in such matters made me thus appreciative at once. It made me positively spoony, so to speak, before the mental superiority of Miss Hart had developed itself in half a dozen sentences about health and weather. The clear, ingenuous smile with which she artlessly regarded me was an inspiration to a gentlemanly languishment denoting the first degree of hopeless captivity, and I became sentimental forthwith.

"You may think me childish, Miss Hart," said I, with interesting gravity, "but this illness of Gwin's depresses me so much that I have really come here to be cheered-up by you. Our other friends cannot feel about Gwin just as I do. He and I were so intimate in childhood that he seems to me like a brother."

"Every one who knows Baby, must love him," was her pensive response, "and I should feel sadly enough, too, if his attack were more severe. So I can sympathize with you, if I cannot cheer you, Mr. Glibun."

"You have sent flowers to him. That was very kind."

"Oh, that was nothing. You know his people, I believe, Mr. Glibun. Are they so proud and uncharitable as Acton Wild appears to think them?"

"I have seen nothing of them since I was a boy," responded I, looking down, "and can only judge them by report. I should not say they were proud, but I'm afraid that they regard Wild as having led Gwin astray, in the first place, and would estimate the rest of us by Wild. Very unjust, of course."

"Ought we to blame them for that?" asked Iona Hart, looking keenly at me as though she would know my real thoughts on the subject. "Would Baby be a sorrow to them now, if he had chosen different company?"

Surprised, if not startled, to hear her speak in that tone, but well aware of the reproachful truth she implied, I was conscious of changing color, and returned an indirect reply,—

"I did all that I could, Miss Hart, to persuade Gwin to return home and be reconciled to his mother and sister. He promised long ago, but kept putting off, putting off."

"Yes, yes," said she, feelingly, "that was the way with Baby,—putting off always. I used to persuade him in that way when he came here to see me. 'Oh, I'm going, 'Ona!' he would say, half-frowning, half-laughing; 'I shall get awful lectures from mother and sister, but I deserve a beating.' But he did not go."

"Do you think it was Wild's influence that made him act so?"

"No more than Church's, or Mr. Fox's, or Mr. Gushington's. It was the influence of the course of life he had fallen into, Mr. Glibun. It was no life for a simple child like Baby. We were not the companious for a weak, easily led young man with a good home and good mother and sister."

"We! Miss Hart?"

"Let us be honest," she earnestly said, clasping her hands and looking at me with a dreamy kind of regret. "We know well enough, in our own hearts, that, if we had brothers and sisters of our own, we would not have them like ourselves. Oh, no, no!"

Giving way to the feelings suddenly aroused in me by her words; drawn closer toward her by the mere magnetism of sincerity; I dismissed all affectation from my face and language, and confessed to Iona Hart more than I had yet confessed to myself.

"This Bohemianism is indeed fit only for the homeless and friendless!" I exclaimed, bitterly; "and who that had any worthy hope or aim in life would adopt it? If I and the others have been pure, good friends to my dear old playmate, why should we all feel ashamed to face his mother and sister, as though we had injured them? I am going there to-morrow with Church; and Mrs. Le Mons and her daughter shall hear me warn my friend to have friends like Church and me no longer."

I lashed myself with such hearty goodwill in the sudden frenzy of remembering my own aimless, outcast condition, that Miss Hart regarded me with increasing wonder.

"You have always seemed different from my other literary friends," she pointedly said. "Margaret Dalen told me how you had spoken to her when she first met you, and we both concluded, Mr. Glibun, that you would not be a Bohemian long. I have taken you to be somewhat like Mr. Dewitt; only coming amongst us occasionally from curiosity."

There was a curiosity in this speech, which, at another time, I might have sought to evade; but now, between morbid self-consciousness and infatuation, I cared only to aggravate my own misfortunes.

"Bohemia is my natural refuge, Miss Hart. Dewitt has a home, and a mother, and home-friends. He has something to look forward to in the world. But I have no home nor friends, nor object of ambition. I have a professional position and can earn a very good living; but as for having claims to any other kind of life than the one you find me in, that is a mistake. I'm nothing but a homeless, hopeless Bohemian!"

There was a short pause after that, during which my right hand wandered to the back of her chair and gave my eyes an excuse not to meet hers.

"Have you no sisters, or brothers, Mr. Glibun?"

"None. — Thank God!"

Another pause, and then, "If I had but a brother, *my* life would be a very different one, I think. After the death of my father, which occurred while I was a child, there was no one left to be a companion and guide to me. My step-mother thought me queer, and neglected me. As I grew older it seemed to me that my step-mother and her friends grudged me a place in my former home; and, as my father had left me a small income, I determined at last to come to New York and seek a new home amongst strangers. After I had been in this city about a year, one who pretended to be a devoted friend induced me to take my money from its investment and lend it. I lost it in that way, and the friend with it. Then, of course, I had to do something for a living, and undertook to write for the press. That made me acquainted with Mr. Church and my other literary friends, and they have always been like so many brothers to me. Still, if I had an own dear brother I should not wish them to be like brothers to him. I tell you all this, Mr. Glibun, because you have spoken so freely of yourself to me, and because *I* would have you think neither better nor worse of me than I deserve."

She spoke in a low, rich voice, with each varying tone of which I regarded her more confidently, and grew happier in a new and glowing emotion. If she had appeared sympathetic and beautiful in my eyes when speaking so gently and regretfully of Gwin, how more tender was the effect when, with drooping head and subdued breath, she so trustfully confided to me her own history. Drawing my chair closer, and leaning toward her until my face nearly touched her graceful shoulder, — until the warmth from my lips must have penetrated that shoulder with the heat of a passionate contact, — I timidly took one of her hands, as though I would thereby express a sympathizing comprehension of more than she had said. The least pulse of an instinct to draw the hand away gave me but the more tremulous pleasure in its possession; the rich color mantling and paling on the velvet cheek like an inaudible sigh, made my breathing quick with a strange, delightful fear.

"Let me call you Iona," I said, in a husky whisper; "will you?"

She slightly averted her face, but bowed her head in silent assent as she did so.

"Let me prove how thoroughly I sympathize with you, — how much more nobly I think of you for the brave womanhood you evince in your false situation, — by offering myself to you as a devoted friend."

"I am not worthy — "

"Do not say that. The similarity of our situation gives us an indisputable equality, or I should not presume to venture as I do. We are both cast out alone upon the world, and fated to lives which we feel to be unlike what they might and should be. Let us have no pride between us; let us understand each other as no others understand us, and be bound to each other in the bond of a sympathy above all around us."

"I should be unkind," she said, quietly, but with eyes still averted, "if I permitted you, in your too generous impulsiveness, to hold me entirely blameless in the things I have told you. I shall prize, and be proud of, you as a literary friend; but for friendship of a higher kind, it may not be wise in you to select such as I. What do you know of me beyond the few words I have spoken of myself?"

"Intuition tells me all I wish, or require, to know!" I passionately exclaimed, my right hand slipping nervously down the back of her chair. "See how instantaneously, as it were, we are drawn so closely together, that a near companionship of years seems to be realized and justified in a moment. Let me regard and treat you as the true sister of my heart; the first human being to whom my nature has ever responded with a love —"

Convulsively her hand closed around mine in an interruption more peremptory than words, —

"Dear friend! we must not speak of love."

"Why not of love, dear, dear Iona!"—I was trembling like a leaf with excitement, and every breath fanned her warm cheek in a warmer gust as my daring hand crept about her waist. "Why not of the true feeling we both experience this moment as our destiny! Look into my eyes; do not turn from me as though we were doing some wrong. See how straightly and honestly I can look at you, dear Iona; even as Petrarch could look at his Laura, when she, in her mistake of his heaven-born sentiment, turned her face aside."

Obedient to the eager summons she turned her grand black eyes — twin midnights with a veiled star in the zenith of each — full upon mine, and, with a gesture commanding, yet gentle, loosened my arm from its caress. Then, as my countenance changed, she said, with deep meaning, "Laura's answer shall be mine. I am not, Petrarch, I am not the person you suppose me."

From the love-chase of Theagenes and Chariclea down to that of the Chevalier W—— and Miss G——, a man battling with the vicissitudes of the tender passion has ever been the feeblest, unwisest, shabbiest failure of the sublime known to human experience. In the full flush of success he is the most weakening and shamefaced of spectacles; but when, under the astonishing shock of disappointment, he smiles a ghastly smile, wheezes consumptively through his nose, and scratches first one arm and then the other in sheer senility, humanity madly revolts from the debilitating exhibition. That Petrarchian bathos of mine had furnished my Juno with the one sentence in all the world that, coming from her, could kill all hope for me. The manner in which that sentence was spoken expressed a volume more, and I lapsed back into my chair the most disconcerted young driveller that ever wished himself dead.

"Then you do not care for me?" I gasped, between a smile and a grimace.

"I do not think it right, dear friend, to let you mistake a momentary fancy for a serious sentiment."

"Madam," ejaculated I, with a bitter sense of my increasing absurdity, "you need not be afraid to tell me at once that I have made a goose of myself."

"Now, Mr. Glibun, please don't be angry with me," she entreated; "I do care for you, and would give worlds to have you for my dear brother. But — Mr. Glibun — I have — already — loved!"

"So I've heard," sneered I, like a ruffian.

If that red flash of indignation on her startled face deserved revenge, she must have seen by the working of my own disordered countenance that resentment could not make me suffer more than I already did. Woman's fine instinct of indulgence and mercy toward the rejected triumphed over her momentary sense of insult, and tears glittered in her pitying eyes.

"May we not still be friends, Mr. Glibun? Let me get you a glass of wine and a cake."

"Cake!" said I, looking sternly at her.

Modestly but very steadily she met my glance, and for the space of a few seconds an ominous rigidity of features prevailed. Then, a something odd in the lines about her lips imparted to my mouth a curious nervous inclination out of all keeping with my dismal state of mind. As I gazed, those lines seemed to be relaxing more and more, like the outlines of clouds breaking away, and I was conscious of a peculiar sensation of the forehead as from the fume of soda-water. Her eyes twinkled, mine winked, and, without the slightest responsibility on my part, I suddenly found myself laughing a spirited duet with her.

Ovid never imagined such a cure as that for love. It refreshed and revived me as a bath does the worn and weary traveller. "Miss Hart," said I, delighted to gain my wits again, "you will oblige me very much by forgetting my recent imbecile remarks, and making the most of what little respect I have permitted you to retain for me. I don't doubt that I have followed the example of many another stupid misinterpreter of your amiability, and been brought to my senses with the same gentle dignity; but I question whether any one of my predecessors had the brutality to repay your most generous conduct with rudeness. If you will just forgive one remark I have made this evening, and promise to regard me as a friend under great obligations to you, I shall have some hope of regaining self-respect."

Oh, but she was a true woman, though, and could have endured a less prompt heroism in my dismissal of the tender spell.

"I'm sure," said she, — and would have pouted had she dared, — "I'm sure there is nothing so very shameful in allowing one's heart to be honest with itself. So far from being foolish in loving, even without hope of return, a person is always the wiser for it, I think."

"May I be an illustration of the fact, Miss Hart!" And I gallantly raised her hand to my lips.

"The discipline of the heart is the experience of the mind."

"I believe with you,—though my own experience has been limited,—that there can be no reliable wisdom in the mind's judgment of things without some practical discipline of the affections and passions. But you have not yet forgiven that rude speech of mine."

"I shall never think of it again, Mr. Glibun."

"You shall never have cause to do so if I can help it. Now let me ask a favor. May I still call you Iona?"

"All my friends call me that."

"Well, then, Iona, what do you say about accepting my escort to the theatre? We shall get there time enough to hear Miss Leggett sing in the third act, and may meet Church."

"I will go, with pleasure." And away she hastened to the toilet.

You say, my friend, that you never heard of such a quickly settled affair of the heart before? Ah, but you have never been in Bohemia.

CHAPTER XLVI.

"FORBEAR TO JUDGE, FOR WE ARE SINNERS ALL."

THE overworked, underpaid day-laborers in the Republic of Letters have all the heart-burnings, jealousies, and enmities of their betters, aggravated, of course, by the ruder freedom of passion and expression pertaining to a lower estate. Embittered by a continual failure to rise above the drudgery of their profession, or rendered callous to every lofty aim in life by the hopeless defeat of a first and cherished aspiration, each views his neighbor with a half-suspicion that the latter is covertly a rival to himself for the scanty rewards of their common toil, or barely tolerates him as a fellow-worker from whose abilities no particular assumption need be feared. It is only the mere demoralization of intellectual habit that inclines them toward any close community whatever; the natural literary instinct being primarily unsocial; but since that inclination does exist, in a feverish, arbitrary way, its gratification is sought chiefly for the sake of an extreme contrast to solitude found rather in personal discords than in harmonious companionships. Hence, while these poorly requited souls exhibit a certain superficial unity in the one pastime of ridiculing and depreciating the very rulers in their republic whom their own past compulsory suffrages helped to elect, there is no genuine cordiality, or co-operation, amongst them, save as it comes of imperative necessity. In the most hilarious gathering of such reapers of a thankless harvest there rankle jealousies from which scarcely one is exempted; in their most intimate associations lurks a seed of enmity. If one of them, by the exercise of an energy not yet sapped by early disappointments, succeeds in elevating himself to a higher rank, his less fortunate former comrades will scarcely stop to decide upon what is most politic before using their every opportunity to detract from his merits. If one amongst them proves to be a good philosopher and apparently aspires to nothing better than a reasonable equality in their company, their appreciation of his philosophy will be more or less tempered by a regret that his likelihoods promise so little help to them in their frequent hours of pecuniary embarrassment. All this while they are all sturdy and stubborn, each able to fight his own way on his own ground and amply return any compliment to its sender. But let disabling accident, or sickness, befall the very brother whom they have railed at the most bitterly, and how touching is the change! From hearts seared and soured by years of fruitless labor for name and competence; from hearts turned hard and reckless under the conviction of irreparable mistake in a vocation no longer alterable; from hearts made bitter and uncharitable by a belief that the world robs true merit to honor worthless pretensions; from hearts wedded to folly, because folly brings much company and few generous responsibilities, —from these sour, reckless, uncharitable, selfish hearts,—there answers a simple, unselfish humanity, tender and devoted as a woman's. All then are brothers to him they so lately mocked as a failure and derided as a dunce. Kind faces hover about his bed; cheering voices tell him pleasant fictions of the great marks he has unwittingly made in literature; poor, shallow, consumptive pocket-books grow more hollow-cheeked to give him comforts; praise is spoken and written of him by twenty surly tongues and pens. He cannot show fight now; but it shall go hard with the other old boys if, by their untiring care and kindness, they do not have him all right on his feet again for a fresh round of very hard ones.

I had not been amongst men like these very long when I discovered that their unanimous tenderness toward Gwin Le Mons was a tribute to his ill-health. That racking cough and the hectic flush appealed to them successfully for genuine affection and approval, where the finest genius would have gained but jeers. He was the merry-hearted, clever, unenergetic sick "Baby;" and, when they knew that he was very ill at last, the brotherly impulse was mighty enough to dare even the terrors of a devout household, with fiddles, cards, terriers, and other amazing Bohemian remedies.

That suddenly soft-hearted reprobate and literary bruiser, Mr. Hardley Church, was at the *Earthquake* office bright and early on the afternoon appointed for the merry visit. He stalked into the compartment occupied by Dewitt and myself with a roll of fresh newspapers under each arm, and as many projecting from the side-pockets of his threadbare coat.

"Well, Glibun," cried he, "I've got pretty nearly all the weeklies here, — begged every one of them, — and it'll do our friend, the Baby, no end of good to read the pleasant mention made of him this week by all our fellows. Have you got your basket yet?"

"Here it is," I answered, touching a basket of assorted southern fruit on my desk.

"So it is. Those bananas look ravishing. I've a mind to try one myself."

"Certainly. Here's a fine one."

"It may look as though I ought to wear bristles; but here goes! I dined on a pipe to-day."

"Then you're very hungry, I suppose. Let's stop at Tick's, on our way up, and try a couple of steaks."

"We'll think about that as we come back. Gushington and Fox have gone up already, and Baby will be expecting us every moment. When you're too hard-up to buy a banquet, my boy, and don't happen to know any one who wants to cash your note of hand. there's nothing like a pipe of cheap, rank Virginia scrap-tobacco. The first three puffs settle all the appetite you may chance to be troubled with."

The poor old fellow looked so thin and shabby in the daylight that his humor had something almost piteous in its effect.

"But is not Dewitt going with us?" he asked, turning toward my editorial associate, who continued writing at his desk, and had paused only long enough to acknowledge the philosopher's presence with a nod.

"I've called there already," said Dewitt, gravely, "and found Le Mons more seriously sick than you think. It will be hardly prudent for you fellows to go there as Wild says you are going. Le Mons is a very sick man."

"Is he dangerously sick?" asked I, alarmed by his serious manner.

"Perhaps not. But he is very weak, and says little. He asked about all his friends, — particularly about you two, — but I doubt that he will enjoy seeing you with dogs and fiddles. He's nervous and low-spirited."

"Then he wants just the cheering up that we've contrived for him, Will Dewitt," returned Church, with a look of triumph. "Suppose one of us were pulled down, and had the blues about it, would he want nothing but glum faces and dismal condolement to make him all right again? Pah! I wouldn't mind betting the entire proceeds of 'Tomyrus' (say half a million!) against Plato Wynne's big diamond, that Le Mons will be well enough to sit up before we leave him."

"He already sits up," observed Dewitt, smiling.

"He does? That's enough! We'll bring him down to Tick's with us! Come along, Glibun."

Not feeling certain that further argument would strengthen the line of conduct to which we were committed. I promptly seized my basket and hurried away with the philosopher. That Dewitt had called upon poor Gwin like a Christian, and been received, apparently, without any marked disrespect to his literary character, was calculated to make me regret my own want of manliness in not following his example. How true is the remark of Kant, that self-esteem is at once the nobility and salvation of mankind! Without it, or even under its impairment, modesty degenerates into cowardice, misfortune becomes degradation, and a morbid jealousy of contempt in others produces a debasing sense of guilt in one's self. For no better reason than the misfortunes of my life, I lacked courage to go to that house in any other way than as a rude defyer of prejudices which my own overwrought self-distrust had guiltily accepted as existing. To be in that condition of mind at all was to be in a fair way of actually meriting the due reward of unworthiness; and, save for the mercy of Providence, I must have truly deserved but cold treatment from any judicious relative of Gwin's by the same rule that accorded it to Acton Wild.

"Don't wear such a church-yard face, Glibun," growled Church, noticing my contracted brows; "and don't assume quite so much the aspect of a sentimental young man under arrest for stealing a basket of fruit."

"I can't help wishing," said I, "that Gushington and Fox had selected other objects of amusement for Le Mons to-day. Your papers and my fruit are well enough; but the violin and dog will look like intentional offence to the poor ladies. We've made a mistake this time, Church, and Dewitt was right."

"Per Jovem!" snarled the philosopher. "Did I ever hear such sermonotonous whining! Cannot the friends of a sick man devise a little innocent amusement for him without provoking all this woe-begone twaddle? Glibun, you're generally the best of fellows, and I owe you several dollars; but if you can't be taken into a little scheme of enlightened humanity like this without prosing so absurdly, it's time for you to go upon some religious paper, and wear a white choker."

"It is absurd," was my petulant answer, "to think of acting the gentleman, when you're only a graceless vagabond in Bohemia!" And, in high dudgeon with him and myself, I walked on more rapidly.

The number of the house having been given us by Wild, we experienced no difficulty in gaining our destination; and, while waiting at the door of the neat dwelling, I could not help sighing my remembrance of Gwin's old home, and our boyish romps together. From basement to roof the shutters were all closed, giving to the building that expression of inward quietude and trouble which the most indifferent visitor cannot observe without a presentiment of calamity; and simultaneously with my imagination of the pale, despondent young man within, came the recollection of a hardy, laughing boy, whose invincible good-humor went so far to lighten the shadows of my own unlovely childhood. Not much time, however, was allowed for meditation in that vein, our use of the bell being promptly answered by a very sad-faced female servant, who, without a word, permitted us to enter the hall, and closed the door noiselessly behind.

"How is Mr. Le Mons to-day?" asked Church, in a nervous whisper.

"No better," she said, and looked down.

"Can we see him?"

"Are you the gentlemen expected by the other gentlemen upstairs?"

"Yes."

"Then you are to please walk up."

She led the way up the stairs so softly, that Church and I involuntarily trod softly, too; and I could see that my companion was as much discomposed as myself, at these appearances of trouble, although he whispered his belief that "this sort of business in a house was enough to make any sick man 'no better.'"

As softly the woman unlatched and pressed open a door on the upper corridor, standing silently aside to give us way, and we passed into a room where dead stillness invested the human forms therein with a fearful tribute to some awful spiritual presence. As I stepped carefully and with swelling heart behind Church, and marked the sinking change in every line of his form at the instant when the door ceased to break the interior view, a sickening dread fell upon me, and I instinctively gave my first glance to a bedstead against one of the walls, in full expectation of reading a terrible explanation there. But the bed was unoccupied, save where the bowed head of poor Mrs. Le Mons was clasped in her hands on the pillow. Beside it, however, with back toward us, was a chintz-covered easy-chair, in the full golden glow of the declining sun; and its story was told in the figure of a pale, rigid, tearless girl, who sat watching it with rapt intensity, and in the concentrated, staring dismay of Fox, Gushington, and Bird, who had seats between it and the radiant window. There, indeed, rested my old playmate, his thin, transparent hands lying nerveless upon his knees, his colorless face turned aside against the cushioned back of the easy-chair, and his sunken eyes closed as though he slept. No one spoke to us; the mother kept her countenance hidden; the sister moved not her eyes from the face of the sleeper; the Bohemians avoided our startled glances of inquiry by looking to the floor.

"I—I—had no idea he was so sick," stammered Church, huskily, his wrinkled face turning old and pallid in a shocked surprise. "I expected to find him quite well. I—I never dreamed of this."

Working his hands unconsciously over and over each other, he looked from the chair to the Bohemians, and from them to Constance, in painful entreaty for at least one word of reassurance. I touched his arm and indicated a couple of chairs which the servant had drawn near to that of the invalid; but, before we could occupy them, Gwin wearily opened his eyes, and looked at us with a faint expression of recognition.

"My dear old Baby!" cried Church, catching the look. "You've had quite a nap. Don't try to shake hands; a little weak yet; I understand."

I, too, approached and bent over him, nodding, and showing the basket of fruit; but, to my deep sorrow and humiliation, he scarcely seemed to notice me after the first glance. Steadily at Church he gazed, with a kind of hungry fear growing in his thin white face; and that gaze continued, as he spoke,—

"Sit down by me; close—close."

The voice was low, hoarse, and indistinct; the short, laborious breath dying on each word.

"So you go to sleep over literary company, do you, young man?" said Church, drawing his chair closer, and striving to appear cheerfully composed. "I don't blame you for being affected in that way by Bird and Gushington, whose poetry would make a black-fish yawn; and Fox's physiognomy is always enough to make an oyster duller; but the subscriber's celebrated vivacity, and Glibun's tremendous intellectual spirits—" Checked by something in that unchanging, searching face, he discarded his trifling manner in an instant, and went on in a far different vein. "Le Mons, you are very sick, I see, and not in a condition to be amused with folly. The boys and I are here in all good feeling, as you know, of course, and we feel more like crying than laughing over you; though we did hope to make you merry. What can we do for you, Baby? We feel like brothers toward you, all of us, and wish we'd been better brothers, too. Are you well enough to say a few words to us before we go?"

"Is there a God—to save—me?" came in startling accents from the bloodless lips.

"I—I—believe there is, dear fellow," was the halting answer.

Struck aghast by the awful question, Church trembled like some palsied old man; while we, his younger associates in conceited irreligion, sat dismayed and self-reproachful around the poor young questioner, like guilty witnesses before some dread tribunal. A half-suppressed groan from Mrs. Le Mons; a sinking to her knees beside her brother's chair of the still voiceless, tearless Constance; and all was silent and motionless again. Then the hollow, gasping, unnatural voice sounded once more,—

"Pray for me!"

If there had been a dreadful fascination in the face of the sufferer before, another face was more awful to look upon then. Every feature of Hardley Church was haggard and working with the torture of affrighted helplessness; perspiration beaded his wrinkled forehead and rolled down his cheeks like tears; and he placed one of his claw-like hands upon the arm of the sick-chair with an uncertain gesture of suppli-cation.

"I'd pray if I could, my dear, dear boy," he mumbled in his miserable despair; "but I don't know how; I don't dare; I'm afraid of insulting the Almighty!"

The eyes of the dying Bohemian had been feverishly bright with an inner radiance of the mind's last terrible concentration; but now they contracted and grew dark with a gloom which seemed to fill the whole wan face with a gray, ashen horror.

"God have mercy upon me! have mercy upon me!" cried Church, frantically press-ing his hands to his own tortured eyes. "I cannot pray; my tongue would cleave to the roof of my mouth. But I — I can sing."

And then, in a harsh, cracked voice, made shrill by the inexpressible misery of the moment, he commenced singing, to the fa-miliar air of Pleyel's Hymn, —

> "Jesus, lover of my soul!
> Let me to thy bosom fly;
> While the billows near me roll,
> While the tempest still is high!"

The poor, shrill, quavering voice had scarcely gone thus far, like broken wings bearing upward a beautiful dove, when other trembling manly voices joined the strain : —

> "Hide me, O my Saviour, hide,
> Till the storm of life is past;
> Safe into the haven guide;
> Oh, receive my soul at last!"

Gushington, with a dog in his lap; Fox, with the violin-case under his arm; Bird, with a pack of cards slipping from his pock-et; I, with my basket of fruit; — thought-less, careless, sinful young souls; — all in-voluntarily joining, with remorseful hearts, in the hymn we had none of us forgotten!

While we sang thus, the mother of our fallen brother left the bedside, and, stooping over the back of the invalid's chair, kissed his hair and forehead. Tears flowed from the eyes of all of us at the sight, and Church fairly sobbed for a moment. It seemed, however, as though the singing had, in a measure, calmed the latter; for when he again spoke it was in a steady and more solemn return of his usual tones.

"*Mea maxima culpa!*" he said, gravely and softly, as communing with himself. Then, affectionately regarding Gwin, whose eyes were closed again, he added, — "In the miserable pride of vainglorious intellect, I have uttered many wicked follies to you, Baby, about the Almighty and his worship; but, as I was ever false to my own instincts and natural convictions in uttering them, you, I believe, never had the wicked, the mad, strength to as greatly outrage your nature by forcing them deeply into it." He shrank suddenly back, as he spoke, quickly

catching his breath, and exclaimed, "Mad-am — Miss Le Mons — look! there is some change here!"

We heard the despairing wail of the moth-er, as she sank fainting to the floor, and sprang from our chairs in shuddering af-fright. Church, too, was on his feet; but what seemed most eloquent of grief and horror in that paralyzing moment was pre-sented by Acton Wild, who had entered the room unnoticed, and now, with the face of a spectre, stood mutely staring at the scene. He had loved Gwin, — not with a love the wisest and least selfish, but, still, with a love to wring a heart at the touch of death. It was hard for him that he should be too late for one parting word from the friend who had chosen him above home and kin-dred. It was hard for him that the sister of his lost friend should arise from her knees beside the dead, and say, slowly and clearly, — her bosom heaving, and her eyes terrible with relentless accusation, —

"You have killed my brother!"

Draw the curtains close. With God, alone, the Merciful and Just, is wise and pitying judgment of the partial wrongs our loves, not less than our enmities, in blind self-will commit. He, only, can tell what answer there should be, when one of us, feeling some vague reproach within himself at the death of an erring fellow-mortal to whom his love has been a destiny, asks of his own conscience, — Am I my brother's keeper?

———◆———

CHAPTER XLVII.

WOLFTON MARSH.

WITH hearts lying heavy in our bosoms, we followed poor Gwin to his last home in the Marble Cemetery; or, rather, we re-paired from our rooms to the place of sep-ulture at the hour appointed for the inter-ment. After the scene narrated in the last chapter, none of us felt like visiting the house again. Acton Wild's cause was, by obvious implication, more or less our own, and in the stern, unforgiving speech which had been so strangely addressed to him by the sister of the dead, we, his comrades, recognized an implacable reproach to his whole fraternity. But on the afternoon of the funeral we awaited the arrival of the body in the cemetery, and stood in sad con-course at the foot of the grave when dust was committed to dust. Mrs. Le Mons and Constance were accompanied by a tall, cler-ical young man, who proved to be the offi-ciating clergyman of the occasion. With heavy black veils between the world and their grief, they stood beside the final rest-ing-place of their beloved and wayward one, like the blackened columns of a once happy home whose prop and support against the storm had fallen to ashes. I would have given worlds to have relieved my sinking heart by going passionately to the side of that self-contained, unbending girl, and telling her how earnestly I had urged her brother to return in penitence to her, his mother, and his home, before it was too late. For a moment it was my impulse to seek the mother and daughter thereafter in the first calm of their great grief, avow to them my identity with Gwin's early playmate, and mingle my tears with theirs in the conciliation of a common sorrow; but quickly came the reflection that they must have become aware of my father's infamy; quickly came the thought that it were something cowardly to shrink from classification with those whom I had elected for every-day associates; and the temptation to vindicate myself was conquered, with a sigh.

That evening, while I sat sullen and alone in my darkening room, thinking gloomily of past and present, and rebelling, more bitterly than ever before, against the fate of a homeless outcast, the ingenious Mr. Fox presented himself at my door, with the suggestion that I should join him, *pour passer le temps*, in a visit of observation to Plato Wynne's.

"As well there as anywhere else, I suppose," was my answer; and, from no stronger motive than a feverish desire to gain temporary distraction from sombre thoughts, I accompanied the stuttering journalist to the locality designated.

Famous throughout the whole country, and no less renowned because involved in an audacious kind of mystery for nine people in ten, the storied Temple of Golden Chance presented a gravely unostentatious front on Broadway, about mid-stream between two of the then-principal public parks. Often, during my long experience of clerkship with Cummin & Tryon, had I passed the place where Fortune was reputed to exhibit her grandest caprices. Often had I glanced curiously at the unrevealing door and windows, wishing that I might gain one glimpse of the master-gamester, whose defiance of law, political daring, and courtly personal address were the elements of a celebrity permanent and unique. The building was an old one, and of brick, rising by two stories to a peaked roof of slate, from the foremost slant of which projected two dormer windows. It had been partially rejuvenated, however, with a coating of brown paint, in imitation of stone, and a pair of ornamentally grated front doors in green and gilt bronze. Recurring midnights found mobs of hackmen and private coachmen gathered about the light stone stoop, and funereal lines of hacks and coaches stretched along either side the street in dark array; but at the earlier hour of our visit the building and its surroundings suggested nothing but severe domestic retirement, and might have been taken for the substantial residence of some rich and steady veteran citizen, who had obstinately refused to be ousted from his old home at any price the world of storekeepers could offer.

A tug at the silver bell-pull summoned an alert figure into view at the grating of the double doors, and my conductor and I, after a nod and a word from the former, were promptly admitted to the presence of a man in footman's livery. Him we followed to the first door in the hall, and were thereby ushered very quietly into what the before mentioned supposititious veteran citizen would have styled his front parlor. It was a room of medium size, furnished with crimson damask curtains, a heavy Turkish carpet, chairs and sofas in yellow satin, mirrors, and paintings. Thence, between green silk curtains, held aside on either hand by the extended marble arm of a pedestalled Venus, we passed into a companion-apartment, where a number of well-dressed gentlemen lounged upon sofas and triple chairs, in luxurious idleness, dozing, smoking, chatting, or consulting the evening papers. Thus far the house gave no positive signs of its true character. In fact, this one particular house at no time harbored a more guileful purpose than was evinced in the harmless relaxations of the company then present; but, through two windows, descending to the floor and opening upon a balcony, you could look over a long, narrow garden to another building, on the back street; and there it was, as my companion told me, that one might expect to see — what he came to find. To this second edifice we made our way, descending by a broad flight of steps from the balcony into the garden, and thence along a path between neat flower-beds. In the various well-lighted rooms now open to us we found luxurious appointments for all the fashionable games of chance, including even a pool billiard table; while in one particular apartment there stood a table superbly spread with every luxurious detail of a cold feast, and glittering with silver liquor-stands, wine-coolers, cut-glass cigar-caskets and decanters, and immense medallioned vases of flowers and fruit. Here were two gentlemen, of foppish attire and sinister countenance, refreshing themselves from dish and decanter alternately, and flavoring their accompanying table-talk with divers pleasant oaths. They had but recently "got up," it seemed; their business cares of the preceding night having delayed their hour of retiring to somewhere about the late breakfast-time of other people; and the oaths had particular reference to the exasperating noises which all creation will persist in making while gentlemen thus delayed are endeavoring to woo tired nature's sweet restorer. To these fine fellows Mr. Fox seemed disposed to address himself, as to valued and distinguished acquaintances; but, my own mood being averse to such company, I whispered my refusal of an introduction.

"But that need not deter you from joining them," I continued, in the same suppressed voice. "As Wynne does not seem to be upon the premises yet, and my curiosity to see him being really the only motive I had for coming here, you may as well attend to your own affairs without further reference to me. I will take a quiet saunter by myself for a while."

Finding me determined to follow this unsociable plan, the stammering squire of theatrical dames left me to my own way, which presently led to the garden again.

Multiplying stars overhead, and the rays of some half a dozen lanterns just lighted on either fence of the latter limited *rus in urbe*, afforded enough illumination for a cogitative promenade along one of the paved paths, and, with arms folded and head slightly inclined, I began to pace back and forth between the two buildings. Here, thought I, it may be my fortune, if I remain long enough, to meet Allyn Vane and Hastings Cutter once more; for did not the former, at our memorable and last interview, inform me that he and the latter were familiars here? And this Plato Wynne,—this lately all-powerful master of political destinies, this daring and matchless double-gamester,—is the husband of Elfie! Is there a fatality in my coming here, where every memory and mystery of my own incomprehensible history presses upon me like a choking presentiment? Who am I? Where are my natural belongings? What will be the end of this confused, inexplicable, haphazard existence of mine? Am I here, fresh from the graveside of a misspent, ruined, youth, to take a lower step in the same downward course, and prove myself worthy a felon father by turning gambler?

Thus tempting myself to untold evil by inwardly torturing unto death all chance and hope of good, I did not at first give much heed to the fidgety little figure of a man, which had appeared on a parallel path of the garden soon after my march began, and occasionally flitted toward me by a cross-walk, and then back again, as though either particularly attracted, or repelled, by my presence. Finally, however, in one of my turns, it came suddenly face to face with me, and I halted, at a timid touch from one of its hands.

"I beg your pardon," said I, in no amiable humor.

"The walk's very narrow," returned a thin, weak voice. "I suppose you belong here, sir?"

"I am a visitor, sir."

"Yes, yes, of course; that's all the same. Do they play in this rear house?"

"I believe they do."

"What games in particular?"

"My good sir," said I, impatiently, "you probably know quite as well as I. You are at liberty to play what you please." I stepped aside to pass him but he caught my arm.

"Then if two persons," rejoined he, in a strange, nervous kind of voice, "wanted to play a private game of all-fours, for small stakes, they could do it?"

The question and manner of asking it struck me ludicrously, but I replied, gravely enough, "Oh, undoubtedly."

"Would — you — mind — trying me — a game?" asked the poor little man, in a tone of mingled fright and desperation.

"My dear sir," said I, amused in spite of myself, "I am as verdant in such matters as you seem to be. Simple curiosity brought me here, and I feel no desire to play."

"If you think I've no money," he exclaimed sharply, "you're mistaken. As for my verdancy, try me! I'm no chicken, let me tell you, young sir! Come, come, let's try one game, for a small stake."

The oddity of the man's conduct made me not unwilling, at the moment, to see more of him; and, as he seemed so curiously bent upon a gaming acquaintance, I indulged the whim without further consideration.

"Well, sir," I remarked, "since you persist in making me a gambler whether I will or not, you shall have the satisfaction of a game with me. We will call for a pack, and make ourselves at home in one of the private rooms."

With an alacrity savoring of childish impatience he at once hooked arms with me, and I was precipitately drawn into the gaming-house and to the first vacant room, where chairs, tables, and a variety of gambling adjuncts awaited the general company not yet arrived. A silent attendant of the establishment brought cards to us, not a feature of his discreet countenance expressing the surprise with which he must naturally have regarded our excessively countryfied proceedings; and, by the brilliant light of four gilded gas-jets I was enabled to observe more satisfactorily the appearance of my new acquaintance. He was, as before remarked, a little man; but I was hardly prepared to find his hair almost entirely gray, and his eyes dancing with an excitement that gave a cast of partial defiance to a countenance otherwise meek. For a few moments I believed him to be under the influence of drink, and heartily "blessed" myself for yielding to his absurdity; but, as we played, and his excitement increased, he seemed more like a madman. He lost; insisted upon playing again; lost once more; flew into a violent rage at my wish to leave the table; and, at last, literally forced me to be the winner of nearly two hundred dollars!

A sense of the comicality of the affair now gave way to a genuine feeling of alarm on my part, and, casting the cards upon the floor, I resolutely refused to play any more.

"Whoever you may be, sir," I exclaimed, energetically, "you certainly act like a maniac. I joined you in this foolish child's play merely for amusement, and have not the remotest intention to take your money. There it is."

"H-have you cheated in your play?" he cried, in a high, shrill voice, his whole face working nervously and the perspiration streaming down his cheeks.

"Take back your money, sir," I reiterated, quietly. "You are excited and forget yourself."

"And you insult me by daring to offer me a charity!" returned he, glaring at me with a wildness more despairing than wrathful, and twisting the cards in his hands to pieces. "You've won the money, — keep it. Don't dare to talk to me as you would to a beggar! You needn't think I'm a beggar!"

No, thought I to myself; but you're as mad as a March hare, and I was a precious goose in not discovering it at once.

He had risen to his feet, leaving the money on the table. I now arose, also, and, money in hand, had approached to compel his acceptance of it, when, with a quick gesture, he pushed me rudely aside and fairly ran from the room. Half-dismayed, half-inclined to laugh, I stood staring confusedly at the door for a moment, and then, hastily donning my hat, followed in pursuit. Gaining the garden, I discerned him moving up the central path toward the front building in hot haste, and after him I went, with the bank-notes still in my hand. The balcony was now brilliant as day with light from three great hall-lanterns, and I gained the foot of its steps just in time to see my lunatic pause and shrink back before a gentleman who was at that moment stepping out through one of the door-windows of the parlor.

"Luke Hyer! Can it be possible!" were the words of this gentleman, as I reached the balcony.

If I did not know the voice, I was too thoroughly a New Yorker not to know the person, of him whose name was a synonyme for the loftiest commercial prosperity and integrity of the Empire City.

"Mr. Goodman!" ejaculated the other.

"Your son followed you to this wicked place to-night," said the great merchant, in a low but distinct voice, "and came to me with the prayer that I would save his father. And you are here, indeed, Luke Hyer, in a gambling-house! My old friend, why is this?"

"Mr. Goodman," I said, stepping up to them, "will you oblige me by walking this way?"

He turned his fine, benignant face toward me, and, to my inexpressible surprise, gave a very perceptible start. Nor did he remove his subsequent intent gaze from my face when following me beyond the view of the persons in the parlor behind him.

"Who are you, sir?" he asked, quickly.

"I am the unwilling winner of Mr. Hyer's money, Mr. Goodman. Under the influence of an extraordinary, and, as it seemed to me, insane, excitement, Mr. Hyer fairly forced me into a farcical game with him this evening. Persisting in playing, he also, I may say, persisted in losing; and when I finally refused to continue the folly and endeavored to return his money, he violently resented my intention as an insult, and was actually running from me when he met you. Here is the money still in my hand. It is hardly necessary to add that I have not a thought of retaining it."

"What is your name, sir?" inquired the merchant, his fixed look filling me with strange sensations.

"That," said I, assuming hauteur, as a disguise of my perplexing discomfiture, "can scarcely be of consequence in the matter, sir. I know you by sight, Mr. Goodman, like every New Yorker, and can claim no other excuse for addressing you by name."

He bowed slightly, and turned again to the poor little man standing, helplessly silent, between us.

"Mr. Hyer," said he, "the young man wishes to perform an honorable act, and you must accept it, as much for his sake as for your own. If there has been anything in your circumstances to arouse one thought of such a terrible resort for help as this, you should have told me long ago. Your children—"

"My children! my children!" whimpered Mr. Hyer. "Don't speak of them here, Mr. Goodman, for God's sake. Luke is a good boy, but the extravagance of my girls is just what has driven me, and driven me, until I'm—here! I'm in debt; I don't know which way to turn. I borrowed the money to come here. I told Luke I must do it at last; and now look at me!"

"When I was a boy," said I, "one of my playmates was named Luke Hyer. If he chances to be your son I shall have all the more pleasure, Mr. Hyer, in appearing to you as something better than a swindler. You will take the money now?"

Like an automaton he took the notes, and turned them over and over in his hand; and again I found Mr. Goodman watching me intently.

"And now, gentlemen," said I, willing to escape from such extraordinary scrutiny, "I will bid you good-evening."

But, as I lifted my hat, a speaking look from Mr. Goodman caused me to hesitate, and, with mingled gratification and embarrassment, I respectfully grasped the hand he frankly extended.

"Since you decline giving me your name," he observed, still kindly studying my countenance, "I will take your conduct to-night as a warrant for at least believing it to be unblemished by the baser associations of a place like this. I could have wished to find a face like yours in a different scene, and I cannot forbear regretting its apparent familiarity here. Young man" (warmly pressing my hand), "your appearance interests me strangely. If the counsel and assistance of an older, and, possibly, wiser, friend can be of use to deter you from a perilous course in life, you have but to call upon me at my place of business, and allow me to tender both. The proposition is unusual, but so are the circumstances evoking it."

Such words, from such a source, gave me almost equal occasion for tears and for the indignation of resentful shame. While yearning to pour forth a torrent of grateful extravagance for an interest so unexpected and honoring, a consciousness that I was taken for a gambler, and had myself rendered an explanation impracticable, made my answer one of pride rather than gratitude.

"In the event of such an exigency as you have mentioned, Mr. Goodman, I shall thankfully remember the remedy you so generously suggest."

Disappointment, if not positive regret, was the expression of the great merchant's countenance as he slowly relinquished my hand. With grave dignity he bade me "Good-evening," and, in the company of the man he had come to save from ruin, passed in through the two parlors, and so from the house.

The luxurious idlers on the chairs and sofas had all recognized the unusual visitor, and observed enough of his actions to judge pretty accurately the object of his visit. True and well-known gentlemen had been there before to rescue wayward sons and friends from the most dangerous of temptations. Mr. Goodman had come amongst them, they knew, intuitively, on some mission of the kind, and, with that polish of manners and well-bred imperturbability which come of the habitual self-control and superficial associations of men in their calling, they refrained from the least sign or expression of either surprise or curiosity.

When I stepped into the parlor, from the balcony, two or three pairs of steely eyes were directed to me for a moment, as though in covert inquiry of my relations with those who had just left me. They were promptly averted, however, on perceiving that I was a stranger; nor did I observe any of that whispering or exchanging of glances which might have attended a much less sensation in many a pretentious drawing-room.

New guests were now beginning to arrive, and the famous King of Diamonds himself was likely to appear in state before another hour had passed; but my adventure had effectually deprived me of all further interest in either king or court. If not angry with myself for being there at all, I was certainly in a dismal temper with the perverse fate which had, as usual, placed me in a false position before others. The peculiar agitation I had experienced under Mr. Goodman's searching observation, could be attributed only to the protests of pride against misjudgment. I could account for it in no other way; nor was I disposed to remain longer where a merely casual appearance of evil had already subjected me to a penalty for evil itself. With hat pressed down over my eyes I returned to the garden, and passed thence to the farther building, intending to leave the premises by the back street. Truth to tell, Mr. Goodman's face haunted me like a reproach, to which my instinct, in

utter defiance of my reason, pleaded guilty. I could not shake off the tormenting sensation; I could not help feeling an acute sense of humiliation, and a cowardly shame against being seen to leave the Broadway door. So, in petulant haste, I sought the "private entrance," as it was called, and gave the porter a fee to open the secret latch for me. But Fox had caught sight of me on my way through the house, and scarcely had I emerged into the open air when he appeared in the doorway.

"I say, Glibun, are you g-g-going?" called he.

"Yes!" snapped I. "And you should have too much sense to bawl-out my name in that way from such a place!"

"Oh, v-very well!" retorted he, "if that's y-your humor you may go, and be hanged!"

In high dudgeon at my rebuke, he slammed the door. Not sorry to be rid of him thus briefly, I descended the four stone steps leading to the pavement, and was about to pursue a homeward way, when a gaunt, rough-looking man stepped out from under a street-lamp directly before the stoop, and simultaneously addressed me, —

"Is your name Glibun — Avery Glibun?" The voice was husky and the tone eager.

"What is that to you?" asked I, drawing back.

"He called you Glibun," said the man, pointing a thumb at the door; "and if your first name is Avery you ought to know me. How you've grown!"

There *was* something familiar in that voice! By the flaring light of the lamp I could see that the speaker had a thin, pale face, and a long, tangled, rusty beard, and that his hat and coat were miserably shabby.

"My name is Glibun," said I, confused and wondering; "but I certainly do not know you. Where have I met you?"

He leaned against the lamp-post, and gave a short, dry laugh.

"Why, if you're the genuine young Avery, you met me once in an old warehouse that my pipe made fireworks of; and once in the street, when you were coming from a young-folks' party; and the last time, when I knocked the school-master over with a bullet from his own gun, and carried you down-hill on my shoulder. Now, who am I but Wolfton Marsh?"

I stared at the man in blank amazement, and not without a vague presentiment of coming evil.

"I remember you now," I said. "You saved my life."

"I fired the shot, to be sure; but it was Elfie made me do it. She gave me the gun and told me to watch. Thank her, and not me. I might not have done as much for you, alone, as I'd do for my daughter."

"Your daughter!" I exclaimed, utterly bewildered; "Elfie your daughter!"

He gave the short laugh again, and pulled at his beard.

"Why, where are your eyes, and ears, and brains, if you don't know that?" said he. "I don't look much like the father-in-law of the King of Diamonds, and don't expect his general relatives to cultivate me much; but, as you still stick to your old name, it may be that all Plato Wynne's fine ideas are not law to you. I'm the father of that man's wife and of your step-mother."

"In Heaven's name. man, what are you saying?" I cried, half wild with his crazy ideas. "What have I to do with Plato Wynne? I never entered this house before to-night, and have never even seen your daughter's husband."

"Never seen your own father?" exclaimed he, as though doubting his own ears.

Black was the night above, and dark the street around; but at the sound of those words, there flashed upon my soul a light so searching and so blasting that it reached far into years of the past and blighted endlessly into years of the future. Blind fool that I had been, not to see the truth when Allyn Vane's story held it so plainly before me.

Clutching Wolfton's arm until he winced. I thrust my tingling face close to his and whispered my answer, —

"I believe what you say. I have never once seen this man, nor your daughter. since I was at school; but I know now that Plato Wynne is my father —God help me! You must not leave me until I know all you can tell me of him and of myself. I saw you once when you did not see me, and when that man mocked you with your own ruin and his possession of some paper of yours." — He started, and made an effort to break away from me, but I held him tightly. — "I don't know what that paper was. I only know that I was detected in the room after you had gone, and sent mercilessly to school to be —as I firmly believe — murdered by a madman! Providence has brought you here, at the threshold of this house, above all others, to tell me what it is my right to know."

"The street is no place for the story," he sullenly muttered.

"My lodgings are not far from here. You can go there with me."

He regarded me silently for a moment, and then said, in a very earnest undertone, "If I tell you what may help you to right yourself, will you promise to do what you can to right me?"

"I solemnly promise it."

"Then show me the way to your place."

Language cannot portray such feelings as were mine during that walk with Wolfton Marsh to Benedick Place; nor can they be appreciated by those whose lives have no ordeal histories. The street was one of Broadway's near parallels with the least of its light and life. It might have been a path through a wood, for all the people we met; and the few lamps were like bleared reflections of the stars in a turgid stream where none would come to look at them. I thought of the night when the fireman walked me to sleep in streets like it; of the nights when the glowing pipes of the gipsies were like feeble stars; of the night when the fireman was again my protector; and of the night when I went through such streets in a carriage to see Roderick Birch lay where I once had lain. The forms and scenes of my adventurous, unguided past all came back to me in the most unlovely by-ways of night, as though darkness had ever claimed me for its special sport; and now they seemed but so many sunless, gas-bleared radiations from the black and covert starting-point of an infamous paternity.

Upon reaching the house in Benedick Place, by this unfrequented way, I hurried my silent companion to my room; and there, with door locked and chairs drawn closely together, implored him to tell me all he knew of my misfortunes.

Now, that his misshapen hat was off and the light fully upon him, he appeared but a deplorable wreck of the sturdy wanderer of the past. His reddish hair, thickly tangled with gray, hung down nearly to the shoulders in matted locks; his whitening beard covered his breast; and between locks and beard glared a face pallid and haggard as want and woe could make it.

"Then it's true that you've never been home since that morning when I had to cut away from you across lots?" he said, staring about the room, after a long look at me. "You've really thought all the time that your name was Glibun, and didn't know who your father was?"

"How could I learn more than I knew on the morning you speak of, when to seek further knowledge was to invite another attempt upon my life? I have been a continual fugitive from the unnatural anger of my father, thinking of him only as a peril and a mystery, and hoping but to keep beyond his sight and knowledge while I lived. There was a time when a vague, unreasoning conviction of my own fitness for better things deluded me with the chimera of some great wrong against nature yet to be righted, and an honest name and position yet to be restored; but at last the story was brought to me that my father had been a felon, a leader and associate of counterfeiters; and, without pausing to inquire between rumor and fact, I at once resigned all hope of anything better. The thought that my unnatural parent might be *dead* has, I now feel, been my last wretched relief from unnerving apprehension! There was fate in my going to that house to-night, and fate in my meeting with you. Tell me what you can; give me some clear ground to stand upon in my own defence ·against an unparalleled outrage of years; and rest assured that I will readily forgive any part you may have taken, voluntarily or otherwise, in the iniquity of Plato Wynne."

"Any part I may have taken!" exclaimed Wolfton Marsh. "You forgive me? Rather say that you need my forgiveness for the ruin your devilish father has brought me to. You sit there in good health, in good dress, in your own comfortable room. You're young and strong, and can outlive all the troubles *you've* got. But look at me,—sick, ragged, homeless, old, and ruined. Who saved you from a broken neck? I did. Who made me what I am? Your father. If there's to be any forgiveness in the case I'm not the one to ask it!" His eyes gleamed fiercely, and he tore at the ragged collar of his coat as though choking with despairing anger.

"I did not mean to do you an injustice," I said, quietly. "Only give me the information I ask, and you shall find me both just and grateful."

"I'll tell you my own story; that's all I can do," returned he, drawing a long breath and casting his look to the floor. "Part of it may help you, and part of it may not; but I may as well tell you the whole. At the time when I first met your father, Elfie and I kept a little school, or academy, as we called it, in a village about twenty miles north of Milton. No matter about the name of the village. It was a small place, and the school gave only a poor support to my daughter and me. She commenced teaching there at twelve years old; but I only undertook it because her mother's last sickness took all the little money I had, and left me so poor that I had not much choice. Your father came into the neighborhood with two other gentlemen, one September, to hunt; and, as he and his friends kept their traps and horses at the village hotel, I became acquainted with him. He called himself Mr. Glibun then. One evening I took him home with me to show him a fine English gun that had belonged to my father; and, as he pretended to think much of my little place, I asked him to stop and smoke his cigar with me. There he saw Elfie; and from the moment his wicked eyes rested on her, she was like a bird bewitched by a snake. He didn't have much to say to her;—not more than if she'd been a tame, pretty bird; —but what he did say was such an artful mixture of patronage and flattery that the young creature became a woman at the very sound of it. (If you don't understand that now, you will when you're older and have seen more of women.) She seemed afraid of him at first; wouldn't sing for us when I asked her to; and left the room before he went back to the hotel; but he had her in his toils already, and knew it, too! He didn't patronize nor flatter me; but he took pains to make me believe myself too good a man to be playing the poor pedagogue in a Jersey village, when I had abilities to make something of myself in another field. I was expert with a pen. I could write almost any hand handsomely. It seemed to come naturally to me and was really the only gift I had for teaching. In the hotel there was a specimen of my writing framed and hung up;—a burlesque petition to the legislature for a new turn-pike, with imitated signatures of celebrated names. Your father continually spoke of that as a wonder, and rarely came to my house of a night without dropping something about the great things I might do with my pen."

Here I interrupted the story, to ask if some of those early details could not be as well omitted? My impatience to hear of other things could scarcely brook such delay.

"I must talk in my own way," was the answer. "You may not care to hear about a time when I wasn't an outcast and a vagabond; but it's what I like best to remember. However, I'll make as short work of it as I can. When the shooting was over, and the shooting-party ready to go back to town, I was wholly under the influence of Plato Wynne, ready to follow him to the end of the world, and anxious to be anywhere else than where I was. A mortgage on my little place had fallen due; and, as I couldn't raise the money to clear it, the place had to be sold. That, of course, made me all the riper for my new friend's use. And Elfie, between defying and adoring him, was the bewitched bird over again. Well, well! we went to Milton, as he ordered us, and there I was introduced to two or three of Wynne's creatures, —all men who had been ruined by him! —and was drawn by degrees into dark doings with them. The whole party were counterfeiters, and had their den in an old mill, some distance from the village. Two-thirds of the people about — farmers and villagers — had an interest in the rascality, and helped to keep the others from prying about the mill, by pretending to believe an old story of its being haunted. Your old school-master was one of the gang. A strange fellow, named Reese, was another. A Yankee, named Easton Sharp, was another—"

He paused, because I had uttered a half-exclamation; but I told him not to mind me; I was only a little nervous.

"The school-master, Birch, took Elfie and me to board, in the school-house, with him and a step-son of his, for a while. He was a widower, and a poor, weak specimen of a creature, who had been beggared and drawn into crime through gambling. His own boy did'nt know that he was one of us, —so closely was the secret kept from those who hadn't interests with the gang. Cursed be the hour when I left my old home for such hell-born company! Cursed be the moment when that smiling devil incarnate —but there's no use in talking of that now, —no use. When the true character of our destroyer became known to Elfie; when he stood revealed to us as the counterfeiter, gambler, scoundrel that he was, such a change came over her that her whole nature seemed altered. She became silent, sullen, and fierce toward me, and contemptuous to the school-master, but to Wynne, when he came amongst us, she was like a spirit-broken tigress, hating him, as

I thought, with her eyes, yet minding him like a dog. Birch finally asked her to be his wife; and, in my presence, she asked our owner if she should accept the offer,—looking awfully into that devil's face, as she did so. To me, her father, she said not a word about it; but, in my presence, asked that of Plato Wynne! And his words were,—'If I were not already married, myself, Miss Marsh, the answer to your question would be selfishly evasive. As it is, I shall esteem you more, if possible, as Mrs. Birch, than as Miss Elfie.' I don't believe that she had known of his marriage before then. At any rate, she turned white as a sheet, and fell down in a fainting-fit. In a week from that day, she married the school-master, hating him all the time. The one child born of this marriage died almost at birth; and thank God it was so! You must know what the end of the marriage was; so I needn't go over all that misery. If the school-master is in the madhouse yet—"

"He is dead," interrupted I.

"Then peace be with my brother in misery!" exclaimed the narrator, shaking his head. "The same soul-killer drove both of us; and what wrong I did him by that shot on the cliff was to save him from going past God's pardon. When your mother was about to be confined, my daughter was ordered to go to the city, and be her nurse. What could she, or the school-master, or I do, but submit? She went, sternly, but like a slave; and from that time began a scheme of villany more daring than all before it. Your unhappy mother's father, who lived somewhere toward Harlem, died of apoplexy,—hastened, as it was told me, by the bad conduct of a runaway son,—before your mother's marriage. Before that, though, the Mr. Glibun whom your father represented himself to be, had established himself in the poor girl's good graces,—I speak of your mother,—much against the will of her parent, who distrusted the wily suitor. The old man's sudden death took place before he could prevent the match; but, with forethought of the worst, he had willed to your mother only the interest accruing from her share of his estate; bequeathing the principal, in trust of his brother, to such male child as might, in any future marriage, be hers; or, in default of such issue, to his brother's family. That was the true will of your mother's father; and that property would be yours now, but for a false will, forged by Plato Wynne, and bearing later date, in which the principal was bequeathed to your mother, subject to *her* last will and testament."

"Merciful Heaven!" cried I, "how could you know this?"

"From the lips of Plato Wynne, himself!" exclaimed Wolfton Marsh, clenching his hands upon his knees. "He told me of it with a wicked laugh; showed me the forgery in his iron safe,—because he knew me to be in his power; me and mine!—and made it an argument to lead me into as base a fraud on a dying woman. See what a wretched slave I was to that monster of iniquitous power! Although he had not *yet* touched the money, himself, your poor young mother had a suspicion of the forgery, I think. At any rate, when, with a presentiment of her coming fate, she wished to make her will, and I—miserable tool!—was brought to her bedside, as a lawyer, she dictated a testament by which the property should go to her unborn child, should it be a son; or, to her husband in trust, should it be a daughter. I know not whether such a will would, or would not, have stood law, had it really been drawn. I do know, however, that, while pretending to draw it thus, I really worded it so that the birth of a daughter would make the property wholly Plato Wynne's. I read it aloud to her,—as she had dictated, *not* as I had actually written; and she signed it, and my daughter and a man named Ketchum signed as witnesses. You may well draw back from me, after hearing that. But listen to this: Degraded and lost to all honor as I was, the villany was perpetrated by me, on the express condition that, should a son be born, and the mother die, the false will should be returned to me. You were born, and your mother died in the same hour; but when I called upon your father to fulfil his promise, the answer was, that he *would* return the document, for destruction,—when he chose! What little manhood had mingled with my guilt before, deserted me then; and, with terror and despair bursting my heart asunder, I sank hopeless and desperate to the lowest depths of coward vagrancy. I never went back to Milton. I haunted the house by day, and dogged the steps of my destroyer by night; ever begging and begging for the paper witnessing my damnation. And then I became the companion of other lost wretches like myself; and finally joined with those who prowl and row about the docks and piers at night, for prey. After your birth, my child, she who had lost her soul was kept most of the time as a guard over you,—I know not why. And at intervals, I would still dog Plato Wynne with my prayers, and still hover about the house where Elfie was. One day she came out to me in the street, and hurriedly asked where I slept. I told her—in the old warehouse. 'To-night,' said she, 'I will take the child there, and leave him to be hidden by you, until I can come to you and him myself.' I asked her, fiercely, why I should be burthened with the whelp of the man who had made a devil of her and a hunted brute of me. 'You want that writing of yours,' said she, coldly. 'Do as I tell you, and we may get it, and even repair some of the wrong we have done. I will bring *his* forgery with the child, sewed in the lining of the cloak I will leave with him. Whatever happens, secure that cloak. When the child and I are far away, you may make your own bargain for an exchange of papers with the man who holds yours.'

Those few wild words were all the preparation I had for finding you, that night, in the old warehouse by the river. You know how the fire gave you into the devil's hands again. From what you have told me to-night about being hidden in the room, when your father mocked my last prayer, you must also know that Effie's intended flight and its circumstances were all known to the tyrant-fiend; that a creature of his, a detective named Ketchum, had followed her, as she carried you from the house; and that he hunted me down in an hour after the fire, and executed his master's order to carry back the cloak. Poor whipped hound that I was, I obeyed. . . . . When Effie was sent back to her soulless husband at Milton, for good, I got the news from you, yourself, that night of the young folks' party. I went there, and haunted the school-house. as I had before haunted your home; sleeping in barns, or under trees, and taking food and orders, secretly, from my demented child. She was a good friend to you. When you were at school the first time, she kept me at the door night after night, to save you, as she said, in case Birch tried to harm you. I looked in through your window one night, and frightened you into a fever. When you came the second time, she seemed to know that there was murder in it. She was going to leave, then, herself; but on the very night of her flight she gave me her husband's own gun, and told me what I must do. You know what followed. I thought I'd killed Birch; and after I'd quitted you that morning, on the Newark road, I hurried to New York, to find my daughter, and make her hide me. Ketchum found me wandering in the steets; told me he'd been on my track all through the murderous work, and threatened me with the gallows if I did not leave the country. He gave me money, from Plato Wynne, to pay my way; and, in a frenzy of fear, I fled to Havana. In two months I was back again! Remorse, desperation, — a thousand goads and horrors drove me back; and I swore in my heart that I would deliver myself to the law, reveal my crimes, and those of Wynne, and expiate my offences with the death I coveted. I came back, to learn that Birch was not dead; to hear, with my own ears, the promise of my infatuated child to become the wife of the arch-demon; and to fly again from the scenes of my damnation, in still wilder despair. With money given me by the wife of Plato Wynne, I've travelled far and wide; I've been an outcast and a vagabond all over the broad earth; I've sought forgetfulness only to find that it will never be mine this side the grave; and now I'm here again to settle the long account with your father at last, if I die for it! I will! I will! I was watching for him there to-night. I'll watch for him when I go from here. I'll have that paper if his life comes with it!"

Chilled to the heart by the astounding revelations of the miserable creature before me, I could yet feel a kind of stern pity for him even then.

"This is a black and awful story," said I, with a composure born of inexorable determination," and you will find that it has not been told in vain. I sincerely pity you, and if, in the immediate measures I shall take to gain justice for myself, I can revenge, without injuring you, be assured I shall do it. It is plain to me, though, that the false will you are so anxious to regain is but the most stupid and harmless of frauds. Whatever may have been its temporary evil purpose in the hands of my father, your own diseased imagination has exaggerated it into an enormity quite beyond the fact. While you were speaking, I was resolving; and now I tell you that I am determined to call my unnatural parent to account, at once, for all *his* iniquities toward me. You shall not be molested. Give up all thought of the worthless paper; let me be at the expense of keeping you comfortably and privately in some out-of-the-way place for the present, and you shall aid me in my righteous work without being known."

"No!" exclaimed Wolfton Marsh, starting to his feet. "That can't be. Give up that paper! Give up what took the last grain of good from my soul, and has kept that soul in the flames of eternal fire ever since! There was hope for me — vile as I was — before I put that wrong and crime upon the dying; but since then, I have been all accursed. I'll have it! I'll have it if I die for it!"

The man's eyes rolled and glared in the red fever of madness, and he stamped and ground his teeth like a tormented beast.

"At least stay here until morning," said I, rising, and placing a hand kindly on his ragged arm. "What can you do, in your present situation, against a man like Plato Wynne? Stay here until morning. You shall sleep on my bed, or sofa, as you prefer. Besides, by attempting anything desperate, now, you may put your enemy upon his guard against what I intend for him."

The miserable creature threw off my hold as though it had stung him, and turned upon me a face livid with scornful fury.

"I'll not hold back an hour for you," hissed he. "You'd have me lose my chance just to help your game, would you? Well, then, I won't! I've told you what you asked to hear, and I don't feel the better for telling it. I'm dangerous to one of your blood, after calling up such things again, and he'd better not cross me."

In vain I expostulated. The relation of his miseries had indeed made him dangerous; and, with an abrupt "good-by to you," he went forth into the black streets again. An hour later found me at the conclusion of all temporizing considerations, and pretty firmly committed to the resolve first inspired by the story. Drawing my chair to the writing-table, and seizing a pen, I wrote as follows: —

"No. — Benedick Place, May —, 185-.

"To Mr. Plato Wynne, —

"Father, — The secret of your unnatural "violation of every parental obligation is "known to me at last. Wolfton Marsh, the "most implacable, as he is the most miser- "able, of your victims, has been with me "to-night. If conscience survives the death "of natural feeling in your breast you need "not be told what I have heard. After "darkening and tainting my tenderest child- "ish years with all that could repel and "pervert the sensitive affection and inno- "cence of a child, you deliberately doomed "me to destruction at the hands of a poor "wretch whom your snares and insults had "driven to reckless despair. The Father "of the fatherless decreed that another of "your unhappy dupes should at once save "me from murder, and you from the guilt "of the only crime not yet recorded by "God and man against you. What your "course toward me has been since then, is "best shown by the fact that, until to-night, "I have believed Glibun to be my true "name, and my hereditary shame the legacy "of a parent only less audacious in every "infamy than Plato Wynne. From the "lips of one who will henceforth follow "you in all your ways like an avenging fate, "I have learned no less of my rights than "of my wrongs, and now demand the "former, with a full determination to exact "them by the means most likely to bring "reparation for the latter. It is my mis- "fortune to be your son; but outraged na- "ture spurns a tie made unholy by a lifetime "of unparalleled abuse, and I prefer to still "call myself

"Avery Glibun."

CHAPTER XLVIII.

A WINDFALL.

After breakfasting so late at Mr. Tick's, on the following morning, that none of my Bohemian associates were in my way, I despatched the letter, by penny-post, to the gaming-house. Scarcely, however, had the missive gone into the box, when I began to question myself about the wisdom of sending; and the more I reflected the less satisfied I became. The more direct and manly plan of obtaining an immediate per- sonal interview with my father had not occurred to me before; but now I commenced regretting having not adopted it. He may toss the letter aside as a forgery by Wolfton Marsh, thought I; or, he may take it for proof that my courage avows itself on paper, for the first time, because it is un- equal to a demonstration in person. A man of his practices must be frequently in the receipt of threatening communications by mail, and why should I hope to move him, beyond, perhaps, a momentary supercilious surprise! In short, I soon tormented my-

self into a determination to go at once in quest of him, wherever he was, and let him hear me in advance, if possible, of my angry letter. Even at that moment he might be in his luxurious den, still lingering over the prey of last night; and why should I not hasten boldly thither? To think was to act. Ready for any rash deed I hurried to Broadway, and had I but crossed that thoroughfare, to the side on which stood the gaming-house, no further reflection would have intervened to restrain me from an act of mere boyish rage and futility. But there was a funeral train of hearse and carriages passing between me and the opposite curb, and, while waiting for it to go by, I received an inspiration from my better genius. First came a sudden wish for the counsel of some trusted and judicious friend; then came a bright recollection of Mr. Goodman and his parting words to me. The great resolutions of our lives are those taken without forethought and in the re- action from resolves long considered. Instinct, in such cases, seems to delight in first permitting reason to perfect her fabric of argument with the very last of her re- sources, and then annihilating the whole structure in an instant with some unrea- soned and irresistible opposing impulse. Instead of crossing the street, I hastened directly along toward the lower part of the city, nor paused to consider again until the stately shades of Goodman & Co's. great establishment had received me from the crowded highway. Then, indeed, it was time to remember what I was about, and the imposing mountains of cloths and silks between which I had entered did serve to remind me of my audacity. The quiet twilight of the mercantile temple, the ten- der gravity of numerous attendant gentle- men who looked like fashionable clergymen, and the air of delicate remonstrance with which one Episcopal divine came gliding out into my aisle from a broadcloth chapel, would have awed me into faltering insig- nificance on any other occasion; but the spirit of my mission made me bold to in- quire for Mr. Goodman without much propitiatory abasement, and I had the honor of my clerical friend's distinguished usher- ship to the very door of the private office.

"This gentleman wishes to see you, sir," prefaced my introduction, and then I found myself standing in the presence of the fa- mous merchant. In a handsome revolving chair he sat at a desk whereon laid a morn- ing paper; and now that the light of day, tempered as it was, fell upon his counte- nance, I again experienced the inexplicable discomposure produced by the same coun- tenance the night before. On rising to re- ceive me, he, too, evinced a perturbation which was not wholly that of surprise, and, for a moment, I knew not what to say.

"You recognize me, I think, Mr. Good- man?" was my first remark.

"I am happy to do so. Please take a seat."

"Thank you. Last night, sir, as you may remember, a peculiar circumstance brought me to your notice, and you were kind enough to place your counsel and aid at my disposal when I should need them."

He bowed, smiled encouragingly, and kept his eyes intently upon me.

"Well, sir," continued I, "my hour of need has already come; and so pressingly, too, that I have presumed to take you at your word thus early."

A sadder look came into his face; but, in a voice all kind and sparing, he said, "I feared, from your presence there, that you would too soon suffer some evil. In what can I advise or help you?"

"Mr. Goodman," returned I, warmly, "you must allow me to correct the misapprehension under which you seem to be laboring. I never entered a gambling-house before last night; and then, as I firmly believe, the will of the Almighty led me thither for a just and righteous purpose! Curiosity, and a willingness to be diverted temporarily from depressing thoughts, were what I supposed to be my sole occasion for going; but, sir, when I have explained to you the need bringing me here, you will admit that something more than chance, or idleness, drew me to that house at that particular time. Excuse me for asking if we are perfectly private here?"

"Perfectly, sir. I am glad to hear what you say."

"Then, sir, to further excuse myself for coming to you upon such extraordinary business," I went on, conscious of a strange and growing eagerness to confide my story to him, "I must first inform you that, from early childhood to the present time, I have been the sport and victim of extraordinary domestic adversity. I am really without one capable friend in the world to advise me regarding the most momentous interest of my life."

"If you need any further assurance of my inclination to befriend you, young man," observed Mr. Goodman, with gentle gravity, "I will repeat what I said to you last night. Your appearance interests me to a degree for which I cannot account. I have thought much of you since our meeting; what you say now impresses me favorably; and if you choose to tell me, frankly, who you are, and what your exigency is, I will endeavor to justify your confidence."

"My name," said I, "is Avery Glibun—"

To my great alarm, Mr. Goodman's face turned pale as death, as I spoke, and his sturdy frame seemed to sink and contract in the chair as though wrenched with a mortal pain. Vague fancies of apoplexy flashed through my brain, and, but for a quick restraining gesture from him, I should have called for assistance."

"You are sick, sir," I cried, nervously.

"How wonderful are the ways of Providence!" he solemnly exclaimed, gazing fixedly at but not addressing me. Then, as the blood came back in deep suffusion to his countenance, he drew himself up with an air of disturbed pride, as I thought, and met my look of anxiety with a forced smile. "Do not mind my momentary indisposition," he said; "it will not return again. Be good enough to touch that spring-bell on the mantel near you."

I did so, and the sound was promptly answered by the entrance of a porter.

"David," said the merchant, turning to him, "see that no person is brought here until I ring again. I shall be privately engaged for some time."

"Very well, sir," said the porter, and disappeared.

"And now, my dear young man," resumed Mr. Goodman, with a fervor of manner that touched me deeply, "you have but to speak unreservedly of yourself, as you would to a father."

"To a father!" echoed I, my lips quivering. "O sir, it is against a father that I am compelled to speak."

"That is a sad necessity, a very sad necessity."

"It is, sir; but not through any evil-doing of my own. Your kind manner, sir, almost encourages me to impose my whole unhappy story upon you; for, without knowing it all, you will scarcely understand what I have to tell of last night."

"My dear young man," repeated he, fervidly as before, "you will do well to confide in me, as you say. Let me know your true history from the beginning."

The last intensification of worldly trouble is an added restraint from seeking the humane indulgence and sympathies of others for it; and only those who have long borne misfortune without the sweet relief of lightening confidences can rightly understand the eagerness with which I hastened to relate my wrongs. Not angrily, nor despondingly, did I tell the tale; for in the calm, steady eyes and benevolent demeanor of that dignified and benignant Christian gentleman was that which made the rehearsal of my friendlessness a conscious and progressive acquisition of a friend. So, with such quietude of heart as had seemed hopeless for such a task, I gave Mr. Goodman the full account of my life, without amplification or comment. Not a word did he interpose, as, with elbow resting on the arm of his chair, and head leaning on his finger-tips, he sat and studied me while I talked. But when, after about an hour of rapid confession, I finally concluded with a description of the letter to my father, he drew a long breath, shook his head, and repeated the words, "How wonderful are the ways of Providence!"

Then, with impressive gravity, he added, "Your story, my young friend, is truly astonishing; and your need of careful and judicious advice is even greater than you suppose it to be. You appear to have acted with surprising discretion thus far in your anomalous situations. A mysterious, overruling Providence and an instinct superior to your apparent condition seem to have strangely protected you through all. In your present crisis, however, there is need of more heads than one. Are you willing to yield implicitly to what I shall counsel, without argument, or question?"

The last condition sounded oddly to me, but I was only too eager to say, "The honor you do me, sir, in offering your counsel, would be unworthily returned, indeed, by anything less than my closest obedience."

"Then, sir," he continued, with a bright smile, "you shall be advised to your heart's content! If my judgment is not greatly at fault you are very near a satisfactory understanding with Mr. Wynne. Why I think so, will yet be evident to you. It will be your best policy to wait patiently for some result of your letter, in the mean time avoiding any personal intrusion upon the unscrupulous and daring man with whom you have to deal. It does not seem to me that you can, with propriety, continue in an avocation which, as you tell me, obliges you to defame your father in print. Consequently, as you have already had some store-experience, I would advise you to accept, for the present, a clerkship which I shall place at your disposal here. Are you willing, without doubt or question, to adopt such views and advice?"

My misfortune seemed to lessen at the very sound of his voice, and the words overwhelmed my senses with a delightful surprise and gratitude too great for verbal expression. I could only bow, and dash my handkerchief across my eyes.

"Very well," resumed he. "Then you may consider yourself a member of my Establishment from to-day. And now let me ask you a question. While you were with that man, Reese, at the — the — Five Points," — he certainly flinched as he named the locality, — "did you see anything of a father and daughter named Grey?"

"Yes, sir," replied I, in fresh amazement. "They were in the same house with me. The father died while I was there."

"I asked the question," said Mr. Goodman, "because I happen to know that the poor little motherless girl of that fearful scene of crime and misery is now a rich and admirable young lady in the best society, and has not yet ceased to speak of a strange and kind lad called Avery, to the few who know her real history. My own first name being Avery may have helped to impress the fact upon my memory."

"April Grey!" was my wondering ejaculation.

"That is the name. You see, I might well remark, at the mention of yours, that the ways of Providence are wonderful. I had heard of you before last night."

"I do not know what to make of it all, Mr. Goodman," I replied, rising; "but then every event of my life has been a mystery at first, and I can only show my heartfelt gratitude to Providence and to you by trying to deserve what comes to me now as a

blessing undisguised. I shall follow your advice in everything, resign my editorial occupation, and thankfully accept the position you offer me here."

"Well spoken!" he exclaimed, extending his right hand. "To-morrow night I shall expect to see you at my residence, number —— Broadway, opposite Union Park. You will meet an old friend there."

I looked for some explanation, but Mr. Goodman seemed determined to leave that point a greater mystery than all the rest; and, with mind more dazed than ever, I took my leave.

If the ways of fate and fortune are capricious to all men, thought I, as I wended my way to the *Earthquake* office, how positively mad are their turnings for me! Here am I fresh from the discovery of a heritage of infamy, and yet in the dawn of what looks like the very climax of good fortune. No sooner do I learn that I am worse than fatherless, than the most fantastical chance in the world gives me a warm friend and protector in one whom the most blessed of young men would be proud to call sire. Who knows what new bewilderment the very next turn of the wheel may bring me? I will not look forward an hour. I will not undertake the least guess at what will be my situation, sensations, or even name, one hour hence! It was well for my own sagacity that I determined thus; for scarcely had I reached the *Earthquake* sanctums, when Dewitt handed me a note which read as follows: —

<pre>
            "LAW OFFICE, No.—, }
        "Nassau Street, May —, 185-. }
</pre>

"MR. AVERY GLIBUN: *Sir*, — From infor-"mation lately come into my possession, I "am induced to believe that you have a "legal claim to certain property held in "charge by me. Please call upon me at "your earliest convenience, and believe me,
            "Your obedient servant,
                    "I. SEWALL,
            "Counsellor and Attorney."

After reading the above three times over, and saying resignedly to myself, "Oh, of course!" it suddenly occurred to me that my filial appeal to my guilty father must have acted with magical celerity, and induced him to take instant measures for my pecuniary satisfaction. Mr. Goodman had expressed the opinion that I was near a satisfactory understanding with my parent; and behold this early proof of the merchant's correct foresight.

"Why, Glibun," cried Dewitt, laughingly, "you don't look particularly intellectual over your mail. Does your tailor take this means of assuring you that he won't stand it any longer?"

"Not exactly," returned I, thrusting the note into my pocket. "Something better than that. I must go around to Nassau Street, now, to transact a little business, and will be back in about an hour."

Forth I started again, not much nearer mental bankruptcy than became an enterprising young man who was working out more of destiny in a day than his fellows achieved in half a century. The law-offices of the reticent Mr. Sewall were not far away, and I traversed the distance and mounted four flights of stairs without any distinct cognizance of street, people, or difference between starting-point and goal. The door of the elevated legal den, however, with its warped panels and bruised tin sign, was a grim limit to everything but the most practical state of mind. I paused before it long enough to withdraw the note from my pocket, and then stalked boldly into what I did not doubt to be the office of my father's attorney.

Two desks, many shelves of law-books, and half a dozen very old chairs were the prominent furniture of the apartment, and near one of the desks sat a mild-eyed old gentleman, with bristling gray hair and whiskers, and a coat and standing-collar of old-fashioned amplitude.

"Mr. Sewall?" I inquired.

The old gentleman promptly turned down upon his knees the law-book he had been reading, and assured me that he was the man.

"You sent me this note, sir, I believe?"

He took the paper, glanced over it, and favored me with the most severe cross-examining scrutiny.

"Ah, yes! Take a chair, sir; take a chair. You are Mr. Glibun?"

"I have answered to that name for some time, sir; but, as you may already know, it is not mine by inheritance. My father's name" — I faltered and blushed as I spoke it — "is Wynne."

"Precisely so. There is some misunderstanding between you and your father, I believe?"

"Mr. Sewall," said I, "you must excuse me if I decline answering any question of that nature until I know for what purpose it is asked. If you are Mr. Wynne's legal adviser, he should have given you sufficient information upon that point, I think."

"Mr. Wynne's legal adviser!" repeated the old gentleman, glaring at me through his spectacles. "I'm no such thing!"

"Indeed!" was my exclamation. "I really beg your pardon; but I inferred from your note that you were about to act for my father in a matter at issue between him and me."

"Not at all," protested the lawyer; "not at all. The matter of this note has no reference to your father, except as it involves your family-identity. The property in question is the estate of your deceased uncle."

Here was another hopeless puzzle for me. I might as well inform the venerable sorcerer, at once, that I hadn't the remotest idea of what he was talking about.

"You may think the assertion a strange one," I observed, feebly; "but I was not aware, before, that I ever had an uncle."

Contrary to my expectation, Mr. Sewall looked quite pleased at this, — settled his spectacles, leaned back with folded arms, and regarded me with some emotion.

"Of course you didn't," assented he, chuckling. "How should you? I'll be as frank with you as you have been with me, and let you know at once, that Mr. Ketchum, the indefatigable detective who hunted you out for me, has told me enough of your adventures and experience as a son, to explain your lack of family-knowledge. Excuse me; I'll finish my story first, and then receive your comments. Your mother had an only brother, who was such an incorrigible scapegrace that his family never knew anything of him, nor he of them, after the time when he was quite a lad. He ran away from home, plunged into every extravagance and vice, worried his father (your grandfather) into apoplexy, and was the same as dead to his sister and remaining relatives from that time forth. By his father's will he was very properly disinherited. But, his sister, your mother, was left under the guardianship of a rich, unmarried brother of her father's, from whom your father, Mr. Plato Wynne (or Mr. Glibun, as he then called himself, by-the-by), took her by marriage; and that guardian finally dying intestate, and without nearer relatives, *his* property went by law to your mother, your scapegrace uncle, their heirs, administrators, and assigns. But your mother was also dead by that time, and I, having been an old and close friend of the intestate-deceased, was appointed to ascertain whether your worthless uncle still lived, or procure some certain proofs of his death. You follow me, do you? Ketchum, of the Independent Detectives, was recommended to me for his sagacity in what is called working-up difficult cases; and, in my first interview with him, I was surprised and pleased to find that he was deep in the secrets of your father, and could discover you, if not your uncle. Upon giving him certain facts for his direction, however, — the name, for instance, which your uncle had assumed at the outset of his evil career, — the detective suddenly declared that he knew where to find his man, and would produce him within a week. He did find the man, hiding in a den of the Five Points, and going by the name of Reese."

"Merciful Heaven!" cried I, scarcely crediting my ears; "was that reckless man my uncle?"

"Beyond all question," answered the lawyer, who evidently found great enjoyment in confounding me.

"And did he know me to be his nephew?"

"He did not, I should say. As I have already told you, his whole family were dead to him from the time of his father's decease. He knew nothing of his sister's marriage to your father; nor was her death known to him until Ketchum mentioned it incidentally while telling him of his uncle's death and his own heirship. As you were with Reese in his hiding-place, you probably knew that he was a counterfeiter, and that the arrest of a gipsy confederate had led to revelations involving him deeply, and his chief, Plato Wynne, more than vaguely. By political influence, however, shameful to say, he might have escaped all punishment and come freely forward to receive his fortune; but God's justice triumphed where man's failed, and Reese was killed in some low broil before he could leave the Five Points. This last event made you the heir, and I sent Ketchum to ferret you out; but all he could ascertain, for the time, was, that at the death of your uncle you had mysteriously disappeared from the Points. Indeed, the detective lost all trace of you, until a day or two ago, when some one happened to name you, in his presence, as an editor of General Cringer's paper. That, I believe, is the whole story. You have but to prove your identity, and step into a very pretty little estate."

After a brief silence, to collect my thoughts, I managed to realize my position, and make the expected response.

"If this is so," said I, studying my words as I spoke them, "I can only request you, sir, to keep the whole matter in charge until I have advised with my friends. As you seem to know what my peculiar lot in life has been so long, you will not be surprised when I confess myself quite unprepared for the information you have given me, and unfit to take any decided step at present. I will consult with one who has lately become my benefactor, and see you soon again."

"That's right," said the lawyer, appreciating my feelings; "take time to comprehend your good luck, and then call here again. Your case is as strange as any I have known in my thirty years' practice. There has been great villany somewhere. However, we'll talk of that next time."

"As you say, Mr. Sewall, next time."

So, I went back to my newspaper office, to hurry through the labors of what I intended should be my last week there; and committed such enormities of abstraction with pen, scissors, and paste-bottle, that the dramatic editor advised "a little soda for a change."

CHAPTER XLIX.

HONOR.

' WITHOUT other provocation than the rankling memory of an old affront; without other justification than the quickness of wine to make all times and places fit for the prosecution of an instinctive personal enmity, Allyn Vane had proclaimed the King of Diamonds a common cheat at the very table of the bank-royal, and dashed a glove into his face before all the sleepless peers of golden Chance! Well might the wild perpetrator of such astounding treason glide, pale and voiceless, from the paralyzed midnight court, while yet all loyal throats and arms were stilled and transfixed by the amazing sacrilege of the act. Well might he take long strides, in his flight from the face struck into something whiter than anger by the touch of an empty glove.

He fled, yet thought the flight to be the last refinement of defiance to the death; for such apparent cowardice would right quickly, he knew, bring a pursuer in its track, to test the fugitive at bay. Instinctively, and without calculations of time, he even glanced backward over either shoulder now and then, as he strode along the night-dead solitude of Broadway, whose lonely watch-lights seemed to flicker with the tread, but revealed not the form, of a swift follower. On he hurried, his hands — one of them ungloved — swinging clenched at his sides. Onward to his hotel, and up to the mere covert of a room where home was but the soulless spectre of unguarded refuge. That was the only home of Allyn Vane; without one sanctity to awe the furious tempest in his mind; without one hallowed influence to lull the fever in his blood; without one forgiving heart to welcome him tenderly at the very climax of his unworthiness, and guard him from the penalty of his supreme offence.

Panting and disordered, he entered the chamber, turned the spark of gas to a full yellow flame, and threw himself upon a dingy easy-chair beside the bed. He knew what would certainly follow; it was his business to listen — not to think — for a while; and, with hat still unremoved, he waited for a guest. Less refinement of hearing would not have caught the cat-like tread of Mr. Hastings Cutter, who had really tarried not far behind his old tutor, and made his appearance soon enough to spare the latter any protracted anxiety.

"Ha, Cutter!" was the greeting, "I can guess what has brought you! I've worked him to it at last, have I?"

"You're right, there, I reckon!" assented the Carolinian, his African nose and lips growing coarser with half a smile. "Mr. Wynne solicits the honor of your early company to the suburbs, and hopes you will excuse a verbal transmission of the invitation. Who do you think of selecting for your friend?"

"No one at all, Mr. Cutter," answered Vane, tossing his hat upon the bed. "The only friend I want is one of English importation which I shall carry in a case."

"Talk sense, Vane, if you're sober."

"And you criticise when you're asked!" was the suddenly fierce rejoinder. "Tell Plato Wynne that I'll be in the Castle Point wood at sunrise."

"Without a second?"

"Yes. Alone."

"Why, it will look like murder, if anything happens! I reckon Bilk, or Dodge, would act for you at five minutes' notice."

"See here, Cutter," exclaimed Vane, leaning from his chair, and glaring savagely into the dissipated face of Cutter, " I intend that it shall be murder! I'll kill him if I can. You know perfectly well what there is between us. And look at this mark." (Touching a peculiar diagonal scar on his forehead.) "For giving me this, I challenged him in the regular way; and he laughed at me! Now I'll have my own terms."

" Well, you'll give me credit for performing my mission, in regular order, I suppose," said the Carolinian.

" You've done your duty."

Hastings Cutter went softly to the door to satisfy himself that it was closed, and then came back as cautiously to the chair.

" Vane," said he, in a suppressed tone, " I'm an infernal deal more your friend than his in this matter, and I want you to tell me, as a friend, if there was really any cheating in the game to-night?"

" No!" was the short reply.

" Then, what under heaven made you fly at Wynne in that wolfish way?"

" I'll tell you," responded Vane, in a hoarse whisper. "When I was going into his house to-night, I caught sight of a face like that of the she-fiend who ruined me. It brought all that I owe to Plato Wynne before me like a mocking picture, and freshened my hatred to a pitch it had never before known."

" A face!" exclaimed Cutter. " You don't mean to say that his wife was in the house?"

" No. It was a man's face. The face of a hungry, crazy-looking old vagabond who was loitering about the 'Private Entrance.' I don't know who he was; but he had a face that set me on fire."

" Vane, my boy," said Cutter, drawing closer, and fixing a sinister look upon the flushed countenance of the other gamester, " I know pretty well what your account is with Wynne, and you may add mine to it! He has always treated me, too, like a dog! In sending me after you to-night with his message he gave me the order as he would have given it to some servant. He's squeezed me dry; he's had the price of two plantations from me, and now I may go to the d—l. I was afraid, when I came here, that you were drunk, and would want to apologize; but, since you know what you're about, I'm with you, heart and soul. Only KILL him, — *in any way you can*, —and I'll swear you clear; swear that he followed you from town to kill you for holding some dangerous secret of his, and that you only defended your life from an assassin!"

" He shall have his shot," retorted Vane, hastily. " I'll be no tricky murderer, Mr. Cutter, if you please."

" Of course; I meant that, I reckon," stammered the other, in momentary confusion. " I only advise you to be cool, and fire straight. I hear that he had two or three affairs some years ago, and never hit his man. Don't trust to that, though. Keep your nerves steady, and remember the school-master's wife!"

A fierce scowl and a convulsive clutch at the arm of the chair were sufficient answer to this friendly advice.

" If you saw the look on Wynne's face when you struck him with the glove," continued the Carolinian, " you know that he'll not fire into the air. But it's past three o'clock now, and will be sunrise in two hours. I must be off."

" Yes; go," was the moody answer.

The treacherous messenger of Plato Wynne glided from the room as snakishly as he had entered it; leaving its revengeful and unhappy master to make preparation for vindicating by crime what he had never gained by virtue,—the honor of a gentleman.

Honor! Instinct vague and lofty as the blue of heaven, steadfast and profound as the native virtue of a soul; gentleness in man, courage in woman; the noble humility of power, and the protecting dignity of powerlessness; nature's predilection for enlightened goodness in the darkened mind of the generous barbarian, and religion's indomitable chivalry of martyrdom in the great Christian heart: be thou a divine despotism, or a Christ-like example; be thou the nobility of the savage, the morality of the sinner, or the ecstasy of the saint; how is thy very sound profaned when red-handed murder makes a warrant of thy name to throw boldly off his accustomed covert of the night and strike down a brother in the sunlight!

Day was pallidly breaking in a gray and feverish haze, as though nature's eyelids were still languid and heavy from the red wine of sunset, when a small boat containing two passengers and an oarsman put off from the side of a private pier, not far below the foot of Canal Street, and headed for the New Jersey shore. Of the two passengers, he who was the shorter in stature and the younger in general appearance sat at the stern of the boat and carried a square, thin article of some kind, wrapped in paper, under his right arm. The other, whose handsome black beard and taller figure distinguished him very strikingly from his companion, preferred a standing position, with his back to that companion, and one foot braced upon a seat. Both were well-dressed, and wore glossy silk hats and grayish spring overcoats; and both, it may be added, had that strained, dry look about the eyes which follows a sleepless night. The sturdy boatman, who, when briefly engaged for a handsome price to row these early gentlemen to Hoboken, had been keeping himself in readiness to board a Hamburg steamer expected up the bay with the first tide, must have felt some curiosity to know what pressing business made them such liberal passengers for him at that hour, when they might have crossed as well by the ferry; but, as a ten-dollar bill had been handed to him in advance by the taller stranger, and a something in the unsociable demeanor of both forbade any thought of familiarity, the fresh-water mariner discreetly gave all his attention to his oars and asked no presumptuous questions. Swiftly over the vigorous blue current of the Hudson sped the little craft, bearing Mr. Plato Wynne and Mr. Hastings Cutter to such business as the honest boatman dreamed not of. Urged by brawny arms it soon accomplished the distance between the shores of the two States, and, avoiding the ferry slip and ship-yards, touched land near the point where Third Street now terminates. As the two gentlemen stepped ashore, the boatman touched his hat, and, with a look toward that place in the stream where the expected steamer was likely to cast anchor, made bold to ask how long they would be gone.

"An hour," was Mr. Wynne's short and decided answer.

"Do you reckon we'd better go back with him?" whispered Cutter, hurriedly. "If anything unpleasant should happen, you know, he might be—"

"You will wait here for me just one hour," repeated the other, addressing the boatman, and not even looking at his cautious companion. "If I am not here again at the expiration of that time, you may go about your business."

And, without further remark, the imperious speaker turned immediately upon his heel and walked away, leaving Mr. Cutter to follow when he chose. Discreet as the boatman was, he ventured to favor the Carolinian with a parting grin, which said very plainly, "Your governor is a high one;" nor did the same observing Aquarius fail to note that the follower involuntarily clenched one of his fists as he started on, and moved his lips to the measure of a sentence expressing anything but affection.

As lion and jackal thus took their way along a dusty and deserted road, within pistol sound of which nearly five thousand of Jersey's parsimonious sons and daughters were enjoying their delightful climacteric morning nap, how readily would the meaner brute have dashed out the brains of the nobler, but for the cowardly hope that a keen hunter would presently revenge every slavish wrong with a bullet. In all that swift walk of two-thirds of a mile, not a word, not a look did the King of Diamonds vouchsafe to his scowling "second," but strode silently on ahead of him as though equally contemptuous of his office and his presence.

In an open space just within the edge of the appointed wood, which was finally reached by crossing a newly ploughed field, Allyn Vane awaited the coming of master and man, and greeted their appearance with a slight nod of his head. Leaning against a tree, his hat in his hand and his flushed face exposed, apparently to catch the faint breeze, he looked, in the cold morning light, like all that dissipation leaves of manhood to mock the fresh color, free air, and dauntless glance of youth. With hair and dress still

in the disorder of last night's reckless passion and abandonment; with eyes gleaming red with sleeplessness and excitement; he stood there to win the gallows if he could, and end a night of madness with a dawn of blood.

Plato Wynne had paused at a distance while Cutter advanced to examine the weapons brought by his antagonist, and as the Carolinian stooped to open the pistol-case upon the sward, near the feet of the latter, he asked, in a shrill whisper, "Are your nerves steady?"

"Steady!" echoed Vane, with a forced laugh. "They're as steady as half a pint of raw brandy can make them."

"It's really very awkward for you not to have a friend here, Mr. Vane," spoke Cutter, aloud. "If we were down in South Car'lina I shouldn't mind it so much; but up North, here, where a parcel of Yankee policemen are likely to interfere in a gentleman's affairs, I could wish to have the thing regular. But there's no help for it now, I reckon. I'm a double second and will do my best. Mr. Wynne gives you a choice of his shooting-irons, Mr. Vane."

"I'll use my own weapon," said Allyn Vane; and again he forced a short, unnatural laugh.

If Wynne had not actually overheard his second's last proposition, and the terms of its reception, he must have guessed what it was from some gesture or look of the speakers; for, advancing toward the pair at a leisurely pace, he now decided the point himself.

"Mr. Cutter," he said, with look and tone suited to the words, "I supposed that you understood your business. The question of whose pistols are to be used, must be decided, of course, by drawing lots."

The coarse face of Hastings Cutter became coarser by the distortions of mingled rage and mortification. "I know that, Mr. Wynne, I reckon," he retorted, clumsily hastening to prepare slips of paper. "I meant that Mr. Vane, as the challenged party, could take his choice from the pair drawn."

Paying no apparent heed to this explanation, the elder duellist turned his gaze to the flushed, defiant face of Vane, and met the fierce, answering look with an expression half contemptuous and half pitying. The two thus confronting each other, under circumstances peculiarly calculated to epitomize the real character of each, presented the strongest contrast that may exist between men of the same moral level. One, at the last delirious pitch of exasperation under fancied wrongs, was all unreasoning, murderous, and brutalized; the other, coolly coming to extract "honor" from an insult, was collected, observant, and even compassionate! The hazy light of that early morning, rendered clearer if more subdued by its passage through the leafy network overhead, gave a sharp distinctness to the two faces; to the wild eyes and working lips of Vane, and the unrevealing features and mask-like beard of the challenger. Cutter, throwing furtive and sullen glances toward them, as he prepared the pistols and slips, grew nervous at the contrasted bearings of the two, and impotently wished for the daring to charge one weapon in each pair without ball.

"Vane," said Plato Wynne, after a moment of silence, "as you have chosen to bring no friend with you, it is particularly incumbent upon me to offer an apology for instructing *my* — companion in your hearing. But, as you see" (with a sneering approach to a smile), "Mr. Cutter is rather unnerved by his double duties, and needs prompting in the details. We need not trouble him, I think, to go through the form of asking whether our difficulty cannot be settled amicably?"

"No; we need not!" was the rude answer; and after it came the short, hysterical laugh once more.

"Because," continued the first speaker, with perfect deliberation, "you are not in a fit condition for the business bringing us here, and I am no longer in the mood to make cold blood a remedy for an offence given in the heat of wine."

"You are very magnanimous, sir," sneered Vane, folding his arms and rocking upon his heels.

"Having indulged too freely last night," pursued the other, quite unruffled by the comment, "you temporarily forgot yourself, and affronted me in my own house, and in the presence of my guests. From your language and appearance *now*, I am the more convinced that you were not yourself *then*. As a gentleman, you can scarcely refuse to offer a reasonable apology in the same house, and before the same witnesses."

"Plato Wynne," exclaimed Allyn Vane, with an evil smile, "I have heretofore known you to be a matchless villain; but, upon my soul, I never before thought you were a coward!"

A momentary flash of the eye and tinge of the cheek told that this insult had not altogether missed its mark; but the spoken answer was indifferent.

"That is nonsense, Vane."

Indifferently as it sounded, however, the disordered younger gamester burst into an ungovernable frenzy of rage at its utterance, and half lifted his hands as though about to clutch the throat of his intolerable tormentor.

"Nonsense, is it?" cried he, in a voice at once shrill and hoarse with passion. "Keep beyond my reach, you incarnate devil, or I shall strike you again! You coward! You pitiful poltroon! You second-hand husband of—"

In the midst of his delirious fury he broke the sentence at the swift bidding of that upraised hand! Not that a blow was threatened; not that there was supplication to his manhood in it; but because there

was a *Soul* in the gesture that even madness had not the hardihood to smite in the face!

"You know well what you've done to me," he went on, panting as from a blow. "You know well that my account with you dates years back of last night. You married the woman I had wooed and won. Yes, — *won!* This man you have brought with you knows that I speak the truth. He knows that I took her from the besotted pedagogue whom you had given her to, and that she is more mine to-day, than yours, — and shall be mine to-morrow, if I can kill you!"

The last sentence was spoken in a shriek; and, as he uttered it, the infuriated speaker struck with both hands at his enemy, and hurled him reeling to a tree.

Even Cutter stood appalled at this crowning and ferocious outrage, and stared confusedly from one to the other until recalled to his senses by a voice still firm enough to command.

"Measure twelve paces," said Plato Wynne, pale as death. "Give him any pistol he wants. Don't waste a moment, — a second!"

Knowing that, as challenger, his principal had the right to name the distance, Hastings Cutter hastily measured the paces. Then, with equal precipitation, he carried both pairs of pistols to Vane, who, with an eager, ravenous air, selected one of his own. Wynne took its mate with scarcely a glance at it; and, in another moment, the two duellists were at their stations, ready for the murderous sign.

Then, taking *his* position, handkerchief in hand, the Carolinian spoke, —

"Gentlemen, are you ready?"

The leaves rustled softly overhead, the birds chirped on twig and bush, and the morning sun, firing the haze at last, gave long ghosts upon the ground to men and trees alike.

"Fire. One — two — three."

Two explosions were simultaneous with the fall of the handkerchief. Allyn Vane sprang into the air, and fell limp and motionless upon the dewy grass.

Uttering such a cry as might have followed a wound in his own breast, Hastings Cutter darted to the side of the prone figure, and as quickly shrank from it.

"Through the brain!" he muttered, hoarsely.

The King of Diamonds, still standing where he had fired the shot, hurled his pistol far away amongst the trees, and returned the ghastly stare of his second with a harsh, intolerant look.

"I meant to kill him," he said, casting a sinister glance toward the body. "I could kill two like him for half of what he said."

"What shall we do with — it?" asked the affrighted accessory, with a gesture sufficiently explanatory.

"Leave it to the dogs!" was the fierce answer, and Plato Wynne turned to go. "Are you coming?"

"No!" shouted Cutter, who, between fear and bitter disappointment, was bolder than himself. "I'll not go with you. *My* friend is killed, and I've done with you, Plato Wynne."

He might have said more in his rage and dismay; but the murderer saved him the trouble by stalking away toward the river without further heed or delay, and he was left alone with the dead. Then, recollection, anger, regret, departed also, and cowardice only remained. He dragged the yet warm corpse, its hand still clasping the pistol, into a clump of bushes; he ran from it a distance, and paused to wipe, if he could, the white horror from his face; he started at the fall of a leaf; he hurled the remaining pistols after that which had done the deed, and caught his breath when they crashed among the brush; he looked here, there, — everywhere but upward, — and fled away through the trees like a belated shadow of the night.

CHAPTER L.

THE ADOPTED DAUGHTER.

As I was about leaving my room on the morning after the interviews with Mr. Goodman and the old lawyer, a janitor of the house confronted me at the threshold with a letter, which, he said, had been left for me a few minutes before, by a man who looked like a gentleman's servant. I received it indifferently, and did not even glance at the address until my door was closed again and the janitor gone. "From my father!" was the instantaneous thought, accompanied by as quick a jealousy of any emotion rising to my countenance. For some moments I held the letter face-downward, feeling a strange reluctance to look for the first time upon the handwriting of one against whom my whole nature rose in irritable defiance. When, at last, however, I threw myself into a chair and doggedly held the thing before me, I was rather surprised to find the superscription quite different in its penmanship from what I had fancied must be that of a man like my uncompromising parent; for, instead of a bold, heavy, and masculine inscription of my name, I beheld the delicate, though firm and legible, character of a feminine hand.

At once dropping all speculation I forthwith tore open the envelope, extracted a trifolded sheet of Bath note, and, with new sensations, read thereupon as follows:—

"No. — UNION SQUARE.

"AVERY GLIBUN,— My husband has trans-
"ferred to me your recent note to him,
"thereby appointing me to answer you.
"Come to the address above given, at eight
"o'clock on Friday evening, and you shall
"have at least some portion of the repara-
"tion you demand. In whatever estimation
"you hold my husband, you may justly
"bestow the same on

"ELFIE WYNNE."

So despairing and arrogant, so cold and passionate,—how vividly did those brief and characteristic words bring before me the face and manner of the writer! Few, unrevealing, and almost awkward as they were, my fancy detected in them much of that mingled rebellion and fascination, fierceness and abjectness, which had made the protectress of my infancy alternately a fear and a wonder to me. The note, from address to signature, contained no more evidence of generous feeling than I might have expected from my father himself; yet I doubted not for an instant that it meant the sternest justice, despite every consequence.

Resolving, however, to submit it to Mr. Goodman before deciding to obey its summons, I carefully consigned it to my pocket; and, after an economical breakfast at the first restaurant, proceeded down-town to my journalistic business.

I had my final European letter to write that day, and naturally anticipated much difficulty in adapting my overwrought mind to the peculiarly cool and deliberate task of minutely describing the last reception at the Tuileries. It was, of course, incumbent upon me, in that connection, to dwell upon the marked attentions of the French Monarch to the American Minister, and I doubted my intellectual power that morning to make the sovereign's overheard remarks as epigrammatic as such remarks always are. But, as upon former occasions, I found in literary composition a quick relief from all worldly cares, and, in less than fifteen minutes, was glowing over my imaginary Europe without a thought of anything else in the world. If imaginative writing had no other use than to divert the vexed and jaded soul of a life-worn mortal from the hourly goadings of this practical sphere to the ardent and untiring incitements of ideal adventure, it would still be richly worthy the cultivation of any capable man. The sharpest exasperation, the intolerable dead-weight, of harassing or disastrous circumstances in the actual world, are due chiefly to the unphilosophical but very common habit of regarding those circumstances as tyrannically arbitrary, and ourselves as entirely guiltless of having in any manner contributed to bring them about. The real discouragement and enervation come from the idea that we are the victims of conditions and occurrences which we have had no hand in creating; and hence the stimulating relief of an appeal to the world of imagination, wherein we can create our own circumstances, and thereby attain that energetic sense of power which is the only effective solace for every trouble. Possibly some future enlightenment will show mankind that the government of human nature is republican, and that each man's controlling circumstances are of his own election; the predominances logically made such by the unconscious suffrage of a majority of his natural traits; but, until then, the fancied iron despotism of such conceptions as fate and destiny must often drive the wearied mind into that sleep of its own, called imagination, to find recuperation in dreams from the exhaustions of reality.

My letter from Paris, and regular weekly editorial upon the certainty of an early and general war between the effete monarchies of Europe, were just the free imaginative labors to divert my mind from all its worldly perplexities, and make me forget for a while the hopeless tangle of conflicting circumstances in which my whole existence seemed to be snared; but when I finally turned to the latest southern newspapers, and commenced writing up "The Shooting Season" for the week, it was coming back to stern actualities again,—my own distractions among the rest. Hence my mood and pen experienced a sudden loss of elasticity at this latter point, and I was halting miserably in an effort to put together the commonest of sentences properly, when Will Dewitt came into the sanctum and observed what I was about.

"Doing the 'Shooting Season,' eh?" remarked he.

"Yes; and I'd give something to be through with it."

"If you want something fresh for it I can give you the article."

"Let me hear it," I said, without much interest.

"I'll give it to you in reporter style," replied the dramatic editor, "and you can romance on it for yourself. This morning a couple of laborers who had gone into a piece of woods in Hoboken, about three-quarters of a mile from the ferry, to cut brush, found amongst some low bushes the dead body of a well-dressed man, apparently about thirty years old. A bullet-hole through the forehead, and a discharged pistol still grasped in the right hand, explained the fate of the unfortunate mortal, who is supposed to have sought that retired spot for the purpose of self-destruction."

"Pooh!" interrupted I, impatiently: "that's merely a common affair. There's no point to it that I see."

"Let me finish," added Dewitt, in a significant tone. "From papers found upon the person of deceased, his name is believed to have been Allyn Vane."

I laid aside my pen and surveyed Dewitt in mingled distress and wonder.

"Can it be possible!"

"So it appears. A reporter brought the news into the *Daily Bread* office just now, while I was there, and the name attracted me. You don't seem to doubt that it means *our* Vane, of the old school."

"It must be the same," said I, musingly. "I met him at a theatre some time ago, and learned, from his own lips, that he was going to the dogs on a full run. I suppose you know that he turned gambler?"

"Yes, I knew that," observed my old school-mate, gravely. "Poor Vane! That tigerish runaway wife of Birch's made a clear fool of him, they say."

I darted a sharp look at the speaker, half suspecting that he might know more of the latter matter than I had supposed; but his countenance gave no indication beyond the bare meaning of his words.

"Vane never had much strength of mind," remarked I, not caring to argue, "and his real ruin was some money left him, as he told me, by his mother. It is easy to imagine such a man losing heavily to sharpers in a gaming-house, and then blowing out his brains in a fit of despair."

"That may have been it," assented Dewitt, thoughtfully. "What an unwholesome, ill-fated concern that school seemed to be! Always more of the lunatic asylum than school about it. I wonder what has become of all the fellows? I wonder if Reed has gone to preaching yet?"

I made no answer to his wonderment, preferring that he should think me no wiser in those particulars than himself; but now that his practical and inquiring mind had been drawn back to the days of our early association, he was willing to talk on.

"Do you know, Glibun," said he, after a brief pause, "that *you* have always struck me as being a curious genius?"

"Have I?"

"Why, yes. At school we were always wondering what there was between you and Vane and Mrs. Birch; and since you first came upon me so unexpectedly in this office, and slid so easily into an editorship, you've puzzled me more than ever. I've taken it into my head that you could tell a story of your own if you chose to."

He said this in something like his old, boyish style, and without any appearance of rude curiosity; so I answered him in good temper,—

"Every one has his own story, I suppose, even if he has nothing else. Poor Vane has just ended his. As for mine, it has just reached the time when I am about to leave hackney literature and enter another business."

"You surprise me," exclaimed Dewitt, his looks justifying his words; "what is your new wrinkle?"

"A dry goods clerkship."

I thought that piece of information would check whatever desire he had to know my "story;" and it did. A poorly-repressed expression of deep disgust came over his face on the instant, and was very plain in the tone of his voice,—

"Leave journalism to deal in tape and muslin! Why, that's worse than herding with the Bohemians."

He was certainly very much disgusted at such a coming down from the intellectualities, and had no further care about the personal adventures of one who could be capable of such deterioration.

"It is true," said I. "Next week I shall be amongst the tapes and muslins; in which I've had some experience, by-the-by, already."

"Well, you know your own business," returned he, making ready to commence work at his desk. "I shall be sorry to have you go." And thus our conversation ended.

By dint of sturdy persistence I worried through my sanguinary Southern department, each tragic incident suggesting to me the prone figure of Vane as one of its features, and rendering my pen still less ready in the work. Satisfied, however, if I but wrote coherently, and not attempting to elaborate much beyond the bare facts as they were given by my authorities, I completed my work by sunset; and then, with a parting word to the dramatic editor, took my way back to Benedick Place.

Chance had favored my inclinations during the past two days by saving me from contact with any of my Bohemian friends during that length of time, and I was particularly glad to accomplish a dinner at Solon Tick's, and get into my room again that night with the same impunity. Occupied as I was with the thickening surprises and mysteries of a culminating destiny, I shrank from companionships associated almost wholly with my frivolous hours; and, as I have said, chance seemed to favor the feeling by keeping the fraternity temporarily away from me. In short, to farther explain the matter, it may as well be stated here that the shockingly sudden death of Le Mons, and the remorseful scenes accompanying and following that reproachful event, had cast a gloom and a chill over Bohemia, and put an end for a time to the livelier sociabilities of its volatile sons.

While carefully attiring myself for my visit to the house of my new and Heaven-sent friend and guide, I reflected that I must presently resign my literary company altogether; for with my change of business I had determined to change my place of abode, and the two changes would pretty certainly carry me quite out of the literary circle. To say that I contemplated such alienation with no regret whatever, would be exaggeration, since I really felt an odd kind of attachment for Church and two or three others; but in all my experience of such company and their ways I had never been able to divest myself entirely of a certain feeling of strangeness, as though I were very far from being "to the manner born;" and Gwin's example and death had carried the sensation very near to impatient aversion. Thus it was that I could so easily consent to even go back again to a clerkship, when the latter offered as an alternative to the occupation no longer tasteful to me. I was no genius; that was the amount of it.

Saying as much to myself while taking a last view of my profile in the little mirror on my dressing-bureau, it simultaneously occurred to me that my forehead was neither high nor broad enough to denote the literary man, and that my fastidious tendency to dress like a Christian was in itself a death-blow to the last hope of intellectual eminence. So far, however, were these discoveries from covering me with humiliation, that I positively regarded my reflected self with some complacency. The mirror gave a cabinet-portrait of a well-shaped young man, rather above the medium height, with curling chestnut hair, regular features, an expression of countenance at once mild, earnest, and boyish, and a general air of quiet respectability. It is not generally a source of satisfaction to know that one does not bear the remotest resemblance to his reputed father; and that I secretly rejoiced in such a conviction may look very much like a proof of incorrigible demoralization; but I make the confession without reserve, and offer it as my last observation before setting out for Mr. Goodman's.

An omnibus carried me to Union Park, and there alighting I quickly found the merchant's residence. It was a plainly handsome house, fronting the Park about midway, and, with its two noble shade-trees on the curb, and little green cemetery within the iron railings, had somewhat of the twilight stateliness of the great Establishment down-town. So much I could discern by the light of the street-lamps and the stars, and it prepared me to find my benefactor the same at home as in his temple of trade. A sumptuous building of the ornate modern style would have filled me with embarrassing expectations of all those royal pomps and ceremonies with which the successful tradesmen of the republic are apt to astonish the friends of their wealthy days. But here there were no architectural pretences, nor obtrusive elaboration of front doors, to make time-honored respectability pass for the rank growth of yesterday. The house, like its owner, had a character to be known without a purchased livery of state; and, in the consciousness that my own right to admittance there would be neither questioned nor degraded by the special social insolences of upstart grandeur, I felt that respectful confidence which true dignity only can inspire.

A servant, whose neat black costume and subdued demeanor were placid reminiscences of his employer's salesmen, conducted me through a fine old hall to a small reception-room opening therefrom on the left, and, having taken my card, left me to make his announcement. I had barely time, however, to realize where I was, before he reappeared with the request that I should follow him to the parlor. Resigning to his care my hat and gloves, and recrossing the hall, I was next bowed into a lofty, well-lighted apartment, furnished handsomely, but in the substantial, old-fashioned style, where Mr. Goodman stood conversing with a stout, short, vivacious gentleman, in gold spectacles and very obvious wig, who seemed to be in the act of taking leave. The merchant was looking toward the door as I entered, and welcomed me so heartily, with both hands, that his parting guest was palpably surprised.

"My young friend, you are punctual," said Mr. Goodman, and added, "Mr. Spanyel, Mr. Glibun."

"Happy, sir," said Mr. Spanyel, politely. "A relative of yours, I infer, Mr. Goodman."

The merchant smiled at the mistake, and I hastened to regret that I could not claim the honor.

"I beg your pardon," rejoined Mr. Spanyel, slightly dashed; "but I thought there was a likeness. I should be pleased to see more of Mr. Glibun, but must really be going now. Mrs. Spanyel may depend, I hope, upon the pleasure of your presence, with Miss Goodman, on the occasion I have mentioned."

"I may venture to promise for the young lady, I think," replied Mr. Goodman; "and if I should not be able to act as her escort, you may permit me to transfer the compliment of your invitation to a substitute?"

"Certainly, Mr. Goodman, with pleasure," answered the gentleman, who thereupon bade us good-evening and departed.

Ungallantly as the confession may sound, I must admit that the mention of a Miss Goodman gave me a sensation nearly akin to jealousy, though why it should affect me in that absurd way I could not have explained to myself.

"Now, sir," said my benefactor, quite unconscious of my emotion, "you may take a chair, if you please, and inform me at once how your affairs are progressing. I judged from the expression of your countenance, when you entered the room, that you had something new to tell me."

In his own house, and with all the light and refined comfort of a generous home about him, he was still more the courtly gentleman of the old school than in the tempered shade and formalities of his counting-room. But in any place or circumstance, in the saloon of the gaming-house, whither he had gone to rescue a soul from destruction, as in his parlor where he sat to dispense elegant hospitality, that natural dignity which was the free expression of his whole benevolent character rather than the jealous pride of a few lofty traits, would have invited as irresistibly the trust and confidence of modest merit, as it would have abashed and silenced the familiarity of vulgar presumption.

"I have, indeed, sir, something new to tell you," said I, in reply to his conjecture, "and hardly know whether to regard it as favorable to myself, or otherwise. Within two days I have been notified of my right as heir to the property of an uncle, whose relationship, while he lived, was never suspected by me; and my step-mother has sent me a written request to visit my father's house to-morrow night."

Wonder was plainly depicted on the countenance of the merchant, nor did it abate when I carefully repeated my conversation with the lawyer.

"This is certainly a development I was far from anticipating," said he, "and requires early and judicious action. Have you brought the lawyer's note with you?"

"I have, sir," said I; "and also that from Mrs. Wynne." And I handed both to him.

Opening Mr. Sewall's first, he read it attentively, turned it over several times, and, after a long pause, observed very deliberately,—

"I will retain this, if you are willing, and attend to it myself."

I was thankful to have him do so, and expressed myself in terms of grateful assent.

"Do you think," asked he, "that the present Mrs. Wynne, formerly your nurse, had any knowledge of the man, Reese, in his true relationship?"

"No, sir, I cannot reasonably think so. If my uncle, himself, did not know me to be his nephew until the very last day of his life,—if he did even then,—how could she be better informed? It seems, indeed, that my father, even, was as ignorant."

"I would advise you," said Mr. Goodman, after another pause, and with his eyes still upon the note, "to place very little stress on this matter. I have good reason to believe that, as regards yourself, it will prove to be a mistake."

If the feeling excited in me by his idea was that of disappointment, it assuredly had but shallow depth. Curiosity, rather than gratification, characterized my sentiments regarding Mr. Sewall's revelation, and, without any keen sense of regret, I heard my benefactor arbitrarily discredit what had seemed so like my good fortune.

"It seems too strange for truth," replied I; "but the same may be said, Mr. Goodman, of all that I know about myself."

"Excuse me a moment," said he; and, going to a strong mahogany escritoire, he placed the lawyer's note in a drawer. Then, returning again to his chair, with a less absorbed expression of countenance, he prepared to examine the second missive.

"Your curious family-history, after being a sealed book to you so long," he observed, "may well bewilder you now by the abruptness, disorder, and rapidity with which its secrets are coming to light. It is the less explicable, however, because you know but a part of it yet. At least, that is my inference. And this brings us to Mrs. Wynne's note."

He opened the latter as he spoke, and read it at a glance, apparently, and returned it to me.

"Mr. Wynne's house," he said, "is almost directly across the Park from here. You should, by all means, obey the summons you have received, for I do not doubt that it will be in the highest degree to your interest to do so. And now, my dear young man," he added, kindness and interest beaming from every feature of his face, "you must give me a frank answer, when I ask if my own conduct and language toward you have not seemed nearly as strange as the rest of your puzzling experiences?"

Not stopping to consider how I really might have regarded them had my nature been less eager for the immediate protection and guidance they supplied, I passionately told him, and truly, too, that I had thought of *him* with my heart only, not with my mind; that, from the moment when he first addressed me, I had, without knowing why, regarded him with a mixture of grateful reverence and implicit trust which left me neither need nor disposition to reason about what he did or said.

"My dear young friend," he replied, as warmly, and with a pleased look, "your words give me much pleasure, — more, indeed, than you can imagine. There could be no better proof that your enforced associations in the past with ignorance and depravity have failed to contaminate you; for reverence is one of the first traits lost in the contraction of vice, and the youth that takes lessons from matured ignorance will seldom heed the wisdom of gray hairs. I think, however, that, despite your implicit lack of curiosity, you should have some explanation of my emotion at hearing your name, my immediate interest in your welfare, and the foreknowledge by which I have been enabled to advise promptly in the complicated matters you have submitted for counsel."

"Am I to understand then, sir," cried I, greatly struck by his words and manner, "that you had foreknowledge of me prior to our first meeting?"

"Such was the case," responded Mr. Goodman, smiling. "Some time before that eventful evening, the writer of this note in my hand, had, in this very house, related much of your story to me, and besought for Avery Glibun my protection and friendship, whenever the young wanderer bearing that name should be found again."

Now, indeed, my benefacter was a puzzle to me; and I am afraid that my countenance betrayed the fact to him by the least dignified of stares.

"I see that I am a source of incomprehensibility to you at last, young sir," he went on, in a still sprightlier voice; "but you must not suppose that Mrs. Wynne and I are old acquaintances. On the occasion of a masquerade ball here, not very long ago, in honor of my adopted daughter's birthday, Mrs. Wynne, in mask and domino, succeeded in gaining admittance and persuaded me to a private interview. Withdrawing with her, as she requested, to a conservatory at hand, I there learned the name of my strange guest and the object of her visit. Of the latter I will tell you no more at present than that the lady related

your misfortunes to me, and with such an argument in your behalf that I did not hesitate to promise what she required. If you could be found, or if you should voluntarily make your appearance where either she or I could know you, I was to take you under my protection. I will tell you no more because it is plain, from this note, that Mrs. Wynne wishes to tell you the remainder herself. Go to her to-morrow night, as she desires, and, when you leave her, come to me again."

My heart melted toward Elfie while he spoke; and in imputing to her a motive almost heroic for boldly asking in my behalf the protection of one whose well-known justice and benevolence were a guaranty that her petition would not be in vain, I willingly concluded that her share in my father's unnatural schemes against me was no more voluntary than it had been when she was my only refuge from him, and that she would still dare every peril to preserve me from further wrong.

I was about to assure Mr. Goodman that I would see her as she had appointed, and rest satisfied until then with what I already knew of her character, when the door of the parlor was hastily pushed open, revealing the figure of a young lady who was palpably surprised at finding me with the merchant.

"Come in, my dear," said the latter.

The fair apparition advanced modestly, but with well-bred ease, revealing to my first admiring glance a face of exquisite girlish beauty and sensibility, and a lithe figure ripe with the earliest symmetry of womanhood; but, as I arose to pay decorous homage, and caught a nearer view of the deep, thoughtful eyes in the shade of her fair forehead and luxuriant dark hair, my heart suddenly received a new sensation and throbbed at a familiar touch.

"My adopted daughter. Mr. Glibun," said Mr. Goodman. "My dear, you come upon us like a spirit."

I had sufficient self-possession to bow and utter the usual commonplace; but my bow was a nervously oblique one, and after the salutation my mouth had a wonderful tendency to remain half open. In short, I had a vague consciousness of having seen the young lady before, and stood an awkward victim, so to speak, of imperfect and incredible memory.

"Perhaps," said the merchant, noticing my perplexity and her confusion thereat, — "perhaps you would feel better acquainted, my dear young people, if I should introduce you again as — April and Avery!"

"April!" ejaculated I. "April Grey!"

"Are you, can you be Avery?" asked the unchanged voice, while the cheeks so lately flushing took the pallor by which I knew them best.

Despite the womanly form, the rich attire, the long, lustrous hair, whose curling cascade had not yet carried over the single white rose-bud to break on shoulders whiter than itself, I recognized the daughter of Olden Grey.

Appreciating our emotions, Mr. Goodman had the tact to perceive that neither of us knew what to say, and came to our relief with ready sympathy.

"There is some excuse for your incredulity of your senses at this meeting, Mr. Glibun," said he, laughingly, "although you had been informed, already, if I remember rightly, that Miss April Grey had brilliantly outgrown the unfashionable circumstances under which you once knew her. But as for you. my dear," he added, laying his hand tenderly upon her head, "there can be no possible pretence for any prolonged amazement on your part. I told you all about Mr. Avery yesterday; and, although you may not have expected to find him here to-night, you must not appear to be astounded at his very existence."

"But I should not have known him if you had not mentioned his first name," said April, regaining her composure at the sound of his voice, and blushing the welcome her little hand was already confirming.

"I should have known you anywhere!" cried I, with an unceremonious ardor proportioned to my recent perturbation.

"And we shall all know each other as well, if we all take seats," said Mr. Goodman.

Forgetting everything in the world save what was before me, I set a chair for the young lady; and, when we were all seated, my benefactor continued, —

"As you already know the sadder portion of April's story, Mr. Glibun, I shall briefly tell you the remainder at once; for in this matter, at least, you should find no mystery. Have you a distinct recollection of all the principal circumstances related in Mr. Grey's written statement?"

I assured him earnestly that not one circumstance narrated in Olden Grey's legacy had escaped my memory, and April cast down her lovely eyes to hide the emotion excited by the pitiful theme.

"Then," proceeded Mr. Goodman, gravely, "I need not repeat that melancholy story. The Honorable Captain, Mr. Grey's father, was an old friend of mine, and on the occasion of my last visit to England, about twelve years ago, I found him upon his death-bed. In the confidence of friendship and with a full realization of his condition, he told me how rigorously he had dealt with his only son, and confessed that he had allowed himself to be unjustly inflamed against the hapless young man by Brighton Keene and the designing mother of the latter. Upon discovering the treachery of Brighton, the discarded son made a fierce attack upon the traitor, and, believing that he had killed him, fled at once to this country. But Brighton Keene lived long enough to confess his iniquities under fear of death, and the dying father spoke only with remorse of his own cruel folly in being the dupe of such a wretch. Knowing that I would soon return to America, he earnestly besought me to trace out his son, or that son's child, and named me trustee, as I may term it, in the last will and testament by which he bequeathed his entire property to Olden and Olden's heirs. Soon after the captain's death I came home, and at once instituted a search for the wronged child of my old friend. My efforts, however, were all in vain, until I had almost relinquished hope; but, finally, by the merest chance, one of the city missionaries who had called upon me for a charitable donation, mentioned the greater success of Catholics than Protestants with the lowest orders of the poor, and told about a little girl, named Grey, who, upon the death of her father, an English unfortunate at the Five Points, had been spirited away, as he termed it, to a convent in H—— street. I lost no time in applying for information at the convent named, and there found April. Her religious protectors were ready to prove her identity, and produced the written statement of the child's father, witnessed by the priest who had brought April to the institution. Her presence here as my adopted daughter explains the rest. That, I believe, is the whole story."

"No, not the whole, dear guardian!" added April, quickly. "You have not said a word of your own noble kindness — "

"Which becomes a very tiresome topic in that little mouth. my dear," he interrupted. casting an arm fondly about her, as she drew closer to his side, and regarding her with such a fatherly, protecting air as he had not before exhibited.

I reverenced him the more for the terse, rapid manner in which he had explained his precious trust without once allowing his own generous part to appear save as a mere incidental agency. And in the conversation following it was no effort for me to join with April in her loving deference to him in everything.

It was hard to leave them at last, and go back to solitude and reflection, to a lonely hired room and gloomy presentiments of the morrow; but the heart with one firm stay to lean upon can take hope against a thousand treasons, and the same sleep that follows the weariest despondencies of the night may bring dreams brighter than the morning.

CHAPTER LI.

THE room was superbly luxurious with dainty furniture and lavish ornament; and if the pretentious front of the house had suggested a strong contrast to the repellant air of neglect and desolation so marked in my old home, how much wider was the difference between the glaring, sumptuous parlor in which I then stood, and that dim, comfortless den of an apartment where my father had successively frightened me with his contempt, consigned me to the unwilling custody of the wretched Birch, and discovered me in that involuntary act of eavesdropping which precipitated the most monstrous of his unnatural designs. Heavy curtains of crimson stuff marked the unlighted entrance to the front parlor; fine canvas, fastened to the walls by gilded half-pillars and to the ceiling by an immense cornice of gilt, bore delicate oil paintings in imitation of tapestry; but what particularly caught my eye was the well-remembered iron safe, set in the wall as it had been before. One glance at that made everything else indifferent to me, and held me sternly fixed in the resentful memories justly mine.

I might well have been confused to find my father himself there, when I had expected to see no one but my step-mother; I might well have felt startled and shocked at the hard, fierce expression of my step-mother's altered face, and at the presence of an over-dressed stranger who had followed stealthily after me into the house, and who, as he stood beside me before my parent and the lady, had yet a familiar look. Had I gone thither the friendless and hopeless mortal that I was but a week before, I must have derived nothing but final discouragement from such a scene, and retreated unmanfully from it after a wild word or two of mad reproach. But I had friends now; there was a strong arm behind me, and I confronted the authors of my misfortunes with the resolute air of one who had come upon no questionable mission.

"Madam," said I, recognizing my step-mother, only, and unhesitatingly extending my hand, "you find me obedient to your note."

She met my grasp coldly and mechanically, letting her hand fall almost immediately to her side again by its own weight.

"And I, Mrs. Wynne, am also as prompt to answer your written request," cried the stranger at my side. "Mr. Wynne, I'm your most obedient."

If I had ignored the presence of my father he was certainly capable of returning the compliment with complete artistic success; for he placidly looked through me at the person who had addressed him, and nodded his acknowledgment without seeming at all aware that I stood in the way. Sitting near a table, on which he indolently rested an elbow and slowly twirled a book, he was not a day older in appearance than when I had last seen him. Time could not stale, nor custom wither, such imperturbable self-possession as his; nor was there any progress of age for face and demeanor, which but passively transmitted an eternal tranquillity of egotism.

The stranger and I took chairs in obedience to a half-contemptuous motion from Elfie; and the latter, surveying me intently but without kindness, replied at last to my equally intent look.

"You expected to see me, only, here," said she, "and fancied perhaps, that I would be meek and humble after what you have heard from my father."

"That you are not alone to receive me, madam," replied I, quite coolly, "is apparently the effect of your own wishes, and I need not trouble you about my expectations. I am truly sorry, however, that you seem so indisposed to meet me in that spirit of kindness which assuredly characterizes my feelings toward you."

"You have no reason to feel kindly toward me," she rejoined, in the same tone, "and this is no time for foolish compliments."

"I understand you," said I. "You are too proud to shrink from the responsibility of things in which you have been seemingly an active sharer, and which have been cruelly unfortunate for me. I can tell you, however, that I know precisely what your share has been. I have no resentment against you. I know all that I owe to you, and am here to-night with every inclination to regard you as a friend."

She was dressed plainly in black, as in the old time, and looked, when her unkind eyes were turned from me, so much like her old self, that my voice trembled with gentler feelings as I spoke. But she paid no apparent heed to what I said; her look was fixed upon my father before I had finished, and she kept it there though still addressing me.

"I have induced my husband to be present," were her words, "because something of what I have to say to you will be a confession new to him."

"That is true, Mrs. Wynne," observed my father, as though she had spoken exclusively to him. "I have the honor to be here at your particular request; and, in view of the fact that it is likely to be my last opportunity for enjoying your society, I wish to be as much your slave as possible. But would you mind informing me why Mr. Ketchum, there, has been summoned to a company which can scarcely offer him the liveliest entertainment?"

I studied the stranger with new sensations, on thus hearing his name, and was favored by him with a peculiar and rather comical wink of recognition.

"I desired him to be here," said Elfie, "because he can substantiate what I affirm."

"It's the only return I can make for my own share in working-up a jolly bad business," explained Mr. Ketchum; and added, with much suavity, "Mr. Glibun — not to say Wynne, junior, — you're much changed since the times when I saw you with the tramps in Jersey and with poor Reese in Cow Bay. Upon my soul, you're improved a bit."

My father gave a slight but politely-submissive bow, expressive of his entire satisfaction with the whole arrangement of our pleasant evening-party; and my step-mother once more turned her repelling eyes to me.

"What has my father told you?" she sharply asked.

"Everything, madam."

"He does not know all."

"He told me all he knew."

She paused a moment with a hand over her eyes, as though collecting her thoughts, then boldly met my look again, and proceeded. —

"I have always known that it would come to this. I have known it for years; and if at any time my strength failed at thought of it, that man — my husband — knew how to cure me of the weakness. He knew that love would make me weak, and gave me contempt to keep me strong!"

She looked at him again; and for an instant her white face was tremulous in all its lines with something pitiful and womanly.

"I have been truer to him because of his contempt!" she cried, in a sudden burst of passion. "For every sneer, and lash, and spurning with the foot, I have, from the first, been the more abject creature of his will. What are women but servile spaniels, to fawn upon the hand that strikes them oftenest!"

"Say, rather," urged my imperturbable father, in an airy tone, "that all women are natural aristocrats, and love a despotism."

He looked the very ideal of handsome wickedness as he uttered the courtly sarcasm, — the very ideal of him who could easily be President if women had but votes.

A fiercer light came into the glance of the wife, and her words hurried faster and more bitterly.

"Do you think, you boy! that I am confessing, from hatred for him, and love for you? Why, what a fool's idea is that! Am I a mighty, boastful man, to sink into cowardly, drivelling rage, ruin, and insanity when Plato Wynne commands; or am I, a weak, timid woman, to grow calmer, stronger, and firmer in mind, by the love that feeds on contumely? I care nothing for you, Avery. I'll have none of your gratitude. *He*, only, owes me gratitude; for, even now — I say it before the God who may charge my soul with it! — I do what I do for love of him!"

And he was pleased with the tribute to his excellent matrimonial policy. He indulged in the old, familiar gesture of sweeping his glossy beard with the jewelled hand, and smiled complacently to himself as, with the other hand, he twirled the book.

"You have told me nothing, yet," I said.

"And suppose that I choose to tell you nothing!" was her angry retort. "What right have you to dictate to me? Are you anything to me? Am I to speak at your bidding?"

"Mrs. Wynne," returned I, meeting her fiery glance with one of inquiring deprecation, "are you not aware that this interview is of your own appointment and characterization? If its purpose is unpleasant to you, it is scarcely more agree-able to me, and I have not the remotest wish to extort anything from you against your free will. You are not the one I hold responsible for my wrongs. I must ask permission to retire if you continue to find my presence a source only of irrelevant irritation."

"To me you *do* owe the only real wrong you suffer," cried the capricious woman, "and you shall not retire until I have forced the proof upon you."

Not knowing how to interpret this wilful assertion, I merely bowed, and assumed an air of submissive attention. Once more she hid her dilated eyes with a hand, and appeared to be collecting her thoughts; nor was this repetition without some suggestion of a mind overtasked by its burden.

"When Plato Wynne's late wife was about to bring a child into the world," she abruptly commenced, fixing her look as abruptly upon Mr. Ketchum, "the man who is now my husband commanded me to become her sole attendant and nurse. If, by his will, I had married a man I despised, it did not become me to resist that will in the second instance. I went as I was called. The woman seemed likely to die in her last act of servitude to the house of her master; and if the soul that came into life when hers went out should be that of a boy, the master would curse the hour of its birth. I learned that very soon; and while I was learning it I saw my father meekly acting a part which made him as fully the puppet of another and bolder man, as myself. I felt the snare drawing closer, and exulted in it, for I loved the hand that drew it and wished to be powerless in its grasp. Well did Plato Wynne understand me, when, without one word of preparation, nor even lowering his voice, he plainly and briefly unfolded to me a project in which I was to take unquestioning part. Across the street lived a lady who, by some fatal chance, was likely to be confined at about the same time with Mrs. Wynne, and whose husband had been called away from the city by urgent political business. If the child in our house should be a son, and the child in that house should be a daughter, the infants were to be changed."

"Stop!" ejaculated I, starting from my chair in uncontrollable astonishment. "What are you telling me? Have you gone mad?"

"Ask the man beside you," responded she, with a contemptuous laugh; "ask him."

"The bill is a true one," said Mr. Ketchum, affably. "I was very much at Mr. Wynne's — or Glibun's — service myself, at that time, and had an acquaintance with the agreeable female acting as nurse to the lady across the street. That agreeable female was a jolly young widow, you see, and destined to become the present Mrs. Ketchum."

Darting a glance at my father, who mildly returned it without at all seeing me, I sat down again in a hopeless state of incredulity.

"You and I," continued Elfie, speaking directly to the detective now, "had our orders, and our master left us until they should be obeyed. *I* had two motives for obeying. I loved the father and hated the mother! and yet—O me! O me!—I did shrink from that deed."

Bowing her head, and clasping her hands tightly across her bosom, she rocked to and fro in a momentary passion of regret.

"You need not be startled yet!" she cried, turning suddenly upon me. "Both children were boys; both mothers died without knowing their children."

I know not what I had expected; but that sentence seemed to tear some of my life away.

"You fell to my care," resumed my stepmother, "and I cherished you as though you had been my own. Do you know why? Because I saw that in the eye of Plato Wynne, when he looked upon you, from which I would have saved him. I stood between you and what would have made him dreadful, even to me. As you grew older, he hated you the more, and I dreaded the more that he would—kill you. From this dread was born a brief, wild wish— God knows how strangely mad it was—to save you and myself together. I was trusted by him, then,—perhaps in very contempt of me he trusted so,—and, availing myself of that trust, I took from his safe a paper, of which my father must have spoken, when he told you all he knew. One evening, I gave you laudanum, to make your sleep secure, and carried you to my broken father's miserable haunt by the river, wrapped in a garment which contained the first of the false wills. My father had blindly promised to bear you away to some secure hiding-place, and then let me know, that I might follow. I left you in the warehouse, and returned, as I thought, unobserved. But I had been watched—"

"By me," interrupted Mr. Ketchum, quickly. "I can't deny it. Mr. Wynne had some reason to suspect the lady's intention, and directed me to watch her closely, he being but seldom at home. I followed her when she took you to the warehouse; and followed her back; and then returned to the warehouse again, and found it on fire. If you have any recollection of an enterprising Yankee who came up the ladder to you just before you got out, and asked your fireman-friend to invest in the Salamander Life Insurance, you must recollect me. I was that jolly credit to the Salamander. I was after you when you got out, and tracked the fireman when he took you home. I picked up your cap, and have it in my private museum now."

"And perhaps you also recollect what treatment was mine for that failure," proceeded Elfie, hurriedly. "I was called to account before you, like an unfaithful servant; charged sternly with abusing the generous confidence reposed in me by a trusting father, and sent back to my pitiful husband, like a dog to his keeper! And then, to show how well he knew his power over me,—to prove how craven he knew I would be after such contemptuous punishment, he sent you straightway into my hands again, and finally bade the school-master make away with you, almost in my very sight! I saved you again, to save him. Yes, Plato," she exclaimed, in a piteous voice, appealing to the figure at the table, and expressing mingled fear and defiance in her pale countenance; "I did it only to save you from — murder. From a murder which would have profited you nothing!"

The King of Diamonds arose slowly from his chair, and, advancing to a low stand under the iron safe, lifted from it a glossy silk hat, deeply banded with crape.

"Madam," said he, his whole manner changed from the perfect indifference of a moment before, to an exact counterfeit of the lofty sternness with which he had received her on the day after my rescue by Hosea Waters,—"your first act of deception was detected, and thwarted, and suitably resented by me, as you have already affirmed. You may remember, too, what I said to you then,—where I had once been deceived, I never trusted again?"

"I do remember it," she replied, in a repressed, breathless way; "and if any ignominious blow, or wrench could have broken my chains, they had been shivered then."

With a motion of his disengaged hand, he dismissed the sentimental comment.

"The badge of mourning on this hat," continued he, "is evidence that I did trust again. You told me that my son was dead; and to this day I wear the memorial of the falsehood."

"It was not your fault that I lived!" came angrily to my lips, but was not spoken.

"I believed that every additional year of the young man's life, would strengthen your motive for committing a mad, self-destructive crime," said Elfie, no longer fearful in either look or voice. She seemed to gather strength and determination from his presumptuous self-possession; and met his sinister gaze with unshrinking resolution. "As in the first falsehood,—call it that if you will,—so in the second. I stood between you and what would have brought God's justice on your head. I am not vindicating myself to your mercy, Plato Wynne; I am not revenging myself for your scorn; I am not pretending to have won the gratitude of a motherless and persecuted child; but I *am* vindicating a love that has borne years of scorn, distrust, and shame to save its object from blood-guiltiness and retribution."

My father replaced the hat upon the stand, with great care not to ruffle the lustrous nap, and then leaned against the stand, folding his arms.

"I could have wished, Mrs. Wynne," returned he, "that you had not deemed it necessary to call in a gentleman of the police, as sharer in our little confidences. But since such has been your taste, and the gentleman is already in possession of the entire stock of family information up to this point, his presence need not deter me from reminding you of the conditions upon which I consented to be entertained by your charming dramatic recitations this evening. I felt obliged to stipulate that your eccentric devotion should, from this night forth, be exercised from a distance sufficiently great to lend the enchantment to which I have hitherto been unfortunately blind; while you voluntarily promised to tell me something new. After giving your remarks my utmost attention, and sharing Mr. Ketchum's edification at your rather pertinacious romancing upon love and murder, I am still without the anticipated sensation of novelty."

His manner of ignoring me, recognizing the detective as the only auditor of their conversation, and tranquilly disregarding every possible provocation to shame or anger in my step-mother's pitiless confession, was a perfection and polish of hypocrisy beyond the most subtle ideal of acting. It fairly fascinated me by its stupendous hardihood, and I stared at him with a vague incredulity of his humanity.

The mocking nicety of his last cold-blooded speech stung the tormented woman into some show of passion again, and she retorted, bitterly, — "Do you think I would speak of my love as I do, had I not already determined to speak of it no more forever? You are not more resolute in that, Plato, than I am."

"Pardon me, Mrs. Wynne, but you are not speaking to the point. I mentioned your promise of a new revelation."

"Must you be heartless and contemptuous with me to the very last?" she rather moaned than said, with another characteristic change of feeling. A kind look, or word, from him, even then, would have made her a tigress to me. The haggard prayer in her face said that.

"No, madam; not contemptuous. When a gentleman hears what I have heard to-night, — that his wife's dissimulation is commended to his favor as a protection from the temptations of crime; his feelings, as a gentleman, can only be those due to the incongruities of an unbalanced mind."

"Matchless villain!" shouted I, no longer able to endure such unparalleled audacity. "With me before you, do you dare make pretence to one natural or manly virtue? If, for any unknown reason, you suppose me to be powerless against you in law, do you think to refine your outrages upon me by an assumed unconsciousness of any guilt whatever? You may have the theatrical skill to unnerve a woman, who, in her infatuation, offers her heart to be wrung; but you cannot impose upon me. If you do not fear God, if you jeer at the law, you shall feel what it is to have your inconceivable villanies proclaimed to the public by your own son. The world shall know you, and what you have done; and the world's judgment shall make even you answer for your iniquities with shame and disgrace!"

Still leaning against the stand, he first regarded me with a mild surprise, as though momentarily taken aback by such freedom from a very young gentleman who had not yet been introduced to him; but, as I went furiously on, a derisive sneer curled his thin upper lip and gleamed in his wicked eyes.

"The world?" said he, in a voice of tolerating inquiry. "It may be wise for you to remember, my impetuous young friend, that your eye is oval and the world is round."

The cool intellectual arrogance of the brief reply was scarcely less baffling than his perfect moral impassibility; and, while I was panting for words to speak, another voice addressed him, —

"You may go too far, you know, Mr. Wynne," cried Ketchum. "I know the whole ground of this little trouble pretty well, and would advise you to draw it milder. You're not so safe, you know, as you used to be before that slip-up at Albany. Your friends, the judges and the district attorney, might go back on you now (if you don't mind the expression), and make bad work for you in court. They think you're down, now, and Cringer is up. You know how such things go. I'm one of the regular detectives now, after leaving the Independents, and will let you into a secret for old acquaintance' sake. I'm after your friend Gamble, who'll 'peach' upon your mill business in Jersey as sure as I catch him. And I'm bound to have him, you know. Here's his portrait that I'm going to send to the western detective agency this very night by express, — I got it from the pocket of a coat that Mr. Avery, here, left in Cow Bay once, — and I shall follow it myself to-morrow. I'll have him, if he hides in the middle of a prairie fire! Now you know your danger, Mr. Wynne, and oughtn't to carry things too far."

He actually drew from a pocket of his fanciful vest the very miniature which the gipsy girl had shown in the pail of water, and which the indignant mother of Aloize had returned to me.

"Madam," said the King of Diamonds, sublimely oblivious to the friendly warning, "these people of yours presume upon the character you have been pleased to give me, and I must decline remaining here if you have no more to say."

"I am not joined with them in any thought or project against you!" exclaimed Elüe, in a sharp tone.

"Spare yourself, madam. I am not to be deceived again."

She rose from the chair on which she had been sitting, and, going to his side, laid a hand upon his shoulder.

"Plato Wynne, the last words I shall ever speak to you in this world are to be spoken to-night. Such is your will, and it is mine. I have loved you better than my soul; and you, in your own soul, know it. I have deceived you. Whatever you are, you are no murderer. You will thank me for that, — thank me in my grave for that, — when you have to die."

Looking into her eyes with a look that might have shamed the most merciless of devils, he slowly extended before her his right hand, on which blazed the diamond.

"Elfie," he said deliberately and with a sinister smile, "if you can say that this hand is not stained with human blood on your account, you can say more than I."

She shrank aghast from him with her own hands clenched convulsively against her bosom; and the detective and I, by one impulse, started in our chairs.

"Now finish your act, madam," continued Plato Wynne, letting the hand fall, "I have spared you a few unnecessary passages."

Elfie grew quickly calm again under the cutting sneer, but withdrew a few paces toward me.

"I do not know what you mean," she said. "I have not much more to say; and yet it means all. I have deceived you; but I spoke only the truth when I said that your son was dead."

I was on my feet at the word, but the detective was before me and scarcely less excited.

"Don't say it, Mrs. Wynne!" cried Mr. Ketchum, gesticulating wildly. "I've got nearly as much to atone for in the young man's case as you have, and I've done him more than one good turn since he got away from the school-master. Stop where you are, and he's safe for a good property, at any rate. He knows that! He knows who Reese was! I've been on your side and his for some time, you know, and I'd advise a snug estate, against a father who might not care to own him."

"I will tell ALL, as I have prepared for all!" exclaimed the woman, laughing hysterically. "Now, Plato Wynne, learn that you were deceived, indeed. The children of the dying mothers and absent fathers WERE changed! Ask this man — "

"Since you will out with it, I can't deny what I know," said Ketchum. "By the aid of the lady now my wife we made the exchange one night. — But I'm afraid this will make bad work."

"And your child died," proceeded Elfie, with increasing wildness. "Do you hear me? — it died the next morning in its false home. I never dared tell you after that; for by my act I had put it beyond your power to reap, without wrong, the benefit of that death. I changed the children because I believed that you would kill a son of your own; but, with power to prove that the child was *not* your own, I could, in the last extremity, make known the truth and keep your hand from murder. For you — for YOU, more than for myself, I have repaired the wrong, and saved you no less from the guilt of a useless crime than from the ven-

geance of him whose child I stole away. You can turn pale now, Plato Wynne. You can show some human feeling now, when you find yourself a victim of deception indeed! When I gave the child its true father's first name, you did not suspect me; when you took me to that mirror in yonder room to show me who you loved and who you hated best, you did not suspect that your culminating contempt would send me to the true father of the boy you thought your own, — to confess all the guilt as mine, to beg that the father would seek out his son in secret, and to save you from retribution! All the misery and real perils of my deception have been mine; none yours. I have delayed this confession until it must be made, — until my act of reparation to the youth we both have wronged has become my vindication and my farewell to you."

I had listened to her half-delirious words, with the heart in my bosom throbbing, and rising in my throat. They were but incoherent sounds after the one tremendous thought given me by the first sentence; yet I stood paralyzed until she was silent. Then, seeing no one but her, and her only as a figure that could tell me the one thing I dared not anticipate, I grasped her by a wrist and spoke, —

"I am not the son of this man?"

"No."

"Who is my father?"

"Avery Goodman."

I was a strange apparition to appear hatless and gasping at a merchant's front door at night, and burst madly into the hall the very moment the latch was turned. I was an alarming apparition to ask a deaconly servant where his master was, and almost choke him on the spot for taking so long to say, "In-n-n the l-library." I was a most muscular, agile, and presumptuous apparition to fairly carry that deaconly servitor up the broad stairs before me, and then brush spectrally past him into a grand room of book-walls where sat the gravest, most benignant watcher that ever waited ghosts from the dim past.

"My father!" I cried, my whole heart and soul moving to their first sanctified utterance of the name.

"My boy! my son!" spoke the loving lips and outstretched hands; and I threw myself into his arms, crying like the petted child I was at last.

"My dearest son," came the words of joy and blessing, "I heard all from the strange, unfortunate woman who has opened your eyes to-night. She has been my visitor even since I first saw you; giving me proofs of what she revealed, speaking remorselessly of herself; pleading for the ignorance of her unworthy husband, and making me promise to let her be the first to tell you of her crime. God help her! she has sinned deeply. But in realizing this wonderful happiness made ours at last, — in resolving to forget what has been darkest and evil in the past,—we shall have none but charitable thoughts for the erring and unhappy one who, in your helpless days, stood to you in the place of a — mother."

The loving voice trembled with emotion. I lifted my head from his breast and followed his glance to the portrait of a woman on the wall. A tall and queenly woman, with tender eyes and curling golden hair, looking down upon us; the pensive face taking a semblance of life from the quivering radiance of the study-lamp.

CHAPTER LII.

A SACRIFICE.

Mr. Chucks, the famous boatswain of Captain Marryatt, had such strong aspirations to gentility, such inveterate detestation of the plebeian condition and associations to which he was confined by lowly birth and education, that when a train of fortuitous circumstances suddenly raised him to high rank at last, the transition seemed too natural to cause him one awkward or overbalancing sensation. The one arbitrary conclusion, that I was the son of a gentleman, went far, as I have shown in earlier pages, to sustain the courage and self-respect of my boyhood against a host of sinister family mysteries. Acting as an instinct, it was the unrecognized providence ever deterring me from assimilation with the coarse and vitiated elements of my fugitive life with Reese; and only when its refutation, through the researches of the Reverend Mr. Beeton, seemed incontestable, did I have my first experience of real demoralization. The loss of personal tone and pitch following that refutation did not, however, quite lower me to absolute content in a vagabond existence. I never could feel entirely satisfied, or at home, in the life which my calmest reason still told me was the best I could hope for. And when, finally, one unannounced and blinding flash of truth blazed through the thick clouds of a life-long delusion, to reveal to me the fullest consummation of the hope so long buried alive, I but closed my dazzled eyes for a moment and then looked upon the translation as something quite natural and exactly suited to my merits. Whether the presence in my veins of the colonial Goetman's blood had anything to do with this facility of adaptation and its preceding phenomena is a sanguinary question for whoever chooses to consider it. Having known the genealogized vital current of an expatriated English horse-thief to produce the most aristocratic and unbearable peculiarities in more than one modern Virginian and Carolinian, I feel a certain delicacy about claiming an advantage over Mr. Chucks by virtue of my sanguineous legacy from the original High-Dutch grantees of Terrapin Island. It still remains true, however, that, like the memorable boatswain, I marched suddenly from comparative nonentity into positive gentility without any embarrassment whatever; and arose from my first night's rest under the roof of a long-lost father with sensations not much more violently strange than might have visited any vivacious young gentleman after his first night home from the country.

Such being the case, I am spared the task of detailing the rather tiresome emotions generally awakened by an abrupt transition in life, and may return to the progressive business of my narrative without farther sentimentalizing.

Behold me, then, on my last trip to that seat of tremendous power, known as the *Earthquake* office; there to resign all share and title in the literary pride of the age, and relinquish a quill which had done average credit to its native goose. Scarcely more gratified with my altered fortunes than with the opportunity to teach Mr. Easton Sharp that the editor he had presumed to neglect somewhat of late could afford to decline the further honor of his employment, I held my head unusually stiff as I walked, and worked my mind into a goodly contempt of everything below wholesale dry goods. But the additional presence of a truly great man was fated to rather qualify the superiority of my demeanor toward the former postmaster of Milton; for I found General Cringer earnestly consulting, pen in hand, with that versatile personage. Both being interested in the paper, however, their consultation did not deter me from entering the compartment where they sat, and nodding familiarly to them as one who really found himself quite well, he thanked them.

"Ah, Glibun!" cried Mr. Sharp, before I could say a word, "you're the very one we want to see."

"That's very true," added the General; "and you're looking remarkably well."

"And I am here particularly to see you, gentlemen," said I; "so we have a coincidence."

They were sitting on either side a table, General Cringer having some sheets of paper before him; and it occurred to me at once that some important project must be under consideration.

"Perhaps, then, you have heard of the change we propose making?" insinuated Mr. Sharp, reaching into a pocket for the jack-knife without which he was conversationally nothing.

"I am aware of no other change, sir, than the one I design making myself."

I said it pretty loftily, that attention might be paid to my purpose at once; but, after one jab with the knife at the arm of his chair, Mr. Sharp crossed his knees, tilted his chair back from the table and his tall hat over his nose, and addressed me as though I had answered nothing.

"Mr. Glibun, we propose turning the *Earthquake* into a Demolition evening journal, to support Mr. John Bull, now President of the Board of Councilmen, for the Mayoralty."

"Demolition!" I ejaculated, surprised into temporary forgetfulness of my own business. "That *is* a change, to be sure. I shouldn't think it would suit the most fastidious."

"Why, no." struck in General Cringer, with a fatherly smile; "it may not strictly jibe with the narrow prejudices of the violent partisan, or the illiberal fanatic; but when a great principle of local government is to be sustained, and the civic rights of our large alien population secured, it becomes a duty of incorruptible journalism to soar above all traditional party trammels and support him only, who can — in fact — who can command the Irish vote."

That "Sir, said Dr. Johnson" air of his, made me conclude, as on former occasions, that he could be enunciating nothing but the most sonorous moralities, and I exchanged smiles of admiration with Mr. Sharp.

"If I, in my capacities of republican citizen and journalist, can facilitate the elevation of a self-made man to the most important of municipal offices and emoluments," pursued the great oracle, pointing modestly to himself with his pen, "it is my duty to forget every past political affiliation at war with that object, and remember only that the Noble Workingman, the fugitive from British tyranny abroad, chooses to make this great metropolis a Demolition city, and will have a Mayor of no other stripe. Mr. Editor Graham says in the *Daily Bread* of this morning, that Mr. Bull was once an extensive dog-proprietor in the purlieus. I regret to oppose Mr. Graham, with whom I have hitherto labored humbly in unison; but I cannot admit that humble origin and a fondness for the honest watchdog's bark are disqualifications for office in a land like ours. Such monarchical sentiments, as I state in an article now under my pen, will cause the great Irish heart of America to throb with indignation."

"Well, gentlemen," said I, "accept my best wishes for the success of your policy; but I —"

"Exactly," interrupted the pure-minded friend of the people, nodding as intelligently as though I had completed and rounded my sentence to the last degree of harmonious lucidity. "We shall facilitate the success of Mr. Bull on the broad principle of justice to our alien population. But what we intend shall be the permanent policy of the *Evening Earthquake*, is relentless exposure of the Inadequacy of the System. No man of average penetration and love of country can fail to be aware that the System — the System, gentlemen — is totally Inadequate."

Being obtuse of intellect at the moment, I horribly committed myself by feebly asking, "What System?"

"The whole System, sir!" thundered General Cringer, thumping the table with such force as to arouse Mr. Sharp from a gentle doze. "When we look abroad over this land, and consider everything in all lights whatsoever, are we not immediately impressed with the Inadequacy of the System? The idea is vast, elastic, and comprehensive, and will apply satisfactorily to everything for which there is no other explanation. Why does not the United States Government at once say to Great Britain, Give down-trodden Ireland her freedom? Because the System is Inadequate! Why are not our Indian wars at once ended by an immediate conversion of all the Indians to Christianity and the cultivation of maize or Indian corn? On account of the Inadequacy of the System. Why are our worthy poor less gifted with pecuniary superfluities than the rich? For no other reason than the glaring failure of the System to be Adequate. Why is anything what anybody could call defective? Solely in consequence of a System far from Adequacy. In fact," continued the incorruptible sage, in a glorious burst of enthusiasm, "the Inadequacy of the System is an answer to every possible conundrum; and in a conscientious hammering upon it, day after day, I behold the most deadly bore that ever wooed success to a leading daily journal — "

"Never offending the most fastidious," murmured Mr. Sharp, in soft and sympathetic ecstasy.

"Giving a mellow tone to public sentiment," urged General Cringer.

"Advertisements pouring in," piped Sharp.

"And the progress of American civilization facilitated," concluded the General.

It seemed a pity that I could not take part, subordinately, even, in this admirably original scheme of public edification; but there was really no choice for me in the matter, and I felt compelled to tell them so.

"When you interrupted me a moment ago, General Cringer, I was about to remark that I could no longer continue in this office. Owing to what I may call family-reasons, my future vocation will not be literary. In short, you will please accept my resignation — you and Mr. Sharp — from this week forth, and allow me to withdraw from a business no longer congenial either to my position or tastes, without detriment to our agreeable personal relations."

"Sir!" said General Cringer, elevating his eyebrows, "you are sacrificing a rare opportunity to make your mark upon the age. We had counted upon you for a series of thoughtful epistles from Ireland, upon the connection between British landlords and the potato blight."

"I am sorry to disappoint you, General; but must incur the sacrifice, notwithstanding."

Mr. Easton Sharp, who had exhibited passing symptoms of surprise at the first mention of my determination, now elevated both his feet to the top of the table, and regarded me over the toes of his boots with a mildly pitying smile.

"You propose leaving us this week?" said he, working the blade of his knife with his thumb.

"Yes, sir!"

"Perhaps a couple of dollars a week extra would be about your figure?"

"No, sir!" said I, in great indignation; "nor two hundred dollars; even though they had been manufactured by the late Milton Bank-note Company!" He turned pale at the unexpected shot he had provoked, and could only stare helplessly at me when I added a curt "Good-morning, gentlemen."

At the door I cast back a hasty glance over my shoulder to see whether General Cringer betrayed any signs of discomposure from my rather peculiar farewell; but could detect no change whatever in the contemplative serenity of that great man. He was writing again; his pen ploughing fields of paper and drawn by ox-like thoughts.

Dewitt received me in the second office with a look denoting his knowledge of what had just occurred, and we parted, with many good wishes on his part and a pledge of future friendship on mine.

Another resignation—that of my room in Benedick Place—was the next in order. Some compunction at deserting my literary brethren of Bohemia without verbal leave-taking afflicted my conscience as I hurried up Broadway, and nearly induced a call en route at Solon Tick's; but, upon second thought, it seemed hardly necessary to practise so much social ceremony with gentlemen who would, probably, regard my intellectual retrogression with more contempt than regret. So, I finally gained my old apartment tolerably reconciled to my own last Bohemianism, and proceeded to pack my effects for transportation to upper Broadway, with that not unpleasing flutter of spirits which might have accompanied similar concluding preparations for a first trip to Europe, Asia, or any other geographical dream-land.

"You're off, are you?" said a familiar voice, blending with the creak of the door. "What were you doing with yourself the last two evenings?"

Looking up from the trunk, I beheld the shambling figure of Hardley Church in the doorway, his sharp eyes twinkling inquisitively, and the eternal pipe in his mouth.

"Come in and sit down," said I; "you won't mind my going on, will you? I slept up-town last night."

The literary disciple of Seneca made himself comfortable on the two nearest chairs, and, after a tremendous puff of smoke, asked if he could not help me.

"No, thank you, Churchy. My effects here are not numerous enough to require more than one pair of hands in their packing."

"I hear from Will Dewitt that some domestic reconciliation or other has put you in a way to make your fortune, and you've concluded to neglect letters and cultivate the yardstick."

"I am about to forswear the pen, at any rate," was my guarded answer.

"And all its votaries?"

"That's not a friendly question."

"It's friendly enough as coming from the subscriber," retorted he, with edifying gravity. "I don't know just what change in your circumstances has occurred, Glibun; but if you've found a good home, and relatives who will help you forward in life, I'd advise you to drop me and my kind. I'm in earnest. I like you well enough to hold myself up to you as a 'frightful example.' After you're once out of Bohemia, stay out."

"Why, what has put you so much out of sorts?" I asked, at a loss to account for such language.

"I'm not out of sorts."

"Your talk sounds like it."

"Never mind how it sounds, if you can understand what it means. Since poor 'Baby' died, I've thought more than little about you, Glibun, and made up my mind to talk to you like a father. You're not at all the style of fellow for our kind of life. In the first place, you haven't got the philosophy for it; and, in the second place, you're just the one to find in it, at last, the fate of Le Mons. I don't want to sing hymns over another ruin of youth, and I'm glad that you're not to be such a one."

I sat upon the edge of my trunk and stared at the impecunious philosopher with new interest; for it was plain that he spoke from feelings unusually deep.

"My dear old comrade," said I, "there must be some particular reason for your doleful strain to-day. Have you been 'respectfully declined' this week by any of the papers on account of a press of European matter?"

He gave a laugh and a puff, shook his head, and, to my unspeakable surprise, drew forth a pocket-book which actually seemed to contain money.

"There!" said he, tossing me a couple of bank-bills. "There are the twenty dollars I owed you, and I'm not broken yet. It makes the subscriber serious to have a month's board in his pocket. That's what ails me."

"My dear old Churchy," cried I, "it does my eyes good to see you afflicted in this way; and if you would only let my debt stand until I called for it—"

"You would take it as a friendly favor," added he. "Sorry to disoblige you, but—keep what's your own." A long puff. "Of course you've heard the news?"

I certainly had heard my share of news since last seeing him; but was, nevertheless, impelled to ask, "What news?"

"Of the marriage of our apostolical friend, the bruised Reed."

"Marriage!" I ejaculated, all amazement. "I've heard nothing of it. When did he marry, and whom?"

"At five last evening," answered Church, "and Mag. Dalen."

"Impossible!" was my breathless exclamation. "Some one has been hoaxing you."

"If my senses have not related to me the most astonishing fiction of the age, my boy, I went down to see the happy pair off on their western bridal tour last night; the bride, herself, having invited me; and, by special request from the same artistic source, called at this room to take you along. If my memory is not the particular failure of the century, I wished health and happiness to the departing twain, not forgetting a venerable African servitor in their train, and received from Mrs. Reed my full pay for the dramatic gem called 'Tomyrus.' You've seen the money for yourself, and it is only left for you to hear that both Daphnis and Chloe charged me with their kindest regards."

"Then," rejoined I, vehemently, "my early antagonism to Ezekiel Reed was just, and he has always been a canting hypocrite. Married to an actress! Upon my word, Church, it's the most astonishing thing I ever heard."

I really felt it like a personal injury, and spoke with hot indignation. Perhaps I felt it as a disappointment, too; for, in spite of my early hostility, the apparently saintly turn of Ezekiel's character had worked its sympathetic effect upon me.

"I thought the business would end so, when I saw them together at the hotel, that night," said the philosopher, smiling cynically through a smoke-wreath. "He was too much the proselyting saint, and she too much the penitent sinner (until supper time) to be very far from a partnership. Oh, but she's an actress! Nothing could be finer in a professional way than the simple manner in which she said to me, just before they started, 'I've taken your play Mr. Church, but I shall never act again. Tell your friend, Mr. Glibun, that I've a friend now who will make me good.'"

"And do you believe she ever will play again?" inquired I, beginning to feel regretful.

"In less than six months. I know her."

"Reed must be insane."

"There you hit the mark," said Church. "But his is an insanity with which you and I will never be afflicted. All I know of him personally is what I saw of him at my sickbed; but a son of old Sewall, a Nassau Street lawyer, tells me that Reed studied law in his father's office and gave some signs of his lunacy there."

"I've seen Mr. Sewall," interrupted I.

"Let me finish my story. Reed had a sister, it seems, whose little property from her deceased mother did not make her altogether comfortable; so what does Reed do, but make over his share to her also, by aid of the lawyer, and nearly starved himself to death until the sister died. Sewall says that the salary from the law-office barely paid for the young man's lodging; and that, as the old man afterwards discovered, he would sometimes have nothing to eat but crackers for days. The crazy part of the business was, that our friend Ezekiel made his sister believe the money came from some distant uncle, so that she might take it; and then came near going mad with melancholy at thought of having practised a falsehood."

"But there is no such spirit as that — call it what you please — in the coarse folly of marrying a dissolute player," I burst forth again, freshly irritated by the conflict of ideas. "Could such a stern morality as Reed has pretended to, have any sympathy for a nature impure, I may almost say, by profession? Such miserable infatuation now, indicates hypocrisy of some degree in the past. Ezekiel Reed marry Mag. Dalen!"

"When you are as old and as wicked as the subscriber," answered the father of Bohemia, "you will find less to surprise you in the vagaries of saints and sinners. There's no fool so invariably foolish in his life as the man of genius; and what is our evangelical young friend but a moral genius? The moment I looked at him last evening, I knew that genius had made an ass of itself, as usual; I knew that he had deliberately thrown more than his life away on an impracticable idea. The hungry, pleading loneliness was in his eyes still; there was no love-sickness about him, I assure you; but in both look and demeanor was the spell of an infatuation worse than any love you ever heard of. The man thinks to save a soul by what he has done. He glories in winning public contempt, and the scorn even of his own straightlaced kind, — in sacrificing the best hopes and best name of youth, — for the sake of a woman whom he thinks to save thus from the devil. He's mad, of course; but there's a methodism in his madness."

<hr>

CHAPTER LIII.

UNCONQUERED.

My social début in the proper name and character of which I had been so long defrauded, created a very pretty sensation. There were those at first who evinced a disposition to be preternaturally sceptical over the long-lost son theory, and plume themselves upon a vaguely-hinted knowledge of some by-gone romance in the great merchant's history; but they were chiefly the lately-enriched fashionables of the day, who, being still on probation, as it were, and not yet admitted to the full confidences of the standard élite, found great provocation to such scepticism in the very meagre explanation they had obtained respecting the older mystery of the adopted daughter. With a free, unembarrassed air; with a demeanor expressing nothing more than calm paternal satisfaction and a frank readiness to be congratulated, my father introduced me simply as a son who, from infancy, had been unfortunately lost to him; adding, in reply to the allowable inquiries of intimate friends, such particulars of my story as were necessary to prevent extravagant misconceptions. At the same time, he judiciously and incidentally divulged such further facts concerning his lovely ward as were requisite to remove all remaining uncertainties as to her identity; and the near friends favored with these confidences lost no time in repressing the more impertinent quips and questions of the gossips.

Thus was I enabled to become a highly interesting "lion" without subjection to the close criticism, or investigation, which might have afflicted me under a siredom of less assured immaculateness; yet the sensation occasioned by my appearance was unmistakable, and the most decorous of people regarded me with a curiosity not to be excluded from their eyes, however silent upon their tongues.

The irrepressible enterprise of journalism could not, of course, be expected to overlook my case, and the *Sunday Tap* displayed its usual delicate interest in the higher social occurrences by promptly publishing a most romantic version of my adventures. "Remarkable Haps and Mishaps of the Son of a Merchant-Prince," was the piquant caption of this choice biographical revelation, in which the excellent Mr. Jenkins, Reporter, politely refrained alike from full names and veracity. "As the parties to this o'er-true tale are all living," wrote Mr. Jenkins, with rather needless accuracy on that point, "we shall carefully refrain from giving names, contenting ourselves by merely stating, that our hero, Mr. A--ry Gl-b-n, as he called himself for a time, is not entirely unknown in literary circles under a *nom de plume* playfully significant of cranial vacuity; that the famous personage to whom from infancy he rendered mistaken filial regard may be fancifully represented either by the letters Pl-to W-nne, or the formula K-ng of D--m--ds; and that the mercantile celebrity regaining a son whose very existence came not within his previous knowledge is sufficiently disguised from annoying recognition by the imperfect word, G--dm-n." The sensibilities of all parties being thus thoughtfully saved from the rude shock of notoriety in print, Mr. Jenkins's masterpiece of fashionable intelligence at once developed into a perfect marvel of fragmentary fact and diseased imagination; an entirely new adventure, of a trip to Europe as cabin-boy, being added to my narrated vicissitudes.

But the most trying penalty of my sudden good fortune was yet to come. One morning, about a fortnight after the above feat of journalism, the daily papers informed all New York that Plato Wynne was a murderer! Readers were requested to remember the finding, by some laborers, of a dead body in a wood, at Hoboken, several weeks before. A verdict of suicide had been rendered by the coroner's jury, deceased hav-

ing been found still holding a recently discharged pistol proved to be his own. Soon after the rendering of the verdict, however, one of the finders of the body confessed to the police that he had also found a gentleman's handkerchief near the fatal spot, and, supposing it belonged to the dead man, had intended no harm in keeping it. Upon learning, however, that the name of the supposed suicide was Vane, whilst the name of "Hastings Cutter" was worked upon the handkerchief, he had thought it best to make known the discovery. Cutter being the name of a young man notoriously frequenting one of the most luxurious "club-houses" in the city; deceased having also been an habitué there; and covert report hinting that an exciting rencounter had occurred at said "club-house" recently; the police authorities believed that the handkerchief would prove a clue to some new development; and, carefully avoiding such publicity as might tend to defeat the ends of justice, proceeded to make close and secret search of the wood in which the body had been found. Three other pistols (one still foul with a recent discharge), and two cases, were discovered among the undergrowth, as though hastily deposited there for temporary secrecy; and it then seemed plain that Mr. Vane had not fallen by his own hand. Next followed a police search for Mr. Cutter, who, however, was not to be found in the city. A description of him was sent to other cities; with the recent result of his arrest in Boston by a detective named Trackum, and his return to New York in close custody. Upon being interrogated by the proper magistrate, the prisoner had at once volunteered to turn state's evidence, and confessed having acted as a kind of "second" in a hasty duel between the unfortunate Mr. Vane and Mr. Plato Wynne,—the fire of the latter proving instantly fatal.

Such was the wording of this startling piece of news, and tremendous was the popular excitement kindled thereby. The King of Diamonds — the monarch of chance — the all-powerful leader of the great Demolition party — the rival of the mighty Cringer for absolute possession of the Empire State — a man to be vulgarly arrested for crime? Could the mighty maker of aldermen, mayors, congressmen, legislators, governors, and senators, be amenable to the police? No wonder the people were electrified; no wonder that Mr. Graham, with a political magnanimity quite uncommon in a partisan, at once declared, in the first editorial column of his *Daily Bread*, that he stood ready to be bailsman for Mr. Wynne as soon as the latter should be arrested. It was hinted by the wags that the amiable editor's fastidiousness in dress was an explanation of his super-political sympathy with the best dresser in the city; but graver thinkers credited a loftier sentiment in the case, — until it suddenly flashed upon everybody that the King of Diamonds had grievously failed to make a senator of the Honorable Mealy O'Murphy! With that spasmodic recollection came an amazing and instantaneous popular reaction: Plato Wynne was *not* so great a power as he had been; he had lost his prestige; had he not lost even that great all-night game at Faro? After him! hunt him down! let no judge fear him! let no district attorney dread his political vengeance! Try him, convict him, hang him!

I could not avoid a very evident agitation of mind at such an explanation of the last ominous words I had heard from him who so long had seemed to be my parent; and, with a characteristic thoughtfulness in my behalf, my good and true father at once suggested the only relief that seemed practicable.

"My dear Avery," he said, after watching the changes in my countenance as I read the startling news, "I see that you feel this terrible business keenly. But endeavor to strengthen yourself with the reflection that it is likely to be your last trial from that quarter. The race of this audacious man is surely run; the time when political autocracy could save him from the penalty of any crime has gone by; and you may regard this last, crowning wickedness, as the end of his dark career. I can sympathize with you, however, in your natural dread of the annoying interest which will attach to yourself from this new exposure. I have been proud of the wonderful discretion you have shown thus far in meeting the ordinary embarrassments of your new position; but do not expect you to be equally composed under a trial so much greater. Perhaps, my dear boy, it will be well for you to travel abroad for a while, until the first excitement of this miserable affair is over, and public curiosity has lost its edge."

I was sitting with my father in his own room when he spoke thus to me, and took time to reflect upon my situation and his words before answering, —

"That would leave you, sir, to bear much curious impertinence for me."

"I shall not mind it," said he, smiling; "but I am glad to have a son so thoughtful of me."

"I should prefer what seems to me the manlier course," returned I, inspired by his tranquil dignity. "With your consent I will remain in the city, and lessen whatever ordeal may be in store, by boldly challenging it at once. I should be scarcely worthy to call myself your son, sir," I added, in a quite heroic glow, "if I adopted any other plan."

"My dear boy! you make me prouder of you every day."

"And, my dear father, to show you that I am in earnest, I shall go at once to call upon Mrs. Fish."

He laughed so heartily at my energy that my courage became something desperate, and I could scarcely make haste enough to confront the inquisitive world at once.

Mrs. Cornelius O'Doricourt Fish, a lady of style in one of the fashionable cross-streets just below Union Park, had recently inaugurated a series of informal morning receptions, the scene being an elegant little upper room which she delighted to call her boudoir. There, enthroned upon a delicate pink sofa, did Mrs. C. O'D. Fish dispense curtain-tinted smiles and conversational piquancies to such morning callers as were not too stately to be "entirely unceremonious for once in life;" and there had I more than once, already, received the welcome due to my romantic fame. To go thither at such a crisis was to face and confound Queen Gossip on her very throne; and hence my quick resolve.

I had but just said "good-morning" to my father however, and was hastening, hat in hand, through the lower hall, when a servant informed me that a gentleman desired to see me in the parlor, at the same time handing me a card. Not waiting to look at the latter, I strode immediately into the room designated, ready to give the untimely guest a cool reception; but all my irritation vanished at sight of my old and poetical friend, Mr. Coffin. There he sat upon a chair, in a crab-like attitude of self-distrust, his fiery brain sustaining its usual combustion of smoky-yellow hair, and both hands hanging into the hat between his sharp knees.

"I — I — really beg your pardon, Mr.. Gl—, I should say, Mr. Goodman," stammered he, tumbling up to meet me. "I should not have intruded but for —"

"Not another word of apology from you, my old friend Coffin," interrupted I, as I shook hands and forced him back into his chair, "or I'll conclude that you take me for somebody else. I'm glad to see you, though you've not been very friendly since we were store-mates."

"I'm glad you're glad to see me," replied the lace-salesman, still in a nervous flutter. "I'm proud to hear it from a man of your mind. I congratulate you, Mr. Goodman, and am delighted to find you enjoying an eminence suited to your intellect."

In looking at him I had an odd consciousness of receiving a very anxious return-look somewhere about the middle of my face instead of in my eyes; and I could not help asking the good old fellow if he found my features much changed.

"If you'll excuse an old friend for saying it," said he, still maintaining the glance, as though fascinated in it, "I don't find your — *will* you excuse it? — your nose, just what I expected."

"My nose, Mr. Coffin!"

"Yes-s," he faltered, raising his eyes to mine, by a desperate push, as it were.

In some alarm I passed one of my hands over the honorable feature in question, to make sure that it had undergone no startling metamorphosis.

"I — I feared," stuttered Mr. Coffin, his own face in a blaze, "I — I — feared it might be (pardon an old friend's apprehension), it might be a little — red."

The honest, friendly anxiety of his manner and tone were too genuine to excite indignation, and I laughed aloud.

"What ever put such an idea as that into your head?" was my first comment.

"Why, do you know, Mr. Goodman, if you'll permit me to say it as a brother, I'd understood, sir, that the ways of fashion and of fame had caused you to plunge into the — ruby bowl?"

Again I laughed, and begged him to give me his reason, or authority, for believing that.

"I heard it, sir, in the social halls of a friend. Since your elevation to your present pinnacle, Mr. Goodman, you have been, as you probably know, an object of respectful interest to the gleaming throng. While mingling in a portion of that throng, sir, on a late occasion, when you were a subject of — let me say admiring wonder, I heard a very gentlemanly person sigh profoundly. He also shook his head regretfully, and his words concerning you were, 'Ah! it's a pity he — drinks.'"

"I'm infinitely obliged to the gentleman," said I. "What is his name, Mr. Coffin?"

"Mr. Benton Stiles. Quite a celebrated character."

"I shall avail myself of the first opportunity to undeceive Mr. Stiles. But you need have no farther anxiety about me on that score, Mr. Coffin, and we will dismiss the whole nonsensical subject, if you please. Do you ever hear nowadays from our friend Job?"

"It's on Job's account that I've taken the liberty of calling," said he, apparently much relieved, and drawing from one of his pockets a letter. "Here is a letter I received from him yesterday, and, as it encloses a sum of money in payment of his old debts to you, I have come to you with it. Here is the money, Mr. Goodman, and the letter, too, if you would like to look over it."

The epistle stated that Mr. Terky was doing well as secretary of an Insurance Company in Chicago, and concluded, after referring pleasantly to me, as follows : —

"My only trouble just now is a want of
"new clothes; and, as I can't get them here
"to suit my particular taste, I may have to
"trouble you, some time, my dear friend,
"to express me an outfit from New York.
"The fine coat I've got already would do,
"if my wife only had time to mend the tear
"she made in it the other day by trying to
"hang it on a nail by the pocket. She sits
"near me while I write, working a pair of
"fire-screens for a friend, and hasn't a mo-
"ment's leisure for the old clothes of
"yours, gratefully, dear Coffin,
"JOB TERKY."

"You notice that last sentence, do you, Mr. Goodman?" asked the lace-salesman, observing my countenance.

"Yes. Poor Job!"

"But she loves him so!"

"No doubt of it."

The laureate of Cummin & Tryon softly put away the letter, shook his head, and smiled feebly. "Those were pleasant times around the family hearthstone."

"So they were, so they were," I answered, particularly remembering some of the catastrophes. "By the way, though, Mr. Coffin, how are you all getting on at Cummin & Tryon's?"

"Nothing new, sir. The same unintellectual round of sordid exercises. Our friend Trust, though, is about to seek hymeneal chains."

"In whose company?"

"A Miss Becton's. Daughter of an intelligent clergyman."

"Ah!"

"And I'm engaged, Mr. Goodman!" exclaimed Mr. Coffin, in a great burst of confidence.

"Not to the widow of the gentleman with a glass — "

"No, sir!" interrupted he, rubbing up his hair with both hands. "That ideal of my youth expired when I saw her eating tropical fruit — or you saw her — on a public gangway. She who established the first mutual bond between you and me is the prize of my riper years. I was introduced to her by Mr. Trust, and her name is Miss Aloize Green."

"Coffin," cried I, "accept my heartiest congratulations. I once had the pleasure of a brief acquaintance with the lady, and shall expect an invitation to the wedding."

Being in a rather sheepish and lover-like confusion after his impulsive confession, the salesman was too modest to risk another word about so delicate a theme; and, having feverishly chased his hat around several chairs, and thumped his head against a table, begged leave to retire.

"I'm going down a couple of squares," said I, "and will bear you company that far."

We went out together, and, when we parted, I saw him dart one last, unspeakably satisfied look at the feature with which I had so agreeably disappointed him.

Now for a trial of my nerves, thought I, pulling on my gloves as I turned into the street where reigned the matron-royal of small talk; now for a prize exhibition of that proud confidence which illustrates conscious innocence and loses nothing by a little preparatory practice in Bohemia. If you have callers before me this morning, most amiable lady, you are probably discussing my case already, and I hope you will not risk your reputation for intuitive sagacity by predicting for me too much discomposure at the latest exploit of my late putative sire.

The presentation of my card by a servant in footman's livery procured my immediate admittance to the luxurious matinal lair of Mrs. Fish, whose manner of welcoming me was so elaborately impressive that I at once detected a disguised perturbation in it.

" Mr. Goodman, I am most happy to see you."

" You honor me, Mrs. Fish. Have I the pleasure of finding you entirely recovered from your recent indisposition? " (Reported as the loss of a false tooth.)

"Quite recovered, thank you."

And then followed my formal presentation to a Miss Keeter, a Miss Meeta Hyer, and a French-looking gentleman, introduced as M. Adam Feuil, who were also callers.

"Minette, place a chair for Mr. Goodman." This to an attendant lady's maid, with a fluttering top-knot of pink ribbons to match the sofa.

The sofa, by the way, stood at an angle between the wall and a window overlooking the street, and, as I wished to carry my assurance to the highest perfection, I promptly drew my chair so near to the window that I almost touched the lady as she sat with studied negligence upon her bank of roses. Furthermore, I occupied my hand with the crimson window-curtains in an elegantly indolent way; experimenting, as it were, with their transfixed blushes, upon the brown locks, hazel eyes, and faded cheeks of Mrs. Fish, alternately.

" Really, ladies," said I, buoyantly, " were it not for M. Feuil's presence here, I should accuse myself of having interrupted some delightfully private consultation on the fate of mankind as affected by the latest inspiration in bonnets."

" Fie, Mr. Goodman!" cried the hostess. "I didn't expect a repetition of that wicked old libel from you." And she giggled.

" It ces slandaire, I think," remarked M. Adam Feuil, evidently convinced that he had said something neat.

"Perhaps bonnets do affect the fate of mankind," simpered Miss Hyer, not unaware that she wore a rather fatal one herself.

Miss Keeter said, " Oh, you!" and tapped her with a parasol.

"I intended nothing ungallant," said I, producing a red focus on Mrs. Fish's nose. " Since ladies are so tyrannically excluded from all active interest in matters of utility, they cannot do better than devote themselves to the details of the beautiful."

"There! We can forgive you after that, Mr. Goodman."

" Forgiveness so charmingly given, Mrs. Fish, is a temptation to err often for the sake of it."

"Oh! Oh! Oh!" Angelic chorus.

" To air is humane, to forgeef deevine," quoted M. Adam Feuil, with some knowledge of English literature.

" Don't you think, Mr. Goodman, — he! he! " (from Miss Keeter) " that ladies might vote? "

" Ah, why do you ask me that, Miss Keeter? Shall I lose, hopelessly lose, your good opinion, when I answer in the negative? You ladies are so delightfully impulsive in all your ways that you would vote for a handsome beard, or a pair of piercing black eyes, at sight. I positively fear that the first full female vote would send Mr. Plato Wynne to the White House."

I said it purposely, and with a smiling countenance, determined to show them at once that my coxcombry was proof against any possible revival of my past associations; and the little screams with which they answered had as much real surprise at my audacity as affected horror of my sentiments in them.

But, not to let that subject go a word farther, I cast my glance through the window, intending to say next, " What a fine view you have here! " and I saw, —

A shabby, decrepit old woman had caused an omnibus to stop for her, and was stooping to lift her heavy basket from the sidewalk. At the moment, a gentleman appeared beside her, lifted the burden from her hands, and, motioning for her to follow, carried it to the vehicle. She seemed to protest against such condescension, and to utter thanks until she had entered the omnibus and received her basket again. Then the omnibus started on, and, after lifting his hat, the gentleman, instead of returning to the sidewalk he had left, kept on across the street directly toward the house in which I was.

With womanly quickness, Mrs. Fish had noticed the change in my countenance as I looked, and, upon moving along her sofa to the window, was as effectually enchained by the sight.

" He's coming here — he's actually coming here!" was her first exclamation, as she turned, pale and dismayed, from the window.

" Who? Who? "

" Mr. Wynne!"

The announcement struck them all dumb. They could only look at each other, and (covertly) at me, in mute helplessness.

"My dear love," said Mrs. Fish, in sheer desperation, addressing Miss Keeter, the youngest of the party, " won't you run down and tell him I'm not at home? I daren't trust Minette to do it; but he don't know you, and you could say it naturally. I wouldn't ask such a thing, my dear, but I'm nearly fainting."

Poor little Miss Keeter blushed and then lost all color, but finally hastened from the room like a heroine; and, as she left the door open, we all instinctively held our breath to listen. We heard the bell tinkle, the street-door open, and the sound of a subdued manly voice, followed by a feminine murmur. Silence ensued for an instant, and then we heard, deliberately and very distinctly spoken, the words, —

"My dear, how prettily you lie! "

In two moments thereafter the foot of Allyn Vane's murderer was on the sill of the boudoir, and he entered, as he had done more than once before, with his irreproachable bow and smile.

Mrs. Cornelius O'Doricourt Fish might have been a vain, weak, trifling woman when vanity, weakness, and trifles were her only incitements; but she could be equal to an emergency, too, and the present one found her no less capable because her first device had so signally failed.

"Mr. Wynne," she said, rising as he came in, and speaking very haughtily, "I am pained to see that you have disregarded the message I sent to the door. I am not at home to you, sir. Minette, show Mr. Wynne the way down."

Approvingly glanced the King of Diamonds at the lady's maid for an instant, and then back at the mistress, as though worshipping her taste in everything.

"Madam," he said, with courtly ease and readiness, "if I am compelled to leave Eden, it is in accordance with illustrious precedent that a member of your sex should show the way."

Then bowed most airily to us all, and went forth a conqueror.

----⁅----

CHAPTER LIV.

THE select circulation in society of about a dozen yellow cards, mysteriously announcing that Mrs. Charles Spanyel would give a yellow dinner-party on such an afternoon, at the Spanyel Place, Todeville, Huckle-bury-on-Harlem, caused a social flurry allied to dismay. A dozen cards would not, of course, go quite around the upper circles, and non-receivers were at liberty to pretend supreme indifference; but, upon those who did receive, it was incumbent to understand what a yellow banquet might be. Its European character seemed evident, from the facts that the Spanyels boasted great English ancestors who came over with King Charles, and that the entertainment was known to be partly in honor of a European daughter of Mr. Spanyel, who had just arrived from Great Britain with her husband, Mr. Lord. Therefore, a failure to comprehend what a yellow dinner-party might be, was equivalent to a confessed ignorance of the most illustrious imported usages of New York society, and dire was the consternation of the invited at finding themselves thus vulgarly unenlightened. Before the day of the jaundiced meal, however, an aged lady who was descended from one of the first families of Washington Market, and had gone the whole round of the most exclusive high life in her day, allowed herself to be coaxed into the statement that the aristocratic old Von Rumsellers had once given a pink supper in her time, founded upon the colored feasts of the Dowager Lady Cork, so famous in literary annals, and that it was true to its hue in dresses, table-covers, china, liveries, and wines.

What a flood of light came with that reminiscence; what a relief to a dozen despairing minds! Orders for yellow dresses were issued immediately; the uninvited were delicately tantalized with aggravating bits of semi-intelligence concerning the coming Event, and sallow complexions became enviable.

But the Spanyels intended something more than honor to Mr. and Mrs. Lord by their stylish little entertainment. They also, and quite particularly, designed it as a pleasant intimation that the wooden house, once their only home, was now but their suburban villa, whither they resorted for the summer alone, and where a select little dinner-party was a tasteful inauguration of their out-of-town season. For Mr. Charles Spanyel had greatly prospered since the days when Todeville knew his homeward step every day in the year; had successfully gone into business for himself, making comfortable sums by the fluctuations in imported hosiery, and had purchased a nobby town-house for occupation in fashionable months.

April and I were among the recipients of the yellow cards (my father having regretted his inability to accept with us), — our romantic celebrity making us invaluable prizes for such an occasion; and the paternal carriage bore us through Hucklebury-on-Harlem, past the cosey "Spanyel Arms," and so to Todeville, at about an hour before sunset on the day appointed. Perhaps the temptation to appear publicly as the especial cavalier of my beautiful companion had rather more to do with my journey thither than the attractions of Todeville itself; yet the opportunity to gratify a family of historical European antecedents was not to be despised, even by a Goodman!

"Little did I think, April," observed I, as we rode on between green fields and suburban woods, — "little did I think, when I met Mr. Spanyel in the parlor on that first evening, and heard him asking for your company at Mrs. Spanyel's dinner, that I should be your escort thither."

"Ah, I was wiser about you at that time, Avery, than you were about yourself," answered April, laughingly, "for your father had told me half the story that very day."

"What an experience mine has been!" ejaculated I.

"And how happily concluded," she said, more seriously. "What a father you have found!"

"I am blessed indeed, dear April. I think my calmness under such happiness may be partially owing to my incapacity for realizing it all. To find you again, as you are, is in itself like an incredible dream."

"I could wish to be much better than I am, dear brother, for then I might hope to make worthier return for all the noble goodness of my guardian."

"You will never leave him, April?" cried I, taking one of her hands, and looking earnestly into her gentle eyes. "You will never leave us?"

"Your father must determine that, Avery."

"And why not let me determine it, dear girl! Why not become a daughter to him you love and honor so, by — "

But we were at the villa of the Spanyels too soon for the remainder of that impassioned question; and, as I hastily relinquished the warm and tremulous little hand, a servile yet lofty being, in a gorgeous yellow coat and shoulder-knots, opened the door of the carriage and ushered us to a shady piazza and hall. What could we do but surrender to this untimely sun-flower at discretion, and follow him to where a brother-blossom of equal size and glare received our names for announcement? Surrender we did, with a most hypocritical pretence of being merely upon polite terms with each other, for if sentimental appearances are ever unspeakably out of place, it is when a dinner impends.

Behold us, then, following our names into a room already lively with ladies in yellow dresses and gentlemen in yellow cravats and gloves, where, upon a yellow sofa, a yellow Mrs. Spanyel fervently received us, supported by her affable lord and master. Then came introductions to Mr. and Mrs. Lord, from London; Mr. and Mrs. Gannayee (as the name sounded); Miss Rose Spanyel, Miss Lily, Mr. Benton Stiles (whom I eyed sharply), and a petite Miss Peller. I also had the pleasure of greeting Mr. and Mrs. Cornelius O'Doricourt Fish, Mr. Luke Hyer, junior, and Miss Meeta Hyer; and, in a few moments thereafter, witnessed the arrival of the stately and venerable Mrs. Heroldun, escorted by a tame young clergyman from Cambridge, named Reverend T. Spooner.

"I hope you found your drive pleasant, sir," said Mr. Spanyel, when I had resigned April to the hostess.

"Charming, sir; and I have seldom enjoyed a ride to a more charming spot than Todeville."

"Excuse me, Mr. Goodman, — Toe-der-veal," corrected Mr. Spanyel, mildly, yet firmly; for I had unthinkingly pronounced the name as though it were closely concerned with that familiar reptile which, although ugly and venomous, is poetically credited with wearing yet a precious jewel in its head.

"I beg your pardon, sir, — Toe-der-veal."

Before I could say more, the very obese and very florid Mr. Gannayee was good enough to step in between us; for the purpose, undoubtedly, of giving an agreeable topic for our discussion.

"Is it thrue, now, Misther Spanyel," said he, with Tuscan accent, "that you bought this place, as I'm towld, from Plato Wynne?"

"Ah-b-h, yes, Mr. Gannayee, y-yes, sir," stammered the other, aghast at the awkward question. "You'll excuse me, if I ask you once more, Mr. Gannayee, what your exact majority was, last week, for comptroller? You probably know, Mr. Goodman, that Mr. Gannayee is our new comptroller?"

"I am happy to congratulate him," returned I, coolly enough to allay Mr. Spanyel's agitation on my account. "You received some thirteen thousand more votes than your competitor, Mr. Gannayee, if I remember rightly?"

"Sure, and Knickerbocker was a fool to run against me," replied the eminent official. "He was bate wance before, running for Congress against O'Murphy; and now he's caught it again."

Which bit of political history suddenly revived a dark political recollection of my own, and ended my share of the odd conversation.

"Miss Hyer," said I, turning to that young lady, "have you heard Stefanone in 'Lucrezia,' yet?"

"Yes, Mr. Goodman. And isn't she exquisitely divine?"

"Her dramatic art is very effective in that character; but her voice is not what it must have been once."

"You gentlemen are such perfectly horrid critics about everything! I think she's deliciously lovely in any character."

But let me repeat no more of the conversational horrors always incident to that dreadful half-hour before dinner, when manly wisdom invariably produces abject drivel, and feminine vivacity becomes little more than hysterical entreaty against positively dead silence.

"Dinner waiting," came at last from the lips of a yellow benefactor at the door, and immediately the company divided into such couples as approved usage and Mr. Spanyel dictated.

I was honored with the privilege of escorting our matronly hostess; the Reverend T. Spooner solemnly guarded April; Mr. Stiles protected Miss Spanyel; Mr. Lord squired Miss Lily; and the rest of the company came on in such order as happy accident, or hasty choice, directed.

The scene in the banquet hall was faithfully yellow. The walls were hung with plaited yellow silk; the sideboard of yellow oak was surmounted by the Spanyel arms in very yellow gilt; table-cloth and napkins had unquestionable yellow borders; yellow china and yellow hock-glasses decked the board, around which stood three servile gentlemen from Ireland in yellow coats; and if any impulsive guest had chosen to yell "Oh!" at the sight, there would have been a poetical aptness in that otherwise indecorous burst of feeling. The soup was also yellow; likewise such vegetables as peas and potatoes, which were placed upon yellow mats. The complexions of some of the ladies, too, looked faintly yellow, — but that must have been a reflection from the yellow walls.

By the yellowish light of a swinging lamp over the centre of the table, — for the yellow silk of the walls covered every window, and excluded the nobler radiance of the setting sun, — I was enabled to take my first careful view of the party in detail, and could not but regret that a more becoming tint had not been selected to set off so many fleshy members of polite society. Mrs. Spanyel, Mrs. Lord, and the two Misses

Spanyel, were all of that rotund school of female loveliness which is liable to produce a rather Chinese effect upon the unaccustomed eye when arrayed in yellow silk. Mrs. Gannayee, being adorned, like the comptroller, with a lurid countenance, resembled some huge flower of the dahlia type blooming above a bank of clustered sunflowers; Mrs. Fish, with her flossy brown hair and colorless cheeks, was a lily in the sear and very yellow leaf; and Miss Hyer and Miss Peller were like a pair of plump fairies in the mellow light of an autumnal moon. Of all the ladies, April alone had ventured to appear in colors reconcilable with the tastes most prevalent in her simple native land; and her disregard, in this respect, of high European precedent made her none the less charming to me.

"Wellington," said Mr. Spanyel, addressing Mr. Lord by his first name, "do we strike you as getting along here? Do we seem to have spread on this side the water, after one returns here from a sojourn in the European capitals?"

"You grow; you grow a little all the time, I assho' yo'," returned the son-in-law, who, as Miss Hyer privately informed me, was a British sea-officer.

"You think we do, eh?" continued Mr. Spanyel, earnestly. "You think we expand socially, too, do you?"

"O pa, 'ow perfectly absurd!" remarked Mrs. Lord, languidly. "It's like going into the country to come from London to New York."

"You'll excuse me, Mrs. Lord, if I can't agree with you there," cried Mr. Stiles, with a travelled and philosophical air, at the same time stroking his goatee with a hand on which glittered a vast locket-ring. "I'd agree with you if I could, really; but London don't strike me in that light."

"'Ave you ever parst any time there, Mr. Stiles?" inquired the lady, in a tone of supercilious surprise.

"Once; several years ago."

"It must be perfectly heavenly to cross the absurd ocean," interpolated Miss Hyer, with irrepressible girlish enthusiasm for the grander works of nature.

"And you saw the Tower, St. Paul's, and hother varst edifices?"

"Not that I remember, ma'am."

"No?"

"No!"

"Why, Mr. Stiles, you must be charfing me?"

"Never was more serious, Mrs. Lord."

"And you've been in London?"

"Once; several years ago. But perhaps I should have been more explicit," added Mr. Stiles, smiling agreeably; "perhaps I should have said London—Canada West."

"You ridiculous creature!" exclaimed Miss Rose Spanyel; and we all laughed at the joke.

"It's quite a *mot*, I'm sure," giggled Mrs. Fish.

"Our churches in America," said Mrs. Heroldun, "have neither the dignity nor the support enjoyed by evangelical worship in England."

"Nor the national recognition, madam; nor the national recognition," urged the Reverend T. Spooner, gloomily.

"Now that you're speaking of churches, Mrs. Heroldun," said Mrs. Spanyel, "what has become of that spiritual-minded young clergyman, Mr. Harry Lewyer, who used to be Mrs. Purser's pastor?"

"Going to be married, my dear," sighed the veteran trainer. "Next week he leads a Miss Constance Le Mons to the altar."

"You must look to the thrue Catholic Churruch, ladies, if ye'd find young prastes sinsible enough to forswear matrimony and the divil together," chuckled Mr. Gannayee, whose particularly coarse manners so greatly disgusted me that I could not forbear from whispering indignantly to young Luke Hyer, who sat on my right,—

"What sort of fellow is that, to be in the company of ladies?"

"Used to keep an Irish liquor den, lowest kind. Notorious political striker, as they call it," whispered Luke, disjointedly, in return. "Spells his name Guinesse, now, if he *can* spell. Used to call himself Macginnis."

"Ah? I've heard of him."

Wrongs of Erin! hoary tyrannies so long fating the fine instrument in Tara's hall to inglorious silence, and forbidding its rightful players to go bragh! Crush the Macginnis, if ye will, in the beautiful isle of his birth, and behold him rising again, like a giant refreshed, on a kindlier side of the ocean, to rule the first-cousins of the very same hated Saxons who murdered him entirely at home (which remarkable resurrection may owe some of its credibility to the fact that an Irishman's death is *not* a sleep that knows no "waking").

The banquet drawing to a close after much agreeable talk of the kind related, our fair companions put their lips to dainty goblets of champagne, wherein inverted snow-storms raged in yellow atmospheres, and then returned in glaring procession to the parlor; leaving us, grosser mortals, to revel a while longer over Cliquot, Sherry, and Madeira. Then it was that I hastened to improve my acquaintance with a gentleman of considerable temporary interest to me, leaning across the table to him while our other friends were hotly discussing some political question, and entreating his attention in a stage-whisper,—

"Mr. Stiles, may I ask you to join me in a brief stroll and cigarette out-doors, before we rejoin the ladies? I hear that you drove up from the city this afternoon with a choice animal, and, if there is still light enough, you may not be unwilling to let me see your prize. I have a weakness for horse-flesh."

To which proposition Mr. Stiles assented with alacrity, incidentally observing that the name "Dame Trot" but feebly expressed the progressive genius of the quadruped; that she had the limbs of an expeditious deer, and that —

> "Thus formed for speed, she challeng-ed the wind,
> And left the Scythian Arrow far behind."

"By 'Scythian Arrow,'" added Mr. Stiles, with pardonable pride, "you will understand any square trotter that presumes to try a brush with the 'Dame.'"

But after fairly beguiling my gentleman to a sloping lawn behind the villa, where early twilight refined the landscape to a dreamy sentiment, and made our glowing cigarettes big brothers to the fireflies, I paused with him under the first tree I could find, and spoke as follows, —

"Mr. Stiles, my object in soliciting your company now is *not* to see your horse. I will take your word for the merits of the animal, and am also inclined to compliment you upon the originality and independence you have displayed in coming to a dinner-party in a trotting-wagon *with* yellow wheels. But, to be frank with you, sir, the subject on my mind at present is not equine."

"I shall be happy to give you my attention for any subject of a dinner-party nature," returned he, disdaining to show surprise. But he rather injured the dignity of the remark by adding, — "So you may lay on the gad and holler."

"Then allow me to ask you, sir, upon what grounds you have presumed to circulate an absurd report derogatory to my character for sobriety?"

"Mr. Goodman," responded Mr. Stiles, pushing aside the flaps of his coat, and inserting a thumb in either arm-hole of his white vest, "the grounds upon which you ask the question are so very damp with dew, that a proper regard for my health will not permit me to answer you here. I cannot consent to be catechised under the present dewy circumstances."

"Very well, sir," I retorted, contemptuously; "you choose to evade the inquiry with impertinence. I shall take an early opportunity to exact an explanation by means which may be better adapted to your comprehension."

I turned from him, intending to say no more; but with remarkable quickness of action, he skipped into my way.

"Stop, sir!" cried he, plunging at my right hand with both of his own, and shaking it violently, despite my resistance. "I see how it is, Mr. Goodman; your romantic story, your high position, the heavy odds on you in aristocratic circles, have tempted me to run into you. We'll say no more about it."

"Your jockey-phrases are quite out of place," retorted I, dragging my hand from him by main force; "but you need not fear that I shall *say* anything more on the subject to you. I shall take the liberty of acting, however, and without ceremony."

"Stop, sir!" cried he again. "I have sighed and shaken my head at mention of your name, adding an expression of pity for your intemperate habits."

"Yes, sir. You have been guilty of that slander and impertinence, on one occasion, at least."

"I know I have," rejoined Mr. Benton Stiles, with delightful— I may say enthusiastically trustful —frankness. "I have a confession to make to you—as a friend." Here he swiftly linked his arm in mine and leaned against me in utter abandonment. "Mr. Goodman, you see in me but the wreck of a former top-sawyer—"

"Be good enough to sustain your own weight, Mr. Stiles."

"Certainly, sir, —overpowered by my feelings. As I was saying, former top-sawyer. Once, when fewer years sat lightly on my brow (you'll notice there's a curl there now), I was a man of ton, and a legitimate favorite, sir, of the Fashion Course. Wall Street recognized me as one of its thoroughbreds by day; and, where the lights of evening shone o'er fair women and brave men, I was universally respected as the voluptuous swell of the poet. But, sir, adversity overlapped me on the home-stretch, and crossed the score a neck ahead. I had been too confident, and paid the penalty in being suddenly ruled off the track. I had gambled on the green to a too great extent, and became a broken broker. Then, sir, in the bitterness of my heart I sought to drown reflection in the glass of fashion, and kept myself damp enough for a while to experience a mould of form. I went down, down, until a cheap clerkship completed my humiliation and restricted me to peanuts for lunch."

Here Mr. Benton Stiles brought his hat aslant over one eye by a jerk of his head, and breathed heavily. "Mr. Goodman, how do you suppose I have recovered from that sub-cellar of misfortune, and climbed the ladder of society again? I'll tell you. By saying of every tip-top fashionable character of whose acquaintance I could not boast, but who happened to be named in my presence, — 'It's a pity he drinks!'"

"And have you never been knocked down for the outrage?" I interrupted, hotly.

"Not to my knowledge," replied Mr. Stiles, pleasantly. "Quite the contrary; I've been gradually lifted up for it. Somehow, the remark always proved to be true. It gained me great credit as a disinterested and intimate friend of all the high-spirited young nobs in society; and many of those nobs, having heard what I had said of them, have cultivated me after it, on the supposition that *I* must have been of their party some time or other when they went down among the dead men disgracefully early. Upon my soul, you know!" exclaimed Mr. Stiles, with friendly warmth, "I've said it of fifty elegant young men of fortune, and you're the very first that ever bolted."

There was something so whimsical in the idea and the man, that all my indignation vanished in an irrepressible fit of laughter.

"Really, Mr. Stiles," said I, "it can do me no credit to quarrel with such an ingenious gentleman as yourself. Since you know me personally, now, you can have no reason to use your magical phrase on my account again; and, as you have already suggested, we'll say no more about it. Let us rejoin the ladies."

And we returned to the parlor together, like two of the best friends in the world.

Yellow wines not being the table nectars over which masculine diners care to linger longest, the other gentlemen had already reappeared from the banquet hall; and there was even some talk of a breaking-up of the party, when an agitated yellow Mercury almost swooned open a door, evidently of recent construction, in the wall opposite the piano, and revealed the artistic use of a small wing lately added to the villa.

"Ladies and gentlemen," said Mr. Spanyel, going mincingly to the doorway, and waving a hand toward the interior, "you must favor our little collection before leaving us."

Here was a tasteful surprise, indeed. Even Mrs. Lord and her sea-officer appeared to take it as such; the former condescending thereupon to partially relinquish the contemptuous expression of countenance with which she had hitherto depreciated her presumptuous native land. With April upon one arm and Miss Hyer on the other, I followed the gratified company into the handsome little picture-gallery, where the rays of three illuminated glass globes were reflected from as many triumphs of European art as there were square yards of wall. There was a "Scene in the South of France," by Widger, R.A., showing that the South of France is marvellously like the lower end of Staten Island and commands a miraculous view of Sandy Hook; a "Sketch in Holland," by Skeggs, of Brussels, giving promise of great future eminence for Skeggs if public sentiment should some day induce him to try his hand in the pictorial window-shade line; "Infant Bacchus," by Perugino, being a bronze babe in an attitude at once inviting and favoring approved parental flagellation; a "Turner's Ferry, Devonshire," by Ruskin, R.A., depicting Spuyten-dyvil Creek before it was removed to its present American location by some unprecedented convulsion of nature; "Landscape, with herdsmen driving cattle," by Titian (A genuine original Titian, gentlemen, and I'm only bid twelve dollars and a half for it,—twelve and a half, only twelve and a half, half, half,—do I hear thirteen? twelve dol-lars and-a-narf, 'narf, 'narf,— the frame's worth ten,—twelve and a harf! Going at twel-ve 'narf! last call! Goin-g-g! Gone!—to Mr. Spanyel at twelve and a narf. If you're not satisfied with your bargain, Mr. Spanyel, bring it to me to-morrow and I'll give you six dollars for it myself.) This rare work was the gem of the collection, and had the Spanyel arms and crest carved at the top of its new frame. At least a dozen choice bits, representing such exciting subjects as corner fruit-stands ("Still Life"), views up a chimney (called "Flemish Night Scenes"), and a study of sunset from a slice of water-melon, were worthy of rapture; but a majority of the company evinced their cultivated and critical tastes by clustering before the glorious Titian.

"That stormy sky is so divinely exquisite!" exclaimed Miss Hyer.

"And see that ridiculously sweet little angel of a goat behind the last herdsman," murmured Miss Rose Spanyel.

"There don't seem, love, to be enough of that last herdsman's —— legs," tittered Mrs. C. O'D. Fish; who was instantly ready to die of shame for saying it.

"The 'ead of that 'erdsman is too 'eavy, ye know. Too much 'air; and all that sort o' thing." From Mr. Lord.

."I admire to see that streak of white on the left hand corner of the mountains," observed Mr. Cornelius O'Doricourt Fish, with his eye-glass and nose nearly touching the canvas.

"The perspective of that Painted Thought," sounded the melancholy voice of the Reverend T. Spooner, "is in itself a terrible ideal of that Measureless Abysm of Eternity, of which the Human Soul has intuitious in metaphysical moments. The blending umbra, penumbra, and arbitrary blackness; the vast stretch over village, field, river, forest, and mountain into an illimitability just touched by the sun, are all rife with the Titanic spirit of the great, mysterious Eterne."

"O Emerson!" murmured Mrs. Heroldun.

O prig! thought I to myself. But what I really said, was,—"And what do *you* think, April?"

"I think," whispered she, smiling rather wearily up into my face, — "I think — that your father must be wondering what keeps us so long."

That instantly became my own private opinion; as I quickly proved by-heading a return-party to the parlor, and proceeding with April to take leave of our hostess. The demonstration proved contagious; the remainder of the company came in from the gallery with like intent, and presently my sweet companion and I were leaders again of a party stepping into carriages.

During the ride back to the city I renewed the conversation interrupted by our arrival from thence, and have, from that time, regarded a carriage with feelings not to be expressed to a coachman. If, from this confession a delicate confidence is understood, I shall not refuse the congratulations of the understanders; but there my revelations must end. If excellent Mrs. Keyes, the house-keeper, can explain why, upon our arrival home that night, April fled away from me, like a bird, to her own room, the very moment the street-door was opened, and I, with a particularly self-satisfied air, repaired immediately to my father in the library, she is at liberty to use her own discretion about making the explanation public.

But Todeville was not quite forsaken by the yellow diners at the close of the fine-art exhibition; for, as has since appeared, Mr. Benton Stiles lingered about the Spanyel villa after all the other guests had departed, and finally invited Miss Rose Spanyel to grant him a brief private interview in the little grove down by the river.

"Rose," he said, in a tragic tone, as the maiden stood beside him on the piazza, "it is too dark here, or you would see that I am very pale, and have a wild look about the eyes. If you will get your bonnet and accompany me down to the grove, we may be happy yet. Otherwise — but no matter."

"You dreadful creature!" ejaculated Rose. "Why can't you come into the parlor? Pa, and ma, and the rest of them have all gone upstairs, and I've got to take my mixture yet."

"I cannot re-enter that scene of recent gayety, feeling as I do," was the sad rejoinder; "I cannot endure to feel like one who treads alone that banquet-hall deserted, — as I should in that European saloon. Come with me to the grove, where the cool evening breeze may play upon my heated brow. Grant me this request — it may be my LAST."

He stepped slightly aside, that he might have room to smite his forehead without knocking off her head-dress, and, in so doing, stumbled over an iron scraper representing the Spanyel arms. "Dam!" — "ascus," he added, "never produced a blade sharper than the pain now existing in my — bosom."

"I'll go with you, Benton," cried the impulsive girl, "though you frighten me to death. I'll be back in a moment."

She hurried into the house, really alarmed by his passionate words and manner; and quickly returned with her bonnet on and a faint druggy fragrance hanging about her.

Arm in arm they descended to the carriage-sweep before the door, and, passing around to the back of the building went down a grassy slope to a small cluster of trees near the smallest of rivers. Here Mr. Stiles handed his fair companion to a rustic settee under one of the trees, and, standing, hat in hand beside her, seemed notifying the evening breeze before mentioned that his brow was quite ready for it.

"Rose," said he, after a pause, "does your heart tell you why I have sought this interview? — or is that palpitation, which I noticed when you were on my arm, chronic?"

"Don't talk in that way, you wicked thing!" entreated Miss Spanyel; "it makes me utterly miserable."

"Rose, 'tis years ago since first we met, as I remember well. On several occasions, the intervals being about three years, I have ventured to tell you the state of my feelings. On the first occasion you assured me that I

was a 'horrid creature;'—which I bore; on the second occasion you seemed more moved, and said that I was 'so perfectly absurd;'—which I bore; on the third occasion, last month, in town, you observed, with deeper feeling, that I was 'utterly ridiculous;'—which I bore. And now the question arises," continued Mr. Stiles, vivaciously forgetting himself for a moment, "if I venture once more, shall I be considered a bore?"

"Why don't you go to the lady in that ring of yours?" pouted Rose.

"Because," said Mr. Stiles, affably, "she was anywhere between France and Constantinople when last heard from."

"How ridiculous!"

With the greatest deliberation Mr. Stiles spread his handkerchief upon the grass at the feet of his beloved, and then knelt upon it.

"Rose, — (don't be afraid, I won't look at your feet), — I have a secret which should have been confessed before. I'm a humbug! Years ago, on a festive occasion, you heard a coarse grocer say that he had seen the face in this ring on a prune-box. It was true. I saw this face on a box of that imported description, and had it daguerreotyped for this bauble on my finger. Forgive me and let me get up, for I think I'm kneeling on a pebble."

"Go 'way, you dreadful creature."

"Rose," — his voice grew softer as he arose, — "your elder sister is married. Her babe is really the smallest excuse for a name I ever saw; but *she* likes it. Your sister Lily is engaged to young Hyer. You are the last Rose of summer, left blooming alone; all your lovely companions are married, or about to be. Will you be mine? Will you become a Rose of Sharon by sharin' my hand and heart?"

"O Mr. Stiles!" cried the pretty blossom, trembling violently; "how *can* you be so awful!"

"I see how it is," exclaimed Mr. Stiles, speaking desperately, and seeming to become so suddenly feeble that he was obliged to sink upon the rustic seat and cling to her for support, "you still hesitate because I am an American. But I'm one by birth only; and I'm ready to live with your father until his example makes me a regular King Charles Spanyel. Shall I ask him?"

"O Benton! if it wasn't *so* perfectly absurd!"

"She's mine!" exclaimed Mr. Stiles, crushing her bonnet under his chin with both arms, and cordially addressing the nearest tree. "I'd be set up for life now, if I only knew who that fellow, Mugses, was. — Let me see; where's your mouth?"

"Oh — h — h! you're mussing my back hair."

"Maid of Athens, ere we part, — just one more."

What happened then seemed to possess an interest for the very skies; for, just at that moment, the full moon popped out from

the lips of a cloud, like a roguish and quizzical O!

------◆◆◆------

CHAPTER LV.

THY HAND, GREAT ANARCH! LETS THE CURTAIN FALL.

My wedding-day,—you have all foreseen
from the very first paragraph of this vera-
cious autobiography that such would be the
inevitable ending of the story; that my
many haps and mishaps, tarryings and adventures, would be, after all, but steps in
some one of those innumerable roads leading to the hymeneal Rome. Yet I, myself,
could scarcely believe in this consummation of my destiny, even on that balmy
summer day formally appointed for it. To
breakfast alone with my father, and be
treated by him with a kind of delicate
reserve, as though I must naturally wish to
make but the most superficial show of
interest in every earthly subject save that
which was rather understood than mentioned; to notice the modest hush there
was upon Mrs. Keyes and one of the most
decorous of footmen out of livery, while
they performed in the great mystery of
packing my trunks; to be conscious that a
rustling little breeze of mysterious preparation pervaded the whole house, yet affected
everybody like the sensitive lull before
some astonishing phenomenon; to feel
airily separated, myself, from the whole
human race, but still with a bewildering
presentiment of being presently in closer
fraternity with mankind than ever before,
—all these and many other incomprehensible
experiences made me sufficiently sympathetic with the Awful and Unfathomable
German Mind (as affected by metaphysical
philosophy) to discern a hopeless difference
between *Ego* and Me.

Something of the vague and misty character of things, as they appeared to me that
day, shall rest like an intangible bridal veil
upon the few remaining words I have to
say about myself; giving the outer world
but hazy glimpses of that coronation of a
life to which all may advance through romances of their own.

Late in the afternoon, when the sun kindled silver and golden torches in every
casement-pane above the street, and scores
of birds—those singing meteors of the
woodland sky—poured fitting music from
leafy clouds in the park across the way, we
emerged in dainty procession from the
home henceforth to know but one name and
family, and stepped royally into the glorified vehicles which should convey us to the
church. Then came the ride that seemed
but around the corner; the holy edifice,
like a great Ear that heard our very
thoughts, and made us tremble with the
organ and blush with the arched and
painted window behind the altar; the pews
filled with people sinfully dissatisfied at

having only two eyes apiece; the main
aisle radiant with the figures of all the
fashion-plates; the clergyman and his
assistant in their robes; the ceremony; the
instant of silence; the growing bustle and
hum; the congratulations,—and home again.

Willing to show any manner of favor to
the last male descendant of the Goetmans
of Terrapin Island, scores of dear fashionable friends, whom I had never seen before
in my life, brought such bridal presents as
can only be imported from Europe; and
these, displayed upon a table draped with
blue velvet, furnished half a column of
adulative enthusiasm to the very genteel
editor of the *Court Plaster*, who was one of
the guests. Standing in that plainly rich
parlor as the young and happy bridegroom,
with my precious darling on my arm, my
father close beside us, and the many givers
of the gifts thronging about us in a perfect
ecstasy of congratulation, I felt my lonely,
friendless past much more a dream than
ever, and deemed its wildest vision the
meeting with the poor old outcast and his
ragged little beggar girl in Rack-and-Ruin
Row.

The wedding dinner over, and my young
wife donning her travelling apparel for the
bridal tour before us, my father drew me
away from the brilliant company for a moment, to one of the open windows overlooking the street. From thence I could see
the carriage waiting to convey April and
myself to the late Washington train, and I
said,—

"If you were only going with us, sir—"

"Ah, Avery, my son, you have one, now,
to go with you all through life and permit
you to want no other. In seeing you true
and tender to her, I shall realize my own
highest blessing as a father; for all these
forms and ceremonies have not made her
the more a child of mine than she has ever
been in my deepest affections. She is the
purest, worthiest, noblest prize man ever
won for wife, and in yielding her to you I
have been permitted to really bless you as
son is rarely blessed. May God be with
you both."

"Best of fathers!" I ejaculated, greatly
moved, "we love each other, I trust and
believe, with a love to end only with life;
but if we needed another bond to make
surer our perfect unity of thought, feeling,
and aspiration, it would be found in the
great debt of life-long reverence and affection we doubly owe to you. When, after a
few weeks, we return here again, it will be
to leave you no more; to be your dutiful,
loving children indeed; and to know no
higher pleasure and privilege than those of
making you as happy as ourselves."

"God bless you both!"

"He *will* bless us, sir, while we deserve
it by our filial truth; and if we ever fail
in that, whether from thoughtlessness or
ignorance, you must tell us where we err.
To you—"

A sharp, crashing sound, as of an explosion, cut short my sentence with a start, and made us both look quickly across the Park in the direction from whence it apparently came.

———

He had been lurking about the front of the house ever since the first lamp upon the curb was lighted, and if passers-by gave no heed to his stealthy, slouching movements, it was because his tattered clothes, rusty tangle of beard, and dismal face, confounded him with the forlorn mendicants who haunt areas for broken victuals. Prowling from the curb to the foot of the white marble stoop; from the latter to the end of the basement railing; from there across the street, and then back again, he seemed to be continually frightened from his purpose, whatever it was, by the passing of a woman, by the sound of a wheel, by the flashing of a light from a window many yards distant,— by any sound, or form, or sight, of mortal watchfulness.

How his long, dingy, talon-like hands worked all the time, whether shivering into his mere rag-holes of pockets, or twitching out again and picking at the jagged tufts where buttons should have been! How his cracked lips moved, and sunken eyes flashed about, each time he turned from the stoop in guilty fear? Oh, for but a second when foot would not fall, nor wheel turn, nor window stare with face or light, on that short block!

It came at last; one infinitesimal point of time when a hare would have seen or heard nothing to startle her along the line *his* eyes and ears watched; and in that instant he was up on the iron balcony before the parlor windows, like a cat; tearing open a shutter, like a wolf tearing the thatch of a winter fold; and into the house, like a thief.

In the cold darkness of the room he stumbled upon a chair with a noise that was thunder to his ears; and, while he stood there holding his breath, the rats in the wainscot were so many footsteps on the carpet to answer the alarm. A pause long enough to banish that terror, and then the man softly felt his way past unseen tables and sofas to the marble mantel-piece. There he struck a match, shading it in his hand until he could draw from his breast and light one of those flat tin cans, stopped with wick, which plumbers use. The pale blue, dancing flame just made the room and the man ghastly without dispensing radiance enough to be seen from the street; and, holding it before him, the stealthy bearer lifted the heavy curtains hiding a second room, and passed into the latter. There he cautiously drew a table against the drapery and placed the flaring can upon it; the light still being too dim to shine through the interstices of the blinds on the farther windows, though clear enough to reveal an iron box, or safe, set in the wall

near by. Going close to the object thus especially disclosed, and scrutinizing it with great care, he seemed to be justified thereby in some foregone idea; for, with much more decision of manner, he gave two quick nods of his head, drew a battered powder-flask, and a short, tin tube from some place of concealment about his waist, and, by the aid of the tube, proceeded to pour the contents of the flask into the key-hole of the safe. This curious task completed, and the stem of a fire-cracker inserted as a slow-match, the man repassed the curtains into the front room again, and peered through the shutters to the street.

The evening had grown darker and he could not see distinctly if the opposite walk, along the Park, was deserted; but no sound of steps or voices was audible, and he stole swiftly back to his grim work. It took him but a moment to apply the blazing can to the end of the slow match, replace it on the table, and go with a shambling run to a far corner of the room. It took but another moment for the charge to explode, with a sharp, cracking report, shivering a great, ragged hole in the iron door, and hurling half a dozen bits of broken metal in as many directions.

Uttering a strange, hoarse cry, the man bounded forward toward the safe at the sound, heedless that the can upon the table had been struck by one of the fragments, and its contents cast in a spray of liquid flames upon the curtains. Grasping the shattered door, on which a murky light now flared through the smoke, he pulled it open with one hand, while the other was thrust eagerly within.

Papers! papers! dragged forth at random, while the fire ran up the curtain and spread with merry speed upon the painted canvas on the wall. Smoke could not suffocate nor flame consume him until he had found what he sought.

But the smoke, drawn by the draught, went curling out through the broken street window by which the incendiary had entered; and a chance-passer whom the noise had stopped, and who now knew what to do about it, bawled the one word, "Fire!"

That devil's watchword of the night is terrible when it cuts the ear in places where the poor have their miserable homes; and falls upon the heart like a first stroke of death where tricked and painted men and women glorify folly in gaudy masquerade, to throngs whom a single narrow hall, or staircase, in flames, may consign to an awful destruction; but in the stately squares of the rich it is only a rallying cry of the vulgar mob, and will scarcely cause one well-bred gentleman or lady to look from the nearest window. So it was, that the distinguished families of the block in which this smoking building was an admired corner, did not compromise their gentility by any hurried demonstration at casements and doors when the cry was first uttered in their neighborhood that night; but contented themselves for the nonce by languidly wondering what that crash could have been. The men of the streets heard it, though, with less apathy, and came scudding across the Park, and down the Avenue, and up from Broadway, with that same insatiable fiery infatuation which, unrestrained by reason, causes horses and moths to plunge into the flames in spite of all restraint. These, however, were not the uproarious spirits who dash into blazing piles with watery serpents that are forever shedding their skins and overpowering the fiery dragon by their mere power of tireless continuity. They were the connoisseurs and dilettanti of conflagrations, who always arrive early to get good places, and never think of such a thing as checking a spectacle which excites their admiration and improves their critical ability in proportion to its extent.

Hence the first popular assemblage, before the windows of the burning parlors, saw no immediate reason for interfering in the matter; and were even exchanging noisy congratulations upon the probability of a spirited display presently, until the shutters enclosing one of those same smoking windows were suddenly dashed open, and a goblin figure could be seen standing in the murky glare of the interior. It stretched its head toward the crowd, threw up its arms with a fierce cry, and seemed to run back into the very heart of the fire.

"There's a man in there!"

The shout was repeated by a dozen tongues, with an energy quite different from the reckless jesting of a moment before; and now the unanimous roar of "Fire!" went up with such mighty earnestness that it set the bells ringing, and brought all the genteel families to their windows and stoops in sudden affright. None were now so eager to have the bells clang louder, and the firemen hurry faster, as those who so recently had thought only of the stirring sight; but precious minutes had been wasted; and as the red-shirted companies came thundering into the swaying multitude, with their glittering engines, colored lamps, and savage clamor, the flames began to show at the front sashes on the lower floor of the doomed house in fitful tongues and spirals.

It was at that moment, too, when a carriage, furiously driven, came up from the direction of Broadway, and stopped nearly opposite the scene of excitement. A gentleman of fine appearance alighted therefrom, and seemed about to make his way through the dense throng in the centre of the street, when a man, who had appeared near the carriage door simultaneously with the stoppage of the vehicle, darted after him, and placed a detaining hand on his shoulder.

"Well, Mr. Ketchum," said the gentleman, turning at the touch, "what do you wish?"

"Sorry to say that I want you, Mr. Wynne," was the answer, in an undertone. "I'm appointed to take you for that Ho-

boken affair, and I thought it might be pleasanter to have the thing done away from your Broadway house. I knew you would be there to-night, and, happening to see this fire, — and give the alarm, too, — before any one else did, I sent a messenger post-haste to bring you. You've been away for some time?"

"In Washington," was the sententious reply.

"To be sure," said the detective, agreeably, at the same time linking arms with him in the most friendly manner. "I hadn't the least possible thought that you'd given us the cut, although some people said so. Pity to see that house over there going so!"

"Yes."

"It's likely to burn up a tiresome old friend of yours, though, Mr. Wynne; for if my eyes are what they used to be, — and they were jolly sharp once, — I saw a man come to one of those red-hot parlor windows about five minutes ago; and that man was — Wolf."

"By the way, Ketchum," asked Plato Wynne, as though he had heard only one word, "where did you pick up that term, 'jolly?'"

"I think," returned the other, thrown off his guard, "that I must have caught it from an officer from London, who worked up a runaway-cashier case with me some years ago."

Mr. Ketchum had not more than cleared his tongue of the last syllable, when, to his unspeakable astonishment, he found himself twisted swiftly around, and thrown against the carriage with such violence that he slid to the ground.

Like a strong swimmer the King of Diamonds plunged into the sea of heads and shoulders, over which lay a hot glare from his own parlors; sweeping fiercely from before him successive waves of startled men, and forcing his way in a nearly straight line to the marble stoop of his house. As he gained the street door in two bounds, and placed a key in the latch, the firemen called to him that the hall was in flames; but before the warning could be repeated, he had disappeared from view, shutting the door again behind him.

Something between a laugh and cheer broke from the hundreds of eager spectators and firemen who had witnessed the incident, and an active figure in the helmet of chief engineer was heard to say something very emphatic about "the real old pluck," before overtopping all other noises with a positively hideous roar through his trumpet. Ordinary ears could detect sounds of no known language in that roar; but certain sophomore students of the Fire Department were more skilled in translation, and came driving through the illuminated crowd with a long ladder on their red shoulders. Up it went against the building, which now smoked ominously from every stifled opening, despite the steady streams pouring into the lower story. Up it went, seeming to those at a distance to raise its skeleton length by some independent power of its own; and, axe in hand, a sturdy monkey in red shirt and leathern helmet mounted the frail steps with surprising agility, and dashed open the blinds of an upper window at one wrenching blow. The gush of dense smoke and bits of glass which followed made the invader retire hastily down half a dozen rungs into the very arms of two likenesses of himself coming after him with hose; and while the three paused in momentary indecision, the window grew luminous and a frightful form peered down at them from the sill.

"There he is again!" rose in a hoarse scream from the surging and shining mob below.

The goblin shouted, shook his fist, and waved defiance with a handful of papers. He even strove to push the ladder from its place, and was showering incoherent curses on the paralyzed climbers, when another dark figure suddenly sprang upon him from within, and the two were seen grappling and struggling in the light of the flames at their very elbows.

For a moment, dead silence and inaction fell upon the astounded lookers-on, the unnatural horror of the spectacle clogging every tongue and nerve. Then, with the howl of a tempest unleashed, hundreds of daring spirits rushed toward the ladder.

"One hundred dollars to the man who brings Plato Wynne out of that house alive!" cried one who wore the dress of a citizen, but mingled frantically with the foremost of the ladder-men.

"The second one is Plato Wynne, boys!" resounded the chorus, and a score of firemen clung to the ladder.

But, with a muffled burst, torrents of flame answered the cry, from every window above their heads, and even shot above the roof. Down stumbled the climbers, one over another, like singed flies, the thunder of a falling floor and a storm of blazing flakes accompanying their flight.

The scene and actors of that infernal death-struggle seemed to have been swallowed-up in one great flash of destruction. With one of those instantaneous, awful changes which the demon of Fire so loves to produce, the entire edifice flamed over its whole front in a moment, bathing street, and park, and men, and clouds in a flood of shapeless radiance.

It shone far across the park upon the carriages into which a wedding-party were just stepping; it glared in the thoughtful face of a chief engineer, who believed that he had once done good service to the son of the man who called that house his home, and never dreamed of the strange explanation yet to come to him and his Milly, accompanied by a present worth having. And it was destined to be the death-light of a silent, fair-haired woman, far away in a convent of Canada, long after its avenging fire had all gone out.

Gone out,—and His unshriven, daring soul gone with it! Gone out, — like the last rebellious flames of sunset from the black city of the storm, when the defiant ship no longer battles with engulfing fate, and darkness crouches to the guilty bosom of the deep.

END OF VOLUME II.